LAWS OF PHYSICS

HYPOTHESIS SERIES BOOK #2

PENNY REID

WWW.PENNYREID.NINJA/NEWSLETTER/

LAWS OF PHYSICS

HYPOTHESIS SERIES BOOK #2

PENNY REID

WWW.PENNYREID.NINJA/NEWSLETTER/

COPYRIGHT

DEDICATION

For nerds who aren't a Bohr.

AUTHOR'S NOTE

If you have read the Elements of Chemistry trilogy (Hypothesis Trilogies #1), the action of this book (Laws of Physics: MOTION) occurs one year prior to the action of Elements of Chemistry: CAPTURE

If you have read Knitting in the City series, the action of this book occurs the summer between Love Hacked and Beauty and the Mustache (and one year prior to the action of Dating-ish)

If you have read the Dear Professor series, the action of this book occurs two years prior to Kissing Tolstoy

If you have read none of these books, ignore this note.

LAWS OF PHYSICS
PART 1: MOTION

CHAPTER 1
PHYSICS IN A PERSONAL AND SOCIAL CONTEXT

"You are receiving a collect call from *ACCEPT THE CHARGES, MONA!* at Cretin County Jail. If you accept the charges, press one. If not, disconnect," the robot—apparently the love child between Alexa and Baymax—announced via my cell phone, the sound an odd amalgamation of her voice and his cadence.

No. Strike that. Inaccurate.

Most of the words were announced by the robot. But the words "ACCEPT THE CHARGES, MONA!" and the voice that whisper-shouted them belonged to my twin sister, Lisa. I didn't press one and I didn't disconnect. But I did stare at nothing, probably making my about-to-sneeze face, and attempted to parse through what I'd just heard.

"Is everything okay?"

Dr. Payton's perfectly reasonable question hijacked my attention and reminded me that I wasn't alone. I was in a restaurant. The planetary astrophysicist's eyebrows inched upward as we stared at each other, his last bite of steak left forgotten on the tip of his fork.

Fraught and feeling illogically harassed, I sputtered, "I don't know."

This was one of the very few times in my nineteen years that I'd said *I don't know*. I didn't like not knowing. I preferred *I'll find out, I'll figure it out,* or *I'll know soon.*

If he'd asked me the same question just thirty seconds ago, I would've known how to answer. Prior to my cell ringing seconds ago, today had been a great day. I'd meditated as soon as I'd awoken. I'd journaled. I'd located and eaten a perfectly ripe avocado for breakfast. The best. Avocados in Chicago and Cambridge, Mass were so seldom perfectly ripe, or they were ripe for only 4.4 seconds. Whereas California had all the ripe avocados.

Traffic on the I-5 had been light while my driver transported me from the Pasadena Marriott to the Palomar Observatory. I'd spent most of my day elbows deep with my best friends: the gorgeous symmetry and chaos of relativistic equations, infrared array imaging, and spectroscopy data.

Late afternoon, I'd gone to the dentist for a teeth cleaning, X-rays, and exam where I'd been told that my home regimen of flossing and brushing was exemplary. Praise from the dentist always put me in a good mood.

Presently, I was having dinner with Dr. Poe Payton, a second-year fellow in planetary astrophysics who was as intelligent as he was handsome and charming, which was considerably. Not that his handsomeness or ability to charm was relevant. As with all my prospective colleagues, nothing was relevant about Dr. Payton other than his ability to keep up.

Afterward, my plans included swimming in the hotel pool, showering, and finally an hour of scheduled fiction reading before bed. Although, now that I was living on my own, and finally free of Dr. Steward's daily oversight, I sometimes read for an hour and a half.

"You are receiving a collect call from *ACCEPT THE CHARGES, MONA!* at Cretin County Jail. If you accept the charges, press one. If not, disconnect," the Alexa-Baymax hybrid announced again, startling me a second time.

Flustered, I pressed one and brought the phone back to my ear. "Uh, hello? Hello?"

"Thank God!" My twin sounded far away, like the connection was bad or she was speaking in a tunnel.

"Lisa?" I whisper-asked, my eyes darting to Dr. Payton's curious and concerned expression.

"First, don't freak out. Second, I don't have a lot of time, so don't ask questions. Just do what I say, okay? I've been arrested."

Arrested.

Oh God. Oh my God! Okay . . . OH MY GOD!

Clutching my forehead, heart racing, I dropped my gaze to the napkin on my lap. "Are you okay? I—what? Where are—"

"Listen," she said firmly, "I need you to listen to me."

"Should I call—"

"No! Don't call anyone. I already have a lawyer, and—if everything goes according to plan—I should be released by next week."

What? "What?"

My eyes darted up, snagging on Dr. Payton, who was now looking at me with some alarm.

He asked, "What can I do?" But this time he mouthed his question.

I didn't answer, I couldn't. Lisa was still talking in my ear, my mind accelerating to a million miles per second.

". . . so I need you to go home and pretend to be me. Otherwise, they'll know what happened and I'll be so, so screwed."

I lifted a finger, motioning for Dr. Payton to give me a minute, and turned my body toward the window on my right. "Uh, pardon?"

"Mona, focus." My typically imperturbable sister's voice trembled. "You have to get to Chicago—*tonight* if possible—and be me."

Go to Chicago? Impossible. But one thing at a time.

Taking a deep breath, I closed my eyes and asked the most pertinent question. "First, tell me if you're okay. Are you hurt?"

Lisa heaved a watery-sounding sigh. "I'm not hurt. But, no. I'm not okay."

Lisa. My lungs constricted, I rubbed my sternum with my fingertips. We weren't particularly close, not anymore, but right now that didn't matter. This was my sister, my twin. There'd been a time when I'd thought we shared one-half of the same heart. Our brother Leo used to tell us this story and we'd believed him.

No. Strike that. Inaccurate. I'd believed him. Lisa had never been as naïve or gullible or susceptible to fictions and romanticism as me.

"What can I do?" I asked, opening my eyes.

"Get to Chicago. Pretend to be me for a week. And—"

"I can't. I'm in California for my visit with Caltech. I'm interviewing for their PhD program."

"Oh please. You mean *you're* interviewing *them*. Everyone wants you. They wouldn't care if you left, they wouldn't care if you did a striptease on the dean's desk while snorting coke off his letter opener. Hell, he'd probably love it."

"The dean is a heterosexual female."

Lisa grunted. "Whatever! Please, please, please listen, Mona. This is serious. This is life and death for me. You have to wear my clothes, my makeup, sleep in my room, act like me. Mom and Dad can't know I'm in . . . shit. I can't believe this happened."

I shook my head. "Lisa, no. No. Listen to yourself. This is crazy, even for you. Mom and Dad will know I'm me."

"Obviously, Mona!" she whispered harshly. "But you don't have to fool Mom and Dad. They're still in Greece. Abram is watching the house. You just have to fool him until I get there."

She was talking so fast, I was having trouble keeping up. "Who is Abram?"

"Abram. You know, Abram, Leo's friend? You don't know Abram? Oh, good"—she sounded relieved—"in fact, that's great! I've only sorta met Abram once, so this'll be super easy. Pretend like you don't remember him or anything about the night we met, which is actually pretty accurate, because I don't remember much. We'll switch places before your BFF Dr. Steward arrives, and no one will know about this nightmare."

Overwhelmed by my confusion and her sense of urgency, I couldn't organize my thoughts into any logical order, asking questions as they occurred to me. "Wait, Dr. Steward is coming?" Dr. Steward had lived with me and served as my guardian for most of my undergrad; this arrangement had lasted until I'd turned eighteen. "And why do I have to go to Chicago if Mom and Dad are in Greece? Shouldn't I come to where you are and—"

She made a short growling sound. "They're planning to cut me off, okay? They said if I wasn't home by tomorrow, and if I didn't hand over my phone to Abram when I got there, *and* if I don't cut off all contact with Tyler, then they'd close my bank accounts and credit cards and that's it."

I struggled anew with this information, mostly because I thought Lisa had already ended all contact with Tyler. Our family had been living the last few months under the assumption that she was safe from his influence, that they were finally over-*over*. She'd sworn it was over. She'd promised.

"You're still with Tyler?"

An epic scoff-snort sounded from the other end of the call. "Not anymore. God, never again. Not after this. I am so done with that lying, cheating, massive piece of shit!"

I had to press the cell closer to my ear to hear her. Unlike most people, both Lisa and I became quieter when we were angry rather than louder.

"Lisa, this is crazy. I can't be you." I kept my voice low, turning in the chair as far from Dr. Payton as I could. "No one will buy it." We hadn't been raised together past the age of eleven. Both my older brother and I had stayed home with private tutors—he studied music, I concentrated on math and science—while Lisa had been sent to boarding school.

"They will buy it. We're physically identical. All you need is a makeover."

I struggled with how to phrase my next objection, but ultimately decided I didn't have time to be tactful. "Lisa, I love you, but I wouldn't know the first thing about acting like you. I don't know you." Most of what I knew about my sister's life was deduced from chance encounters with the gossip sections of newspapers and magazines.

Exotica and DJ Tang's youngest daughter spotted at New York hot spot

Exotica and DJ Tang's youngest daughter in trouble again

Exotica and DJ Tang's youngest daughter rumored to be dating Pirate Orgy's front man, Tyler

Exotica and DJ Tang's youngest daughter partying at fashion week

Exotica and DJ Tang's youngest daughter wrecks Tesla

"That's not true." She sounded exasperated rather than hurt.

"I call you once a week, you never pick up. And when you respond it's with a text message."

"Mona, you never returned my letters when I was sent to boarding school, so what's the big deal?"

What? Why was she bringing this up? Again! Lisa had been bringing this up to excuse treating me poorly for *years*. It's how she justified her jokes and pranks, none of which were funny.

"I did return your letters. How many times—"

"I'm not going to argue with you about this again. You didn't return my letters, which is why I stopped sending them. So, again, why does it matter if I text you back?"

"Because when we do talk on the phone, it's for less than five minutes. You think my life is boring and we have nothing in common." I tried—and succeeded—to keep emotion out of my voice. This was my superpower, a skill I'd honed as a fifteen-year-old girl, entering a field dominated by not fifteen-year-old girls. "You were right. We have nothing in common. And now you want me to pretend to be you? It won't work."

For better or worse, I had more in common with my musician older brother than I did with my twin.

"Yes. It will. Like I said, Abram has only met me once, and he didn't seem impressed, and I hardly remember it. So as long as you're wearing my clothes and your impersonation is passable, he'll leave you alone and we'll be golden. I've already set everything up with Gabby. She's expecting your call. She'll meet you in Chicago, dress you to look like me before you go to the house."

Gabby. My nostrils flexed, flared with annoyance (I hated it when they did that).

Gabby was Lisa's best friend and used to be mine, once upon a time. The three of us had been inseparable as kids. We used to pretend we were triplets, with Gabby being our long-lost sister. Noteworthy, Gabby and Lisa had always been more interested in pretty dresses and painting their nails than I had; and I loved reading in a way they both eschewed; but our differences hadn't seemed to matter at the time. I would paint my nails right along with them, and they indulged my love of stories by listening to me read out loud.

Things started to change around the age of nine. Gabby and Lisa's interests moved firmly from imaginary games involving being dragon tamers—or being astronauts, or being stranded on a desert island—to imaginary games involving being famous and important in the *real* world, calling the games I wanted to play "baby stuff."

But pretending within the confines of "the real world" made no sense to me. It's like they were speaking a different language, one I couldn't understand, and one that seemed horribly . . . well, *boring.*

Anyway.

Our official friendship separation (Gabby and Lisa versus Mona) could be traced to one night when we were eleven. I'd alerted our nanny that my sister and our friend had snuck some whiskey from the liquor cabinet after asking them repeatedly to put it back. Lisa had been sent to boarding school not long after, but when she was home, I'd played on my own and they'd been virtually inseparable.

Fascinatingly, eight years later, Gabby still held a grudge—let me repeat, for *eight years*—related to my snitching on her when we were eleven. I'd never snitched again. On anyone. For anything. Ever.

Understatement: I'd learned my lesson about snitching.

I'd tried (and failed) to get in their good graces for years after the whiskey-snitching incident until Gabby introduced Lisa to Tyler. Now Gabby's dislike of me was entirely mutual. I didn't know how to forgive her for introducing my twin to that scumbag.

Conclusion: At this point, I worked under the assumption that Gabby was quite possibly mentally unhinged and strongly disliked—if not outright hated—me.

But back to now and Lisa being in jail and me being shocked and awed and making my about-to-sneeze face.

Lisa continued, "When you get there, all you have to do is wear designer clothes, eyeliner, and make terrible life decisions." She laughed, the sound both hysterical and sad. "Plus, you have to do this for me. You don't have a choice. Unless you plan to do nothing—*again*—and let Mom and Dad disown me."

What the what?

"Doing nothing? What are you—"

"Forget it, Mona. Now isn't the time. If you care about me at all, go to Chicago and pretend for Abram until I get there."

"But who is Abram? Why is he at the house? Why would Mom and Dad trust him to do this? And how can I—"

"God! Look, I don't have time to argue with you about this." Her tone was tired, strained, frazzled. "Are you going to help me or not?"

I wanted to say, *This will never work!* But when I opened my mouth, no words came out.

"Call Gabby, she's expecting your call. Go to Chicago. Get a ticket for tonight, okay? My cell phone has been mailed to Chicago and should arrive tomorrow or the next day. If Abram asks you for my phone when you get there, just tell him you left it behind and are having it mailed to you. Sit tight and let your inhibitions go—for once—until I get there."

"Lisa—"

"Promise me, Mona. Promise me. I swear, I'll be so good. I'll be so fucking good. I'll go back and finish high school, I'll never touch drugs again, I'll never see Tyler again, I'll be the best sister and daughter, I'll forgive you for everything, we'll create a special handshake for when the next NASA thing lands on Jupiter or whatever, I will never call physics boring, and I will make this up to you. I will never, ever lie. But if you don't do this for me, I'm dead. I'm so, so dead." Her voice caught on the last sentence, adopting a decidedly watery edge, and that sobered me more than anything else would have.

My sister didn't cry. Ever. What a messy mess.

"You don't have to worry about paparazzi or anything like that." Her breath hitched, and that told me she was now unable to stem the tears. "Gabby hooked me up with the best lawyer, she specializes in this kind of stuff, keeping it out of the papers. This won't make it out to the press. And you know they only care about the overachievers in the family."

I resisted the urge to huff and remind her that she was the lucky one, the one the press didn't follow at all, the one who was able to live her life out of the spotlight. But every time I told her this it just seemed to piss her off.

"They don't care about me unless I fuck up . . ." she added quietly.

"Lisa—"

But then she said, "Please."

The single word sounded so desperate, so broken, it struck a chord deep within me, a bond I'd assumed had dissolved, but now understood had merely been dormant. She hadn't asked me for anything since we were kids. How could I say no?

I couldn't.

"Of course. Yes." Even though it was complete madness.

"Thank you, thank you. And when I see you, I'll tell you everything, don't worry. You won't be sorry. You are the best sister in the world. I love you!" she said just before the line went dead.

Removing the cell from my ear, I stared at the blank screen, my mind in chaos. I was unsure what to do, or on which problem I should focus.

Am I really going to do this?

Hastily, I made a list of the most basic action items. Getting a ticket to Chicago shouldn't be a big deal. If I left directly from the restaurant, I could probably catch something tonight, stay in a hotel by O'Hare. I'd call Gabby on the way. Assuming my parents didn't insist on speaking to me—well, "to me" meaning Lisa—then I might be back in Pasadena by the end of the week.

Am I really going to do this?

"Hey." Dr. Payton's soft voice cut through my list making. His wide brown eyes moved over my face, concern etched between his eyebrows. "Hey, is everything okay?"

"I'm sorry. That was rude. I should have left the table," I said on autopilot, my brain still working through next steps. I felt his eyes on me as I returned my phone to my backpack. His stare felt assessing, but not in the usual way. Usually, when people stared, I knew exactly what they were thinking.

Depending on the person and context, it was either, *Isn't that the girl whose research on Bose-Einstein condensates improved the reliability and power of infrared arrays? Wasn't she twelve when that happened?* Or the person was thinking, *Isn't that one of Exotica and DJ Tang's daughters? Is that the cool crazy one or the weirdo math prodigy?*

"Don't apologize," Dr. Payton said unexpectedly, drawing my gaze back to his as he reached a hand across the table and covered mine.

I pulled my fingers away. Immediately. On instinct.

Tangentially, I noted his skin had been warm and that this was the first time he'd touched me other than a handshake. In fact, other than my one friend, Allyn, this was the first time someone had touched me to offer comfort since . . . well, since longer than I could remember.

"What's wrong?" he asked, his voice gentle and interested. "How can I help?"

"Wrong? Help?" *What?*

"All the color left your face." Dr. Payton paused to study me, the intensity of his frown increasing. "Mona, what happened? Who was that?"

Mona? The informality was a bucket of ice water, cutting through the haze of confusion. I blinked at him and the use of my first name. For these last two weeks he'd been Dr. Payton and I'd been Ms. DaVinci, which was how interactions within my world worked. Always.

As the youngest person by far in any given room—and the room was typically full of men with PhDs fighting for prestige, tenure, and grant dollars—I'd learned early and often that informality meant being taken advantage of. It meant being the second or third author instead of the first on a scholarly article of my own original ideas. It meant opening a door to borrowing (i.e. stealing) my work and intellectual property.

Nothing was more sacred or worth protecting in academia than intellectual property, and everyone wanted to take credit for mine.

"Dr. Payton, I'm very sorry to cut our meeting short." When I stood, he stood, giving me the impression his good manners were ingrained. "I hope we can continue our discussion on Illustris soon, but I have to go." Once again, I flexed my superpower, removing all emotion from my voice.

Clearly surprised by my coolness, Dr. Payton rocked back on his heels and stuffed his hands in his pockets. "Absolutely. I understand," he said, though it was obvious he didn't understand.

Placing my backpack on the chair, I furtively studied him as I zipped and unzipped it, searching for my wallet. I noted the cautious yet concerned way he continued to examine me, at the tense set of his jaw, like he was engaging in an internal debate. I had to swat away a pang of guilt and doubt.

Dr. Payton—Poe—had been nothing but gracious since I'd arrived, but not overbearingly so. Overbearing and overly solicitous faculty had been my experience at the other institutions I'd visited during my quest to find the right PhD program. Even his willingness to collaborate and share, discuss and troubleshoot had been unpretentious. Poe's ideas and approach were unique and refreshing.

The man was certainly brilliant, seemed to be a genuinely good guy, and I was curious about his thoughts on Illustris, the universe-scale simulation project, which was why I'd agreed to dinner. Yet, tempted as I might be to soften my rules about informality and friendly fraternization with colleagues, I wouldn't.

"Do you need a ride anywhere?" he asked stiffly, quickly adding, "No pressure. It's just, my mother would be appalled if I didn't offer."

His slight confession, and how he referred to his mother with deference, made me pause my furious zipping. "Thank you. I have a driver."

He cleared his throat and nodded, seemed to stand straighter. My gaze flickered to his then away, and I dug for my wallet. Finding it, I placed a fifty-dollar bill on the table to cover the cost of my dinner.

"You don't need to do that." He frowned, reaching for the money and offering it back to me.

I shook my head and swung my backpack into place on my right shoulder. "My advisor told me I should pay for my own meals during the recruitment process so as to not unduly influence my final decision."

He flinched subtly, like I'd surprised him again. "I see," he said, then huffed a little laugh. It was amused, but also sounded a tad incredulous. I got the sense I'd offended him somehow . . .

A renewed wave of flustered urgency crashed over me. I didn't have time to think about Dr. Payton. I had to call Gabby, get to Chicago, and figure out how to behave like Lisa and not like me.

"I'll be gone for a few days," I said, not understanding why I felt the need to explain anything. "There's been an unexpected emergency. I'll email Dr. Clarence and the team to let them know."

"Fine." He pressed his lips together, a flat line, his expression now neutral.

I hesitated for a split second, knowing I was doing something wrong yet unable to put my finger on what. But exigency—for my sister's sake—spurred me to move. Giving him a final head nod, I left the restaurant.

With any luck, I'd be in Chicago before midnight.

* * *

"We're going to have to get you a blowout." Gabby pursed her lips at the sight of my single braid, sighed dramatically, and marched past me into my hotel room. "And Lisa's hair is a little shorter I think, so we'll also need a cut. But the color is fine, she went back to her natural dark brown too, like, I don't know, a few months ago, when she pretended to split from Tyler. Do you own any makeup at all?"

Turning, I allowed the hotel door to shut behind me and faced my former friend. "Hello, and yes I own makeup."

Of note, Gabby's real name was Lyndsay. Gabby was a nickname she'd earned because she talked too much and had no filter, always saying whatever popped into her head. This worked for her because her parents were massively wealthy movie stars and had no problem bailing her out of whatever trouble she—and her mouth— found herself in.

Ignoring my greeting, she set a bag on the bed. "I bet it's the wrong kind of makeup. Whatever. There's a Sephora on the way to your house, we'll go there. Lisa said you don't know how to do your eyes, so they can teach you there. Lisa *never* shows her face without mascara and liner, so make sure you do that every day. And here"—she gestured to the bag—"I brought some of Lisa's clothes from the last time she spent the night at my house. We got *soooo* drunk. And it was tequila drunk, not vodka tonic drunk, you know what I mean?" Gabby laughed and gave me a commiserating look.

I didn't know what she meant, but I could extrapolate. Regardless, I did not return her look.

Her amusement vanished.

"Anyway." She paired the single word with an eyebrow lift, a sure sign of exasperation. "This should have everything you need for now. Feel free to thank me at any point here."

No thanks was forthcoming, but she already knew that.

I hadn't returned to my hotel in Los Angeles last night. There was no point in packing clothes before leaving via LAX. Other than underwear and socks, I was supposed to wear Lisa's clothes anyway.

Everything I needed was in my backpack—my laptop, my research notes, my journal—so I sent a text to Gabby and hopped on the next plane to Chicago. We touched down just after 1:00 AM and I spent the night at the Westin near O'Hare, wearing the same clothes to sleep that I'd worn to the dentist.

There's something liberating about sleeping in clothes instead of pajamas, I'd mused the next morning as I brushed my teeth with supplies hastily purchased from the lobby store. The thought felt rebellious, so I pushed it aside and waited for Gabby to show up.

Which brings us to now.

Am I really doing this?

Not for the first or the thousandth time since hanging up with Lisa yesterday, I took stock of this messy mess and how I'd arrived at this moment, peeking inside a bag brought by Gabby. Speaking of the Gabster, she was staring at my profile as I peered in the bag.

Abruptly, apropos of nothing, she said, "You're boring."

My eyes lifted to hers. "Okay."

"You look boring, I mean. Like, I know you and Lisa are supposed to be identical, but if you were in a club you'd be invisible. You'd be wallpaper. Doesn't that bother you?" Though the words might've been interpreted as harsh, the question sounded honestly curious.

Nevertheless, it aggravated me. This was my chance to find out why Lisa had been arrested and Gabby was already getting under my skin before I could ask any questions.

"No," I answered, just as honestly, withholding all emotion from my voice and expression.

"Haven't you ever wanted to be noticed? Be . . . interesting?"

"Not really." I turned my attention back to the clothes and spotted a black lace bra tucked to one side.

. . . Am I really doing this?

"How is it possible you are still such a Mary Sue?" She poked my shoulder. "Haven't you heard? Nowadays, being nice is unlikable. It's all about the rebel. You should do something unexpected, mean, selfish, and don't apologize for it. Be bad for once and tell everyone to fuck off."

I sent her a quick glare. "I just ditched a PhD program interview. I'm about to lie and impersonate my twin sister for several days so my parents won't disown her. Maybe save that question for later, when it might be more accurate."

"Well, you kind of owe her, don't you?"

"Owe her? Owe her for what?"

"For getting her sent off to boarding school? For ratting us out to your nanny? Ring any bells?"

I was so proud of myself for not punching her in the face, and even more proud for keeping my voice level and calm. "We both know Lisa wasn't sent to boarding school because I told our nanny that you had taken whiskey from the cabinet."

"Oh? Really? That's not how I remember it."

"Yes. Really. The only reason Leo and I stayed with Mom and Dad was because of his music and my research."

"Whatever you need to tell yourself so you can sleep at night." Gabby studied her nails. "And you know what I mean about being a Mary Sue. Helping Lisa is just part of the same saintly shit, different day."

Why was she giving me grief about being helpful? *Oh. That's right. Because she's unhinged.*

"While you're standing here telling me to be bad, Lisa is in jail. Aren't you at all concerned about her?" As much as I despised interacting with Gabby these days, we were both here for one reason: to help Lisa because we loved and cared about her.

Gabby rolled her eyes. "Of course I'm concerned about her. I'm terrified for her, okay? And I'm doing everything I can to get her out and save her ass, including putting up with you."

"Putting up with me?" Arg! She was so irritating, all my questions fled my brain.

"You heard me." Talking to her was like arguing with a flat-earther. *Ignorance plus arrogance is why we can't have nice things!*

Best just to get straight to the point. "Why was Lisa arrested?"

Gabby's flippancy morphed into a severe scowl. "Does it matter? She needs your help. What? Now you don't want to help her?"

"I didn't say that."

"Then help her, and put on these clothes, and stop making this about you."

"I just want to know why—"

"Classic Mary Sue behavior. Even when you're being bad, you're still looking for a way to be the do-gooder center of attention. Where is the fun in always being the good one when it means you have no friends? Why must you ruin fun for everyone else?"

"Oh, you know, I think the fun is in not being arrested for doing something stupid and selfishly forcing your sister to clean up your giant mess." Despite my best efforts, a hint of bitterness entered my voice, and that flustered me.

Rattled by my uncontrollable, unexpected, and uncharacteristic show of feelings, I cleared my throat and dropped my eyes. Apparently, my ability to speak truth without emotion was on the fritz. Best not to speak to her at all. Pulling out the black bra and shirt Gabby had brought, I held the top up to me. Scowling, I wondered where the other half was, it seemed to be missing the section that covered the stomach.

Gabby snorted and rolled her eyes. "None of Lisa's clothes are boring. You're going to be noticed."

Reaching for a bunched-up pile of black leather in the bottom of the bag and realizing it was pants, I heaved a sigh. "Whether or not I'm boring is irrelevant. Whether or not I'm likable or nice or good or a Mary Sue is irrelevant. The fact is, I am boring and unlikable by your standards. That's never going to change because I don't subscribe to your standards. So, moving on, is there anything else I can wear other than this?"

Gabby turned her grumpy expression to the scrap of the shirt, black lace bra, and the black leather pants. "What's wrong with this?"

"Nothing," I mumbled, resigned, and scooped them up before turning for the bathroom. "I'll go change."

"Too bad you can't actually change," she called after me. "Too bad putting on Lisa's clothes doesn't also give you some of her badass mojo and rebel spirit."

Unable to help myself, I mumbled, "You belong on Venus, Gabby."

"You mean, because it's, like, the planet of love?" she asked with fake sweetness.

"No. Because it's, *like,* our solar system's analog to hell." And with that, I closed the door to the bathroom and changed. Into my sister.

CHAPTER 2
INTRODUCTION TO ONE-DIMENSIONAL KINEMATICS

"You actually look . . ." Gabby snorted, as though she couldn't believe what she was about to say, and then said, "You're fucking gorgeous."

We'd left the Westin near O'Hare via taxi and were now downtown in the Old Town Triangle area of Chicago, near my parents' brownstone. We'd already visited the hair salon and were now finishing up at the makeup store, during which I'd said less than ten words total. I didn't want to fight with Gabby. Even though we only saw each other about once a year, I was *so tired* of fighting with her.

But now the moment was imminently upon us. Soon we'd be walking the few short blocks home. Time flies when one is fretting about impersonating one's twin sister.

While I'd been getting my "blowout" as Gabby called it, I'd received a call from someone who identified herself as Lisa's lawyer. She'd left a voice message, detailing her strategy for getting Lisa released, the projected timeline—still one week —and that Lisa's phone had been sent via priority to the Chicago house.

What she didn't reveal was why Lisa had been arrested in the first place. I'd tried calling her back, but it went straight to voicemail.

Currently, I was staring at my reflection; at the copious waves of dark brown hair falling over my shoulders, how wearing it down brought out the olive tone in my skin more than wearing it back; at the red stain and gloss accentuating the fullness of my lips; at the dark liner and mascara and eye shadow emphasizing the thickness of my lashes and honey color of my eyes. Paired with the half shirt and leather pants, the entirety of everything together made me look . . .

I look hot.

With a resigned sigh, I accepted that Gabby was correct. "I look like Lisa." Which meant I also looked like our mother. Even at fifty-two, our mother and Lisa were often confused by the press.

"Exactly." She grinned. "Like I said, you're gorgeous. You work out, right?"

I gave her a noncommittal shrug. I swam daily and used a standing desk, which probably didn't meet her definition of working out. Lisa and Gabby, I was pretty sure, both had personal trainers. Theoretically, I wanted a personal trainer—because wouldn't that be nice? Someone to plan my workout, keep it interesting, keep me engaged, think about my health so I didn't have to—but in reality, I didn't want one.

I'd tried it once. The guy touched my arm to reposition it without asking me first. I flinched, which caused me to drop the dumbbell on his foot. I never went back, but I did pay his doctor's bills and sent him a year's supply of protein bars.

She walked to the other side of the chair, and the Sephora external aesthetic-modifier technician (which is what I decided they ought to be called) stepped back, giving Gabby room to inspect my face from a new angle. "Wow"—her eyes swept over me, from the black and white Converse on my feet, up to the leather pants, to my bare midriff, chest, collarbone, neck—"you really do look like her." She sounded surprised.

I bit my tongue so I wouldn't point out the obvious, that we were identical twins. Of course I looked like her. But Gabby wasn't being insulting for once and I had enough on my mind. No need to pick another fight. Hopefully, merely looking like Lisa would be enough to convince Leo's friend that I was Lisa, because I had no idea how to act like a normal person, let alone like my sister.

Gabby cocked her head to the side, her gaze growing thoughtful. "Why don't you wear your hair down ever? Or do your eyes? You're beautiful, or would be if you put in the effort."

"We already talked about this."

"Because you want to be a nerd-girl stereotype, Mary Sue?"

"Human beauty is irrelevant in physics," I mumbled. Not wanting to get into it, but beauty was more than irrelevant. It was a liability.

"Okay, Borg." She lifted that eyebrow. "It doesn't matter."

"Then it has no mass," I said automatically.

"What?"

"If it has no matter, it has no mass."

Her stare was blank. "What are you talking about?"

"It's a physics joke. If something has no matter, then—never mind." I pressed my lips together.

"No more physics jokes!" Gabby stabbed a finger at my shoulder.

Leaning away, I lifted my hands in a show of surrender.

She administered one final exasperated eyebrow lift before turning and giving the external aesthetic-modifier technician instructions on what items we were going to purchase.

Meanwhile, I stood from the chair and tried not to lick my lips. The lip stain wasn't flavored, but the gloss the employee had applied over it tasted like bubble gum. In a word, delicious. I'd had a minor addiction to cherry flavored ChapStick at one point and it had taken a year to break the habit. Thus, I vowed to throw away the bubble gum gloss as soon as I left Chicago.

Or as soon as I landed at LAX.

Or, at the very latest, as soon as I made it back to the hotel in Los Angeles.

Maybe I'd keep it for a week, *what's the harm in that?*

"Let's go, Mona Lisa." Gabby nudged my arm, pushing me toward the door as she handed over the bag with all the makeup. I gave her the side-eye, accepted the products, but said nothing.

Once outside, she nudged me again. "Get it? *Mona Lisa?*"

"Yes." Hil-AR-ious.

My parents had decided naming my brother Leonardo, me Mona, my sister Lisa, and giving us the last name of DaVinci was a really great idea. It could have been worse. They could have named my brother "Michel," me "Ang," and Lisa "Elo," which had been their original plan. Over the course of my life, I'd come to understand that my parents had named their children as a reflection of themselves rather than as a reflection of their hopes for us. Based on my informal sampling of celebrity children, it was always thus for superstars.

I glanced at my watch, it was only 1:00 PM. I considered calling the lawyer to check on the status of Lisa's release even though she'd just touched base a few hours ago and I'd left her a voice message already.

"Your backpack." Gabby flicked my bag. "What are you doing with that? Where will you put it?"

"Um." My steps faltered. "I hadn't thought about that." I was bad at this. *What other lying logistics had I not considered?*

She continued to eye it. "What's inside? Clothes?"

"My computer, research notes, wallet, phone."

Gabby started shaking her head before I'd finished speaking. "Ah, no. You can't bring that to the house. Lisa said Abram was supposed to take her phone as soon as she got there, right? Well then, he'll definitely take—and probably search—your backpack. If he searches your backpack, he'll know you're you and not Lisa. Plus, he'll find your phone, and you're supposed to pretend like you left it behind."

I scowled even though she was right. None of her valid points had occurred to me. "I guess I could go back to O'Hare, bag check it at the Westin, and pick it up on my way out of town next week." I didn't like the thought of being separated from my research or my journal.

She inspected me. "When we get to your block, give it to me. I'll carry it the rest of the way and say it's mine if he asks."

I shifted away from her, distrustful. "What will you do with it?"

She made another of her give-me-a-break faces. "I'll put it in your room—in *Mona's* room—when we go upstairs. By the way, don't forget, your room is Lisa's room. Because you are Lisa and you don't tell physics jokes. You tell peen and poop jokes like all self-respecting feminists."

"You're not going to take it?" I lifted my chin, scrutinizing her dependability in this particular situation. "If you try to take my backpack out of the house, I'll break character right there and tell Abraham the truth."

"You have trust issues. Don't worry, I won't take your precious backpack. It doesn't match my ensemble. And it's Abram, not Abraham."

Speaking of not-Abraham. "Have you met him?"

Gabby gave me a meaningful look and kept on walking. Unfortunately, I'd never been gifted at deciphering meaningful looks.

I tried again. "So you do know him? Or what?"

"Abram?" Gabby blinked, once, hard. "Lisa didn't tell you about Abram?"

I shook my head.

"Leo didn't introduce you? They're, like, best friends."

"No. Leo never mentioned him." When Leo and I talked, it was once every six months and typically focused on him telling me about his upcoming gigs as well as questioning me about girls—how they thought, why they did certain things, etc. He rarely mentioned his friend group, if at all. I'd tried to explain that I didn't understand girls. Or people. He persisted. As such, I did my best to offer generalizable theories about female behavior.

Gabby stopped, blinking several times as though her brain was having difficulty accepting my words. "Oh, Mona. You are in for a *treat.*" Flipping her braids over her shoulder, she'd placed special emphasis on the word *treat.*

I glanced from side to side. "Why? Does he abhor superstring theory?"

She made another face of distaste, or at least tried to. I caught the tail end of a suppressed smile as she said, "I know him a lot better than Lisa does, because sometimes I hang with Leo when he's in town. Abram can be uptight, for sure, but he's also a big flirt. And woman, he's so gorgeous it hurts. I mean, it physically hurts my hoo-hah to look at him in the best, hoo-hah happiest way. He's so gorgeous, I've already forgiven him for being mean to our girl. And he's a musician."

She paused here to bite her bottom lip and look at the sky. "Writes his own music," she moaned, "plays the bass guitar, and the piano, and every other instrument, and he sings. And when he sings, it makes my panties want to melt right off my body. Just *whoop*"—she made a swooping motion with her hand, gesturing from her crotch to the sidewalk—"they want to melt right off."

"Is he smart?"

"Uh, what?" Her gaze flickered over me, leaving me with the impression I'd disappointed her. "Here I am talking about his fineness, and you have to rain on my parade by asking about his brains?"

"Is he smart?" I repeated.

"Does it matter?"

Don't make another physics joke about matter! "It's relevant if his level of intelligence means he'll deduce I'm not Lisa."

"Okay, first of all"—she lifted a finger between us—"you can't speak like that."

"Like what?"

"Don't use words like *deduce* or *relevant.*" Gabby overpronounced the offending words, obviously attempting an impression of me.

"Fine." A flutter of disquiet hit my stomach, which I hid. "Maybe I won't speak at all."

"That works. Don't speak. Or, just give one-word answers. For example: no, yes, what, who, when, whatever. If in doubt, saying *whatever* usually works." Gabby turned back to the sidewalk and we both began walking again.

While interacting with people about nonacademic topics, I'd experienced my fair share of difficulty knowing how to segue into a new subject, or how to end a conversation, or knowing what to say when people over-shared. When I was fifteen, I stumbled across a list of phrases that mostly worked for any occasion, and I'd put them into practice with varying levels of success.

Phrases like *But at what cost?*

Or *In this economy?*

Or *So . . . it has come to this.*

Or *So let it be written, so let it be done.*

Or my personal favorite for when I didn't know how to end a sentence or complete a thought . . . *And then the wolves came.*

These phrases seemed to work best when attempting to diffuse a tense situation or confuse the other person long enough for me to make my escape. Regardless, in the same spirit, I appreciated Gabby's tip. I could default to saying *whatever*. That would be fine.

"Just don't say anything obviously Mona-like," she continued. "You look so much like Lisa, I don't think the possibility that you're Mona will even occur to him."

"But he's met Lisa."

"Yes, but for like five minutes. He doesn't really know her. Lisa only met him the one time, when we crashed one of your brother's parties." She paused here, sighing wistfully, as though remembering the encounter, and then added, "And even though they barely interacted, he was kind of a dick to Lisa."

He'd been "a dick" to her? That triggered the ingrained protective-sister sonar. Regardless of how close (or not) we were, sister-sonar meant I would automatically dislike anyone who'd been "a dick" to Lisa, no matter how much hoo-hah happiness he inspired. Hoo-hah happiness was irrelevant.

"What did he say to her?"

"They didn't really, uh, talk."

Even with my paltry conversation-nuance detection skills, I picked up on the weird way she said *talk.* "Expand on that, please."

Gabby waved her hand in the air, dismissing my question. "Whatever, it's not important. Getting back to your original question, Abram might be smart, I don't know. But he doesn't know Lisa well enough to tell the difference between the two of you *as long as* you don't go around telling physics jokes and asking him to deduce or expand on things."

"Fine." I turned and continued walking toward the house, wondering if Gabby would fly off the handle again if I asked about Lisa's arrest. Not wanting to inspire another round of insults, I tried a different—but related—topic. "So, why Abram? Why did my parents choose Abram to keep an eye on Lisa?"

"Uh, I don't really know. According to Lisa, when I talked to her yesterday on the phone and we discussed the plan, she made it sound like he just happened to be in the right place at the wrong time."

"Was she okay? When you talked to her?"

Gabby sent me a sharp, irritated glare. "How do you think she was?"

Okay, fine. *Don't ask Gabby about Lisa.* Got it.

"Anyway." Gabby flipped her braids, her tone growing lofty. "Lisa said that your brother was supposed to be at the house this summer, but that he went down to Florida for a thing."

"I think he has work in Miami." The last time I spoke to Leo, he'd mentioned spending part of the summer in south Florida, playing a few clubs.

"Yeah, something like that. So, I guess your guardian lady was supposed to step in and watch the house. What's her name?"

"You mean Dr. Steward? She can't, I think she's in China." I was nineteen now, but the day after I'd turned eighteen, Dr. Steward had taken off to travel the world. She'd been planning the trip for as long as I'd known her.

"That's right. So, until Dr. Steward comes back, your brother suggested Abram keep an eye on the house. I think he's being paid to house-sit. So when your parents issued the ultimatum that Lisa had to go home and wait for their return, they asked Leo to ask Abram to keep an eye on her."

"Do they even know Abram? Why do they trust him?" I felt like I already knew my parents well enough to know the answers to these questions. But I also felt like they needed to be asked, just in case this would be the one time my parents surprised me.

"I don't know." Gabby shrugged. "I guess they figure, if your brother trusts the guy . . ."

I released an irritated puff of a breath, shaking my head, now absorbed in second-hand anger on my sister's behalf. "That's great."

So, not surprised.

It had been the same way with Dr. Steward. The woman was a friend of a friend, an adjunct professor at a college in the Northeast. They hadn't even interviewed her in person before sending me to the Northeast to live with her full time as a teenager. She'd been . . . fine. Strict and considerably more interested in the money she was banking than in me as a person, but fine.

"What?" Gabby poked me lightly, presumably to get my attention. "Leo wouldn't recommend someone to watch the house who isn't trustworthy, would he? Plus, like I said, they're best friends. *Plus*, like I said, Abram is super uptight."

"And uptight is trustworthy?"

"Exactly. Just look at you."

I grumbled but said nothing to that.

Earlier, Gabby had said, *He was kind of a dick to Lisa,* and yet she saw nothing wrong with this guy keeping an eye on Lisa?

Nothing about Abram, or spending the next week in the same house as him, sounded treat-like to me. Another almost-stranger my parents trusted with one of their daughters. Granted, this guy was Leo's good friend, and Leo did seem to have better judgment about people than either me or Lisa.

Am I really going to do this?

Yes. Yes, I was. We were about two blocks away now, I wasn't a snitch, my sister needed help, and I'd promised. There was only one logical path forward.

But mostly, I refused to be another person in Lisa's life who let her down. Gripping my bag's strap tighter, I imagined the moment I'd have to hand it over to Gabby. Just the thought of trusting her with my backpack for any length of time was making my hands sweat.

"What?" She bumped me with her shoulder.

I shrugged, irritated I couldn't wipe my hands on my pants. Wiping sweaty hands on leather just made for visibly wet leather and still sweaty hands, and wet leather was never a good idea. Never.

"What is that face you're making?" She pointed to my face with her index finger, moving it in a circle.

"I don't know, I can't see myself." There was just something about Gabby that grated, brought my emotions closer to the surface. Or perhaps it was this entire situation. Whatever it was, I couldn't wait for this week to be over and return to the world I understood.

"Here, I'll make the face you're making." Gabby caught my arm and I immediately maneuvered out of her grip. My reflexive reaction didn't seem to bother her, or she didn't notice. Regardless, she cleared her features of all expression except her eyes. She'd narrowed them subtly, and seemed to peer at the world with a hypercritical coolness. "This is the face," she said robotically.

Trying to stuff my fingers into my pockets and failing—because the pockets were sewn shut—I scratched the elbow she'd grabbed and started walking again. "It's just my face."

"Well don't make that face around Abram. Lisa doesn't make that face."

"Okay." *How the hell am I going to do this for a week?* I pasted on a big, fake smile. "Is this better?"

"God, no. Don't do that either." She looked horrified. "What the hell was that? Was that a smile? Was that you smiling?"

I neither confirmed nor denied her speculation, keeping my attention forward as I twisted my lips to the side, trying not to smile for real. Gabby was a nebulous assemblage of unscrupulousness and exasperating nonsense, and we'd likely never be friends again, but she was undoubtedly charming when she wanted to be. There'd always been something about her timing, her delivery, that veered into the territory of funny.

"Okay, hand it over." She touched my arm again, stopping me, and this time I had the wherewithal to not yank out of her grip. Instead, I removed my backpack with *extreme reluctance*, which elicited an eye roll from Gabby. "Oh, give it a break, Mona. Just hurry up. I have other things to do today."

With continued *extreme reluctance*, I eventually handed her the backpack. She carried it the rest of the way to our brownstone while I continued to carry the makeup bag. Every so often, she'd pretend like she was going to toss my backpack in the road, snickering when I tensed.

"Relax, *Lisa.* I wouldn't do anything to jeopardize the happiness and well-being of my BFF."

Gabby batted her eyelashes as I punched in the gate code, all nerves and thumbs. Our brownstone had a tall cast-iron fence facing the sidewalk. I wasn't surprised by the lack of paparazzi. Everyone assumed the DaVinci family members people cared to gossip about—my parents and my brother mostly, me sometimes, Lisa only when she did something crazy—were elsewhere.

After three attempts, I finally got the code right and opened the gate for her. She preceded me up the stairs while I glared at the back of her head. When we reached the door, I reached for my backpack. She twisted away.

"What are you doing?" she hissed.

"I need my keys to open the door."

"No. Your keys aren't in my ugly backpack, *Lisa.*" Gabby sent yet another meaningful look to the house.

Oh. That's right.

Giving my backpack one more longing look, I stepped away from Gabby and rang the doorbell.

"Good." She moved closer to me as we waited for this Abram person to open the door. "That face you're making is very Lisa. Pouty. I approve."

Before I could respond, the door swung open, revealing . . . well, revealing an extremely handsome guy. Upon my initial cursory inspection, I noted that he was tall, had brown hair and eyes, was both startlingly attractive and visibly displeased. One might go so far as to call him irked.

The guy—dressed in a faded black T-shirt and worn blue jeans—pushed a hand into a fall of shiny hair, lifting the long strands away from his forehead. Most men look sloppy in faded T's and worn jeans. But he did not. He looked hot.

Oooohhhh. Okay, I get it.

Yep. I understood at once what Gabby had meant. Abram had won the genetics lottery. Or Powerball. Or whatever. The point was, this guy probably received congratulations cards for his face. *Noted.*

"Lisa," he said to me. A muscle at his defined jaw jumped, visible even beneath the few days of stubble covering the lower half of his face.

"You're Abram," I said, because who else could he be? This statement was made to his distracting chin. His chin—like the rest of him—was pleasingly formed, but his stubble was remarkable. A shade lighter than the hair on his head, it was just as thick.

If he ignored it, he'd likely have a hell of a wizard beard in a matter of months. The only thing I truly envied men was their ability to grow wizard beards.

Lifting my hand for a shake, Gabby intercepted it before I could bring my fingers parallel to the ground. "As always, a real pleasure to look at you, Abram. What do you have to eat? Lisa left all her stuff behind—including her wallet—so we're starving." Using my mistakenly offered hand, she pulled me inside the house, brushing past Abram.

Oh, right. Why would Lisa shake his hand? I sent Gabby a glance of gratitude and wondered again how in the helium I was going to fake being not-me for a week.

"There's leftover Chinese food and pizza in the fridge." His tone blatantly hostile, providing additional proof that he wasn't happy to see us.

Gabby steered me into the kitchen and sat me on a stool, giving me a hard look before turning for the fridge and pulling out a box of pizza. I placed the Sephora bag on the counter and waited, unsure what to do. If I'd been me—Mona, not Lisa—I'd have made myself mint tea. But I had no idea if drinking mint tea was in character for Lisa. *Maybe I should pour myself a glass of whiskey?*

While I was stuck debating my beverage choice, Abram appeared in the doorway. He opted to hover by the entrance to the kitchen, leaning his back against the doorframe and shifting his irked glare from me to Gabby. Even scowling and visibly inimical, he was hot.

"Where's your phone?" he asked, his attention coming back to me, lifting his chin as his eyelids drooped.

"Like I said, gorgeous"—Gabby walked into his line of sight, blocking me from view—"she left all her shit behind, even her phone."

"How'd she board a plane if she left everything behind?"

I was used to people talking about me in the third person, like I was a calculator. *These numbers make no sense, how did she arrive at these values? Did she do this part in her head?*

It didn't bother me.

"Well, if you'd let me finish, I would tell you. She left it all at security. She was almost late for the plane and had to run to the gate," Gabby lied smoothly, making me envious. "We'd already arranged to have me pick her up from O'Hare. Don't fret, though. My mother's secretary called the airport and they're sending her phone and stuff. It should get here tomorrow or the day after."

Gabby's lies were so persuasive, spoken with such artlessness, I almost believed her.

Conclusion: I required lying lessons.

Abram leaned to the side to peer around my sister's friend, his eyelids still droopy, his gaze still irritated and distrustful. "You don't have your phone?"

One-word answers. One-word answers. One-word answers.

"Nope," I said, both proud and disgusted with myself for the lie. Needing a distraction, I picked through the fruit bowl in the center of the island, hunting for the perfect apple.

In my peripheral vision, I watched as Abram stepped away from the door, walked around Gabby, and stopped four feet from me just as I took a bite from the apple. *Honeycrisp.* I chewed and he studied my face. Meeting his inspection directly, I concentrated on the taste of the apple and hoped I was making a Lisa-face.

Lifting his chin toward the Sephora bag, he asked, "You had money for makeup but not for food?"

"Priorities, Abram," Gabby spoke for me.

He ignored her. "You don't mind if I search you for it?"

Before I could catch it, I felt my eyes squint and my lips curve into an unfriendly sneer. *Like hell* he was putting his hands on me. I didn't care who he was, whether or not he was Leo's best friend, or whether my parents trusted him, I didn't like being touched by *anyone.*

Abram's glare sharpened, as though my reaction surprised him, or he found it confusing.

But Gabby laughed, taking the stool next to mine. "Yeah, sure. Go for it, handsome. Where is she going to hide a cell phone in that outfit? But, okay. I'm sure you'll both probably enjoy it, so go ahead."

I glanced down at myself, at my boobs on display in the tank top and black lace bra, my bare stomach, and the second skin of Lisa's leather pants. Once again, Gabby made a good point. There was nowhere to hide anything in these clothes, the pockets were sewn shut for Bohr's sake.

Returning my attention to Abram, it was my turn to be surprised. An expression of mild repugnance passed over his features as he looked me over, like the thought of giving "Lisa" a pat down was just as distasteful to him as it was to me.

Well, okay then. Maybe nineteen-year-old, olive-skinned, heavily makeupped, athletic with big boobs, long black hair, and brown eyes wasn't his type.

Crossing his arms, Abram leveled me with a severe stare. "As soon as your stuff arrives, you give me the phone."

"Fine." I shrugged and took another bite of the apple while Gabby selected a piece of pizza from the box.

My calm capitulation seemed to increase his irritation. "No drinking. No drugs. No parties. No sneaking out. No one comes over until your parents get home in two weeks, or Dr. Steward arrives, whichever comes first. And no leaving the house without me. Anywhere you go, I go."

I stared at him evenly, because—other than having him escort me out of the house— he was basically reading my Christmas list. Total seclusion and quiet for the next week? Where did I sign up?

But staring evenly with no reaction must've been the wrong thing to do, because the force of his eye-squint escalated, his gaze flickering over me with suspicion. "Did you hear me?"

"Yep," I said, wishing I'd thought ahead and brought books to read. I'd already read all the ones here. *Maybe I can go to the library? Wait, no. Shoot! No card. Bookstore?*

Abram continued to examine me, his frown intensifying, his suspicion now edged with confusion. "Are you . . . feeling okay?"

I sensed Gabby's restlessness before she stood from her stool and stepped in front of me again. "Okay, Dad. What are you, like only three or four years older than us?" She huffed, rolled her eyes. "Whatever. We got it. No fun."

Successfully disguising my disapproval at the petulance in her tone and the instinct to distance myself from her puerile response, I continued to give him my very best blank-face. To be clear, I'm not against sass or sarcasm. Both definitely have their place. But Gabby's dramatics felt immature and superfluous.

Given the situation, the fact that Lisa was currently in jail and had been lying about being with Tyler for months, this Abram guy's rules made complete sense. If I'd been left in charge, I would have set similar limitations.

"We'll just be upstairs." She pulled me from the stool, and I had to consciously force myself to allow Gabby to lead me toward the back stairs. "And just so we're clear, we'll be doing absolutely *nothing*," Gabby spat, the venom in her voice—again— striking me as childish.

"No." Abram shook his head, moving quickly to block our path. "No, Gabby. You're not staying."

I was relieved to see the earlier suspicion and confusion pointed at me had faded, replaced with a hard look for Lisa's friend.

"What?" she screeched, her mouth falling open. "What the hell, Abram? You're cute, but you're not *that* cute. Stop being such an asshole."

Abram rubbed his face tiredly, his jaw ticking again, his eyes now almost black. "Do you think I want to spend the next few weeks babysitting Lisa? No. I'm doing this as a favor to Leo." He said this last part to me, his animosity a palpable thing. "So, if you could just, you know, not do anything stupid or crazy for the next two weeks, that would be really great."

"Wanting to talk to her best friend is neither stupid or crazy." Gabby inched us closer to the back stairs.

He moved to counter our progress, a big wall of lean muscle and unyielding determination. "Gabby, time for you to go."

"Lisa isn't a prisoner!"

I tried not to smirk at the irony of Gabby's statement.

"Gabby," he said, the single word a warning.

"This is such bullshit!" she continued to protest, but it was evident Abram wasn't going to bend.

Turning my arm, I encircled Gabby's wrist with my fingers and tugged her lightly, encouraging her to face me. "You should go. I'll be fine."

Her moss-green eyes moved between mine, hot with anger, but also tempered with worry. She made a frustrated sound in the back of her throat, like a grunt, and pulled me into a hug.

I stiffened in her embrace, baffled by the action and feeling a familiar reflexive suffocation, but then she whispered, "The backpack is under the stool I was sitting on. Don't let him see it or we're all dead."

Gabby released me and leaned away to administer one of her meaningful looks. This one I read perfectly.

Nodding once, she turned back to Abram, looked him over, and promptly walked to the kitchen exit. "You're still hot, Abram, even if you are an uptight asshole."

"I'll walk her out, you stay here." He exhaled a harassed-sounding breath, turned, and followed Gabby from the kitchen.

I watched them go. As soon as they were out of sight, I dashed to my backpack, grabbed it, and . . . hesitated. Would I have enough time to run up to my room, deposit it within, and be back in the kitchen before Abram returned?

Probably not.

Which meant I needed to hide it before he returned. There were many, many options as the kitchen was expansive. Did I hide it in the pantry? Or beneath the double oven? Or above the fridge? The unmistakable sound of the front door shutting made my decision for me. The pantry was closest, so that would be its home for the time being.

Rushing, I shoved the bag behind baking supplies on the bottom shelf. Unless Abraham—*Abram? Abraham? Damn. Which one was it?*—was secretly a pastry chef, I felt like it was the safest place.

"Lisa?"

He'd returned.

Panicking, I reached blindly for a bag of something on the snack shelf and poked my head out of the walk-in pantry.

Following Gabby's advice, I said, "What?"

The guy's gaze found me, his slashing dark eyebrows pulled low, giving him an air of being thoroughly . . . *I'm going to go with the word* irked *again.* "What are you doing?"

"Getting"—I held out the bag of whatever I'd grabbed in front of me, reading the package—"prunes."

Ah jeez. Prunes. Why'd it have to be prunes?

He blinked. Some of the severity in his glare seemed to dissolve into confusion as he looked between me and the bag. "Prunes."

I nodded. What else could I do? I was holding a package of prunes, now I just had to *commit* to the package of prunes.

"Yes. Prunes. As you see." Tearing it open and walking out of the pantry, I reached into the bag. Slimy, larger versions of raisins were waiting for me inside.

"You're going to eat . . . prunes?"

I nodded, struggling to find a lie that sounded as plausible as Gabby's had been. "You don't know anyone who eats prunes?"

"My grandpa," he said flatly, still splitting his attention between me and the bag.

"Smart man. They're high in fiber."

"Fiber."

"Yes." I lifted the bag to scan the nutritional information, hoping they were actually high in fiber. Though I had a suspicion, I wasn't 100 percent certain. After reading the package, I released a relieved breath. "Twelve grams of fiber per serving. It says so right here. That's a lot. And I need my fiber."

"Why do you need fiber?"

"Flying makes me"—*oh God, don't say it!*—"makes me"—*oh noes, here it comes*—"constipated." I nodded at my own assertion, quickly stuffing my mouth with three prunes so I wouldn't be able to speak.

His confusion persisted, but he said nothing. Holding perfectly still, he watched me with a frown that teetered on dismayed.

Meanwhile, I had to stop chewing. Each prune had a pit. *Shit.* There existed no graceful way to remove pits from one's mouth. I would have to spit the pits.

Holding his gaze, which now seemed to be fascinated in addition to dismayed, I spit the pit into my palm. I then gave him a tight-lipped smile while I continued to chew, because that's what I did when people stared at me. *I wonder what Lisa does when people stare at her?*

One of his eyebrows lifted and he gave his head a subtle shake. "Okay. Right." He glanced at the ceiling and then around the kitchen, as though trying to figure out where he was. "I'm going to have to call your parents' assistant, Dr. Steward, right? And let her know you don't have your phone."

Luckily, I was still chewing the prunes, which gave me a few moments to think about how to respond to this statement. As an aside, carrying around a bag of food and stuffing my face whenever he asked me a question was a solid plan. It would give me an opportunity to stall, to think.

Stating that Dr. Steward was my parents' assistant wasn't entirely accurate. More like, she had incidentally become one of the various team of people my parents called upon when they needed a problem handled. But I didn't need to clarify that with Abram. Trying to explain the complexities of staff and their unofficial roles to people who didn't understand celebrity was time-consuming and typically yielded even more confusion.

Moving on.

Even though I dreaded the possibility of speaking to either of my parents while pretending to be Lisa, his logic made sense. I couldn't see any way of talking him out of calling Dr. Steward as I could form no compelling—i.e. logical—argument against it.

Therefore, after swallowing, I said, "Whatever, Abe."

I'd decided to say *whatever* since Gabby had indicated it would always be a safe choice, and I'd called him Abe since it was short for both Abram and Abraham. For the life of me, I couldn't remember which was correct. I'd never been good at remembering names. Or remembering faces. Or people.

This must've been precisely the right thing to say—and by that, I mean it was the wrong thing to say but in the right way—because his eyelids lowered again to half-mast and his mouth flattened. He looked perturbed, which was good. Perturbed was much better than suspicious or confused. Perturbed meant he saw me as Lisa and not as a potential imposter. So, in summary, *woot woot!*

"Forget it," he grumbled, turning from me and running a hand through his longish brown hair. "Just, hand over the phone when it arrives, okay? I'll be in the basement. Let me know if you need to go out for anything. Otherwise just . . ." His gaze flickered to me and I spotted that same hint of repugnance as before, like he found my presence unsavory. "Just don't do anything stupid."

I wanted to respond with *In this economy?* But instead, and without thinking too much about it, I saluted, still gripping the pits in my hand. Why I did this, I had no idea. Luckily, the action didn't faze him. With one last irked look, Abe walked out of the kitchen, leaving me with my prunes, their pits, and an immediate sense of relief.

CHAPTER 3
DISPLACEMENT

Prunes would be my constant companion for the next week, the means by which I delayed answering or speaking to Abe. *Good plan.* The fiber consumed would be a bonus.

Tossing the pits in the garbage and rinsing my hand, I zipped closed the bag, tucked it under my arm, and glanced at the pantry. The backpack would stay put for now. Abe didn't trust Lisa. Best to move the bag in the middle of the night, or at some point when I could be 97 percent certain we wouldn't cross paths.

So, what did I do now? Read? Exercise? Going for a walk was out of the question. Watch a movie in the theater downstairs? I hadn't seen a movie or TV show in months, but Abe said he'd be in the basement, so that was a no-go . . . *How about a shower?*

Yes. Shower. A shower was the answer. I hadn't showered since yesterday. Plane rides didn't make me constipated, they made me feel grimy. A shower sounded divine. Hydra environments were deeply within my wheelhouse.

And yet, I was faced with a quandary: I wanted a shower, yet I couldn't get any part of my head wet. Gabby had been adamant about not allowing Abe to see me without Lisa's hair and makeup. Protecting my hair and face from the shower spray was necessary.

A waterproof implement was in order, one that allowed me to see and breathe, and ideally large enough to cover my entire head. A shower cap wouldn't cut it, I had too much hair and by design it left the face exposed. The more I thought the issue over,

37

the more I realized I would need something reusable. I didn't want to have to reapply makeup all the time, or redo my hair.

Conclusion: What I needed was a shower helmet. I was fairly certain a shower helmet didn't exist. I'd have to make one.

Biting the inside of my bottom lip, I searched the kitchen drawers closest to the gas range and found what I sought: aluminum foil, parchment paper, tape, scissors, and plastic wrap. Laying my materials on the kitchen island, I used the aluminum foil to make a mold of my entire head. I lined the inside with parchment paper, cut away spaces for my eyes and mouth, and finally covered the outside with several layers of plastic wrap.

I did have to make a few minor tweaks: air holes, increasing the size of the eye area for better range of vision, expanding the crown section so that I could wear my hair up and out of the way. Once I was satisfied, I carried my shower helmet and bag of new makeup to the bathroom, making a pit stop in my actual room first to grab underwear.

When the house was remodeled before we moved in, my parents had installed an elevator. Since my room was only one flight up, I typically took the stairs. Lisa and I shared the bathroom off the main hall on the second floor.

Leo's room was on the third floor, he shared his bathroom with the two guest rooms on that level. My parents had their own bathroom and living space on the fourth floor, a giant master suite that took up the entire level.

Stripping out of the tank top and leather pants, I twisted my hair into a bun and fitted the waterproof helmet into place. Three minutes into my shower, I was generally pleased with the results of my efforts. The helmet succeeded in its purpose. My hair and face were dry. The only downside was the interior acoustics, which seemed to amplify the sound of the shower tenfold. Ah well. I would have to make notes for a second prototype, should the need arise.

Toweling off, I studied my image in the mirror as best I could given the limitations of the helmet, and debated how to best dry the contraption. Leaving it outside was the obvious choice, just not in direct sunlight. I didn't want the plastic to melt. The small balcony off my room should work and had the added bonus of giving me an excuse to access "Mona's room" whenever I wanted.

Decision made, I pulled on my underwear. I left the helmet on—enjoying the novelty of feeling like a Storm Trooper, or perhaps a member of Daft Punk—wrapped an oversized towel around myself, and opened the bathroom door just in time to almost collide with Abe. But we didn't collide, thanks to my eyeholes and his veering to the left at the last minute.

"What the hell?" he said, staring at me aghast. "What are you doing?"

Bah! I forgot my prunes.

Lifting the towel closer to my neck, I met his stunned gaze through the plastic sheeting of my helmet, and debated how best to answer. In the end, I decided the truth would have to do. "I'm walking to my room. What are you doing?"

"No, I mean, what are you wearing?"

I glanced down at myself. "A towel and underwear."

"No. On your head." He touched his temple and I mimicked the movement, my fingers coming in contact with the plastic outer layer. "What's that thing on your head? Is that aluminum foil?"

"Oh. It's for the shower. To keep my hair dry and, you know, my face also." An image of me, of what I looked like in the helmet, flashed into my brain. I guess I looked silly. Removing it, I gave him another of my tight smiles. "Is that better?"

I could see him more clearly now. His forehead was scrunched, like I, or my shower helmet, or both of us together were inconceivable.

"That's actually . . ." His expression cleared and he blinked, shifting back a step as though to get a better look at me. "That's actually really smart."

Now I frowned at him. The way he'd said *smart* irritated me on my sister's behalf, as though the mere idea of me—Lisa—doing anything smart was outside his understanding of reality.

So I lifted my chin and said, "Well, *you* would know."

He must've detected the undercurrent of sarcasm in my tone because his head moved back an inch on his neck, his gaze flickering over me. "What?"

"Clearly, you're a foremost expert on what qualifies as 'smart.'" I tugged my towel higher.

"Are you"—his eyes narrowed—"are you giving me shit for complimenting your —your—"

"Shower helmet."

Abe pressed his lips together in an obvious attempt to curb a smile, but the presence of faint indents on either side of his mouth, the beginning of dimples, betrayed him.

"Shower helmet," he said, eyes—which I'd just this second realized were the color of amber when he wasn't irked—glinted with amusement.

"Yes, I'm giving you shit regarding your paltry compliment about my shower helmet, because it was wholly eclipsed by your incredulity that I am capable of doing something 'smart.'"

He gave up the fight against his grin. "Oh? Really?"

"Yes. Really."

Abe huffed a disbelieving laugh, looking at me like I was a puzzle. "Well then, you know what would've been *actually* smart?"

"Please enlighten me."

"Taking a bath."

I opened my mouth to volley a new sarcasm, but then promptly snapped it shut, blinking in astonishment. He was right. Taking a bath would have been the simplest and smartest course of action. But taking a bath hadn't occurred to me. I hadn't taken a bath since Lisa and I'd taken them together as children.

"Unless you don't like baths." Abe's left eyebrow tilted upward a hint, as did his mouth.

Scowling, because I wasn't going to admit that taking a bath hadn't occurred to me, I deflected by asking, "Why are you here? I thought you were in the basement."

"I'm staying in one of the guest rooms on the third floor, I'm on my way up."

"Oh. That makes . . . sense."

We traded stares for several seconds, neither of us moving. I debated what to do or say while I watched all the good humor slowly leach from his features, leaving a mantle of renewed hostility. My stomach fluttered, startling me, and I pressed a hand against it.

You're having butterflies because he's pretty, I told myself. But the hurried explanation felt woefully inadequate.

Let the record show, Abe really was extremely attractive in a cool, aloof, tall, dark, and handsome kind of way—if you go for that. For some strange reason, I couldn't help but compare him to Dr. Poe Payton, who was also extremely attractive. But although Poe was tall, dark, and handsome—objectively, perhaps even more handsome than Abe—he wasn't aloof. He was friendly and brilliant.

That's the problem, a voice inside my head informed me, *has anyone brilliant ever been nice to you without having an ulterior motive?*

Releasing a silent sigh, I wallowed for a split second in the sudden cold nausea curdling my stomach, fighting a duel with the flutters. It might have been the hastily eaten prunes, but I didn't think so. More likely, it was the realization that I was more inclined to trust someone who disliked me than someone who liked me.

Which was probably why despite Abe's apparent dislike for all things Lisa (and therefore me) in that moment, while standing so close to his handsomeness, I felt a small kinship with Gabby and her hoo-hah. Abe openly disliked me/Lisa, and I found him and his dislike attractive as evidenced by the increasing fluttery activity in my abdomen. How messed up was that?

Needing to break the moment, I considered saying one of my anytime phrases.

My first instinct was to use *Is this why fate brought us together?* but immediately dismissed it as an option. I usually employed this one when I spotted something I wanted, like chocolate gelato or fingerless gloves. So, nah.

Perhaps, *Be that as it may, still may it be as it may be?* Eh. No. Too random and too much time had passed with us just staring at each other.

Eventually, I channeled Lisa and flicked my wrist, moving my hand in a dismissive out-of-the-way motion I'd seen her use the last time we were together.

"Move. You're in my way."

His lips curved, definitely more of a smirk than a smile. Hinted at dimples made an appearance, deeper on the left side than on the right. But that might've been because his mouth hitched higher on that side. Licking his lips, his eyes dropped to the ground, the radiant amber irises now hidden by his long black lashes. He stepped to the side, lifting his arm in a go-right-ahead gesture.

So I did. I walked to my room. I opened the door. And then I closed it.

Not three seconds later, he knocked.

Gritting my teeth, I opened it, once again coming face-to-face with his smirking smile, dimples, and amber eyes, which—for the record—held no amusement.

"What do you want?"

"Isn't this your sister's room?" Abe crossed his arms and lifted a dark, challenging, irked eyebrow.

Ah! I was in my room! But that was okay because of my shower helmet plan. Which meant I didn't even need to lie.

"This is Mona's room." *Truth.* "This room also has a balcony, which I plan to use to dry my shower helmet." *Also truth.* Turning from him, I walked to the single French door leading to the small balcony and unlocked it, opened it, and placed the helmet under the small table so it wouldn't get direct sunlight.

Shutting the door to the balcony, I was surprised to see that Abe had followed me into my room. His gaze moved over the interior of the space, seemingly taking in or cataloguing the objects within. His unexpected inspection made me look around as well. I attempted to view my sanctuary from his perspective. What must it look like to a stranger?

The walls were white. I liked rooms painted white, especially if I spent any period of time within the room. Books. Lots of books on four giant shelves lining the wall closest to the door. Two floor-to-ceiling windows on either side of the French door dominated the far side and flooded the space with light. The bed was twin-sized with a night-sky print comforter and one white pillow. I preferred the small footprint of a twin over surrendering valuable floor space to a larger bed. A drafting table that served as my desk sat against the fourth wall. Books and papers were stacked beneath.

"'Heisenberg may have slept here,'" Abe read the sign over my bed, his tone thoughtful. "What does that mean?"

Since I didn't have my prunes, I didn't pause to think before asking, "You're *uncertain* who Heisenberg is?" and then immediately grimaced, because *no physics jokes.*

Abe's gaze moved to mine. "The name sounds familiar."

"Have you ever taken chemistry? Or physics?"

"Yeah. In high school."

It was on the tip of my tongue to explain who Heisenberg was, and that the Heisenberg Uncertainty Principle related to the fact that everything in the universe behaves like both a particle and a wave at the same time, which meant no one can ever simultaneously know the exact position and the exact speed of an object at any given time. Furthermore, just the act of measuring anything—or attempting to measure— changes the object being measured.

But then I remembered I was Lisa. I was Lisa, not Mona. And Lisa had never understood or cared why the sign over my bed was funny.

Taking a breath, I swallowed and shrugged. "It probably has to do with something like that. Mona likes, uh, physics. A lot."

"Leo said she went to some big deal, Ivy League school."

I cleared my throat and nodded once. "Correct."

"When she was fourteen?" Abe's gaze moved back to the sign.

"Fifteen." The fine hairs on the back of my neck prickled, probably because I was still standing around wearing nothing but a towel and undies. But maybe also because I was discussing myself like I wasn't me.

He made a dismissive, scoffing sound and moved to leave. "That would suck."

I scowled at the back of his head, following him into the hall and catching myself before saying, *Pardon?*

Instead I said, "What?"

He glanced at me, his expression one of clear aversion to the direction of his thoughts. "Going to college at *fifteen*? Never getting to experience high school? That would have sucked."

My throat felt oddly tight and a bizarre restlessness stirred in my chest. "Some people say that high school sucks." I didn't know why I was arguing with him about this. I should have been avoiding him. And getting dressed.

"High school does suck." Abe nodded, tilting his head to the side, his eyes growing fuzzy as though he was recalling a specific memory. "But fifteen-year-olds are still kids. High school is your last chance to make mistakes without huge adult consequences. Missing out on that chance would suck. That's like losing four years of your childhood."

His gaze returned to mine and seemed to be guileless, as though we were just two random people having a random conversation about a random topic where neither of us had an emotional investment. It was the first time since I'd arrived an hour ago that he'd looked at me without being irritated, or confused, or—as he'd done just moments ago upon finding me with my shower helmet—freaked out with a hint of good humor.

Meanwhile, I was still scowling.

Abe blinked, apparently what he saw on my face confused him. But then his expression cleared, as though he'd just realized something significant.

"You dropped out of high school." He said this with no malice, but rather as though this fact—Lisa dropping out of high school—explained my persistent scowl.

"Yes," I said stiffly. And just for good measure, I added, "Whatever." *So . . . it has come to this.*

His gaze moved over me, assessing and yet surprisingly free of judgment. These amber eyes of his were making me tremendously self-conscious as I sensed something new behind his inspection. Something like interest, but not quite. Whatever the something was, it also made me acutely cognizant that I was wearing just a towel and underwear.

I gathered a deep breath, about to walk around him to Lisa's room, when he said quietly, "So did I."

"What?"

"I dropped out of high school."

I flinched, astonished. "You—you did?"

He nodded, biting his lower lip, a faint smile in his eyes. "That surprises you?"

"Why would you do that?" I asked this as myself, as Mona, because dropping out of school made no sense to me. To have access to knowledge and to reject it made no logical sense.

Abe's left dimple appeared, his pretty eyes—yes, they were pretty, but *alluring* might have been a more fitting word—seemed to glow.

Instead of answering, he countered, "Why did you drop out?"

"My parents couldn't find a high school that would take—take me. I was kicked out of ten schools by my junior year." I thought everyone knew this story. It had been in all the papers.

He made a low whistling sound. "Ten?"

I nodded, remembering the phone call I'd had with Lisa after number ten. She'd seemed proud, like it had been an accomplishment. I didn't understand her.

"So, technically, I didn't drop out," I said, repeating what she'd said to me at the time.

"Right." He looked less than impressed, which echoed how I'd felt about Lisa's statement.

Before I could catch the impulse, I rolled my eyes, a small smile tugging at my lips, forgetting for a moment that we weren't commiserating over Lisa's recklessness because, you know, I *was* Lisa.

Abe looked at me like I'd again surprised him.

Oh. Oh no. He thinks I'm being self-deprecating. Yikes.

"Yeah. Well. I'm the funniest person I know, and then the wolves came." I forced a light laugh, knowing I'd messed up. Lisa was many things, but I'd never known her to be self-deprecating. If there was one thing my sister took too seriously in this world, it was herself.

"Wolves?" His gaze traveled over my face, a smile lingering even though his eyebrows had pulled together. The dichotomy of his expression had me wondering whether he was enjoying our conversation, or if perhaps he was confused about the fact that he was enjoying our conversation.

"Anyway." I took a step to the side, and then another. I needed to extract myself. I needed the prunes to chew on before I could be trusted to speak. "I'm cold. I need clothes. Goodbye."

With that, I crossed to Lisa's room, stepped inside, and shut the door behind me. I counted seven seconds until I heard footsteps on the stairway leading up. Shaking my head at how incompetent I was at lying, I moved to Lisa's dresser.

As I searched for something to wear, I admitted to myself that I failed at pretending to be someone else. Everything that had just happened—except for me saying *whatever* and flicking my wrist at him—had been completely out of character for my sister.

Avoiding Abe was the only way to salvage this week and allow Lisa to slip back into the house without raising suspicion.

Avoidance. I would avoid him.

Complete avoidance.

Yep.

CHAPTER 4
VECTORS, SCALARS, AND COORDINATE SYSTEMS

When someone asks where I'm from, I say Chicago. I'd spent less than one sixty-fourth of my life here and yet, of all my parents' houses all over the world, the Chicago house was the one I considered home. Perhaps because my parents were both born on the outskirts of Chicago, or maybe because it was also the only house without permanent live-in caretakers. As a kid, I'd thought the other houses belonged to the caretakers and we were merely their guests.

Which is all to say, I knew where the best hide-and-seek places were in the house.

Upon waking, I checked my hair—as far as I could tell, it still looked fine—reapplied the makeup as faithfully as I could, and crept from Lisa's room early in the morning. The questions I'd been asking myself since hopping on a plane thirty-six hours ago still whispering between my ears, *Are you really doing this? Are you really going to impersonate Lisa for up to a week? Are you really okay with pretending to be her?*

I had no answers. Furthermore, I was frustrated that the questions persisted. The decision had been made. Lisa was in trouble and probably scared out of her mind. As much as the situation gave me a sour stomach, I was more worried for her than for me.

And anyway, allowing myself to be swept up and along by momentum was normal for me. Momentum was good. It made sense. It existed for a reason. It helped people stay on the right path.

Second-guessing my decisions was not normal. It, the impersonation of my sister and the lies, was already happening. I was already doing this. I'd promised my sister. I'd *promised*. And I never snitched.

So, defeating the impulse to check my phone and call the lawyer, I hid.

My hiding spot was the mudroom off the back door. The light was excellent for reading, and it housed a cozy cushioned cubby built into the wall, a space that had likely been a small closet at one point. There was no chance of being happened upon as no one used the back door.

I read my book, *Moby Dick*, while ignoring the whispers of doubt until they faded. I also listened for Abe. Once he was up and about, I'd make an appearance in the kitchen just after he finished his breakfast/when he was on his way out. That way he would see me, but there'd be no loitering and or making of further chitchat.

Maybe I'd pretend to be on my way to the bathroom.

A while later—a long while later—I came up for breath and glanced at my surroundings. The earlier post-dawn diffused glow now felt like midmorning sunlight. I frowned, worried that Abe had grabbed breakfast at some point, I hadn't heard him, and I'd neglected to check in. Chewing the inside of my bottom lip, I set my book to the side and tiptoed to the kitchen, searching for any sign of life and checking the clock mounted above the wood-fired pizza oven.

I experienced a shock. It was now past 1:00 PM. I then experienced a spike of alarm, hoping Ahab hadn't gone looking for Lisa, given up, and called my parents.

"Doom, doom, doom!" I murmured, dashing toward the back stairs. I would have to find Ahab and convince him I'd been home all morning, and then I'd—

"Did you just say 'doom doom doom,' or 'zoom, zoom, zoom'?"

I stopped short and was forced to take several steps backward. Ahab was walking down the stairs, his longish hair in messy disarray, his voice roughened with sleep, and his eyes squinted like the room was too bright.

"I . . ." Incredulous, I inspected his rumpled attire. He was still wearing the same T-shirt and jeans he'd been wearing yesterday. "Did—did you just wake up?" *And he slept in his clothes?*

Yawning, his gaze moving down and up my person, he nodded. "What time is it? I think I left my phone down here."

My eyes bugged. Wasn't he supposed to be watching Lisa? Wasn't he supposed to take her phone and ensure she didn't call Tyler and didn't leave and didn't do anything stupid? And he was just now waking up? I could have been out all morning. *I could have met with and had sex with and dropped acid with Tyler ten times by now!*

To be fair, I didn't know how long it took to drop acid, but based on various data sources and movies I'd watched, I could extrapolate.

"You—did you—your—" I couldn't figure out which question I wanted to ask first.

"Is there still pizza?" he asked, walking past me and making a straight line for the fridge.

Confounded, certain I was missing something critical, I stumbled after him. "I can't believe you're just waking up."

I'd never slept until 1:00 PM. Never. Not after a long international flight, not on the weekend after pulling several all-nighters the week prior, not even when I'd been sick with the flu. Never ever, ever.

Sending me a quick, small, sleepy smile, Ahab opened the fridge. "Why? When did you wake up?"

Crossing my arms, I wished for my bag of prunes or something else to chew. I suspected this was one of those situations where telling the truth would make a negative impact to my Lisa-credibility. It was a safe bet to assume my sister didn't often wake up at 6:30 AM.

Rather than outright lie, I decided vague was just as good. "A while ago. When did you go to sleep?"

"Around five."

I started, blinking several times. "Five? AM?"

"Yep." He pulled the pizza from the fridge and placed it on the island, flipping open the box.

"That's insane, Ahab. What were you doing until five AM?"

He'd been lifting a slice of cold pizza—*COLD PIZZA!*—when I spoke, but his hand halted midway to his mouth and he glared at me.

"What did you just say?"

"I said, that's insane." Frowning at him and the slice of cold pizza in turn, I had to ask, "Do you want me to heat that up for you?"

He returned the pizza to the box, staring at me like I was a curiosity. "My name is Abram."

Dammit. Abram!! Why didn't I just call him Abe?

I blinked some more. "Uh, I don't mind heating up the pizza." Maybe if I ignored the slipup, he'd let it drop?

"You just called me Ahab."

Oh noes! He wasn't going to let it drop.

"Pardon? I mean, what? I mean, no I didn't." I laughed, backing away, stuffing my hands into the back pockets of Lisa's only pair of semi-tight jeans instead of boa-constrictor-tight jeans.

"Yes, you did." His eyes narrowed, moving over me.

I tossed my thumb over my shoulder. "Would you believe that I was just reading *Moby Dick*?"

He shook his head, and I didn't know how to feel, because that was good, right? I mean, it wasn't good that I'd messed up his name, but it was good that he didn't believe I'd been reading *Moby Dick*. I felt a level of certainty that Lisa wouldn't read *Moby Dick,* so he must've still believed I was Lisa . . . right?

"Ahab?" His voice dripped with irritation.

"Why would I call you Ahab? I don't think that happened. Your name is Abram. You heard wrong. You're an unreliable witness." I glanced behind me, not knowing where I was going. I only had three feet until my back hit the wall, so I pivoted, still walking backward but aiming for the arched doorway.

"Unreliable witness?" His left dimple reappeared followed by the right, and he was doing that smile-frown thing again. It was cute. How irksome.

"Yes. You just woke up. You're muddled. Go eat your disgusting cold pizza. Whatever!" I was almost to the arched doorway, which would lead me to the back stairs, which meant I could hide for the rest of the afternoon. It would probably take all afternoon for my heart rate to return to normal.

"Fine, I will." He lifted the pizza to his mouth and added, "And then we're going out, *Liza*."

That had my feet coming to a halt. "Pardon?"

"Your name is Liza, isn't it?" He said this with a sardonic twist to his lips.

But I didn't care what he called me as long as it wasn't Mona. I was more concerned with the first part of this statement. "We're going out? Where?"

Abram didn't respond right away, instead he took a bite of pizza and chewed. My attention dropped to his jaw and neck and, for some inexplicable reason, I was entranced by the sight of his jaw working, flexing, and the action of his Adam's apple as he swallowed. I can honestly say, I'd never noticed the way someone chewed before, because why would I? But in his case, I don't know . . . It was just all extraordinarily man-like.

"I'm looking at a guitar, the guy is holding it for me until three."

"Why do I need to go?" I forced my eyes back to his and crossed my arms, bewildered by my preoccupation with his chewing. *So weird.*

"I can't leave you here by yourself." He said this like it was obvious.

I regathered the threads of the conversation just in time to find critical fault in his logic. "But you'll sleep until after noon? What if I'd gone out this morning?"

"Did you go out this morning?" He asked this like he already knew the answer.

"That's not the point. I could have."

"But you didn't."

"But I could have. You trusted me to stay put this morning, but not this afternoon?"

"This morning is in the past, this afternoon is now. You're coming."

I glared at him and his stunning lack of sense. "You make no sense."

"I don't have to make sense." He stalked around the kitchen island holding two pieces of pizza, his grin smug, slowly regaining the steps I'd placed between us. "I just have to keep you from doing anything stupid until your parents' assistant shows up. You're coming, *Liza.*"

Giving me another second of his smug grin, he walked around me, bumping my shoulder with his arm as he did so, and walked up the stairs.

Once I was fairly certain he was out of earshot, I mumbled darkly to myself, "So . . . it has come to this."

Full-out avoidance was now no longer an option. At least not for the next few hours. Since I had no choice but to accompany Abram on his errand, my new plan was to avoid conversation. I would do this by taking Gabby's advice regarding single-word answers.

While Abram showered and changed on the third floor, I crept to the kitchen pantry, pulled my phone from the hidden backpack, and checked for messages from Lisa or her lawyer. There were none.

But my good friend Allyn had messaged, and so had Gabby. I ignored the Gabster for now and opened Allyn's thread.

Allyn: *How's it going in CA? Remember, you're eating avocados for two. I am living vicariously through you. Also, send pictures of the avocados before you eat them.*

Allyn: *PS I love you for more than just your avocado pics!*

I grinned, because she was so weird and cool. We'd met my senior year, which happened to be her freshman year, and we'd clicked instantly. I'd begun to doubt clicking with anyone in any sort of situation was ever going to happen. And then I'd met Allyn, in the cafeteria, picking through sad avocado flesh. We'd shared a sigh over the substandard options and she'd taken that as an open invitation to become my best friend. I had no objections, because she was everything I was not—funny, open, engaging, comfortable in her own skin—but definitely wanted to be.

I sent her a quick text, promising to send her photos when possible—probably next week—and, with *extreme reluctance*, navigated to Gabby's texts, a series of messages beginning last night and through this afternoon.

Gabby: *I will be over tomorrow evening to check on you. Stay strong, nerdy grasshopper.*

Gabby: *Don't forget to apply makeup in the morning. Heavy on the liner.*

Gabby: *And do your hair.*

Gabby: *Good morning, sunshine. How are things?*

Gabby: *Since you haven't responded, I'm assuming you're sitting on Abram's face and I totally applaud this development.*

I stopped here, sucking in a small, startled breath as a lurid flash of an underwearless me sitting on Abram's face suffused every millimeter of my consciousness and sent pinpricks of tingling awareness racing beneath my skin. It was like being assaulted with hot honey, leaving me flushed and sticky and confused, because why would someone assault another person with hot honey? That would be strange.

"Jeez, Gabby," I murmured to my phone, fanning my shirt and blinking away the vivid image, though the visceral effects lingered. I endeavored to not dwell on the fact that none of my initial, secondary, or tertiary reactions to the thought had been displeasure or disgust.

No. Best not to dwell on that.

But I did dwell on it, how could I not? Thankfully, my brain rescued me, reminding me that my last quasi-sexual encounter with another person had been several months ago, after which I'd definitively determined that sexual partners were optional— often superfluous—to the sex act.

Abram had an attractive exterior and therefore I was attracted to it, and that was normal. My body had physical urges that I'd neglected, and that was also normal.

Yet being attracted to someone's exterior and having neglected urges did not mean taking action with that exterior was a foregone conclusion. I wasn't a slave to my physical urges and attractive exteriors. I could, and would, simply ignore the attraction and attend to myself when convenient. Maybe tomorrow. Perhaps even tonight.

But where . . . ?

Plugging my phone into the portable USB charger I always carried in my bag, I stuffed both into the backpack, and stuffed the backpack back into place. I'd taken too much time already, I'd have to call the lawyer to check on Lisa another time.

Wiping clammy hands on my pants, I stood and searched the snack shelf for something quick to eat. Granola bars seemed like the best choice, given my options, but I did note that there were four more bags of unopened prunes near the edge.

The discovery made me feel a modicum better about grabbing one of the bags earlier. Of all the snacks, prunes were in the greatest abundance. Statistically speaking, I'd been more likely to grab prunes than anything else on the shelf. But as I left the pantry, granola bars in hand, I couldn't help wondering why we had so many prunes, and who had bought them.

I made quick work of the granola bar and washed it down with water, setting the glass by the sink for later use. Checking the time, I meandered to the front door and searched the shoe cubby for footwear. I found some of my old Birkenstocks and a pair of Lisa's flip-flops—Vera Wang, black soles with bejeweled straps. Gazing longingly at the Birkenstocks, I pulled on the Vera Wang sandals.

But then, when I stood and tested them, I was *shook*. Fantastic arch support, supple leather straps, soft soles. They were the most comfortable sandals I'd ever worn.

"Huh," I said to my feet's reflection in the mirror as I rocked back and forth, testing their flexibility. "Nice." Maybe I'd have to invest in some fancy Vera Wang sandals.

"Is that what you're wearing?"

Abram's question pulled my attention away from my feet to his approach. I noted his hair was wet and his clothes were different.

"Yes." Glancing down at myself, at the semi-tight jeans and plain black tank top I'd been wearing all day, and then back to him, I asked, "Why?"

Abram lowered a pair of aviator sunglasses into place, blocking his eyes. "No reason."

"Should I change?" I tossed my thumb toward the kitchen stairs. "Is this a rococo guitar shop? Is there a dress code?"

"What's *rococo*?" Abram walked to the front door, stopping directly in front of me.

His approach and proximity made me tense, so I believe I can be excused for not thinking before responding, "Rococo is characterized by an elaborately ornamental late baroque style of decor prevalent in eighteenth-century Continental Europe, with asymmetrical patterns involving motifs and scrollwork."

His left dimple made a brief appearance, a very brief appearance, but I almost didn't notice because, just then, I caught a whiff of soap and shaving cream and something else I couldn't identify. It—he—smelled *SUPER* amazing. Wet and fresh and warm and clean. It smelled so good the tension in my body dissipated, leaving goose bumps and a languid kind of stunned relaxation instead. From a smell.

"No. Not rococo. Let's go," he said flatly, opening the door and motioning for me to exit.

I didn't move. I lowered my eyes to scan his clothes while also maybe inhaling deeply. I told myself I was comparing his clothes to mine to determine if I were dressed appropriately while also breathing normally. I was not sniffing.

Upon completing my perusal and inhaling the glorious scent of him—but not sniffing—a few more times, I could see no deficit in my outfit. In fact, after his shower he'd changed and now we were similarly attired: jeans, black shirt, he was in dark sneakers, I was in dark sandals. One might even say we matched.

Lifting my chin to peer up at him, I found him gazing down at me. Right there. Super close. Still smelling super good. My breath caught and any comments I had about the similarity between our attire scattered. I could feel the heat from his body.

Time seemed to slow as my mind sluggishly wondered how I'd arrived at this moment. I could mostly make out his eyes behind the dark lenses. They were lowered, focused somewhere on my face. I didn't think it was my eyes.

Did he move? Or were we always standing this close? And why wasn't I cringing away? Goodness, his face would be nice to sit on.

AAHHHH!

"Um." I flinched, startled by the direction of my thoughts, and stepped back, scratching my cheek. Frowning, flustered by how flustered and hot I suddenly felt —*flustered squared*—I sputtered, "I, uh, yeah. I go. Out. The door." Unnecessarily, I pointed to the open door, and then dashed through it, my heart swooping between my throat and cervix.

Shading my face from the afternoon sun, I took two large breaths and endeavored to regain my dismantled composure. It was hot, even for August. I replaced the lingering exquisite smell of him with the city air, a heady aroma of pavement and steadily rising temperature. Pushing open the gate, I darted through it and began speed walking up the street.

"Where are you going? That's the wrong way," Abram's voice called after me.

I turned, rubbing my forehead. I had no idea where we were going.

"There's no escape from destiny," I mumbled one of my anytime-occasion phrases to myself, jogging back, and keeping my attention pointed at the sidewalk behind him. "I'll follow you."

He didn't move, and I felt his scrutinizing gaze travel over me. I thought about tossing out *whatever* while also actively biting back the urge to say another of my anytime-phrases, such as, *As the prophesy foretold* or *So . . . it has come to this.*

The less I spoke at this point, the better. Clearly, Gabby's text had lit a spark, and that spark had flared, and now oxidation of a nearby fuel source had occurred. I needed to keep my head down, be quiet, and stop thinking about sitting on his face. The flames must not be fanned!

Damn Gabby and the power of suggestion!

Perhaps this was something odd about me, but when my physical urges were like this, sometimes they made concentrating difficult. I'd discovered that a tangible, present partner wasn't necessary for satisfying these urges, yet space, quiet, relaxation, and time to think of fantasy situations were essential. But for right now, and likely for the next week, I could do nothing about it. Satiating measures would have to wait until I returned to California.

Ignore him. That's the only logical course of action. Good, solid plan.

CHAPTER 5
TIME, VELOCITY, AND SPEED

I gnoring Abram proved difficult.

On the way to the shop, I walked slightly behind him. This made sense since he knew the way. I distracted myself by counting the number of houses we passed instead of staring at his ass, and I deserved a medal for this because he had a super great ass. Super. Great.

I also distracted myself by cursing out Gabby in my head. I rarely noticed man parts, and usually only as a *Well, look at that nice thing. Huh. Moving on.* Presently, however, I was on the precipice of full-on man-part appreciation. Frustrating.

Once the houses gave way to shops, I counted the bus stops, but continued to curse out Gabby.

Overall, my coping strategies kept me from fixating on his very attractive form, backside, confident stride, and how he stopped at every intersection to walk adjacent to me, as though he were a gentleman from a bygone age of lusty ankles and jaunty carriage rides. Afterward, he would motion that I should precede him. I refused with a tight shake of my head, a flat smile, and no eye contact. With a sigh, he would lead the way once more until the next intersection.

It was just after the fifth intersection that he attempted conversation. Not allowing me to resume my position behind him, he slowed his steps such that we were shoulder to shoulder.

"Do you play?" he asked.

I knew what he meant and I had no reason to lie. Both Lisa and I had taken piano, oboe, singing, and violin lessons. I nodded.

"What do you play?"

"Several instruments."

Out of the corner of my eye, I saw him tilt his head to one side, as though leaning closer so he could hear better. "Like what?"

"Violin."

"Do you still?"

"No."

He was quiet for a moment, perhaps contemplating this information, before asking, "You don't like to play?"

"No time."

Abram made a small grunt that sounded both derisive and amused. "Too busy managing Pirate Orgy's social calendar?"

Pirate Orgy was Tyler's band and Tyler was the grossest human ever. Unthinkingly, I glanced at Abram's sunglasses and caught my reflection. I might as well have had a marquee on my forehead that read *INTENSE DISGUST*.

Get control of your facial expressions, Mona!

His eyebrows shot high on his forehead. "You split from Tyler?"

Nodding, I wiped at the beading sweat on my forehead with the back of my wrist. "Yes."

"Huh."

I felt his eyes on me, so I glanced at him again. "What?"

"I'm surprised. When Leo asked me to watch you for the week, until that Steward lady gets here, he said one of the reasons your parents were so pissed was because you kept seeing Tyler behind their backs."

I nodded even as my wheels turned, realizing that this conversation had presented me with a unique opportunity. "What else did Leo say?"

"About Tyler?"

As I studied Abram, the curiosity floodgate I'd sealed shut hours ago sprung a leak. Due to the urgency of Lisa's predicament, I'd agreed to lie for her. And though I'd been playing along and doing my best, justifying my role as sisterly duty and worry for her and *Whatcha gonna do? Decision has already been made*, nothing about this hatched plan sat well with me.

The whispers of doubt I'd suppressed this morning were now asking different questions: What had Lisa done that made my parents so angry? Knowing my parents, it had to be something that had the potential to make them look bad or damage their carefully constructed images of having it all: a happy, well-adjusted family; beautiful houses and clothes and art and things; cultural relevance; respect of the industry; living their best life of ethical hedonism.

She'd done a ton to make them vaguely annoyed, but what could have possibly galvanized them into acting? It couldn't be just Tyler. And why was she in jail?

Up to now, I'd endeavored to ignore my curiosity about the subject, reasoning that curiosity with no source of reliable information was pointless. Gabby had been either unsurprisingly vague or outright hostile when I'd asked her. I couldn't question Lisa or Leo or my parents, and I had no idea when I'd be able to get in touch with Lisa's lawyer.

But Abram? . . . *Possibly.*

Choosing my words carefully, I asked, "What else did Leo say about my parents and why they were—or are—upset?"

"Trying to find out how much they know?" He seemed to be scrutinizing me. I couldn't see his eyes, but I could feel them.

Rolling my lips between my teeth, I said nothing, hoping he'd fill in the answer for himself.

Abram watched me for a bit longer, and then released a short laugh. He shook his head. He sighed. "Um. . ." He sighed again. "According to Leo, it was the drugs that really freaked them out."

"Hmm." They were upset about drugs? That made no sense.

My parents' attitude toward illegal substances was that nothing should be illegal. To say they were progressive would be an understatement. They'd always done a variety of drugs, even when we were little, making no secret of partaking in what they called "creativity enhancers," like ecstasy, marijuana, and mushrooms. They'd even talked about it openly in interviews.

That said, my dad had "the drug talk" with me and Lisa when we were eight. The message had been: wait until your brain is fully developed, and then consider them like a rich dessert: fine on birthdays, bat mitzvahs, Christmas, and when you want a rare treat, but avoid more than one serving at a time.

I'd never touched anything—not cigarettes, not alcohol, not marijuana—mostly because any curiosity I might've experienced ended after I took a series of MIT OpenCourseWare classes on the brain and cognitive sciences, including neurochemistry. I'd subsequently decided that if I was going to put chemicals in my body, then they better be pharmaceutical grade, produced in a lab overseen by the FDA, and prescribed by a medical professional.

While I was still pondering the puzzle of his response, Abram added, "I guess they didn't want their baby girl selling cocaine to sixteen-year-olds at concerts." And that's when I choked on air. Hard.

What. The. HELL?

LISA!

Oh man. Oh man oh man oh man. Cocaine? To *SIXTEEN-YEAR-OLDS?*

I had to stop walking or risk falling over. Standing in the middle of the sidewalk, I was coughing so hard, tears formed in the corners of my eyes and I wheezed when I inhaled.

Cocaine was right up there with opiates as the most addictive, life destroying substances. When I saw her next, she would give me answers. All the answers. I would settle for nothing less. And if what Abram said was true, if she'd been peddling to kids, I was going to blow the lid off this deception. *I was going to—*

"Are you okay?"

Abruptly, I became aware that we were stopped in the middle of the sidewalk. Abram was still there, once again standing close enough for me to feel the heat of his body even though it must've been eighty-five degrees Fahrenheit in the shade. Interestingly and confoundedly, his hand was also rubbing circles on my back and I hadn't noticed.

But as soon as I became aware of his touch, I stepped away. Sucking in a raspy breath and holding it, I let my eyelids fall. I tried to swallow. My throat felt gravelly and raw.

No wonder my parents had freaked. If this got out to the papers, their pedestals might not survive.

"I guess it's not true?" His words were halting, like he was speaking his thoughts as they occurred to him.

What could I say? One of my anytime-situation phrases popped in my head (*And thus, I die*), but I quickly pushed it away. Opening my eyes, I glared at my reflection in his aviators and said nothing. I didn't know what she'd done to land behind bars. I had no idea!

"Where's this guitar shop?" I asked, glancing up and down the sidewalk, my voice extremely rough.

Abram hooked his thumbs in his jeans' pockets. "We're about a block away."

Clearing my throat, I motioned for him to proceed. Irritatingly, his initial footfalls were slow, which made it awkward for me to follow without walking next to him. I didn't want to walk next to him. I wanted to quietly fume and make plans for how I might uncover the truth as soon as possible.

But I couldn't do either because he was talking again. "So, the Tyler stuff is true, but the drugs stuff is not." He nodded at his own statement. "Good to know."

Staring forward, I erased my face of expression. *The drug stuff better not be true . . . OR ELSE!*

"But—" He scratched his cheek, seemed to hesitate before finishing his thought, "But you and Tyler are split? For good?"

"Yes."

"You've broken up before though, right?"

I nodded, only half paying attention. *If Lisa was selling cocaine to teenagers, I will go to a nerd-con and, posing as her, I would make out with a B-list celebrity and ensure we were photographed.* She would be horrified and might never recover. I felt certain of this in my bones.

"What's different this time with Tyler?"

Preoccupied by my perdition plans, I tried to remember my sister's response to this question when I'd asked two nights ago. "Never again. I'm done with that floating trash island of whale excrement."

Whale excrement? Where had that come from? Once again, I blamed *Moby Dick*.

Abram's chuckle was a burst of air, like my answer had caught him totally off guard.

"'Floating trash island of whale excrement,'" he quoted, sounding contemplative, drawing my eyes to his profile.

Since I was walking on his left, I caught the flash of his dimple and it—paired with his super handsome profile—was enough to distract me from my thoughts of revenge. "That's right."

"That's an interesting description." Abram's steps slowed, stopped, and he reached for the door of a shop, holding it open for me. "You have a way with words. You should write song lyrics."

I grunted, scanning the front of the building. The window facing the sidewalk showcased a two-by-ten array of guitars, all held aloft by a heavy-duty black wire cage display. Through the wire and guitars, the interior of the shop was scarcely visible. But, no matter. Clearly this was our destination.

"Why whale excrement?"

Abram's question drew my attention away from the guitars. He'd taken off his sunglasses and was folding them with one hand, holding the door open with the other. His gaze felt different. Oddly piercing.

"Because it's got to be the biggest piece of poop. Right? Whale poop should be massive."

He seemed to be fighting another smile and he opened his mouth as though to respond, but a voice called from the interior of the shop, "Are you coming inside? You're letting all the AC out the door!"

"Whoops!" I hurried past Abram and quickly found the owner of the voice. Giving him a little wave and conciliatory smile, I said, "Sorry about that."

"Yeah, yeah." The man didn't look up from where he stood in the far corner, one foot on an amp, the other on the floor, a Martin D-45 Fire & Ice Dreadnought in his hands. Based on his level of preoccupation, he seemed to be tuning the acoustic guitar.

"It's expensive."

I turned to Abram, giving him a questioning look as the door shut at his back. "You mean the guitar he's tuning? The Martin D-45? Yes. It is. My mom has one and she never let us touch it."

His rich brown eyes seemed to glitter. "No. I mean"—he shook his head, now fully smiling—"Yes, the Martin D-45 Fire & Ice is expensive, but I was referring to whale excrement."

I wrinkled my nose at him. "What?"

"Have you heard of ambergris? It's found in the digestive tract of sperm whales."

"Pardon?"

"Yeah. They use it to make perfume—real perfume, not the fake stuff—it's expensive," he said conversationally, like this was true.

Crossing my arms, I waited for the punchline. Based on interactions with my brother, I was sure the joke's end had to do with both poop and sperm.

But when he continued to stare at me steadily with a small smile on his lips and those intense brown eyes while leaning a few centimeters closer, butterflies re-awoke in my stomach.

I was flustered again. *Stupid, distracting pretty man parts.*

Shaking my head, I lifted my chin and hid behind a frown. "That's the most ridiculous thing I've ever heard."

He leaned even closer, splitting his attention between my eyes and my mouth. "It makes scent, perfume, last longer. And some people believe it allows a person's pheromones to comingle with the perfume, increasing the intensity of both."

I said nothing. The butterflies swirled. He still smelled so atypically delicious, I fleetingly wondered if what I was actually smelling were Abram-specific pheromones mixed with fancy sperm whale poop instead of cologne.

"Look it up if you don't believe me." His statement sounded like a dare. His dimple and voice deepening, Abram's stare seemed to dance as it traveled lower, from my eyes to my nose, mouth, chin, and neck. And then, he smiled.

I turned abruptly—needing . . . away, from all *that*—walking aimlessly forward. "Aren't we here to get a guitar?"

"You really don't believe me?" He was trailing close behind and I didn't need to look to know he was shadowing my steps.

"I don't believe you."

"Why would I lie?" Abram's voice held his smile and was still deep and lovely. For some reason this caused a shiver to race down my spine.

"It was an acoustic, right?" Meanwhile, my voice was tight, held a hint of betraying nerves, and why was my neck hot?

Abram chuckled, like he was enjoying himself, and the sound—close to my ear—gave me new goose bumps. "No. It's a bass. You want to make a bet?"

NO BETS! Right then and there, I solemnly promised myself I would never make a bet with Abram as long as I lived, *with the universe as my witness.*

"I want to get your new bass guitar so we can get back to the house," I said stiffly, pretending to be interested in a used Rogue RA Dreadnought. How had a discussion about whale excrement turn into something that made my body temperature go wonky? And wasn't I supposed to be giving one-word answers?

Needing to hurriedly analyze the situation, I listed the facts: I'd just discovered my sister had—allegedly—been selling drugs to minors; I'd been roped into unwittingly covering for her; I was upset and flustered and off-balance and Abram had very pretty man parts I shouldn't be noticing, because they're irrelevant.

Conclusion: DEFLECT!

"How about if I'm right, then you—"

I spun, glaring at him towering over me. "Fine. Then Tyler is whale vomit. Happy?"

Abram sucked in a breath between his teeth while also—blatantly—still grinning. "Actually, whale vomit is also expensive."

"Now I know you're making this up."

"I'm not." He pressed a hand to his chest, laughing. "Partly indigestible beaks of squid cause sperm whales to have indigestion, and their vomit also contains ambergris."

Partly indigestible beaks of what? Scrunching my face, I shook my head, rejecting his nonsense.

He mimicked my headshake and face-scrunch while still smiling. "The indigestible beak causes irritation in the intestines, and this results in a build-up, like a rock, to form inside the whale. Ambergris is expelled."

"No."

He was laughing again. "It's like an extremely rare, smelly rock."

"Smelly rock. Riiiiiight."

Now he was laughing harder. "And they wash up on shore."

"You are full of *ambergris*."

Now he was laughing so hard, he was forced to take a step back and was holding his stomach. *Goodness, that smile.* My heart thumped and stuttered; my chest ached; my mouth curved into an answering grin (against my will). *That smile is lethal. Wow.*

However, before basking in or allowing myself to comprehend the full effect of his smile, it was tempered by a sudden thought: was he laughing in good humor or laughing at my expense?

I'd never been gifted in the art of solving situations for this unknown variable. There'd been many incidences—especially during my freshman year of college—when I'd thought my classmates and professors were laughing in good humor. As it turned out, it had been the other . . .

"I will prove it to you." He reached for my arm.

I backed away before his hand could make contact, the butterflies ceasing abruptly, my stomach turning cold.

What did I know about Abram? He'd lucked out in the genetics lottery with his face and body and voice. He slept past noon. He'd dropped out of high school for reasons unknown. He wasn't a fan of consistently applying logic. Like my parents, he was a musician (ugh). He smelled like the Orion Nebula looked (beautiful). He didn't like Lisa. *He thinks I'm Lisa.*

He was probably laughing at me.

A lump formed in my throat.

So what if he was laughing at me? So what? Technically, he was laughing at Lisa. But that didn't make me feel better, either. I didn't want anyone laughing at my sister *—unless she's been selling cocaine to sixteen-year-olds. Then all bets are off!*

"Whatever," I said, glaring at him, trying to find fault with his maddeningly attractive face.

"I insist. I will prove it." He didn't see my glare, he was too busy pulling out his phone and swiping his thumb over the number keys to unlock it.

"Your source better not be Wikipedia. I don't trust crowd-sourced data. You could have created the page and edited it." These words came out more hostile than I'd intended. I told myself to relax.

"Fine." He peered at me, big fat grin on his face, eyebrow raised in a challenge, looking arrogant and tremendously attractive and standing too close. "What do you trust?"

"Peer-reviewed publications," I whisper-croaked, dropping my gaze to the glass case on my left and giving him just my profile.

Why couldn't he just pick up his guitar so we could leave? And why was my throat so tight?

His eyes were on me, I felt them. Mine were studiously focused on the glass case, but I wasn't looking within. A few seconds ticked by, during which I meditated on slowing my breathing and concentrated on pretending he wasn't there, pushing his presence and the echoes of his laughter aside.

Swallowing against the tightness, I ventured to my happiest place, picturing the concave dome of a planetarium above me, a blanket of deceptive white dots overhead, planets and galaxies and solar systems masquerading as stars. And between the white dots? Black matter. What we could not see, what we did not yet understand.

The universe—in all its infinite complexity and beauty—struck me as an apt reverse allegory for human interaction. We are deceived by the white dots. We label them stars. Often, they're so much more. Layered. Complex. Important. Surprising. Beautiful.

This was, I found, the opposite of people. In both cases, we label stars based on first impressions. The universe never disappoints or fails to inspire wonder, but people usually do.

Or maybe—maybe it wasn't a reverse allegory. Maybe it was exactly correct. After all, the brightest object in earth's night sky was usually our little moon. Whereas the majority of the dim, twinkling lights in the distance, the ones we barely noticed, were not only stars but something altogether more awe-inspiring once you took the time to investigate. To *know.*

"Hey."

The softly spoken word pulled me out of my reflections and I glanced at Abram. He was standing close, like before. His face was still unreasonably handsome, his scent still captivating, and his eyes appeared warm and interested. He was no longer (outwardly) laughing at me.

"Pardon? Did you say something?" I felt none of the earlier chaos or discomfort. Both had been replaced with cool dispassion. *Abram is a moon, most people are.*

His eyebrows pulled together as his attention flickered over me. "Are you okay?"

"Fine. You?"

He blinked, like I'd blown dust in his eyes, and he seemed to rock back on his heels. Abram's lips parted, perhaps intending to speak. But then he snapped his mouth shut, frowning like I'd done or said something to confuse him.

Giving him one more cursory glance, I twisted at the waist and called to the man in the corner, "This is Abram. He's here for a bass guitar. I believe you're holding it for him?"

* * *

As soon as we returned, I left Abram in the entranceway and reclaimed my seat in the mudroom by the back door. Picking up my book, I opened to the bookmark and stared at the words. I did not read them. My earlier cool dispassion hadn't lasted long. During the silent march home, I'd felt increasingly . . .

Hot. And aggravated. A vicious recursive loop of being aggravated at being hot and getting hotter by being aggravated.

Huffing, I set my book down once more and left the reading cubby, heading for the kitchen stairs and Lisa's room. I needed to cool down while also blowing off steam.

Conclusion: Swimming.

Opening and closing Lisa's drawers, I searched for a bathing suit. My choices were slim, literally. She owned nothing but string bikinis. Huffing again, I selected a plain white one with the tags still on. If I was going to put on a string bikini, I might as well use one my sister had never worn. Undressing, dressing, and then covering myself in her oversized terry cloth bathrobe, I made my way to the back-garden pool.

We didn't have a huge backyard, but the fact that we had one at all in this neighborhood was remarkable. My parents had bought a dilapidated brownstone on one side of theirs and torn it down, cleverly keeping the tall cast iron fence and the façade facing the street. From the sidewalk, one would never know a garden, a small shed, and a pool lay behind the wall instead of a house. The garden had been specifically designed to provide coverage and privacy from the neighbors while also allowing areas of sunshine for afternoon sunbathing.

Since it was just past three in the afternoon, the pool and its perimeter were dotted with sunlight peeking through the trees. That was fine. I'd never been a fan of spotlights.

Discarding the bathrobe, I walked to the water's edge and incidentally into a swath of sunlight, but then hesitated.

I still had on makeup. I needed goggles from the pool shed to see underwater. And what about my hair? If I went swimming, I'd have to do it again. Makeup was one thing, but I wasn't sure I could style my hair again on my own.

"Hmm." I dipped my toe in the water. It felt nice. And I missed swimming. And it was hot outside. And I was hot *inside*. . .

"Lisa, wait!" a voice shouted.

I stiffened, looking toward the house and spotting Gabby walking quickly toward me. At first I thought she was also wearing a bathing suit, but upon closer inspection her outfit turned out to be short-shorts and a tube top.

"What are you doing?" She dropped her voice to a harsh whisper as soon as she was close enough to be heard, her eyes wide and questioning. Not waiting for me to answer, she glanced over her shoulder hastily and stepped closer. "Please tell me you're not about to go swimming."

Movement at the bottom of the stairs leading up to the house caught my attention and I spotted Abram coming to a stop at the end of the railing. As our gazes connected, he stood straighter. But then his attention swept down my body and he took a step back. His eyes seemed to grow rounder, his dark eyebrows inching up his forehead, his lips parting.

Not thinking too much about the instinct, I shrunk backward toward the shade, away from the pool, placing Gabby in front of me so I wouldn't be as visible.

I wasn't shy about my body. I was wary. About everything. There's a difference.

For as long as I could recall, I lived with an ingrained undercurrent of discomfort in most social situations, including exposure of my façade. Did I wish I were more like Gabby and my sister? That I didn't dislike people looking at my body? Sometimes. It would be one less thing to be weird and anxious about.

But my ingrained undercurrent of discomfort in most social situations also carried over to my area of study. It made me a meticulous researcher. It meant I checked and double-checked and triple-checked. It meant I was always certain before I challenged others, which meant I was always right, which had led to my reputation of being credible, listened to, and taken seriously.

Funny how the very weaknesses that cripple us in some situations are often the foundation for our greatest achievements.

"I am about to go swimming, but first I need to get goggles," I whispered in answer to her objection. "By the way, how did you get in?"

"I have the gate code, and I ran past Abram when he opened the door." She waved this away like it was a minor thing. "You can't go swimming. You can't get your hair wet. I had to call in two favors to get you the blowout yesterday with George on such short notice. This hair has to last you for the next week."

"Would it really be a big deal if I wore my hair in a ponytail or a braid?" I split my attention between her and the bathrobe I'd placed on the chair.

"Yes. It would be a big deal. All the pictures in the house are of Mona with her hair back and Lisa with her hair down. What—what are you doing?" She followed my line of sight to where the bathrobe lay. "No, no. Do not put it on. Lisa would not cover herself. Do not put that bathrobe on."

Releasing a hissing breath between my teeth, I glared at my sister's friend, feeling increasingly antsy the closer Abram came. "Me putting a bathrobe on is not going to be a red flag for Abram."

"Yes. It will." An odd kind of urgency entered her voice. "The only time Abram and Lisa met, she was naked, okay? You covering up now would be weird."

What? Naked? What? I sputtered, my mouth opening and closing.

Giving me no time to recover, Gabby pasted a smile on her face, glanced over her shoulder again, laughed a fake laugh that sounded real, and turned back to me just as her expression switched to stern. "Act like a hot girl who is proud of her hotness, he's coming!"

CHAPTER 6
ACCELERATION

"What do you mean she was naked?" I whisper-hissed.

"Shut up."

"Gabby—"

She didn't respond, instead looping her arm through mine and turning to face an approaching Abram. I flinched automatically and moved to withdraw. Gabby countered quickly, holding my arm in a tighter grip. My only excuse for not tempering my pulling-away instinct was that I remained stunned by her latest revelation. Indeed, my mind was still running through possible scenarios which might explain why Lisa would need to be naked in front of someone she didn't know.

Perhaps she'd stepped in an ant pile and they'd crawled under her clothes and she'd needed to rip them off? Or someone poured anthrax down the back of her shirt? Or . . . *what the heck?*

I was so entirely in my own head that it took me a few moments to realize that Abram and Gabby were speaking.

"I found her. You can go away, Abram, unless you're planning to join us by the pool." Gabby's tone was light and playful.

"You're not staying." His voice was like granite.

Distractedly, I glanced at Abram, found him examining me with wary eyes, like he half expected me to pounce on him. He was also a good ten feet away, pointedly keeping his distance. Even so, his gaze did move over me—legs, hips, stomach, and so forth—with the scarcest visible glimmer of appreciation, giving me the impression he was irritated with himself for noticing at all.

I had to wrestle with the impulse to step fully behind Gabby or otherwise use her to block myself from view.

"I can't stay long, I have to be somewhere," Gabby said, obviously pretending to misinterpret his meaning. "But if *you* put on a bathing suit, I'll cancel my other plans."

Abram crossed his arms, his wary gaze returning to mine. It seemed to soften. Or . . . maybe it didn't? Or maybe some plotting, rebellious part of me wanted irrelevantly attractive Abram to look at me differently than he looked at Gabby?

Yes. That's probably it. It's all in my imagination.

But then he asked "Lisa, are you going swimming?" and the tone he used was undeniably softer than the one he'd used with Gabby.

Oh.

So I croaked "Yes" and hated that the majority of my insides melted at the irrefutable evidence: Abram's expression and voice had gentled as he addressed me. Fact.

Gabby squeezed my arm.

I quickly put an end to the internal organ melting and came back to myself, adding firmly, "Preferably alone. Don't feel like you need to stay, Gabby."

She gave me the side-eye and a saccharine sweet smile. "You're funny. I do have to be someplace, but we have so much to talk about. I wouldn't think of leaving quite yet. Plus, I brought you dry shampoo. For your *hair.* You know you can't get your hair wet or else Abram will have to take you back to George."

"Who is George?" Abram took a step forward, glancing between us.

"George is Lisa's stylist in Chicago. Her stylist in New York is also George, but it's spelled G-O-R-G," Gabby answered, like it was the most natural thing in the world for a person to have a stylist with a name pronounced *George* in every city.

My upbringing meant I hadn't truly understood until undergrad how unusual it was for a person to have a stylist in every city, or even one in one city. My superstar mother was followed by a beauty and health entourage everywhere she went. When she and my father had taken Leo and I to movie premieres, or award shows, or wherever they'd be photographed with their two prized prodigy pedigrees, her life had been my initial baseline.

I'd spent the last four years readjusting my expectations of normal. Even so, since my Ivy League past and living with Dr. Steward were now my secondary baseline, I knew I was still hugely out of touch about many, many realities of the typical, normal, or average experience.

I didn't know what I didn't know, but I was working on it.

Abram lifted an eyebrow at Gabby's explanation. It looked judgmental. "You can't do your own hair?"

"Apparently, not in Chicago or New York," I said dryly, unable to help the note of sarcasm given my level of frustration. I just wanted to go swimming and cool down! Was that too much to ask?

Gabby shot me a dirty look, her elbow digging into my side.

But Abram's judgy single-eyebrow lift became a double rise of surprise, his gaze moving over me, his mouth curving into another of his reluctant grins.

"Given how much Abram loves your company, I'm sure he won't have any problem taking you to George to get your hair done." Gabby met my sarcasm and raised me a dose of mockery.

"Or maybe Abram could just change his name to George?" I appealed to Abram, pulling my arm from her grip.

"Sure. I can do that." He nodded, surprising me by playing along.

"There we go. I have my George. I can go swimming. Gabby, you can rest easy about my hair. And now you can both leave."

Gabby's mouth dropped open, and I could feel the squawking protest building inside her.

But Abram spoke before she had the chance. "Oh no, George can't leave. George has to go swimming."

Those statements earned him an intense eye-squint. "Why does George have to go swimming?"

"Don't you want a George nearby? Just in case there's a hair emergency?" He was grinning. Apparently he'd decided to stop hiding his smiles, just this once.

"No." I frowned, confused by the smile he was sending me. "Never mind. You're Ahab again."

Abram dropped his chin to his chest and covered his mouth with a hand, clearly trying to hide the fact that he was laughing. The maneuver didn't work because his shaking shoulders gave him away.

I sensed Gabby glance between the two of us, I also sensed her incredulity, but I didn't give her any of my direct attention. I was too busy battling warm feelings because Abram was laughing at my Ahab joke, which meant he was laughing *with* me. Which meant I was melting again.

It felt . . . good.

Eventually, he shrugged, his arms falling to his sides. When he lifted his head, his eyes were glowing, and he'd pressed his lips together as though to erase his grin. It didn't work, his dimples betrayed him.

"Too bad, *Liza.* George will be right back."

Scowling to hide this burgeoning warmth in my stomach and chest, I shouted at his back as he jogged away, "Where are you going?"

He turned and walked backward, looking very pleased. "To change into my swimsuit."

"Well take your time!" I crossed my arms, raging against some new, hotter emotion I didn't dare identify.

"I won't!" he yelled in return, giving us his back again as he climbed the stairs. "See you in a second."

I grunted, grinding my teeth, and not understanding why I wasn't more irritated. I should have been. My pool plans had been disrupted. Cooling down while blowing off steam would be impossible with Abram around.

The combination of Gabby's ill-timed text and his superfluously handsome man parts were responsible for making me hot!

Yeah, but now you'll see Abram shirtless. Worth it.

ARG!

Dammit, internal monologue. STFU.

"Well, well, well, *Lisa.*"

I moved my eyes to Gabby. Something about her tone made the hairs on the back of my neck rise. She sounded . . . pleased. *That can't be good.*

"Pardon?"

"You don't waste any time, do you?" Yes. She was pleased. Her gaze moved over me appraisingly and she nodded, as though agreeing with unspoken thoughts.

"What are you talking about?"

Gabby leaned close, her green eyes sparkling. "Abram."

"What about him?"

"What did you do?" She wagged her eyebrows.

"What are we talking about?"

"Look at you! He's vibing on you." Grabbing my wrist, she forced me to give her a high five before I could react. "Get it, girl!"

We were clearly having two different conversations. "I'm so lost. I know you're speaking, because your mouth is moving and sounds are coming out, but I don't understand a word you're saying."

She rubbed her hands together. "Oh, this is so good. I can't wait to tell your sister you got him in his swimsuit." Her eyes moved down and then up my body. "Or his birthday suit."

I flinched. "Gabby!"

"What? Did you see how he was looking at you?"

"Gabby."

"Maybe you will be sitting on his face after all."

"Gabby!" I covered my ears with my hands and shut my eyes. It was no good. Again, the sexy images, the spark, the flame, the fire. "Keep your power of suggestion to yourself."

She pulled my wrists away from my head. "I'm just saying, I've seen Abram work it before when he's surrounded by his harem, but a boy don't flirt like *that* unless he's thirsty for a girl's milkshake."

Harem? Flirt? Milkshake? *What?*

My eyes flew open and it took several seconds for me to decide which of her statements to contradict first. "He wasn't flirting with me."

She gave me a snort of disbelief and an eye roll. "You're kidding, right?"

"Why would he flirt with me? It would be completely inappropriate."

"Oh my god, Mary Sue, try to keep up. He wants your baa-day!"

"He shouldn't." I glanced at the back door to the house, dreading his return.

"Why the hell not? Have you seen him? Have you seen yourself in this bikini? I mean, yeah. You need a wax, but you two would be *hot*." She shrugged with her entire body. "I would kind of want to watch, to be honest."

"Oh my God!" A shock of two conflicting emotional states—one completely expected and logical, and one dark and secret and troubling—had me turning away from her and reaching for my bathrobe: repugnance and fascination, revulsion and curiosity, disgust and temptation.

She grabbed the terry cloth before I could and tossed it in the pool. "There. It's gone. Stop trying to cover up. Now give me one good reason why you two shouldn't take advantage of this fortress of solitude for the next few days."

My temper was lost along with the bathrobe and undammed feelings surged forth, coating my voice in viscous *emotion*. "Because he's in a position of authority over me. He could tell my parents lies about me—about Lisa not behaving, or seeing Tyler—if he wanted, and it would be my word against his. He could try to blackmail me into physical intimacy, if I don't do what he wants. So, no. He absolutely shouldn't be flirting with me!"

By the end of my tirade, Gabby was staring at me with wide-eyed confusion, but it quickly morphed into narrowed-eyed suspicion.

"Mona," she whispered.

"You mean Lisa."

"Mona," she whispered more insistently, her eyes moving between mine. "Did something happen to you? Did someone . . . did they do something?"

"No," I said, unable to hold her gaze. "I mean, no. Not really."

"What do you mean, *'Not really'*?"

"I mean, nothing *happened*."

She bent and moved her face in front of mine, forcing me to look at her. "But someone tried to make something happen? While you were in college?"

I shrugged, waving my hands around. "No. It wasn't like that. I overreacted."

"About what?"

"Does it matter? If nothing actually happened?"

"I don't know, why don't you tell me what didn't happen?" She squinted until her eyes were nearly closed.

"It's not a big deal." Again, I glanced at the back door. *Shouldn't he be back by now?*

"Then it shouldn't be a big deal telling me what happened, or what didn't happen."

"I—" Now I felt silly. It wasn't a big deal. Every girl or woman I knew had gone through something similar, where she misinterpreted an innocuous situation, let her imagination get the better of her. If it happened to all women, then it wasn't a big deal, right? "It's stupid."

"I love stupid. Stupid is my favorite. Go on. And hurry, before the hottie gets back."

I vacillated, feeling inexplicably out of breath. I didn't want to tell her. "Fine. I'll tell you what happened if you tell me about Lisa being naked with Abram."

"Deal. Tell me."

Oh. Okay. Damn. I hadn't expected her to agree.

"You're going to be disappointed."

"Tell me."

I rolled my eyes at myself. "Fine. There was this postgrad TA. And he used to, you know, get touchy with undergrads. Give back massages or hug us from behind. I didn't like it, so I avoided him. Really, no big deal."

"That's it? How old were you?"

"That's not it. I was fifteen."

"Hmm. So what happened?"

"He . . ." *Why are you telling Gabby, of all people?* Why was I telling anyone? It was no big deal. No big deal.

"Mona."

"He cornered me—once—when I was alone in the chem lab. Made me feel uncomfortable." *Stop talking.*

"What did he do?"

"He"—my eyes lost focus as they drifted over her shoulder—"came up behind me and put his hand over my mouth. I didn't hear him come in, so I freaked out. I thought . . ." I shook my head at myself. "See? Stupid."

I didn't want to talk about this. My heart was galloping at the memory. Just like then, I couldn't seem to get my pulse under control. *So stupid.*

"And then?"

"I was kicking and elbowing him, because I didn't know it was a joke," I said, my voice growing quieter, more robotic. "But he was bigger than me, it didn't even faze him. When he let me go, he laughed. He said, 'You should see your face.' And then, when I finally calmed down, he acted like he wasn't going to let me leave again, and I got scared. Again."

Gabby, frowning, nodded slowly, apparently absorbing every detail. "What did he do next?"

This is Gabby. You don't trust her. STOP TALKING!

I hadn't even told Allyn about this, and I didn't stop. I met her stare and finished the story calmly. "He chased me, grabbed me again and pinned me against the wall. When I started to cry, he laughed again and let me go, said I didn't know how to take a joke, that I was easy to tease, like his little sister. And then he left, and it was over."

"Did you report him? Tell anyone?"

Her question cracked the shell of outward calm I'd erected. I looked at her like she was nuts. "Tell them what? That I got scared like a little kid?" I whispered harshly, because I was upset. I hated that this still upset me.

"Nooo." She drew the word out, but her eyes were tender, patient. "That he assaulted you. That he put his hands on you without your permission and frightened you. And when you told him to stop, he did it again."

"Come on, Gabby. It was a joke." Resurrecting cold reason to distance myself from the memory—*nothing happened, no big deal, nothing happened*—I took several deep breaths and my heart began to slow. The story was done, it was over, but for the life of me, I couldn't figure out why I'd said anything to begin with. Especially to Gabby.

"It was assault. You should have reported him."

"And then what?" I asked, once again employing my calmest, most rational voice. "I was fifteen, and he was the son of someone important. No one would have believed me. There was only one logical path forward, and that was to forget about it."

"Are you kidding? You were the perfect victim. Young girl genius, daughter of DJ Tang and Exotica, Mary Sue do-gooder, everyone would have believed you."

"First, there is no such thing as a 'perfect victim.' No one is ever perfect enough when there's no hard evidence of wrongdoing. Add to that, when the truth or identity of the alleged perpetrator—"

"'Alleged perpetrator?' Can you hear yourself?"

"—is inconvenient, no one wants to listen, no one wants to know the truth, let alone do anything about it. Second, I might have been terrified, but nothing actually happened. They would have told me it was no big deal, because it was *no big deal*. I wasn't hurt, I was just scared." Inexplicably, despite my determined sensibleness, my eyes stung.

Gabby glared at me for several seconds. Whatever this expression was on her face, I'd never seen it before.

I was just about to speak, to reiterate how minor of an event it had been, when she said, "No. Not hurt, just scarred."

I blinked against the hot sensation behind my eyes and labored to form a complete thought for a few moments before finally managing, "Pardon?"

She gently—but suddenly—encircled my wrist with her fingers and I winced, instinctively yanking it back without thought.

"See? Scarred." Her smile was small and sad.

My face flushed anew, my tongue tasting like ash. "Just because I don't like—"

"You didn't think I noticed? You don't think Lisa noticed? You've changed. Not answering Lisa's letters from boarding school is one thing, but cutting her out completely?"

OH MY GOD! The letters. The damn letters!

"I had no control over the fact that her school didn't allow emails or internet. And I answered her handwritten letters. I answered every single one of them, and yet she continues to point to them as a reason to be mean-spirited."

I'd answered them as soon as I'd received them, which was months late. As an eleven-year-old, I'd begged my tutor to stop holding them, parsing them out as prizes for accomplishments. When that didn't work, I'd asked my parents to intervene, but they agreed with my tutor (which really meant they didn't want to rock the boat). I'd even asked Leo for help and discovered his teacher was doing the same thing to him!

When would Lisa and Gabby get it through their brains that there'd been nothing I could have done?

"You responded months after she sent them. Months and months, Mona. She was sent away—because of you—and you were too busy to respond. And she's never been mean to you, not as far as I know."

"That's so untrue! You know she can't stand me."

"False."

"Oh yeah? What about that prank? With the university newspaper? Plus, as I've explained a hundred times, I didn't get the letters—"

"Whatever, that prank was a joke. You're just too busy thinking the worst of her to realize it." She flicked away this fact with a wave of her hand. "The point is now. You don't even like it when your twin sister hugs you. What happened changed you."

"That's preposterous." I was sputtering again, "I—it—what happened didn't change me. I've never liked . . . I just don't like not knowing when—when—nothing—"

I didn't get a chance to complete my thought or reiterate my objection because Abram chose that moment to exit the house, the sound of the door drawing my attention. I watched him, some forty feet away, as he descended the stairs dressed only in board shorts.

I flinched.

"Good. Lord. That man is gorgeous." Gabby's breathless exclamation felt like sand in my bathing suit. My eyes still stinging, I frowned at the back of her head for a beat before glancing again at Abram.

Perhaps it was the recounting of my no-big-deal story just moments ago and the strange emotional toll that had taken, but as my attention moved over Abram, all I experienced was an aloof observation of a fact.

Objectively, I could admit that Abram was, his body was, breathtaking. Big, wide shoulders—linebacker shoulders, but still lean—on a tall frame, defined stomach, narrow hips. He wasn't just strong, he was exceptionally formed. He was perfect proportions and elegant lines and exquisite angles.

He was gorgeous. However, my accompanying thought was, *so what?* Abram was gorgeous, so what? The sky was blue, so what? I have no idea why my damn eyes are still stinging, so what?

And then he looked up. Met my gaze. A whisper of a smile curved his lips and I experienced an odd sort of tunnel vision as he approached. His warm brown eyes didn't stray from mine though his smile waned, and the focus, the concentrated intensity of interest obvious in his stare seemed to increase the closer he came.

Suddenly, he was there. Standing in front of me.

"Hey," he said softly, those warm eyes of his moving over my face, a concerned-looking wrinkle appearing between his eyebrows. "Are you okay?"

Am I okay?

"Of course," I said automatically, feeling oddly flustered by the question.

The wrinkle between his eyebrows deepened and he shifted closer, confusion and urgency behind his gaze. "Are you—have you been crying?"

CHAPTER 7

MOTION EQUATIONS FOR CONSTANT ACCELERATION

It was 2:47 AM. I couldn't sleep. *Maybe I didn't get enough exercise . . .*

I hadn't gone swimming, and I had only myself to blame. More specifically, my wonky emotions were to blame. Or maybe it was Gabby's fault and her potent power of suggestion. Whatever it was, I was paying the price now.

Instead of getting control of myself like a sane person, Abram's intensely gentle concern for my well-being freaked me out and drove me away from the pool. I'd made some lame, hurried excuse about needing to wash the bathrobe, fished it out of the water, and sprint-walked to the house. Then, feeling like a fool, I brought the robe upstairs to the bathroom, tossed it in the tub—planning to wring it out and dry it later—and ran into Lisa's room.

Any plans I'd had of going swimming or cooling off were forgotten, which was fine. After recounting my stupid, ridiculous story to Gabby, I'd no longer felt hot anyway. I'd felt nothing.

I'd wanted to go to my own room but didn't. That wouldn't have been prudent. Changing back into day clothes, I searched my sister's room for something to do, something—anything—that might occupy my mind and time. After a short hunt, I discovered one of our old violins in the back of her closet along with a pile of early workbooks and advanced sheet music.

I took it all out, attempted to tune the instrument, reacquainted myself with how to hold the bow, where to place my fingers on the fingerboard, and began playing. I started with "Twinkle, Twinkle, Little Star." I played it ten times and then flipped the page of the Suzuki Method, Book One to the second piece, "Old MacDonald."

I'd just made it to page eighteen when I thought I detected someone approaching, reverberating footsteps on the stairs, on the landing, coming closer. Closing my eyes, I replayed the song from the previous page—which I had memorized at this point—and silently chanted in time to the music, *Please go away, please go away, please go away.*

Whether it was Abram or Gabby, I would never know. Whoever it was, they left after two stanzas, continuing upward to the third floor. *So, probably Abram.*

I played and I played until my neck ached, and my wrist cramped, and my fingertips stung, and I suspected the violin had given me hickeys on my neck. And then I played some more. When my arm started to spasm, I put the violin back in its case, but didn't place it back in the closet. I left it out for tomorrow.

That had been hours ago and I'd only left Lisa's room to sneak into the bathroom twice. I spent the rest of my evening going through her record, cassette tape, and CD collections. Despite living in the digital age, my sister still collected hardcopy forms of music.

Where my shelves were stuffed with books, hers were stuffed with music, vintage devices used to play the music, and fashion magazines. She owned an old boombox with a double cassette player, an AM/FM radio, and a CD player; a Sony Walkman; a record player; and several sets of quality Bose headphones. I'd listened to various and sundry music until late, lying on the carpet, my feet in the air or against the wall.

Then, at 1:00 AM, I'd gone to the bathroom to wash my face. There, on the counter, I found a note from Gabby folded under a brown plastic bottle with a pink label.

Hey you,

I'm leaving dry shampoo here, use it. I'll check on you tomorrow.

Love, Gabs

PS Sorry if I upset you

She'd also wrung out and hung up the bathrobe.

Numbly setting her note to the side and promptly pushing it from my mind, I washed my face, braided my hair, and changed into a pair of pink tank top and boy-short PJs. I then tried to go to sleep.

Maybe I can't sleep because I'm hungry? This was a distinct possibility, given the fact that I'd eaten only a granola bar yesterday.

My stomach rumbled, long and loud, and I pressed my hand against it. Grunting into the darkness, I tossed off the covers and stood from Lisa's bed. Food on my mind, I slipped out of the room and down the stairs. The kitchen was dark, but instead of flipping on a light—which might've alerted Abram as to my whereabouts . . . which he probably didn't care about so long as "Lisa wasn't doing anything crazy"—I crept on quiet feet to the fridge and opened it.

Momentarily dazzled by the bright light within, it took several seconds of squinting and blinking before the scant contents became visible. I frowned. In addition to the pizza box, two suspicious-looking containers of Chinese takeout, and various condiments, I found: shredded cheddar/jack cheese blend, a zucchini, a half a pint of mushrooms, and hot salsa. Opening the hot salsa, I smelled it, and then I dipped my pinkie inside and tasted it while examining the lid. It looked, smelled, and tasted fine.

Placing my finds on the island counter, I shut the fridge. The sudden extinguishing of the bright light meant that the kitchen was now pitch black. Shrugging off my lack of sight, I extended my arms and blindly felt my way over to the pantry until my hands connected with the torso of a person.

A person.

A PERSON!

I jumped back on instinct, my leg hitting one of the stools at the island counter and sending it crashing to the ground. My heart in my throat, I screamed, turned, and darted forward, but my feet tangled with the felled stool and I pitched, bracing myself for a gravitational collision with unseen wooden bars and a granite stool top.

But then strong arms caught me, deftly spinning and lifting me into the air. Cold dread rushed through my body, tensing every muscle. I couldn't think. I didn't think. Instinctively, my legs and fists pumped, fighting against my captor. Rocks in my throat as I readied another scream, a hand covered my mouth just as I belted it out.

"Whoa! Calm down. It's me." Abram's voice at my ear soothed, his bulky arm a tight band around my torso, my back to his front, my feet not touching the ground. "Calm down. Shhh. Calm down."

Hot breath teased my hair and neck, and I stilled, relief at discovering it was Abram didn't quite chase away the viral panic still attached to my hemoglobin, coursing through my veins. I shook. I was shaking. And I was gasping through my nose, greedy for air.

Perhaps he heard or felt my strained breathing because his arm loosened, lowering my feet to the ground, and his hand covering my mouth slid away. "Are you okay? Are you hurt?"

"I'm fine," I said, not sounding convincing. Truth was, I felt like throwing up. "Can you, uh, let me go?"

His arms immediately fell away and I stupidly rushed forward, once more crashing into the stool.

I heard Abram mutter a curse under his breath just as he caught me again, lifting me off the ground again, and saving me—again—from another gravitational collision. This time he turned us away from the stool and carried me across the room.

I didn't fight him this time. In fact, I relaxed into him. Wired and exhausted, but mostly embarrassed, I allowed myself to be transported without protest. We left the kitchen and I was finally able to see dim outlines of furniture and walls, courtesy of the streetlamp illumination spilling through the windows of the living room.

Abram carried me to my mother's favorite piece of furniture in our house, a gold velvet chaise lounge said to have once belonged to Napoleon's sister, Pauline Bonaparte. Depositing me on the soft surface, Abram crossed to one of the Tiffany lamps and pulled the chain, bathing the room in soft blue and yellow, colored light filtering through the stained glass.

He then returned, knelt in front of me, one hand on my leg, the other cupping my cheek. "Are you okay?"

"Yes," I said, cleared my throat, unable to lift my eyes higher than his black T-shirt, and said again, "Yes."

He blew out a breath, pushing his fingers through my hair. By doing so, he forced my chin up and caught my gaze. That wrinkle of worry appeared between his eyebrows, and his very pretty eyes—which glowed and sparkled like polished amber cabochons —moved between mine.

"You really freaked out."

I stiffened, gritting my teeth and yanking my head back, out of his reach. "I didn't know you were there."

Watching me with watchful watchfulness, he let his hand drop slowly until it rested on my left leg, next to his other hand which covered my right knee. "I said your name—twice—when I walked in."

"I didn't hear you." I glanced from his eyes to where his palms were hot on my skin. "And I couldn't see. I'd just shut the fridge, my eyes hadn't adjusted."

"Did you think I was a robber?" His left eyebrow lifted as did the side of his mouth, just a hint.

Clearly, he was trying to lighten the mood. Unfortunately, I still felt shaky. And embarrassed.

"I—I didn't think," I admitted, releasing an unsteady breath. "I wasn't thinking. Sorry I fell."

"No need to apologize. It wasn't like you could help it."

"Yeah. Gravity can be such a downer."

He made a light, laughing sound. "What?"

"Uh, nothing. Whatever." *No physics jokes!*

His frown returned, his fingers flexing slightly on my legs. "Are you sure you're okay?"

Reaching for his hands, I removed them from my knees, setting them away. "I'm really fine. I just don't like—"

He glanced at my knees. "Being touched?"

"When it's unexpected." I crossed my arms.

"That makes sense. But your reaction, even after you knew it was me—" He paused and sat back on his heels, as though debating how to continue and finally settling on, "It was a big reaction." Abram continued to study me with his big, pretty, knowing brown eyes. "Hey, I would never hurt you."

I winced, just a little, my gaze falling to my knees where his hands had been. I wanted to huff a laugh and roll my eyes, maybe say something like, *I know, don't be ridiculous.*

But the word "Okay," small and fragile sounding, slipped out instead. I immediately wished it back, because I didn't understand it. I didn't know why I'd said it, and I hated not knowing.

Get ahold of yourself, Mona. Pull it together. You are fine. Nothing happened.

Meanwhile, he continued his examination of me. I felt his stare, assessing my down-turned face. "Out of curiosity, and no big deal if you don't want to say, but did something happen to you this last year?"

My back straightened and I sucked in a slow, deep breath before asking calmly, "Like what?"

"You're very . . . different than you were before."

"Because I don't want you touching me?" I tried to infuse my words with challenge, strength—wanting to shake off any earlier impression of weakness—and mostly succeeded. Peeking at him, I gauged his reaction from behind a hastily built wall of dispassion.

But then Abram dropped his chin to his chest, a massive grin lighting his features, and the fragrance of him hit me. My lashes fluttered as though he'd blown dust in my eyes, penetrating my wobbly wall of dispassion and sending it crumbling to the ground.

God, he smelled so good, and—unlike visual stimuli—I couldn't stop whatever cascade of relaxing, soothing, melting awareness smelling his scent set off. Unthinkingly, I leaned forward an inch, chasing and inhaling the smell of him while he cleared his throat, like he was trying not to laugh.

Why he was fighting a laugh, I didn't know, but the apparent genuineness of Abram's struggle to subdue his grin only served to increase his attractiveness.

A moment later, he lifted his eyes and they connected with mine. He'd conceded to a shy smile. It was *quite* a smile.

"Yes," he said.

"Yes?" I parroted dumbly. *What were we talking about? And would it be weird if I buried my nose in his neck?*

"Yes. You not wanting me to touch you means that you are very different now than you were before," he explained.

I appreciated the completeness and thoroughness of his sentence.

My cheeks were hot. I pressed my hands against them while I examined him with suspicion. What was he doing to me?

"How so?" I asked, hoping to keep him talking so I could hunt down the splintered pieces of my concentration.

His eyebrows pulled together as his shy smile became a smirk. "You're telling me you don't remember?"

"Tell me your version of events," I demanded, side-stepping a lie and still holding my cheeks.

"Uhh . . ." He scratched the back of his neck, peering at me like I both confused and amused him.

I was used to confusing people, but not amusing them. My cheeks burned hotter.

"Do *you* even remember?" I pushed, knowing my tone was belligerent.

He made a sound like he was choking on a laugh. "Yes. It's hard to forget waking up to a naked girl in my bed."

Jaw dropping, my eyes grew to their maximum diameter.

Naked. Girl. In . . . bed?

"Are you serious?" I whispered, my mind darting in all directions, attempting to form a reasonable hypothesis for Lisa's behavior and coming up completely empty. Suddenly, I couldn't catch my breath.

He shook his head, giving me an astonished once-over. "You honestly don't remember?"

My mouth opened and closed as I struggled to speak, but it was no use. I was too . . . I was too many things. Shocked. Confused. Incredulous. ANGRY.

LISA!

What had she been thinking? She'd been eighteen! How would she have liked waking up to find a strange, naked, eighteen-year-old boy in *her* bed?

I was beyond shocked. I was horrified. I was electrocuted by the reality of my sister's brazen-slash-creepy quotient, because I couldn't imagine doing anything in the same sphere of possibility. I was beginning to believe that if my twin and I were represented by a Venn diagram, our only areas of overlap would be physical. A minor sliver of shared corporal characteristics, and that was absolutely it.

"Lisa?"

Blinking at Abram, and promptly becoming tangled in his searching gaze, I realized he was still there. And I was still here. And my hands were still pressed against my cheeks as I warred with what I now identified as hot mortification.

What else could I do? I shot to my feet and marched out of the living room, dropping my hands and running up the main staircase.

She owed him an apology and . . . and . . . a voluntarily executed restraining order, a promise to stay one hundred meters away at all times. I clutched my forehead as I made it to the second floor, pausing only for a second when I registered the sound of his footsteps rushing up the stairs behind me. Sucking in a large breath, I jogged to my room—*dammit!*—and pivoted as soon as I realized the error, turning to Lisa's room just as Abram crested the top stair.

"Hey, wait. Wait." Abram stepped in front of Lisa's door and held his hands out as though to catch me by the shoulders, but I rocked back before he could make contact. He looked bemused and amused.

"You think this is funny?" I asked, though it was really an accusation.

"I guess I do." His gaze traveled over my face, and—like before—he was looking at me like I'd surprised him, delighted him, like I was something new.

I was too angry at Lisa to worry about what this look might mean. Did he suspect I was Mona? I didn't think so, but I couldn't be sure because I couldn't concentrate. My attention was split between my disgust with my sister's actions and trying to shake off all the damn noticing I was doing of Abram's every damn mannerism.

Plus, his current obvious amusement did not help.

Gritting my teeth, I was having trouble holding his gaze but forced myself to do so anyway. "How can you think this is funny? I think it's horrifying."

Abram lifted an eyebrow. "You think it's horrifying?"

It was a miracle he'd been so nice to me—to Lisa—up to now. His standoffishness when we'd first arrived made complete sense. No wonder he'd looked at me with such hostility. If I'd been him, I would have refused Leo's request. *Abram is a saint!* A SAINT!

And Gabby knew about it this whole time . . .

"You're owed an apology." Crossing my arms and lifting my chin a notch, I nodded my head. "On behalf of—on behalf of that Lisa, who did that to you, who behaved in an unforgivable way, I apologize."

His eyes softened, the focus of their warmth shifting from inward amusement to outward . . . something else.

"You're forgiven," he said in a way that was a little breathless, dazed. His stare had turned hazy, velvet and hot. I felt the words and the weight of this new look straight to my heart, and now I was also breathless.

What is happening?

We passed a moment, staring at each other, where all I felt was confusion and chaos and a frenzied sort of all-directional momentum. Though I know it is theoretically impossible, which really just means improbable, time slowed until it merged with the physical plane, and I lived every infinite possibility that touched this second: leaving, staying, staring, kissing, shaking hands, touching, grabbing, high-fiving, walking backward to a bed—

But then Abram leaned closer, his attention dropping to my mouth. He blinked dazedly, and whispered, "Lisa."

Lisa.

. . . LISA!

Her name was a vomit pie to the face and merged all the infinite possibilities into just one inescapable path forward.

The bizarre moment broken, I huffed a shaky laugh. Unable to maintain eye contact, I backed away. I didn't believe in predestination, but Abram and I were predestined to be less than friends, hopefully not even acquaintances. For order to exist and be maintained in my universe, we must be absolutely nothing to each other.

"Don't forgive me," I said, my voice gravelly, surveying the space between Abram and my sister's open door behind him, looking for a way into the room that wouldn't bring our bodies into contact. Finding none, I turned for the stairs, calling over my shoulder, "In fact, do us both a favor: hold a grudge."

* * *

I slept in my parents' room, but not in their bed. Their bed was huge and huge beds had never held any allure for me. Since going to college, I'd been a nervous sleeper, waking up several times a night, tangling myself in my sheets. I never make my bed because it would be an inefficient use of time, and big beds with big sheets give me drowning dreams.

The cushioned window seat was my bed for the night and I used one of the many plush blankets piled high in the linen closet. They smelled of geranium and rose. The housekeeper had layered the blankets with linen squares scented with essential oils, as per my mother's instructions. She had a sensitive nose and had always been very particular about how things smelled.

Other than my looks, I'd never considered that I might share any traits with my mother. She was very glamorous, vivacious, and charismatic.

I was . . . not.

But as I tossed and turned on the cushioned seat, and despite the aroma of geranium and rose, I couldn't stop thinking about Abram and how delicious he smelled and how the fragrance of him fogged my brain.

I'd always enjoyed good smells—fresh baked bread, warm cookies straight out of the oven, cinnamon, donuts, apple cider, orange blossoms, lavender, and lemon—but I'd never thought of myself as being sensitive to them. Until now.

Thoughts of Abram's heady scent on my mind, I forced my eyes closed by laying a forearm over my eyelids. I must have eventually fallen asleep because I dreamt of him. I dreamt of that moment in the hall and all those infinite possibilities.

I looked into his eyes, hazy and velvet and trusting. Instead of saying my sister's name, he'd said, "Mona . . ."

And knew what I wanted with a clarity that, even though I was merely dreaming, it was jarring.

In general—in my experience—good decisions were always made by default. Living your best life wasn't about active choice, it was about the risk/benefit ratio, an equation that balanced the greatest good against the least harm. The logical path forward was the only path forward.

But I wanted him.

So, I made an active choice to be reckless.

I placed my hand against his cheek without an invitation. I dropped my eyes to his lips and thought of nothing but my own selfishness and how much I wanted to taste them. I stepped closer, into his warmth, absorbing his heat, pressing my body to his without asking for permission, and finally—*finally*—took his beautiful lips with mine.

And then inexplicably, just as an explosion of heat and taste invaded my mouth, he said, "Rise and shine, sleeping beauty."

The soft slide of fingers brushing loose strands off my forehead paired with his soft, grumbly whisper made no sense. We were kissing. How could he be speaking when we were kissing?

But we aren't kissing, not really.

Rousing reluctantly, I turned my face toward his voice, stretching languidly, feeling relaxed and calm and inhaling a chest-expanding breath.

"What time is it?" I asked, brushing the back of my knuckles against my lips.

"Ten," he said.

He said . . .

Who said?

Abram.

And just like that, I was awake. But I didn't open my eyes. Nor did I tense, or shrink away. Instead, for reasons unknown, I held perfectly still.

His hand made another pass over my forehead. His fingertips, rough and callused, pushed into my hair gently, curving back around so that his knuckles skimmed over my upper cheek, down my jaw, the pad of his thumb caressing a little circle around my chin. It felt like he was tracing me, drawing me into wakefulness, and—once I stopped attempting to calculate the risk/benefit of this moment—it felt really, really nice.

"Sorry I have to wake you," he said, sounding sorry, and sleepy, and extremely close. "But we have to go."

"Where are we going?" I asked, still not opening my eyes, hoping he'd trace my face again.

He did, his fingers followed the same lazy path. "To Michigan."

"What's in Michigan?"

Finished with his third tracing, his hand paused on my shoulder, and then slid slowly down my arm. That felt good too. The rough spots a surprising texture, his touch a three-dimensional, complex experience. He had nice hands.

"My parents' house."

My eyes flew open, reacquainted themselves with his big, pretty ones—which were currently smiling down at me tiredly—and blinked. "Your parents' house?"

His warm hand made a return trip up my arm and came to a rest on my shoulder. "Yes. It's my mom's birthday. We have to be there by two thirty, so we have to leave soon."

"We?"

"I let you sleep as long as I could, and I didn't sleep." He stopped here to yawn, taking his hand away to cover his mouth. "Sorry," he said around his display of exhaustion. "But we have to go."

I shook my head and squinted at him, at the circles under his eyes, at the ashen quality to his skin. "You didn't sleep? Why didn't you sleep?"

"I couldn't." He smiled, plainly happy, standing and shrugging.

"You couldn't?" I sat up and held the blanket to my chest, tracking him as he backed away.

Abram pointed at me with both index fingers. "Too many ideas, my muse!"

"Ideas?"

"Be ready in a half hour." He yawned. "You're driving. I'll sleep in the car on the way. I'll be fine."

I'm driving?

How could I drive? I had my (Mona's) driver's license, but I didn't have Lisa's. Obviously, I couldn't take mine. Wasn't it illegal to drive without a license? And what if I were pulled over? Who would I say that I was?

"Abram." I stood, shaking my head at the tangled strands of information he'd just dropped in my lap. "Wait. Stop. Let me get this straight. You want me to go to your mother's birthday? What if I promised to stay put?"

"Where I go, you go."

"I won't leave the house."

"I don't have a choice, and neither do you. I promised your brother."

I couldn't argue with that. "So, we're going to your parents' because it's your mother's birthday? And you have to be there by two thirty, but you haven't slept, so you need me to drive, and you're expecting to sleep on the way?"

"Correct." He was almost to the door, his steps shuffling, like he was too tired to pick up his feet.

Hastily discarding the blanket, I followed him. "Do you have a present?"

"I'll pick something up on the way." He yawned again. "Maybe a card. She likes flowers."

Frowning at his blasé comment, I persisted. "No, no. Don't get her flowers on the way. We have—I mean, my mom has—a stash of stuff. Designer bags, perfume, silk scarves for last minute gifts. Let me put something together."

Abram stopped walking backward, but he also made a face. "Silk scarves?" he slurred, his eyes blinking like he was having trouble keeping them open.

"Trust me. Just, go get ready. I'll get the gift and meet you downstairs in a half hour." I walked around him, pressing the call button for the lift. "And take the elevator. You're exhausted."

"I'm fine. It's just one floor down." He waved away my comment, but promptly had to cover his mouth again for another yawn.

Thankfully, the doors opened immediately, and he didn't protest as I pushed him onto the elevator. In fact, my pushing seemed to amuse him.

"Okay, see you soon." I ignored the way my skin heated at his warm expression, focusing instead on what needed to be done. "And if you use the stairs, promise me you'll hold onto the rail. I don't want you falling down."

"Yeah, gravity can be such a downer," Abram mumbled, repeating my words from the prior evening, and that gave me pause.

I watched him closely as he leaned backward against the wall of the car, as though standing upright took too much energy. His sleepy, half-lidded gaze moved over me. His smile grew.

"You look . . . nice," he said, his voice dropping an octave.

Frowning in confusion, I glanced down at myself, at my braless chest in the skimpy pink tank top and boy-short PJs. Awareness caused a shock of pinpricks beneath my skin and I lifted startled eyes, catching the tail end of his transparently hot and appreciative look just as the doors slid shut.

CHAPTER 8

FALLING OBJECTS

I assembled a birthday package for Abram's mom, pulled on one of my—Mona's —dresses as it felt more appropriate for the situation; unbraided and brushed my hair, ignoring the bottle of dry shampoo; applied the eye makeup; and grabbed two granola bars. The bars I washed down with a glass of milk just as Abram called Lisa's name from the foyer.

"That's a nice dress," he said, leaning against the front door and watching me as I entered.

Glancing down at my somewhat fitted skirt, I shrugged. His gaze persisted, but I ignored it, instead turning to the mirror and pretending to fuss with my appearance.

"Very librarian chic." His voice was deeper than usual, probably because he hadn't slept at all. "All you need now is glasses, a ruler, and a very disapproving scowl."

I fought against the sudden urge to scowl disapprovingly—just to see what he'd do—and said, "It's Mona's."

Telling the truth here made the most sense. I'd never worn it before, so I didn't have to worry about any pictures of me (Mona) in this dress somewhere in the house. Yet, it definitely wasn't Lisa's style: "boring" navy blue cotton, capped sleeves, a conservative neckline with a little collar, and an equally conservative hemline that fell just past my knees. However, it was form-fitting, which was why I'd never worn it, but was why I thought maybe it was a good compromise for today.

Abram pushed away from the door and strolled to my shoulder. "You'll need this."

Avoiding eye contact (and speaking and smelling), I turned to him and accepted the phone he held. Google Maps was already pulled up, and an address in Michigan was already mapped out.

Wordlessly, he guided me out the door, ten meters to the right beyond our gate, and to his car, a 1999 Honda Civic. Good thing I knew how to drive a stick shift. But, unfortunately, the stick shift also meant I had to hike my fitted skirt up a bit to use the clutch. Feeling acutely self-conscious—especially after the look he'd given me this morning before the elevator doors closed—I had difficulty swallowing until I glanced at my companion.

Abram had already fallen asleep, zonking out as soon as I'd pulled away from the curb. Seeing this, I laughed at my silly self-consciousness, hiked my skirt up a little more for ease of clutch-usage, and released a giant sigh.

I must be in an alternate dimension. My brain has officially gone off the rails.

I felt . . . lost. Not geographically lost, thanks to Abram's GPS, but mentally and emotionally and physically muddled. Since talking everything over with Allyn was out of the question, I used the long, quiet drive to sort through the tangle of thoughts in my brain and the bundle of nerves in my stomach without her help.

First and foremost, I was nervous because I'd never operated a motor vehicle without my driver's license before. If sleeping in my day clothes felt disobedient, this felt exponentially disobedient. I couldn't relax. I felt the illegal nature of my actions like an elusive hair in my mouth, but instead *IN MY BRAIN*. Which was why I drove ten to twenty miles under the speed limit the entire way, with both hands on the steering wheel. At all times.

Second, there was that dream from last night and *that look* from this morning. I tried to talk myself into believing *that look* had been imagined. But then I'd recall the image of his hot eyes in his super handsome face, staring at me daringly, brazenly.

No matter how much I tried, I couldn't talk myself into believing something false. Abram had been ogling me. Fact.

No. Not me. Lisa.

Except, in that moment, I wasn't Lisa. But, I also was her. *Confusing.*

Which brings me to the third item: everything else. The tense moment between Abram and I last night in front of Lisa's door and whatever that meant; the revelation that Lisa had appeared naked and uninvited in his bed last year; the fact that I'd told Gabby about that stupid story with that stupid TA my freshman year (*Why oh why had I done that?*); the possibility that Lisa had been dealing drugs to teenagers; the unknowns surrounding her arrest; and the fact that I was a lying liar, pretending to be her, right now. What a mess.

I didn't like all the unknowns.

My life had been supremely tidy up to now, by design. And Abram was the definition of messy—from the way he dressed to how infrequently he shaved to eating cold pizza, sleeping at random hours, approaching his responsibilities with a laissez-faire nonchalance, waiting until the last minute to get his mother a birthday gift, and *did the man even have a job?*—and liking him had the potential to be incredibly messy.

And yet, I did.

I liked him.

Talking to him was confoundedly easy. One might even say *seductively* easy. Seductive because, when we spoke, I was constantly forgetting to lie, or speak in one-word sentences, or try to be Lisa-like. I couldn't help but default to being myself.

I liked, now that I understood the situation better, that he'd shunned Lisa (I know, I know, I'm strange) and firmly rejected her BS, setting down rules and laying out expectations with both her and Gabby upon our arrival. Lisa had behaved horribly to him in the past. Still, he'd agreed to help my brother and had forgiven her—me—as soon as I'd apologized.

Also, I was now mostly convinced he hadn't been making fun of me during the sperm-whale-poop conversation at the guitar shop. He'd been teasing me and, upon recalling the conversation, I liked how his teasing had been clever and informed. He'd caught me by surprise with something I hadn't known. I liked that his sarcasm was funny and quick-witted rather than biting and mean-spirited. Clearly, he was intelligent, though it was a species of applied, pragmatic intelligence mostly foreign to me.

But! He's a slacker. And you've only known him for two days, Mona.

True. Very true.

In my world of faculty and fellows, data and research, practical smarts weren't a requisite. In fact, I'd been told they were an impediment to expansive thinking. Theoretical intelligence was all that was needed, application of theory was for capitalists and corporations.

And yet, I couldn't help but enjoy Abram's pragmatism, like when he'd told me to take a bath instead of engineering a shower helmet (he'd been right!).

And finally, I liked how gentle he'd been last night when I'd freaked out. He'd been comforting and concerned. Of course, there was this morning, and how he'd woken me up with more gentleness. Even though there'd been unexpected touching, I'd liked everything about it.

But, again, you've only known him for two days!! And Lisa will be home very, very soon . . .

Also true. Very true.

When Lisa arrived home, ideally, she'd continue the lie. Abram would have to believe we were the same person. Which meant any friendly overtures, or clever teasing, or any looks of appreciation he sent my way would all eventually be shifted to her.

Twisting my lips to the side, I removed one of my hands from the wheel just long enough to rub my sternum. My chest ached, a strange expanding tightness against my lower ribs, and the thought of Abram teasing Lisa made me want to pull over and punch that stupid guy in his stupid hat on that stupid billboard I kept seeing all along I-94.

Once or twice, when the highway was free of other cars, I gave into the temptation to glance over at Abram's silently sleeping form. Entirely quiet and motionless, his stillness verged on eerie. At one point I debated whether or not to pull over and check his pulse. That would've necessitated touching him, which I had mixed feelings about—he couldn't give consent, but then again, he might be dead—which was ultimately why I didn't do it. However, if I'd had a mirror on me, I probably would've pulled over to hold it under his nose.

Who sleeps like that?

Not me.

But back to Abram. I snuck another look and my stomach flip-flopped. He'd called me sleeping beauty, but the label firmly belonged to him and his dark lashes, his gently parted, gorgeous lips, the angle of his strong jaw, and the perfect curve of his bicep supporting his head. This was all transposed against tousled hair and rumpled clothes.

He was a messy Adonis and, despite myself, I just . . . really liked him.

But why?

To what purpose?

What are you doing, Mona? Stay on the path. Liking him is irrelevant.

My chest flared with another ache. Indigestion? I probably should have eaten something more substantial than granola.

Conclusion: I needed a healthy meal, and I needed to get control of this situation.

More precisely, after today, I needed to redouble my efforts to avoid Abram, and I needed to take care of my physical urges. Because that's all this was really.

Embrace the null hypothesis, Mona!

Liking Abram was madness. It would never lead anywhere. Therefore, there was no decision to make. My choice was made by default. I didn't actually like Abram. I had physical needs. Thanks to Gabby's insidious text yesterday, I was having trouble concentrating. I thought I'd be able to wait until I made it back to California, but that wasn't going to work. I'd have to take care of the physical urges now.

I glanced down at my form-fitting skirt hiked up to my mid-thigh. Well, not *now now*. More precisely, this evening *now*.

Maybe once that box was checked I'd stop noticing the prettiness and amber color of Abram's eyes, and how great he smelled, and how the man chewed, and how achingly gentle and sincere he was with me when voicing his concern for my well-being, and I would be able to properly avoid him. Yes. This was a good plan. The moment we returned to the house? I was definitely going to avoid him and . . . do something.

But first, I needed to get through this expanse of highway, operating this vehicle without my license, his mother's birthday, and the drive back to the house. After that, it would be all avoidance, all the time.

Four hours into our journey, just when a rest stop sign appeared and I was seriously close to pulling off and placing two fingers against his neck—not because I was itching to touch him, but because who wants to drive not only without a license but also with a corpse?—Abram finally stirred.

Without meaning to do so, I exhaled a large sigh, mumbling one of my anytime-phrases, "As the prophesy foretold," and felt my shoulders relax.

In my peripheral vision, I saw Abram lift his head, rub his eyes, and peer out the windshield. "Hey. What time is it? Where are we?" His voice—deep and sleep-sand-papery—slid over me, making me sit up straighter. His voice was pleasing all the time, but newly awake Abram-voice was real nice.

But irrelevant.

"On I-94." I cleared my throat, glancing at the car's clock before remembering it was broken.

"What time is it?" he asked, peering at his phone where it was held suspended on the dash. "It's after three? Did we—did you miss the turn off?"

"No. It's still a few miles away." I gestured to the looming green sign. "We passed Kalamazoo twenty minutes ago."

I sensed rather than saw his stare. "Did you pull off for a while? Take a break from driving?"

"No."

"No?"

"No."

He waited a beat, and then asked, "Is there something wrong with the car?"

"No."

"No?"

"No."

Again, he waited a beat before questioning me further, but this time I felt a mood shift. "Then what happened? We should have been there an hour ago." He grabbed his phone from the dash, moving his thumb along the screen. "My mom has texted me five times."

"Your mom texted you five times?"

"Yes. Haven't you noticed the messages?"

"Yes, but I didn't read them or know they were from her. I hid them when they came in."

"You didn't read them?"

"They're not my messages, it would have been an invasion of privacy." I gave a weak shrug. "Why? Why did she text?"

"Lisa, we're very late and she's worried." He said this like it was obvious, as though all parents worried and texted their kids when they were late. "We've gone a hundred and fifty miles in four hours, why are you driving so slow?"

"I don't have my driver's license."

He waited, like he expected me to continue. When I didn't, he asked, "So?"

"So, I didn't want to get pulled over." I glanced at him, found him staring at me. "Hey. Don't give me that look. You're not the one operating a motor vehicle illegally."

"It's not illegal to drive without a license. It's illegal to drive if you have no license."

Sending him a quick glare, I readjusted my hand placement on the steering wheel. "Is that some kind of riddle? If I say your name backward three times, will you drive?"

Abram barked a laugh, drawing my attention. I found him looking at me with glassy eyes, his hand over his mouth, hiding his smile while shaking his head. His shoulders shook with quiet laughter.

"You are . . ." he started, stopped, sighed, then chuckled. "I should be mad at you."

"You're mad at me?" I felt equal parts indignant and contrite, which was a weird, new combination for me.

"But I'm not. You are so much different than I thought you would be."

Unsurprisingly, that had me gripping the steering wheel tighter and flailing for something to say that might sound Lisa-like.

But then I stopped flailing.

If my actions and our conversations over the last few days hadn't made him suspicious, then he wasn't going to be suspicious. At all. In fact, now I had a suspicion Abram wasn't ever going to be suspicious of me.

Conclusion: No need for me to worry about acting Lisa-like, because—to him—I was her.

Which, I conceded with a good measure of uneasiness, when she arrived, she'd have to act like me.

* * *

I'd never been to a suburb before.

Driving through Abram's parents' neighborhood was like visiting a movie set. The houses all looked remarkably similar, the front lawns were perfectly maintained, US flags flew from flagpoles, wreaths hung on doors. I even spotted a few picket fences.

Honestly? I loved it.

"You grew up here?"

"Yes."

"What do your parents do?" I asked, making a left onto another street that looked just like the last street. Everything was so delightfully tidy.

He didn't answer immediately, so I glanced at him. He looked uncomfortable.

"What?" I split my attention between him and the street. "Do they run a grow house?"

Abram coughed a laugh, now staring at me. "No! My parents don't run a grow house!"

"This neighborhood reminds me of that show, *Breaking Bad*. Of course, we're in Michigan, not New Mexico, and the house styles are different, but the neighborhood has a similar feel. Have you ever watched it?"

"No." His tone held amusement, but also maybe defensiveness. Or something like defensiveness.

"It's a good show. The chemistry stuff is spot on," I said distractedly. A house with a picket fence, a rooster weather vane, *and* a towering flagpole with a US flag snagged my attention. The outside was painted white, the shutters were trimmed forest green, the door was red. A summery-looking wreath with yellow flowers was affixed to the door. It probably had a welcome mat.

I want to live there.

"How would you know about the chemistry stuff?" he asked, also sounding distracted.

Instead of being flustered or worried that I'd made a mistake by mentioning chemistry, I saw his question for exactly what it was: a way to avoid answering my earlier query about his parents.

So I said, "Mona knows chemistry stuff," which wasn't a lie, but rather a true statement meant to deflect, and then asked again, "So, what do your parents do?"

Abram released an audible breath, shifted in his seat, and then finally said, "They're retired."

"Retired?"

He nodded.

"What did they do before they retired?" I lifted my eyebrows expectantly. When he didn't answer, I suggested, "Run a grow house?"

"No."

I peeked at him, found him grinning and trying to hide his grin by covering the bottom half of his mouth with his hand, his elbow propped on the window sill. He was giving me an amused side-eye.

Finally, he answered, "My dad was a general contractor and my mom ran the business part. They had my sister late, and me even later."

"Oh." I made a right. "How late?"

"Mom was forty when she had me and dad was forty-seven."

"Oh." I made another right, scanning the scrolling numbers on the side of the mailboxes. We were four houses away. "How old are you?"

"Twenty-three."

That's right. Gabby had said something about him being three or four years older than us.

"So she's sixty-four today?"

"Yes."

"Oh." I slowed as we approached the address, studying the two-story yellow house.

I found myself swallowing against a pang of longing as my gaze greedily noted the details of Abram's childhood home. Navy shutters, white drapes, maroon door, and a wreath of pink and white flowers. No picket fence, but it did have a stone path leading to the front door which was lined with abundant rose bushes, all fully in bloom.

Forget that other house. I want to live here.

"Is this why fate brought us together?" I mumbled another of my anytime-phrases, the one I typically reserved for inanimate objects I desired.

"What?" Abram's question brought my attention back to him.

"It's so pretty."

His eyes narrowed. "What?"

"Your parents' house. It's so pretty."

His eyes narrowed further, moving over me in a way that felt apprehensive, like he didn't believe me, or he thought I was making fun of his family, or he was waiting for me to add a *but*, or a *for a plebeian's house,* or something equally judgmental and pretentious.

Shifting my gaze back to the house, I allowed the envy in my features tell the truth of my words; tall yellow rose bushes flanked the porch; adjacent were several shorter bushes with lavender-colored blooms.

"Are those Blue Moons?" I lifted my chin toward the purple flowers. I didn't know all the different varieties of roses, just a few of my favorites: Princess Anne, Boscobel, Blue Moon, but Eden was my absolute favorite. They smelled like how heaven must feel.

"I honestly don't know. But my mom will." Abram seemed to hesitate, and then mildly surprised me by placing his hand on my bared leg, drawing my gaze back to his and causing an immediate swirling heat low in my stomach.

But not alarm. *Interesting.*

When I looked at him, I found his eyes were uncharacteristically—insomuch as I knew his character—somber. "Hey, one more thing. And promise me you won't freak out."

I lifted my eyebrows at the irony of the situation: here I was, trying to ignore how very, very nice the heat of his hand felt on my thigh and he was asking me to not freak out. Meanwhile, I'd usually be freaking out about an uninvited hand on my leg.

But I wasn't. I *liked* it. And I was just barely holding the door closed on all sorts of odd, inappropriate hopes. Like maybe he'd pull the hem of my skirt just a little higher, or reach underneath . . .

Pushing those thoughts back behind the closed door, on a rush I said, "I can't promise you I won't freak out until you tell me what I'm not supposed to freak out about."

His lips quirked to the side. The left side. My gaze dropped to the dimple I felt certain would make an appearance. I wasn't disappointed, even though it was promptly hidden again.

"Okay, makes sense." He breathed in, he breathed out, his fingers flexed on my leg and I swallowed thickly. "Here goes: my sister, who is probably already here, is a journalist."

My eyes cut to his. All inappropriate heat and hopes extinguished. *A journalist?*

"Pardon?" My single word was sharp.

"My sister, Marie. She's an investigative journalist." He seemed to be watching my reaction closely. "Leo said you guys—your family doesn't like journalists."

An investigative journalist? Of the exposé variety?

I didn't freak out, outwardly. I freaked out inwardly. "What does she investigate?"

"Whatever she finds interesting or whatever she's assigned." He shrugged. "She's freelance, part of the AP, so she does all kinds of things."

A member of the Associated Press? She was the real deal. So many questions, none of which I could voice, and most involving worst-case scenarios.

What if this is a setup? Unlikely. His mother's birth date wasn't something Abram's sister had any control over.

But, what if his sister knows who I am? Or, I've met her before now? What if she's interviewed me? What if this benign birthday party leads to exposing Lisa's arrest? Like most professions, the world of professional journalism was a lot smaller than people realized.

"What's her name?" I asked.

"Marie Harris. She's awesome, and I told her she wasn't allowed to ask you anything on the record."

"Hmm . . ." The name didn't sound familiar, but that didn't mean anything.

"Also, she just broke up with her boyfriend recently, a few months ago. He was a chef in Chicago, kind of a dweeb, actually. She deserves *a lot* better. Don't bring up anything related to that. I think she's still sensitive about it."

I was only half-listening to him. Leo had been right. My family had a love/hate relationship with the media. According to my parents, none of them could be trusted. Ever. But they served a purpose.

For my part, I hypothesized that there were three types of journalists: those who wanted to do another fluff piece on music's most beloved power couple's "odd-ball, genius daughter" (say that ten times real fast), or those who wanted dirt, or those who wanted both.

Having been interviewed countless times, the interviewers always seemed content to follow the same, predictable path, painting me using the same brush, prosaic questions the brush strokes: What's it like to be so smart? What's it like to have DJ Tang and Exotica as parents? Are you dating anyone? Blah blah blah.

However, having been interviewed countless times *and* having never been surprised meant I rarely remembered the interviewers' names. In summary, I'd never met a journalist who pleasantly surprised or impressed me.

"Any stories on, uh, the children of celebrities?"

Abram shook his head. "No. Politicians are more her speed." His gaze lost some of its focus as it moved over my shoulder. "She also writes some weird stories too. Stuff that gets her in trouble."

"Trouble?"

"Yes." His gaze came back to mine and he smirked. "Ask her about bodybuilders."

"Bodybuilders." I relaxed. A tad. My gaze flickered over him. "Okay. So . . . what are we going to tell her? What's the story?"

"The story?" He turned a little in his seat. His hand slipped from my leg and he pushed his fingers into his hair, moving the dark mahogany strands off his forehead.

"What's the story about why I'm here? With you? What are we telling your sister and parents?"

"Uh . . . the truth?"

I sat up straighter while having a minor heart attack. "The-the—"

"That you're Leo's sister and you came home while I was house-sitting your parents' place in Chicago. We've shacked up together for the summer, you're my muse, and I've fallen madly in love with you over the last"—he grabbed his phone from the dash, glancing at the clock—"forty-eight hours."

With that tornado of an esoteric suggestion, Abram opened the passenger door and exited the car. Unhurriedly unfolding his long form from the Civic, he stretched. I stared at the band of back, side, and stomach skin (and muscles) left exposed as he lifted his arms over his head and twisted at the waist—first left, and then right.

In love? Muse? Is he . . .?

He's . . .

I shook my head in an effort to rouse my brain. Tearing my stare from his body, I chuckled and rolled my eyes.

He was joking, of course. *Oh, Ahab.*

I decided right then, that whenever Abram said or did anything nutso, I would think of and refer to him as Ahab.

"Ha ha ha," I said to myself, adding for good measure, "and then the wolves came."

I guess we were winging it. I didn't like the idea of winging it, but I trusted Abram . . . insomuch as I was capable of trusting anyone I'd just met two days ago.

Finished stretching, Abram sauntered around to my side while I turned my attention back to the likelihood of having met Marie Harris in the past, talking myself into, and then out of, a freak-out.

Worst-case scenario: She'd interviewed both Lisa and me at some point, but so what? If she had, it had been only once. How much could a person remember from a ten-minute interview? And what could she do? Call me Mona and sew a scarlet M to my chest? Nah.

As Abram opened my door and extended his hand, which I accepted distractedly, and then allowed him to pull me from my seat, I reasoned that—even if his sister was a journalist of the dirt-digging variety—she couldn't expose me as Mona in the span of an afternoon. I would just . . . not talk much. Speak only when spoken to.

Keep my answers polite, but vague.

Yes. Good plan. *I can do this.*

CHAPTER 9
INTRODUCTION TO TWO-DIMENSIONAL KINEMATICS

"Ah!" Glancing between the bundle Marie had placed in my hands and the woman herself, I added the apt anytime-phrase "Is this why fate brought us together?" because it was perfect for the situation and needed to be said.

Marie tossed her head back and laughed. And then Abram's mom was also laughing. And then I was laughing, because the Harris women's laughter was contagious. For reals, it was an airborne illness of awesome.

Marie reminded me of my friend Allyn in some ways—how open she was, how friendly and engaging—but without the naïve awkwardness I found so charming in my friend. Marie was . . . well, she was a woman. Or, how I thought a woman should aspire to be. Knowledgeable. Confident. Kind. Reasonable. Empathetic. Inclusive. An adult. There was so much I could learn from her. Basically, Marie was who I wanted to be when I grew up.

But Pamela reminded me of no one. I'd never met anyone like her, and therefore I felt like I could learn a lot from her as well.

Perhaps I should have been disappointed in myself for not sticking to the plan. But try as I might, I could not stop talking. I was having too good of a time to care about the logical path forward. It was official: I loved both Abram's mom and his sister and I wanted them both to adopt me.

Here's how it happened: Abram and I had walked in, and I'd been determined to be on my best rigid behavior. But then Pamela—Abram's mom—pulled me into a hug, kissed my cheek like I was something precious, and slipped me a cookie under the premise of wiping lipstick from my face. She also winked. Stunned, I ate the cookie. It was shortbread and it was so good I wanted to cry.

I handed off the present I'd brought to Abram and, with her arm around my waist, Pamela walked me into the kitchen where Marie—who was Abram's opposite in coloring and willingness to show her smile—also gave me a hug and gave me a cookie. Another shortbread.

Is this all it takes to earn my trust? Cookies and smiles?! Can I be bought for so little?

Apparently, yes. Which I felt was the right answer. Besides, who is to say cookies are cheap? Cookies are priceless! (Don't @ me.)

Anyway, Marie promptly confided that both she and Pamela were Hufflepuffs, but that Abram was a Gryffindor with Slytherin tendencies, and then asked me which house I was in.

It all happened so quickly. One moment I was discussing how I preferred the blue and bronze scheme from the book to the blue and silver combo in the films (for the Ravenclaw house colors), and commiserating on the absence of Peeves in the movies, and in the next moment—really, six hours later of near constant enthralling conversation—Marie was showing me her hand-knit collection of fingerless gloves and asking me if I wanted a pair.

Which brings us to now.

"You are hilarious. 'Is this why fate brought us together?'" Abram's sister quoted me, wiping at her eyes. "They're just fingerless gloves. Take them."

"I will. I will take them." With no shame, I clutched the gloves to my chest. "Thank you." Not only were they warm, they were blue and bronze, *my real house colors.*

Since I worked and spent most of my day in cold offices sitting in front of a keyboard, my fingers were often cold. I'd tried full-fingered gloves to various degrees of failure. Explaining my cold finger lament to the ladies over peppermint tea—leaving out any particulars that might reveal me as Mona—Marie had immediately offered me a pair, volunteering that she was a knitter and had several spare sets in her old room, along with scarves, blankets, hats, and so forth.

"My apartment in Chicago is too small to hold everything I make, so I store a lot of stuff here. And you're welcome," Marie replied warmly, her face and her smile sunshine. "Thanks for giving my mom such generous gifts for her birthday, they were very thoughtful." Her gaze flickered over to her mother.

"Yes, thank you so much." Pamela placed her fingertips on her chest, immediately flustered all over again, just like she'd been when she'd first opened the presents.

I wanted to tell her it was no big deal. My mother received free luxury goods from all the major names, so a Burberry bag, scarf, and bottle of perfume had been—quite honestly—nothing from my perspective. But after seeing how Pamela had been almost afraid to touch the bag, scarf, and perfume upon opening them, and how agitated and grateful she'd been, I decided to keep this information to myself.

"I hope you enjoy them" was all I'd said then—which had earned me a soft smile from Abram at the time—and it was all I said now.

"Well, I absolutely will." Pamela sent me another affectionate gaze of gratitude, which only made me want to change the subject.

I wasn't comfortable with her appreciation. It wasn't deserved. Plus, I'd intruded on her birthday celebration. I was the one who needed to express gratitude.

"Thank you so much for having me today. Thank you for letting me crash your party."

"Oh pshaw. You didn't crash anything. You're welcome anytime. Did you get enough to eat?" Pamela motioned to Marie's bedroom door. "Do you want another piece of cake?"

I laughed. "No, thank you. I think two is enough."

"And you're assuming, Mom, that Abram hasn't already finished it off." Marie crossed to her bed and sat on the end of it, motioning that I should do the same. "I don't think we've ever had a birthday cake last twenty-four hours in this house."

"He's always been a good eater," Pamela said proudly, lowering herself into the chair in front of Marie's desk.

Marie glanced at me, giving me a closed-lipped smile. "Does he finish your food when you go out to restaurants? I swear, he only visits me in the city when he's hungry."

I straightened my spine, the question catching me unprepared, and opened my mouth to respond, but said nothing. This was the first time since I'd arrived that either Marie or her mother had asked me about Abram or made any reference to the possibility that he and I existed as a unit.

I'd been partnered with Marie and Pamela all day while Abram had gone off with his dad. We'd reconvened for a leisurely dinner, during which Abram sat across from me. The seating arrangements hadn't done much to settle the knots in my stomach, but they had strengthened my resolve to avoid him upon returning to the city.

First of all, I caught him staring at me. More than once. And worse, he'd caught me staring at him, *a lot* more than once. Each time it happened was like cymbals crashing between my ears as our eyes collided, snagged, and were hastily ripped away. After the crashing came the hot flare of mortification in my chest and up my neck.

And yet, I did it over and over, almost compulsively, like my free will had been hijacked. It was the most maddening thing, but my eyeballs drifted to him, seeking out his face, wanting to watch his features as he conversed quietly with his dad, or sparred good-naturedly with his sister, or told his mom how pretty she looked on her birthday.

I was mesmerized during these little interactions; how he demonstrated affection for these people he loved; how they in turn showed their affection for him. This family seemed to know each other intimately, and—for some inexplicable reason—Abram's attractiveness increased exponentially as I watched him love through quiet, small gestures. It made . . . *it makes me . . .*

It gave me heartburn.

Wonderful, dizzying, problematic heartburn.

And, yes, I also found myself once more mesmerized by the action of his jaw and throat and lips as he chewed. *Why am I such a weirdo?*

Dessert and presents followed, but then we split again. While the men did the dishes, the women sipped tea and talked.

Over the course of the afternoon and early evening, we'd discussed books, movies, historical events, current events, recipes, and even scientific advances, but neither of them had asked me a single thing about Abram. Or why he'd brought me. Or who I was.

Presently, Marie's eyes moved over me as I struggled to answer her question, her gaze feeling remarkably patient. "I'm sorry. I didn't mean to make you uncomfortable."

"You didn't," I said automatically, wanting to reassure her. "It's, uh, just that he's never finished my dinner at a restaurant because I've never gone to a restaurant with Abram."

Pamela made a clicking sound with her tongue and teeth. "What is he thinking? I swear, I raised him better. I know I did."

For some reason, her irritation made me chuckle even as I sought to clarify that Abram and I weren't a unit. "Oh, no. No, no. Abram and I aren't—"

"It's just, this is the first time my brother has brought anyone home." Marie leaned closer to me, her voice lowering, like she was confiding something important. "It's been great to see him smile so much."

"Smile?" I looked between the women. "He doesn't smile?"

Pamela nodded. "He was my stoic little deep thinker growing up and wasn't what you would call a happy baby. Or child." She sighed.

"Or teenager, or adult," Marie added, laughing.

"But that's okay. If I wanted sunshine, I'd spend time with my Marie." Pamela sent her daughter an affectionate smile. "That's not to say Marie isn't a deep thinker—she is—but she doesn't rain all over your parade with her deep thoughts."

Marie laughed harder and shook her head at Pamela's obvious frustration with Abram. "I think what my mom means is that Abram has always been one to push back, question authority, and has a deep sense of right and wrong. He often expresses his opinions as sarcasm and his sarcasm can be difficult at times."

"You mean his sass-back." Pamela's eyes narrowed, her lips compressing as though she weren't impressed.

"I mean his *sarcasm*," Marie said diplomatically.

It was at this point I should've clarified that Abram and I were not a unit, we were not dating. I shouldn't have allowed these fine women to believe otherwise. Continuing to sit quietly and listen without correcting their misconception was dishonest. I knew that.

And yet, I sat quietly, my eyes ping-ponging between the two women, my pulse quickening, my mind arguing with itself.

Speak up! You are lying by omission.

A voice that sounded suspiciously like Gabby's shushed my altruistic instinct, *Don't you say a word. Just go with it, Mary Sue.*

"Well, you know what that's all about, don't you? The sarcasm?" Pamela asked, sounding exasperated, but I couldn't tell which of us she was addressing or if she was merely speaking to herself. "It's what he does to hide that big, sensitive heart of his. That's all that is. Abram has always been extremely sensitive. He wasn't a cheerful child, but he was a cuddly one, always needing hugs. And the world isn't nice to sensitive little people, so they learn to hide it, unfortunately."

"Mom—"

"They withdraw behind sass—uh—sarcasm, and pretend not to care, act like nothing matters. But when they do care"—Pamela puffed out a breath and lifted her eyebrows meaningfully, glancing between Marie and me with rounded eyes—"watch out, 'cause when Abram commits that heart to something—like he did with his music when he dropped out of high school, leaping without looking—he doesn't know how to hold any part of himself back. Good or bad, even if he crashes and burns."

I won't ask questions about Abram because I am not at all curious, because knowing more about him is pointless.

Okay, okay. You got me. I *was* curious.

Apparently, I was exceptionally curious, because I was now sitting on the edge of the bed, gluttonously gorging myself on this incredibly fascinating glimpse into Abram's history and personality courtesy of his mother, greedily coveting and storing and consuming every single word, detail, and insight.

I wasn't, however, ready to admit how ravenous I'd been for information about Abram. Nor was I willing to cross the snooping line. Passive listening was one thing, allowing them to misunderstand the nature of my relationship with Abram through a lie of omission was also one thing, but actively drilling them for information on this man I liked—but shouldn't like—was a gamma ray of a different wavelength.

So, I refused to ask any questions, accomplishing this Herculean task by gripping my new fingerless gloves very, very tightly on my lap, holding my breath, and rolling my tongue to one side within my mouth.

"But mostly good, right, Mom? Abram's choices are mostly good?" Marie cut in and her tone held an undercurrent of hardness, one my sister and my mom used on me and my brother when they didn't want us embarrassing them in public.

Clearly, Marie was trying to be a good sister. I adored her for it, but I also wanted her to mind her own damn business and let her mother spill all the Abram beans.

"And he's like a big thundercloud when he's upset." Pamela sighed again and set her chin in her palm, obviously not taking Marie's hint, but she also wore a soft smile. "Won't listen. Stubborn."

"Mom—"

"Remember when he found out about Santa Claus?" Pamela pointed at her daughter but didn't wait for her to respond. "Took him a year to forgive his dad and me. A year! Even longer to forgive Marie, since she knew before he did. Said the trust had been broken and we'd all lied to him. He was seven. Thank God we never did the Tooth Fairy or Easter Bunny with him, he might've sought emancipation! Always been that way." She made that clicking sound again with her tongue and teeth. "And so broody. Quiet. Keeps everything bottled up, like his dad. Won't talk. And once he sets his mind to something, doesn't matter how nonsensical and foolhardy, there's no changing it."

"*Anyway*, I think today is the most I've seen him smile. Ever." Marie tried again to shift the conversation back on track, adding softly, "He's clearly smitten with you."

Again, she'd caught me off guard. Again, I opened my mouth to respond, to explain that Abram and I were not a unit, or together, or dating, or anything of the sort. But this time guilt kept me from speaking. I'd let them talk and talk and talk about Abram, revealing things they may not have revealed if they'd known the truth about us.

There was no *us*.

And admitting that we weren't a unit now would certainly crush me under the weight of confession-awkwardness. So, I closed my mouth, and I returned her smile.

And I said nothing.

CHAPTER 10
VECTOR ADDITION AND SUBTRACTION

Abram was the one who drove us back to Chicago through some unspoken, implicit agreement.

But then, once we were on the highway, he said, "You don't mind if I drive, do you? I'd like to get back before my next birthday."

Glaring at him from the passenger seat, I asked, "When is your birthday?"

"In a few months."

I rolled my eyes, pressing my lips together, pretending to be irritated. This made him laugh, a good, deep sound. I liked the sound, and I liked the way a smile looked on his face, which was why I'd pretended to be irritated. He seemed to enjoy teasing me. And, you know what? I liked it too.

Lisa's teasing hadn't been actual teasing—but rather passive aggressive barbs—in a very long time. Leo used to tease me, but we'd been speaking so infrequently these days and our calls had grown shorter and shorter.

Other than Allyn, no one teased me. I'd been in very real danger of taking myself too seriously, a personality trait of my parents' I'd never wanted to share. I firmly believed that good-natured teasing was good for keeping the ego in check, and therefore, it was good for the soul.

We drove in silence for a while and I thought about the day's events, feeling a small smile on my lips wax and wane at intervals. My brain kept snagging on and returning to one short conversation during dessert where Abram's dad, a man of few words, had questioned Abram about his music.

"How's the song writing going?" He sounded genuinely interested and I found this enthralling.

As far as I could piece together, Abram had dropped out of high school to pursue music. Where most parents would still be holding a grudge about potentially being embarrassed by their child's rash choices (in front of their friends and colleagues), Abram's parents seemed more interested in having a relationship with their son.

Fascinating.

The attention evident in Mr. Harris's voice was one of the main reasons I'd kept smiling at the memory. How would that be? To have a parent interested in what brought you joy? To have a parent who valued the actual relationship over the value of having the relationship?

The other reason I kept smiling had to do with Abram's response.

"Great," Abram answered immediately. But then, as though needing to clarify, he added, "*Now* it's great."

"Now?"

Abram lifted his chin in my direction, his gaze sliding over me in a way that had my breath catching before his eyes dropped to his cup and he cleared his throat. "Since Lisa, it's been going great."

"Really?" I sat up straighter, equally confused and surprised by this news.

"Yes." He rolled his lips between his teeth, not raising his eyes from the surface of his coffee. "Really."

I'd felt myself smile in wonder, still confused, but also flattered. An enjoyable, spreading warmth had expanded in my chest, a feeling I couldn't seem to stop chasing on the quiet drive home.

I appreciated the quiet. Finding other people who also liked quiet, with whom it wasn't strained or awkward, seemed to be a rare occurrence.

I thought I'd be spending the time grappling with residual guilt instead of trying to relive the best parts of the day, but I didn't. In retrospect, passively plying Abram's mom and sister for information about him didn't feel like such a terrible thing.

Sure, in the moment, I'd worried that all my morals and ethics were crumbling around me, that failing to correct someone else's misunderstanding today would undoubtedly lead to running for a US senate seat and golfing with big tobacco tomorrow.

The slope wasn't nearly as steep or as slippery as I'd assumed.

But then randomly, an image of Lisa stripping off her clothes and climbing into bed with a clueless and sleeping Abram flashed in my mind's eye. I frowned, shifted in my seat, and glared at the unpleasant image.

Or . . .

Or is the gradual steepness of the slope exactly the problem? Was this how Lisa's lies had started? By her own admission, she was now a serial liar. One trivial omission had become a white lie, which had become a gray lie, which had become a Tyler-trash-island whopper?

"What's going on over there?"

Abram's question didn't quite pull me from my musings and I said distractedly, "Incremental temperature increases."

"What?"

"If you boil a frog slowly, it doesn't notice."

I felt his eyes move over my profile, which finally stirred me from the morbid reflections. "Sorry. Just thinking."

"About boiling frogs?" His voice did a cute little catch thing at the end of his sentence, like he was worried that boiling frogs might lead to boiling bunnies.

I slid my eyes to the side, clandestinely peering at him and wondering what he thought—what he *really* thought—of Lisa's behavior last year. He'd been pissed at me (her) a few days ago, but when we'd discussed it last night, he'd forgiven me (her) easily.

"Do you mind telling me about the night I, uh, the night we met?"

Abram's eyebrows climbed a half inch on his forehead. "You really don't remember anything?"

"Humor me."

He glanced at me once, twice, three times before saying, "I guess—I mean, you *were* pretty drunk. Do you remember the party?"

"The party," I said vaguely, using a tone I typically employed when my professors or classmates would suggest something foolish and I didn't want to sound judgmental, but rather wanted to give them the time and space to correct or withdraw their faulty suggestion.

"Yes. You and Gabby showed up at Leo's party?"

"Ah. Okay. Yes. Then what happened? I mean, from your perspective. What happened from your perspective?"

He shifted in his seat, placing his elbow on the window sill, his index and middle finger lightly brushing against his lips as he stared out the windshield. "Let's see . . . You came in and your brother pointed you and Gabby out. It was dark, there were a lot of people, so I didn't get a chance to officially meet you. Plus, I was preoccupied with the upcoming set."

"Ah, yes. The set." I assumed he meant a music set, i.e. he must've played a set of music for the party.

Abram cleared his throat. "I thought it went well, given I'd never played for that many people before." A hint of uncertainty edged into his voice, which had me smiling at him automatically.

"The set was great," I said unthinkingly, the falsehood slipping out of my mouth and sounding sincere. I didn't know whether to be disgusted or impressed with myself, nor did I know why I'd said it.

But then he looked at me again and smiled, another hitting-me-right-in-the-center-of-my-stomach grin, melting my brain with fuzzy feels. And I understood at once why my subconscious had decided to lie so convincingly.

Conclusion: My subconscious wants to see him smile.

Abram's gaze flickered over my face, his eyes warm and appraising as he said quietly, "You have a really nice smile."

I blinked at him, and then turned my attention back to the road, surprised to discover that I'd been smiling as well. Surprise was accompanied by a rush of flustered heat to my cheeks at his unexpected compliment. It's one thing to admire a person in the comfortable privacy of one's own thoughts, but for those thoughts to be reciprocated *out loud* was highly disorienting.

Struggling in the ensuing silence for a response, I finally settled on, "Thank you. Also, your smile is also nice. Also." Instead of wincing at the stilted quality of my response, I cleared my throat and expression. "So, after your excellent set. What happened next?"

I anticipated the next words out of his mouth with both dread and anticipation, but he didn't leave me in suspense for long. "Leo introduced me to this guy named Broderick—a producer out of New York—and the three of us talked 'til late, calling it a night around four. I went to bed, fell asleep, and then . . ."

"And then?"

He sighed. "And then I woke up and you were there."

"Naked."

"Yeah."

"Yikes."

We were both quiet for a short moment, and again the image of Lisa crawling into bed—okay, maybe she didn't crawl, but crawling is skeevy and therefore in my imagination, she crawled—flashed within my brain. I was so irritated with her. Irritated and disappointed and . . . *wait? Is that jealousy? WHAT?*

"You were pretty drunk."

"Don't make excuses for—for me." I swallowed around a lump of unpleasant feelings constricting my throat. We'd just exited the highway and Abram had to stop at a red light.

He opened his mouth, as though to argue, but I cut him off, "How did you even recognize me? It was crowded at the party, we weren't even properly introduced."

Abram's eyelids lowered and he gave me a *cut the crap* look that reminded me of Leo.

I shook my head. "What?"

"Come on, Lisa."

"What?" I glanced left, I glanced right. What was I missing?

"You know you're crazy beautiful," he said, not sounding happy about having to say it.

Startled by this explanation, and confused about how irritated it made me feel, I straightened my spine and glared at him. *He thinks Lisa is beautiful.* Which, I reminded myself calmly, meant he thought I was beautiful. Because we were identical.

. . . I hate that he thinks she's beautiful.

Shaking my head again, I mentally swatted away the irrational thought just as the light changed and he turned his attention back to the road. "Right, well—"

"It's impossible not to notice you," he interrupted gently. "Even in a crowded room."

Suspended on those words, I felt my glare dissolve, again not knowing what to feel. Or, perhaps more importantly, why I was feeling anything at all. Settling back in my seat, I refocused on the questions I wanted to ask and the information I was lacking.

"Right, so," I started again, concentrating on balling my hands into fists. "You knew it was me. What did you do next?"

"I tried to wake you up. When you didn't wake up right away, I checked your pulse and breathing. You seemed fine." His tone was flat as he told the story, giving me the impression this memory was not one that he enjoyed. "So I got dressed, put a T-shirt on you—I didn't look!" He added this last bit sharply, sending me a hard glance. "And then I called your brother."

"You called Leo? Did you wake him up?"

"No. He was with Gabby. They were both frantic, looking for you."

"Gabby was looking for . . . me." I thought about that. I turned it over in my head. I examined it from many different angles.

"I guess you disappeared on her and she freaked out, because she knew you were drunk. Haven't you talked to her about this?"

"Of course." Crap. I was going to need to be more careful with my questions. "From your perspective, though, what happened next?"

He sent me a questioning glare as he readjusted his hands on the wheel. "Gabby and Leo showed up, you were mostly awake by then, climbing all over me. I was trying to keep you from hurting yourself, but also . . ." He paused and shook his head, making a face of intense irritation.

"Oh no." I covered my face and peeked at him from between my fingers, frustration and anger nearly choking me. "I groped you, didn't I?"

He shrugged, not looking at me, but there was a palpable mood shift. He suddenly felt very distant, faraway. "Anyway, I wasn't too happy. Gabby and I got into it. Leo carried you to your room. Gabby left. The end."

With more force than necessary, Abram flipped the turn blinker and made a right onto our street while I sat perfectly still. I felt so . . . so . . .

ANGRY.

How could he forgive her? What was wrong with him? He should have—should have—*I don't know. But he should have done something.*

Wordlessly, he parked in front of the house, turned off the headlights, and cut the engine, all the while staring forward. I let my hands drop from my face to my lap and also stared forward, now nauseous.

But then, just as the stillness and silence settled around us, he faced me, drawing my eyes to his, Abram's features now mostly in shadow. "Can we just forget about that? Can we just pretend it didn't happen? I mean, what did happen? Nothing happened."

Nothing happened.

A bubble of laughter erupted from between my lips and I shook my head, closing my eyes. I sighed.

"Lisa." He placed his hand over mine.

I didn't yank it, but I did slide it away and turned to open the door. "Come on. Let's go inside."

Exiting the car, I took a moment to fix my skirt before walking to the keypad and punching in the code. I heard Abram's door close behind me and he opened the gate just as it unlocked and buzzed. I walked through it and we climbed the stairs side by side, his hands in his pockets, my arms crossed over my chest.

When we reached the top stair, he side-stepped, cutting me off, stopping directly in front of me, and forcing my eyes to his.

"Listen, I was pissed at the time. But I'm not upset anymore."

"If the roles had been reversed, if I'd found you, an unknown person, naked in my bed. And then you groped me? Should I forgive you so easily? Should I not be upset?"

He frowned, looking frustrated. "I'm not saying what you did was okay, and I'm really glad—I mean, really fucking glad—you feel remorse about it. You apologized. I forgive you."

I scoffed, shaking my head.

His tone turned stern. "No. I get to decide what and who I forgive, and I forgive you. But, fine, forget about that for a minute. There's one fundamental difference between what happened that night and the hypothetical, role reversal situation you're proposing."

"Oh yeah? What's that?" I lifted my chin a notch.

"At no point was I afraid of you." His gaze seemed to narrow, as though watching my reaction very carefully, and he added slowly, "But I'm guessing, whatever happened to you, was scary as hell."

I didn't flinch. But holding his eyes, I felt mine sting. A searing numbness settled in my stomach and I found I had to swallow before I could speak.

"Nothing happened." I parroted his own words, my voice gravelly, and then stepped around him, walking calmly to the front door.

I remembered I didn't have any keys just as I spotted two slips of paper tucked into the door jam. Retrieving them, I read the first.

Hey you,

I stopped by. Wanted to see how you were doing. I found this postal service slip just inside the gate on the cement so I brought it up to the door.

I'll be by tomorrow. Maybe we can have breakfast and catch up.

Love ya, Gabby

I handed her note to Abram when I finished and glanced at the second slip. Sure enough, it was one of those orange United States Postal Service slips.

Sorry we missed you! We tried to deliver your package. It is now being held for you at Wicker Park Commons on N Ashland Ave. Please stop by with a photo ID to collect your package.

"Must be your cell phone and stuff," he said.

I turned my head and found him at my shoulder, reading the postal service slip.

"Yeah. Must be." I handed it to him as well and stepped to the side so he could unlock the door.

Abram shoved the notes in his back pocket and retrieved the keys, his eyes on me the whole time, his features mostly clear of expression. But he didn't unlock the door.

"Hey," he said.

"Yes?" I said.

"So, can we forget it happened?" He took a shuffling step toward me, dipping his chin.

"Are you going to unlock the door?"

"Can we forget about it? Start over?"

I didn't have to think much about his request, because the only logical path forward was obvious. "No. We're not going to forget about it. You're going to hold that grudge."

He exhaled a frustrated-sounding breath even as his lips tugged to the side. "Oh yeah? Why would I do that?"

I told him the truth, "Because you never know when *that* Lisa might come back."

CHAPTER 11
NEWTON'S FIRST LAW OF MOTION: INERTIA

I needed coffee.

I didn't usually drink coffee, but I awoke the next day with an insatiable desire for coffee. And donuts. Okay, actually, it was a Stan's chocolate cake donut I wanted. But donuts always tasted better with coffee.

Regardless, I needed both. And a shower.

Last night, after returning home and our short—albeit uncomfortable—discussion on the front porch, he'd wordlessly unlocked the door and we'd both retreated to our separate spaces: me, upstairs to play the violin; him, wherever he went.

It was for the best. No other choice. Lisa would be arriving any day now, we would be switching places, and Abram could never know I'd been Lisa this week. Any like or regard or respect I had for my messy Adonis was as irrelevant as it was inconvenient.

Therefore, I put him firmly from my mind, played my violin badly for a few hours, went to sleep, and then woke up with an insatiable craving. For donuts.

Presently, checking the clock next to Lisa's bed and discovering it was still quite early, I decided to take my time getting ready while I waited for Abram to wake up and escort me to get donuts. The plan was: I would speak to him as little as possible on the way, and I would avoid him for the rest of the day.

In the meantime, I debated whether or not to take a bath, but ultimately decided against it. I already had that shower helmet. Plus, I suspected a bath would just make me think of Abram, and I definitely didn't need to be thinking about Abram while taking a bath. BIG NO.

Retrieving the awesome helmet from my room, I took a shower. I then turned the showerhead off, sat on the edge of the tub, removed the helmet, and turned on the main faucet. Since I had plenty of time before Abram woke up—given his slackerish history of sleeping until whenever—I shaved everything that was appropriate to shave. Usually, I didn't. Fanatical grooming was pretty low on my priority list. But, given my present predicament, how else was I going to pass the time?

Once finished, I turned my attention to the dry shampoo Gabby left two days ago. I'd never used dry shampoo before, and I had plenty of doubts about its effectiveness. I was pleased to discover it worked superbly. *Huh.*

After brushing my teeth, toweling off, and dressing in Lisa's clothes—a flowy, silk pink tank top tunic, a brand-new white lace bra, and a pair of tight jeans—applying makeup, and checking my appearance a few times, I was disheartened to discover that a mere forty minutes had passed since I'd woken up. And yet, the hunger had only intensified. For donuts.

7:53 AM.

Slowly, I descended the back stairs, strolled into the kitchen, sauntered to a stool, and sat. Sadly.

Sigh.

Man. I really wanted it (a donut). One of those colossal cravings held me in its grip, where you can almost taste the thing you want, your mouth waters just thinking about the coveted item, and you get this sense of restless injustice, like the world is conspiring against you, keeping you from the object of your desire . . . which was a donut.

Tapping my fingers on the quartz countertop, I glanced at the clock over the double ovens.

7:57 AM.

That's it.

Standing, I speed-walked to the pantry, pulled my wallet from my bag, pulled a twenty from my wallet, pushed the wallet and the bag back in their hiding place, and tiptoed to the front door. I couldn't wait. Abram was probably going to sleep until after noon, and I refused to be denied (A DONUT!).

Slipping on Lisa's Vera Wang comfy sandals, I crept to the door, opened it as quietly as possible, and closed it just as quietly.

The walk to the Stan's Donuts was speedy and uneventful, and the ordering process was efficient and swift. I was more than halfway home when I realized, in my rush, I'd forgotten to order coffee.

No matter. *I can just brew a cup when I—when I . . .*

Yikes!

I stiffened, stopped, and sucked in a breath.

There he was. Abram. Sitting on the outside steps, his elbows on his knees, his hands clasped in front of him. Glaring at me like I'd just deleted his LHC simulation data without making a backup.

Releasing the air in my lungs, I bit my bottom lip and approached the gate with caution. I shouldn't have been noticing how crazy attractive he was when he glared, but I did. How could I not? He glared at me as I punched in the code. He glared at me as I opened the gate and shut it firmly behind me. He glared at me as I approached. By the time I made it to the bottom step, I wasn't sure if the warm blush heating my cheeks was remorseful embarrassment at having been caught, or merely a reaction to the stern severity in his gorgeous dark eyes.

Either way, I tried to ignore both, and smiled. "Want a donut?"

His glare flickered to the bag I held, and then back to me. "You left." Abram's voice was cold steel, had cold steel been able to speak and was alarmingly good-looking when it glared.

I shifted my weight from one foot to the other. "Yes. Yes, I did. And I'm sorry."

"You broke your promise."

"I needed coffee, but I forgot to get coffee, because what I really wanted was a donut. And here, see?" I lifted up the bag. "I got enough for you too."

Nothing about his expression altered, which caused a thrilling little shiver to race down my spine. *My goodness.* Was it hot outside? It was hot outside, right?

He blinked just once. "What kind of donuts?"

"Uh, all kinds. A virtual cornucopia of donuts, if you will. They usually give people a box for this many, but I asked for a bag." Peering into the paper sack, I began listing all the options.

But as I rattled off the list, Abram stood, descended the steps until less than five decimeters separated us, and used his finger to hook the top of the bag open further, peeking inside. He was so close, I could smell him, his fragrance, and it had that melting effect on me as usual. But I also smelled the donuts, which meant I was now melting and trying not to drool.

Abram glanced between me and the interior of the paper bag. "Which one is your favorite?" he asked quietly, an edge of something treacherous in his tone, maybe even sinister.

I blinked up at him. "Why?"

"Because I want it." The softness of his response only served to underscore the meanness.

My mouth dropped open. "Why don't you just take the one you actually want and leave my preferences out of it?"

He lifted his eyebrows, giving me a pointed look, but otherwise didn't respond. It was response enough.

"You're unconscionable."

"Which one?"

"Fine. It's the chocolate cake donut. Happy?"

"Yessss." The flash of a grin also meant a flash of his dimples, the combination momentarily discombobulated me, just long enough for him to snatch the bag from my hand.

"Hey!"

"There are two chocolate cake donuts in here." He turned away and walked up the stairs.

"Yes. One for me and one for—hey!"

He'd extracted both chocolate cake donuts and carelessly handed off the bag to me, as though discarding it, walking through the front door. I chased him into the house and to the kitchen, gasping in horror when I saw he'd already finished one of the donuts and had just taken a bite out of the other.

I don't know what made me do it, but I tossed the bag full of inferior donuts onto the kitchen island and grabbed his wrist. Actually, I do know what made me do it: fury and hunger. I wasn't hangry, I was *furngry*.

Before he could react and holding his eyes, I guided his hand to my lips and took a giant bite, shoving a full half of the remaining chocolate cake deliciousness into my mouth.

His eyes grew round with shock even as he laughed. "You're going to pay for that."

I didn't respond. I was too busy chewing, giving him my dirtiest look, holding his wrist in place with a death grip, and ignoring the excited, hot, electric shiver dancing down my spine. He flexed his arm, as though to raise his fingers and finish off my precious. I couldn't let that happen. Plus, I wanted to see his arm flex again.

Grabbing his forearm, I shoved it down with all my might, and I swallowed. He chased his hand, his mouth open and ready to bite. So did I. A brief struggle ensued, during which our foreheads knocked together as we both reached the shared target.

"Ow!" I said, but I didn't back down. I refused to cede my grip on his arm, because doing so would mean surrendering my breakfast, and the loss of watching him strain, and listening to him grunt. Twisting and trying to jump, it was no use. He was bigger and stronger and taller, so much taller, and he smelled so, so, so good. *Olfaction satisfaction.*

Momentarily distracted by (what else?) Abram-fragrance, his forearm slipped from my fingers and he held the remainder of the donut above us both, turning his face toward mine.

"Give it to me." I clawed at his raised bicep, breathing hard, headless of how this pressed my body more completely against him. Or how every time I jumped for his arm, my chest bumped into his and I slid down his front.

I am so hot right now.

"What? Give you what?" he whispered, tilting his head to the side, liquid brown eyes shaded beneath those dark lashes.

No matter how I pushed against him, he held firm. So firm. So very, *very* firm.

Out of breath, I ignored the swirling butterfly field in my stomach, determined to reach the donut, no matter what it took. *Mine! Mine mine MINE!*

"You know what I want, *Ahab*." I lunged against him. I didn't know what made me do it—

Actually, I do know what made me do it: fury and hunger and horniness. I was no longer *furngry*, I was *furnghorngry*.

Despite my lunging, he didn't even rock back on his heels.

Ugh. Damn him. Why was he so immovable? He was in my way, keeping me from what I wanted, and—in that moment—my throat burned with how much I despised him. SO MUCH!

But Abram did lower his arm at the last minute, holding the donut behind his back. As I reached around him blindly, my lips accidentally grazed his jaw, our bodies sliding together, the friction causing an immediate straining and awakening within my own. Flinching as though burned, I retreated, working to subdue this destructive awareness fragmenting my composure as his arms came around me, the donut now behind my back.

"Too bad, *Liza.* I didn't get what I wanted either." He was breathing hard. *Good.*

"Oh yeah? What's that?" I ground out, also breathing hard.

"You . . ." he said, his voice a gruff whisper, his mesmerizing gaze darting between my eyes and mouth.

I sucked in a short, surprised breath, blinking furiously as pinpricks of heat pulsed just beneath my skin. But before I could connect too many fantasy-fulfillment imaginary dots, he leaned even closer.

I felt his breath on my lips as he finished the thought, "You . . . are not allowed to leave the house without me."

"You were asleep."

"You know the rules."

"You can't lock me up."

He nudged my nose with his, the barest of touches, a gentle slide, whispering darkly, "But I can *tie* you up."

Oh.

My.

GOD.

I held perfectly still despite being out of breath, my eyes on his, my heart in my throat; the sensation of being launched into the air and falling all at once; my lower abdomen a swirling, twisting, universe of activity. Because I wanted it.

I wanted it.

I wanted it.

I want it. So. Bad.

His eyes held me transfixed, turning impossibly darker, hotter, half-lidded monsters, mirrors of my darkest desires, and they lowered slowly—so slowly—to my lips. He licked his bottom lip, also slowly. And he leaned. And I exhaled an incomplete, hitching breath of sweet anticipation. And I let my eyes flutter close. And—

"Hey! Why is the front door open?"

The sound of Gabby's voice followed by the front door closing had the same effect as a gunshot.

We jumped apart. I scrambled around the kitchen island, placing it between us. He backed up to the kitchen table. Our eyes met—his dark and piercing, mine probably frantic and disoriented—and crashing cymbals sounded between my ears just as Gabby walked into the kitchen.

"Hey you . . . two." She'd started her greeting with a smile, but ended it with a frown, glancing between us. "What's wrong? What happened?"

Abram, the muscle at his jaw jumping, pushed his fingers into his hair, his eyes sliding to the side and giving the full weight of his glare to Gabby. "What are you doing here?"

Holy hadron collider, he sounded pissed.

She retreated a step, visibly alarmed. "I left a note. Yesterday? On the doorstep?" When he continued glaring at her without speaking, she lifted her palms. "Jeez, Abram. What the hell? You look like you want to murder me."

Abram's glare flickered to me for the briefest of instants, and then dropped to the floor. He lifted his hands to his hips, but he still held the partially eaten donut, a fact he didn't seem to realize immediately. Giving his fingers a stern double take, he studied the donut for several seconds before taking a deep breath and placing it on the kitchen table behind him.

During this odd moment, Gabby sent me a wide-eyed look. I knew it was supposed to impart something to me, but I had no idea what. I wasn't yet thinking clearly, still recovering from my *furnghorngry* moment of madness.

Make no mistake, it was madness. Gabby had saved me—saved us both—from making a colossal and intractable error in judgment.

"Gabby," I said, my voice breathless and quiet because my thoughts were too loud. I gestured to the bag on the island. "I picked up some, um, donuts, if you want any."

"She's not staying." Abram said this firmly, his hands now fully on his hips, shifting his scowl from her frown to my face.

I stared at him, working hard to catch my breath and keep my eyeballs from broadcasting how badly I still wanted . . . I still *wanted.*

He stared back. He blinked. Aggravation dissipated, becoming something else entirely—conflict, concentration, fervor—and I experienced that bizarre tunnel vision again.

Eventually, Abram took a deep breath. He closed his eyes. He shook his head.

"Fine. She can stay for an hour, and that's it. And she has to leave her cell phone on the kitchen table." Eyes still closed, he rubbed his forehead like he had a headache.

Gabby's mouth dropped open, and she seemed to be on the precipice of saying something—likely cheeky and inappropriate—so I shook my head furiously, making my eyes as large as I could, hoping to impart to *her* that saying anything at this moment would likely result in her being expelled from the premises.

She started, rolled her lips between her teeth, and shifted her eyes back and forth between Abram and me. Clearly a struggle for her to keep quiet, she appeared to be almost bursting with the need to speak her mind. Come to think of it, I'd never known her to hold her tongue. Ever.

It must've been a real character-building experience, not getting what she most wanted in that moment; even if it felt like a compulsion; even if it would have been a terrible, terrible mistake.

I know how she feels.

* * *

If someone had asked me for one word to describe myself prior to Lisa's phone call earlier in the week, I would have replied, *rational.*

But no person is just one thing, one label, one facet of their personality or single characteristic or decision they've made. This was a fact that could sometimes be super inconvenient. Like now.

"What's going on?"

My eyes cut to Gabby's. Held. I couldn't believe she'd been quiet for so long. It must've been a full five minutes since she left her phone on the kitchen table and we climbed the stairs to Lisa's room.

Gabby sat on the low bookshelf at one end of the room, her legs extended in front of her, her ankles crossed, her false fingernails tapping on the wood. I sat on the bed, my feet flat on the floor, my arms crossed over my stomach. I'd been slouching and staring at nothing since entering the room.

When I didn't respond, because I was still debating what to say, she whispered, "Does he suspect?"

"Suspect what?" I whispered back.

Her lips formed a flat, frustrated line and she crossed to the bed, sitting next to me and leaning her head toward mine. She smelled like sweetness and flowers. "Does he suspect you're you?"

"No. Of course not."

"Well, that's a relief. Because, man, he looked pissed when I got here." She breathed out. Now she was slouching too. Her gaze turned assessing as it moved over me. "So, what's going on then? What did I interrupt? And don't say nothing, because I definitely interrupted something. Were you two fighting?"

I stared at her, wondering where I'd placed those prunes.

"Mona!" she whisper-hissed.

I stood, waving my hands around my face, feeling harassed. "I don't want to talk about it."

I didn't even want to think about it. That person in the kitchen? That wasn't me. I wasn't her. She wasn't rational. And I didn't know how to be rational about it. Or rationalize it.

Gabby breathed out again, a huff this time. "You're so frustrating." She stood and shadowed me around the room. "Just tell me what happened. I will die of curiosity if you don't. Do you want me to die? Don't answer that!"

Upon reaching the corner of the room, I spun, my hand nearly knocking over the pile of CDs I'd yet to put away. "Gabby. I don't want to talk about it."

Her nose scrunched and her lips became impossibly small. "Fine."

"Fine." My arms were crossed again, but I didn't remember crossing them. "Now, tell me—"

"If you tell me what's going on between you guys, I'll tell you what happened with Lisa and Abram last year."

I laughed, it was a tired sound, and I shook my head at her. "You already promised to tell me about Lisa and Abram if I told you that stupid story about my TA." *Blarg!*

Rocks of emotion in my throat. *Ignore!* "And besides, Abram already told me what Lisa did."

Gabby flinched and stepped back. "He did?"

"Yes, he did," I said through clenched teeth, feeling angry all over again on Abram's behalf. "How could Lisa do that? What the hell was she thinking?"

Gabby exhaled loudly a third time, closing her eyes. "Okay, well, first of all, she was drunk."

"Not a good excuse."

"And she was angry at Tyler." Gabby paced away, her tone resigned. "And Abram—I mean, you would've had to be there—was just the most delicious thing, so hot. And during his set? Talent is such a turn-on, you know? And that voice . . ." Her tone held a dreamy quality and she was staring at nothing, clearly thinking about my messy Adonis.

So, I snapped my fingers in front of her face. "Snap out of it!"

She flinched, coming out of her daze, and glared at me. "What was that for?"

"You've already expressed how happy he makes your hoo-hah. I don't need to hear it again. Tell me what happened—from your perspective—with Lisa that night." I fought to suppress an irrational flare of jealousy. Some primal part of myself wanted to claw her eyes out for thinking thoughts about Abram.

NO THINKING THOUGHTS ALLOWED!

Placing a hand on her hip and waving the other through the air, she continued. "Fine. After his set, I'm trying to get her upstairs, so she can sleep it off, and she gives me the slip. I freak out, because—you know, she's shit-faced and *somewhere*—so I call Leo. He and I start searching the house, calling everyone, and then Abram calls Leo, says she's with him." Gabby paused here to wince and peek at me. "Naked."

The flare of irrational jealousy was now more of a campfire, every word out of her mouth building it higher. "What happened next?"

"We race to his room and"—Gabby's wince intensified—"he'd put a shirt on her, but she was all over him. And instead of laughing it off, or keeping her occupied—which is what would have made sense to me—he looks *pissed* and is pushing her away. I mean, he looked like he was about to lose his cool." She stopped here to give me a look like, *can you believe this guy?*

I couldn't believe her.

"Leo was all, like, apologizing. But I didn't appreciate how Abram was kind of rough, you know? Pushing her away."

That had me straightening my spine. "He was rough with her?"

Gabby's eyes lost focus and moved to the wall behind me. "He wasn't, like, rough *physically*. He wasn't pushing her, he was pushing her hands away. But his words were totally disrespectful *and* he threatened to file charges."

"File charges. Wow." Good. "What did he say?"

"I don't even remember. Something like, *Don't fucking touch me!* And he kept telling her to get away from him."

I was so confused. How was Abram telling Lisa to back off disrespectful?

"Did he call her names?"

"Well. No. Just like I said, *Get out of here!* That kind of thing. Like I told you before, he was a dick to her. She wasn't herself. She was drunk, and he wasn't cool. And threatening her with calling the police, also not cool."

"Gabby." I waited until I had her attention. I erased all emotion from my voice, because otherwise I was going to scream. "How would you have felt if you woke up and a strange guy was naked in your bed? And then he began touching you, *groping you*, and no matter what you said, he wouldn't stop? Wouldn't you want to file charges? And isn't that what you said I should have done? Even though what happened to me, which was nothing, didn't include—"

"It's not at all the same thing! You can't compare the two." Her lips flattened and a frown pulled her eyebrows together. "Firstly, it's not like she could've hurt him, Mona! Or made him do anything he didn't want to. Abram is three times her size."

I shook my head, wanting to scream, and instead closed my eyes. "I can't believe you don't think what Lisa did was wrong."

"Of course it was wrong!" Gabby's voice lowered, now laced with an edge of seriousness. "Lisa felt like an asshole the next day, okay? And she wanted to apologize, but he was already gone, not to mention it was so embarrassing, alright? She regretted it immediately. The two situations are completely different! You can't treat all these kinds of things like they're the same. That's stupid. She made a mistake. And I hate to break it to you, Mary Sue: people—other than you, obviously—make mistakes."

Leaning my shoulder against the wall, I rubbed the back of my neck and opened my eyes, a picture on the shelf snagging my attention, a moment in time forgotten until now. A shot of the three of us—of me, Gabby, and Lisa—from when we were eight leaned against a collection of dusty magazines. Gabby, in the middle, wore a dark brown wig to cover her red hair.

"I make mistakes," I mumbled, studying the photo, feeling strangely lethargic and heavy as well as a powerful sense of loss.

Gabby didn't respond at first, merely studied my profile. But then she came to stand next to me, presumably to peer at the shelf.

"Ha," she said, the smile in her voice drawing my attention. "I remember that day. I wanted to look like you and Lisa, so Leo got me that wig as a joke." She turned her face to mine. We were standing so close, I could make out the dark blue flecks in her moss green eyes. "I wore it every day for a year," she added softly.

"I remember." My lips curved into a small smile, some—most—of my anger dissolving as nostalgia took its place, and I remembered how she'd cried when Leo told her she couldn't take the wig home. I'd hugged her then, comforting her, and telling her she would always be my second twin.

As I gazed at Gabby now, I tried to chase the anger, to hold a new grudge, to judge her for excusing Lisa's shoddy treatment of Abram so easily. But I couldn't.

What did I expect? This was Gabby. Gabby made mistakes. Gabby walked through life with blinders on either side of her face and a mirror in front. Gabby wouldn't understand because she couldn't. Did I expect anything differently? No. There was nothing to learn from Gabby other than how not to behave. *That's just how she is.*

And yet, did nostalgia mean I'd made excuses for her because I'd known her all my life? Definitely. Behold the power of nostalgia.

Cursed nostalgia!

What was it about nostalgia? I despised it even as I longed for it, often suspecting it was the most powerful emotion, eclipsing even grief and fear. Nostalgia seemed to make everything, no matter how large the offense, forgivable.

Clearing my throat, I returned my attention to the photo. "What happened to the wig?"

"I think my mom burned it after I tried to wear it to that movie premiere." Gabby chuckled.

But then she grew silent so suddenly I looked at her again. Her lips were pulled down at the corners and she seemed to be trying to swallow.

"What? What is it?"

She glanced at me and smiled. It didn't reach her eyes. "Nothing."

"Nothing?"

"Nothing my therapist hasn't already heard." She turned and strolled away, stuffing her hands in her back pockets. "Speaking of which, I could give you her name. If you want."

Pushing away from the wall, I straightened the stack of CDs I'd almost knocked over. "What for?"

"You know I've been going to therapy for, like, ever, right? Well . . ." Gabby sat on the low bookshelf again. "I think maybe you should go to therapy and figure some shit out."

I couldn't help but screw up my face and give her the side-eye. "I do not need therapy." I rejected the mere notion on a visceral level and repeated words that Dr. Steward had said to me on any number of occasions: "We—all of us—are extremely privileged and lucky, and I recognize my privilege. I've been given every opportunity to succeed, and I recognize that I've grown up with virtually no hardship in my life."

My sister's best friend watched me with wide eyes, her mouth hanging open, her eyebrows high on her forehead. "Wow. I—*wooow*." Gabby leaned back, her gaze moving over my face as though she were seeing me for the first time.

"Therapy would be a misuse of time and energy that could be spent attending to others who are actually in need of help." This last statement hadn't been one of Dr. Steward's frequent reminders, but I could extrapolate. My discomforts were *nothing* in comparison to what other people lived on a daily basis, and I wouldn't waste my time—or a therapist's time—with my small concerns.

Gabby and I stared at each other for several long seconds, during which she appeared to be stunned. It was clear she didn't know what to say, but she had an abundance of thoughts on the subject. Conversely, I didn't need to give the issue any additional consideration. I knew my thoughts, and therefore I knew what actions to take and how to behave.

Eventually, the lack of conversation or action made me antsy. I turned from Gabby's stare and reacquainted myself with our surroundings. Picking up the violin I'd left on Lisa's desk, I carefully returned it to its case.

"You are . . ." Gabby paused, and I looked at her. Her expression was free of judgment. "You are . . ." Again, she didn't finish her thought. This time her mouth opened and closed, as though she were hunting for the most-accurate descriptive phrase possible, her eyes narrowing as her focus seemed to turn inward.

Closing the violin case, I secured the latches and leaned it against the wall near where Gabby sat conducting her mental word search.

I'd just straightened when Gabby asked, "Are you a virgin?"

CHAPTER 12
NEWTON'S SECOND LAW OF MOTION: CONCEPT OF A SYSTEM

I froze, shifting my eyes to her face. She'd asked the question evenly, thoughtfully, as though merely questioning whether I'd ever baked a turkey in the spatchcock position, and did I recommend it or have a good recipe.

I shook my head. "I'm not answering that."

"Come on. Tell me. I'm seriously trying to help you."

"Oh yeah?"

"Yes."

"Gabby." I leveled her with a glare. "You don't even like me."

"That's not true. I like you, but you are also so freaking irritating."

"Which means you don't like me."

"Because you became a Mary Sue. But I love you."

I snorted, shaking my head, and returned to Lisa's desk. Picking up the first half of the music books stacked there, I walked to the closet.

"If you search your coldly rational soul, you will see that I am telling the truth." She watched me for a few minutes as I ignored her and piled the sheet music neatly in the corner of Lisa's closet. Eventually she added, "Mona, we've known each other almost our whole lives. I will always want what I think is best for you."

"You want what's best for me? Which is what?" I returned to the desk, grabbing more music books.

"First and foremost, a life of fulfillment. Secondarily, security, peace of mind, comfort, and companionship."

Her response surprised me to such an extent, I lost my grip on the second stack of music as I knelt, and they fell to the floor in a haphazard pile.

"Did I *surprise* you?" She asked this feigning a British accent.

I huffed a laugh, but said, "Yes. I find your answer surprising."

"You can thank my therapist." She sauntered over and shoved my shoulder again with her fingers. "So, are you a virgin?"

"No," I ground out reluctantly, rearranging the pile.

"And I assume you lost your virginity to a boyfriend?"

I shook my head. "No. I've never had a boyfriend."

"Really? Now you've surprised me."

"How so?"

Gabby was quiet for a bit. I heard her take a deep breath. Release it. Take another. Meanwhile, finished stacking the music, I stood and returned to the bed, reclaiming my seat at the end of it.

Finally, she said, "But, I guess, it does kind of make sense."

"What makes sense?"

"You've never had a boyfriend, and that makes sense. It would require you asking someone to put you first."

I gritted my teeth. "Gabby—"

"But how does that work? I mean, you yank away when I touch your arm and you've known me forever."

I tried to hide my wince by studying Lisa's bedspread for lint. "So?"

"*Soooo*, you don't like to be touched. At all. How does sex work if you don't like touching?"

"I don't like uninvited touching, when it's a surprise." I believed these words when I said them. But after they were out of my mouth, I discovered they weren't entirely accurate—not recently, not with Abram—and worked to suppress a blooming yet distressing warmth low in my stomach.

"I don't get it. What do you do when you have sex? Announce what you're going to do before you do it?"

"Not all sex requires a lot of touching. I'm extremely clear regarding my expectations before sex, what I want out of the experience, what we will and will not do, what I hope to achieve. I ask my partner for the same information. If the guy does anything unexpected, I simply end it."

"*Reeeeeeally?*" Gabby plopped down next to me on the bed, the intensity of her gaze told me she was absolutely fascinated. "Like, you talk about the sex before you have it? What you're going to do? What's going to happen?"

"Exactly." How else was I supposed to determine whether or not sex with a partner was necessary? The scientific method existed for a reason.

"That's so interesting!"

I squinted at her. "You don't?"

She shook her head.

"Not at all?"

She shook her head again.

I scrunched my nose. "If you don't talk about it, about the plan, then how do you give consent?"

She scrunched her nose in return but also laughed. "Uh, through my actions."

I turned away and stood before she could see my expression, walking to the desk. Consent through actions? Like people expected each other to read their minds and know what each person liked without talking about it first? And that assumed the other person would be mindful enough to ensure climax was reached? What about boundaries? Limits?

Sure. Right. Okay. NOPE! Not for me.

"I have more questions about your pre-sex discussions. But first, how many partners have you had?" Her voice adopted a tone I associated with academic discussions. For some reason, it helped me relax a bit, made the conversation feel less personal.

Sitting on the edge of the desk, I crossed my arms. "Seven."

"Seven?" She stared at me, her eyebrows arched high on her forehead. "Oh. Okay. Wow. Also surprising."

"Why? How many have you had?"

"One," she said quietly, giving me the impression that her *one* had been meaningful. Clearing her throat, she continued, "Was any of the sex enjoyable?"

I paused to mentally thumb through all relevant encounters. "Some."

"Were they all one-night stands?"

"No."

"Some were multiple-night stands?"

"Yes."

"But none became a boyfriend?" A renewed hint of curiosity edged into her voice.

"No."

"Why not?" she asked.

"It wasn't necessary," I said with a sigh, tired of this discussion.

"Necessary?"

How could I explain this to Gabby in a way she'd understand? I'd sought to answer a question. The question had been answered. Case closed.

Eventually, I decided on, "I don't have time for that."

"That? What is 'that'?"

"You know"—I waved my hand in the air—"calling, texting, having conversations about mundane things, making plans. That." Not when I could achieve more satisfaction on my own than with a partner. It was simple math.

Gabby blinked at me several times. "It's like I don't even know you, Mona."

My chuckle caught me off guard, so did my lingering smile as Gabby and I looked at each other. Her eyes were intent as they moved over my face, like she was trying to solve a puzzle.

"You need help," Gabby said at last, causing my smile to vanish.

I frowned at the floor. "Help with what?"

"You have a distorted view of reality, and what you deserve," she said softly.

"No. I just don't believe romantic relationships are necessary."

"You think you deserve less."

"It's not about what people deserve, Gabby." I sighed. Again. Hadn't it been an hour yet? Shouldn't she be leaving soon? "It's about what people need. I don't need—or want—a relationship."

"Because you don't have time?"

That wasn't precisely true, but—as Lisa would say—whatever. "Sure."

"Because you're so busy being a genius and doing the math, you don't have time for people?"

"I have time for people, just not a boyfriend."

"Even if that boyfriend was awesome? Even if he built you up, supported you, loved you, adored you, and made it his life's mission to ensure you knew—every day— how amazing and special you are?"

"That's not a boyfriend. That's a dog."

She waved away my sarcasm. "You don't need love? Companionship?"

I hesitated, searching the air around her head for the right words.

"Fine," she said before I could assemble a response. "Then you think you *need* less than other people."

I shot her a questioning glance, but before I could respond, she snapped her fingers.

"I have an idea!" Gabby scooched to the end of the bed closest to me and leveled me with an intent and wide stare. "Abram."

I returned her stare, giving nothing of my thoughts, or my feelings, or my body's betraying, quantum reaction at the mention of his name. "What about him?"

"He's hot, right?"

I shrugged and confessed to the understatement of the century, "His exterior is attractive."

"Yeah, but what do you think of him so far? You two were flirting up a storm the other day. Is he a guy you might want to get to know better? If you know what I mean."

"I don't know him very well," was what I said, but my thoughts on the subject were: *I LIKE HIM SO MUCH!*

"Ah ha!" She pointed at me. "You didn't say no, which means you've pictured him naked."

I sighed for the hundredth time. Speaking of, where the heck was Abram? Shouldn't he be kicking Gabby out?

She grinned, wagging her eyebrows. "You should let him touch you."

I choked. "Pardon?"

"Let him touch you. I'm not saying—you know—let him do whatever he wants or anything. I'm just saying, *if* he touches you, and *if* you like it, you should let him. And also, you shouldn't interrupt the touching with discussions of consent and expectations or whatever."

I looked at her askance. "You're kidding."

"I'm not. You should just—you know—give a guy the opportunity to read you, see if he can figure out what you like without giving him printed directions. And a map. And a contract to sign in triplicate. See if you can enjoy not knowing what will happen."

I was already shaking my head before she finished, planning to tell her how ludicrous of an idea this was.

First, no.

Second, also no.

Third, what happens when Lisa arrives?

And fourth, an encounter without explicitly communicating expectations, hard limits, and goals? What was the point? The data wouldn't be generalizable!

Except . . . the times Abram has touched you without asking, you've liked it. Mucho.

My pulse jumped. *Just the thought of all that—all that touching me without . . .* I rubbed my chest, at a hot tightness there, and tore my stare away to scowl at the wall. Gabby's suggestion was on repeat in my head, and it wasn't just anxiety or fear I was feeling.

"You're thinking about it!" Gabby jumped up from the bed and crossed to the desk, standing directly in front of me.

"Gabby, you're mentally disturbed."

"Don't deny it, you're definitely thinking about it. You should make the Mona-moves on him."

I gave that suggestion a firm mental shove. "And what happens when Lisa gets back? Would she pick up where I left off with Abram? Pretend to be me pretending to be her? Gross and cosmically wrong on so many levels."

She sighed impatiently. "You think too much. She'll just call things off."

"Just like that?" I snapped my fingers. "And he won't care?"

Gabby shrugged. "I mean, probably not? Look at him. He's a hot commodity in this town. If he wants some, he doesn't usually have to work too hard to get it. He's a goodtime guy."

I shook my head lightly, squinting at her, a flare of something uncomfortable in my chest. "A goodtime guy? What does that mean?"

"It means he's experienced, and he'll show you a good time, but you don't have to worry about him getting clingy." When I continued to stare at her she huffed and lifted her eyes to the ceiling, exasperated. "Let me put it this way: I've never seen him with a girlfriend, but he's always surrounded by girls."

"And you know for a fact that he has relations with all these girls?"

"You sound like a lawyer, Mona. This isn't a trial." She studied her nails. "Guys like him always have—"

"Guys like him? Guys like what?"

"You know, insanely hot, talented, always single and keeping his options open. He's not going to care when Lisa calls it off."

I could feel myself making my about-to-sneeze face. What Gabby was saying was diametrically opposed to the Abram I was coming to know, especially after talking to his mother and sister. He just didn't seem like that kind of person—

Wait. What kind of person? You mean someone like you?

I flinched, frowning, not liking this thought. And it wouldn't be the same, would it? Yes, I'd had relations with several men without any intention of making any of those men my long-term partner, but that was all in the interest of testing a hypothesis. Totally different.

Okay. Whatever you need to tell yourself to sleep at night.

"Why are you making that angry face?" Gabby lifted an eyebrow, her gaze moving over my features. "Don't get mad at me for Abram being easy. I'm trying to do you a favor here. Get in there and use him to have a good time."

Pinching the bridge of my nose, I took a deep breath, irrationally offended on Abram's behalf at him being labeled a 'goodtime guy.' That wasn't Abram. It just wasn't. Don't ask me why, but I knew this was an unfair estimation of his character.

Anyway! I couldn't think about this now. Therefore, I ignored this discordant assertion.

"Whatever. It doesn't matter, because nothing is going to happen between us. I can't ignore that Abram is in a position of authority over me, over Lisa." I said this mostly as a reminder to myself. After our donut encounter this morning, I couldn't and shouldn't forget that *nothing* was ever going to happen between us. He and I weren't even friends. Lisa's well-being was his responsibility. "He's been tasked with ensuring my safety. How inappropriate would it be for me to, as you say, make moves on him? I would never put him in that position."

"Oh, come on. I'm sure he wouldn't mind being put in *any* position with you if—"

I interrupted her mid-eye roll. "No. I think he's already been through enough. Lisa did enough damage last year, don't you think?"

"It's not like being with either of you would be a hardship." Her hands fell to her legs, smacking her thighs as she completed the eye roll. "See? This is what I'm talking about. Why can't you understand how beautiful you are? Anyone, including Abram, would be lucky to—"

"He's not an object! Even if he's been with the entire female half of Chicago, he's still not an object!" I whispered harshly, straightening from the desk, causing her to rock back on her heels. "People are so much more than what they look like, what is wrong with you? He's not disposable. He's not here to use and amuse. He is more than 'like, super hot.' He is a *person*, with thoughts and feelings and a family who loves him, who he also loves. He is funny and sweet, and irritating and witty, and doesn't like to show his smile. He writes music and sleeps at crazy hours, he eats pizza cold—who does that? So gross—and knows too much about whales, and steals donuts, and should really invest in a new razor . . ."

I stopped there because Gabby was giving me a sideways look, the rest of her face frozen, the fire of suspicion behind her eyes.

"What?" I asked sharply. "What is it?"

"I don't get it. You've slept with like, seven guys, right? And never wanted a relationship with any of them."

"We didn't sleep together, we had sex as a means to determine specific aims. And that doesn't mean I've treated them like objects." I hadn't. I really hadn't. It had been a mutually beneficial arrangement, where we'd both used each other's bodies to answer—*You know what? Never mind.*

"You . . ." Her eyes narrowed. "You're into Abram," she said and nodded, slowly at first, but then faster after a second. "Like, way, way, *waaaaay* into him."

I pinched my nose with my thumb and forefinger again, closing my eyes. "Just because I recognize that Abram isn't an object, doesn't mean I'm into him."

But, for the record, she was totally right. I was into him. Way, way, *waaaaay* into him. And now I had a headache.

"Oh girl, you know what? I take back my suggestion. Avoid him. You don't want this goodtime guy as your first crush. He's the caviar of goodtime guys. Avoid him at all costs."

Peeking at her, I frowned, because she was contradicting herself and her expression looked so entirely earnest. "You make no sense. A minute ago, you're telling me to use him for his body. But now that you think I like him, you're telling me to run the other way?"

"Yes." She nodded, her eyes large and sympathetic. "Lisa will be back in a few days, and Abram can *never ever know* that you impersonated her this week. He will totally *flip out* and tell the world about it. His sister is a journalist, you know? It'll be everywhere."

I studied her, her words, her expression. Clearly, she believed what she said, but I couldn't help offering a counterpoint. "Really? I don't know. What about Leo? Wouldn't that make things awkward between them? And when I apologized on behalf of Lisa for what happened last year, he accepted the apology, no problem."

"You have to trust me on this. He has mad respect for Leo, but this guy is ridiculous about lies. I know him much, much, much better than you do. Remember? I hang with him and your brother and their group when Leo is in town, so I know Abram. When I say he's uptight, I mean it."

"But—"

"He hates lies. Hates them."

It was a struggle not to roll my eyes. "Everyone hates lies."

"He has ended friendships, both long-term and with powerful people who could help him in his music career—like, a lot—because they told a stupid lie and he found out about it. Ask Leo, you don't lie to Abram. And knowing Leo, how laid back he is, he probably wouldn't be surprised if Abram ratted you both out to the press. Now, I'm not saying Leo would forgive him for it, but he wouldn't be surprised."

"Hmm." She looked so serious, I decided to stop pushing the issue. For now.

"So, yeah. If you like him—like, if you like *him,* as a person—if you're crushing on him at all, pretend he doesn't exist and push him from your mind. Avoid him like the plague or whatever. Even if you weren't already lying to him, I'd say the same thing. He is definitely *not* someone you want to have feelings for."

Giving me one more nod, she stepped back, glanced around the room, and sauntered to the door. "I'll be back tomorrow to check on you."

"Gabby," I called to her as her hand touched the doorknob. "You confuse me."

"I know." She shrugged, a flat smile on her lips. "But honestly, babe, I'm just looking out for your heart. Learn from your sister's mistakes: don't go chasing musicians or windmills."

I stared at her, unable to believe my ears.

Windmills? Had Gabby just made a *Don Quixote* reference? *Did that just happen?*

Before I could ask or clarify, she opened the door and strolled out of it.

* * *

I'd wanted to ask Gabby about the drugs and whether Lisa had been selling them to teenagers. I'd wanted to uncover why my sister had been arrested and what the deal was with Tyler. But I hadn't. I'd been too distracted by Abram, and talking about Abram, and thinking about Abram.

What is happening to me?

Taking a pain reliever for the headache, I lay on the bed, staring at the ceiling for approximately twenty minutes, and gave myself a pep talk.

FACT: He can never know you are Mona. Ever.

FACT: You must avoid him for the REST of your LIFE.

FACT: Your interactions serve no purpose. They have to end.

FACT ACCORDING TO GABBY: He's a goodtime guy.

And, most importantly, stop noticing the way he chews. It's not okay.

But traitorous little objections searched for cracks, issuing rebuttals and trying to bargain—

Why can't he know you're Mona? Maybe Gabby was overexaggerating about his loathing of liars. Once you explain the situation, he'll understand. What if he'll keep it a secret too? What if he helps you?

If I have to avoid him for the rest of my life, why avoid him now? Shouldn't I make the most out of the time we have left?

All interactions serve a purpose, even if they're not immediately apparent. Right? What if Abram has something to teach you? What if not knowing him puts you on a path of inexorable ignorance?

And what's the harm in watching him chew? It's not hurting anyone. I can hide and watch him chew, right? He won't even see me.

And, I'm sorry, but he just doesn't seem like a goodtime guy. He just doesn't. Being surrounded by women doesn't mean he's a goodtime guy, it just means women like him. And I don't blame them!

—and this was concerning because: why?

Why was my heart doing this to me? Why was I arguing with myself? I'd never allowed a crush. I'd been tempted once or twice, but the most logical path forward had never included time for a relationship. Therefore, crushes were (are!) irrelevant.

So why him? Why now? Why? Why? Why? WHY?!

What a mess.

Going in circles, and growing increasingly frustrated, I decided there was no point in continuing this discussion with myself. Facts were facts. What I needed was a distraction. So I snuck down to the kitchen. All was quiet, and Abram was nowhere in sight. But because I was a loony bird, I also sniffed before taking another step, searching for smells. The aroma of donuts permeated the air, but I detected no trace of Abram-fragrance.

Heaving a large sigh, I meandered to the kitchen table, hoping against hope that the remainder of my chocolate donut was still there. It wasn't. Instead, I found a plate in the center of the table with—*one, two, three, four, five* . . . thirteen chocolate cake donuts.

!!!!!!

I stared at them, not understanding how it was possible to have so many emotions at once.

He went out and bought me donuts.

I was rubbing my chest, massaging the warm, tight ache there, before I realized what I was doing.

He bought me donuts. My favorite donuts. Thirteen. A prime number. A baker's dozen.

As I stared at the pile, I was distressed to discover that my mouth was now dry, which ultimately necessitated a swallow. My mouth should have been watering at the sight of all that deliciousness, but it wasn't. And, worse, I suddenly had no appetite. It's hard to think about eating when you're panicking.

However, the panic did help me close the door on my traitorous thoughts. I didn't want messy, and the only way to avoid more messy was to put all dissenting opinions on lockdown. I would focus on the facts, as they were, and stay the course.

I made myself tea, crept to the mudroom, and found my old dog-eared copy of *Moby Dick* waiting for me. It felt familiar, and paired with the aroma of peppermint tea, it felt like an oasis.

But my brain was not quiet and would not allow me to absorb the story when I opened to the bookmarked paragraph where I'd left off a few days ago. Taking several calming deep breaths, I flipped open a random page—which happened to be chapter one, the first page—and forced my eyes to read the words.

Whenever I find myself growing grim about the mouth; whenever it is a damp, drizzly November in my soul; whenever I find myself involuntarily pausing before coffin warehouses, and bringing up the rear of every funeral I meet; and especially whenever my hypos get such an upper hand of me, that it requires a strong moral principle to prevent me from deliberately stepping into the street, and methodically knocking people's hats off—then, I account it high time to get to sea as soon as I can.

A little huff of wonder slipped past my lips and I blinked at the black ink. What were the chances? *This!* This was what I needed to read. It was a sign. It was magic. It was the universe telling me—

But wait.

My eyes drifted to the top of the page and I was no longer surprised or convinced the universe was telling me anything at all. Opening to this very page was no accident. I'd triple folded the corner, because it was my favorite passage. Like all mysteries investigated thoroughly, there was a perfectly reasonable explanation.

Mystery solved, I took Melville's advice in any case.

Closing my eyes, I went to space. I visited the safety and calm of my brain-planetarium—my own version of Melville's sea—and distracted my mind from small cares with the complexity of creation. From the Sloan Great Wall to a single quark, the whole and the individual pieces, working within the constraints of laws, of beautiful order.

No wonder I was frazzled and confused. Since starting undergrad, I'd never taken such a long break from academic pursuits or my research interests. I'd traded order for chaos, knowns for unknowns, equations for unsolvable conundrums.

This wasn't my world. I didn't belong here. Here was Lisa's reality, not mine. Here were decisions based on desires, not facts and risk/benefit ratios.

Also here, footsteps approaching.

My eyes flew open just as Abram rounded the corner. Acting on some crazed instinct, I shoved *Moby Dick* between my legs (ha! . . . *that's what she said)* and picked up my mug, holding it over my lap to obscure the book from view.

My ruckusy and flustered movements immediately drew his attention, his handsome face turning toward me, his eyes scanning over my form as his thumbs hooked into his pockets.

"Hey," he said, sounding and looking totally normal, where normal for us was now apparently defined as friendly and interested. "There you are."

"Yes. Here I am." I was attempting to hold the mug *just so,* which made my elbows feel awkward.

His eyes dropped to my lap. "Is that a book? What are you reading?"

I clenched my thighs around the novel, my voice higher pitched than I would have liked as I said, "Nothing."

"Come on." A faint smile on his lips, a delightful little crooking of his eyebrow, he wandered closer, making no attempt to hide his blatant inspection of my lap. "What's the title?"

His voice dropped a half-octave. It had a flustering effect on me. *Why must he be this way? Where are his flaws?!*

"Hair removal for dummies," I sputtered stupidly, moving the tea to the side so as not to spill it on me and *Moby.*

But before I could manage settling the tea on the seat, he reached between my knees and withdrew the book. CURSES!

Instinct told me to launch myself at him, like I'd done this morning, and take it back by force.

I didn't. I balled my hands into fists, threw my legs over the side of the bench seat, and crossed my arms to keep from reaching for him or the book. Another tussle with Abram would lead nowhere good—depending on one's definition of the word *good* —and there'd definitely be no interruption just in the nick of time.

Tossing me a triumphant side-eye and a smirk, he lifted the book and read the title. And then his head shifted back on his neck and the smirk disappeared. He blinked. He frowned. He squinted.

"*Moby Dick?*"

I cleared my throat, searching for a plausible lie. "After our discussion about whales, it looked interesting." As I said this, I stared at my feet, but then I peeked at him to see if he bought my untruth.

He gave his head a subtle shake. "You're lying."

Lifting my chin, I kept my mouth shut. *See?* Lying was at the bottom of my failure pile, along with matching my socks and telling the difference between Taylor Swift and Katy Perry and Lorde; they all looked identical to me, but then I'd never been good with faces.

"You're lying," he said again, like this discovery was fascinating rather than worrying. "You didn't pick this book up because of our discussion about whales. You've read this book before."

"Fine. Yes. Guilty." I glared at his chin and the ever-present potential for a wizard beard. *I hope he never buys a new razor.*

Abram laughed like I was strange, coming to stand directly in front of me and holding out the book. "Why would you lie about reading *Moby Dick?*"

I accepted it, careful not to touch his fingers, and asked a question instead of answering his, "Have you read it?"

"No," he said softly, tilting his head to the side as though to ensure I didn't break eye contact.

"Really? And after all your whale facts, I'm a little disappointed." Goodness, he had pretty eyes. So pretty. So very pretty . . . *I bet he uses those eyes on all the girls.*

Bah.

Once again internal monologue, STFU.

It was a struggle to keep my face free of revealing expression, but I managed it. Not that I thought he was, but what did I care if Abram was a goodtime guy? It wasn't my business. And if it was true—which my subconscious seemed to be pondering—good for him.

To the point: Abram's goodtime-guy status was irrelevant to me.

Okay. Good. That's settled. Now all I had to do was leave. *Time to go. Get up, get up, get up!*

I didn't get up. I couldn't seem to make myself move. What I needed was an exit strategy. Brain-tussling with Abram about my favorite book was likely to be just as dangerous as body-tussling with him over a donut.

"I only know that stuff about whales because of my sister's friend, Janie. She knows a ton of random facts."

Perking up at the mention of Marie, I wanted to say, *Tell me more!*

Instead, I tried to think of something Lisa might say while searching for a way to extract myself from this assuredly captivating conversation. "She sounds boring."

"She's not." A hint of irritation entered his tone. "She's awesome."

"Awesome?" I asked before I could catch the question, knowing I sounded interested. Marie had been just the best person ever, of course I was curious about her friends. Specifically, how would one go about being friends with Marie?

One of his reluctant smiles made an appearance, his eyes dancing, like he knew how curious I was. They were so very bright and engaging as they moved between mine. "Yes. Amazing. Brilliant. Surprising. Funny. Fascinating. Beautiful. She reminds me of you, actually. She—"

ALERT! COMPLIMENT ALERT!

I jumped up, bumping into his chest before maneuvering around him. It couldn't be avoided. He was standing so close and I had to leave. Now.

"Okay. Well. See you later." I tucked *Moby* under my arm and darted for the back door, a wave of warm pleasure rushing up my cheeks.

He thinks you're beautiful and fascinating and surprising and—Wait, why was beauty the first thing I was happy about? Shouldn't I be focusing on brilliance? And funniness? Beauty was irrelevant, *irrelevant I say!*

"Wait, where are you going?" He caught my arm.

I spun, my eyes going to where his hand encircled my wrist. He immediately let me go.

"I thought I might practice the violin again," I said while rubbing my wrist. An arm grab had never felt so good.

His attention flickered to the door behind me. "You're going to practice outside?"

Bah! My overthinking about his indirect compliments had me all turned around.

"No, uh, obviously not. I'm going upstairs. To my room." Taking a pivoting step, I aimed in the direction of the back stairs, and said, "Fare thee well."

And then I grimaced at having said *fare thee well* while endeavoring to keep my pace unhurried.

He shadowed my steps all the way down the hall and into the kitchen before calling suddenly, "I guess you don't want to go to Anderson's with me then."

If I'd been making tracks, I would have stopped in them. Anderson's? The bookstore?

But if I go, I'll be spending time with Abram, which is a bad idea.

I swatted away good intentions and sense and I turned completely around. "Anderson's? As in the bookstore?" I asked, doing nothing to mask the naked hope of my expression or in my voice.

I couldn't hide them. No one was that good at lying.

"Yeah." He sighed, sounding regretful even though his brown eyes were glittering mischievously. His lips remained flat, but that left dimple winked at me, a slight indent in his cheek. *No wonder he covers his mouth when he smiles, that dimple is his tell.*

But I didn't care if he thought it was funny to dangle a bookstore visit as a carrot, I didn't care if he was inwardly laughing at me. I wanted to go. I wanted to go very, very badly.

"I was going to drive over, and then grab some food"—he shrugged—"but if you want to practice violin instead, then—"

"Let's go!"

CHAPTER 13
NEWTON'S THIRD LAW OF MOTION: SYMMETRY IN FORCES

Unsurprisingly, Abram insisted on driving to Anderson's Bookshop.

On the way, we discussed options for a post-shopping meal. What he didn't know was that I planned to spend as much time at the bookstore as possible, so most of the lunch places he suggested wouldn't be open by the time we left. I didn't correct him. Let him believe what he wanted, we wouldn't be leaving that bookstore until after closing if I could help it.

Upon arriving, I made a beeline for the nearest display, not caring about the genre. I planned to go through every single section, every shelf, every book. When I went back to being Mona, I would never take for granted the ability to go where I wanted, when I wanted, ever again.

Abram and I stuck together most of the time, him pointing out books he thought were interesting, or ones he thought I might like, or asking me what I thought about a title or a cover or a blurb. Eventually, I began doing the same with him.

It was . . . fun. I was having a great time, the comradery, the quiet, the whispers, and the inevitable snickering when we made it to the romance section. (My snickering, not his.)

"What are you laughing at?" he whispered, trying to get a good look at the cover of the book I was holding.

I pressed the cover to my chest. "Nothing." It was the most ridiculous cover—a cross-stitched beard—with the dumbest title I'd ever seen—*Grin and Beard It.*

Abram glanced between me and the back of the novel. "You read romance?"

"Um, no," I said, tucking the book back where it belonged. Serious people with serious thoughts didn't read romance novels.

"Why not?"

I gave him a look. "Why would I?"

"You like to read, right?"

"Uh, yes. But—"

"You should try this." Abram selected a novel from a nearby shelf and showed me the cover.

I scanned the title, glanced at Abram, and then placed it back on the shelf. "No, thank you. I don't read that kind of stuff."

"What kind of stuff?" He grabbed it again, leaning a shoulder against the shelf, giving me the sense of being caged in (but not in a bad way).

I made a face as I inspected him, unable to discern whether he was poking fun at me, or the author, or what, so I said, "I'll read it if you read it."

"Deal." He handed it to me again. "I like this author."

I reared back, shocked, stunned, shocked again. "You read romance?"

"Yes."

I blinked at him several times; apparently my eyes couldn't believe my ears. "No, you don't."

"Yes. I do." He leaned closer, smiling down at me like he thought I was cute, or my disbelief was cute, or something like that.

"Prove it. What else has this author written? And no looking at the shelf or the book I'm holding." I hid the novel by twisting away, but my attention remained on Abram's face, enthralled. I still couldn't tell if he was joking.

"Let's see, uh, *Devil In Winter*—that was a really good one—and the other book I really liked was *Love in the Afternoon*. The main character was obsessed with animals." His smile grew as his eyes drifted over my shoulder. "She cracked me up."

Captivated, I stared at him. I didn't know what other books this author had written, so I couldn't fact-check his statements. Nevertheless, I was now convinced Abram read romance.

His gaze returned to mine. "What?"

"I'm so confused."

"Why?"

"When would you have come across romance novels? Did your mom read them?"

"No." He wrinkled his nose—just a little—at this question. "My mom reads gardening books and science fiction. But my sister reads everything." He tapped at the cover of the book I clutched. "I read whatever she recommends, and she recommended this author, highly."

"Your sister is so . . ." I was in love with Marie. No use denying it. *Teach me your ways, Marie-Wan Kenobi.*

"What?"

"Amazing," I said on a sigh.

His grin was as quick as it was massive, but then he dropped his chin—as though to hide his smile again—and cleared his throat. "She is, but don't tell her I said so."

"Why wouldn't you tell her yourself?"

"You know how it is between siblings."

My eyebrows inched upwards. "How is it?"

"They live to torture each other."

"They do?"

"Of course." His eyes moved between mine and he looked truly confused by my confusion. "Come off it, Lisa. Leo doesn't talk about you and your sister much, but he's told me a few stories about you. You love to piss him off."

Oh! . . . *yeah.* I'd forgotten for a moment who I was supposed to be. Okay, I'd forgotten for longer than a moment. Actually, I'd been Mona all day.

"Ah! Hahaha. Yes. That is true." I turned and promptly winced.

He was not finished. "The time you texted Meghan using his phone, but called her Melissa? Classic."

I glanced at Abram, who now walked at my shoulder, and gave him a noncommittal shrug. I didn't know anything about a Meghan, or a Melissa, so it was probably best neither to confirm nor deny his statements.

"Actually, I should thank you for that one."

I stopped. "You should thank me?"

"Oh yeah." He nodded, looking serious. "Did you ever see them together? She wasn't good for him."

Frowning, I nodded—again vaguely—making a mental note to ask Leo about this Meghan person the next time we spoke. And then I'd ask him why he'd never told me about this Meghan person.

"Well, see? That wasn't torture. I was helping Leo make good life decisions."

"Sure." He gave me another little smile, now squinting. "And what you did to your sister before her graduation? With the newspaper? What was that?"

Staring at Abram, I became very, very still. *How did . . . ?*

"How do you know about that?" I whispered the question. My hands suddenly felt clammy, my throat hurt, and my heart was beating like mad.

"Leo told me. He thought it was hilarious." Abram had picked up a book and was browsing the back cover, apparently not noticing the shift in my demeanor.

Leo thought it was hilarious?

Coming to myself just enough to realize it probably wasn't a good idea to continue staring as though shell-shocked, I turned. Nodding faintly, I grabbed the first book I found and pretending to read the cover, I worked to regain my composure.

Upon arriving two days before my graduation, she'd given an interview to the university's newspaper pretending to be me. Luckily, the student reporter called to double-check one of my statements and I'd discovered the "prank" before they'd published the story.

It wasn't that big of a deal to anyone but me. And—I reasoned—from the outside looking in, I could see how it might be funny. She'd told the reporter I planned to give up physics for a career in performance art, that I'd discovered my true passion and that passion was nude interpretive dance.

Hilarious.

Except not. Not when you've spent four years struggling to be taken seriously.

"It's a small world." Abram's statement brought me back to the present, and I worried for a moment that he'd been speaking and I'd missed some of it.

But then he said, "What are the chances that you go to boarding school with this girl, and then she goes on to the same university as your sister, and she's on the news-paper the same year your sister graduated."

I blinked, processing his words, and asking before I could catch myself, "Sorry, what?"

He glanced at me, his lips curved to the left. "Leo said Mona freaked out, thinking the whole thing was real, thinking you actually gave the interview." His gaze moved over my features and warmed, softened, his mouth gave in to a real smile. "Your sister must not know you very well, to think you'd do something so mean."

* * *

"What are you doing?" Abram's attention flickered between me and the book I'd just opened. "Are you starting? Now?"

"Yes." I flipped to the page that read *Chapter One.*

My plan to remain at the bookstore until closing didn't come to fruition, mostly due to a Julius-and-Ethel-Rosenberg-level betrayal by my stomach. It had growled so loudly, Abram gave me the side-eye, paid for our purchases directly, and pushed me out of the shop.

Silly with starvation, I had a fantastical thought: had I not been so hungry, I would've liked the afternoon to last forever.

I'd had the best time. The BEST time. *THE BEST TIME!*

Other than that one minor uncomfortable reminder of Lisa's practical joke and his bizarre statements that followed, good feelings reigned. I hadn't been able to figure out how to ask him about the prank without blowing my cover—was he saying that Lisa hadn't actually given the interview? That the interviewer/reporter had been in on the joke? Or what?—so, I ultimately decided to let it go. For now. *Something to ask Lisa or Gabby about later.*

It had been somewhat difficult to push it from my mind. But my continued proximity to Abram while browsing at the bookstore meant his mysterious man-scent had been easily accessible. Loose and wonderfully fuzzy headed, anytime I thought of Lisa's prank, trying to parse through what he'd meant by "Your sister must not know you very well, to think you'd do something so mean," all I had to do was move closer to Abram. I'd pretend to reach around him for a book, or brush past him when the space between aisles grew tight—and take a big sniff.

Instant olfactory sensory relaxation.

Presently, we were sitting in a booth at a small Italian place not far from Anderson's. We'd just ordered—lasagna for me, steak of some sort for him—and then I'd opened the romance novel he'd bought me.

"I thought you were hungry?" He poked at the book with a breadstick.

"I am. But my brain is also hungry. For stimulation."

"What? My conversation isn't stimulating enough?"

I smirked, because he was just so darn cute sometimes and it made me smile.

"I didn't say that." I cleared my throat in an effort to erase the smile from my face, lifting the book higher to hide the persistent grin as I mumbled, "But you said it and you're very perceptive."

A surprised-sounding laugh emanated from his side of the table.

Impulsively, I lowered the book and peeked at him, anticipating he would do something to hide his happy expression. Like clockwork, he covered the bottom half of his face with his hand. My heart gave a little tug at the sight. For a big, strong, tall, dark and manly musician, he sure was super adorable sometimes.

"Fine." Abram shook his head, turning it away from me and pulling out the book he'd bought for himself. Setting it on the table, he opened it. "Go ahead and read."

Lifting my book, I grinned secretly, and read.

I had doubts that I'd be able to concentrate, which were initially well-founded. A few times, struck by a bizarre compulsion, I snuck a glance at Abram. He would either: a) already be watching me, which would cause us both to hastily return our eyes to our books, or b) I'd steal several seconds of watching him before he caught me, which would cause us both to hastily return our eyes to our books.

After a few minutes of this unfathomable behavior, we both settled, reading quietly, absorbed in our books.

Sometime later, the arrival of our food surprised me, and I blinked dazedly at our server when he set my dinner down. Despite being hungry, I found the sudden presence of our food inconvenient. Setting the novel aside with a sigh, I placed the napkin on my lap. Apparently, for a moment there I'd forgotten I wasn't in nineteenth-century England.

"How's the book?"

"It's really good. Really good," I said distractedly, picking up my fork and knife, cutting into the steaming plate of lasagna and adding, "She paints a vivid picture."

"I have some more suggestions, if you want—"

"Yes. You should write them down."

"Even if they're romance novels?" Abram leaned forward to cut his steak, sparing me a quick, amused look.

"But is it really a romance novel?" I lifted my chin towards the book. "It reads more like fiction."

"Romance is fiction." He punctuated this statement by taking a bite of steak, and then chewing.

"But it's—it's—" Interesting? Well researched? Engaging? Well written? *All of the above.*

"Not what you expected?" he supplied, smirking around his bite. "What did you expect?"

Shrugging, I lifted a small rectangle of lasagna on my fork and blew at the steam. "I guess something brainless." I didn't add that I followed *The New York Times Book Review* and they'd had more than their fair share of articles calling the romance genre "fluffy."

If you couldn't trust *The New York Times Book Review*, who could you trust?

"Why? Because it's about love and has a happy ending? And only stories of unhappiness with tragic endings are important? Because a struggle that leads to something good isn't worthwhile?"

Taking a bite and avoiding eye contact, I shrugged again because he'd just hit the nail on the head. His questions challenged my preconceived notions and made me sound like an idiot. I wasn't used to feeling like an idiot. Or being challenged. *Then again, I usually never deviate from my appointed lane . . .*

It was both an uncomfortable and exhilarating experience.

I felt his stare linger for a moment before he spoke. "Glad you like it."

Grateful he'd decided to let the subject drop, I said quietly, "I do. Thank you for recommending it to me."

"No problem." I heard a smile in his voice. "Is it better than *Moby Dick*?"

"I don't know. I just started." I gave the cover a wistful glance before giving Abram my eyes. "But *Moby Dick* is one of my favorites."

"Really?" His face screwed up. "Why?"

"It's about dealing with disappointment and putting things into perspective. Everyone should read it."

His weird look persisted, like my words made no sense.

So I laughed. "I know, not a very modern concept."

"You like reading books about disappointment?"

I nodded, agreeing before thinking too much about it.

"Why?"

I hypothesized out loud. "It's comforting."

This earned me a single-eyebrow lift. "How so?"

Again, speaking without considering my words, I said, "Think about it. Stories of expectations, hopes, and dreams not being met are confirmation that life is—fundamentally—a . . ." *Disappointment.*

Staring at him, and realizing what I was just about to say, my chest tightened. I was officially unnerved. Did I really think that? Did I really think that life was a disappointment?

I guess I did.

Abram lifted both eyebrows. "A what?"

"Um," I stalled.

How could I possibly think life was a disappointment? I lived a charmed life, right? I'd never wanted for anything. I'd been given every advantage. I had the use of all my limbs. I had my health. I'd been told by many people, many times how beautiful I was (if I'd only make an effort). I'd traveled extensively. I'd worked hard to be recognized as a content expert in my field, to be taken seriously, and now I was being courted by all the top research programs in the world. I had everything I'd ever wanted. *Everything.*

Right?

My gaze moved over Abram, his artfully messy hair, his scruffy beard, the twinkle in his amber eyes, the dimple at his left cheek, the curve of his generous lips. I'd almost kissed those lips earlier in the day.

Or maybe, suggested a mutinous little voice, *I have everything I've allowed myself to want.*

"Life is a what? A series of unfortunate events?" he prompted, snapping me out of my contemplations. "A whale hunting trip?"

There was no way I was going to tell the truth of my thoughts, but I had to say something. I decided on, "A challenge."

"Hmm." Abram's eyes narrowed. That paired with the small smile still on his lips gave me the sense he suspected I wasn't being honest.

We stared at each other for a long moment until he speared a bite of steak with his fork. "You should get a new one."

"New what?" New perspective on life?

"New copy. Of *Moby Dick*. Yours is all torn up." He placed the bite in his mouth.

I averted my attention before I could indulge in my weirdo desire to watch him chew. "Then what would I do with the old one?"

"I don't know, give it away?"

"What?" I reared back. "Absolutely not!"

"Why not?"

"Books are friends. You don't just—just—just give away friends!"

Abram, his elbow propped on the table, covered the lower half of his face with his hand, but his shaking shoulders gave him away.

Squinting at him accusingly, I crossed my arms. "You're laughing at me."

"Yes. I am."

"How would you like it if someone gave you away?" I muttered, indignant.

"Well, since the question infers that I would've had to give myself to that person before it would be possible for her to give me away, I wouldn't like it."

The temptation to ask *Have you? And, if so, what happened? And who is this stupid woman who gave you away?* was nearly overwhelming. If anything was true in the universe, it was that anyone who could willingly give Abram away was stupid (and also Newton's Laws of Motion).

Locking eyes with Abram, the questions were at the forefront of my brain, that mutinous little voice pushing them to the tip of my tongue, but the server chose that moment to swing by to refill our waters, saving me from making a critical error in judgment.

After ascertaining all was delicious and well, the server left. I did my utmost to ignore the curiosity pressing uncomfortably against my skull, and instead took a bite of lasagna.

I felt Abram's attention move over me, and eventually he said, "So, you read a lot," giving me the impression he was trying to get me talking again.

Since this was a benign, previously established fact, I confirmed it.

"Every night before bed, for about an hour. If I don't have a busy day the next day, I'll read for an hour and a half."

"Oh. Really busy day? Like what? Getting a blowout from someone named George?"

I was about to ask him who George was when my slow brain finally caught up. *Double yikes.* Again, I'd forgotten who I was supposed to be. *I blame Lisa Kleypas's excellent novel.*

"Well . . ." I worked for a moment to identify an appropriate response to his teasing. Luckily, I was able to stall by taking a bite of my food. Once I finished chewing, I said, "Who is to say how I spend my time isn't any more or less important than how you spend your time?"

"Good point." He nodded eagerly, like he'd been hoping I would respond this way. "So, tell me, how do you spend your time?"

Taking another bite, I chewed for longer than was necessary, my eyes moving up and to the left, because—since I was not in fact Lisa—this was a tricky question. I had no idea how my sister spent her time. Furthermore, I couldn't help but feel I'd just fallen into a verbal trap of some sort.

Unable to delay responding forever, I eventually decided on, "I sleep." This was true for Lisa, me, and humanity.

"You sleep." His voice was deadpan.

"Yep. Speaking of which, did you, uh, sleep well last night?"

Abram's gaze flickered over me, as though he thought I might be leading him into a trap of my own. Little did he know, I was just trying to change the subject.

"Yes," he said reluctantly, "I slept fine. Why?"

"It's just, you were up early." His sleep patterns were so sporadic, and this facet of his personality fascinated me.

Abram finished chewing a bite of steak before responding. "You were expecting to make it to the donut shop and back before I woke up?"

I shrugged, but also shot him a guilty look.

He chuckled. "I came down the stairs just as you walked out the front door."

"Why didn't you try to stop me?"

He ignored my question and asked one of his own, "Any regrets?" The speculation behind his eyes made me think maybe the question had a double meaning, but I was too distracted by the memory of this morning's tussle to parse through what the double meaning might be.

The grabbing, the teasing, the friction of our bodies as I jumped and slid down his, the touching, the staring, his scent . . .

Instead of answering directly, I cleared my throat and said, "It's important to live in the present." I said this mostly to remind myself, but also, due to the limits of the space-time continuum, living in the present was the only option. Wishing for a different past or an impossible future was pointless. "So, uh, did you write any music last night?"

"No, but I did get some lyrics written earlier today. You're playing the violin again?"

"Yes. I can almost play 'Twinkle Twinkle Little Star,' which means 'Old MacDonald' is next, and that's my favorite, with all the *bock, bock, bocking*, and *moo, moo, mooing*, and then the wolves came, as the prophesy foretold, in this economy." I forced myself to take a deep breath here so I would stop talking. Something about the way he was looking at me with those intense, deep brown eyes made me feel fidgety.

But Abram grinned, and the flash of dimples made my knees happy I was sitting instead of standing. "Why do you do that?"

"Do what?"

"You say weird stuff sometimes. Like, 'and then the wolves came.' What is that?"

"It's just a thing I do . . . when I don't know what to say." I'd been caught without prunes and my lasagna was finished. Might as well tell the truth.

"So you speak nonsense?"

"It's not nonsense. These phrases, they're special. They're special phrases that work for almost any occasion. They're evergreen."

"If you say so." During dinner, his left dimple had become a permanent fixture on his face and it was hugely distracting.

"They are." I rubbed my forehead, feeling somewhat harassed by his attractiveness. "Here, say something and I'll use one of my phrases."

"Fine. Let's see. Um—" Abram's gaze moved beyond me. "Okay. Want to go see a movie?"

"In this economy?"

A short, surprised laugh shook his shoulders and lit his eyes. "You're nuts."

"So let it be written, so let it be done."

"Oh no. You're not going to stop, are you?"

"Be that as it may, still may it be as it may be."

He was fighting a massive grin. "Please stop."

"There's no escape from destiny."

"What can I say to make you stop?"

"Wise words by wise men write wise deeds in wise pen."

"You are so fucking weird sometimes." He shook his head, his shoulders also shaking, losing the fight.

"As the prophesy foretold."

"Oh my God"—he clutched his stomach, tossing his head back to laugh—"I love you."

I sucked in a breath, my heart doing a strange, twisting thing. I kept my eyes affixed to the table so he wouldn't see my illogical and sudden turmoil, because it was illogical and it was turmoil. I told myself that his words had been an expression, nothing more.

Abram is a goodtime guy, he probably loves everyone.

Yes. Exactly.

. . . Wait! No. No, he is not a goodtime guy! Stop thinking of him that way.

The explanation was much simpler: he didn't *love* love me. It had been a figure of speech.

I lifted my gaze—just for a single second—to peek at him. But then I couldn't look away because something distressing happened.

The laughter and resultant smile lit up his face, casting everything else in the room in bleak shadow, and he wasn't hiding either this time. However, it wasn't just the smile that was distressing—I'd seen him smile several times at this point—but rather my new and completely involuntary physical reaction to it. The sight hit me in the stomach, an unexpected blow, jarring my teeth, a little painful and a lot uncomfortable. At first.

And then the pain dissipated, became an expanding warmth, a hum of kinetic energy —even though I was sitting perfectly still—radiating outward to my fingertips and toes, clouding my brain, and wrapping my whole person in a lovely, tight, cozy cloud.

Holy shit.

What the hell was that?

A microcosm of the big bang *but in my body!*

Disoriented and mesmerized, I couldn't take my eyes from his face where the effects of his laughter still lingered, giving his features an attractiveness that was four-dimensional. More than physical, it was an allure that permeated both space and time.

"What?" Abram's laughter had tapered while I'd been having a mini freak-out. "No more phrases left?"

I pretended like I needed to scratch the back of my neck as I quickly sifted through the possible anytime-phrases remaining:

Just like in my dream.

But at what cost?

And thus, I die.

They all felt a little too . . . accurate.

So I shrugged, glancing at him quickly and offering a tight smile, murmuring, "And then the wolves came."

CHAPTER 14
NORMAL, TENSION, AND OTHER EXAMPLES OF FORCES

Recovering from the mini big bang took some serious concentration. Luckily, Abram's mood had turned contemplative on the drive home and neither of us spoke.

Although, halfway through the drive, while we were stuck at a stoplight, he turned to me and said, "Thank you for coming with me. I had a great time."

I was trapped in the sincerity of his stare, caught in the velvety cadence of his voice, only able to nod dumbly and mutter stupidly, "Great time. I had . . . also."

He grinned, his features softened by the glow of nearby streetlamps and the red light of the traffic signal, his four-dimensional attractiveness growing to ten dimensions, where the tenth were those pesky infinite possibilities and I was suffocating in the tenderness of his big, gorgeous, ten-dimensional brown eyes.

Oh my heart.

But then the light changed and he gave the road his attention, leaving me to my entropy. Thank goodness we still had several blocks before the house. I required both the dark and the quiet to order my thoughts.

Closing my eyes, I frantically tried imagining the vastness of space. Like earlier in the day, I worked to put facts first and events into perspective. I reminded myself that I didn't belong here, that this was Lisa's reality and not mine. That helped.

I reminded myself of Gabby's advice, that he wasn't the type of person I wanted to have feelings for. That also helped even if I didn't 100 percent believe it.

The crack had widened, the mutinous bargaining voice had grown more persistent, leaving me with an undercurrent of agitation instead of peace, and wishing instead of acceptance.

As soon as Abram pulled into the street parking outside our house, I was out of the car, walking to the gate and punching in the code. By the time he'd sauntered to where I stood holding the gate open, I had a plan. Once we made it inside, I was going upstairs and going to bed. I hadn't been sleeping well, and lack of sleep could lead to poor decisions.

Abram said nothing as we walked up the stairs to the front door, and I kept my eyes firmly fixed forward, my jaw clenched, my hands fisted at my sides. *No matter what, you will go upstairs and go to bed. By yourself.*

He withdrew the keys and unlocked the door; I felt his eyes move over me just before opening the door. "You want to watch a movie?"

I waited until we were inside and I'd slipped my shoes off before answering. "Um, no thanks." Without turning, I added, "I think I might go to sleep."

I sensed that this answer seemed to take him aback, as though it had been exactly the opposite of what he'd been expecting. I took advantage of his momentary confusion and turned for the kitchen, my brain telling me to *go, go, go!*

Even so, my movements were sluggish. The logical path was forward, I knew that. Nothing could ever happen between us, I knew that too. Watching a movie with Abram would undoubtedly lead to *not* watching the movie while still *being* with Abram.

But to what end? The way he'd been teasing me all day, the easy banter, how I caught him looking at me in the bookstore and over dinner, how I'd undeniably been looking at him in the same way. I wasn't stupid. All the variables plugged into an equation that equaled mutual attraction.

This wasn't a crush, this was requited desire and reciprocated like. Kissing, unscripted touching, gazing, whispers . . . I was near dizzy at the thought. But in this specific case, that also totaled certain disaster.

He's not a person you want to have feelings for.

And yet, I wanted.

Something is wrong with me.

"You're tired?" he asked, following me into the kitchen and to the back stairs.

Offering just my profile, I shrugged noncommittally, because I wasn't tired enough to sleep and I didn't want to lie to him anymore, not even a white lie. Placing my hand on the banister, a twisting in my stomach made me pause just for a moment as I prepared to launch myself up the first flight.

But before I could climb the first step, he covered my hand, stopping me. A warm, electric current traveled up my arm, weaving itself into my bloodstream and brain. I glanced at his hand on top of mine, and the mutinous whispers returned. Another something terrible had happened: I officially liked it when Abram touched me.

Meanwhile, he hesitated for the span of a breath, and then stepped close. So close, I felt his chest against my back, his thighs against my backside. Abram pulled my hair to the side and the fall of hot breath against my neck caused the most potent and delectable involuntary shiver of my life.

Holy hadron collider.

I was a solution, he was a solute, and total saturation was on my mind.

"Care for company?" he whispered before I'd recovered, his lips just barely against the shell of my ear.

Holy hadron collider, indeed.

The fragrance of him invaded my good sense and for a moment I lost my breath. My breasts swelled, heavy and needy and hot, my nipples tightening into little beads, pressing against the lace bra. I felt the silk of the shirt everywhere it met my skin. He was close, so close, touching, right there and my eyelids fluttered under the weight of such heavenly sensory overload.

And yet, even under attack, my good sense held firm, buffered by a grim sense of certainty: I didn't believe Gabby, that Abram would be fine with a fling. I didn't. He liked me. This was as real for him as it was for me. What was happening between us wasn't something Lisa would be able to just call off when she took my place.

And that meant I would not be able to live with myself if I allowed him to believe *anything* between us was a possibility. That would be the same as leading him on, as using him.

My foolish heart, however, thought his idea was great. In fact, it had decided to hatch an escape plan and was currently attempting to beat itself out of my chest. *Oh please oh please oh please say yes!*

I cleared my throat, concentrating on the grim resolve. "Company?" The question was just above a whisper, because I couldn't manage much else. Gravity had seemed to reverse, or become centripetal in nature, pulling me in all directions at once.

"I could read you a bedtime story, from your new book." Knuckles brushed softly against the skin of my neck, the silk of my shirt, and then down my bare arm, raising goose bumps in their path. "Or I could sing you a song."

Oh no. *Do not want!* If Gabby was to be believed, I wouldn't be able to withstand an Abram talent-assault in addition to the rest of what I knew about him. Usually, musicians held no allure for me. But Abram was breaking the mold on all my *usuallys.*

Grasping that grim resolve, I slid my hand from beneath his on the banister, folded my arms over my chest (to conceal *that* situation), and turned to face him.

Swallowing the rocks in my throat, I asked, "Are you flirting with me?"

Two dimples, an unhidden smile given freely, gorgeous brown eyes caressing my face.

This is hard. So hard.

"You have to ask?" he said. Flirtatiously.

Despite the disobedient—and therefore destructive—thrill his nonadmission elicited, I cleared my throat and forced myself to say, "Do you think that's appropriate?"

He blinked, his grin faltering, but only a little. "Appropriate?"

"Yes." Crowbarring indignation into my voice I didn't feel, I narrowed my eyes. "Aren't you supposed to be the adult here? Ensuring I don't get into trouble or harm myself? For all intents and purposes, you're in charge of me, reporting back to my parents about my behavior. They trust you with my well-being. Leo *trusts* you. Therefore, let me ask you again: do you think flirting with someone you're in charge of is appropriate?"

Abram flinched back, taking two shuffling steps away as I spoke. At first, his eyebrows lifted, but then they lowered into a severe line over his darkening eyes.

"Are you . . . are you kidding?"

I glared at him, saying nothing, because I didn't trust myself to speak. *This is so hard.*

He shook his head, just slightly, as though to clear it, his eyes searching. "Or are you serious?"

"Serious," I parroted immediately, grasping at the word. Then I swallowed. Because I had to. *This is the hardest.*

Abram flinched, his lips parting, giving me the impression that a very loud objection was on the tip of his tongue. But then he snapped his mouth shut, staring at me for several seconds, perhaps expecting me to say *just kidding!* When I continued glaring in silence, he glanced at the ceiling. He then glanced at the wall to his left. His hands came to his hips. He exhaled a light laugh, shaking his head and covering his mouth.

He'd gone back to hiding his smiles, even the bitter ones.

I waited, watching him, feeling . . . horrible. And enormously uneasy. Also, immensely remorseful, wishing I could take the words back, but knowing it was for the best.

By the time his eyes had traveled around the kitchen and returned to mine, they were shuttered, dim, remote, and hit me with a force that felt physical.

"Yes. Absolutely. You're right." His tone matched his expression, and the combination made me wonder if my heart had just sustained a serious injury somehow. It would've explained why it was suddenly so hard to breathe.

I think it's hard to breathe because this is hard.

"I, uh, that's okay." My voice wavered along with my resolve and I took a step toward him. Apparently, at some point over the last several days, I'd become magnetized to Abram.

Or maybe it's gravity, he is quite big.

Or maybe it's one of the four fundamental forces, working on an atomic level: weak, strong, electromagnetic, gravitational.

Or maybe—

But he held up his hand, staying me. "No. It's not okay. Please accept my apology. I . . ." A flicker of something ignited behind his eyes, a vulnerability that crippled my brain, there and hidden in an instant. He dropped his gaze to the floor, and gave his head another shake before adding quietly, "No excuses. It won't happen again."

CHAPTER 15
PROBLEM-SOLVING STRATEGIES

The potency of my self-doubt and regret was a new experience.

When Abram left me at the bottom of the stairs with a polite departing head nod after my duplicitous speech about the appropriateness of his actions, I felt a large part of myself go with him. It felt like a physical separation, being split into two distinctly different versions of myself—one followed the logical path, and one followed him—and that was nonsensical.

The one that followed him wanted to tackle him to the ground and spill my guts. I almost did.

The rest of me retrieved my dirty cup from earlier in the day and made a new cup of tea, blinking away tears. I was the worst kind of hypocrite, acting like I had all this moral authority. Meanwhile, I was a lying liar of lies, sitting on a throne of lies, eating lie soup and liar cake.

Try as I might to be rational, I couldn't shake the sense that something was very, very wrong with me. This sense was only heightened by the near constant ache in my stomach and heart, both of which felt like an overreaction.

I never overreacted. Underreaction was where I lived my life.

You cannot deny he was behaving inappropriately, given what he knows to be true of the situation, a shrill little voice reminded me, one that sounded suspiciously like Dr. Steward.

Unable to navigate this strange labyrinth of emotional upheaval, I spotted the bag from the bookstore on the counter, grabbed my new book, left my new cup of tea in the sink, and went upstairs to play the violin. Unpacking it, I tried to play. I couldn't play. My fingers weren't working right. Setting the instrument on the desk, I picked up my new book. I set the book down. I didn't want to read.

Making a split decision, I changed into the bikini from the other day. I then marched down to the back door, intent on the pool—my hairdo and Gabby and George-the-stylist be damned.

But before I opened the back door, I spotted movement. It was now dark outside, but the pool light illuminated the water. Abram was swimming laps. I didn't press my face against the glass, but I did watch him without meaning to, tracking him, unable to look away, admiring how he paired gracefulness and power. He wasn't a perfect swimmer, his technique could use some help, but he was strong and fast and clearly determined to swim forever.

I must've watched him for a half hour, probably longer. My feet grew tired of standing in the same place, necessitating that I shift my weight and flex my calves. Still, he swam. It wasn't until he stopped and straightened, breathing hard and wiping away excess water with his hands, his eyes seeming to move directly to the window where I stood, that I tore my gaze away and stepped back.

Spooked—because clearly I was still overreacting—I sprinted to the back stairs. But then, a thought occurred to me. Pivoting, I jogged to the pantry, grabbed my backpack, and hastily climbed to the second floor, running into Lisa's room after a short moment of hesitation, closing and locking the door.

Eureka!

I had my laptop and research notes. Yes. Yes, yes, yes!

Why I'd neglected to retrieve my backpack prior to now, I couldn't fathom. I'd had opportunity and means—plenty of both—and yet I'd left everything there, hidden in the pantry, out of sight and out of mind. *There is something wrong with me. Why did I wait so long? This behavior isn't normal.*

Powering up my laptop, I took a deep breath, some of the earlier ache dissipating as I entered my password and navigated to connect to the Wi-Fi. That's when another disaster struck.

"What? What's this?" I asked the little yellow exclamation point next to our Wi-Fi network.

It's not working.

The Wi-Fi was down. I plugged my phone in and unlocked it to double-check. Sure enough, my phone couldn't connect either.

"Shoooooot!" I made a fist and shook it at the sky. And then I sighed, letting my hand drop.

Using the cellular hotspot, I could connect my laptop to the internet. Sadly, it wasn't fast enough for me to run my analyses, or access my data in any meaningful way. But I could check my email and browse the internet.

So I called Lisa's lawyer, left another voice message noting that she'd never called me back, and connected my laptop to the substandard hotspot.

I searched for any news of Lisa's arrest. I came up empty on *arrest,* but I did find recent links pairing her name with Tyler's. Bracing myself against the sliminess, I clicked on a story from TMZ, timestamp three hours ago.

Front man from Pirate Orgy spotted getting cozy with an unnamed female who was definitely not his longtime ladylove, Lisa DaVinci, DJ Tang and Exotica's wild-child youngest daughter. The pair were making out at a . . . and then blah blah blah.

I clicked through a few gossip sites, all telling the same story: Tyler had been photographed and filmed at a club with someone who was not Lisa, though there was no word from Lisa and no sightings of her. Neither my sister or Tyler were considered big names or newsmakers. She and I seemed to exist on the outer rim of celebrity culture—me because I actively rejected it, her because (I hypothesized) she tried too hard to be a part of it.

After I tired of searching for news on Lisa, I clicked through several of my bookmarks, checking to see if the latest editions of my favorite peer-reviewed publications had been published. They had not. So I busied myself by reading random news stories until doing so made me want to stab someone. I closed my laptop.

And then, debating and dismissing all my non-Abram-related options, I realized I was officially bored.

* * *

It was 6:03 AM and I was awake.

Despite falling asleep after midnight—after spending the remainder of the evening wandering around a silent house, in a boredom funk, eventually watching slowly loading, low-res YouTube videos on how to do makeup and hair—I could not go back to sleep.

As dawn gave way to day, I lay in bed, wondering what the last Hawaiian tree snail was up to these days as well as how I could arrange things such that Abram was told the truth about me, about Lisa, without everything going to Venus (hell).

By 7:00 AM I accepted the fact that I had just as much insight into the thoughts of the last Hawaiian tree snail as I had into fixing my present predicament. Therefore, best not to think about either.

The next hour was spent taking a meticulous shower. I—gasp!—washed my hair. And then I tried to give myself a blowout. I did okay, but more practice was needed, and more understanding of what product to use, how much, and at what stage. I added this knowledge deficiency to my list of videos to watch for the day.

Once the hair was done-ish, I (quietly and clandestinely) followed the tutorial I'd saved to my phone for how to do "day eyeliner." Apparently, there was a difference between day and night eyeliner, as well as occasion eyeliner and non-occasion eyeliner (aka everyday eyeliner). Basically, there was an eyeliner strategy for all possible situations.

Are you meeting your boyfriend's parents? There's an eyeliner for that.

Are you going to an office party, during the holidays, but not a Christmas event? There's an eyeliner for that.

Are you flying to Hawaii to view the last Hawaiian tree snail? . . . there was no eyeliner for that. But, should I survive the remainder of this week, I was tempted to record a tutorial for it.

A full hour and a half later, I was dressed and 100 percent ready to do absolutely nothing productive all day. Giving my laptop's new hiding place one last longing look and mentally cursing the lack of high-speed internet, I meandered downstairs. I hadn't appreciated how much I would miss having meaningful tasks to occupy my mind until they were no longer an option.

Striding into the kitchen, I didn't even sniff the air. Honestly, I was sorta kinda hoping to run into Abram. I hadn't seen him since spying on him from the window yesterday. The house had been quiet, like I was completely alone, its sole occupant. I'd been tempted to venture into the basement last night, where the recording studio was housed, or to the third floor, where he was occupying a guest bedroom. I didn't.

This morning, however, the temptation felt more like an incessantly prodding urge and I used food to justify it, arguing with no one about the fact that I was hungry. I'd noticed he'd cleared away the chocolate cake donuts at some point, so I couldn't even eat those. There'd been no decent food in the fridge for days, so of course I must find him and force him to go out with me for food. And if, incidentally, we had to share a meal and talk to each other . . .

But then I opened the fridge, as though to prove what I already knew to be true, and discovered it was now stocked with essentials: eggs, butter, cheese, a variety of vegetables, hummus and several kinds of healthy-ish dips, both raw and cooked chicken breasts. I could easily make a healthy and hearty breakfast, lunch, and dinner. No problem.

Stupid food.

I made myself eggs and toast. I ate them. They were delicious. My stomach was happy with the best breakfast I'd had since arriving in Chicago, but my heart still felt sick and my brain still felt bored.

The discombobulation persisted throughout the day as I wandered the empty main and second floors, checking the clock, wondering when Gabby would arrive. Eventually, I watched a few more tutorials on hair product usage. One of my bookmarked peer-reviewed journals uploaded their monthly publication; I read it from start to finish, jotting down a few thoughts in the composition book that held my current research notes.

I made a big salad for lunch and used all the cooked chicken. I also made four cups of peppermint tea which necessitated four trips to the bathroom. After my late lunch, I managed to read a few chapters of *Moby Dick*. If ever there was a time to remind myself of life's disappointments, now was that time.

All the while brain-bored and heartsick. *Or maybe I'm heart-bored and brain-sick?*

Afternoon finally, *finally* crept into evening with no sign of Gabby. Okay. Yes. I was actually looking forward to her visit, and not just because I'd be grilling her for answers about Lisa's arrest. I . . . liked talking to her. *I know!* It was like I didn't even know myself anymore!

The light in the mudroom had dimmed to a soft yellow and then the orangey-pink indicative of sunsets. Staring at the evocative color, I realized it had been a while since I saw a sunset. Several months at least.

Placing my book on the bench seat, I dragged myself to the elevator and punched the call button several times. Yes, I could have taken the stairs, but apparently a by-product of being discombobulated was a general sense of lethargy. I didn't want to take the stairs. I wanted to be sad and lazy.

Leaning a hand against the wall, I waited, twisting my lips to the side as I contemplated how best to view the sunset. My parents had a balcony that was more of a deck leading off my dad's office. It faced northwest.

My mind was on the sunset when the doors slid open, which was probably why I didn't immediately realize Abram was standing in the elevator. But when I did, I gasped. Cartoonishly. And then held perfectly still, staring at him with wide eyes.

Why I did this, I don't know. My body had officially become weird around him. I was on the verge of disowning it and all its crazy Abram-related flutterings.

Meanwhile, he leaned against the back of the elevator, his arms crossed, looking at me with bland indifference. He was wearing all black. Black T-shirt, black jeans, black boots. *Wait. Why is he wearing shoes?*

"Are you going up?" he asked. Eventually.

"Uh . . ." I twisted my fingers. Debating. Debating. My attention lowered to his shoes again. *Is he going somewhere?*

The doors started to slide shut and he made no move to stop them. So, of course I launched myself into the scant space at the last second. The thing about small, private elevators is that their safety measures aren't as responsive as the big, corporate building ones. Which meant I was knocked around a little by the closing doors.

Visibly alarmed, Abram reached out, one hand sliding around my waist, the other gripping my upper arm as he pulled me further into the small lift. This was presumably to either: a) save me from the jaws of death, or b) keep me from clumsily crashing into him.

With comical belatedness, the doors opened again, like, *Oh. Did you want to get on? Sorry about that, old chap.*

But I was already on the elevator, now pressed against the back wall by Abram; his back to the opening as though shielding me from any further door-related injuries; his eyes on mine, a mixture of concerned and confused.

"Are you okay?"

I nodded hurriedly, breathing in through my nose because I missed how he smelled. *Soak it up, buttercup. This might be your last opportunity.*

As usual, the fragrance of him had an inebriating, relaxing effect. But for some reason, this time it also made me want to . . . lick . . . something.

Abram continued to stare down at me. "Are you sure?"

"Yes. I'm fine." I took another breath through my nose. "How are you?"

Abram's grip loosened a little, like he planned to release me.

So my mutinous mouth lied, "But I think I banged up my shoulder a little. Oh. Oh, ouch." I lifted my right shoulder, making a wincing face, even though no part of me hurt. *Pathetic.*

"Is that where the door hit you?" His attention shifted to my offended shoulder and he inspected it, his eyebrows pulling together.

Huh. Clearly, he believed me, and I couldn't believe he'd fallen for that. *Perhaps I no longer require lying lessons.*

"This is where it hit, yes." I leaned forward a smidge, the doors behind him finally slid shut, and the elevator made a *whirring* sound as it slowly ascended.

I could only assume he'd pressed the button for the third floor when he'd originally stepped onto the elevator from the basement and that's why we were moving. I hadn't pressed the fourth-floor button yet, I'd been too busy liking how his body cocooned mine; liking how close he was and how that meant I could feel the warmth of him; liking how his hand slid up my arm to gently prod and smooth over my shoulder, checking for injury; liking how he hadn't seemed to notice that my hands were on his biceps, enjoying the solid strength and size. Or if he'd noticed my hand placement, he didn't seem to care.

Basically, continuing to gaze at Abram, I liked everything about the moment, and this was odd because he was—essentially—taking care of me. If you didn't count medical professionals, I'd never experienced *taking care* with anyone but a nanny, my sister, and Gabby, all incidences which had occurred many, many moons ago.

He frowned at my shoulder. "I think it's fine. But if it bothers you, we should ice it."

"Okay," I said softly, feeling inclined to agree with just about anything he suggested.

But then he stilled, his eyes cutting back to mine. Abram lifted an eyebrow, his gaze narrowing, assessing, examining.

He let me go. He removed himself to the adjacent wall. He crossed his arms.

Clearing his features of expression, his gaze dimming once more to disinterested and reserved, Abram stared forward and cleared his throat. A renewed pang of regret bounced around inside my ribcage as I watched this transformation, amazed at how much distance he was able to put between us in such a small space.

Clearing his throat again, he glanced at the digital floor readout, and then back to me. "Which floor?"

"The, uh, the fourth floor. The top floor." The pang of regret sunk to my stomach. Knowing why he'd stepped back and not at all blaming him for putting distance between us, I rubbed my shoulder.

Though it was my heart that felt injured.

CHAPTER 16
FURTHER APPLICATIONS OF NEWTON'S LAWS OF MOTION

I watched the sunset. By myself. Wondering when Gabby would finally show up. Feeling like the personification of a bookmark.

Bookmark was the perfect descriptive word for this restless paralyzed state of being. I couldn't think. I couldn't do. I was a placeholder with no power or free will. My only utility was the fact that I existed. A bookmark.

No longer feeling lazy, I jogged down the stairs to the second floor and changed into the white bikini I'd worn twice but had never used. In record time, I was ready to move. I needed exercise so I could sleep. I needed sleep to set my brain in order. *I'll feel better, more myself, after a good night's sleep.*

Again, taking the stairs, I marched past the kitchen, down the hall, and to the mudroom, determined to expend some energy. Alas, just before opening the door, movement in the pool caught my attention.

Abram. In the pool. Swimming. Déjà vu.

Staring at his form, I was breathing harder than I should've been. But that was because I was truly torn. *What should I do?* My brain was getting a rare workout.

We had a gym in the basement. I could change—again—and use the treadmill.

He couldn't swim forever. I could wait until he was finished.

I didn't have to exercise at all. I could go upstairs and read my new book, or good old *Moby Dick.* A voice that sounded a little like Gabby's whispered between my ears, *It's the only dick you're getting any time soon.*

Growling at the window, I shoved the crass—albeit true—thought to the side. There were several logical paths available to me. But instead of taking any of them, I gathered a deep breath, squared my shoulders, and opened the door. No doubt I was being stubborn and stupid.

But I wanted to go swimming.

Abram using the pool was not a reason for me to avoid swimming. We could be friendly. We were adults, at least in the eyes of the US government. We would be able to manage a civil conversation. Why would he care if I went swimming? He wouldn't.

He won't . . .

Strangely, this thought did nothing to make me feel better.

Still breathing harder than I should've been, I opened the door and left the house. Making a short detour to the little pool shed tucked against the façade of the brownstone my parents had torn down, I grabbed a pair of goggles and a towel. And then I approached the pool, my eyes following Abram as he continued his laps, ignorant of my arrival.

Setting the towel on one of the nearby lounge chairs, I cleared my mind of all dissent and stepped into the pool, hustling to the side he wasn't using. But he must've seen my legs or sensed a shift in the force, because he stopped swimming mid-lap and stood, wiping his eyes and frowning at me.

He was also breathing hard, which was to be expected given the fact that he'd been swimming for an eternity.

Giving him a tight smile and a head nod, but no eye contact, I dipped the googles into the pool and ignored the frantic beating of my heart. Goodness, I'd forgotten how perfectly formed he was up close with no shirt, and this time rivulets of water were dripping from his perfectly formed . . . form.

"Lisa." He moved a step closer.

"Abram." The end of his name caught in the back of my throat, necessitating a thorough throat clearing.

He waited until I'd finished clearing my throat before asking, "What are you doing?"

"Uh, well, you see, if you get the goggles used to the temperature of the water before you wear them, they won't fog as much." I rubbed the lenses with my fingers, staring at the action of my hands with an intensity of concentration more befitting rocket science. *I would know.*

"Not the goggles." He moved again, the ripples of water caused by his body now meeting mine. "What are you doing?" he asked, slower this time.

"I'm going to swim some laps." Finished acclimating the goggles, I pulled them on, correcting the suction around my eye sockets.

I felt his eyes on me. I felt them as assuredly as if he'd touched where he looked. That meant I had the urge to lower myself into the water up to my neck before he spied what my nipples thought about being the subject of his attention.

Spoiler alert: They liked it.

But I didn't lower myself, even though they'd tightened into traitorous stiff beads. Given historical data, everything about this situation and my body's reaction to it should have alarmed me.

First, I wasn't usually scantily clad while around another person.

Second, if I was, it occurred in near or complete darkness, and only after a great deal of discussion surrounding expectations. On the off chance that it wasn't dark, my nipples didn't typically have an opinion about being gazed upon one way or the other.

However, as Abram drifted closer, I discovered my well of wary was running distressingly low. Some reckless part of myself encouraged the rest of me to remain standing, betraying boobs be damned. Abram wanted an eyeful? Fine with me.

Actually, great.

Fantastic!

My irrational thoughts were as follows: I liked him looking. I *wanted* him to look. I wanted him to like what he saw and think about me later. I couldn't talk to him; I couldn't kiss him; I couldn't touch him. But I could stand here, in this bikini, and give him a memory. Hopefully a nice one.

And inexplicably, if I were being honest with myself, Abram looking at my body made me feel absolutelyfuckingfabulous.

See? Clearly, I was sleep-deprived and veering into Gabby's mentally unhinged lane.

"You're going to swim laps in a bikini?" he asked, his voice a little rough.

"Yep." I adjusted my hair so the rubber strap of the goggles didn't tug uncomfortably.

"In a string bikini?"

"Yep." The pool was cool, my cheeks were hot. I dipped my head all the way under-water, getting my hair and face wet while sneaking a glance at Abram's glorious torso, illuminated to perfection by the pool light, and made a nice memory of my own.

I am an Objectifying Olivia. I am Hypocritical Helen. I am a Lying Lisa. I am Winnifred the Worst.

Breaking the surface, I wiped my nose and lips of water, and backed up to the edge of the pool. Freely accepting that I was behaving irrationally, I smoothed my hair away from my face with both hands, the action probably doing great things for my chest headlights.

Abram made a huffing sound, which morphed into a low growl. "You can't wait until I'm finished?"

"You don't need the whole pool." I glanced at him from behind my goggles. And then I stared at him from behind my goggles. And then I ogled him from behind my goggles, which felt most appropriate because goggles were probably designed for ogles, hence the name.

"I'm almost done." He said this through his teeth, his dark glare continuing to blatantly travel over my body. He needed goggles.

"No. You're not." I set my hand on my waist. "Yesterday you were in here for an hour or more."

His eyes narrowed. "How do you know that?"

Stiffening, my hand dropped from my waist. I took a deep breath as a stalling tactic, perversely pleased when his eyes dropped to my chest—as though compelled—before he closed them. The muscle at his jaw jumped. His nostrils flared. He looked pissed. Or frustrated. Or both.

"I wanted to go swimming yesterday," I finally admitted, seeing nothing wrong with telling the truth. "I waited for you to finish. It took forever. I'm not waiting today."

Now he gathered a deep breath and my eyes dropped to his chest and stomach, the sparse smattering of hair and definition of his muscles were hypnotic. Once again, I had that urge to lick . . . something.

Shaking his head, he opened his eyes. They were focused on a spot behind me and to the right, giving me the impression he was purposefully averting his attention.

"Fine. I'll leave." Abram began wading through the water, aiming for the pool steps.

"Fine." I frowned, not liking this development and tearing my ogling eyes from his body. Focusing on the far end of the pool, I muttered childishly, "Good idea. I don't want to embarrass you."

That stopped him. "What?"

"I mean, when I lap you," I said matter-of-factly. "I don't want to embarrass you by how much faster of a swimmer I am. Than you."

Abram's eyelids lowered, a spark of irritation—but also something else—seemed to change them, turn the typically light brown irises the color of smoldering embers. Even in the pale, cyan illumination of the pool light, and from behind the lenses of my goggles, I saw the transformation.

"You think so?" His jaw worked and his words sounded like a dare. Both made my skin erupt in goose bumps of anticipation.

If I thought his glare had been sexy, this look paired with his bare chest and ticking-time-bomb jaw was cosmically erotic. *Another nice memory.*

"I know so," I said, just as darkly, lying. I wasn't certain I could beat him, but I was certainly up for giving it a try.

"Fine." He spat the word, moving his big body through the water and to the edge of the pool. Placing himself three feet from where I stood, he didn't glance at me as he barked, "Here's the deal: two laps—there and back two times—winner stays, loser leaves."

Oh jeez. Okay. Hmm . . .

I'd previously promised myself never to enter into a bet with Abram. *You promised the universe. You promised—*

"Five laps. There and back five times," I said, ignoring the recollection of my promise even though doing so gave me a niggle of discomfort.

I'd suggested five laps partially to be contrary. But also, partially because five laps were more than two. If he won, at least I'd get *some* exercise. And also, partially because I wanted to see him wet, angry, and breathing hard up close again.

"Okay." He drew out the word, still not looking at me. "Five."

"Good. Ready?" I lifted my hands to the edge behind me, gripping it and bracing my feet against the wall.

He did likewise. "On the count of three."

"One," I said.

I felt him glance at me, but all he said was, "Two."

"Thr—"

He pushed forward, BEFORE I'D FINISHED SAYING THREE!! UGH!!!!

Furious and, yes, turned on, I launched forward, pumping my arms and legs as though my life depended on winning, which it kind of did.

Since I'd promised I wouldn't make a bet with Abram, I decided to change it into a bet with the universe, in my heart, a secret bet. If I won, I would tell him the truth, about Lisa, about me, about how I felt—even though I didn't have complete clarity on that subject—but if I lost, I'd keep my mouth shut.

Lactic acid burned my muscles, my quads ached, my lungs felt like they might explode, but I made it to the far side of the pool and back in record time, narrowing Abram's cheating lead. After the second lap we were neck and neck, after the third I was slightly ahead.

But as we pushed off against the deep-side wall, marking the middle of the fourth lap, Abram surged forward. His hips were next to my face, which meant he was a half body length—a half *Abram* body length—ahead, and I was swimming as fast as I could. There was no way I would catch up. No way.

Despair and frustration gripped my throat and heart and lungs. I felt like crying. I think I did cry because I couldn't see out of my goggles anymore. Heading into the fifth lap blind, I gritted my teeth, telling myself this was it. This last lap was it. Even though I didn't believe in such things, I told myself, if I lost, it would be the universe communicating with me. I'd made a binding and irrevocable bet: I could never tell him the truth and there would always be lies between us.

I turned at the far wall just a second after he did. Head down, eyes closed, I put every joule of energy, every milligram of mass, every newton of force in my entire being into propelling myself to first.

Lungs on fire, my hand touched the wall and I immediately popped up, ripping off my goggles and looking to my right, to where Abram should have been. For a second, for a single, solitary moment in the eternity of time, my heart swelled with so much happiness and relief, I thought I might die. He was not there. He hadn't yet finished. *YES!*

But then, after two more seconds and no Abram, I frowned. Glancing around, searching for him, I found him treading water in the middle of the pool.

I blinked. Shocked. Stunned. Horrified. "What—why?" I didn't know what I wanted to ask first, and I was still struggling to catch my breath.

He was also breathing hard, also working to catch his, watching me with veiled eyes, too far away for me to search his face for answers.

"What are you doing?" I asked, my voice pitched high and slightly hysterical.

He shook his head. "I forfeit."

"You—you—you what?" Unthinkingly, I waded toward him, my dismayed stare transfixed on his extremely cool one.

"You win, I'll leave." Shrugging, he gave the water a languid stroke, bringing him closer, but only incidentally. I could see now that his destination was the pool steps, not me.

"No!" I darted to the side, putting myself in his path, forcing him to backtrack so as not to collide with me. "No, I don't win! It's not winning if you give up."

"What's the problem? You win." His glare had returned, his dark eyebrows descending over equally dark eyes.

"You forfeit, that's giving up. Not the same as me winning!" My voice was now a frantic, enraged whisper. I slammed the water with my hands, splashing it every-where. I didn't care, angry tears were making it impossible for me to see.

God, I just . . . *I just* . . . I couldn't remember ever being so angry before.

"What the hell is your problem?" Once again, Abram was speaking through his teeth.

"You're my problem." I shoved my face into his. "You don't forfeit—i.e. *give up*—in the last leg of the last lap. That's a shitty thing to do."

"Oh? Really? Was that shitty of me?" Likewise, he shoved his face forward, not that he had much room to move.

"Yes. Very shitty," I whispered, but then swallowed the last word because the current of the water—waves caused by our race—pushed me forward. My front knocked into and then slid against his, the slippery friction like a KO punch to my good sense and a wake-up call to everything else.

Him. His eyes. His body. Just . . . *yesssss*. Yes. The texture, the warmth, the hard planes, the everything. My eyes fell to his lips, pink lusciousness framed by the black shadow of his scruff, a blushing rose among thorns, and I could not look away.

Abram sucked in a hissing breath, his hands immediately coming to my arms and separating us by gently—and firmly—moving me away. But he only moved me six or seven centimeters. We were still plenty close. *But not close enough.* But still plenty.

"What. Are. You. Doing?" he growled, sounding frustrated and furious. But the question also sounded like a plea.

Still transfixed by his mouth, I shook my head, blinking, breathing just as hard as I'd been when I'd finished the race.

Lie.

Walk away.

Say one of your anytime-phrases.

These were all signposts on the logical path forward. But I didn't do any of these. I couldn't. I was caught in some unknown field, propelled and shredded by an unidentified force, not contact, neither gravitational, magnetic, nor electrical.

Struggling against it made it worse. Ignoring it made it stronger. The only thing I hadn't tried was accepting it. *But I can't.*

"I can't . . ."

"You can't what?"

A wrinkle appeared between his eyebrows, something flaring behind his eyes as they drilled into mine. He released my arms, pushing his fingers through the fall of hair on his forehead, pushing it away with both hands, and then he waited. Glaring at me, his arms falling to his sides, standing still while his chest rose and fell with his slowing breaths.

He waited. He waited for me.

And I was such a mess, wanting to rage and laugh and cry; wanting him to pull me close, and dreading what would happen if he did; wanting to rewind time to the moment he'd stopped swimming so I could also stop and scream at him to finish, so I could win, so I could tell him the truth.

Now we were here and "by forfeit" was not how a bargain with the universe was won. This was not winning. This was neither winning nor losing, which meant I was back at square one. Which was losing.

I felt my chin wobble and I firmed it, pressing my lips together to stop the revealing involuntary waver, but it was too late. He'd seen it. I knew at once because he took a deep breath, the force of anger in his glare dwindling to merely mystified uncertainty.

"Lisa. What are you doing? Why are you doing this?" he asked with impossible tenderness. "You win. You don't want me. I'm done. I'm leaving."

"It doesn't feel like winning." My voice was unsteady and my words were unplanned, so were the hot tears that spilled over my cheeks. *I'm a mess!*

I hoped they'd be camouflaged by the residual pool water but knew at once this was not the case. Abram's gaze watched their progress, gliding down my face. His features were restive, betraying his indecision, his uncertainty. But the hesitation didn't last.

Lifting his hands to cup my face, his thumbs brushing away the tracks of saltwater, Abram's gaze softened. All contrary emotions dissolved, replaced by resolute concern.

"Don't cry." He pressed his forehead to mine. "Please don't cry."

"I'm not crying." I sniffled, closing my eyes, more tears leaking from beneath my lashes, my stupid chin wobbling. *Why did he have to forfeit?*

He chuckled. "Why are you crying?"

"Why did you forfeit?" I'd been aiming for accusatory, but the question came out sounding watery and just plain sad.

"You're crying because I forfeit?" His voice held humor and incredulity.

"No. That's not—" I sniffled again, taking several deep breaths, and then said firmly, "I'm not crying."

"Stubborn."

"I'm not—"

"Shh." Against my lips I felt his shushing breath, which made me hold mine. The ever present, simmering desire low in my belly twisted, but the paralyzing restlessness within me thawed. How my body could respond in this dichotomous way, at once relaxing and tightening when he touched me, I had no idea.

Abram's fingers pushed into my wet hair, curling around my neck, and his nose slid against mine, nuzzling.

"You have to tell me what you want," he whispered gruffly. "If you don't want me, tell me. But you have to know, you must know, I only want to make you happy."

CHAPTER 17
ELASTICITY: STRESS AND STRAIN

S igh.

My heart.

I opened my eyes. Our gazes didn't clash, they mated. Instead of cymbals between my ears, I heard the gentle lapping of the pool against the tile, the sounds of the city, the hum of summer insects in our little garden oasis.

I breathed out, lifting my chin by a millimeter, licking my lips. *Kiss me.*

His gorgeous stare never wavered from mine, he didn't move, not to close the scant distance between our mouths, not to push me away. No.

He was waiting. Again. Waiting for me.

Please. Please kiss me.

I wanted him to end this torture because I couldn't be the one to end it. Telling him the truth was not an option because it would jeopardize my sister, and I refused to be another person who let her down. But kissing Abram without telling him the truth was also not an option, a line I absolutely couldn't cross.

However.

If he kisses me, I reasoned and bartered with the universe, searching for a new deal, *I'll have to tell him the truth, right? I wouldn't have a choice. The decision would be made.*

"Lisa," he said, a gentle whisper, the single-word reminder of reality breaking the spell so completely, it jarred me to my core. The seismic equivalent of telling a roomful of kindergarteners that they would never have candy again. And then following that devastation with a forty-five-minute lecture on taxes.

Stepping away, I dropped my head and closed my eyes, feeling the weight of air and dark matter and cosmic dust press down on my shoulders. I wanted to hit the water again. I wanted to throw a giant tantrum.

Instead I whispered, "Fuck."

A moment later, I heard Abram sigh. A moment after that, I heard the telltale sound of him moving through the water, leaving. My stomach sunk and I swallowed around the rocks in my throat, but I wouldn't cry. It was an unfair situation, of my own making, and he deserved better. So, so, so much better.

Let him go. And let this be the last time.

But then I felt his palm slide against mine, his fingers entwined my fingers, and he squeezed. My eyes flew open and, wide-eyed, I looked up at him. He wasn't looking at me. Jaw set, Abram's eyes were on the stairs leading out of the pool. Without pausing, he pulled me after him.

I found my voice as I crested the last step. "Where are we going?"

Releasing my hand, he passed me my towel, only glancing at me briefly. "Here. Dry off."

I accepted it, wrapping it around my body and reflexively folding the top over so it wouldn't unravel.

Abram wiped at his face, neck, and torso with forceful strokes, and then wrapped his around his hips. Reaching for and grabbing my hand again, we were on the move.

To the house, up the stairs, into the mudroom, down the hall. He stopped in the kitchen, turning to face me, but not releasing my hand.

"We should watch a movie. You like movies?" The words were abrupt, direct, and had an edge of impatience.

"Movies?" I parroted dumbly.

"Yes. Movies."

Inspecting him, I searched his face for some sign as to his thoughts, what he hoped to accomplish. He didn't look angry.

Disappointed? Yes.

Angry? Not at all.

But you know what? Of the two, the disappointment felt worse.

Gathering a deep breath, I couldn't help what expression my face was making, but I assumed it was something like dismayed remorse. "Abram, I am so sorry. I never—"

He waved away my apology. "Nope. No apologies. No explaining. No talking. No."

"No . . . ? No talk—"

"Go upstairs, change, shower, whatever. Come down when you're ready, to the basement. We'll watch a movie."

I shook my head, feeling my eyebrows pull together, not understanding what was happening. *He won't close the distance of three centimeters to kiss me, so he wants to watch a movie?*

He must've read the confused anguish in my eyes and on my face, especially since I was unable and disinclined to hide them, because his left dimple made an appearance.

"Look." He brought my hand up, pressing it flat between both of his. "I trust you, so trust me. I just want to spend time with you. We don't have to talk. You don't need to apologize for anything. We can sit together, watch a movie, share popcorn."

A little breath escaped me, one of wonder and distress. How was he so consistently perfect?

"There's nothing wrong with watching a movie, people do it all the time," he prodded gently, tilting his head, his hand coming to my hair, smoothing over the wet strands and down my back. "It doesn't have to mean anything."

* * *

It meant something.

Lying next to Abram on the big, red, plush love seat, tucked under his arm, my cheek on his chest, smelling his man-fragrance while we watched *The Blues Brothers* on the home theater screen, it definitely meant something.

But that didn't make him a liar, because it hadn't started out meaning anything.

After I went upstairs and showered, haphazardly blow-drying my hair and applying minimal makeup, I changed into a pair of yoga pants and a tank top. My brain on self-destruct autopilot, I didn't think about the logical path forward or fretting about my actions. I thought about popcorn.

We'd begun the movie in the chairs, with the popcorn between us on a buffer seat. He'd given me a polite smile, saying nothing, and motioned that I should take the chair on the other side of the popcorn. The theater seats were a good size, but Abram was taller than average. He shifted in his chair several times, crossing his legs at the knee when he couldn't stretch them out fully in front of him.

But ten minutes after the movie started, Abram sighed, picked up the popcorn and moved to the love seat at the front of the room, reclining on his back, a hand behind his head, his feet and legs stretched out toward the screen.

The love seat wasn't a typical love seat, which was a smaller version of a sofa. It was the width of a love seat with a pull-out ottoman piece extending towards the screen that turned it into a giant chaise lounge, basically a full-sized bed with sofa cushions at the back.

"Hey," I called out disgruntledly after he settled in, raising my voice over the action of the film.

He lifted on his elbow and twisted his neck to look at me. "What?"

"You took the popcorn."

He held out the bag with his other arm. "Come take it if you want it."

My frowning gaze flickered between the bag and his face. He'd made the popcorn. It didn't make sense for me to take the whole thing. I could go to the kitchen and get a bowl so the popcorn was split evenly, or I could take several trips (up to where he held the popcorn hostage) several times during the movie to grab handfuls, or I could—

"Or just sit up here with me. Whatever."

Well. Since he suggested it.

Clearly self-destruct autopilot was still engaged, because I crossed to the love seat, scooched back until I rested against the sofa cushions, my legs stretched out in front of me, and stuck my hand in the popcorn bag between us.

Around the halfway mark, my eyes glanced over at Abram. The popcorn was gone, so the bag wasn't between us. His ankles were crossed. He had a hand on the T-shirt covering his stomach and an arm behind his head. His eyes were on the screen and a smile was on his mouth. A sliver of skin where his T-shirt hem had lifted away from his jeans was visible, as was the gray-and-black waistband of his boxers (which might have been boxer briefs, more data were required before a definitive classification could be made).

He looked comfortable, relaxed, happy, and I felt an answering desire to an unasked question: I wanted to be as he was.

In his own way, but in a way that was entirely alien to me, Abram was stunningly pragmatic and rational. Here he was, in a state of disappointment, and yet also in a comfortable, relaxed, and happy state. How did he do that? How could one state follow the other so seamlessly? Or exist in tandem?

I formulated no hypothesis, because a second later, he caught me staring.

As usual, I quickly tore my eyes away, a blaze of self-consciousness rushing to my cheeks. His eyes were on me. I felt them, but I also confirmed this sense with a quick glance in his direction. His eyes were on me and it wasn't a quick scrutinizing. Now he was staring. Unabashedly.

"Hey," he said after a protracted moment, lifting his hand from his stomach and placing it on my back. His palm moved in a slow circle over the thin fabric of my tank top. "Are you comfortable? You wanna lie down?"

I wasn't comfortable only because I wanted to lie down. The logical path was to remain in my present position as lying down felt a little stupid and dangerous, like acknowledging the slipperiness of the slope and attempting the slope anyway.

Even so, self-destruct autopilot engaged, I nodded and lay down. His arm behind me didn't move as I readjusted myself, which meant my head rested on his bicep when I finally reclined. The butterflies in my stomach made concentrating on the film difficult, so when his arm came around me, squeezing me to his chest during a particularly funny part, I only knew it was funny because he was laughing so hard.

That was the moment my head ended up over his heart. Instead of listening to Dan Aykroyd and John Belushi tell me about their mission from God, I counted Abram's heartbeats, slowing my breathing to see if I could match his pulse to mine.

Tangentially, I realized that listening to Abram's heart had been a terrible idea, a critical error in judgment. Now—even with the tempo still filling my ear—I knew with absolute certainty I would never tire of the sound. In fact, I would crave it for the rest of my life, from this moment forward.

Our society warns us from an early age to eschew drugs that might be addictive, or habits and hobbies—like gambling or video games or fantasy worlds—that employ Skinner box tactics meant to target addiction-causing pleasure centers of the brain.

But no one tells you to avoid the sound of a heartbeat.

This was also *the* moment. Lying here with Abram was the memory I would keep, the one I would retrieve on rainy days, the one that would inspire wistful daydreams.

And as beautiful as he'd been in the pool, as utterly perfect of an exterior he possessed, I wouldn't be thinking of his body when I missed him, I would be thinking of his heart.

By the final musical act, the entire length of me was pressed against Abram's body, one arm draped over his stomach, my other arm tucked between us, our feet tangled, his hand lazily moving up and down my side. When the end credits rolled, I didn't notice.

"Hey," he said eventually after the final credit had scrolled, the screen had faded to black. "The movie is over."

"Yep." I tightened my arm around his torso, holding on and squeezing my eyes shut. Maybe if I refused to acknowledge the existence of reality, reality would cease to exist. *All hypotheses are worth exploring! Even the crazy ones.*

He took a deep breath, his chest rising and lifting my head as he filled his lungs with air. I clung to him.

"Lisa." I felt him shift, his hand that had been supporting his head came to my forearm and he caressed the length of it with his palm. "Do you want to get up?"

"No."

He chuckled, and then sighed. "Okay. Do you want to talk?"

"No."

Seven. Eight. Nine. Ten . . . I was counting the beats of his heart between questions and noted with some interest that his pulse had just increased. His heart was beating faster, which meant mine—which had been in sync with his for the last quarter of the movie—also began beating faster.

"What do you want to do?" His voice deepened, and there was no mistaking the grumbly, suggestive quality to it.

"So many things," I whispered. My leg constricted over his thigh, my arm around his waist now squeezing, I scrunched my eyes tighter.

He waited, his breath becoming shallow.

Twenty-nine, thirty, thirty-one, thirty-two . . .

And then he waited, his breath returning to normal.

Forty-seven, forty-eight, forty-nine . . . Inexplicably, his heart rate slowed. Mine fell out of sync, because mine was still racing.

Abram took another deep breath, speaking as he exhaled, "Okay. We have time. When you're ready, I'll be here." His arm around me tightened briefly and then relaxed. He kissed my forehead. "I'll always be here."

As his words sunk in, a small, silent huff of bitter amusement escaped my lungs.

Time?

No. We had no time. Lisa was due back any day. There was no more time. Time was up.

Here?

Here he was. Here we were. Here was I. Experiencing the first and only time in my life where I didn't want someone to ask permission or for instructions prior to touching me, and that's exactly what he does.

Oh. The *IRONY!*

Hot tears of frustration pressed against the back of my eyelids, stinging my nose and throat. I rolled my lips between my teeth, firming my chin to keep it from wobbling. Meanwhile, Abram's heart had returned to its steady beat, his hand still smoothing languidly back and forth along my forearm, his breathing regular and even.

My mind worked to extinguish this reality and replace it with an alternate one, one where he knew I was Mona, but we'd still found ourselves at this singularity in time.

I wanted it so badly, *so badly*. If wanting were a means by which travel between dimensions was possible, surely my want would have carried us there. But the gulf between wanting and reality was just as vast as the chasm between wanting and action.

Not insurmountable, but well beyond my reach.

Unless . . .

Unless I actively made a choice to betray my sister by telling Abram the truth, or betrayed Abram by taking what I wanted with the lies between us. Those were my options. Neither were the logical path forward and both would fundamentally change who I was, thereby changing my reality.

These were the circular thoughts in my head as I fell asleep in Abram's arms. I didn't remember falling asleep. But I must have drifted off, because I was awoken from delightful dreams of alternate realities—where I told Abram the truth and he forgave me at once, offering to help with Lisa's plight just before removing my clothes—by someone holding my nose closed.

It was a peculiar thing, something Lisa and Gabby and I used to do to each other during sleepovers as children. As such, I wasn't able to incorporate it into my now deliciously dirty dream and it woke me at once.

Blinking scratchy eyes open, I squinted at the face above mine.

Gabby.

Her eyes were wide and she was mouthing something. I frowned, not understanding.

She huffed and then pressed her index finger to her lips, tilting her head to my right, her left while shifting her eyes meaningfully. Clearly, she was indicating to something on my right, so I glanced that way.

Abram. Asleep.

Oh. Oh yeah!

Understanding at once that she wanted me to be quiet so as not to wake my sleepy, messy Adonis, I nodded faintly, lifting the hand that rested on his stomach to gesture that I was getting up. This seemed to immediately relieve whatever anxiety she was feeling, because the crazy quality behind her stare eased and she nodded.

Rubbing my eyes, I scooched to the end of the couch as unobtrusively as possible, making careful movements so as not to disturb Abram. I met Gabby just outside the entrance to the theater, where—again—she pressed her index finger to her lips and waved me forward toward the hallway that led to the stairs.

Fuzzy headed, I followed, up the stairs, past the kitchen landing. It wasn't until the second flight that I spoke, asking and thinking at the same time, "How did you get in?"

Gabby glanced at me briefly over her shoulder. "Lisa has her keys."

I stopped.

Every cell, every atom, electron, neutron, positron, and quark within me stopped.

Time might also have stopped. The ability to see and hear certainly stopped, my brain and heart and body all aligning to become a void of absolute nothingness, which was accompanied by the strangest thought.

I no longer exist.

LAWS OF PHYSICS

PART 2: SPACE

PROLOGUE: LINEAR MOMENTUM AND COLLISIONS

L isa was there . . . *here.*

At the house.

In her room.

And so was I.

We were sitting on her bed and she was talking about the arrest, explaining what happened, how Tyler had known she was calling things off for good, so he set her up to make it look like she'd been selling drugs to kids, but that—though she'd been arrested—the charges were dropped when the witnesses changed their stories. She used expletives and insults to describe Tyler, her voice growing quieter and quieter with rage.

Now she was thanking me, and her eyes were wide and open, and she looked like a different version of herself, one I actually knew rather than the stranger she'd become. She was saying that she forgave me for what happened when we were younger, and that she'd been stupid to hold on to the grudge for so long, and that she missed me when she'd been sent away after I'd tattled on her and Gabby to our nanny, and that seeing media images of Leo and me with our parents at events and movie premieres and award shows while she was at boarding school alone made her feel like she was trash, unwanted, forgotten.

But she realized now that I had nothing to do with that, she realized I was just as trapped as she had been. And she was so sorry. So sorry. She'd expected Leo and me to protect her, but she knew we'd been powerless, and she was working on accepting being abandoned and wanted to move on.

Now she was saying it was all in the past, and I'd protected her now. I'd protected her and she would never forget it. I'd protected her and it meant the world to her. I'd protected her and now she felt like she had another chance at life and I was responsible for changing her life.

Now she was next to me on the bed, hugging me, apologizing for hugging me because she knew I didn't like it, but saying she couldn't help it, and thanking me, and telling me how much she owed me and saying that, if there was ever anything she could ever do to help me, I should ask. I should always ask. She promised that all the bad choices were at an end and that she was going back to school, she was done being selfish, she was done being destructive.

Now she was staring at me like she was confused, or she was worried, and then glancing at Gabby. Gabby shrugged, shaking her head quickly, wearing an identical frown to Lisa's, her eyes coming back to me.

Now they were both looking at me like they expected me to say something.

But I didn't know what to say. I didn't know what to do.

I didn't know . . . *I don't know.*

"Mona!"

My name sounded faraway, as though it had been spoken through a tunnel, or underwater. I felt a small shake. Someone was shaking me. I heard a sudden snap, like the crack of a whip. I blinked, abruptly surfacing to the present, the last half hour and all of Lisa's words rushing over me, flooding my brain.

Lisa.

"Hey, snap out of it." My sister was here, kneeling in front of me, snapping her fingers in front of my face, sounding frightened. She turned over her shoulder. "What is wrong with her? Did something happen? Oh my God, he didn't—did he hurt her?" Lisa appealed to Gabby, who shook her head.

"No, no, of course not. Not all guys are like Tyler, Lisa." Gabby was sitting on the desk, watching me with a worry-rimmed stare. "They got along really well. When I went downstairs, they were—"

"I can't do this." My hoarse voice brought Lisa's attention back to me. Her eyes darted between mine. I gripped her forearms. "Lisa, I can't do this. I can't leave."

"What?" My sister whispered. "What are you talking about? Are you okay? Did something happen?"

I shook my head, my thoughts a mess. "Yes. I mean, no. Not like that, not something bad. But it's-it's terrible."

Tightening my hold on my twin, I didn't get a chance to explain further because Gabby gasped.

"Oh my God! Oh no. Mona! I swear to God, Mona DaVinci. Did you fall for him?" Gabby had straightened from the desk, her eyes now a little crazy, rimmed with panic and accusation.

I sighed helplessly.

She groaned and covered her face. "No! No, no, no, no! I told you to stay away if you liked him! Why didn't you listen to me?"

"What is going on?" Lisa was glancing frantically between Gabby and I, looking completely perplexed.

Gabby abruptly dropped her hands from her face, setting them on her waist and shaking her head at me, her look one of intense frustration. "You are so smart, and yet so impossibly stupid. What are you thinking? That you're going to tell him the truth? Tell him about Lisa? If you do, you're *insane*. Insane!"

"What?" Now Lisa's eyes returned to me and she looked completely lost. "What is going on? Will someone tell me what's going on?"

I licked my lips, skootching forward on the bed, desperate to make her understand. "Listen, he won't tell Mom and Dad, okay? I really think he and I—"

Gabby's hard laugh interrupted me. "No, Mona. Abram *will* tell your parents. That'll be the first thing he does. Then he'll call his sister and give her a good scoop. Then he'll tell you to get lost."

"You don't know that!" I whisper-yelled.

"I do know it!" Gabby yell-yelled. She took a few rushing steps forward, causing me to lean back. "You think he has feelings for you? Well, guess what? That doesn't make you special. I tried to warn you, this is what he does! Everyone is in love with him. He doesn't care about you. You're just another one to him. But, I can guarantee you, he'll definitely care about being lied to. He'll be super pissed about that. And if you think he'll ever forgive you, you're out of your mind. He'll hate you forever."

My heart was beating out of my chest, each thump enormously painful, and I was breathing like I'd just run a race. It was on the tip of my tongue to reject her words, because I knew Abram. He wasn't like that. He'd forgive me. He'd keep—

"And for what? To clear your conscience?" Gabby asked shrilly, laughing again. "Typical Mona Mary Sue bullshit. You think you're doing the right thing? Well, you're not. You're doing what you think is the right thing *for you.* You couldn't care less about what will happen to Lisa, but it's going to blow up in your face. You've known him for six days. Six days! And you're choosing him over your twin sister? You're the one who is selfish. You're the reason Lisa was sent to boarding school when we were kids, and you'll be the reason she's banished now!"

"Okay, enough!" Lisa had stood at some point and she paired this proclamation with a double hand swipe, cutting her arms through the air and sending Gabby a fierce look. "That's enough, Gabby. I know you're trying to help, but you're not."

I blinked against hot tears, berating myself for all this confounded crying. I'd cried—or wanted to cry—more in the last twenty-four hours than I had in the previous ten years.

Something is wrong with me. I don't know who I am, but I'm not myself.

"Just . . ." I heard Lisa sigh and I looked at her, she was shaking her head tiredly. "Be quiet for a minute and let me talk to Mona, okay?"

Gabby nodded stiffly, and then sent me a cutting look, turning and pacing to the other side of the room. Meanwhile, Lisa sat next to me on the bed and pinched the bridge of her nose. I took a moment to look at my sister, to really look at her.

Her hair was dull, lifeless. She wore eye makeup, but more concealer than liner. Even with all the concealer, I could still make out the dark circles under her eyes. Her lips were thinned, pale. She looked exhausted, overwhelmed, and my thumping heart twinged painfully.

Was Gabby right? Was I being selfish? And why was I so sure of Abram? *You've known him for six days, and you're choosing him over your sister.*

I couldn't think. Everything was a mess. *This is why I hate messes!*

Lisa was taking deep breaths, frowning at whatever internal thoughts she was having.

"Lisa," I said unthinkingly, wanting to explain before she made up her mind about anything. But when she lifted her eyes, all I could think to say was, "I'm sorry."

Her shoulders sagged and the side of her mouth tugged upward in a sad smile. "Don't apologize, Mona. God, don't ever apologize to me. I—" She sighed, a full body sigh, her eyes glassy. "Listen, I don't know what happened, or what's going on with you. I'm tired. I'm so tired, I'm trying to think. But I do know one thing: I hate the person I've become."

She blurred in my vision until I blinked, two fat tears rolling down my face.

She shook her head at me. "Don't be sad, and please don't be sorry. I'm sorry I put you in this position, and I'm sorry you're upset now. This is my fault, not yours."

"Lisa—"

"No, listen. If you want to tell him—Abram—the truth, that's up to you. I've done a lot of thinking over the last week and I can't keep living like this, being like this. I trust your judgment a hell of a lot more than I trust my own. I just want you to know, I won't be upset. I won't blame you, no matter what happens. This is my fault, these were my choices, and you shouldn't have to pay for them."

I heard Gabby make a scoffing noise, like a growl, and Lisa turned to frown at her friend. "Gabby!" Her voice held a warning. "You need to let it go too."

Gabby crossed her arms and shook her head in a quick, jerky movement. "No. This is bullshit, and you know it!" And then she turned to me. "I don't trust your judgment. Your judgment is why the three of us were separated and Lisa was sent away." Her tone wavered, had turned quiet and earnest, her eyes were watery with unshed tears and her nose had turned red, her skin splotchy. "You think Lisa is the only one who lost her family after that? What do you think happened to me? I lost you both. I lost everything. Just . . . don't. Please don't do this again."

A sudden pain seized my chest and I winced at the raw helplessness in her voice, at the pleading I heard in her words.

But she wasn't finished. "Your judgment is telling you that Abram will forgive you when I'm telling you—since I actually know him—that he will not. He. Will. Not. He is the most unforgiving person I've ever met. I have been trying to tell you from the start not to trust him, and—"

"That's it, Gabby." Lisa cut in, standing and walking to the door. "You know I love you, but you can't put this on Mona." My sister opened the door and gestured to the hall. "Can you wait downstairs?"

"Yes—" Gabby sniffed, swiping at her eyes "—if Mona keeps her promise and I'm taking her to the airport, I'll wait for her." Walking to the door, she said to Lisa, "But if she tells Abram the truth, then I'll wait for you and I'll take you home with me. I don't know how my parents will react, but I don't care."

Maybe Gabby didn't think her words made an impact on me, but they did. She was willing to do whatever it took to keep Lisa safe, whereas I was not. Fact.

And I believed her about Abram. Rather, I believed she believed what she was saying. Also fact.

But I didn't know what to do. I didn't know what to think. I was lost. So lost. The logical path forward had been erased by my stupidity. Now, no matter what I did, I was making the wrong decision.

Did I tell Abram the truth? How could I? Even if I was convinced he wouldn't hate me, that what was happening between us was real, Gabby believed he would tell our parents the truth.

Did I leave now, like Gabby wanted? I would never see him again. But this was not a shock. I'd been preparing for this all week.

So why does it feel like the end of the world?

"Mona." Lisa had claimed her seat on the bed again and only hesitated for a second before grabbing my hands and cradling them; her fingers were freezing. "It's clear you've been through a lot this week."

I huffed a bitter laugh, abruptly angry with myself. "I've been through a lot? Lisa, you've been in jail."

"Yes. But that was my fault."

"That wasn't your fault." I gripped her hands tighter, willing them to be warmer. "That was Tyler."

"I chose Tyler. I lied about being with him. That was my decision. This, none of this, is your fault. And you—" She took a deep breath, her eyes dropping to our hands, like she couldn't look at me and say this next part. "You need to do what you think is right. But you also need to know that, no matter what, I won't be mad. You are my sister and I love you. I can't lose you again, and . . . I'm sorry. I'm so sorry."

This last part she said brokenly, tears finally falling. My imperturbable sister was crying. And not just quiet weeping. Massive, body-wracking sobs. My heart bled for her, for she was the other part of myself.

Pulling Lisa into my arms, I held her. I rocked her. I told her how much I loved her. I pet her hair and promised to always take care of her, because the path had revealed itself and I knew the answer.

I knew what I had to do.

* * *

Abram

Reaching for Lisa, my hand encountered only a cold, vacant couch. I'd hoped to find her next to me, to curl myself around her. But she wasn't there.

Opening my eyes, blinking at the darkness, I listened for a sign of her presence. A ballooning disappointment deflated hope. When it was clear she wasn't anywhere close, I flexed my jaw, stood from the sofa, and stretched while yawning. Discontented. Frustrated. She was gone, she'd taken her sweet softness, and—

Gone, and she took all softness with her.

Gone, and emptiness takes shape.

Gone, and summer is winter.

Gone, and... And?

Cassette tape? Fate? Concord grape?

Scowling for many reasons, I pushed the hair out of my eyes and left the dark theater in search of my lyric book, a toothbrush, and the exceptional woman constantly on my mind.

I wouldn't use "fate" to end the fourth line of this new stanza, and obviously not "concord grape." The first part was useable—her/winter wasn't a textbook rhyme, but that only made it more perfect—yet I couldn't work out what word to use with *shape.*

Gone, and I browse the internet using Netscape? No.

Gone, and where did I put that videotape? No, but it made me grin.

Gone, and something about a great ape? Ha ha!

Great ape. Funny. Perhaps I was the ape? . . . *worth considering.*

Stopping by the basement bathroom, I brushed my teeth and splashed my face with water. This was my usual waking-up routine, whenever I might wake up: absentmindedly going through the motions while words played musical chairs in my mind. Since agreeing to house-sit for Leo's parents, I'd been sleeping mostly in the recording studio on the couch. That's where all my lyric notebooks were as well as my guitars.

Before Lisa came, I'd found it was easier to write while in the studio, trying and testing lyrics with background accompaniment via the soundboard. But now that she was here, writing music, poetry, lyrics had been just like sharing her company: effortless.

Gone, and she took all softness with her.

Gone, and empty (or emptiness?) takes a shape. . .

Shape. What else rhymes with shape? My priority was to capture this feeling, that moment upon waking, discovered loss or whatever it was.

I wouldn't force it. If I had to force the words, then they were a lie. Studying words had been a compulsion of mine from a young age. I collected and hoarded them. I thought about how to assemble and arrange them to communicate the most truth in the least amount of syllables. I treasured them when they were real just as much as I reviled them when they were false.

Because of this, I wouldn't force the missing line, and I was certain I wouldn't need to. With Lisa here, the right ones would come to me.

I miss her.

Yes. That was it. I missed her. And missing someone is not just the absence of the person. Distance exists. Separation is real. It is a measurable construct, but also intangible.

This space between us is what? This space of separation is what?

Distracted, I left the bathroom and crossed the hall to the studio, flipping on the light and moving to my pile of notebooks. They weren't organized by anything other than the approximate date, and so I picked up the only one that was neither full nor empty and wrote those first three lines of a stanza that might become a song.

Then, when I reached the fourth line, I frowned at my reflection in the studio glass. I shook my head.

Gone, and . . . what do I miss about Lisa when she is gone?

Potential answers immediately and effortlessly piled upon each other: her eyes when she laughed; her smile; her body in that white bikini; smooth, hot skin; her strength; a silk waterfall of dark hair spread over my chest while she slept; her humor; her eyes when she was angry; her kindness; the color of embarrassment on her cheeks; her voice; her surprising cleverness; her equally surprising awkwardness; how, with each breath last night, the rise and fall of her breasts pressed against my side; her eyes when she was surprised; the weight of her, the warmth, and the awareness where every inch of her touched every inch of me; her mouth; her softness.

Her softness.

Yes.

I don't think women understand how much decent men appreciate softness, not just in the woman they admire and desire, but in the world. I'd had conversations with Leo about this a few times.

"What is it about her?" I'd asked the last time he'd gone crazy for a woman.

We'd been sitting in a VIP room at a club called Outrageous. He liked it because they changed the interior often. This made it feel like we were going to a new place but without the hassle of learning the names of new waitstaff, bartenders, bouncers, and managers.

"She's soft, you know? Like, she's not jaded. Man, my parents and everyone I know are so fucking jaded. It's just nice to be around someone who still has *the wonder*." He took a drink from his beer, smiling an uncertain little smile, his knee bouncing in time with the bass. "That's why I keep you around, Abram."

"Oh yeah? Do I have the wonder?" I didn't smile. I wasn't convinced.

"You so do, man. Yeah, you're also an abyss of deep thoughts and depressing shit, but—" he leaned forward, hit my shoulder "—you still make me feel my age, not . . ." His eyes drifted to the crowd beyond the wall of glass separating our VIP box from the club. "You don't make me feel like I'm ninety years old all the damn time."

I'd smiled. I knew he was referring to Charlie, our other good friend, drummer, and frequent co-conspirator. Where Leo was an optimist, Charlie was an eternal pessimist. I fell somewhere in the middle. They were both good guys, and unlike many of our mutual acquaintances, neither Charlie nor Leo needed to be high or drunk to have a real conversation.

"You have the wonder too, Leo." I returned the compliment, because I thought maybe he needed to hear it.

"Thanks." His eyes grew big, solemn. "Seriously, thank you, man. I try. I try to stay soft, but the world makes it hard."

I try to stay soft, but the world makes it hard.

I'd written down Leo's words about softness because they were true. It was maybe the truest thing I'd ever heard. What he'd said was brave and a difficult thing to live.

I respected Leo for trying to be soft, but I respected him even more for never forcing it.

Presently, staring at the studio glass, I didn't sit on the stool by the soundboard. But I did flip through the last few pages of my notebook, letting my eyes skate over the iterative versions of a poem I knew would eventually be a song entitled, *Hold a Grudge.*

I wasn't finished. *Hold a Grudge* needed a chorus and structured stanzas, I still needed to figure out where to put the bridge, how often to repeat the chorus, and how to end it. But first, it needed the right melody. I was a much better lyricist than a composer. I found myself nodding at the accuracy of the poem, and then I flipped back to the new lines I'd just written.

Gone, and . . . What sounds like shape? Manscape? *God, no.*

I rolled my eyes at myself, and then read the three lines of this new poem again. I repeated them silently until they were fully memorized. And then I closed the book and returned it to the pile, certain the last line would come to me sooner rather than later. But right now, I was anxious to see Lisa, so I left the studio in search of her.

The longer I was awake, the more urgent the need to be in her company. This had been the case since the morning we drove to Michigan. At the time, I'd assumed it was because I was worried about her, because of how shaken she'd been that night before we drove to my parents' house. But now there was no mistaking it or explaining it away.

I was in love with her.

I didn't lie, not even to myself, not even when the truth felt impossible to explain. I could almost hear my friend Charlie and his jaded view on everything, "Don't be a dumbass. People don't fall in love in a week."

To which I would say, "Fuck people."

Over the last six days, Lisa and I had clicked seamlessly into place. I'd considered fighting, resisting the enormity of giving into wanting her so completely. But even when she'd pushed me away with talk of 'appropriateness' and 'power dynamics,' giving into the potentially impossible daydream of her felt better—so much better—than the idea of anyone else.

I'd fallen in love with Lisa, and all her contradictions, and all her beauty and character and strength and softness. She'd become my place. With her, I never had to force the wonder, and being soft hadn't seemed so hard.

Now, ascending the final step to the kitchen level, I spotted Lisa and it was like my body and mind finally became fully awake. She was on a stool at the island, her lovely profile to me, her waterfall hair sweeping the center of her back, and the whole stanza came to me at once:

Gone, and she took all her sweet softness with her.

Gone, and emptiness takes a shape.

Gone, and summer is winter.

Gone, and I sleep.

But when she's here, I'm finally awake.

A barren landscape,

Now beauty in her wake.

With Lisa, vibrancy. Without her, emptiness took shape, a barren landscape.

I filled my lungs with the sight of her, energized by the deprivation of desire—to see her, touch her, listen to her, engage with her—and reminding myself to take it slow. Wait. Tread carefully. I was certain of what I wanted, how I felt, but she wasn't someone to rush. The truth was, I had no idea when or if she'd get there. Though that was somewhat terrifying, it didn't stress me. Especially when she made the waiting and anticipation so much fun.

Lisa's eyes were on a magazine spread flat on the kitchen island and she was hunched over a bowl of something, distractedly eating spoonfuls while reading.

I loved that she read so much. I loved, even though she'd dropped out of school, that her brain was obviously hungry for knowledge, debate, and philosophy. I loved that she'd been kicked out of school but seemed to be an unbending rule follower. I loved that once you knew her, nothing about her past made any sense.

Leo had been worried about his youngest sister for a while, specifically that their parents had "fucking ruined her." According to Leo, Mona, the older twin, had never needed much from anyone and automatically knew what to do and how to behave in all situations.

I'd never met Lisa's sister, but there were pictures of her in the front room. From what I'd seen, Mona and Lisa didn't resemble each other much. In the family photos Leo had pointed out to me from Mona DaVinci's recent college graduation, I never would have guessed that the two women were twins if I didn't already know. She was shorter than Lisa in all the pictures of them together, and seemed smaller, fading into the background, always smiling with a closed mouth, and definitely lacking

Lisa's vibrancy. To be blunt, the older twin looked like she'd stopped aging at twelve.

"Mona is smarter than all of us combined," he'd said when he asked me to keep an eye on Lisa over a week ago. Leo didn't usually talk about his sisters, but he'd wanted to prepare me for her arrival. "I'm Mona's older brother, but I go to *her* for advice. She's like a superhero, I swear. Doesn't need or take shit from anyone, doesn't care what anyone thinks, not even me, not even my parents. But Lisa . . ." Leo had sounded worried. "I know you don't like her, man. And I'm sorry for what she did last year, but she needs people, you know? She needs community. She needs someone to take care of, someone to take care of her. Some people don't need that, but Lisa does."

Presently, I stuffed my hands in my back pockets so I wouldn't reach for her. I wanted to. I always wanted to touch her. But something had happened to Lisa since last year, something she didn't yet feel comfortable confiding, something that made every first touch difficult. Maybe more time together would fix it for her. Maybe not.

Whatever she needed, because I knew exactly what Leo had meant about Lisa needing people.

My sister and I had been born with this same curse: *Someone to take care of, someone to take care of me, an inescapable desire for codependency.* Another song lyric. I wasn't happy with it, it needed work, but that was basically the gist of why I didn't fuck around with my time or with people.

Lisa didn't look up as I approached, so I said, "Hey," not hiding my smile.

From now on, all my smiles belonged to her.

Her eyes flickered up, and then dropped just as fast to the bowl of what I now saw was cereal. She straightened her back, closing the magazine and clearing her throat while I studied the bowl. *Note to self, she likes Lucky Charms.*

"Abram," she said, swallowing, tucking hair behind both her ears. "Good morning."

Immediately, I heard the guarded, distant, and particular quality to her voice. But it was the *particular* that resonated like an out of tune piano. I ignored it, eager to remove that barren landscape between us.

"Good morning, Lisa." I leaned my elbows on the island, making my tone ironically formal and bending at the waist to bring us eye level. "And how did you sleep last night?" I hoped this would make her blush. She was so very exquisite when she blushed.

She didn't blush but she still wouldn't look at me. "I, uh, didn't sleep very well, honestly." Lisa lifted her chin but not her eyes. "We should talk."

I frowned at the persisting particular quality to her voice, my eyes moving over her. It was at least eighty-five degrees outside and she was dressed in a baggy black hoodie and yoga pants. On her feet she wore socks and she'd stuffed her hands into the pockets of her sweatshirt. She was also wearing a lot of makeup, darker than usual, like the day she'd come home last week.

"Are you okay?" I dipped my head to one side, hoping that would encourage her to meet my eyes, hoping she'd let me take care of her.

Someone to take care of, someone to take care of me.

I couldn't shake those words. Spending time with Lisa, they resonated in a new way, one that was 3-D and in color, with softness and wonder and not just black ink written on a white notebook page.

She didn't meet my eyes, instead speaking to my forearms. "You have been very nice to me. Thank you. This is a difficult time, and I'm going through a lot, so I'm sorry if I've been acting weird."

As she spoke, I felt a chill. Something was . . . wrong. Her voice continued to hit the wrong note over and over.

Mystified, I said, "No need to apologize. You haven't been acting weird until just now."

Her eyes cut to mine and I started, flinching back and standing. *What the hell?* The chill became a sense of freezing dread I couldn't explain. Something was most definitely wrong. I couldn't identify the problem, but there was a problem.

". . . Lisa?" I asked like a fool, but—seriously—what the hell? This wasn't her. Her eyes were different. Not the shape or color or size, and yet unquestionably different. Lisa was there, but she also wasn't, like she'd been possessed. Or she was absent. It was freaky as hell.

Her eyes widened for the briefest of seconds, and then her lips flattened, her gaze moving to the closed magazine. She picked it up. She stood from the stool, glaring at the wall behind me, looking irritated and therefore the closest to acting like herself since I'd walked in.

"Look." Her voice was hard but also soft, quiet; I prepared myself for a whisper since she was visibly upset; an odd quirk I'd noticed about her, when she was upset, she always whispered. "Why are you doing this?"

"Doing what?"

"Pretending like you care about me." Her gaze fell to the floor and she sounded angry, but not at all hurt.

Were we playing this game again? The Push Abram Away Game? I didn't like games. I had a low tolerance and I'd never put up with them. Maybe it wasn't true for everyone, but I couldn't keep the wonder while also fucking around and playing games.

I made too much of things, I gave words too much weight, I searched for meaning where none existed. For me, there was no such thing as casual friends; you were my good friend, or you were an acquaintance. Likewise, there was no such thing as a meaningless hookup. An action, a touch was sacred, or it wasn't. Maybe that's why Leo thought I wasn't jaded? Because I didn't play games?

But with Lisa, I seemed to have an infinite reserve of patience that extended to game playing. Even when she was sour, she was still so intoxicatingly sweet, it was like being caught in a web of cotton candy.

So instead of giving into the building apprehension—even though she did sound off —I said, "Pretending."

She needed to push me away again? Okay. I could give her space. As long as later today, when she came to her senses, she also came to the pool, wearing that white bikini.

"Yes, pretending," Lisa said, her tone hard. "Gabby is my best friend, remember? She has my back."

"What are you talking about?" I needed to keep my head, but it wasn't just her words that unsettled me, or how she wasn't meeting my eyes. She was speaking to me like we were strangers.

Lisa gave her eyes a half roll. "You're a player, Abram. So whatever act this is, drop it."

The accusation angered me, and therefore distracted me from the discordant tone in her voice. Needing space was one thing. But believing and then spouting lies was another.

"This isn't an act." I tried to conceal the spike of temper by lowering my voice.

"Yeah. Right."

"And I don't know what Gabby told you, but she is misinformed." But obviously Lisa trusted her, and that had a shot of adrenaline clouding my vision.

"Okay. Sure. She just imagined the depth and breadth of your harem at gigs?"

Is that what this is about? I relaxed a little, breathing out. "Come on Lisa, this is nuts. I have female fans, yes. But I'm not dating any of them. Do you honestly think—"

"You don't date *anyone*. You just flirt with everyone and lead them on."

"I absolutely do not." *Fucking Gabby.* I could strangle her for filling Lisa's head with this shit.

She crossed her arms and shrugged. "I don't, for one minute, think that I'm special to you. Sure, whatever, we'll be friends, fine. But can you be cool and cut the act?"

She doesn't think . . . ? Was I hearing her correctly? How could she possibly think that?

The adrenaline returned, full force. "Then you're wrong, because you are special to me. And what happened last night was special, and dammit Lisa—would you listen?"

She'd turned and marched away. I reached for her arm, which she shook off. I let go immediately and stepped back. I shouldn't have touched her. Shit, I knew that. But I couldn't just let her believe Gabby's lies.

Knowing I'd fucked up, I pushed my fingers through my hair and tried to calm down. "Here is the truth: I have all sorts of fans, both male and female. They like my music, they come to my shows, maybe they like me. I don't know, I haven't asked them. I don't hang out with my fans and I don't lead people on, I don't flirt. The only thing Gabby told you that's true is this: I do not date. If you don't believe me, ask Leo."

Her eyes remained steadfastly on the floor and she mumbled, "You don't date because you're a player."

"No," I ground out. "I don't date because I don't believe in wasting time treading water. When I know, I know."

"What does that mean?"

"That means, I'm in love with you."

Finally, finally her eyes came back to me. They widened, her jaw slackened, and she stood silent like a statue. I couldn't believe this news stunned her as much as it seemed to. Maybe I could allow for some surprise, but she looked completely shell-shocked.

Hesitating only a second—partly because I wondered if it would be taking advantage, but also because she was acting so strangely—I closed the distance between us. Everything was wrong, but this might be my only chance to make things right. I slid my hands around her back. I held her. I kissed her.

She flinched and didn't respond at all, at first. But then she responded by twisting her face from mine.

"No, no, no!" She pushed me.

I let her go and grabbed fistfuls of my hair, turning away and pacing the length of the kitchen. Fire in my chest. My thoughts in disorder. *What the fuck was happening?*

I glanced at her. She'd covered her face and was shaking her head. And then she sniffled, the unmistakable sound of a sob rending from her chest that tore at mine.

Please don't cry. "I'm sorry. I shouldn't have—"

"Goddammit! You don't love me! I hate—" She cut herself off, shaking her head harder.

I watched her, helpless and so fucking confused, my mind all over the place, unable to see straight. *What is happening?*

"Lisa—"

"Just fucking listen," she shouted, surprising me, her hands dropping and revealing a face that looked like a stranger's. "I'm not who you think I am, okay?"

Despite hearing these words from her before, this time I believed her. I didn't argue, just watched her and waited for . . . I had no idea. A sign? A glimmer of my Lisa? The woman I couldn't get enough of? The woman I'd written twenty poems about in six days?

"But before I say anything else—" she swiped at her eyes leaving dark smudges on her cheeks, sucking in a deep breath "—I have to ask you something."

I waited, promising myself I wouldn't cross to her or try to touch her until invited. Strangely, this promise didn't seem as big as it had yesterday when we were in the pool, or when we were on the couch. Last night I'd promised myself not to touch her, and it had been torture.

Today? It was self-preservation.

When she didn't say anything, I prompted with forced calm, "Fine. What do you want to ask?"

She licked her lips, shifting her weight from one foot to the other, a nervous habit I hadn't noticed before. "If I lied to you, would you forgive me?" she finally blurted, shutting her eyes.

Lied to me? I straightened my back.

"About what?" The question slipped out, unplanned.

"No. I'm not—it could be about anything, okay?" Her eyes opened again and she stared forward at my neck. "If I lied to you at any point this week, would you be able to forgive me?"

My mind was racing with worst-case scenarios, my stomach sinking. "Did you sell those drugs? To those kids?" More unplanned questions, but what could I do? She was acting so crazy.

"No." She was back to whispering again, giving me a clue that the question had upset her. "I didn't do that. I would never do that."

I believed her. But the next obvious choice made my throat tighten with the urge to rage.

"Are you back with Tyler?" I asked roughly, determined not to raise my voice, but I was already so jealous. I didn't want to be jealous. I'd never been jealous. But I was so fucking jealous in that moment, the cloud around my vision turned red.

Fuck.

I'd never experienced anything like this before.

I hated it. *Hated it.* It felt like being branded with a million tiny hot pokers.

"No." Her glare turned distracted. "But it's something like that—" her eyes came to mine, still guarded, still off, still wrong "—something just as bad as that. A lie that big."

I'd never been so frantic before to recall previous conversations. I went through every day, every interaction, every word that I could remember. I came up empty.

"What is it?"

"Would you forgive me?"

I nodded but didn't answer out loud, trying to convince myself while also dealing with this insane jealousy. I would. I would forgive her anything. I would—

"Hypothetically, what if I told you that I've been lying to you every day, this whole week, about something important. You say you love me, but would you forgive me?"

I stopped nodding. "Have you?"

She remained silent, her eyes now narrowed, searching. "You wouldn't forgive me, would you?"

"I don't know!" I exploded, not understanding her or why she was doing this. "You haven't told me what it is. Fuck, Lisa. I don't even know what we're talking about."

"Forget it." She gave her head a small shake, her eyes dropping to the kitchen floor.

She looked exhausted and sad, and seeing her this way should've made me want to break all her unspoken rules about touching. I should've wanted to hold her, but I didn't. If this had been yesterday, I would've promised to forgive her anything and everything, and I would've meant it.

But now? I had no clarity. Making promises now would be a lie, and I never lied. If she'd been seeing Tyler this whole week while spending time with me, falling for her, I wouldn't forgive her. It wasn't in me. I would despise her.

Clearing my throat, I grit my teeth to keep from yelling again. "Forget what? What should I forget?"

"Forget me. You don't love me. You might think you do, but you don't." She sounded tired, but also as though she were trying her best to be compassionate, gentle. "Believe me, you'll get over this—whatever it is—so fast, I'll be a blip, a nothing. Seriously, forget it. You don't want to know me. I promise you, you don't."

"So you keep saying." I pushed back against a creeping numbness climbing up my ribs, stalling, needing a way to fix this.

"Then what's the problem? Why don't you believe me? I'm messed up, okay? I don't know who I am." Like a switch, her mood and manner turned exasperated. "I don't know what I want. I'm all fucked up. I am telling you the truth, but you refuse to believe me!"

In a huff, she turned and stomped to the back stairs.

"I don't understand what's happening," I called after her, another unplanned statement of my thoughts.

She stopped on the third step, turning halfway, giving me just her profile.

I walked to the bottom of the stairs, not seeing her or anything else, but wading through a general sense of everything crumbling to dust, a barren landscape.

"What changed? Between last night and this morning, what changed? What did I do wrong?"

Lisa swallowed, shaking her head. "I'm two different people, Abram." She pulled her sleeves down to cover her hands, turning completely away and crossing her arms. "I'm the person I want to be and the person I currently am, and if my parents disown me, I feel like I'll sink to the bottom of the ocean and drown. I feel like it'll be the end of the world." Initially her voice had been strong and steady, but it grew quieter and quieter as she spoke.

I stared at the back of her head, working through my own bitterness and this trail of crumbs she was leaving. I couldn't believe what she was saying. I couldn't believe this was the same person I'd spent the last week with. But there she was, looking just the same.

I'd thought her trust was a beautiful thing. I thought her values unbendable. But now? I couldn't see what had been right in front of me the whole time, I'd been blind to the truth: she had no trust in me, maybe not in anyone.

Swallowing around the vice tightening my throat, I glanced up at the ceiling. "Let me see if I have this right: you lied to me, about something big, and you think I'll tell your parents if I find out. Is that right?" The bitterness snuck into my voice.

We were now broken. This wasn't like before, where she'd used logic and ethics and temperance to push me away. I could forgive that. In retrospect, it had almost been cute.

But this?

Maybe it's for the best.

No. Fuck that. It wasn't for the best. Us together was for the best.

Eying her back, her stiff shoulders bunched around her neck, I felt myself soften.

What happened to make her this way?

I couldn't let her go without trying one more time.

"Lisa." I placed a hand on her arm, keeping my touch light.

She tensed and I swallowed fear. I ignored my drumming heart, the taste of sand, the uncomfortable tightness in my chest that made taking a complete breath unbearable, and I reminded myself of Leo's truest words: *I try to stay soft, but the world makes it hard.*

Be open. Be brave. Be soft, for Lisa.

"I told you yesterday, I just want to make you happy. Do you believe me?"

I watched her back rise and fall with a deep breath, and the barest glimmer of hope had me curling my fingers around her forearm.

But then she shook off my hand. "You can't *make me* happy, Abram. People can't *make* other people happy. I've tried that. It doesn't work. The truth is, I'm still—I'm still in love with Tyler and—" She took another deep breath, and when she spoke next, I could barely hear her, "And sorry for dicking you around but nothing is ever going to happen with us, so just give me some fucking space."

CHAPTER 1

ELECTRIC CHARGE AND ELECTRIC FIELD

TWO AND A HALF YEARS LATER.

Mona

"You left."

Shifting my eyes from the computer screen to the doorway of my office, I blinked at Poe's sudden appearance. "Pardon?"

"The reception." He pushed his hands into his pockets, strolling to the chair in front of my desk and helping himself to a seat. "You left before the speech." Poe smiled at his own statement, though it was clear my leaving the reception was what he found amusing.

"I guess I did." I leaned back in my chair and returned his smile. "She always gives the same speech."

"You mean, she always brings up that she's mentoring the infamous genius, Mona DaVinci, and you find that irritating." Poe said this as he studied his nails, still smiling.

Stinker. He knew me too well.

Lifting my eyes to the ceiling, I shrugged. "Irritating is such a strong word. But yes. It feels a little condescending."

"Because your mentor doesn't actually mentor you, or why?" Poe leaned his elbow on the arm of the leather chair, stretching his legs in front of him as though getting comfortable, his brown eyes still bright with amusement.

He already knew the answer to this question, so why was he asking? I folded my hands over my stomach and inspected him, deciding that he was just in a teasing mood.

Therefore, I made myself sound lofty. "You know I would never say my mentor doesn't mentor me."

That made him laugh, a good, deep, belly laugh, and he shook his head. "You would never say it, even though it's the truth."

We stared across the length of my desk, smiling at each other, good feelings and trust and respect between us, and I couldn't help but wonder—

A moment flashed behind my mind's eye, a dark room, my cheek pressed to a soft T-shirt, the sound of a heart beating beneath my ear. Arms—Abram's arms—were around me. Reality and time felt fuzzy around the edges, as though I might be able to touch the past . . .

Sigh.

In the present, my hand reflexively moved to the folded envelope in my front pocket and I felt my smile fall, likely due to the ache in my chest. Despite my attempts to be rational about the short—*extremely* short—time I'd spent with Abram, memories of him used to cause a brutal, violent stabbing sensation in the vicinity of my heart, scatter my brain, and send a burst of heat up my neck and over my cheeks.

I'd written him a letter a month after returning from Chicago, hoping to dispel some of the near-constant torment; I'd placed it in an envelope; I'd addressed the envelope to his parents' house in Michigan and I carried it with me every day, folded in my front pocket. Writing the letter hadn't helped dispel anything, but it had given me something to hold, to touch when I felt like I couldn't breathe in those early days.

The ache I experienced now—over two years later—was a huge improvement. I hoped soon it would be a mere small twinge. Yet, I still carried the letter in my pocket, every day, though I was unsure why. Habit maybe?

Despite the nonsensical and lingering physical symptoms and resultant mental quirks, I didn't regret my decision to help my sister. How could I? She'd kept her word, I'd kept mine, we were so much closer than before, and she was flourishing. Even Gabby and I were friendly more often than at odds. Her latest birthday card to me sat on a bookshelf at my right, proudly inscribed, *Donuts before bronuts. Love you forever, Gabster.*

Work, my research was good. Great even.

Things with my sister were good. Great even.

I had good friends. Great even.

However . . . *however.*

Taking a deep breath, working to disperse the ache and the image of Abram, I brought Poe back into focus. His smile had turned wry and he shook his head, a faint movement. We never spoke about it, about how I wasn't over a guy who I'd known for a blink of an eye, but I was almost certain my friend knew what—or who—I'd been remembering just now.

Poe, his smile slowly giving way to a thoughtful frown, reached forward and picked up the snow globe on my desk, shaking it. "Don't worry, I covered for you at the reception. I told everyone you had a flight and couldn't stay."

I knew he'd cover for me. We always covered for each other, which was why I'd left the reception. When I returned from my memorable one-week trip to Chicago, Poe Payton had been the shoulder I'd cried on the *one* night I'd allowed myself to cry.

It happened two weeks before the fall semester. I'd been nineteen and drunk at a grad school mixer. He'd told everyone I was on flu meds. I'd bawled in his car, telling him the entire story on the drive back to my condo between self-recriminating sobs and rants. He stayed over, spending the night on the couch. He also made me breakfast in the morning, told me a story about his oldest sister's disastrous love life that made me feel better about mine, and then we went for a silent, oddly cathartic walk on the beach.

I shoved the ghost of Abram from my brain and allowed myself to be distracted by the floating bits of white swirling around the snow globe Poe had just given another shake.

"Are you sure you don't want to go with us? To the cabin?" I asked, hoping he would change his mind. "It's not too late to get you a ticket."

"Nah," he said, bringing my attention back to his face. "Who wants to spend a week surrounded by snow, skiing in Aspen when one could be here, surrounded by ocean and sunshine, surfing in Southern California?"

I made a face. He'd tried to give me a surfing lesson once and it hadn't gone well.

"You know I don't ski. Or surf," I added quickly, just in case he offered to teach me again. "And the allure of being surrounded by snow has more to do with the beverages and hermit life than the activities."

"The beverages?"

I began ticking off my fingers. "Hot cider. Hot chocolate. Hot, mulled wine. Hot—"

"I get it. You like it hot."

"Yes. But only in the snow." I didn't mention that the other main attraction was the snow itself.

Hushed, gently falling snow was the closest I would get to the quiet of space without visiting a sensory deprivation chamber. I'd tried that once and had something like a panic attack after two minutes. The walls had been too close, claustrophobic. It had felt oppressive, suffocating.

But I'd grown a bit preoccupied with the concept of complete silence, a recent occurrence after testifying before Congress on climate change last summer. There'd been subsequent interviews on cable news outlets during the fall and everyone had been so loud. Why did reporters shout on TV? Didn't they know viewers could turn the volume up if needed?

Stressful.

Summary: The quiet isolation of the mountains, cut off from the world by distance and snow, felt like the only place I could draw a complete breath these days. Whenever I had free time, I went to Aspen.

"So noted." Poe reached forward again, arranging the snow globe on the desk so that the front of the little model cabin within faced me. "Does the cabin actually look like this?"

"Not exactly." My attention flickered to the rustic little log structure encased in water and glass, a memento I'd picked up on my previous return trip from Aspen. "And I don't think 'cabin' is really the right word for it. It's more like a—"

"Mansion?" he asked dryly, making me smile.

"Uh, lodge?"

"A mansion lodge?" His voice was still dry, likely because he knew he was right. All of my parents' properties were mansion-like.

But I didn't like to admit it, not even to myself. I suggested instead, "A small estate."

"A huge estate compound mansion lodge? Something like that?"

I laughed. "It's not like that."

It was totally like that.

"Really? How many bedrooms does it have?"

"Um . . ." I moved my eyes up and to the right, counting silently. "Twenty?"

He made a choking sound and I looked at him just as he'd placed his hand flat on his sternum, like the number upset his delicate sensibilities. "Twenty?"

His expression was priceless. I laughed again.

"You could sleep in a different room every night, and still not sleep in them all."

My cellphone, face down on the desk, started to buzz. "Why would I do that?"

"Because you live your life like the princess in that story, where the bed is never right."

"You mean Goldilocks? She wasn't a princess. And I don't like cereal, not even oatmeal." Glancing at the phone, I saw it was Allyn.

"No. The other story, the one with the pea." He sounded oddly stern.

I swiped my thumb across the screen, whispering just before I brought the phone to my ear. "Don't be ludicrous."

He quickly whispered back, "Ludicrous is awesome, everyone wants to be him."

I gave Poe a glare that was ruined by a traitorous smile, and suffused my voice with friendliness as I answered the phone. "Allyn! Hey! Are you all packed? Is there a problem with the itinerary?"

"No, everything is great! I'm just calling to let you know I'm on my way to the airport and I'm SO EXCITED!" She yelled this last part necessitating that I hold the phone away from my ear.

Poe chuckled, shaking his head at Allyn's exuberance. They'd met a few times and got along wonderfully, almost better than she and I did.

His gaze was warm as it settled on the cell in my hand. It was also full of mischief. "Tell Allyn I say hi," he whispered loudly, clearly hoping she would hear him.

"Wait. Is that Poe?" Allyn asked. "Did you convince him to come?"

He shook his head, but he smiled. "I'm not going."

"Did you hear that?" I asked Allyn, not returning his grin. "He said he's not going because he doesn't like all-expense paid trips to Aspen."

"But if y'all were going to Hawaii . . ." he sucked in a breath between his teeth, moving his head back and forth in a considering motion, making me laugh again. Even though Poe was from Tennessee, he had almost no accent. However, the occasional *y'all* did slip out from time to time.

Allyn asked, "Do your parents have a place in Hawaii?"

"No! I mean, yes. But we're not going to Hawaii. We're going to Aspen to drink hot beverages while wrapping ourselves in warm blankets, avoiding people, luxuriating in silence, and that's that." Once again I tried to glare at Poe. Once again I ultimately failed.

He stood. "I'm just saying, if you wanted me to come, you'd go to Hawaii. That's all I'm saying."

"Next time go to Hawaii!" Allyn urged. "And tell him we're holding him to his promise."

Poe captured my gaze, one of his eyebrows raised in a slight challenge, his lips faintly curved. I felt my stomach flutter.

Another topic we never broached: the possibility that—if we gave it a good try, and if I'd ever get myself together and move on from the impossibility of Abram—there might be something worth exploring between me and Poe.

Unthinkingly, I touched the outside of my front pocket again, my finger tracing the outline of the folded envelope. *Move on, Mona.* How many times had I told myself that? The X-axis was now approaching infinity.

I'd followed every mention of Abram for over a year after leaving Chicago, obsessively checking sources for music news, hunting through social media for information from his shows, pictures, videos, snippets of stories. An interesting byproduct of my investigations was that I'd learned a great deal about him, things I didn't know, most of it definitional in nature.

Where he'd gone to school: Melvil Dewey High School, where he'd been voted most talented his senior year even though he'd dropped out before graduating.

Why he'd dropped out of high school the last half of his senior year: To pursue music full-time after receiving an offer to play bass guitar on tour for an (at the time) up and coming indie rock band named Cyclops Ulysses.

What jobs he'd had: Dishwasher at fourteen for his uncle's restaurant; construction jobs at sixteen and every summer with his dad's old company (which explained his lean yet broad build); bass guitarist for Cyclops Ulysses at eighteen until they'd disbanded; bass guitarist for another, equally promising band named Ink Revolution at twenty-one; bass guitar for hire and solo artist at twenty-three.

His self-professed musical influences: Victor Wooten, Marcus Miller, Carol Kaye, Eddie Van Halen, Tal Wilkenfeld, John Lennon, Tupac Shakur, Tom Waits, Bob Dylan, and Kendrick Lamar.

Shortly after I left, right after I'd written the letter, he'd been photographed with a remarkably beautiful woman. His arm was around her shoulders. In one photo he was kissing her neck while she grinned at the camera, a cigarette held aloft. Seeing that photo had hurt. A lot. It had hurt like being punched hard in the stomach. I'd lost my breath. Admittedly, breathing had been difficult for a while after that.

But I got over it. Or rather, I kept telling myself there was nothing to "get over." *Move on, Mona.*

And yet, I'd still searched for news about him, nightly, religiously, obsessively. His first arrest caught me by surprise, but by the third I almost mailed the letter. All the charges had eventually been dropped as far as I could tell, he'd never been arraigned, but—and I didn't feel this was a controversial statement—Abram seemed to be in a downward spiral. I almost mailed the letter because I couldn't help but wonder if I'd been the cause even as I rolled my eyes at myself.

No, Mona. Abram is not getting himself arrested and into fights and losing weight and taking up smoking because of you. Six days. People change. Don't give yourself so much credit. Move on.

Mentions of him began to taper off around the one-year anniversary of my trip to Chicago. He wasn't playing the club scene, he wasn't signed with or subbing for any bands, he wasn't out publicly for any gigs. I simmered in my uneasiness until finally, sixteen months ago, he'd disappeared. From everywhere. No stories. No bookings. No performances. No arrests.

After three weeks, frantic for news, I'd called my sister and made some bogus excuse for why I was curious. The excuse hadn't been a lie, but it also hadn't been the whole truth. Lisa then called Leo, and Leo explained that he and Abram had lost touch, but he was aware that Abram had changed his last name. After his latest night in lock-up, Abram had told Leo he was worried about tarnishing his sister's journalistic name and reputation. Leo told Lisa he thought it more likely that Abram didn't want to keep embarrassing his parents.

Lisa didn't give me his new last name.

I hadn't asked.

I'd tried to take it as a sign from the universe: move on.

Move. Stay in motion. Keep moving. Move on, Mona.

So that's what I'd done. I moved. I worked. I read. I wrote a paper about the age of the universe, it had been called groundbreaking. I testified before Congress. I gave interviews. I worked some more.

Constantly moving hadn't yet yielded moving on, but it had made me tired. So very, very tired. Sometimes I was even too tired to fret about Abram—what he was doing, who he was with—before falling asleep. Sometimes I even forgot to fret.

But back to Poe and us staring at each other, and all the unspoken 'what ifs' heavy between us. No, we never talked about it. But what if we did? What if I put Hawaii on the table? *What if I actually moved on?*

After a protracted moment—during which indecision refereed a tug-of-war between my irrational longing for the impossibility of Abram and my rational desire to stop being a pathetic lunatic—Poe sighed, dropping his chin to his chest and licking his lips. The flutter in my stomach was abruptly overshadowed by a hint of guilt.

I liked him. What was there not to like? We wanted the same things: kids who we could fuss over and adore, a house in a nice neighborhood with neighbors and neighbor kids and a lawn to mow, a big library, work that was meaningful and inter-esting, a car payment and retirement accounts and more savings than debt. A normal, quiet life of exceptionalism.

Poe was loyal, wickedly funny, brilliant, kind, and so very, very handsome. I liked him.

But do you deserve someone like him?

I was attracted to Poe, *really* attracted. Maybe I could become someone who would deserve him? How long did I expect him to be single? It was a miracle he wasn't already married.

"What's going on?" Allyn whispered in my ear. "Why aren't you promising him a trip to Hawaii? You know he's crazy about you. Promise him!"

Crazy about me?

Studying him now, the dark glitter of hope in his gaze tempered by the stark line of his mouth and jaw, I felt jarring certainty that Poe Payton had remained single for a reason. He'd been waiting. For me. And that was hugely unfair. To him. He shouldn't be waiting for anyone. People should be waiting for him! He—like Abram —deserved better. Much, much better.

Abruptly, the spark in his eyes extinguished and he gave me a polite smile. "I'll be thinking of you while you're snowed in. Have a good time with Allyn." His words were also polite. So polite.

My stomach sank.

"Gaw! You're infuriating!" Allyn huffed.

Poe, seemingly nodding at his own thoughts, pressed his lips together and turned for the door, stuffing his hands in his pockets as he left.

"Say something!" my friend urged. "Don't just let him go!"

Another flash of Abram clouded my vision, this time he was kneeling in front of me in the dark, his hands on my knees, worry etched into his forehead. *Are you okay?*

Before I could fully experience the ache, I shoved the image away and cleared my throat, calling out without allowing myself to think, "Hey Poe."

I stopped tracing the envelope in my pocket. It was time to move on. In fact, it was past time. Really and truly. Abram had disappeared over a year ago. I needed to let him go.

Poe paused, his hand on the door frame, and then turned. His expression was free of everything but mild curiosity.

"How about Hawaii for spring break?" I asked, the question sounding awkward and amiss to my ears. And my heart.

His eyes narrowed. "You're in Europe all next semester."

"Yes."

"You're going to fly back from Europe? All the way to Hawaii, just for spring break?"

I hesitated, because he had a point. I hadn't considered whether going to Hawaii for a week would even be possible, given my commitments in Geneva. Poe's gaze moved over my face, like he was searching for something, a sign, a tell. I held my breath, clearing my features of expression.

Eventually, he bestowed upon me one of his small, patient smiles. "Okay, Mona. Whatever you say. See you in a week."

"See you in a week," I croaked, managing a smile for him in return, even though I felt embarrassed by my clumsy, sudden, and logistically unsound suggestion. Embarrassed and wrong and sad and anxious.

Giving me a slight nod, Poe turned and left. Reaching my hand in my pocket, I gripped the envelope, squeezing it, and breathed out, or at least I tried to. The ache in my chest had returned full force. Yes, I needed to move on. Yes, I'd been behaving irrationally for over two years, holding on to the possibility of an impossibility. But no, I shouldn't use Poe to move on.

I felt like an ass.

Meanwhile, Allyn squealed in my ear, "Yay! Hawaii with Poe! Of course, I'll find a reason not to go so you two can—"

"Calm down, Allyn. It's probably not going to happen." Releasing the letter, I lifted my fingers and rubbed my sternum, so ready for this vacation. So ready for quiet and calm and peace.

So ready for less motion.

CHAPTER 2
ELECTRIC CURRENT, RESISTANCE, AND OHM'S LAW

Mona

My parents' McMansion was built into the side of a mountain. Reaching the property during winter required the traveler to have a certain degree of flexible ambivalence for their own safety. I'd explained the situation to Allyn months ago, perhaps even exaggerating the danger, just to be sure she was fully informed prior to giving her consent. She'd readily agreed.

As soon as my plane touched down, I powered up my cell to message Allyn. The screen told me that my brother had called and left a voicemail while I'd been airborne. Making a mental note to check his message later, I sent Allyn a text, letting her know I'd finally arrived.

The plane had been delayed leaving LAX by an hour and a half, therefore our flights arrived within a half hour of each other instead of mine landing first. After grabbing my carry-ons, darting off the plane and through the gate area to baggage claim, I discovered Melvin—one half of the caretaker team for the Aspen property—had already found Allyn and her bags.

As soon as she spotted me, Allyn—as usual—didn't say hi. She began talking as though we were in the middle of a conversation. "I was hoping to get a good view of the mountains as we touched down, but it was too cloudy and dark. I didn't get to see anything."

Pulling me into an embrace once I was within arm's reach, she didn't seem to notice how I tensed. Allyn never did notice my reticence about being touched, but that was fine. I'd been working on my "touching issues" for a while now and I appreciated her ignorance of my struggles. I didn't want anyone walking on eggshells or making it into their problem.

"You couldn't see the mountains because of the snow," Melvin said, stepping forward to reach for my bag. "This is it? Did you check anything?"

I shook my head, lifting my shoulder to indicate that I'd be fine carrying my backpack. "Just the two carry-ons."

"Good. Let's go." He turned and began power-walking to the exit.

It took me a second to react to his swift departure. I'd expected to hear all the local news, as Melvin was typically the chatty sort. He and his daughter Lila were Aspen natives. He seemed to think of the place as a small hamlet rather than the opulent resort town it had become. The last time I'd visited—just two months ago—he'd told me all about the latest issues with sanitation management and how the mayor's son had been escorted out of Big Ben's Bear Shack after dancing on the bar.

But instead of chatting, Melvin—now ten feet away—twisted his head to see if we were following, and then waved us forward urgently. Following his lead, we were wordlessly and hurriedly ushered out of the airport and into the waiting car.

Once we were packed in, on the road and on our way, I lowered the glass separating Allyn and I from Melvin.

"Can we stop at the store?" I'd been assured via email by Lila—Melvin's daughter, the other half of the caretaker team all year round, and the chef when my parents were present—that the house had been appropriately stocked for our arrival. Even so, I'd wanted to make a stop in downtown Aspen to pick up a few supplies.

Melvin clicked his tongue, not sparing me a glance in the rearview mirror. "We can, but the forecast has another two feet by midnight. If we stop now, there's no guarantee we'll be able to access 82 at all, or reach the house for the next several days. It's a good thing you girls arrived when you did. Lila's been fretting all week. If your plane had been further delayed, you might've been staying the week at one of the lodges instead."

"Does that mean we won't be able to leave once we get there?" Allyn addressed this question equally to both me and Melvin.

"Forecast has snow slowing by week's end, and they plow on Fridays. You should be fine to fly out, assuming the forecast is on target."

"But we can't leave for the whole week?" She didn't sound upset or worried, merely curious.

"That's right. Once we get there, you two will be stuck for the week with the rest of us. But don't worry, we do this all the time, it's not unusual. And Lila has a menu planned. We'll do our best to make it bearable for you."

By 'rest of us' I assumed he meant Lila, me, and himself, but I was surprised that Lila was planning to cook.

"I told Lila she doesn't need to cook," I reminded him, leaning forward in my seat. When it was just me, I made sure she never felt pressured to make anything.

"Mona, don't you make a big deal out of it." Now Melvin did spare me a glance in the mirror, narrowing his eyes. "Just let her be. She likes cooking when there's company. She is a pro chef, after all. And if she's not making her fancy dishes, her talents just go to waste. Think of it that way."

I didn't argue, but I still wasn't convinced. I didn't like to inconvenience people. I could take care of myself.

After driving through downtown Aspen, we took several precarious off-shoots from State Road 82. I tried not to look out the window, but Allyn seemed fascinated by the near whiteout conditions. At one point, Melvin must've been going five miles per hour, it was fully dark by the time we arrived. Even so, I barely noticed the length of the car ride. Allyn had talked non-stop, her pretty, melodic voice filling the car with stories about her difficult last semester, all of which seemed hilarious to her in retrospect.

The three parking garages near the base of the peak served only as a pitstop and storage. A funicular, which was just as fancy as it was functional, had been installed well before my parents purchased the Mountain McMansion. It was the only way to actually access the main house October through April, give or take a month depending on the snowfall.

Melvin pulled as close to the funicular structure as he could, knocking on the back door of the Jeep before opening it for Allyn. "Okay, ladies. Time to get out. You go up first while I clear a path to the garage, must be two feet of snow up here since I left this morning. I'll come after with your bags and the supplies I picked up on my way to the airport. Hurry, it's cold."

White flakes of frost swirled around him, but nothing much else was visible. Happy to do as we were told, my friend and I gathered our backpacks and left the warmth of the SUV. Melvin had been right. The snow came up to my knee, my boots disappearing into two or more decimeters of fresh powder.

Glancing back, I smiled at Allyn's huge grin and laugh, her eyes on where her feet should be. "Follow me," I said. "The funicular is just through here."

"Funicular is a fun word to say." She held her hands out to keep her balance. "It sounds like fun and particular had a word baby."

"Well, this funicular is particular, but I don't know how fun it is."

"Everything can be fun. You just have to want it to be fun," she said, the combination of her bright eyes and wide smile a sunbeam in the cold darkness, laughing as she added, "And, you know, the habit of constantly laughing at yourself."

That made me laugh, though I wasn't sure why. When Allyn was around, I always seemed to be laughing. And, in truth, taking the fancy funicular used to be fun. As a kid, it was my favorite part of visiting the mountain house. I would hang out inside, reading books, breathing against the paned window and drawing designs into the puff of condensation with the tip of my finger.

The benches were a gold-ish velvet and there was space for four comfortably, six if absolutely needed. Our ride up the mountain was uneventful despite the snowfall, but I felt a little badly about the inclement weather.

"I was snowed in here twice last year, but only for about three days. After that, it cleared up. We should have some nice views, assuming the snow stops." I motioned to the darkness beyond the glass. The flakes were so big, they made tapping sounds against the window reminiscent of light rain.

"That'll be nice. Can we do any hiking? Is it safe?"

"If you want exercise, there's an indoor pool and gym. But if you really want to go for a walk outside, you can go snowshoeing through the trails."

"I've never gone snowshoeing."

"It's just very slow walking, with funny shoes. Though it'll feel like you've covered a hundred miles by the time you finish. There's a few Jacuzzis for warming up after, and a sauna near the gym as well as one on the top floor."

Allyn's eyebrows pulled together even as she smiled. "A few jacuzzis? Two saunas? Are you sure this isn't a hotel?"

I rolled my eyes good-naturedly, but didn't respond. I didn't come here for the Jacuzzis and saunas and huge fireplaces and the music room and the sound studio and movie theater. My parents had houses all over the world, and they put money into a travel account for me (and one for each of my siblings) every year, mostly because they never wanted us to have an excuse if they requested our presence at some event. I rarely used the travel account and the mountain house was the only one I ever asked to visit.

"I'll go snowshoeing with you if you really want to go." I breathed on the glass, making a rough oval of condensation, and drew two smiley faces. "But mostly, I'd like to get some reading done."

"Work stuff?" Allyn asked, making her own condensation canvas in the glass and drawing a flower. It looked like a thistle. She was a good artist.

"No, actually. A few novels I've been saving."

"Really? Which ones?"

The funicular car began to slow, and I twisted my neck to peer out the window behind me. The house was now fully in view and all lit up. It looked warm and inviting, though I frowned at how many windows were illuminated. I usually stuck to the main floor, eschewing the larger rooms on the upper levels. *Why would Lila turn on all the lights in every room?* Strange.

"Uh, Lisa Kleypas. Her most recent two," I answered distractedly.

"Oh, you haven't read her latest book?" Allyn sounded anxious, which brought my attention back to her.

"No. Not yet. You know me, I've been saving them."

"When you finish, I need to talk about it. I have feelings!" My friend did jazz hands, wiggling her fingers in the air.

Laughing, I stood as the car came to a stop in the top-side structure. "Okay. Sounds good. I'll probably have feelings too. We can compare feelings notes."

"Yes!" She jumped up and turned to grab her bag.

I unfastened the door and slid it to the side, and then I paused because I spotted a dark figure approaching the funicular structure, silhouetted by the lights of the house. The size of the outline made the person too big to be Lila, and the wrong chromosomal arrangement. Meaning, it was a man. And he was carrying what looked like a shovel over his shoulder.

"Who is . . . ?" I narrowed my eyes, stepping off the car, leaving my bag for the moment, and opened the structure door.

"Mona!"

I stood straighter at the sound of my brother's greeting, ignoring the blast of cold wind. "Leo? What are you doing here?" I had to raise my voice over the gust. It hadn't been nearly as blustery at the parking structures. I gripped my hat to my head, just in case it decided to fly off.

Fully materializing, he grinned down at me, his dark eyes moving over my face. "It's good to see you! Do you need help with bags?" Leo made no move to hug me, not that I expected him to. After putting up with my stiff, detached hugs for several years, he'd stopped trying.

I shook my head, confused by his presence, and also by the uncomfortable prickling at the back of my neck. "It's good to see you too. I didn't know you were coming."

"Did you get my voicemail?" he asked, but then glanced over my shoulder, obviously spotting Allyn. "Oh, hey. Alan, right?" He extended his hand automatically, but then chuckled at himself when he seemed to suddenly remember the work gloves covering his fingers.

"It's pronounced Al-lean," I corrected.

"Oh, sorry." Leo seemed to be apologizing for both his inability to shake her hand and mispronouncing her name.

"That's okay. You can call me Al if you like. And I can wave," she offered cheerfully, coming to stand fully beside me. "I can also salute, but that might be weird."

Her comment made Leo laugh, and he gave her another look, his eyes narrowing slightly as they moved down and then up. "I guess we're saluting," he said, smiling, saluting, his eyes still suspiciously squinty.

I say *suspiciously* because they were sparkly as well as squinty, and I knew that face: Leo had decided she was worth a second look. Allyn and Leo had met just once, separated by many people and meters, and very briefly, at my graduation from undergrad almost three years ago. It had been so short, I don't think he even heard her name correctly and had called her "Alan." Before I could correct his error then, he was pulled elsewhere, and Allyn had disappeared into the crowd.

Presently, they were still smiling at each other, almost like I wasn't there, and the exchange was exponential levels of cute. Under normal circumstances, it would've initiated my innate scheming proclivities (arranging an accidental half-naked interaction, planning their wedding, sending out save-the-date cards, and prepping for her bachelorette party) because who wouldn't want a best friend to marry an awesome sibling? But I was still perplexed by his presence and the sense of being suddenly and inexplicably *on edge*.

I also saluted and stepped in front of Allyn once again. "Hey, what's going on? Why are you here?"

"I called you and left a message. I invited a few—" A gust of wind filled the small structure, pushing Leo forward such that he had to use his free hand to brace himself against the door.

Just before he righted himself, I noticed movement behind him. Another man—a big one by the looks of him—was walking toward us along the path. My stomach tensed. A shivery—yet hot—spike of awareness shot up my spine to my neck. And my heart . . . *my heart.*

I licked my lips, my eyes wide on my brother. "Leo. Is there—is there someone here with you?"

"Why don't you come inside? I'll explain everything."

I grabbed his arm. "Explain now." *Why is my heart beating so hard?*

It was like that moment in the sensory deprivation chamber, I was hot and cold and clammy everywhere.

Leo shook his head, giving me a look of mild exasperation. "Mona, it's freezing and you're doing that whispering thing. I can barely hear you. Let's go."

He easily pulled out of my grip, turning for the house and lowering the shovel, and I reached for him again. But before I could grab my brother, the new person emerged from the dark and snow, and entered the little halo spilling from the funicular structure's overhead lights.

I stopped.

I think even my heart stopped.

I know my forebrain stopped, or was—at the very least—broken.

It was . . .

He was . . .

He looked . . .

How . . . ?

"Abram."

CHAPTER 3
MAGNETISM

"Abram." Leo stopped upon catching sight of me. Most of his face was in shadow, but what I could see looked relieved. "Good. Hey, so I guess I will need you to take the funicular down to the garage level after all."

I nodded, my attention moving beyond him to the two women. The one on the left must've been Mona's friend, Alan. My eyes sought the one on the right.

Huh.

She was shorter than I remembered. Memories are tricky that way, always trying to make the past bigger, more important, more interesting and relevant and meaningful. But memories were so seldom reflective of reality.

And yet, I had to concede that she was just as beautiful as I remembered, even though all the color had leached from her skin. Mona looked like she'd just seen a ghost. This filled me with a perverse kind of satisfaction, because she was staring right at me. I was the ghost.

Even wan, she was still extraordinary. Those honey colored eyes of hers were wide with surprise and her pretty pink heart-shaped lips were parted slightly. The delicate line of her jaw, the gentle point of her chin, the subtle indent just beneath her cheek-bones, it all made me want to hold her face in my palms, push her hat off, thread my fingers into her dark hair, tilt her head back, and—

"My sister didn't get the messages I left earlier. Thanks for your help. I know it's freezing." Leo lifted his voice over the howling wind. "I want to get the girls settled, make introductions, you know."

"Not a problem." I shoved my hands into my pockets, lest they get any ideas, and gave Leo another nod. But my attention remained fastened to the genius astrophysicist who continued to gape at me. I didn't remember her looking at me that way during our week together, nor during any of her interviews, and I wondered if this was a new expression for Ms. Mona DaVinci.

Had she ever been unpleasantly surprised before? Had she ever come face-to-face with a mistake? Leo had once told me Mona never made mistakes. What did that make me?

The opposite of a mistake is intentional action.

I felt my lips curve into a bitter smile at the thought and blinked, moving my carefully bored glare from Mona to her friend. Leo had said the friend's name was Alan, so I'd been expecting a man. Obviously, this Alan wasn't a man. For some reason, the discovery relaxed the tension around my ribs somewhat. I wouldn't think too much about that, if I could help it.

Alan was also staring at me, her lips also parted, but she wasn't looking at me like I was a ghost. She was looking at me like she knew who I was, and she was a fan. *Great.*

Sighing, I dropped my attention to the pathway and moved toward the ski lift house, or whatever it was called. Despite Leo's shoveling, the large slate path was quickly refilling with snow. The old guy down at the garage level would definitely need help. That's what I would think about.

Eyeballing the doorway blocked by the two women, I hesitated before walking slowly forward. Mona's friend wasn't a big person, but I was. Unless she wanted to press herself flat against the wall, there was no way we'd both fit in the tight hallway. Thus, it was no surprise when, at my approach, Alan scrambled out of the way, stepping around Mona and onto the much broader path.

The friend wore a wide, shy smile as my gaze flickered to her. I gave her a single head nod in acknowledgement. I'd learned the value of keeping an air of detachment. Fans preferred the myth that I was inherently aloof to any version of truly knowing me. Who was it who'd said, "Better to shut your mouth and be thought a fool than open it and remove all doubt"? These days, that was basically my mantra.

Unlike her friend, Mona's feet did not move at my approach. Her body still blocked most of the door. But she did lift her chin as I closed the distance between us.

Except, I wasn't closing the distance between *us*. She was in my way, and I needed to move past her in order to continue forward.

Given her inconvenient location, I was forced to slow, stop, and then wait. Clearing my throat, I kept my eyes fastened on the ski lift behind her and waited for her to get out of my way.

"Let me show you the house." Leo lifted his voice behind me, presumably speaking to Alan. "Abram will help Melvin with the bags. We saved the top floor for you and Mona, so it'll be quiet, just like she likes. Do you . . ." His voice drifted off, swallowed by the wind and increasing distance.

I wasn't close to Mona, allowing her plenty of space to walk past me. If memory served, and in this case I trusted memory, Mona didn't like people getting too close. *Unless, that part was a lie too.*

"Hi—hello," she said, stepping forward but not out of the way, drawing my attention.

She was still staring at me, her face still pale, but her eyes had turned searching instead of stunned.

"I—" She stopped herself, swallowing, her gaze dropping to the front of my coat, a cute little frown furrowing her eyebrows. In the next moment, she was pulling off the glove of her right hand. Abruptly, she shoved the ungloved fingers toward me, returning her eyes to mine. "I'm Mona."

I suppressed my disbelief at her small action before it could break my outward mask of calm. I wasn't calm. Just to be clear, I was the opposite of calm.

The fact that she was introducing herself to me now meant that she thought I was too stupid to figure out her lies over the last two-and-a-half-fucking years. She was arguably one of the smartest people in the world, after all. To her, people like me must seem like housebroken pets. So it shouldn't have surprised me. But it did. The tension and tightness around my ribs reappeared, squeezing uncomfortably.

Dropping my attention to her bare hand, I pressed my lips into a tighter line, dismissing the way my pulse jumped at the sight of her wrist, the olive tone of her skin under the yellow string lights overhead. Glaring at her outstretched offering, I considered telling her to go to hell.

I considered it, but I wouldn't.

I didn't trust myself to speak, that was reason number one.

The other reason was harder to explain, or use as a justification, or admit to myself. Staring at her hand, I braced against a sudden flare of hunger. She might consider me a lower life-form, but that didn't change the fact that I wanted to touch her. I wanted to touch her more than I wanted to tell her to go to hell, and that was fucking pitiful.

But there it was.

Acting on the compulsion, I lifted my right hand and tugged off the ski glove, sliding my warm palm against her much colder one. Her hand felt good in my hand, the right weight, the right size, the right texture, and I inhaled freezing air.

Mona also seemed to suck in a slow but expansive breath as our hands touched, held. This brought my eyes back to hers in time to see her lashes flutter. Pink colored her previously pale cheeks. The sound of the wailing wind, the sting of the air and frost momentarily melted away, leaving just her, her soft skin warming against mine, her beautiful face filling my vision.

So beautiful.

She really was. She was stunning. I hated that she was still so beautiful to me.

She looks just like her sister.

I blinked, stopping myself before I shook my head at the bitter thought.

Except, no. She doesn't. Not at all.

About two years ago, when I'd begun to suspect the truth, I'd compared countless images of the twins. The pictures were more contemporary than my fuzzy memories of the photos at the house in Chicago, the ones where Mona had looked twelve, and Lisa hadn't.

I decided they looked identical, especially in pictures taken this last year. Side by side, they looked like the same person. When the suspicion became growing certainty, their similarity in photos made me feel a little better about the possibility of being so completely fooled.

But now, looking at Mona *now*, seeing the physical differences in sharp focus, I felt sick.

I should have known immediately. God, I should have known.

The way she'd looked at me then, the way she was looking at me now, so completely different than her sister. The last question I'd struggled with—the final puzzle piece —snapped resoundingly into place. *She left after the movie.*

I'd suspected, but now I knew with absolute certainty. It had been Mona during *The Blues Brothers,* and Lisa in the morning. That's when they'd switched places.

Riding the wave of nausea, I pulled my fingers from hers and shifted my attention to the interior of the ski lift, no longer wanting to touch her or look at her or breathe the same air as her.

"You're Abram," she said, moving closer, too close.

I sidestepped her, brushing past into the small building. My tongue felt thick and dry, and a pulse of heat radiated from my skin outward, but also pushing back at me, just like the sensation when a rollercoaster takes a dive. *How could I have been so fucking stupid?*

Behind me, I heard the door close, cutting off the sound of the wind, and she said, "You and Leo are—uh—good friends."

Not answering, I closed my eyes against the spike of anger. I took a deep breath. Her boots made noise on the tile floor as she drew near. She was trailing me.

"I didn't know anyone would be here. We thought it would be just us. I . . ." She cleared her throat, then continued, "I hope we didn't interrupt you guys or that us being here is an inconvenience to—to—to—uh, to anything. If you need us to go, we can leave." Her voice had grown quieter as she spoke, sounding like *her*. Even at a near whisper, I heard every word as I stepped onto the little car.

Grinding my teeth, I spotted a backpack through the haze of red tinting my vision. I lifted it. I turned. "This yours?"

She shifted back a half step, her eyes still wide and searching. "Uh. Yes. Mine."

I shoved the bag at her chest. Not hard, just enough to force her to retreat another step, clearing the doorway of the car so I could slide it shut, which I did.

She flinched, blinking at me through the glass, visibly astonished by my closing of the door so abruptly, and she either whispered or mouthed, "Abram."

Didn't matter. I gave her my back and started the car's descent, though she was still visible in the reflection of the glass in front of me. But I couldn't hear her with the closed door between us, and soon I wouldn't be able to see her either.

So fucking stupid.

I shook my head at myself, exhaling slowly, lead in my chest, but relieved to have made it through this initial encounter without making an idiot of myself. Biting the inside of my lower lip, I stared at the snow beyond her reflection until she disappeared, feeling and welcoming the cold.

I'd caught Mona DaVinci's testimony to Congress a few months ago. She'd been as eloquent as she'd been brutally brilliant, passing off cutting remarks as polite responses. Strangely, after watching her make fools of the most powerful people in the country, I felt like I'd also been torn to shreds. She was magnificent. She'd also been completely without emotion.

Still, even then, I doubted. I bargained with myself, I reasoned against the likelihood of such a scheme. Who would do that? And how dumb would I have to be to fall for it? Between the two possibilities of crazy or stupid, crazy seemed like the lesser of two evils. In pictures, Lisa looked like my Lisa. Yet, so did Mona.

But then, during an interview on the news several days after the testimony—I'll never forget—Mona said, "I disagree. Senator Nevelson's question was irrelevant and lacked a fundamental understanding of the scientific method, and then the wolves came."

And then the wolves came.

Sometimes reality feels like a dream. Something happens, and it makes you question everything you know to be true, everything you take for granted about the world, about yourself. When that happens, your surroundings and interactions become likewise warped, like you're watching those around you through a magnifying glass, or in high saturation color, and you can't stop. You can't make the world normal again, you know too much.

I'd spent two years doubting my sanity. Instead, I should have been doubting the fundamental goodness of people, my willingness to trust, and my intelligence.

And. Then. The. Wolves. Came.

So. Fucking. Stupid.

I stopped lying to myself, wishing for a different explanation, wishing *my Lisa* would somehow reappear and miraculously want to be with me. I stopped assuming people had good intentions. I stopped looking for the good. I stopped assuming the best, of anyone.

In that moment, I knew without a shadow of a doubt what they'd done. Nothing about that week had been real. Everything had been a lie.

But shame on me.

I should've listened to her the first time she told me to hold a grudge.

CHAPTER 4
ELECTROMAGNETIC INDUCTION

Melvin reminded me of my uncle. They both gossiped. A lot.

No complaints. Melvin's gossip served as a welcome distraction, as was the biting cold. It's hard to remain focused on being pissed when your appendages are freezing.

Even better, Melvin didn't seem to require any response from me. I let him talk, mostly about Aspen politics and recent local scandals, while we shoveled snow. Apparently, the garage closest to the main road, if you could call a one-lane mountain road a "main road," housed a small snow plow and he liked keeping the area in front of it clear.

"It's for emergencies," he said. "It's good to be ready, just in case we need to use it. And this path between the funicular house and the snow plow gets shoveled too."

"Why don't you just use the plow now? Clear this area?"

"Well, I wouldn't use the plow at night." He lifted the rim of his ski cap to scratch his head. "Yeah, I got those lights up there." Melvin gestured to the high intensity work lamps on each of the garages, illuminating the clearing where we stood and the area around the three garages. "They're bright, but I might not see a big branch or something like it. Plus, it uses diesel, which I don't have an unlimited supply of, and I like the exercise." His eyelashes were frosty, but he was grinning as he said this, his gloved hands resting on the pole of the shovel. "You ever want to come down and help shovel, just let me know. Think about it."

I didn't need to think about it, any excuse to leave over the next few days would come in handy. "I will. You come down here every day?"

"Yes. Sometimes twice, sometimes three times. Snow is easier to shovel if you move it within six hours of falling."

I nodded, knowing this already. Michigan winters were why I never wanted to live someplace where daily snow shoveling in the winter was a requirement for leaving the house.

My dad would wake me up before school with a shovel in hand, saying, "God gave you those shoulders for a reason, son. And today that reason is shoveling snow."

"Hey, we'll clear this here together, and then you got this area?" Melvin gestured to the last few feet before the ski lift. "I'll go get the bags and we can ride up together."

"Bags?" I blinked as freezing flakes fell on my face near my eyes.

"Mona's. And her friend, Alan, or All-lean, or Al-lena, or something like that. These names, I can't pronounce them without practicing."

Glancing away, the white cloud of my exhales following me, I studied the pile of snow near my boots. "Sure. I got it."

"Thanks. You know, if it were just Mona, like last time, she could have taken it all up in one trip." Melvin began shoveling again. "Never met a person who packs as light as our Mona."

I said nothing, but that hot pulse of energy radiated outward again, pushing back, my stomach dropping, a tight band around my throat.

"She's something else." Melvin paired this statement with a chuckle and a head-shake. "You know, she never lets Lila cook for her. Says she doesn't want to inconvenience anyone. And she'd be out here shoveling if I'd let her. One time, she got up before me, at the butt crack of dawn. Snow was coming down like a waterfall and she shoveled half the path before I arrived. Reamed her a new one for being so reckless."

I lifted an eyebrow at that. "You reamed Mona 'a new one'?"

"Yep. Gave it to her, good and hard."

I swallowed, internally stiffening and growing hot at the word choice.

But he wasn't finished. "She said she liked the exertion or some such nonsense. Something about never being worn out, since she sits at a desk all day." Melvin rolled his eyes heavenward. "That Mona, she needs a firm hand, doesn't like to take no for an answer. I've had to lay the law down with her a few times."

A spike of something both pleasant and unpleasant had me shaking my head to clear it. "About shoveling snow?"

"About all manner of things. She wants to do her own laundry. She cleans her own room, vacuums and dusts, even. She likes to stop by the store in town before coming up here, every time, and usually eats only what she brings. Drives Lila bonkers."

"You mean she's picky."

"Nope. No. Not that. Not that at all. She doesn't want to be a bother. Between you and me and this snow here, I like Leo a lot. The parents, I could take or leave, and Lisa hasn't been here in ages, she was a sweet kid when I knew her. But Mona is my favorite."

"Because she doesn't want to be a bother?" I decided Melvin talked too much, and one day his gossiping was going to get him in trouble.

"No. Because she goes out of her way to treat us like people instead of servants. Now, I know, I know." He paused shoveling to make a waving motion with his hand. "We work for them, we're their employees. But Mona checks in before she comes to make sure the dates work for us, since we live here and all. Who else does that? No one. We didn't even know Leo was coming until you people arrived. Don't get me wrong, I'm not complaining, but there's definitely a difference. As an example, one time Lila was sick, so Mona canceled her trip and sent a care package instead." Melvin pushed his shovel forward, resuming his work. "They're all nice people, but Mona is a different kind of nice. You know Mona?"

I was listening so intently, I almost didn't catch his question. It took me several seconds to figure out how I wanted to respond to it, and a few more before I trusted my voice to sound disinterested.

"She seems like she'd be judgmental."

"What?" He scrutinized me, sounding confused. "Mona?"

"Yeah. Isn't she supposed to be a genius?"

"Is she? You mean because of going to that Ivy League school when she was little?" Melvin laughed. "I guess that makes me a genius too. Because I beat her at poker every time we play. Or maybe she's just bad at bluffing."

I didn't respond, clamping my jaw together, taking my frustration out on the pile of snow instead.

"No, Mona isn't judgmental. She's a little quiet, but I think that's because she's . . . well, she's shy."

"Shy?" I asked without meaning to, and then snapped my mouth shut.

"Yeah. Shy. She never did have friends. Lisa was always bringing friends here, kids from those boarding schools she went to, and Mona would play by herself, mostly here, in the funicular, reading books. Leo would also bring friends, he still does." Melvin lifted his chin toward me. "That's why I was surprised to see all you guys when you arrived, since Mona was coming."

I found I needed to clear my throat before asking, "She's always alone?"

He nodded. "Yep. Always alone. Every time she comes, and she comes up here a lot. Which is why we take pity on her and play poker, or Scrabble. She also likes Trivial Pursuit—the one from the eighties, when USSR was still a country—but we just read the cards back and forth to see who knows the most answers. She tried to get us to play this new thing called Punderdome or Punundrum, but it needs an even number of people."

Punderdome? That sounds—

I interrupted the rhythm of my thoughts. Gripping the shovel tighter at the realization we'd just spent the last ten minutes talking about the one person I least wanted to talk about, I shook my head, scowling at the snow.

Stop asking about her.

I'd spent over two years trying to forget about one week. Nothing Melvin said, or was going to say, would help me move on. Clearly, he liked her, respected her. Fine.

Stop talking about her.

"Mona is real good at chess though, never have beat her at that game. But she—"

Enough.

"Hey, I'll move up here and get this taken care of. Why don't you get the bags?"

Melvin's perspective on Mona confused me, unsettled my mind. The man might talk all night about her if I let him, and part of me wanted to let him. But that would've been counterproductive.

Stop thinking about her.

I didn't want to like Mona, nor did I appreciate this urge I'd carried with me, this wanting to know her, the real her, all about her, sketch an accurate likeness of her character. What was the point?

She'd lied to me. She'd pretended to be someone else. Knowing Mona DaVinci better wasn't going to change that.

Melvin paused his shoveling at my abrupt suggestion, but then he chuckled. "Getting cold?"

Stop wanting her.

I forced a quick, tight smile and nodded. "Yeah. Something like that."

* * *

Melvin took me around to the side door of the house, which was much closer than the path Leo and I had shoveled earlier to the main entrance. We both removed our jackets, boots, gloves, and snow pants and hung them up in the mudroom closet.

"Here, I'll take the luggage up. Go get warm by the fire in the big room, go see your friends."

I hesitated, glancing at the small stairway behind him that led to the upper floors, struggling with the desire to seek her out. Bringing her luggage up would be a perfect excuse. Then again, not taking advantage of the opportunity to see her was an opportunity in and of itself.

Stop thinking about her.

"While you're there, do you mind checking on the fire? Might need more wood," Melvin called over his shoulder, already on the fifth stair.

Curling my hands into tight fists, I nodded and stepped back, removing myself from the temptation of the suitcases. Watching Melvin disappear up the flight of stairs felt both good—like I'd finally been successful in flexing that self-control muscle—and not good. I stared at the roller case he'd left behind, a hollow, restlessness in my stomach.

Turning toward the faint sound of a piano, I walked out of the mudroom and toward the music, not looking at the remaining bag despite feeling a pull to return, pick up the case, and take it to the third floor where Mona and her friend were staying.

Earlier, when I'd left the house under the guise of helping Leo and Melvin with the snow, the crowd Leo had gathered were in high spirits. I knew most of them, but not all. Leo had this magical superpower of bringing talented people together and making valuable connections within the community he'd built.

The only valuable connection I'd ever introduced to Leo, and not the other way around, was my songwriting partner, Kaitlyn Parker. Meanwhile, Leo had been the one to introduce me to our drummer when I was fifteen, our lead guitarist five years ago, and our producer three years ago. Our producer was the one who'd eventually helped sign us to the label.

My mind on suitcases and perfect excuses, I slowed as I approached the entrance to the main floor living room, a thought suddenly occurring to me. What if Mona was here, on the main level with everyone else? What if, by attempting to avoid her, I was actually achieving the opposite?

Mouth suddenly dry, I approached the wide doorframe and stopped, taking a moment to scan the room. Leo wasn't there, neither were Mona or her friend, but most everyone else seemed to be. The mood had shifted since I'd left over an hour earlier.

Instead of everyone gathering around the piano, playing music, talking in a haphazard circle, they'd separated themselves into smaller, two- or three-person clusters. They were talking quietly. No one looked especially happy. And the music wasn't helping.

My attention moved to Kaitlyn sitting at the piano, playing a technically brilliant and woefully ominous sounding piece on the instrument. I suspected it was improvised, something she was making up on the spot, as was her habit.

Rubbing my cold hands together, I entered the large living room—which looked more like a medium-sized hotel lobby than a living room—nodding at our drummer, Charlie, as I passed, and declining our guitarist's invitation to join her small group on my way to the piano. I did take the long way around to check on the fire. It wasn't low, but I added another two logs anyway.

Sitting next to Kaitlyn on the bench, I brought my folded fingers to my mouth, breathing hot air into my cupped hands, and bumping her shoulder lightly. "What's that?"

Without stopping her improvisation or looking at me, she said, "I'm providing the soundtrack."

"The soundtrack?"

"Yes. If we were in a movie, this would be the soundtrack for the moment," she whispered. "Earlier, before *the arrival*, everything was light and fun and fancy-free, like a Disney cartoon. C major."

I glanced between her profile and where she depressed the keys. A maudlin tune, with frequent dramatic pauses, reverberated from the grand piano.

"And now?" I prompted.

"And now, D-sharp." She said *D-sharp* in a very deep voice, sounding like Eeyore, pulling a smile from me. Her left hand moved lower down the bass clef, taking the mood from maudlin to morose.

Shaking my head, and despite myself, I chuckled. "You are so weird."

"Thank you," she said brightly, giving me a quick, bright smile.

"Why did the key change?" *The arrival* she referred to was obviously Mona and Alan's.

"Well, let's see. Where to start, where to start . . ." Kaitlyn leaned to the side, extremely close.

With anyone else I would've suspected she was trying to flirt, but not with her. Kaitlyn Parker wasn't a flirter. I doubted she had any idea how to flirt. One time after a gig, when we both played for the same for-hire live band, she did a robot-dance-off on a dare and won after twenty straight minutes of impressively stunted movement and seriously committed beeps and boops. But her lack of flirt-skills didn't matter. She was a brilliant composer, gorgeous, smart, and hilarious both accidentally and on purpose.

She was also engaged to be married, and the guy was a real asshole. A ridiculously rich asshole with an asshole name (Martin) who was a stockbroker or something equally asshole-like. Yeah, he worshipped her. Yeah, he treated her like a goddess as far as I could tell. But he was still an asshole.

"Did something happen?" I whispered close to her ear.

She nodded and lifted her rounded gray eyes to mine, saying in a hushed rush, "Yes. The first one came in and everything was fine—Allyn, very nice, kind of kooky but sweet—and then Leo noticed his sister wasn't anywhere. He opened the door, and then we all kind of heard this screaming sound, and—"

"Screaming?" I sat up, alert and alarmed. "Is she okay? Was she hurt?"

"No, no. Not hurt. Actually, it was more like yelling or growling, not screaming."

I frowned, confused. "What?"

"She was standing on the path to the house, yell-growling."

"At what?"

"Honestly, I don't know. A bear, maybe? No explanation was offered. Anyway, it kind of killed the mood and freaked everyone out. And then Leo went outside to get her."

My eyes drifted to the piano keys, trying to make sense of the story. "Did she stop yelling?"

"Yes. As soon as she saw Leo, she seemed to stop. And then she came inside with him and he introduced her to everyone. One by one. All twenty-one of us. And it was awkward, so awkward, because clearly everyone was still thinking about the loud yelling, she was very . . ." Kaitlyn paused here, now she was frowning, and she turned her attention back to the piano, switching to a new key, no longer the existential angst of D-sharp.

"What key is that?"

"D minor," she said, sounding thoughtful, pensive, just like the music she was playing. "It's actually Requiem in D minor by Mozart."

My eyes flickered between her and the room full of people quietly talking. Everyone seemed to be whispering, still on edge.

"Why D minor?" I asked.

"Because Mona DaVinci seems like a D minor kind of gal." Kaitlyn's response sounded distracted.

The piece she played was growing in intensity, louder but strangely restrained. The song frustrated me. It was like riding a rollercoaster that only went up, building anticipation with no foreseeable payoff.

Swallowing against the aggravation making my throat tight, I covered her treble clef hand, forcing her to stop playing. She glanced at me, giving me a questioning look.

"What?"

I swallowed again, and then cleared my throat, letting my hand drop from hers. "Leo introduced her to everyone?"

She nodded and, still looking at me, began softly playing "Chopsticks." She replied, "He did. And it was weird."

"Weird?"

Stop asking about her.

"Like, we all expected her to be hurt, or injured, or upset, or have slain a bear and painted herself with its blood—you know, because she was just moments prior literally yelling. When she came in though, she seemed fine. Frosty, but fine."

"Frosty?"

"She was about as warm and friendly as a polar vortex. *Super* frosty." Kaitlyn frowned, and then scrunched her face. "I've read that about her. Mona DaVinci, supergenius, personality of fifty below zero. But then, if I had her IQ, I might be the same way. We must all seem like single-cell organisms to her."

I bit the inside of my lip to keep my expression dispassionate and from asking another question, though many scrolled through my mind, *How long did she stay? Did she say anything to anyone? Did she say she'd be back down tonight?*

"Anyway," Kaitlyn continued, "in that interview I read? The interviewer said she was a cold person. Perhaps she's the mythical Snow Queen. And that yelling was her speaking the snow language, giving orders to her minion snowflakes. *ATTACK THE BEARS!*"

Preoccupied and unsettled, I forced a smirk at Kaitlyn's silliness and scratched the back of my neck. I'd read every interview Mona DaVinci had given, or all the ones I could find online, and Kaitlyn was right. If Mona was described in an interview, they used words like cold, emotionless, blunt, and abrupt just as often as they used gifted, intelligent, smart, and brilliant. They'd also called her "the greatest mind of her generation," and, "this generation's Einstein."

The closest anyone had come to 'friendly' was when Rolling Stone had done a profile on the exceptional children of famous musicians. The journalist mentioned something about Mona DaVinci only being animated while she discussed advances in the field of physics with an audience of high school seniors.

According to the article, Mona donated some of her free time to a foundation dedicated to advancing women in STEM fields. Mona flew around the country a few times a year, giving speeches to assemblies in rural areas and underserved schools. Apparently, she was also a philanthropist. I didn't know why, but evidence of her good deeds aggravated me.

However, the rest of the article went on to describe her as single-mindedly focused on her research and the foundation, disinterested in questions about all other facets of life.

At one point they'd asked, "Do you think you'll ever get married?"

To which she'd responded, "Irrelevant. Next question."

Then they'd asked, "Anyone special in your life?"

To which she'd responded, "Yes. The Large Hadron Collider at CERN. Next question."

And that made me laugh. It also pissed me off when her responses in interviews made me laugh.

Kaitlyn pulled me out of my thoughts by bumping my shoulder. "Hey there, Abram. What's going on in your brain? You are behaving in odd and uncharacteristic ways."

I lifted an eyebrow at her. "What do you mean?"

She studied me for a moment before asking, "Why are we here?"

"To write music." *And to assuage my . . . curiosity.*

Curiosity was not the right word, but it was definitely a part of why we were here now.

When Leo had suggested the trip three days ago, I thought he was nuts. I didn't see how I could drop everything for several days and go to Aspen for New Years, just two weeks before leaving for the tour. But then he mentioned we'd have to share the house with his sister. Mona.

We'd left New York for Aspen the next day.

Revenge was a construct I used to actively avoid, the idea of it both repulsive and tempting. Repulsive because my parents had raised me better, and tempting because . . . *Honestly?*

I'd always felt injustice on a visceral level. Fairness was a sore spot, a stumbling block, the wall I banged my head against instead of searching for a door or a window. When I was younger, I'd avoided the temptation of seeking vengeance, made better choices, been a better person, had more restraint and self-control.

Now? *Not so much.*

So, yeah. I was curious. Given what she'd done to me, what would revenge against Mona DaVinci look like? What could I possibly do to this generation's Einstein that would be a just settling of accounts between us? Maybe nothing. Maybe she was too frosty and couldn't be touched. Maybe I didn't want revenge at all. Maybe I didn't care.

I was on the fence, committed to nothing, not a place I spent much time.

Presently, Kaitlyn's eyes narrowed slightly. "You haven't written new lyrics in over a year."

I tilted my head to the side, avoiding her searching glare. "All the more reason for me to write now."

"You're being quiet," she accused.

"Am I?"

"Yep. You've been quiet since we left New York. And you've been pensive. I'm not used to pensive Abram. I'm used to salty, sarcastic Abram. What's going on? Is your manbun too tight?"

I shrugged, forcing another smirk. "Just tired."

"Falsehood. Untruth. Lie." She punctuated the triple accusation with chords, singing the words in a falsetto voice like an opera singer.

My grin this time was genuine. The only thing bigger than Kaitlyn's talent and her vocabulary was her personality.

"Let it go, Kaitlyn."

She removed her hands from the instrument, turned at the waist, and leaned away to inspect me. "Are you nervous? Worried? About the tour?"

I shook my head, my eyes dropping to my hands. "No."

"I would be, if I were you. It's okay to be nervous. You'll do great. It'll be great. You've been playing live for years."

"I'm not nervous."

"But you're not excited either?"

I shrugged again, movement by the big staircase drawing my attention. Leo was walking down the stairs, taking them slowly, a frown on his face.

I sat up straighter, wondering what had happened to make Mona yell and if she was truly okay, or hurt and hiding it, or what?

Stop thinking about her.

"I'm ambivalent about—" I paused, sighed, frowned "—about it," I finally answered.

Kaitlyn made a snorting noise, and then said, "Scoff."

I cut my eyes to her. "Did you just say, 'Scoff'?"

"Yes. Scoff-scoffety-scoff-scoff. You are crazypants, Abram Fletcher. I know what ambivalent means. How can you be uncertain about the tour? You have the number one song in the country—"

"No. *We* have the number one song in the country."

"You know what I mean, it's your song."

"No." I turned to face her. "It's our song."

"It's *our* musical composition, but they're all your words. It's seventy-five percent your song, at least. And the rules of scientific digits mean that it's your song. But that's beside the point. As I was saying, you have the number one song in the country, and two others climbing the charts. That's a BFD."

I let her claim—that it was seventy-five percent my song—go, even though it wasn't true. Most of the words were mine, true. But Kaitlyn had helped me fine-tune the lyrics. Her vocabulary was crazy, which made sense. She had this game, where she'd chant synonyms, when she was nervous.

"By BFD, you mean big fucking deal?" I smiled at my friend, lifting my eyebrows.

Kaitlyn hated curse words, which was why I usually never cussed in front of her. But I did enjoy teasing her for this peculiarity in her personality from time to time.

She wrinkled her nose, right on cue. "No. By BFD, I mean a beautiful fantastic delight."

"Suuure." I crossed my arms, my eyelids dropping.

She mimicked my pose and expression. "Look, all I'm saying is that you are winning at winning. You're in Aspen. At DJ Tang and Exotica's *mansion* with your awesome friends and bandmates. You're about to go on a world tour with said bandmates. Your songs are everywhere. You have everything you've ever wanted."

I frowned, dropping my eyes to the piano, the last words she'd spoken echoing within my mind, sounding lonely and untrue. A memory—*the* memory of Mona pretending to be Lisa I contemplated most frequently—materialized. It was the moment after she'd apologized for Lisa's behavior, standing on the second-floor landing outside Lisa's room, how horrified she'd been, shocked, remorseful.

I replayed it often, the way she'd sucked in a startled breath, the anguish—for me— plain on her features. Everything else, I questioned. Every other interaction, I'd easily convinced myself was false, a charade, part of her act.

But that moment—

Kaitlyn poked my shoulder, drawing my gaze back to hers which was now squinted, her lips a stern line.

"Is this about that woman?"

I stiffened, turning my face and glaring at her from the side. "What?"

"You know. That woman." She gave me a look like, *you know what I'm talking about.* "The one you've been trying to get over since forever?"

I tried to shush her.

She kept talking, "The one you wrote all those songs—awesome songs BTW—about? The someone worth hurting for? The woman—"

"God, shut up." I covered her mouth with my hand, glancing around, because her voice wasn't quiet. I swear, sometimes she was like an irritating little sister.

Arching her eyebrows, she waited, blinking slowly.

Dropping my voice to a whisper, I lowered my hand. "Don't . . . don't bring that up."

She shook her head at me, her mouth a flat line, and then turned her attention back to the piano, playing the theme to the movie *Love Story.* "Oh, the *angst! THE DRAMA!*"

"Shut up," I said, glaring at her, trying not to laugh.

"Come on, Abram. Cheer up." Kaitlyn nudged my elbow, switching to 'The Entertainer.' "Turn that frown upside down. Don't make me say something nice about you, you know I hate it," she teased.

I gave in to a small laugh, shaking my head. "Fine. I'm happy. This is me happy. I have everything I've ever wanted." Sarcasm wasn't technically a lie.

A genuine frown invaded her usually sunny expression while she inspected me. "Yes. You do. Maybe take a moment to recognize how far you've come. No more fist-fights, no more arrests. No more gig weddings and corporate parties. Now you're six months without even a cigarette. And! No more playing Def Leppard covers."

"Those were dark days," I agreed with mock solemnity. "Except for the Def Leppard."

She ignored me, but she did crack a small smile. "You have it all. So maybe, possibly, perchance just . . . enjoy it?"

I nodded thoughtfully. My friend was right. I had everything I wanted.

Stop thinking about her.

Well, everything I wanted, almost.

CHAPTER 5
ELECTROMAGNETIC WAVES

Mona

"Are you okay?"

I nodded, continuing to stare out the window at the flecks of white appearing, and then disappearing. We were in my room—the room I'd be staying in—which was the largest room in the house. It wasn't, oddly enough, the room my parents typically used. My parents preferred the master suite on the main level in this house. I wasn't sure why. I'd never given it much thought.

"Mona." Allyn placed her hand on my knee, and I flinched, my eyes darting to hers. She looked concerned. Really concerned. "You, uh, haven't said anything since Leo brought you inside."

Her statement was accurate, so I nodded. Again.

Allyn's expression grew pained and she did a squirmy little dance in the window seat where she sat facing me. I watched her, though it felt like she was behind some kind of filter, fuzzy, distant.

But then she blurted, "What happened? Why were you yelling? What is going on? Why aren't you talking? Are you sure you're okay?"

Abruptly, Allyn, the room, the cold, time, and my position relative to all four came into focus. Also in focus? The hot, leaden weight on my chest. It was an invisible weight, and I hypothesized that all dark matter were actually feelings, clustering and

265

pressing upon hapless humans during the most inconvenient of times. Perhaps dark matter was attracted to heartache?

"I'm sorry," I croaked, even though I'd cleared my throat before speaking.

She sighed, her head tilting to one side as she examined me. "The yelling? You have to tell me what the deal is with the yelling."

I shook my head. "I wasn't yelling."

"What were you doing?"

Hesitating, I lifted my eyes to the tall, vaulted ceiling, and tried, "Growling?"

"Growling?"

"Yes?"

Allyn made a sound of confusion, and then asked, "Why do all your answers sound like questions?"

I brought my gaze back to hers. "Because they are?"

That made her laugh lightly, but she still looked concerned. Now, sitting here, looking at my behavior over the last hour or so, I understood why she was concerned.

After Abram left, unceremoniously shutting the door in my face, I'd watched the funicular until it disappeared down the mountain. I then stared at the darkness where the small car should (approximately) be for much longer, all the while arguing with myself.

He knows the truth. *He doesn't.*

He does. He definitely, definitely does. *He doesn't know. How could he know? And at this point, why would he care?*

The way he looked at me, like he *hates* me. He knows, and he hates me, and now I feel like becoming one with the snow. I want to make snow angels until every part of me is numb and I can't think, or feel my toes, or my heart. *He doesn't know and stop being so dramatic. If he knew, wouldn't he have reached out? Confronted you? Or told your parents? Or told Leo? Or a million other things?*

Then why did he look at me like that? *Maybe he still has feelings for Lisa? Maybe you remind him of her and that's why he was distant?*

But he wasn't just distant, he was aggressively aloof!

I'd rubbed my chest, wincing. It hurt. It hurt reminiscent of those early days after Chicago, with the searing intensity of sitting too close to a campfire, in a sauna, while severely sunburned, under a heat lamp, and sitting on coals. My brain was a mess—again—and I couldn't draw a full breath no matter how much I tried.

What are you going to do? *I don't know.*

I didn't know what to do. Standing there in the funicular structure, staring at black nothing, I hurt all over and I didn't know what to do.

DAMMIT ALL TO HECK!

Therefore, I'd growled. Glaring at the ceiling of the funicular house and foisting my free hand into the air while I gripped the backpack to my chest with the other, I turned and marched down the hallway, growling. Once I was outside, in the snow and wind, I growled again, raging. This time louder and longer, like maybe a tiger might do, or a mountain lioness. And then I did it again and again and again.

I wasn't thinking because I didn't know what to think. The truth was, I didn't want to think. But I also didn't want to feel, because it hurt, and it was an inescapable hurt. It hunted me relentlessly, except when I growled—or, I guess, yelled—all I felt was the cold beating against my face and the rawness of my throat and the constricting of my abdominal muscles. Yelling had been a relief, until I sucked in another breath and—

"Mo-naaaah!"

I'd stiffened, squinting at the snow around me, wondering at first if what sounded like my name was actually an echo of my growl/yell. But then I spotted movement on the path ahead and heard a second call, "Mo!"

It was my brother.

Exhausted, I'd exhaled a sigh, but then pressed my lips together when the sigh sounded dangerously like a sob. Stumbling forward, I pushed my arms into the straps of my backpack and attempted to gain control or administer some semblance of order over my chaotic thoughts:

I needed to go inside, because I was freezing. I needed a minute, or sixty, to come to terms with the sudden reality of seeing Abram. I needed to figure out whether Abram knew the truth. If he didn't know, I needed to figure out what to do next.

But if he did know? And he hated me?

I can't think about that. If I think about that, I'll start making snow angels and never go inside the house.

The several minutes that followed were a blur, mostly because I'd spent them in my happy planetarium, gazing at the stars, blanketing my awareness with the sparseness and peacefulness and darkness of space. I remembered walking into the house with my brother. I remembered there being a lot of people. I remembered making an effort to look at each of them as they were introduced, but I couldn't quite bring myself to shake anyone's hand.

And then we went up the stairs and I sat on the window seat while Leo and Allyn spoke in hushed tones. Sometime later, Leo left. Sometime after that, Melvin arrived with the bags, but he also left.

Now it was just Allyn, me, and all these horrible feelings. Horrible feelings were the third, fourth, and fifth beings in the room, making the large room feel crowded, suffocating, uninvited guests on what was supposed to be my vacation.

"Did something happen, between you and Abram Fletcher, after Leo and I left?" Allyn's question had me looking at her sharply.

"Fletcher? Who?"

Her gaze was steady, patient. "Abram Fletcher. The guy who went down to help Melvin?"

A strange buzzing sounded between my ears. Abram Fletcher. *Fletcher.* Why did that name sound so familiar?

"Mona?"

I squinted at her. "You know who he is?"

"Yes." She shook her head at me, a small movement. "Of course."

"Of course?"

"Don't you know who he is?"

I thought about how to answer that question and decided there was no right answer that would encapsulate the enormity of the truth, so I settled on, "Why don't you tell me who you think he is?"

"He's Abram Fletcher, lead singer and guitarist—bass guitar, I think—for Redburn."

"Redburn?" *Redburn?* As in Herman Melville's fourth book?

"Yes." Allyn laughed, making a face like she thought I was funny. "Redburn, the band? Haven't you heard 'Hold a Grudge'?"

"Hold a grudge?" The question arrived sounding more like a breath than words, and my right hand drifted to my chest.

"Yeah, Mona. Where have you been? It's been playing everywhere for weeks. You can't go into a coffee shop without hearing his album."

This was . . . this was terrible.

I swallowed around the rocks in my throat and was once more croaking my replies, "You don't say."

For some reason, a very specific teenage memory was summoned. My mother had invited me to lunch at a swanky hotel near my summer camp and I was excited. But when I arrived, she wasn't alone. She introduced me to a man, and when she left to use the lady's room, he told me that he was one of her lovers.

One of her lovers.

One of them.

I didn't believe him, but I'd been twelve at the time. But when I told my mother what he'd said, she confirmed it.

"Monogamy isn't for musicians, honey," she said. Her voice had been gentle, her expression compassionate. "I love your father, and he loves me. Love isn't supposed to be confining, it's about allowing the space for the other to fly. We both have many partners who feed our creativity in different ways. The soul of an artist is too needy. One person could never be enough."

I knew this. This was fact. And Lisa also knew this, which was why—when Tyler hadn't been faithful to her—no one was surprised.

Presently, Allyn lifted her phone in the air above her, as though searching for a signal. "If you were on any social media at all, you would know this. Or watched TV other than those Turkish shows with the hot guys. Or listened to the song lists I send you. I've been following Redburn for seven months, before they released the studio album. I think their next single releases this week—their fifth—let me see . . ."

I was having too many thoughts. Too many. Way too many.

However, the logical path forward decided to do me a solid and reveal itself, a miraculous unveiling of crystal-clear obviousness. If I thought about it rather than bemoaning it, I wasn't surprised by Abram's success, just like I wasn't surprised by my ignorance of it.

"Shoot. I have no connection here and I didn't download the album." She frowned at her phone. "You should turn on the radio every so often, or check out the top ten once a month."

Allyn was right. I didn't listen to the radio. I didn't visit coffee shops. I didn't watch TV. I wasn't on social media and I didn't care to be. I no longer read articles written about me. Ever. Other than semi-stalking Abram's sister Marie's bylines and articles, I didn't read much other than scientific journals.

Popular culture was a world I'd purposefully and systematically eschewed.

It didn't matter if Abram knew who I was. It didn't matter if he'd figured everything out. It didn't even matter if he hated me. He was a wildly successful musician, living on the same planet as me, but now existing within a world firmly removed from mine.

The last two and a half years had been like waiting in a line with no guaranteed destination. It had been a line for the sake of lining up, for the sake of having a spot to stand. Then, abruptly and randomly, I was now at the front of the line. Standing in place and waiting were no longer options.

Abram and I, we were two circles in a Venn diagram that would never overlap.

We were two asteroids on opposite sides of the solar system, ensnared by Jupiter's gravity, destined to orbit the asteroid belt in the same direction, but never together.

We were two magnets with the same polarity.

Conclusion: If he didn't know about my deception, I would tell him the truth. It was the right thing to do. It was time. First, I'd call Lisa and inform her of my decision. And if he already knew, okay. That was fine.

But I knew now, reality being what it was, my logical path forward didn't include Abram Harris (Fletcher), it never really had. The past, our past, and this present random encounter were irrelevant to my future.

Just like my existence was irrelevant to his.

* * *

I slept horribly. But, no matter. That was the thing about sleep, there would always be more time to practice.

As soon as I opened my eyes, the events of the prior evening came back to me. But, again, no matter. I was prepared. The space suit of numbness, my recognition and swift acceptance of the futility of wanting Abram, saved me from a repeat of the searing pain.

Sitting up in bed, I checked the time on my phone, 6:14 AM, my hand knocking the letter I always carried to the floor. Leaning over the edge, I picked up the letter, my thumbs moving over the worn, smooth corners of the envelope, and gently returned it to the side table.

I needed to ready myself for the day. There was still the small matter of telling Abram the truth, assuming he didn't already know. And in order to accomplish that with a clear conscience, I would have to call my sister. And that's what I did.

Reaching for my phone again, I unlocked it, dialed her number, and waited. She'd become an early riser and our weekly phone calls typically took place before 7:00 AM, so I knew she'd be up now. The line rang on the other end, but the connection sounded spotty, broken, like a skipping record.

When she answered, I immediately asked, "Lisa? Lisa? Can you hear me?"

"Yes. Hey, Mo. I can hear you. Where are you? Aren't you supposed to be in—" the sound dropped off, replaced with clicks and scratching sounds, and then suddenly she was back "—thought you were going this week?"

"You're breaking up. Listen, I have to talk to you about something important." I pushed the covers back and strolled to the window seat where Allyn and I had taken up residence the previous evening until close to 2:00 AM. Without any prompting, I'd told Allyn the whole story about my week in Chicago before we'd gone to bed last night, and I do mean the *whole* story.

I figured, if I was really going to tell Abram the truth today—and despite the fact that any interaction with him was ultimately pointless to my future—I would still require some level of moral support after the task had been accomplished. I continued to have alarmingly nebulous and irrational feelings for the man. It would therefore make sense that my subsequent antiphon post-truth-telling would also be likewise irrational.

I wanted to be prepared, so I'd made preparations.

"What? Sorry, you're breaking up," Lisa's voice sounded from the other end of the phone.

"This is important. Can you hear me?"

"Yes. I can hear you now, but there's static on the line or something."

"Okay. I'll make it quick. Listen, Abram is here."

"What?"

"Abram." I whisper-yelled, stepping into a corner of the room, as though facing the corner would keep my voice from leaving the little triangle of secret shame I'd created with my body and the two walls. See? Already, just talking about him made me behave in strange and mysterious ways.

"Oh shit. Abram?"

"Yes. Listen." I clutched my forehead, squeezing my eyes shut. "Just listen."

"You want to tell him the truth," she said, surprising the heck out of me, but also relieved that she'd guessed.

Gripping the front of my shirt, I twisted the neckline of my sleep shirt around my middle and index finger. "Yes. I want to tell him. He's here, at the house, in Aspen, with Leo and other music people of an indeterminate number. It's snowing, and we're trapped. If he hasn't figured it out yet, he definitely will now that we're—"

"You're breaking up again. Before the call drops, if you're asking, my vote is to do it."

My eyes flew open. "What?"

"Do it. Tell him. Mom and Dad will never cut you off, so I think them finding out now won't hurt you. And they aren't looking for reasons to cut me off anymore. I mean, they don't talk to me, but I've let go of ever being a priority to—" She cut off for several seconds and I frowned, willing the line to reconnect. It did midsentence, "—getting to the point where I don't even care. I have a good job, I have school, things are good, I can take care of myself. If that was keeping you from telling Abram, don't worry about me. At this point, it's not like the story would be interesting to his reporter sister. No one would care and it would just make him look idiotic. And if after all this time you still—" The line clicked and hissed, and I only caught skipped syllables of what she said for a few seconds, but then it picked back up, "—and it's still really bothering you, then I say do it. I never should have asked you to lie in the first place. You tell him, clear your conscience, and don't worry about me. I'm good, we're good, I understand why you want to do it. You have my support one hundred percent."

For some reason, my breathing was labored. Instead of feeling better upon receiving her blessing, I felt worse.

I said and thought at the same time, "How long have you felt this way?"

"What?"

"How long have you, I mean, how long ago could I have told him?"

She hesitated, and I thought for a second that the line had cut out, but then she asked, "Wait. Mona, have you had feelings for Abram all this time?" She sounded confused, like it hadn't occurred to her that this might've been a possibility.

I let my forehead fall to the junction of the two walls and confessed the truth. "Yes." As the prophesy foretold.

Yes, I'm not over him.

Yes, I think about him daily.

Yes, I've wanted to tell him the truth since I left and have lived in a state of readiness to do so, carrying that letter everywhere I go.

Yes, I'll never be able to mentally move on until he knows, until that equation is solved, that hypothesis proves null.

I had no choice now but to move on. He was a famous musician, a fact that was inescapable. I had no desire to live in that world ever again. Even if, by some cosmic miracle and warping of reality, he was eventually interested at some point—which he definitely *would never be*—we might as well have existed in different dimensions.

The line cracked, buzzed, but was otherwise silent for several seconds until finally she said, "You should have told me."

"Told you? I thought you knew."

"No! I had no idea!"

I had to press the phone closer to my ear because her voice was quiet, and I struggled to keep my voice loud enough to be heard on her side. "How could you have no idea?"

"You never said anything! I can't read your mind, Mona. You never say anything about how you're doing, how you're feeling, what you want. All you talk about is telescopes and—" she cut out again, and so I counted.

One, two, three, four, five, six—

"—we're all going to eventually use blackholes to power settled planets in different solar systems." She sounded exasperated. "The only time you mentioned him was that one time, when he changed his last name. I kept waiting for you to ask for his new name, but you didn't. And then, when I tried to get you to talk about Abram, you kept changing the subject. I kept expecting you to talk to me about him, about what happened after you left, but you didn't want to hear it and—God, honestly?—I didn't know how to tell you. I didn't want to make anything harder, after what you did for me. But Abram had been everywhere this year, his songs are everywhere, his face is everywhere, and still nothing from you until right now. Until he's there, in front of you, and you have no choice but to confront it."

Yikes.

She had a point. I'd never talked to her about Abram, or what happened the day after I'd left. I'd only told Poe about Abram because I'd been drunk—very sloppy of me —and Allyn knew nothing about my fateful trip to Chicago at all.

"Okay. Yes, it's my fault. You're right."

"That's not what I'm saying. It's not your fault. It's—"

Another break in the line. *One, two, three, four, five, six.*

"—but you have to stop pretending like you don't have any emotions." Her voice was steady now, louder. "If you have feelings for Abram, then tell him. Maybe he feels the same, maybe he doesn't, maybe he'll break your heart, maybe he'll disappoint you, but you can't expect him or anyone else to know what you're thinking if you keep quiet, or if you keep denying your feelings, or pretending they don't matter. You have to stop acting like you don't need anyone. You have to let people care about you, and I'm not just talking about this guy, or whatever guy or person you ultimately—"

One, two, three—I thought about interrupting her, explaining that telling Abram the truth now wasn't about hoping for a future with him, but rather giving our past closure. However, my sister was really on a roll with this rant and I doubted I'd be able to get a word in. At this point, I just wanted to get off the phone, tell Abram the truth, and finally place all this messiness behind me—*four, five, six.*

"—come visit me, you're always invited. I mean it. Okay?"

"Okay. Thank you. Sounds good. I appreciate you supporting me in this decision."

"Uh, no problem? I mean—uh—wait. Are you coming to visit me or what?"

"Sure. Yes. I can do that."

She huffed. "When?"

I closed my eyes again, scrunching them shut tighter. "When?"

"Mona!"

"I'll email you."

"Fine. I'll come to California. I'll visit you." It sounded like a threat.

"How about next week?"

"Next week?" I could tell I'd surprised her with the offer, but I was serious.

"Yes. Next week. I have nothing for the next two weeks but prepping my stuff for next semester in Europe, and everything is basically done. I can come next week."

"And we'll hang out?" She sounded so hopeful and—despite the blanket of numbness to protect me from the Abram-angstravaganza—my heart softened.

"Yes."

"Awesome! Okay. Well." Even with the static on the line, I heard her take a deep breath. "I guess I'll see you next week."

"See you next week." I opened my eyes, sighing, nodding resolutely, and turning away from the corner to face the room.

Step one, done. Step two, after a shower!

"And good luck with Abram," she added. "And though I've never believed he was actually in—"

One, two, three, four, five, six, seven, eight, nine, ten, and so forth. I waited until the count of twenty before the line made a definitive click-off sound, followed by a beeping dial tone.

Frowning, I reselected her number, wanting to ask Lisa to finish her sentence, but also end the call the right way, with *I love yous* and plans to talk about my trip to see her next week. But each time I tried to dial her number again, it wouldn't connect. Peeking out the window, seeing the blizzard-like, whiteout conditions, I understood why.

I gave up, for now. Gathering a steadying breath and placing my phone next to the letter on the side-table, I dragged myself into the bathroom to take a shower.

Soon, all of this chaos would be set to order.

CHAPTER 6
GEOMETRIC OPTICS

Mona

I concocted a plan in the shower.

First, I would write Abram a note, which—after drying off, dressing, and braiding my hair—I did. It went through several revisions.

~~Dearest Abram,~~

~~Dear Mr. Fletcher,~~

~~Abram,~~

Mr. Fletcher,

If you have the time and inclination, ~~I was hoping~~ I would be most appreciative if you would ~~meet with me~~ extend me the courtesy of meeting ~~today~~ sometime this week for a short conversation about ~~what happened in Chicago two summers ago~~ an important matter.

If you have neither the time nor inclination, I completely understand and wish you ~~nothing but the best, the happiest, and the most fulfilling everything, you deserve it~~ well.

~~Please don't hate me.~~

~~Love,~~

~~Sincerely,~~

~~Wishing you the best,~~

~~Best~~ *Regards, Mona DaVinci (Leo's sister)*

Content with the final version, I placed the letter in an envelope, which I sealed and stuffed in the side pocket of my black cargo pants. Of note, I loved cargo pants. They were my favorite due to the plethora of pockets.

My work uniform consisted of a white button-down shirt and either black, brown, or navy cargo pants. If I needed to look more business casual, I'd wear a suit jacket of a coordinating color over the white shirt. No muss. No fuss. No making myself nuts, wondering what to wear.

In addition to my jacket, gloves, hat, etc., all I'd packed (other than utilitarian swim shorts and a swimming top for the pool, underwear, bras, and wool socks) were black leggings, black snoga pants—like yoga pants, but for the snow—black cargo pants, and black drywear long sleeve shirts. Therefore, picking out an outfit for *the truth telling* wasn't an issue.

Walking to the door, I turned and surveyed my room. The bed was a crazy mess, the comforter and blankets a twisted pile in the center as usual. But everything else was tidy. My attention snagged on the other note, the letter I always carried, laying on the side table.

On a whim I didn't bother examining too closely, I strolled to it, picked it up, and placed it in the pocket at my knee. I always carried the letter, why wouldn't I carry it now? Turning back to the door, I breathed in through my nose, told myself to be brave, and then slipped out of the room.

It was early enough that I hoped most of the house would still be asleep, but that Lila and Melvin would be up. Discovering which room Abram occupied should be easy, Lila always kept a chart of who was sleeping in which room, no matter the number of guests. Then it would only be a matter of interacting with the others, acting normal, and waiting.

My suspicions proved right. The corridors were quiet, but Lila was up and moving around the kitchen. After exchanging a bit of friendliness, where I asked after her sprained ankle and she asked about my work, Lila relayed the morning's gossip, like father like daughter, and informed me of a few critical facts:

Number one: I was the second person down for breakfast if you didn't count her or Melvin.

Number two: Melvin and the nice—but rough-looking—young man named Abram had left about forty-five minutes ago to go clear the slate path and the base area around the garages.

Number three: Leo had been expecting more than the twenty-three guests already present, but these extra people—spouses and significant others—were delayed due to the heavy snow.

Number four: She showed me the chart where she'd assigned everyone's rooms. Abram was on the main level, in the green room with teak paneling, as opposed to the green room with ash paneling or the blue room with teak paneling.

Thanking her, and even though I didn't like the idea of her cooking for me, I promised to return in a little bit for a Belgian waffle since she'd already made the batter.

The most direct path, even though it was the most public, took me through the main floor great room. Running into one of Leo's guests wouldn't be the worst thing in the world. I'd behaved oddly last night, I knew that, I regretted it, and the sooner I started smiling at people and making chit-chat, the better. These people were important to my brother, otherwise he wouldn't have invited them. Therefore, they were important to me. I would make an effort!

No one was encountered on my way to Abram's room. I knew he wasn't inside, but I knocked anyway, my heart in my throat. There was no answer. I tried the knob. It turned. I walked in. My plan was to leave the envelope on his pillow, where he'd certainly see it, and then leave. That was the plan.

Instead, I took a moment to stand just inside the doorway and stare like a lunatic at his things, cataloguing them: his phone appeared to have a cracked screen, unclear as to whether it was the screen cover or the screen itself that was cracked. It sat on the side table. Next to it were two quarters and a penny, and a book. I longed to read the cover of the book. I didn't.

Counting his change and noticing the fractured screen of his phone was one thing, but inspecting the title of his novel felt like an invasion of privacy, so I tore my eyes away, swallowing around my aching heart lodged in my throat, and rushed to his bed, endeavoring not to notice the contents of his suitcase open on the floor.

Do not look. Do not look. Do not look.

I looked. Clothes and more books and—

AH! STOP LOOKING!

Screwing my eyes shut, I withdrew the envelope. Peeking just one eye open, I placed the envelope on his side table, on top of his phone instead of on his pillow which I suddenly decided felt too intimate, and turned for the door. Breath held, I made it to the door without any more creeping on Abram's stuff, shut the door, and turned back toward the kitchen for a waffle.

And then he was there.

Startled, I froze.

Head down, he was strolling toward me, wearing a long-sleeved white shirt and green snow pants that did wonderful things for his chest and thighs, which did all kinds of wonderful and terrible things to my chest and thighs.

Regrouping my scattered wits, I drew myself up straighter, squared my shoulders, and faced him.

Okay. This is it. This is it. Be brave like Ahab.

What? No! Ahab was insane, not brave!

Well, honestly, if the shoe fits . . .

Frowning and mentally shaking a fist at my internal dialogue, I shook my head to clear it and allowed my gaze to move over Abram. I hadn't really looked at him last night. The lights of the funicular structure at night were dim compared to inside the house during the day, and I'd been somewhat blinded by shock. But I looked at—and saw—him now.

He looked so different. So astonishingly different. And yet, he was the same.

For one, he was bulkier, which made him seem taller. In the last images I'd seen of Abram, before he'd changed his last name and disappeared, he'd been thinner, not bulkier. Obviously, he'd made some changes. He looked like he'd been working out a lot. Like one of those people who took a healthy gym habit to the next level. Like lifting weights had become a source of mental health more than physical health. The added muscle suited him, looked extremely good on him, but it also gave Abram an air of power and strength that I found both flustering—because, *holy hot specimen of the male species, Batman*—and alarming.

Another change, his scruffy stubble had become a bountiful beard, trimmed and shaped neatly. Also, his hair was much, much longer. It was so long, he wore it in a manbun twisted near his crown. It wasn't a pithy manbun. No, no. This manbun restrained a quantity of thick, shiny brown hair. I wondered tangentially if he'd cut it since Chicago.

Of course, there was also the small matter of his face. He had scars where none had existed prior, presumably from the fights I already knew about—the ones where he'd been arrested but no charges had been filed—and perhaps from a few fights I didn't. Nothing major, just enough to give him an air of wickedness without verging into sinister territory.

But his nose, which had obviously been broken, was different. It looked more pronounced than before and . . . different. Again, I knew about his broken nose already, having internet-stalked him for over a year. Maybe that's why the change in his features from handsome to hardened—but still handsome—didn't faze me much, and maybe he didn't receive congratulations cards on his face anymore. But I hadn't been mooning over his external attractiveness for the last several years. Abram's nose hadn't been the star of my dreams. It was his heart I longed for.

Therefore, the most startling of the changes revealed itself as our eyes met. My heart did a double backflip but failed the dismount, splattering all over and making a mess, while his steps slowed. I held my breath again. No amount of numbing space suit technology, bracing rationality, or accepting the futility of the future prepared me for what I saw.

Gone were the warmth in the amber of his eyes, the knowing twinkle, the sensitive spark. In their places were cool aloofness, sharp intelligence, and stark asceticism. The difference suffused every corner of my being with sorrow, caused a deep, potent ache in my chest such that I dreaded my next breath. I was dizzy.

But Abram, other than slowing his approach, showed no outward sign of, well, anything. His features were wiped of expression, and he seemed to gaze upon my face like I might be a piece of furniture.

Oh. Ouch. Jeez. That hurts. Yikes. What's the temperature in here? Is it set to Venus-hellfire? Or is that just me?

But he did speak. "What are you doing?"

I swallowed my nerves, lifted my chin, and pointed to the door behind me with my thumb. "I was leaving something for you, in your room."

"You were in my room?" he asked, shifting closer.

And that's when I smelled the Abram smell. My pulse hammered against my neck and wrists, my blood somehow made thicker by the fragrance of him. I reminded my bones that they were not made of liquid, but they weren't so sure. Despite recognizing the madness of the impulse, I greedily inhaled through my nose. The memory, the nostalgia left me feeling an acute sense of wonder and subsequent calm.

Some things change completely. Even the rate of change changed, fluctuated. Change was the only true constant in the universe.

But, over short periods relative to the existence of time, some things changed not at all. In this instance, the lack of change, the consistency of how Abram smelled, was overwhelmingly comforting.

"Hello?"

I blinked at him, opening my mouth to respond, but I'd forgotten the question. "Could you repeat the question, please?"

His eyes flickered between mine and I perceived a crack there, a curiosity, a bit of ye-Abram-of-old peeking through. But his tone was flat as he asked again, "You were in my room?"

"Oh. Yes." Coming back to myself, I gripped the material of my cargo pants and nodded. "But, don't worry. I knew you were gone. I would never go in your room if I thought you were in it."

Abram stared at me, his eyes narrowing, his lips parted as though he wanted to ask a question, but my words were so confusing, he didn't know where to start.

Discerning the fact that he was confused, I reviewed my statements, and what might have been confusing about them. I'd spoken on instinct, my goal to assure him that he didn't need to worry about me sneaking in, in the middle of the night, and pulling a teenage-Lisa.

Clarification was in order. "I just mean, you are safe. From me."

He blinked once, slowly, shifting back on his feet and lifting his chin. While doing so, he tucked away his confusion and that sliver of his former self, leaving a half-lidded glare of hostility. "Oh. Really?"

"Yes." I nodded emphatically, experiencing the long dormant sensation of being discombobulated.

"What did you leave in my room?" The question sounded bored with an edge of the aforementioned hostility.

"A letter. Or, rather, a note. It's not long enough to be a letter."

"You left me a memo?"

So discombobulated was I, I didn't think before responding, "Uh, no. Memos usually have dates and subject lines, I didn't include either of those. But I can." I tossed my thumb over my shoulder again, indicating to his door. "If you want to wait here, I can go get. . ."

As I spoke, one of Abram's eyebrows slowly lifted, and I belatedly caught on.

Sarcasm. That was sarcasm.

Poe used sarcasm to tease me, and I used sarcasm to tease him. Our sarcasm-interactions were well-meaning and helped keep my sense of humor (and self) healthy. Without Poe, Allyn, Lisa, and to a certain extent, Gabby to tease me and keep me grounded, I shuddered to think how shuttered I might be.

Poe's sarcasm was friendly. But Abram's statement was the other kind of sarcasm, the unfriendly kind.

My unfriendly-sarcasm detection abilities were usually within one standard deviation of normal, a skill I honed for obvious reasons. Not many, but a sparse few of my colleagues enjoyed making the youngest person in the room feel inadequate and naïve.

Unfriendly sarcasm didn't usually faze me now. I used to visit my brain planetarium or mutter nonsensical phrases as a means of distraction. I still muttered those anytime phrases, but more as a joke with my friends than as a coping mechanism.

Twenty-one-year-old Mona believed the best policy was to ignore unfriendly sarcasm. Being the butt of someone's joke was only funny if I reacted. If I kept my head down, if I stayed focused, if I outperformed and outthought them, if my research was ultimately more relevant and necessary and important than theirs, no one laughed.

I cleared my throat, struggling with an uncomfortable rush of embarrassed heat, and gave Abram a thin smile.

"No. Not a memo. Just a note. It's—uh—on your dresser."

Every word out of my mouth arrived quieter than the last and my gaze settled on his chin covered in a baby wizard beard. I knew he still had the potential to grow one. I wondered if I would ever see it.

"You went into my room without my permission and put a note on my dresser," he summarized, sounding unfriendly and distracted.

I'd thought I'd be safe in my spacesuit of acceptance, but apparently, I wasn't. He was here. Real. Standing in front of me. Smelling like Abram. Looking like Abram, but not. He was Abram, but not. I asked myself a question that hadn't occurred to me before just now, *What do you hope to gain from this?*

The answer was an immediate and resounding, *Nothing.*

That made me feel better. I honestly didn't want anything from him. I wanted to tell him the truth, so he would know, because it was the right thing to do. That was it.

Taking a deep breath, I lifted my gaze to his and met his glare, an action made easier now that my specific aims had been clarified. He seemed to flinch this time as our eyes connected, a subtle wince I might've missed if we hadn't been standing so close.

Abram studied me, and I gave him a polite smile, gathering a breath in preparation for making an excuse to leave.

But then he asked, "What's in the note?"

"Uh . . ." My eyes moved up and to the right as I recalled the note's contents. "I asked—it's very short. I request a time to meet, if you have the time and inclination."

"You want to meet with me?"

"Y—yes."

"Why?"

"To talk to you," I answered honestly, meeting his gaze with equal frankness.

"What about?"

"An important matter," I quoted the note. Since we were standing in a hall with many bedrooms attached to it, I didn't think he'd want me to go into details here.

He lifted the eyebrow again, his lips twisting. "What's wrong with now?"

I swallowed reflexively, startled by the suggestion. "Now?"

"Yeah. Now."

"Okay. Sure. If you follow me, there's a study on the second floor we can use, and—"

He stepped closer, very close, necessitating that I take a step back if I didn't want him to bump into me. For the record, I had mixed feelings about being bumped into by Abram, and with mixed feelings, erring on the side of caution was always prudent.

He reached around my right side and apparently turned the knob, opening the door to his room. "Let's do it here."

"Here?" I squeaked.

"Yes," he said, staring down at me, taking more steps forward. Like before, I stepped back to avoid coming in contact with his advancing form, which had a by-product of carrying us both into his bedroom.

Once we were fully inside, he shut the door behind him without turning, his eyes never leaving mine. And then we stood like that, looking at each other, in his room with the door closed, for several seconds.

In his room.

With the door closed.

Wait.

How did I get here?

I felt suddenly winded, like I couldn't catch my breath, and I couldn't quite pinpoint why. On the one hand, this was how several of my amorous nighttime fantasies started: Abram, a room with a bed, us alone, many sexually explicit moments to follow.

On the other hand, I didn't feel particularly amorous at present.

I felt cold. My palms were clammy. A river of disquiet rushed down my spine. Instead of focusing on Abram, my eyes saw only a big man standing in front of a closed door, two barriers between me and the hall.

In the next moment, I sensed him move and I recoiled, stumbling backward and reaching for . . . something.

He stopped moving.

We stood in silence for another few seconds. I assumed he was looking at me, but I was too busy chasing the abruptly worn threads of lucidity, telling my galloping heart to *chill out*, and blinking against the loss of focus caused by adrenaline.

This is Abram. You are perfectly safe. He would never hurt you.

Before I could discover where my wits had scattered, and why, Abram opened the door again and stepped to the side.

Clearing his throat, he backed even further away. "You said there's a study on the second floor?"

"Yes." I breathed the word, a burst of wary relief radiating outward from my stomach to my fingertips at the sight of the hallway.

"Okay. Let's go there." Abram's voice was soft, even, calm, and he came back into focus for me.

I was mildly surprised to discover he was now leaning against the wall farthest from the door, his arms crossed, and he was watching me with a strange kind of intensity that felt significant. I couldn't deconstruct its meaning.

My mind automatically informed me—even though he was much bigger than me, and stronger, and probably fairly fast on his feet—at his present distance from the door, he wouldn't be able to catch me if I made a run for the exit.

Not that I was going to make a run for the exit.

Because making a run for the exit would be silly.

"Lead the way," Abram said, using that same soft voice and not moving from his spot, his gaze still watchful.

I nodded and unclenched my hands that had at some point balled themselves into fists. Taking a deep breath, I walked forward, my steps calm, normal, unhurried.

When I breached the doorway, I laughed lightly at myself, and continued down the hall. When I didn't immediately hear him follow, I glanced over my shoulder and our eyes met. His features had rearranged themselves into a mask of indifference, I was once again furniture. But he was behind me, and he was following.

Just, following from a distance.

CHAPTER 7
SPECIAL RELATIVITY

Abram

I'd been wrong.

Not everything about Mona was a lie, and this made me want to murder someone.

I kept ten feet away from Mona DaVinci as she walked down the hall, and as she climbed the stairs to the second floor and walked down another hall. Her wild eyes, the way her skin had gone from flushed to waxy in the span of twenty seconds were responsible for my murderous thoughts, and reminded me of another time, when I'd stumbled across her in the dark.

Sitting in the large front room of her parents' Chicago house, pushing her dark hair from her beautiful face, she'd had the same wild look in her eyes. The intensity of her reaction at the time hadn't been part of the lie. *Unfortunately.*

Since her panic wasn't an act, then there was a reason for Mona's freak-outs, her dislike of being touched unexpectedly, closeness, and apparently closed doors. It didn't take a genius to connect the dots: the reason for her freak-outs was a person, and what that person had done to her. This knowledge made me as frustrated and irate now as it had then.

What happened to her?

I'd speculated often over the years. Initially, the mysterious incident was blamed for Lisa pushing me away. As time passed, especially once I'd realized the truth, I'd wondered whether it had been part of the pretense. Did she overreact to distract me? Gain my sympathy? Make me care for her?

No. It was real. She'd been harmed at some point.

Whether it was instinct or what, this knowledge turned my mind to vengeful thoughts, but not against her. Revenge for her, for her peace, for justice. Someone needed to suffer for making her suffer.

Mona reached a closed door in the hallway. I stopped, maintaining the careful distance, willing to do just about anything to avoid seeing her panic again, especially when the panic had been caused by something I'd done. She knocked on the door, paused, and then opened it. Just inside the room, she turned and motioned me forward, her eyes lifting no higher than my chest.

"If you still have time," she said, giving me a smile that touched only her lips.

At my approach she took a small step to the side, providing more space for me to enter. But once I was in, she surprised me by closing the door. My attention dropped to the handle as she moved further into the room. She hadn't locked it.

"Abram."

I lifted my eyes to hers and said, "Mona," before considering the impulse.

That made her swallow, revived the alluring blush she'd worn earlier. Her long lashes fluttered like I'd blown dust in them. I watched her, riveted. She seemed to be working hard to remain calm, but not like she'd been inside my room, not with a feral kind of panic.

This was like before, outside of my door, when I'd caught her. She wasn't freaked out, she was adorably agitated.

My instinct was to put Mona at ease. This instinct surprised me. I was determined to be uncompromising in my distrust of and disinterest in her. *That* was the goal. Thus, I didn't understand this instinct. Therefore, I said nothing. Instead taking advantage of the opportunity to look my fill.

She shoved her hands in her pockets, drawing my eyes down to her hips. Mona DaVinci did not dress like her sister. All black, her clothes were somewhat baggy, loose, definitely not tight, leaving much to the imagination. Unashamed of my imagination, I licked my lips, wondering if she was still as fast of a swimmer now as she had been then.

Yanking my mind back from maddening memories of a certain white bikini, I lifted my attention to her face, a move necessary for self-preservation. She wore no makeup that I could see, and her hair was pulled back into a long braid. It was longer than before, several inches longer, and made me think of shiny, thick rope.

Mona dropped her gaze to the vicinity of the floor, but her voice was steady as she said, "There's something you should know."

I stared at her, at this exquisite face, this face I'd dreamt of and hated and longed for, and knew at once what she was going to say. I felt it in the vibrations of tension coming from her body, the set of her jaw, the dazed but resolute look in her eyes. I felt it in the absence of sound, the stillness, how even the dust seemed to be suspended.

I felt it in myself, how my muscles tightened, my breathing slowed, as though she still had that kind of power over me.

So, I laughed.

Mona's gaze darted to mine, and I laughed harder at her obvious confusion, turning and finding a desk. I sat on the edge of it and faced her, clasping my hands together, one leg braced on the floor, the other dangling at the knee.

The bitterness returned and was powerful motivation, like last night when she'd offered her hand and introduced herself, assuming I'd been *too stupid* to discover her lies. Well, she'd been right about one thing. I *had* been stupid.

But I wasn't stupid anymore.

"I wonder," I said without thinking, still laughing lightly, my concern for her well-being overshadowed by the sour memory of her duplicity. I gave myself fully over to the anger. "I've always wanted to know, did she tell you I loved you?"

Mona flinched, her eyes bugging out of her head. "What?" she asked, the single word more breath than sound.

"When you two talked about it, after you switched places?" I waved my index and middle finger in front of me. "Did she tell you that I loved you? She tell you about that?"

She said nothing, her breaths coming faster, looking visibly stunned.

I laughed again, more of a light chuckle this time. "Was that part of the plan? Or why switch places for the week? I've always wondered."

Like last night, Mona's face was devoid of color. Staring at me, shell-shocked, eyes glassy.

"Abram—"

"You know, I thought I was crazy." I had to cut her off. The way she said my name caused a pulse of heat to press outward against every inch of my skin and behind my eyes. I didn't like it. "For a really long time, I thought I'd lost my mind. It was like . . ." Tearing my eyes from hers, I glanced over her head and finished my thought. "It was like, I woke up that morning and you—Lisa—were someone else. She broke my heart, but she did a good job of letting me down gently, everything considered." Smiling with mock-ruefulness, I shook my head. "See? I even sound crazy now."

Mona made a soft sound of distress. I ignored it. I'd trusted this woman blindly, after knowing some version of her for six days. Just six days. I'd fallen stupid in love with a fictional person, and now here we were.

"What I'm trying to say is: letting that Lisa go wasn't hard. I couldn't stand her voice. It was the same, but it wasn't. It grated, nails on a chalkboard, everything was wrong. But I couldn't stop thinking about *my Lisa*." I stopped here to laugh lightly again.

Moving just my eyes, I studied Mona DaVinci from my spot across the room. Anguish, sorrow, regret played in equal measure over her features. Her nose was red, and several tears had rolled down her cheeks. How much of it was real? Impossible to say. But it did succeed in wiping the smile from my face.

Swallowing, she closed her eyes, but then she clenched her jaw and opened them again. Lifting her chin with a stubborn tilt, Mona affixed her stare to mine, looking dejected but also determined, giving me the impression she was forcing herself to meet my gaze. An inconvenient suspicion, that she was trying to accept my spiteful words as some kind of punishment, as a way to take responsibility for past mistakes, infuriated me, because it also made me respect her.

It doesn't matter. It's too late now.

"When did you find out?" she asked, her voice hoarse and quiet.

"I suspected almost immediately, the month after you left, in fact. But, like I said, I thought I was crazy for a long time. But then, I saw your testimony in front of Congress this summer." I paused here, my attention moving over her face, reprimanding myself again for taking so long to accept the truth. "You were wearing glasses, and your hair was pulled back, like it is now, but in a bun. You didn't look like my Lisa, but your voice . . ."

Mona cleared her throat, sniffed, and pressed her lips together, continuing to hold my glare with admirable self-possession given the fact that tears were still leaking out of her eyes.

So beautiful.

Faking it or not, even sorrowful, even pale and tear streaked, this woman was unbelievably beautiful to me. Ethereal beauty, not of this world, inhuman in its hold over me. There was something else about her, devastating gentleness and strength, ruinous sweetness and vulnerability despite the severity of her intelligence. *Or maybe because of it?*

And a genuineness that was so convincing, despite everything I knew to be true, I believed it.

I knew *for a fact* that she was a fucking liar . . . and yet I believed her to be genuine. How was that possible? How did that make any sense?

Another pulsing wave of heat pushed me toward her, one that demanded action and urged me to go to her, grab her, and finally, finally fucking kiss her. I ignored it by telling myself that she wasn't really the one I wanted. She wasn't my Lisa.

She's not my anything.

Instead, I pulled my bottom lip between my teeth and bit it. Lowering my eyes to my hands, I held the lip in place until the impulse dwindled and I could trust myself to speak.

But when I did, I spoke to my palm because I didn't trust myself to look at her. Not yet. "I thought it was just more of me being crazy, grasping at something that didn't exist. But then, the next day, or maybe the day after, I caught an interview you gave on Fox News, or maybe CNN. You ended a sentence under your breath with, 'And then the wolves came.'" Another sound of amusement escaped my throat, and I admitted softly, "And that's when I accepted it."

She was quiet for several moments. I sensed she was looking at me, but I wasn't ready to look at her. The urge to kiss her hadn't yet fully passed. I waited for calm, for my heart to slow, for my chest to expand enough for me to breathe normally, but it—all of it—never happened.

Sitting there, unable to look at this woman, this *liar* without craving the feel of her in my arms, I confronted the pitiful truth: I still wanted her. Or maybe, I still wanted the idea of what she represented.

My muse. My inspiration. The desire in me to take care of her, and the hope that she'd take care of me in return hadn't diminished. It lived in me, a constant corrupting companion, a foolish optimism that refused to yield. It was the reason my mind drifted to her before falling asleep, the reason she'd appeared in my dreams and was on my mind when I awoke. The reason all my songs were ultimately about *her*.

But why? I shook my head, tracing the lines of one hand with the thumb of the other, asking myself for the millionth time, *Why her?*

Six days. It had been nothing. We'd barely touched. We'd never kissed. Why did the idea of this woman feel so essential? I thought we'd clicked seamlessly into place. Together. Counterweights that balanced a scale. I'd given myself over to the idea fully, without reservation. And she had been a lie.

"What do you want?" Mona asked softly, her voice steadier than before. "What can I do?"

Again, I spoke without thinking, "I don't want to be crazy."

"You're not crazy. You're right. I was . . . it was me. It is me."

No. It wasn't you. It's not you.

I readied myself, and then lifted my chin to level her with a glare. Mona swallowed, but otherwise she didn't move, and she didn't look away. The tears had dried on her face, but her nose was still red, and her eyes were still glassy.

God, how I wanted to touch her, to brush away her tears and whisper words of forgiveness. *Without reservation.* But I wouldn't, because that would make me actually crazy.

Suddenly, out of nowhere, I was exhausted. What was the point of this? Why keep asking questions? Nothing could change the past.

I'd fallen for the contradictions, the surprises, how she'd challenged my expectations. I'd felt the pull, the draw intrinsically, without searching for it, without giving it much thought. With "my Lisa," I'd never had to force the wonder, and being soft hadn't seemed so hard. But this person wasn't her. All of it had been imagined.

And yet, even knowing, I asked softly, "Why'd you do it?" Her reason didn't matter, but I wanted to know.

"She needed my help."

"Lisa? How so?"

"She'd been arrested."

I blinked at that, the puzzle I'd thought was finished suddenly had another piece. "Lisa was arrested?"

"Yes. She called from lock-up the night before I arrived. She asked me to help her, to be her, to take her place until she was released. She promised me it wouldn't take more than a week."

"And you did it." It wasn't a question. Obviously, I already knew the answer.

"She's my sister." Mona's voice broke on the last word and she finally looked away, her eyes moving to some point over my shoulder, her lips forming a stubborn line.

Unable to tear my eyes from those lips, I mentally filled in the rest of the story I hadn't realized were blanks, and it all made so much more sense: Gabby's hovering, the missing phone and wallet that "Lisa" didn't care about picking up from the post office, how exhausted real Lisa had looked the morning after Mona left, why real Lisa hadn't budged on telling me the truth. *She'd been in jail.*

"Abram."

The pleading edge in Mona's voice had me looking at her.

"I wanted to tell you."

A shock of something unidentifiable, but that felt dangerous, had me standing and pacing to the large window. It was the furthest spot from her.

I don't need to think about this.

This new information changed nothing. Mona had pretended to be someone else, and then she'd left. Lisa being in jail and Mona covering for her sister explained the initial lies, but it didn't justify the rest of it, and it didn't change the fact that the woman I'd fallen in love with didn't actually exist.

"Abram, I—"

"Why'd you do it?" I turned to face her. My feet were carrying me across the room while her confused stare moved over me. Again, nothing she could say would make me forgive her, so I wasn't sure why I asked the question.

"Like I said, she needed my help."

"No. Not that. I'm not asking why you stepped in for your sister. I get that. What I want to know is . . . ." I needed to stop advancing, but my feet had a mind of their own. Soon I was upon her, inches away, and this time she didn't retreat. She lifted her chin to maintain eye contact and seemed to sway forward just as I asked, "Why did you pretend. With me?"

Mona shook her head, her attention dropping for a split second to my mouth and then darting back to my eyes. "I didn't."

"You did."

"I didn't."

"You left."

"I promised Lisa I would protect her! You don't know, you don't know what it's like to have parents who don't care about you except as an extension of their reputation. I wasn't going to be another person who let her down."

"I get that, *Mona*." Her name came out sounding like an expletive. "That's not what I'm asking. Why talk to me at all if you knew you were just going to leave."

"I tried to avoid—I didn't—I don't know."

"You don't know."

"No. I don't know what I was—I didn't think—"

"Did you love me?"

Mona snapped her mouth shut, a hint of what looked like terror playing behind her eyes. Her lips parted, and she took several gulping breaths, making me think she was preparing herself to say something difficult.

I decided I didn't want to hear the answer, whatever it was, and guessed, "You regret it."

"I do," she agreed immediately.

My eyelids lowered and I flexed my jaw once, twice, absorbing the blunt force of her honesty, not understanding why her response had hurt as badly as it did. "Okay."

"No. Not okay. That's not what I—I mean, I do regret what happened. I regret so much, but I didn't have a choice, did I? I couldn't not—I couldn't let Lisa down."

"You could have told me."

"Really?" She sounded both curious and disbelieving. "Really? You would've forgiven me for lying to you? You wouldn't have told Leo, or my parents about Lisa? You would've lied too?"

"Yes! You ask for forgiveness, I give it!" I answered honestly, because such was the idiocy of my devotion to this woman at the time. Blind. Senseless. *Without reservation.* "I thought I loved you. I was crazy about you. I wanted nothing but to make you happy."

New tears sprang where the old ones had dried and she pressed her lips together more firmly, working to subdue the unsteadiness of her chin.

"I was an idiot," I said.

She flinched. And then she struggled to swallow, still wincing, like my latest words had a lasting, painful effect.

I wasn't finished. "*I* regret it. No one falls in love with another person in six days, that's stupid. I was stupid and naïve, trusting. *Soft.*" I spat this last word, despising her for not understanding the importance of it.

Mona reached out, as though she might touch me, so I backed away. She used the hand she'd lifted to cover her mouth, her eyes following me, turning as I walked to the door.

I opened it, but I couldn't leave without making one more thing perfectly clear. "Don't worry, Mona. I have no more illusions. I'm not in love with you, because I never really was. I know now, you are no more that woman than your sister is."

CHAPTER 8
INTRODUCTION TO QUANTUM PHYSICS

Abram

"Has anyone actually seen Mona? Since she and her friend arrived?" Charlie spun a drumstick between his fingers, the movement absentminded as he shifted his eyes from me to Kaitlyn, to Ruthie, and then back to me.

Ruthie shook her head and Kaitlyn reached for another of my lyric notebooks, setting it on her lap. Sitting in the large room on the main floor, we were going through my old notebooks with the band, looking for lyrics to pair with her recent compositions. Since the partners/husbands/wives/significant others were delayed—including Kaitlyn's fiancé Martin and Ruthie's girlfriend Maxine—we'd decided to make the best of it.

Or more correctly, I told everyone to meet me in the living room and so they did. I told them we were working on new music and so here we were. I told them to bring their instruments and so Charlie had drumsticks, Ruthie had her Martin D-28 acoustic, Kaitlyn sat at the piano and had a composition notebook on the music stand, and I'd brought a Fender Kingman acoustic bass and the lyric notebooks.

"I haven't seen Mona, unfortunately. But Leo said she's not very social, so maybe she just needs time to warm up to us?" Kaitlyn shrugged and turned her attention to the book of my half-finished poetry, as if being antisocial explained Mona's absence at every meal for the last few days, that she never left the third floor, went outside, or interacted with anyone in a house full of people.

Antisocial didn't quite cover it.

I'd read Mona's note, the one she'd left on my side table, the one where she'd asked me—*if I had the time and inclination*—to meet with her. It was impersonal and polite. It made me angry. I tore it up and tossed it into the big stone fireplace two days ago.

I glanced at the large fire there now, unable to see any trace of the burnt letter. It looked like Melvin made a habit of cleaning out the ashes every day. Good riddance.

"Damn." Charlie frowned.

"Why damn?" Ruthie strummed lightly on her guitar, trying to replicate a melody Kaitlyn had played earlier on the piano.

"I kinda—you know." He glanced between Kaitlyn and Ruthie. "I wanted to get to know her."

"Why?" I asked, the question unplanned. So was the scowl I wore.

Charlie was a nice guy, if not a little cynical and jaded. He was a great drummer, a good friend. I usually liked Charlie.

But I didn't like Charlie right now.

"Because she's Mona-fucking-DaVinci, Abram. How often do you get a chance to converse with a literal fucking genius?" Charlie's attention was on me, so he didn't see Kaitlyn flinch at his use of the F-word.

But because his attention was on me, I made my expression carefully neutral. "What would there be to talk about, Charlie? She's a rocket scientist. Encyclopedic knowledge of Star Trek isn't the same thing."

That earned me a glare from Kaitlyn even though she was fighting a grin. "Hey now, Star Trek is awesome."

"No arguments here." I made *live long and prosper* signs with both my right and left hands. "But you have to admit Kaitlyn, his statement is illogical," I added, doing my best Spock impression, making them all chuckle, and once again successfully hiding my preoccupation with Mona DaVinci and her whereabouts.

I'd been searching for her everywhere for the last two days, except the third floor. Her floor. I had no reason to go up there, and I wouldn't invade her space without an invitation. I'd already invaded her vacation for reasons unclear even to myself.

The house was huge, large enough that you could go all day seeing just two or three of the twenty-seven people currently here until dinner. Everyone ate together at dinner time, except Mona. She hadn't eaten with us yet and her absence had been noticed by more people than just me.

According to Lila, Mona didn't want food to be brought up to her room. Over our meal last night, Charlie had asked Allyn if she needed help making a plate for Mona.

With a bright smile for everyone but me, Allyn had said, "No. No need. She'll come down later and get something if she's hungry. No worries." Then she'd picked up a bowl and in a terrible British accent said, "Oh, what excellent boiled potatoes." Which made a few people laugh.

Taking advantage of the distraction provided by her Mr. Collins reference, Allyn had glared pointedly at me, making me assume two things to be true: Allyn was no longer a fan of mine, and Mona had filled her in on some version of our conversation in the study.

This frustrated me, made me restless, aggravated. I didn't fault Mona for talking to her friend, that made sense. But hiding? Avoiding everyone? Rather than, if she had something to say, seeking me out and telling her side? That struck me as cowardly.

Or maybe she doesn't care.

Maybe she was just as cold and detached as everyone claimed. I didn't know. She didn't give me anything but polite notes and fucking *restraint.*

After dinner, I gave Allyn a wide-berth and I camped out in the kitchen, helping Lila with the dishes, and then reading a book until past 3:00 AM. Mona never came down.

I'd almost convinced myself this urge to seek her out was revenge related. Maybe I really did want to settle a score. If that was the case, if I wanted to get even, then one uncomfortable conversation didn't settle anything.

No, I wasn't finished with her yet.

Except . . . revenge wasn't the reason I'd positioned myself in the library, hoping she'd come down to find a book, or why I'd awoken early the last two mornings to catch her at the pool (Allyn said she still swam laps, usually in the early morning). Knowing she was here but absent was almost as unbearable as it had been the first time, when I'd thought Lisa was my Lisa, and we'd waited for Dr. Steward to arrive in our separate corners of the Chicago house.

Given the murkiness of my motives and how I compulsively sought her out, like a pitiful, lovesick idiot, you might think I'd grow tired of her, of thinking about her, and let it all go. You'd be wrong. If anything, the fact that I couldn't help myself, that she still held this power over me, that I couldn't think straight with her so close, only made me angrier.

"Hey, listen to this." Kaitlyn lifted one of my lyric books, one I didn't remember packing but immediately recognized now that I took the time to scan the front. My hands gripped the arms of my chair reflexively and I readied myself for what she might've found.

"Gone, and she took all her sweet softness with her.

Gone, and emptiness takes a shape.

Gone, and summer is winter.

Gone, and I sleep.

But when she's here, I'm finally awake.

A barren landscape,

Now beauty in her wake."

After Kaitlyn read the poem aloud, silence followed. My friend frowned at the page, and then lifted her gray eyes to mine. They moved over me, searching, thoughtful. But she said nothing.

"Damn, Abram." Charlie hit my shoulder with a drumstick. "That's some beautiful, deep shit. When'd you write that?"

I cleared my throat, glancing at our drummer. "About two years ago." *Two years, four months, eighteen days.*

"How come we didn't use it for this album?" Ruthie reached for the notebook and Kaitlyn handed it over.

I shrugged, standing, and searched for my guitar, wanting to do something other than shrug. I did too much shrugging these days.

"Have you guys seen my guitar?" It wasn't where I remembered leaving it. Strange.

But if I hadn't stood up to search for my guitar, I wouldn't have seen Mona, Allyn, Leo, and a few others walking down the hall toward the kitchen. Stopping short, I stared at them. They were all dressed in snow gear, carrying sleds. Mona had a thick length of rope hanging from her elbow, coiled in a big circle. Leo was struggling under the weight of two large pulleys.

When did she come downstairs? Why now? Did I miss her at breakfast? Was she okay?

Stop wondering about her.

Before I could think or react, Charlie appeared at my shoulder. "It's not here? I swear I saw you put it here by the—oh. Oh, hey!" Charlie jogged forward upon catching sight of the group, placing himself in front of Mona. "Hey. Hey there."

"Hello," she said, stopping. They all stopped.

"I'm Charlie." He held out his hand, grinning down at her, his voice sounding strange (for Charlie).

"I'm Mona."

"I'm so glad to see you." Charlie shuffled closer and grinned down at her in a way I'd never seen him grin at anyone, and I'd known Charlie for going on ten years.

My attention dropped to where she juggled the rope and accepted his handshake with a quick and firm up-down movement. Her arm moved like she was pulling back and his arm followed, his fingers keeping hold of hers.

Flexing my jaw, I lifted my attention from their hands. Charlie was still grinning, and Mona was smiling politely, and I wanted to break his face. I wouldn't do it, but I wanted to break his face, and that was just the way it was.

Leo, God bless Leo, cleared his throat, set down the pulleys, and stepped between them. "You met Mona already, remember? Two nights ago?" When he spoke, I noticed his voice was a little rough, nasally, like he was getting sick or had allergies.

"You were very tired." My drummer continued speaking to Mona, but finally released her hand. He wasn't ceding much room to Leo, leaning over our mutual friend to address his sister. "Where are you going? Outside? Are you having dinner with us tonight?"

My feet moved me toward the group and I nodded at Jenny Vee, Connie Will, and Nicole Mac. The three of them, friends of Leo's, made up the indie rock band, Fin, and seemed to be generally talented, cool, and low-key. Like Kaitlyn and Ruthie, their partners/boyfriends/husbands were supposed to join us yesterday but were stuck in town due to the snow.

And then I looked at Mona.

Her eyes were on me, but her smile had fallen, and she looked pale. Not pale like before, where all the color had suddenly left her face, but pale like she'd been sick for a while. Her eyes were dim, shuddered, bracing, *restrained*, and seeing her this way had my chest tightening. A hot, restive remorse made my stomach twist. I didn't like it.

"I, uh, yes. We're going outside," she said softly, her wary gaze still on me.

"We're going sledding." Leo lifted the two pulleys with effort, finally forcing Charlie to step back. "If you guys want to come, you're welcome. But we only have five sleds and they're all spoken for. You'll need to do some sweet talking if you want to share."

"There's six of you." I glanced at Leo briefly, unable to keep my eyes from moving back to Mona's.

"Allyn and I are sharing." Leo grinned at Mona's friend. She grinned back.

"I'll share with Mona," Charlie said, skipping away quickly, like he was in a rush. "Let me go put on my stuff."

"I don't think so—" Leo didn't finish his thought as he was forced to cover his mouth to catch a sneeze.

Charlie turned and jogged toward the main floor bedrooms, calling back to us, "Come on, man. It'll be fine. She doesn't mind. I'll be right there."

Leo lifted his voice, sniffing. "No, listen. She won't—" he cut himself off, sneezing again, and then making a sound of frustration. Leo glanced at his sister. "Sorry."

She gave him a tight smile. "It's fine. Don't make it a big thing."

"He can share mine," Jenny Vee offered, giving Mona a big grin. "I don't mind."

"He'll share Jenny's and he can deal with it," Leo said firmly.

What is the deal with this sled? I half expected it to be named Rosebud.

I lifted an eyebrow at the exchange, but Connie Will asked Mona before I could, "What's the problem with your sled?"

Mona gave the woman a friendly—but very small—smile, opening her mouth as though to explain, but Leo spoke over her before she could, "Mona built the sled herself, when we were kids, and I broke it. I finally just got it fixed up for her and I don't want it to break again."

The trio said, "Oh . . ." in a chorus.

"It's fine," Mona protested, her eyes darting to me, and then away. "It's really fine. I don't mind. It's just a sled."

"You're telling me you want Charlie to use your sled?" Leo challenged, as though they were talking about something other than just a sled, as though he were referring to Mona herself. "You don't even know Charlie and you want him touching your sled."

Her eyes on the floor, her cheeks turning pink, she whispered, "Can we not make it a big deal?"

Leo gave her an incredulous look, and opened his mouth as though to argue again. Clearly, he saw his sister was uncomfortable. Clearly, she didn't want to talk about it. Clearly, he didn't care.

"What are the pulleys for?" I interrupted, successfully keeping my annoyance with Leo out of my voice.

Again, her eyes flickered to me, and then away, making my next breath painful.

"They're for something Mona set up when we were kids, so we can get the sleds up the hill easier. I'll show you if you want, it's pretty cool." Leo shot a proud grin at his sister, she gave him a quick, closed mouth smile in return.

I stepped forward, lifting my chin toward the stairs ahead of us and addressing Allyn, Mona, and the trio from Fin. "You ladies go ahead, I'll help Leo carry these." And then to Leo, I added, "Wait here a second. I need to let Kaitlyn and Ruthie know we're done for now."

He nodded, rolling his other shoulder. "Go, go. I'll wait here."

I waited another beat before stepping away to tell Kaitlyn and Ruthie the news, wanting to put plenty of space between the group of women and us so Leo and I wouldn't be overheard as we walked.

Ruthie and Kaitlyn seemed fine with the change of plans, and so I quickly returned to help Leo carry his burden.

"You want to get your jacket and stuff first?" Leo picked up the other pulley, sniffing.

"Are you sick?"

Leo shook his head. "No. Just allergies. I'll wait here if you want to get your coat."

I wasn't convinced, Leo looked sick. His face was flushed, he kept sniffing, and his voice sounded raw.

Continuing to inspect my friend, I said, "Nah. My stuff is in the mudroom closet. I've been helping Melvin with the snow."

"Oh. Good. We're headed to the mudroom," he said, using both hands to carry the substantial pulley, laughing as he added, "I think these things are made of lead. Where did she get these?"

"Who?"

"Mona. These are hers."

I nodded, somehow not surprised Mona owned and used seventy-pound pulleys. "What's the big deal with the sled?"

He frowned, pressing his lips together and making a sound of irritation. "I told you, I broke it and—"

"No, no. I mean, what's really going on? What's the deal there? Is it Charlie?"

Leo sighed loudly, tilting his head back and forth, his eyes on his sister's back. "No. Well, yes and no. Charlie has been asking about Mona—a lot—since I told you guys she'd be here."

"Oh." I swallowed this knowledge and the renewed desire to break Charlie's face, and then asked, "So?" hoping I sounded convincingly disinterested.

"He's not Mona's type."

"What's wrong with Charlie?"

"Nothing." He frowned at me, looking confused. "You know I like Charlie."

"Then what's Mona's type?"

Stop asking about her.

Leo's frown intensified. "Her type is no type. She's not . . ." He glanced at me, giving me a face that reminded me of myself when I was worried about my sister. "You know."

"No. What?"

"She's not—she's, you know, asexual."

I almost dropped the pulley, and I turned my face away from Leo so he couldn't see the look on my face. I'd never thought of Leo as dumb, but his sister was as likely to be asexual as Karley Sciortino.

"Your sister told you that?"

Leo huffed again, giving me an irritated side-eye. "Listen, man. I don't want to talk about my sister's sex life, okay? Let's just say, years ago, she told me she didn't believe two people were necessary for getting off during sex, encouraged me to focus on *self-reliance* or some shit like that, and that the modern idea of romantic relationships would soon be considered outdated and irrelevant. She was trying to help me get over a breakup, I think. Anyway, add to that she doesn't like it when people touch her—not even her family—and, yeah, I feel pretty confident in assuming she's asexual."

I nodded thoughtfully, stopping myself from asking *You don't think it might be something else? Like maybe someone hurt her? And how long ago was this conversation? And when did she come downstairs? Is she okay?* even though the urge to question him was overwhelming.

Don't ask about her.

I promised myself I'd stop asking about Mona, but I'd been startled to see her after two full days of self-sequestration. She looked sick. Had she been eating?

Leo paused outside of the door to the mudroom, readjusting the pulley and drawing me out of my thoughts. "I don't want Charlie to get his hopes up is all. It's obvious he's really into her, but she'll shoot him down, 'cause she's always shooting everyone down. And when she does it, it's hard to watch. Brutal."

"Is that why you've never introduced us? You thought I'd make a move and she'd shoot me down?"

He shook his head. "Nah, man. I'm not worried about you. But I've lost friends before. Or acquaintances, I guess. Guys it would have been good to know, keep in touch with. I get it, she's beautiful, unique, interesting. Everyone wants to meet her. That's why I don't talk about her. And I don't want Mona making things bad between me and Charlie."

"Leo, that's bullshit. Mona wouldn't be the one making it bad. It's on him. It's not her job to make your guy friends—or acquaintances—feel good about themselves." I was repeating a general sentiment my sister and her friends had said to me on many, *many* occasions.

Leo smirked, like he thought I was funny, and then he laughed-coughed. "Yeah, you'd be surprised how many guys don't see it that way. But that's why I'm not worried about you. You know better. You've been taught. You have a sister, you know what it's like."

"Not having a sister is a shitty excuse," I mumbled.

"Hey. I agree." Leo's eyebrows lifted high on his forehead, he sniffed again. "But that's the way it is. I'm not saying it's right, I'm just saying you don't make people better by telling them to be better without real life examples, and then it has to be relevant to them, meaningful in some way. Important. Relationships, interacting with someone who has a different point of view, using a mistake as a teaching moment, that's how you make things change. But just saying, 'People should be better. Now, why aren't you a better person? Didn't I just tell you to be better?' That's just lazy."

I laughed. Leo's tangents sometimes reminded me of stand-up routines.

He wasn't finished. "It would be great if stuff worked that way, but it Just. Fucking. Doesn't. It's like saying, 'People shouldn't rob other people. Now why are people still robbing people? Didn't I just say to stop robbing people? Why hasn't this robbery shit magically corrected itself?' Or 'Don't be poor. Now why are you still poor? Didn't I just tell you not to be poor?'" He was laughing too.

"You're comparing being poor to committing a crime?"

"No, man. But, you know, society does. Rich people are good people just because they're rich? Hell. No. I know better. I have a *lifetime* of knowing better. And that's another thing—"

"Okay. Okay. I get it." If I didn't stop him now, he'd be ranting all day while we stood outside the mudroom.

Leo shook his head, smiling at me. "Sorry, sorry. The point is, no. Mona shouldn't let Charlie use her sled. He's a dummy about women, and it'll send the wrong message. She's smarter than he is, she's smarter than all of us, and that means she has more responsibility. That's just the way it is. The greater the gift, the greater the burden."

I could not believe my ears. "Are you fucking kidding me?"

He shrugged, as though to say, *that's just the way it is.*

I scoffed, shaking my head in disgust. "You should win the Brother of the Year Award, really. Nice job."

Leo glared, lowering his voice. "What do you want me to do? I mean, I could talk to him, but then I'll sound like an overprotective older brother and he'll assume I don't like him. I don't want to lose an old friend, I've known Charlie forever. So have you."

"You're an asshole, Leo. And you make no sense."

"Fuck off, Abram. What's the big deal? She should just shut him down now so he's not hoping later. She's going to do it eventually."

Seething at my friend, I walked through the door into the mudroom, too pissed off to say anything else. Charlie was *his* friend. Leo should be the one to step in and set him straight. It shouldn't be Mona's job. Leo, we, all of us weren't even supposed to fucking be here.

At first, I was so frustrated, I didn't notice the other people in the room. I moved to the far wall and set down the pulley, trying to get control of my temper. But as I calmed down—or forced myself to calm down—I glanced around. The women were pulling on their gloves, talking animatedly, laughing. Unsurprisingly, my attention immediately sought and found Mona. Or more correctly, Mona's ass.

She was bent at the waist, adjusting her boot, the coiled rope was next to her on the floor, and her pants were definitely not baggy. They looked like yoga pants, just thicker, and fit her perfectly, though they changed the fit of mine.

I didn't have to use my imagination at all. But I did. Just a little.

Tearing my eyes away before Leo—or anyone else—noticed me staring at the curve of her perfect and gorgeous rounded bottom, I left the pulley by the wall and crossed to the closet to retrieve my coat, gloves, and hat. While I was pulling them on and trying to get control of my blood pressure, Charlie burst through the door.

Upon spotting Mona, who was now standing, her long shirt falling to her thighs, he grinned that grin again and slowly swaggered toward her. I glanced at Leo and found him glaring at me.

On the one hand, I understood his dilemma. Charlie was a good friend, they'd been through a lot together, and Charlie always had his back. On the other hand, just because setting Charlie straight was inconvenient and might be uncomfortable, Leo owed it to Mona, not just because she was his sister, but because it was the right thing to do.

Not thinking about the instinct too much, I crossed to where Mona was standing, not missing how Allyn was glaring at me. This wasn't a surprise. She'd been sending me unfriendly looks since the second day they'd arrived.

Mona's head lifted, her eyes connecting with mine just as I said, "Thanks for letting me share your sled. I'm sure Charlie won't mind using Jenny's."

Mona started, her lashes fluttering, her eyes wide, and she nodded. "No—no problem."

Giving her a flat smile, I nodded, sparing a glance for Allyn. She was still giving me a dirty look.

Sucking in a deep breath, I turned to face Charlie, who was now scowling at me.

Great.

* * *

"What's this for?" Charlie, who was still sending me annoyed side-eyes—which I ignored, he'd get over it—tugged on the rope Mona had just finished threading through the pulley on the top of the hill.

The other pulley had been set in its place at the bottom of the hill. They both hung from sturdy, six-foot poles.

"It's a pulley system. You attach your sled to the rope here, using the hooks welded to the sleds. And then you can pull the rope to send them back up to the top of the hill." She pointed out two metal hooks that had been added unobtrusively to the underside of the five sleds. Apparently, she hadn't just made one of the sleds. She'd made them all.

The hooks were encased in a small tube of the same metal and were retractable. Since the sleds were on ski rails and the platform sat off the ground, the hooks and their tubes wouldn't interfere with sliding down the hill. The tubes also kept the hooks from inadvertently catching a person or their clothes. The design was smart.

"Huh. Smart." Charlie grinned at her. "So you don't have to carry the sled back up the hill."

"Nice." Nicole said, inspecting her sled.

We were at the crest of a hill overlooking the house, the slope and length were just the right for sledding. Not too steep where going ass over ankles was a concern, not too long where walking back up the hill would make repeated rides not worth the effort.

Mona started back down the hill, stomping her feet as she went and bending over every so often to pack down the snow.

"What are you doing?" Jenny asked. "Do you need help?"

"Making snow stairs, for people to climb instead of struggling with the slope. Even without having to carry the sled back up, as you experienced on the way up here, it can be difficult."

I watched her work for a moment, knowing I'd be down there to help her whether she liked it or not. *But first* . . . I turned to glance at the pulley system she'd set up. Reaching for the rope, I tugged, hard. The poles holding the pulley and rope were extremely sturdy. They didn't budge.

"Why do you need the stairs?" I asked. "Couldn't you use the rope to pull yourself up?"

I felt unfriendly eyes on me, so I looked around. Sure enough, Allyn was watching me through near slits, arms crossed, her mouth pinched.

Glancing at the sky briefly, I decided to ignore her, too.

Keeping her focus on the snow, Mona sighed. "Well, not really. Because if you pull on the up rope, the other side—the down rope—moves in the pulley and you'd end up staying where you are."

"Yeah. True. But if you held on to both ropes, both sides, neither would move. And you could pull yourself up the hill, which would be easier, less energy, and faster than either taking snow stairs or climbing."

Mona glanced up and our eyes met. As I'd come to expect, my next breath was difficult.

I wonder when that's going to stop.

She just looked. Her face blank as she seemed to consider me. Everyone else glanced between us.

"And," I added as another option occurred to me, "if you didn't want to use both ropes like that, you could use the pulley. Someone could stand up here and pull people up using the 'down' side of the rope, while the other person holds onto the 'up' rope."

Mona inhaled slowly, straightening fully, her eyes still holding mine, a glimmer of something behind them. The barest of smiles curved her lips. I countered the compulsion to return her smile by scowling, needing a defensive barrier against the admiring look in her eyes and the faint—but no less impactful—curve of her lips.

She nodded. "You're right. Those are both better options—smarter, simpler options, less time-consuming—than the snow stairs." Dusting the white flakes from her hands, she walked back to where we stood. Specifically, she walked back to where I stood, holding the sled we would share. "We should do one or both of those."

The others agreed and made their way to the set-off point in the center of the hill, lining up to take turns. Jenny made some joke about snow in the pants that had Connie and Nicole jogging ahead.

Mona and I didn't move.

She stood about four feet away. It was still snowing, and a snowflake landed on her cheekbone, melting almost as quickly as it touched her skin. I knew how it felt.

"Thank you."

Steadying myself, keeping my features clear of expression, I gave my eyes back to her. "For what?"

"For being so civil."

"Civil." I tested the word on my tongue and decided I didn't like it. "Civil as in civilized? You think just because people aren't as smart as you, they're incapable of civility?"

Her eyebrows pulled together, and she flinched. "I never—I never thought, nor do I think, that I'm smarter than you."

"Then you're an idiot." I glanced over her head at nothing and I chuckled humorlessly. "What does that make me?"

She made a sound of frustration, taking another half step forward, drawing my eyes back to hers. I was surprised to see a bit of fire behind her gaze, like I'd made her angry.

"Then I rescind my appreciation for your civility, and I thank you instead—and in specific—for sharing my sled. Or, I guess, offering to." Her eyes were whiskey colored today and slightly narrowed, staring at me with what looked like simmering annoyance.

Perversely, I liked that I could get any reaction out of her. I'd been thinking constantly about our conversation in the study two days ago and I'd decided it had been one-sided. She'd barely said anything. She'd made a brave face, let me say my piece, and admitted only that she'd *regretted* it. But she hadn't apologized.

And that fucking note . . .

Just thinking about her admission of regret and that note had me grinding my teeth. I shoved my hands into my coat pockets, a crescendo of anger making me speak without thinking, "Leo should tell Charlie to back off, but I don't think he will."

Mona was quiet for a second, and I heard her take a deep breath. "Okay."

"Charlie isn't a bad guy."

"I didn't think he was."

Returning my attention to her lovely face, I studied the dark circles beneath her eyes, the paleness of her lips. But her cheeks were now pink, probably from the cold. *Has she been eating?* I didn't think so.

Stop wondering about her.

"It's none of my business. . ." I said, unsure what I was talking about. Charlie? Or if she'd been eating? Swallowing the impulse to ask how she was, if she was okay, I worked hard to keep my concern for her buried, shielding it behind the anger I was having trouble holding on to.

"Abram." Mona had also stuck one of her hands in her coat pocket, seemed to be fiddling with something inside. "I'm not interested in Charlie," she said gently.

She'd taken another step forward and it felt too close. Her eyes had turned soft, but also restrained. She looked like she wanted to say more. She didn't.

Kaitlyn had been right. Mona DaVinci was a D minor kind of gal. She was all of those adjectives the interviewers used. Cold, brilliant, calculating, aloof. She was not the sunny, funny girl from Chicago that made me laugh, who was so easy to tease, who made me hot with her brains and body and wit. She was not brave. She was not honest, maybe not even with herself.

"Then you should tell him. Tell him, so he doesn't waste time hoping for more," I said, my voice rough, allowing the cold within me to join the cold without and embracing the numbness of disenchantment. "Try being honest for once. You might like it."

CHAPTER 9
PARTICLE PHYSICS

Mona

Try being honest for once.

I couldn't get his parting shot out of my head. *Try being honest . . .* For once.

Even as I checked Leo's temperature and pressed a cold cloth to his forehead, Abram's voice chanted in my head, *be honest, be honest, be honest.*

"That bad?" My brother's unsteady question pulled me out of my musings. He shivered under his covers and his jaw was clamped shut, like he was trying to stop his teeth from reflexively clacking together.

Poor Leo. He'd finally succumbed to his cold about two hours into our sledding adventure and would soon be in a medicine haze. I'd administered a hefty dose of everything we had in hopes it would help him sleep.

Glancing at the readout on the thermometer, I read, "102.4."

"Ugh. This sucks. I just want to die."

Rolling my lips between my teeth to stop my smile, I rolled my eyes at his dramatics. "You're not dying."

"No. But it feels like I am."

Now I did smile, setting aside his thermometer to the side table. On a whim, I placed a kiss on his forehead. "You need to sleep."

As I leaned away, he caught my eyes, ensnared them. Even in his hazy state, my small action seemed to shock the hell out of him.

"Are you feeling okay?" he asked, looking truly alarmed.

"Better than you are." I pressed my cool hand to his cheek. "I'm sorry you're sick, but I'm happy you're not alone and sick."

He coughed, covering his mouth. "I always have friends around, Mona. I'm rarely alone." He had sore-throat voice.

"It's not the same though, is it?" I watched my hand brush hair off my sweet brother's forehead. "It's better with family, I think. You know I'll always love you, no matter what."

Leo frowned, his glassy eyes turning thoughtful. "You love me, huh?"

I smirked at his ridiculous question. "Of course I do."

He shook his head, his frown intensifying, and blurted, "Why don't you like me touching you?"

I stiffened and held perfectly still.

But Leo had more questions. "Was it something I did? I know Lisa had her issues with me, and boarding school. We worked it out and I think we're fine now. But what did I do to you?"

"Nothing," I whispered, straightening to sit upright in my chair, but I didn't completely withdraw. I covered his hand with mine. "You should sleep."

Try being honest for once.

Leo might've been the one who was sick, but Abram's words plagued me.

"There's got to be something, Mona." My brother's eyes, the same color as mine and Lisa's, as my mom's, searched my face. "I'm really sorry, whatever it was."

"It wasn't you," I said without meaning to, wanting to calm him.

It had the opposite effect.

Leo's fingers tightened over mine, his eyes growing wider, suddenly fierce. "Then who was it?"

Try being honest for once.

Swallowing around a knot in my throat that threatened to bring with it a flood of memories, I glanced at the headboard behind him. I told myself for the billionth time that I'd given a meaningless and stupid incident too much power over me, over my relationships with my family, and my friends.

Nothing had happened. I wasn't hurt. I was fine then and I was fine now.

Abram's voice sounded between my ears, demanding, *Try being honest for once.*

I felt my lips curve downward in a frown. "Can we talk about this later?" I slipped my fingers from Leo's, but didn't remove my hand, covering his once again. "When your fever is below 100?"

Leo's forehead twitched, he blinked his eyes, obviously having trouble keeping them open. "If someone hurt you—"

"No one hurt me," I soothed, which I reminded myself was the truth. "But you're going to hurt yourself if you don't sleep."

He didn't believe me, it was written all over his face. "Mona—"

"Go to sleep." I stood, reached for the light on his side table and switched it off. "I'll be back to check on you later."

"Mona."

"Leo. Sleep. Now." I backed away toward the door, punctuating each word with a finger point even though he probably couldn't see me. "And I'll tell you anything you want to know."

"I'll hold you to that."

The shiver of disquiet raced down my spine, causing me to wince, and making me grateful I'd turned off the light. "Sweet dreams, big brother."

He grunted in response and shifted on the bed.

Reaching the door, I stepped backward to close it, and heard him say, "I love you, Mona."

Smiling into the darkness, I answered, "I love you too, Leonardo DaVinci."

He chuckled. I closed the door. I took a deep breath. And, after washing my hands of residual flu-like symptom causing germs, I forced my feet to carry me to the dining room where I knew dinner had already been served.

I craved quiet, but I didn't know if that was because silence had become habitual, or if I actually wished for it. Regardless, I refused to remove myself to my room again, or use Leo's sickness as an excuse to be absent. I could've stayed with him and avoided the crowd under the guise of watching my brother sleep. That would've made me a coward.

After years of wanting to see him, Abram was here, now. At best, he hated me. At worst, he was indifferent toward me. I thought maybe his true feelings fell someplace in between. Everything between us was officially over. Any possibility of a future between us was an asymptote of a curve, approaching zero reaching to infinity but never touching the axis. I was clear on all of that.

But I also recognized these next few days would be my last chance to be near him in any meaningful way. I could avoid him and all the uncomfortable, painful, breath-snatching feelings, or I could experience him and the feelings. Even if he hated me, even if I didn't understand why I continued to feel so strongly about him, even if the only memories I made during this time were agonizing ones, I'd take agonizing over another black hole of nothingness.

And that was honestly the truth.

Walking into the dining room, I scanned the table, my chest seized when I spotted Abram sitting at the head. Next to him were Charlie on the left, and, on his right, the woman Connie Will (from sledding this afternoon) had referred to as Kaitlyn. She'd said they made music together, and they were very, *very* close—whatever that meant. Just thinking about it made my heart beat faster and darkness edge into the corners of my vision.

Indulging myself for a long moment, I let myself devour the image of Abram, tucking it away later for quiet moments, because he was smiling. Sure, he wasn't smiling at me, but that didn't matter. Seeing him happy, smiling, no matter the reason, did wonderful things to my heart. For some reason, his smile made me think of delicious ice cream—rocky road—in a cookie cone, a delectable, decadent, rare treat, best when savored, licked . . .

"Mona! I saved you a seat."

Abram looked up at the sound of Allyn calling my name and our gazes collided, a crash of cymbals between my ears paired with a buzzing, static feedback loop. His smile fell precipitously, but he didn't look away. Peripherally, I was aware of she-called-Kaitlyn turning to look, obviously checking to see what or who had darkened his mood.

Swallowing around another knot, I tore my eyes from his and turned to my friend. Allyn was now waving from her spot at the other head of the table, literally the farthest spot from Abram she could've selected.

I took my place next to her with a *thank you,* and then turned to reintroduce myself to the person I didn't remember meeting at my right and the people across from me.

Once introductions had been made and what I considered appropriate polite chit-chat commenced, I forced myself to take a bite of food. I hadn't been able to eat much since we'd arrived, and I knew lack of sustenance was one of the reasons I didn't feel quite myself now.

"Did you have fun today?" Allyn asked, sounding optimistic.

I gave her a smile that I hoped communicated my gratitude and my remorse. "I'm sorry I haven't been an attentive host."

She covered my hand, not seeming to notice when I flinched. "Oh no, don't apologize. Don't worry about me." Her greenish-blue eyes widened, and she shook her head. "I just want to make sure you're okay. After what you told me—about you and the Captain—if I were you, I would be camped out in my room until the week was over."

We'd decided on *the Captain* for Abram's code name, mostly because of me mistakenly calling him Ahab while he and I had shared the house in Chicago.

"I'm okay," I said automatically.

Try being honest for once.

I frowned, then rubbed my forehead with stiff fingers, Abram's words from earlier still chanting between my ears. "Actually, it's not okay. I'm not okay. I don't understand myself. I can't figure out why I still feel so strongly about a person I knew years ago, and only for one week, and with whom a future is impossible."

"It sounded like an intense week."

"It was intense, kinda. And it wasn't. I mean, we didn't even kiss. Part of me wonders, if I hadn't lied to him, if I didn't feel so guilty, would I still be holding on? Thinking about him all the time? Maybe it's just guilt I'm feeling, and not—"

"Infatuation?"

I was actually thinking more along the lines of love *given the fact that this madness has persisted for over two years, but—*

"Sure, we'll call it infatuation. Maybe I'm infatuated with him because I feel like I owe him? Because I lied?"

"I don't know about that, Mona. If you were going to be infatuated with someone, the Captain is an excellent candidate. I've listened to Redburn's songs on repeat for months now. They're the current soundtrack to my life. And Abr—I mean, *the Captain* wrote all those songs. His words—" Allyn sighed, her gaze flickered to the far end of the table, and then back to me. "I'm a little in love with him, and we didn't spend a week together."

Ugh. She likely hadn't meant her statements to be a reminder of how impossible my feelings for Abram were, but that's what she'd done. No doubt, thousands of women —and men for that matter—had sentiments echoing Allyn's. I'd seen it with my parents, admiration to the point of worship based on their music. He was and always would be adored by many.

Musicians aren't monogamous. And I wanted a picket fence, with a lawn, and a rose garden, and children. We would bake pies in the shape of pi. Rock stars don't have rose gardens, and I definitely didn't want an open relationship. I'd seen my sister make this mistake.

And, even if Abram was monogamous, he doesn't want you.

"Maybe it's a combination of things." Allyn bumped my knee with hers beneath the table. "You feel guilty, yes. But maybe you feel so guilty because you truly do like him. And the guilt plus the like creates these super intense feelings that are hard to move past."

Stewing in discontent, I pushed my food around with my fork.

"You never told me," she started, and I felt her gaze on my profile. "What happened on Saturday? When the two of you talked? I want to give you space, and I don't wish to push you about it. But, do you want to discuss it?"

Although I'd told Allyn about my past with Abram—everything in Chicago, how I'd internet-stalked him for a year after, how he'd given me the cold shoulder in the funicular structure after she went inside with Leo, my plan to tell him the truth about impersonating Lisa, etcetera—I hadn't yet filled her in on the outcome of my conversation with Abram the morning after we'd arrived.

"I . . ." I struggled to recall the incident while also forming coherent words. I couldn't.

My first instinct—when Abram and I were in the study on Saturday, and he'd told his side of our twisted story— had been to say sorry. To bleed my apologies all over the place. To rend them from my lips and my hands and my guts and my heart. But as we'd looked at each other, seeing each other for the very first time, I knew with absolute certainty that he didn't want a gushing apology or excuses.

Gushing, pleading apologies and attempts at justification would've made him angrier, more distant, more certain in his disdain and resolute in his dislike. I was desperate to give him what he wanted, whatever that was. But I didn't know what he wanted, and I wondered if he even knew what he wanted.

I suspected not.

Therefore, I'd stood there and listened, doing my best to *not* explain. I hoped that if I gave him space, then he might give me time later.

And on that note, I dropped my fork and fit my hand in the pocket of my snoga pants, where I'd placed the letter. Feeling it there calmed me, and that was good because simply thinking about what Abram had said, how he'd looked at me, made me feel like crying again. I was so tired of crying. I'd just spent two days hiding in my room with the silence, crying, and I wasn't even a crier!

I didn't want to cry anymore.

Allyn gave me a sympathetic look, squeezing my hand harder. "Should I have stayed with you? This afternoon? I saw you and Abram talking, I didn't know what to do. I mean, he looks intimidating in all the band's photos, and he's bigger and scarier in real life, but even though I love him for his music, I will break his nose—no questions asked—if you wanted me to."

"No, no." I laughed at the image of sweet Allyn breaking Abram's nose, even though it was a weird thing to find funny. Maybe I laughed because I appreciated the distraction the image conjured.

It's not that Allyn wasn't capable of it—she totally was, especially if she caught him off-guard—it's just that she was one of those peace-loving sorts, always trying to mediate, see both sides of every issue, and negotiate a cease-fire.

"It was okay. We were fine. Relative to our last interaction, today was fine."

Try being honest for once.

"It *was* fine," I repeated, frowning at Abram's voice in my head arguing the point. Given where we'd ended things in the study on Saturday, our interaction this afternoon felt almost miraculous.

For no reason whatsoever, I found myself glancing down the table, spying on him. He was speaking to the Kaitlyn woman. Their heads were together. They smiled at each other. They looked comfortable and cozy. I felt my stomach tense like I might be sick.

My attention lingered on her for too long, but I couldn't help it. She wasn't particularly pretty—her lips were an unusual shape, her eyebrows thick, black, too pronounced, her eyes a drab shade of gray, and she had a noticeable gap between her two front teeth—but she, taken all together, was strikingly beautiful, and the sight filled me with restive fury.

Her beauty should've been irrelevant. What did it matter if Abram was laughing and smiling with this woman? What did it matter if her rejoining laughter made me want to singe her eyebrows from her face using a hot poker? I wouldn't actually do it. It didn't matter. *It had no mass.*

But somehow, her striking beauty didn't feel irrelevant. It did have mass, and matter, and weight.

Are they dating?

My stomach twisted tighter, hurt.

Do they have an open relationship? Like my parents? Maybe they're just lovers. He probably has several.

"Are you sure you don't want to talk about your conversation with him on Saturday?" Allyn's question yanked me out of my destructive, pointless musings, and I faced her again.

"No, honestly. But I think maybe I should. How about tonight? After dinner."

She nodded. "Sure. We'll have wine."

"Maybe not wine." I didn't need a wine-haze clouding my judgment with potentially hot pokers nearby. "How about tea?"

"Oh, yes. I will make you my winter tea. I should make some for Leo too." She gave me a shy smile and asked reluctantly, "Speaking of, how is Leo?"

I tried not to grin at the way her voice pitched higher at his name.

Yes, Leo was a musician, but he wasn't like all the others. I knew his heart and he craved monogamy. He craved finding that special someone. He was the exception that proved the rule, but he'd made the mistake of only dating musicians . . . *so far.*

Plans. Lots of plans. *Allyn and Leo will marry in the summer, on a vineyard, and I'll be the maid of honor. The table numbers will all be prime numbers, because I'll be planning the wedding.*

Allyn narrowed her eyes, leaning away. "Why are you looking at me like that?"

"Like what?" I mimicked the singsong quality to her voice. "Like, *You and Leo sitting in a tree, K-I-N-E-T-I-C energy?*"

She blushed, making me happy, and her lips twisted to the side, clearly fighting a smile. "I was just asking if he was okay. He seemed really sick."

"He is. You should go take care of him."

"Mona."

"He would love it."

"Mona."

"Give him a sponge bath."

"MONA!"

"What?" I laughed, delighted with the direction and escalation of my teasing.

Allyn cleared her throat and leaned forward, asking primly, "What happened with Charlie?"

"Charlie?" I sat straighter, blinking at the sudden subject change, and glancing back down the table to Charlie.

"Yes. Charlie. He seemed very friendly before we went sledding. I saw you two talking at the top of the hill, right before we all went back inside. What was that about?"

Unfortunately, instead of looking at Charlie, my gaze was drawn to Abram and Kaitlyn again. They were still talking. And laughing. And looking cozy.

Thank goodness Allyn was here to distract me, otherwise I would've spent half of dinner trying not to spy on Abram and Kaitlyn, and the other half spying on Abram and Kaitlyn.

Mortifyingly, Kaitlyn glanced up at just that moment. She caught me staring.

I glanced away quickly, fighting against the embarrassment heating my face and telling myself not to look again.

No. I want to look. I want to see him.

Then she'll see you.

Does it matter?

I couldn't decide.

"Mona?" Allyn prompted.

"Hmm?" I picked up my fork and knife and cut into the tenderloin on my plate, determined to eat more food.

"Did something bad happen with Charlie?"

I shook my head, shoveling steak, polenta with mushrooms, and the rocket, spinach, goat cheese, and cranberry salad into my mouth. Under normal circumstances, I probably would've requested a second serving. But not tonight. Tonight, even mushrooms tasted like unflavored tapioca pudding. *Mush.*

I felt Allyn's eyes on me. I also felt someone else's eyes on me, and I suspected they belonged to she-called-Kaitlyn.

"Hey, you ladies want anything to drink? I'm making cocktails." Bruce—the guy sitting across from me and next to Allyn—leaned forward and glanced between us. "If I may say so, I make an excellent manhattan."

"No thanks," Allyn answered for both of us. "I'm making winter tea later, so cocktails now would be too much, I think."

"Suit yourself," he said, giving her a smile, me a single nod, and stood from the table, taking his plate with him. I decided, even though I didn't know Bruce, I liked him. Anyone who cleared their own plate from the table without being asked was worthy of my respect.

"I like Bruce," Allyn said, watching him go. "Maybe tomorrow I'll take him up on his offer to make me a cocktail. This is the third time he's asked, and he's always so nice about it. I've never had a manhattan."

"Hey now," I said around my last bite of polenta, "what about my poor brother?"

Allyn laughed, giving me a look like she thought I was weird. "I don't like Bruce *that way.* I—" Realizing what she'd just said, Allyn covered her mouth with her hand and stared at me with big eyes.

JACKPOT!

Pointing at her, I shook my head. "No take-backs."

Her hand dropped, she crossed her arms. "Fine. Fine. Now you know the truth. Leo is a cutie pie and I just want to wrap him up in rice paper and eat him up like an egg roll."

"Weird and gross. Nevertheless, I approve." I'd had similar thoughts about Abram, but instead he was ice cream in a cookie cone.

Grinning, finished with my food, and feeling better than I had in days, of course I glanced down the table again and all the good feelings were chased away.

Kaitlyn was shaking her head at something Abram had said and she hit him lightly on the shoulder. He threw his head back, laughing with abandon, his hands over his chest.

Stop looking.

She'll see you and know you're a weirdo. Is that what you want?

Does it matter? He hates you. Look now, because you'll never be this close to him again.

I still couldn't decide, and I still hadn't decided when she caught me spying. Again. But this time? I didn't glance away.

Try being honest for once.

I held her gaze and allowed myself to just be jealous. I'd never been jealous before, but I knew in my bones that's what this horrible feeling was. I felt it oozing out of me, jealousy-radiation coming from my pores and eyes, and then the weirdest thing happened.

Kaitlyn blinked. And then she smiled.

CHAPTER 10
CIRCUITS AND BIOELECTRICITY

Mona

She smiled.

Smiled. At me.

And not a mean-person smile, or a villain smile, or even a knowing smile.

It looked genuine, friendly, and—infuriatingly and adorably—cute due to the big gap between her teeth. The next thing I knew, she'd stood from her seat and walked down the length of the table, her eyes never leaving mine. And that's when I got a good look at Abram's Kaitlyn. That's when I regretted eating all my dinner because my stomach now hurt. That's when I wanted to rage against the unfairness of life.

Ladies and gents, this Kaitlyn person was a bombshell. Her boobs were ridiculous, and her waist was ridiculous, and her hips were ridiculous, a comic book rendering come to life. She was Betty Boop with longer hair and an intelligent spark in her eye.

If she were Abram's girlfriend or soon-to-be girlfriend, or one of his lovers, I foresaw a lot of jealousy-fueled snow angels in my future.

"Hi. I'm Kaitlyn Parker." She put her hand in front of me, like she expected me to take it.

I did, giving her a perfunctory shake. "Hello. I'm Mona DaVinci."

Her grin widened and she glanced at the empty seat next to Allyn. "Do you mind if I sit?"

I glanced at Allyn, hoping to see a frown of disdain. But instead of an expression that mirrored mine, Allyn grinned at me, and then turned her sunny smile to Kaitlyn.

"Yes. Come sit down. You and Mona should be friends."

WHAT!?

Now I glared at my *former* friend Allyn, the traitor, and she returned my scowl with a look of innocent confusion. But it was too late, this Kaitlyn person was already on the move, claiming the vacant seat. My fingers closed around the handle of my fork for no reason and I held it under the table. I wasn't going to stab her with it. I wasn't.

I wasn't.

Don't look at me with those judgy eyes!

"Sorry if my hand was sweaty," Kaitlyn said, smiling at us both with her adorable smile. "I'm really nervous. I've wanted to meet you for a while. Can I just say, I really appreciated the testimony you gave in front of Congress this last summer. I was glued to my TV. I feel like what you did made a difference, you seem to have swayed public opinion, and I hope it means things will start moving in the right direction."

I blinked at her, feeling inadequate and tongue-tied and jealous. SO JEALOUS. But rather than continue to scowl, especially since she was being so nice, I worked to keep my face emotionless. This was no easy task considering the direction of my thoughts.

They probably kiss. All the time. They've probably kissed today.

Stop it! You don't even know if they're dating.

Are you kidding? I would date her in a heartbeat. She's stunning and her voice reminds me of how honey tastes.

I blinked, sitting up straighter . . . *where did that thought come from?*

Given all this, I was having trouble pulling a response out of my brain that was anything close to situationally appropriate. I absolutely could not say anything like, *Did you kiss Abram today? How long have you two been together? Does he talk about me? Are you two getting married?*

On that pleasant note, my eyes lowered to her self-professed sweaty hands and that's when I saw it. A ring. But not just any ring. A beautiful, tasteful, HUGE light-blue sapphire engagement ring.

"So, it has come to this," I murmured unthinkingly.

"Pardon me?" The obvious confusion in Kaitlyn's voice forced my eyes back to hers.

"Uh, I mean—" *And thus, I die.* "Um, congratulations." . . . *on your engagement to the man I'm obsessed with. And then the wolves came.* She blinked at me, still confused. I indicated with my chin to her ring finger. "That's a gorgeous engagement ring. A sapphire?" *In this economy?*

"Oh! Thank you." She smiled down at the ring, her eyes turning hazy. But instead of lifting it for me to look at—which is what most women, in my experience, seemed to do—she pulled it closer to herself, like it was precious. "It's an aquamarine."

I nodded, my voice coming out weak as I said with a light chuckle, "As the prophesy foretold." Because I was a dork and I didn't know how to *speak people.* Specifically, I didn't know how to speak to the person who was going to marry Abram. *My Abram.*

MINE!

A surge of possessiveness, such that I was unable to breathe or focus for a few seconds, held me in its grip. It choked me, I was dizzy with it, and I regretted not taking that Bruce guy up on his offer of cocktails. That'll teach me to turn down cocktails.

I was only half paying attention when, with a dreamy quality to her voice, Allyn said, "It's so lovely. Aquamarine is a unique choice for an engagement ring, what made you pick it?"

"There's a reason, but it'll sound cheesy." Kaitlyn grinned at Allyn, and then at me.

"Cheesy? What? No! Pshaw!" I forced a grin along with cheerfulness into my voice, but there must've been something wrong with my face because Allyn's smile fell, her eyes widened, and she was looking at me like my head had been replaced with the genitalia of an animal.

Because, let's face it, genitalia—all genitalia, no matter the animal—range from distressing to disturbing to horrifying. Human vaginas look like sea creatures that slurp their food—and probably regurgitate half of it—and penises are startling, no matter the situation. If someone made a horror movie entitled, *Dick Pics* and just showed various dick pics? It would be the scariest, most distressing movie ever made.

The *only* species that does reproductive systems visually right are angiosperms (flowering plants). When you're smelling a flower, you're basically smelling a dick. Let that sink in.

"Uh . . ." Kaitlyn blinked at me, her smile wavering, her expression also wavering between perplexed and terrified at my expression.

What could I do? Usually, concealing my thoughts was my superpower, but Abram was my kryptonite. I couldn't hide my emotions on the subject of his engagement. Randomly, selfishly, I didn't want to. And besides, hadn't that been Abram's parting shot/advice?

Try being honest for once.

Honestly, I was (honestly) insanely jealous. Honestly.

I was just about to break things down for her—something like, *Look, Kaitlyn. I'm INTENSELY in love-lust-infatuation with your fiancé. I know it would never work out between us, but I'd like to lock him away from the world in my basement, lick him nightly like an ice cream, and make him the second member of my two-person book club. I think maybe we can't be friends*—when Kaitlyn turned to Allyn.

She said, "The stone is the same color as my fiancé's eyes. See? Cheesy."

And I said, "Look, Kaitlyn—uh, what?" Now I blinked at her, sitting up straight. "What—what—what was that?"

Allyn shook her head at me. "Are you feeling okay?"

I ignored her, patting the table with my hand to get Kaitlyn's attention. "Focus. The eyes? The eyes. What did you say about your fiancé's eyes?"

"That they're—uh—aquamarine?" Her gaze grew shifty, and she looked to Allyn as though seeking help with the cumbersome task of dealing with the crazy person sitting across from her.

Which, since we're all being honest with ourselves, was a fair assessment.

I breathed out. So much air left my body. All the air left my body with that exhale. And I smiled, this time true and genuine. And I laughed.

"Well. That's the best thing I've ever heard. I mean, I think I've never heard anything better than that. Ever. In my whole life."

Kaitlyn nodded, continuing to regard me with cautious bewilderment. "Thank you."

"Kaitlyn's mom is Senator Parker," Allyn said, giving me a searching look. "And Kaitlyn is a composer. She wrote the musical accompaniment for Redburn's 'Hold A Grudge' as well as a few of their other big singles."

Oh!

Ah. I see!

Abram's huge hit, number one single. When Connie Will had said Kaitlyn and Abram made music together, she must've been referring to the literal meaning of "making music."

Kaitlyn and Allyn looked at me expectantly, like they were waiting for me to say or do something else ludicrous. But I wouldn't. Jealousy had dissolved into self-recrimination with a hefty side-dose of confusion. My reaction to Kaitlyn's hypothetical relationship had been strong—stronger than a gamma-ray burst, stronger than my sense of and commitment to rationality—and that was concerning.

Understatement!

Even so, I did my best to locate my composure before responding genuinely, "Congratulations, that's so, so exciting. So happy for you. And Abram. For the song."

"Mona hasn't heard 'Hold A Grudge' yet." Allyn turned to Kaitlyn, confiding in her like they were old friends. "But it's been my favorite since I heard it the first time. You are so talented."

"Thank you, you're very kind," Kaitlyn said to Allyn, sounding sincerely flattered, but then she shifted a penetrating gaze to me. "You haven't heard 'Hold A Grudge'?"

"Who hasn't?" This question came from Jenny Vee, one of the ladies we'd gone sledding with earlier in the day. She was about halfway down the table and her voice carried, probably because she was the lead singer in her band, Fin. "Who hasn't heard 'Hold A Grudge'?"

Yikes!

I shook my head, sitting straighter, patting the table again, this time to get Jenny Vee's attention. "Wait. Wait. No—"

But before I could say anything substantive, Kaitlyn talked over me, "Mona hasn't heard 'Hold A Grudge' yet. She hasn't heard Abram's song."

My now frantic gaze cut back to Kaitlyn. I found her head turned slightly, her stare scrutinizing as it moved over me. Clearly, she was having many thoughts.

Oh no.

"Abram!" This came from Nicole, the third member of Fin. "Where's Ruthie? Since Mona is the last person in the world who hasn't heard the song, you should play it for all of us, before you get tired of singing it on tour."

OH MY GOD!

The fingers holding the fork under the table began to shake, so I covered it with my other hand. A cold sheen of sweat broke out all over my skin. My heart heaved itself into my mouth.

Meanwhile, everyone present erupted in support of this idea, but their encouragement was drowned out by the sound of blood rushing between my ears. Meanwhile, Kaitlyn and I continued our staring contest, her eyes now slightly narrowed, that rascally spark still present, but so was something else. . . *suspicion.*

But then I flinched, closing my eyes, because I heard Abram's deep voice say, "If she wants to hear it, all she has to do is ask."

I swallowed a knot, or many knots, or perhaps all the knots as cheers followed this news. I felt everyone's eyes turn to me even though mine were closed. Beneath the table, I felt a hand close over mine and I didn't flinch this time. It gave me the wherewithal to open my eyes.

Allyn was looking at me, sympathy and worry in her gaze, and she gave me an encouraging smile, seeming to communicate, *You are a badass. I believe in you. You can get through this without making a spectacle of yourself. And then we will cuddle together while you cry.*

Perhaps that wasn't exactly what she sought to communicate, but I felt confident it was close enough.

The room was still a ruckus of excitement and armchair conversation about the likelihood of my never hearing the song.

"How is it possible someone hasn't heard 'Hold A Grudge'?"

"She must be the last person on earth to hear it."

"I hear it ten times a day, no lie."

"They have their instruments, right?"

"I don't think Charlie brought his drums."

"I hope he plays it. It would be cool to hear an acoustic version."

But one comment in particular carried above the others, reaching me from Abram's side of the table. "I guess rocket scientists don't get out much."

For some reason, the statement gave me the bravery I needed to lean forward and lock eyes with Abram, probably because the statement was true.

Try being honest for once.

I didn't get out much, I got out never. And when I got out, I came to Aspen where I could be snowed in and not go out. I'd been living in limbo, in line, waiting in the silence.

Abram, relaxing in his chair, glared at me. His elbows on the armrests, his fingers steepled in front of him. He looked at ease, like a king holding court, and completely indifferent to whatever I might say.

If he doesn't care, then it doesn't matter.

Clearing my throat, and squeezing Allyn's fingers, I lifted my voice above the hubbub and said calmly, "I'd like to hear your song, if you don't mind playing it for me."

* * *

I sat on the periphery of the main floor living room with Lila, slightly separating myself from the larger group on the other side so that, once the song was over, I could make a hasty getaway. Tomorrow, it would begin again, the turbulent rocket ride orbiting Abram. But as of right now, I'd had enough of turbulence, anguish, and making memories.

After Abram had agreed to my request with a nonchalant shrug and a neutral sounding, *sure*, the entire room fell into rapturous excitement, forgetting about me (to my relief). Well, everyone but Kaitlyn forgot about me. While the rest of her companions celebrated, she continued to examine me as though forming various and sundry theories behind her intelligent gray eyes.

Under the guise of helping Lila with the dishes, I quickly excused myself. Allyn followed and wrapped me in a hug once we reached the hallway, which I accepted, telling myself to enjoy the contact. It wasn't uncomfortable, I didn't hate it, and that felt like a win.

Once the hug was over, we helped Lila and Melvin with the dishes, and then Allyn sent me and Lila into the living room to scope out a seat. "I'll be right there, I just want to make the winter tea first. I feel like you're going to need it."

By the time Lila and I arrived, everything had been settled but Abram was nowhere in sight. Jenny Vee informed us that the members of Redburn would be playing "Hold A Grudge" for everyone. But first, Melvin was helping them bring up the drum set from the basement studio, which they were almost finished assembling.

It would be an unplugged, acoustic performance. Nicole Mac from Fin would play Abram's acoustic bass guitar so he could just sing, and everyone present had to agree not to film it or talk about it on social media. In fact, Ruthie went around and confiscated everyone's phones, including mine.

Not that it mattered. Reception up here was always spotty at best, which was why I hadn't called Lisa back to whisper-yell at her yet. Abram had told my sister that he loved me, and she never communicated that fact? UNACCEPTABLE!!

Never mind that you never gave her a chance, did you?

Go away, reason. *You can't sit here.*

"How are you doing?" Allyn handed me a mug from a tray of three, her eyes full of sympathy. I gave my friend a grateful smile, though it was of a small diameter.

"No, thank you." Lila shook her head when Allyn tried to hand her one of the mugs. "I'm not much of a tea person. But thank you, honey! Here, just leave the extra one right there on the coffee table, in case one of you wants another cup."

"Are you sure?" Allyn sat on my other side, warming her hands on her mug.

Lila stood to take the now empty tray. "I'm not much of a tea person, but I think I will have a glass of wine. Can I get either of you anything while I'm up?"

We both shook our heads, saying, "No, thank you," in unison.

Lila turned to leave, and I brought the tea to my nose, sniffing.

"Thank you for the tea." It smelled like peppermint and . . . I lifted an eyebrow at my friend. "Is that whiskey?"

"Yes. It's whiskey." She gave me a pointed look and leaned forward to whisper, "How are you? Are you okay? You were weird around Kaitlyn, and you've been really quiet since everyone pressured you into asking the Captain to play his song."

I shrugged, wanting to be honest, but honestly not knowing how I was feeling. Terrified? Anxious? Cold? Hot? Confused? *All of the above.*

The song title, "Hold A Grudge" had struck me as strangely familiar when Allyn told me about it a few days ago. If memory served, I'd said those exact words to Abram while we were in Chicago. But I'd quickly dismissed the notion that the song might've been about me. I couldn't contemplate it. How conceited would that make me? Thinking Abram had written a song about me, and that song was now number one on billboard charts everywhere.

So I'd said, *Get over yourself, Mona,* and then I had (gotten over myself) and ignored the lingering, nagging suspicion.

However, after Abram's harsh words in the study, I was now terrified to hear the song. Given everything he'd said, the chances of the song being about me—about us —felt more like fifty percent than zero percent. Did that make me conceited?

I had no idea.

These days, I felt like I didn't know much about anything.

Sniffing the tea again, I endeavored to clear my mind of these chaotic thoughts and just enjoy the marriage-aroma of whiskey and peppermint. I decided it was a superior combination of smells. Then I took a sip and tried not to cough.

Allyn's eyes widened, her sympathy for my emotional well-being replaced with concern for my physical. "Are you okay? Did I add too much whiskey?"

Swallowing tea and air and half of my tongue, I shook my head. "No. No, it's perfect." My voice was raspy. She looked unconvinced, so I took another sip—more of a gulp—and smiled. It still burned, but the second swallow had been considerably easier.

"Are you sure?"

"Yes. I'm sure. I feel . . . steadier already."

Her worried eyes conducted another pass of my face. "Let's talk about something else. I asked you earlier, about Charlie. He hasn't come up to you tonight. He backed off, huh?"

My gaze shifted to Charlie just as he lifted his blue eyes from where he was setting up the drum set. He sent me a small smile full of compassion and I lifted my chin, hoping to communicate a silent thanks. "Yes. He did. He's a nice guy, that Charlie."

"I saw you talking to him at the top of the hill while we were sledding, when it was just the two of you. The conversation seemed intense. What did you say?" she asked quietly.

I sighed, meeting her gaze. "He asked what I was doing later, so I told him what I thought—at the time—would probably be the truth."

"Which was what?"

"That I'd be in my room crying."

"What?" Allyn stopped herself just before taking a sip of her tea, which was good. From the way she'd said *what*, I suspected she would've spat tea all over me had she taken the drink.

"I told him I was hung up on someone who hated my guts, and rightfully so, because I'd lied and treated him horribly."

"Oh my." Allyn stared at me, a hand coming to her cheek. "What did he say?"

"He told me it couldn't be *that* bad, that he didn't think anyone could ever hate me. And thus, I told him more truth."

"Oh no." She shook her head, looking distressed.

"Oh yes. I told him I'd pretended to be my sister to keep her out of trouble—I didn't go into too many specifics there, since it's not really my story to tell—and the guy I fell for thought I was Lisa. By the way, this is really good. Is that just whiskey and peppermint tea? Or do I detect honey?" I took another gulp and licked my lips. "Maybe lemon?"

"Mona, you told Charlie all of that?" She sounded dismayed.

"Yes."

"Jeez." Her forehead fell to her fingers and she peered at me with obvious worry. "You didn't tell me about any of this until three days ago, and I'm your best friend. Why did you tell Charlie?"

Movement by the room's entrance drew my attention and I turned my head just in time to see Abram walk in. Almost immediately, his eyes came to my eyes, held for a protracted millisecond, and then he glanced away. Metaphorical swords of self-recrimination and want—so much *want*—speared me, sliced me from sternum to stomach, and I had to hold my breath for several full seconds, wait for the room to right itself, and the world beneath to resume spinning.

Please, please, please, don't let this song be about me.

"Mona, are you sure it was a good idea to tell Charlie?"

"No," I answered, more breath than words. "But I wanted to try being honest. . . for once."

"Okay." Abram called everyone's attention to him, which was unnecessary. As soon as he'd entered the room the energy shifted, changed, seemed to flow from him as a single source. He was the gamma-ray burst and we basked in his overwhelming magnificence.

Or maybe it was just me that felt that way.

Regardless, all eyes were already on Abram before he spoke. "Special thanks to Nicole for playing bass."

He gestured to her and she smiled widely, curtseying to the room as they clapped devotedly. Abram took his place in front of the other three musicians. He sat on a stool set a little apart from everyone else, and then—as though taking their cue from him—the other three sat on their stools.

"We're going to switch it up a little, try something we want to do on the tour." He seemed to be speaking to the other group, the larger assembly comprised mostly of musicians who sat closer to the makeshift stage. "It'll be slower, quieter. You can think of yourselves as our guinea pigs."

"Will we get carrots?" Bruce—the cocktail guy—asked, making a few people laugh.

"I'm not throwing you a carrot or a bone, if that's what you're asking." Abram's response made more people laugh, and harder.

I didn't laugh. My stomach hurt, so I went to drink more tea. Sadly, I found it was empty. Licking my lips, I set the empty cup down and picked up the new one on the table, the one Lila hadn't wanted, and took a gulp of the lukewarm mixture. It was still good, heartening, and I felt myself settle a little. But then, Charlie banged his drumsticks together to mark the beat. Suddenly, they were playing.

The intro.

Every muscle in my body tensed and Abram lifted his eyes to mine. Immediately, completely, utterly I was ensnared, caught. Him, the infinite dimensions of Abram, and all else seemed to fade into a void, even the music. I couldn't look away. I was trapped, so trapped.

And then he opened his mouth, and he sang,

"She falls, I catch her.
She fights, I let her go.
It starts, she stops it.
She has to know. She has to know.

I stand, I kneel, I sit, I chase,
But it's like we haven't moved.
We're still here, with the past between us,
This place
I hate
I'm left to wonder what I haven't proved.

This is new, for me and for you.
Nothing you say, nothing you do
Can make me hold a grudge.

Whispers in the dark, stealing touches, holding my breath.
Replaying moments between us, wanting more, taking less
But when she asked for forgiveness so sweetly,
She has to know, she must know,
I became hers completely.

This is new, for me and for you.
Nothing you say, nothing you do
Can make me hold a grudge.

You tell me to go,
But you have to know, you must know,
If this is a mistake, I'm making it
And if this is my chance, I'm taking it.
I can't regret
Never giving up on you

Nothing you can do
Nothing you can do
Will make me hold a grudge
I'll never give up on you.

CHAPTER 11
HEAT AND HEAT TRANSFER METHODS

I t wasn't how I wanted her to hear the song, in a room full of people, anger between us.

When I wrote "Hold A Grudge," when we were in Chicago, that night she told me to hold a grudge and I stayed up all night writing poetry about her, I'd imagined myself playing it just for Lisa. I had this fantasy scenario where she'd be the first one to hear it set to music.

But now, staring into *Mona's* captivated and captivating eyes, sharing the finishing note, the last reverberations of Ruthie and Nicole's guitars softly fading, I decided this scenario wasn't so bad either.

We weren't alone. She hadn't been the first to hear the words she'd inspired. But at least, for Mona's first time hearing our song—and I could no longer deny that it was *our* song—I'd been able to sing it directly to her. The words were the same as the version on the radio, but I'd arranged the music in a new way.

She'd inspired that too.

I was still angry. And yet, earlier in the evening, when she'd walked into the dining room and our eyes met, the moment confirmed a nagging suspicion: it wasn't revenge I wanted from Mona DaVinci, it was honesty.

Maybe she wasn't the woman I'd fallen for so foolishly and completely. Maybe she was. I had no idea. She gave me nothing. Her wall built of lies remained a barrier between us, yes. But it was Mona's continued *restraint* and detachment that formed the true impassible chasm.

The applause caught me off guard, stirring me from my reflections. Taking one more look at Mona, as she was now—her lovely eyes misty, unguarded, vulnerable, lips parted, expression open and guileless—and knowing I'd held her attention rapt, I'd had the entirety of her whole being and focus for the span of our song, it felt like enough.

The group assembled, pressed forward, and their rousing appreciation for the new version demanded my attention. Nearly everyone was on their feet, making noise, and I accepted their praise with gratitude. I was grateful the song, and subsequent singles, had done well. I was grateful for the chance to tour with musicians I respected. But that's not why I wrote music.

As soon as the snow cleared enough for me to leave, I decided I would leave. Whatever I'd hoped to find here, whatever I'd hoped to take from Mona DaVinci, or receive from her, it was never going to happen more or truer than this moment. I felt certain that now, right now, was the most honest she'd been in a while, maybe ever. Perhaps she wasn't capable of more, and—if so—that was heartbreaking.

But it's enough.

Decision made, I gathered a true deep breath, my first one in days, and I turned toward Kaitlyn. She'd stood as soon as the clapping started and gave me a smile that was more smirk than grin as she approached.

"You changed the key. D minor."

"I did." I nodded, my gaze flickering to Mona. She was also standing, her hand fiddling with the waistband of her pants. She pulled out an envelope, her eyes were on it, and she unfolded it with what looked like great care.

"Interesting. *Very* interesting," Kaitlyn said, and I shifted my attention back to my friend, she was stroking her chin, looking in Mona's direction. "I have theories."

More people moved around us, telling me how much they enjoyed the new variation, asking Ruthie if she could convince me to play another song, delaying me from responding to Kaitlyn. I turned more fully away from Mona and answered Jenny Vee's questions about our tour dates, Charlie's concerns about the new arrangement, and Bruce's insistent suggestion that he make me a mixed drink, to which I answered no thank you.

Deflecting requests to play additional songs from the album, I mumbled to Kaitlyn when I got a chance, "You always have theories."

"But these theories are provable, and being snowed in is as close to actions occurring in a vacuum as possible outside of a laboratory setting, which is exciting," she whispered on a rush. "I miss doing 'the science.' Ah! Mona! Hello."

My muscles tensed with the knowledge that she was close, but I kept my back firmly to her.

I'd assumed she'd already left. Asking me to play the song hadn't been her idea, she'd been pressured, that was perfectly clear. But we'd had a moment. A meaningful moment. Our beginning and our end had been hers to define, this had been mine. Poetic justice, a way to force closure, whatever it was, that's what I wanted. Now we were done, now I needed it to be over.

"Hi, Kaitlyn." Mona's voice moved over me like a crashing wave, and I closed my eyes for a beat, frustrated because the sound made me hungry.

"Did you like the song?" Kaitlyn asked, tugging on my bicep to turn me around. "If so, which part did you like best? I like the part where he becomes hers completely."

Shooting my writing partner a look I hoped conveyed the full force of my murderous thoughts, I readied myself for the next several minutes and gave Mona my eyes, but *just* my eyes.

Or, that was the idea. But then, I saw she was still misty, her expression still open, vulnerable with raw hope. I had to swallow. The impact of this image, the sight of this woman as she was now, it struck out, overwhelmed.

"Can I talk to you?" She tilted her head toward the uninhabited part of the large room, her typically staid voice laced with optimism.

I nodded, mesmerized by this version of her and mutely followed where Mona led, walking where she walked, stopping when she stopped. She faced me, lifting her chin, her gaze conducting a cherishing sweep of my features. I held my breath.

"Here," she said, giving me a smile that looked brave and nervous. "This is for you."

I blinked at her, confused. And then I glanced down. There, extended between us, was the envelope she'd been unfolding with care.

"What's this?"

"It's a letter."

A letter.

And just like that, all hope, all anticipation, all madness ended. The spell was broken.

"Another letter?" I sounded bitter. I was bitter. The last thing I needed from Mona was another of her letters. The last one might not have been a memo, but it read like one. I didn't want any more fucking correspondence with a salutation of *Regards* or *Best wishes.*

"Uh, yes. But this one is much—much—wait. What are you doing? Wait."

Crumpling the envelope in a fist, I walked to the fireplace.

"Abram." She was right behind me, at my shoulder, her voice edged with panic. "Wait, what—what—oh my God!"

I tossed it in the fireplace, toward the very back where it was hottest, and turned back to her, prepared to tell her where she could shove her memos. The words expired on my tongue.

Her eyes were big, so big, and her mouth gaped wide open with shock, hurt, and what looked like unfiltered rage. I allowed the sight of her obvious pain and fury to slip past my barrier of indifference, because it surprised me so damn much. Mona was looking at me like I'd tossed *her* into the fire instead of her letter.

Jaw working, up and down, big movements, like she might yell at me. Like she might growl and scream at me instead of the snow this time. But she didn't.

At length, she expelled a short breath, I caught the scent of whiskey and peppermint. Using an extremely low voice that sounded barely controlled, she said, "You, Abram Harris—"

"Fletcher," I corrected, noting that she'd slurred *Harris.*

"*Harris,* preside over a kingdom of lies! You call me a liar, but *you* are the liar." The word *lies* was also slurred. *Is she drunk?*

"I'm the liar?" My glare flickered over her, the bright red flush to her cheeks. She wasn't drunk, she was angry and Mona DaVinci looked scorching hot like this. Eyes flashing, a bundle of restless, ferocious energy. I hated that my body took notice, coming to life, the beat of my pulse encouraging me to do unwise things.

"Yes. Your song? 'Hold a Grudge'? It's a lie. You're a siren selling lies to hapless hopeful sailors, where I am the seaman!"

I stepped closer, shoving my face in hers, heedless of the crowd of people on the other side of the room whose voices I could no longer hear.

"Mona," I said, matching her volume, but lowering my voice an octave, "You can keep your fucking memos. I don't want them."

"It wasn't a *memo*!" she said between clenched teeth, her eyes moving from mine to my mouth.

"Oh, it didn't have a subject line?" I taunted, enjoying this, her reaction, far too much, because—*damn*— at least it was honest.

"It. Was. A. Letter."

"I'm sure you can write another one. But you should know, I'll just burn that one too."

Mona looked like she was choking for a moment, and she lifted both of her hands. I thought she might grab me. I thought maybe she might shake me.

Instead, she pointed at the fire. "You, Abram of rotating last names, are a gamma-ray burst! But not in the strong, blinding and beautiful way. Yes, you're that. But I'm talking about the destructive, horrible, chaotic side of a GRB. And you don't deserve honesty, because when it's given to you, you throw it in a fire. You *destroy* it. Here is my official *I bid you good day, sir.*" She turned, slurring *sir*, and released a low, wrathful low growl.

Without thinking, completely on instinct, I reached for her.

"Mona—"

"I say, good day!" she whisper-yelled, yanking her arm out of my grip while doing an absurd little twirling thing with her hand, almost like a salute, and marched away.

Watching her go, my hands on my hips, I slid my teeth to the side, fire in my lungs. Instead of leaving, which was what I'd expected her to do, she rejoined her friend on the couch, Allyn, who was shooting poison darts of dislike in my direction. *What else is new?*

Mona forcefully sat, grabbed her cup of tea, and glared at me over the rim as she downed the rest of its contents. At her side, Allyn made a short sound of protest, her gaze moving between Mona and the cup, and then to me.

Her friend's eyes were wide, rimmed with worry, maybe a hint of panic. Studying the women, I wrestled with curiosity and the impulse to chase after Mona, and to drag her caveman-style into my room. To ignore the pain and the wrong and seize this rare moment of honesty. She was angry? Fine. Let's take our aggression out on each other in ways that didn't hurt, ways that felt good.

Why couldn't *that* be our last moment?

What would it be like to have Mona DaVinci? I winced slightly at the thought, flashes of carnal imagery an assault. It wasn't the first time I wondered. Would she be cold? Rationing her touches? Requiring that I ration mine? Would she tease me? Make me suffer for her? Would she let me tease her?

These were dangerous thoughts to be having with her sitting there, within reach, still throwing knives with her eyes.

Finished with her tea, she reached for Allyn's. Plucking it from her friend's hand, she spilled a little on the couch. Either she didn't notice or she didn't care, because in the next second she was downing that cup too.

The action felt spiteful, like she hoped to punish me by drinking tea, and I couldn't stop the grim smile at her absurdity. I didn't care if she drank tea. I didn't want to care about her. I'd chased her before, I wasn't chasing her again. She was finished with me? Fine.

"Fine," I said quietly, to no one, but knew at once she'd read my lips. Her gaze narrowed, darker, angrier.

So. Fucking. Hot.

Shaking my head at myself, I exhaled a breath that felt like an inferno leaving my lungs and ripped my eyes from hers. Turning aimlessly in the other direction, I commanded my feet to carry me to the far side of the room.

That's when I finally looked up and remembered we had an audience. Kaitlyn—and presumably everyone else—was looking at me like I was someone different, openly gaping, her eyebrows high on her forehead.

We hadn't been yelling. In fact, Mona had whispered every one of her angry words, but our body language must've been unmistakable. Kaitlyn's attention drifted past me to where Mona and Allyn sat, and a small, mischievous hint of a smile tugged her mouth to one side. She started forward, her eyes cutting to mine, her smile growing.

"I'll be right back," she said gleefully.

"Kaitlyn." I made sure my voice sounded like a warning.

She walked faster. "Or I won't be right back."

Gritting my teeth, suppressing a string of curses, I shook my head and sighed. *Great.* Just great. I couldn't wait for Leo to hear about this.

A hand on my shoulder had me glancing over, following the line of the arm to Bruce's sober expression. "Hey, man. Want that drink now?" He held out a glass. "You look like you need it."

I nodded. I took it. I drank it. "Thanks."

"You bet." He gave me a commiserating non-smile. "Let me make you another."

* * *

I didn't have another drink.

I left.

I needed to cool off, and I knew myself. There wouldn't be any *cooling off* with Mona around. Grabbing the snow shovel in the mudroom and not bothering with my coat, I cleared the slate path between the house and the ski lift house. There wasn't much snow, just a few inches, but it was enough.

Calmer, I returned to the house and removed my boots in the mudroom. I was cold, my teeth were chattering, but my skin still felt hot, too tight. Pulling off my wet sweater, I hung it in the closet and took the stairs up to the main floor, intent on my room and the lyric notebook waiting on my desk.

I had no lines, no clear direction, yet something had to give. Even recording the bursts of nonsense running through my mind would be a relief. I'd just climbed the top stair when I heard a loud groan, like a sound of defeat, coming from the living room, followed by sloppy laughter.

"Oh no! Bruce! You're out." Mona's voice stopped me.

It and the words spoken were very un-Mona like.

Swerving from my original destination, I walked slowly toward the sounds, straining my ears for clues as to what I might see when I arrived. More groaning, glasses clinking, laughter, nothing that would have prepared me for what I found.

I absorbed several things at once: only five people remained in the room, playing cards were scattered all over the coffee table and floor, an empty bottle of vodka and a half-finished bottle of whiskey also sat on the coffee table along with too many shot glasses to count, Charlie and Bruce were in nothing but boxers, Jenny Vee and Allyn in their bras and underwear, and Mona.

Mona.

Mona wore the most—wool socks, yoga pants, plain black bra—but her shirt and sweater were gone.

"Hey ya Abram, old buddy, old pal." Allyn lifted her arm and waved, noticing me first, but promptly lowered it, like it was too heavy. She wasn't giving me the stare down. This was probably because she was intoxicated.

"What the hell is going on?" My eyes moved up and down Mona's body, and everything was right and wrong. Right because I missed seeing her skin. I missed her body. I ached for it. But wrong because no part of her body was mine to miss.

"She wanted to play strip poker," Charlie said, pointing to Mona like they were kids and he didn't want to take the blame for getting caught. But the arm he raised offset his balance and he fell over. Laughing. *Drunk.*

Glaring at my drummer—promising, *I'll take care of you later*—I moved my eyes around the gathered circle.

"Where is everyone?"

"They went to bed after the shots." Bruce held his chin propped up with his palm. His chin kept falling off of it. "Armatures." *Drunk.*

"You mean amateurs?" I asked, incredulous, taking several more steps into the room. I'd only known Bruce for a short while, but I'd never seen him drink past his limit.

"That's what I said. Armchairs." He nodded at himself.

Exhaling a short, disbelieving breath, I studied Mona. She was looking at me, swallowing, a glimmer of nerves in the reflexive movement.

But she'd also lifted her chin to squint at me. "You want to play? Bruce is about to lose his shorts, and then he's out."

I flinched, because every word with an *s* sound had been slurred. Gaping, I looked at her, really looked at *her* and not the skin she'd exposed. She was drunk. Maybe not as gone as the others, but she was close. Sitting upright, she swayed. And the eye squint? She wasn't giving me back my glare, she was trying to keep her eyes focused and open.

"Holy shit," I said, shocked. *Shook.*

"No, we're playing five card stud." Mona shook her head, but then kept shaking it, like she couldn't stop once she'd started.

Closing the rest of the distance and kneeling in front of her, I hesitated for a second, and then I placed my hands on either side of her face to stop the motion. "Stop shaking your head. Where is your shirt?" Not waiting for her to answer, I dropped my hands to the cushion on either side of her thighs and glanced around the room. I didn't see it.

"Where *is* your shirt?" Allyn asked, also searching, yawning. "Didn't you throw it outside?"

"That's right. I did."

I looked back at Mona. Her eyes were on me, hazy but hot, moving over my face.

Lifting her fingers, she smoothed them over my beard, up to my temples, tugging lightly at my hair, sending arcing waves of sensation down my spine. Just as unexpectedly, she leaned closer, her lips inches from mine, and whispered, "I want to lick you like an ice cream and eat the fuck out of your cookie cone."

I started, staring, feeling like I'd just been shocked. A throb of energy pressed against my skin, electrifying. Mona's hair was down, pulled out of its braid, and slipped over her shoulders as she straightened, brushing the tops of her breasts. Gorgeous.

But then, holding my eyes, her fingers still tugging at my hair, she wobbled inelegantly. And I remembered.

She.

Is.

Drunk.

Clearing my throat, I ripped my eyes from hers, catching her wrists and removing her hands. I gulped air, released an unsteady breath, and made up my mind.

"Come on." I stood, not looking at her because doing so would've been unwise. Very unwise. *Extremely unwise.* "Let's get you all to bed." Then, before Mona could react or protest, I turned to Jenny Vee. "Do you know where your clothes are?"

CHAPTER 12
OSCILLATORY MOTION AND WAVES

After figuring out just how drunk everyone was—very, but not dangerously—I woke up Melvin and Lila. We put Jenny, Bruce, and Charlie to bed first since they were on the main level.

I asked Melvin to help me get Allyn and Mona upstairs, and Lila to put bottles of water and pain relievers next to each drunk person's bed. I also wanted her to double-check on the ladies, make sure they were all still sleeping alone, and lock everyone's doors—whether they'd been drunk or not—*just to be safe*.

They were both nice about it, which I appreciated.

Giving up on finding anyone's clothes, we wrapped Mona and Allyn in blankets. Melvin carried Allyn up under Lila's supervision, and then they both came downstairs to clean the living room.

"Take Mona up." Melvin pushed me away from the coffee table, where I was stacking shot glasses.

"I can take myself up," she said from where she was crawling around on the ground, trying to pick up playing cards. I had to tear my eyes away from the image of Mona on all fours in just yoga pants and a bra, the blanket we'd wrapped around her forgotten somewhere on the floor.

"Sorry about the mess, Melvin." Mona stretched, her back arching as she reached for a king of hearts.

Kill me now.

"It's fine, sweetie." But then to me, in a quieter voice, he said, "Take her upstairs and we'll clean this."

I gritted my teeth, shook my head, working to sweep away my frustrations and focus. It wasn't just the state of the living room, it was the drunk people who'd made the mess. Mona bending over to reach for playing cards under the table, ass in the air, wasn't helping either.

"Let me get the glasses." My voice was rough. I cleared my throat.

"Don't worry about it." Lila gave me a warm smile as she walked in. "This is honestly no big deal. You should see this place after Kimberly and Troy's parties."

"Who?"

"Exotica and DJ Tang," Melvin answered. "One time we had to replace all the carpets after they left." He amazed me by chuckling, like it was a fond memory. "That was *disgusting.* This is nothing."

I decided I didn't want to know.

"Please." Lila came to me, taking the glasses out of my hands. "You take Mona up. I've already put water and a pain reliever by her bed, and I'll be up to check on her once we get this under control."

When I hesitated, she laughed at me. "Really, it's our job. How would you like it if I tried to record your songs or write your music? Now go."

Heaving a sigh, I reluctantly passed the glasses over to her and nodded, feeling shitty about it. This wasn't how I was raised. It felt wrong to leave them with a mess they hadn't made.

Once I found Mona's blanket, I dropped it over her back and scooped her up.

"Hey. Whoa, wait. Why is the room moving?"

Ignoring her, I turned for the stairs.

She was quiet until we were halfway up the first flight. "What are you doing?"

"Carrying you."

"Why?"

"Because you're drunk and there are many stairs."

"Oh yeah. I guess I am. It's a good thing you're so strong, and have this amazing body, otherwise we'd be shoulder hoofing it."

"Shoulder hoofing?"

"You know, I put my arm around your shoulder, you put your arm around my waist, we try to make it work, but someone is going to fall down the stairs." Her eyes were concentrated on the side of my face. In my peripheral vision I saw her lick her lips. "What do you think about my ice cream idea?"

I stiffened, shoving away thoughts about *that,* and had the wherewithal to change the subject. "Why did you take off your shirt before your socks?"

"My feet are cold. Also, I never told you, I love the way you smell."

My steps faltered. I blinked, flexed my jaw.

"I'm sorry." She sounded sorry. "Did that make you feel uncomfortable? If I'm making you feel uncomfortable, I'll be quiet."

"No. That didn't make me feel uncomfortable."

"Good. Because I need to talk to someone about it, and I've never mentioned it to anyone—the way you smell—because it's not something people talk about, but I always want to talk about it."

"You always want to talk about how I smell?" I paused at the landing, lifting her higher and readjusting my hold before taking the next flight.

"Yes. Sometimes, when people ask how I'm doing, I want to say: better if I could sniff Abram."

I rolled my lips between my teeth to keep from laughing, keeping my eyes forward.

She wasn't finished. "It's like how chocolate, the really good kind, melts in your mouth. That's what you do, smelling you, does to my body. I am chocolate, and your smell is the mouth in this analogy, and I just . . . melt."

I swallowed. "Maybe you shouldn't talk."

"Why? Am I making you uncomfort—"

"No. But you might not remember any of this tomorrow. I don't want you to say anything you'll regret."

"Well, I will remember it tomorrow, so you don't have to worry about that. And, as for regretting it, I don't think I will. I mean, I'll be cosmically embarrassed, *that's for sure*, but I'll take it like a woman."

"Take it like a woman?" I smiled at the way she'd modified the *take it like a man* turn of phrase.

"Yes. I'll accept responsibility, apologize, be sensitive to your concerns, work to modify my behavior in the future, and suggest we try to find a way forward with minimal awkwardness. You know, take it like a woman."

"What would *take it like a man* look like? In comparison?"

She shrugged, sighed, rested her head against my shoulder. "I don't know. I guess, pretend it didn't happen? Put on a brave face? Take you out for a beer?"

I scoffed. "That's what you think of men?"

"What's wrong with beer and bravery? I think very highly of men. Well, of some men. I think highly of you, and Poe, and Leo, and Dr. Goldblatt, and Melvin, and you."

"You already said me."

"But I think very highly of you, so you deserve to be mentioned twice." She paused, seemed to be contemplating the issue, and then asked, "Do you want me to take you out for a beer instead? Because I can take it like a man. We could arm wrestle! FEATS OF STRENGTH!" She shoved an arm into the air.

"Shh. Mona, people are asleep." Again, I pressed my lips together so I wouldn't laugh.

"Sorry. And sorry if I'm making you uncomfortable."

We reached her floor. I could've set her down and sent her on her way, watched her from a distance to make sure she made it into her room.

Instead, I carried her. I was enjoying her honesty, even if it was fueled by whiskey. "You're not going to say anything that will make me feel uncomfortable, so you don't need to worry about that."

"I bet I can."

"I doubt it." I used her feet to push her door open and stepped inside.

"How much do you want to bet?"

"Nothing, because I'll win." Glancing around at the huge space, I decided setting her on the window seat made the most sense. It wasn't as close as the bed. But it wasn't *the bed.*

"Oh. I'm thinking of something right now and it'll take you from zero to the speed of light on the uncomfortable Richter scale."

"The Richter scale measures earthquakes." I paused in front of the window seat, looking at her in my arms, liking her there, the weight of her, and didn't put her down like I should.

"Yes." She smiled up at me, sighing languidly like she was relaxed and enjoying herself. "But this will rock your world so much, it'll send it hurtling through space *at the speed of light.*"

Smirking, I shook my head once. "Nope." It was time to go.

"Do you want to hear it?" she whispered, like the question was the beginning of a secret.

"I do, very much," I whispered in return, bending to place her on the window seat and preparing to leave. "But I don't want you to say anything that you'll regret when you're sober, and I don't think—"

"I loved you."

I stopped.

I'd just set her down, was currently crouching in front of her, poised to straighten, stand, and leave, and I stopped. I couldn't move.

I looked at her and I wondered how she could believe the words she was saying even as I grasped at them, willing them to be true. My heart shoved itself against my ribcage and the suddenness and pain of it made anything other than complete stillness impossible.

She smiled at me, her gaze tracing my features like she was memorizing them, or remembering them. "See?" she asked softly, lightly, the word a little slurred. "Now you're uncomfortable. I win. Yay."

I shook my head, dazed. When I managed that small movement, I tried speaking. "I'm not uncomfortable." My voice was hoarse.

"You are." Her golden-brown eyes inspected me, still cloudy with liquor, but no less intelligent or assessing. "And if that didn't make you uncomfortable, this definitely will. I'm still in love with you. I'm so very, very much in love with you."

I closed my eyes, wondering if this was a dream. Maybe I was the one who was drunk. Maybe she wasn't here, and this was me wishing.

"Either I'm in love with you, or I'm in love with my guilty feelings. I don't know. I've never been in love, so I have no baseline comparison. Six days! All it took was six days. Nothing about this makes sense. But it has to be love, because how else could it survive two-years of no contact? How else!? It won't go away. And I win. I win at this game." Her confused agony compelled my eyes open.

Did she know what she was saying? What was love to Mona DaVinci? What did it look like? Did it open and stretch in front of her like a cavern, with no way around, no alternate course? Just through and through, into the unknown, the absence of it only coming into focus when the breadth of it was revealed?

"I love you," she repeated, firmer this time, but somehow awkward. "And that—if me saying so makes you uncomfortable, I understand." *Still drunk*, her clumsiness of speech a sobering reminder. *She's still drunk, and these are just words absent evidence or action.*

I shook my head, scattering the hope. Thinking about this now, taking her seriously was foolishness. I'd been a fool for her once. If I could help it, I wanted to avoid being a fool for her again . . . *if I can help it.*

With another deep inhale, I stood. "I'm still not uncomfortable."

She lifted her hands as though to reach for me. "Okay, how about if I said—"

"Mona." I caught her fingers before they made contact, pressed them between my palms. "Please stop talking. You are drunk and you don't want to say these things."

"I do." She stood and I backed away, letting her go and bringing my hands to my hips. Her voice was still a whisper as she insisted, "I do want to say them, I want to shout them. They burn me up with the heat of plasma, molecules of transcendent temperatures boiling inside me."

"Mona—"

"You burned that letter, and I guess I know why. You thought it was going to be more tepid and polite requests. But it wasn't. It was the opposite of polite." It was unclear whether she was speaking to me or herself. She pushed her fingers into her hair, gripping her scalp. "It was all these hot feelings. I'm suffocating, choking on air, because it doesn't smell like you. And now that you're here, I'm still choking, because you hate me, and I don't blame you. I hate me too."

These are still just words.

I took another step away, stalling, needing to clear my throat before speaking. "I don't . . . I don't hate you."

"You should." She glanced up suddenly, her stare glassy but fierce. "You should."

"And you should go to sleep." I lifted my hands, palms out, hoping she would surrender. Talking about this now, while she was drunk, was pointless.

It was pointless, and yet my heart beat frantically, like it was true.

Her eyes followed me as I took another step backward, and then another, this new, unexpected connection between us stretching, the growing distance necessary, but painful. Would it last the night? *God, I hope so.* But I wasn't counting on it.

Mona watched my shuffling movements toward the door. I told myself the deliberateness of my steps was about being gentle, easing out of her room. It wasn't about reluctance, or hungrily admiring her disheveled beauty.

But before I made it fully to the door, she darted forward. "Since I've already said too much, and you're not uncomfortable, can I ask for one more thing? And if it makes you feel uncomfortable, then—"

"Mona." I stopped, clearing my throat, my attention tracing the lines of her body in the low light. I needed to leave. *Now.* "Nothing you say, or ask, will make me feel uncomfortable. Ever."

"But you don't want me to talk." She was fidgety, her stare searching.

"Only because I realize you're drunk, and this isn't you."

"This is me." Pressing her lips together, her forehead wrinkled, like she was suddenly in deep thought. "Or, rather, a part of me I don't like."

That struck me, and before I could stop myself, I asked, "Why?"

"You mean, why don't I like the part of myself that vocalized my problems and angst, and then vomited them all over the person I've victimized? You know, I think it's probably because it makes me a total—"

"You didn't victimize me."

"I did. And if you don't think I did, then I should make you a diagram and write you a proof that proves it. I could, you know."

I didn't want to smile at her threat, but I couldn't help myself. "You're overthinking this."

"Yeah, probably. But that doesn't make it any less true. Why don't you hate me? After everything I've done, you should hate me. I hate that you don't hate me."

Swallowing several versions of the truth, I settled on, "You're very difficult to hate."

"But my actions demand it." She hit the palm of one hand with the fist of the other. "If the world knew what I did to you, if social media caught wind of it, I'd be crucified and they'd be right. And then they'd call you weak for not hating me and wanting me crucified."

"Maybe that's more telling of the problem with social media than with you."

"What? How does that make any sense?"

"Love doesn't have to make sense," I said, thoughtlessly, stupidly, foolishly.

Dammit.

She let out a little breath, like I'd surprised her, and then she swayed. Instinctively, I reached for her, holding her steady. Mona's eyes grew hazier as her gaze moved between mine.

I couldn't think. I worked to shut down the part of myself that was anticipating the morning, and the new confrontation, and everything that—hopefully honesty—would come after. She was drunk. I had questions and I had a list of demands, but those would have to wait, when her confessions weren't tainted by intoxication.

And then her attention dropped to my lips, and she made no attempt to disguise what she was thinking, what she wanted.

Oh hell no.

I wasn't doing this now. Nope. *Is that what this was about?*

I let her go. I stepped away and crossed my arms, clearing my throat of the choking anger.

Fuck her.

I should have fucking known better. I should've fucking *known!*

She wanted me, that much was painfully clear. What had she said earlier? *I want to lick you like an ice cream and eat the fuck out of your cookie cone. . .*

Fine. Alright. Okay. I got it. I understood what was going on here. If she'd proposed sex while sober, before pretending to have feelings for me, at least it would've been honest. But this? Telling me she loved me, she still loved me, and then this? Why had I expected more?

Just leave the room.

I didn't. Like a fool, I didn't.

"You wanted something?" I asked, working to keep my voice free of bitterness. I knew, beyond a shadow of a doubt, what she would ask for. But perversely, I needed to hear her say it. This would be my escape hatch from hope. This would be all the proof I needed.

"I did?" Her gaze was still on my mouth, and she'd leaned forward as I stepped away.

I did not reach out to steady her this time. "You did. You said you wanted to ask for one more thing?"

She blinked, her eyes completely losing focus for a second. She frowned her cute frown and my temper spiked. After tonight, I never wanted to see her again.

"Oh, yes!" She tried to snap, failed, and waved an index finger through the air. "I remember."

"What is it?"

"I'm only asking you this because you've claimed it's impossible for me to make you feel uncomfortable at present, and when I'm drunk, I'm selfish and have no filter."

"Mona, what is it?"

"Can I listen to your heart?"

I started, blinked, confused. "What?"

"Can I listen to your heartbeat? Obviously, it's fine to say no. It's incredibly fine. In fact, I expect you to say no. But, since I've already confessed to plasma levels of being hot for you, and still in love with you, I figured I might as well make it a trifecta of selfishness and mortification—a trifecta squared? An exponential trifecta? A tripod of shame? I don't know, fill in the blank—and just ask for what I really want."

What? "You want to . . . listen to my heartbeat? That's what you want?"

"I do." She nodded, her eyes earnest and eager. "I want to lie next to you." She redirected her focus to the left side of my chest, and she swallowed, gazing at the spot with naked longing. "I want to place my ear right there." Mona lifted her hand and stopped just short of touching me, her breath coming faster, making her voice softer.

"And I want to listen to your heart. I want it more than I want to breathe, if I'm being honest. Which I am being honest, as we've established."

I stared at her.

I stared at her, and stared at her, and stared at her. I stared at her and I worked to keep my balance, because the floor and the earth moved beneath my feet. The cavern opened and stretched in front of me. I stared at her and I was afraid, because I knew.

My whole life, from this point forward, I would be a fool for Mona DaVinci.

CHAPTER 13
ATOMIC PHYSICS

"Have you slept?"

Startled, my head snapped up and my neck protested, stars flaring in my vision. I winced.

"You haven't slept." Kaitlyn sounded concerned, and when she came into focus, she looked concerned. "Are you okay?"

"Fine," I said, my voice gravelly, and tested my neck. Slowly, I stretched it. Once I was sure it was fine, I stood from the desk, blinked at the room, at the sunlight filtering in through the windows, and I stretched my back.

Kaitlyn wore a frown of intense concern and I realized at once what was bothering her. "I only had the one drink, okay? I didn't get drunk."

My friend's forehead cleared of concern, obviously she'd been thinking I was hungover. "Sorry. I don't mean to hover. But when you left and didn't say where you were going . . ."

"No need to say sorry." I twisted at the waist, waving away her apology. Kaitlyn had seen the tail end of my downward spiral. She'd been a major source of support for me, helping me climb out of the hole I'd dug for myself. She'd seen me drunk. And when I was drunk, I was disorderly. "Do you know what time it is?"

Her attention moved between me and the open notebook on the desk. "It's just past seven. Have you been up all night writing?"

I nodded, yawning, abruptly feeling the lack of sleep. "I had no idea."

"What?"

"That it was so late."

"You mean early." She smiled, but then it vanished, and she leaned a shoulder against the doorframe. "I'm glad you've been writing."

"Me too." I glanced at the lines I'd been working on for the last hour. Or maybe for the last several hours.

"Abram," she said softly, but there was a note of concern. "Do you want to talk about it?"

"Talk about what?"

"About Mona."

Without looking up, I sighed, and then I laughed, shaking my head. "I don't know where to start."

I felt her eyes move over me before she asked, "Start with when you met her originally. Did Leo introduce you?"

I continued shaking my head. "No. Leo didn't—doesn't—know."

How Leo would react to the news of Mona and me—our past or the potential for our future—was anyone's guess. I'd seen him lose his shit with an acquaintance of ours who'd said that Lisa was "fucking hot." But then I'd also witnessed yesterday how he'd worried about Charlie's interest in Mona, like Charlie was the one who needed protecting.

The sound of the door closing brought my eyes up and I watched Kaitlyn march over to one of the leather armchairs by the window. She motioned to the other. "Please. Sit."

I lifted an eyebrow at her. "Is this a therapy session?"

"No," she said, sitting. "It's a *I'm worried about my friend, Abram* session."

"Really?" I shoved my hands in my pockets, taking my time, strolling to the chair across from her. "Shouldn't you be happy? I'm writing again."

"When was the last time you wrote like this? Staying up all night?" she asked, challenge in her voice. "Was it, perhaps, the last time you saw Mona?"

That earned her a frown. "How did you . . ."

"You said to me once that your ex had messed with your head, made you think you were crazy. But you'd never been more inspired—or written so much in such a short time—than when you had been with her."

"It's not what you think. Mona didn't—" I huffed, pulling a hand through my hair and scratching the crown of my head. I'd taken it out of its binding at some point last night and now it was driving me crazy, getting in my face. "She didn't do anything—"

"You forget, I was there."

That stopped me. We stared at each other.

Her gray eyes looked silver this morning, in the sunlight reflecting off the snow. "I was there to see the after, the crater left by meteor-Mona, if you will."

My jaw working, I slid my teeth to the side and finally sat in the chair across from her. "You seemed to like her just fine last night."

"Oh, I do like her. I still like her, as an impressive person, as a genius astrophysicist, a public figure. But is she good enough for my friend?" Kaitlyn shrugged.

I'd never spoken to *anyone* about Mona other than Kaitlyn. Even then, I'd spoken in generalities. I'd never given her a name, or told our story.

"Fine. I'll allow it. What do you want to say? You think I should steer clear?"

She shrugged again, this time with her shoulders, her face, and her hands folded in her lap. "I honestly have no idea. If you want my advice, you're going to have to tell me the whole story, not just vague bits and pieces."

I chuckled. "You know, just now, you sounded like how Senator Parker does when she's confronting a bullshitter."

"Well, she is my mom. And you are a bullshitter. Therefore . . ." Again, she shrugged with her shoulders, her face, and her hands, but she also grinned. "Come on, Abram. Talk about it. Talk about Mona. Tell me the whole story."

I hesitated, glancing over her head, stalling. Being the object of an elaborate prank, or hoax, during which I'd made a total fool of myself, wasn't something I wanted to advertise. That said, I knew Kaitlyn's concern for me came from a genuine place, which was probably why it was so disarming.

"For the record, I think she's completely crazy."

My eyes cut back to her and I frowned. "She's not—"

"Crazy about you. Crazy weird. All the good crazies."

"You think she's crazy about me?"

"Yes. After you burned whatever was in that envelope last night and left, I sat with her and Allyn. She kept looking for you. And during dinner, when I walked over, I think she'd assumed you and I were together and engaged."

"She did?"

"Yes. The woman was practically seething with jealousy." Kaitlyn widened her eyes, as though still struck by the memory. "I thought she might do me harm."

I was tired, so it didn't occur to me to hide my smile.

"Really, Abram? That pleases you?"

Now I tried to hide my smile. "No. . ."

She lifted her eyebrows.

"Okay, yes. Obviously not the part about her wanting to harm you. But, the fact that she was jealous? I'm not going to lie, I like that."

Kaitlyn tried to look disgusted, but the effect was ruined by the amused curve of her mouth. "It doesn't matter what I think of Mona. What do you think of Mona?"

Studying my friend, I realized what she said wasn't precisely true. "It does matter what you think of Mona, actually."

"What? Why?"

"Because I trust you. I trust your judgment."

Her lips twisted to the side as she studied me in return. "I'll love her just as long as she treats you like the prince you are and recognizes that your heart requires no tenderizing. It's tender enough."

Shaking my head at my friend, I rolled my eyes.

"Don't you roll your eyes at me. You write *poetry* for barnacle's sake. You can't tell me you're not tender. You're like veal, or foie gras, but without the sketchy ethics issues." She leaned forward. "What's the deal? How did you two meet? How did this thing start between you?"

I gathered a deep breath, debating where to start. "It's a convoluted story, and long."

She grinned. "My favorite kind."

* * *

I knew this already, but Kaitlyn Parker was a great listener. She'd asked a few questions when she needed clarification, but otherwise just listened, her features showing only interest.

However, I'd underestimated how much her excellent listening skills would compel me to reveal, which turned out to be everything. Or maybe it was the lack of sleep. Whatever it was, I held nothing back. Once I started, I couldn't stop.

"Wait. What?" Kaitlyn's forehead wrinkled and she gave her head a subtle shake, like she was certain she'd heard me wrong. "She wanted to listen to your heartbeat?"

"Yes."

Her gaze thoughtful, she shifted her eyes to some spot over my shoulder. "That was —is—not what I expected her to ask for."

"Me neither." I leaned forward, resting my elbows on my knees.

My friend's attention returned to me, sharpened, and she nudged my foot with hers. "What happened next?"

I sighed. "I left."

Kaitlyn stared at me, waiting.

I gave her a tight smile.

"You left."

"Yes."

"Without a word?"

"Yes."

Her gray eyes moved between mine, searching. "And then you wrote poetry all night."

"Yes." I studied my left hand, flexing it.

"And now here we are."

"Yep."

She nudged my foot again, more of a kick this time. "What's the plan?"

I exhaled a light laugh, my face falling to my hands. "You know I'm not big on plans. I have no idea."

We were quiet for a minute, separating to steep in our own thoughts. Except, I had no thoughts left. They'd all been transcribed to the pages of the notebook still laying on the desk behind me.

But I was tired.

"You want advice?" she asked, interrupting the silence.

I nodded, rubbing my eyes. "Yes."

"Okay, I'll give you my advice. But first, I need to . . ."

I peeked at her from between my fingers. Her eyes were on me and felt sharp, intent.

"What? What is it?" I let my hands drop and leaned back in the chair.

She inhaled a deep breath, giving me the sense she was preparing herself for an unpleasant task. "But first, I need to provide context to my advice."

"Okay. Shoot."

"You told me once that, before your ex, you used to write lyrics, poetry all the time. It was a compulsion for you, yes?" Her words were blunt, direct, and I expected no less.

I nodded, setting my elbow on the arm of the chair and placing my thumb under my chin, my fingers along the side of my face.

"But then, you broke up."

"As I explained, we didn't break up, and I shouldn't have called her my ex. I didn't have another word, a better word for what—it wasn't—we weren't—"

"Whatever. You obviously thought of her that way at the time, clearly. The issue is the writing. Before her, you wrote. With her, you wrote lyrics that eventually became four hit singles and an album that is on its way to triple platinum. After her, you didn't write. Not at all."

She paused here, as though to let her words sink in, and then she added, "Yes, you revised what you'd already written. You also got yourself arrested a few times, before we met, and made some questionable life choices. As time heals all wounds, those days post meteor-Mona are behind you. But now—" Kaitlyn gestured to the notebook on the desk, punctuating the movement with a truncated head nod. "You're writing again."

"Yes." I was too tired to figure out where she was going with this.

"That's great. I know you missed it. I know it's been a struggle. And I hope all these new poems become number one hits, or I hope they never get turned into songs at all. Whatever you want, whatever makes *you* happy. But . . ." She trailed off again.

Her gaze seemed to waver, grow uncertain, like she already regretted the next words out of her mouth.

"What? Just say it."

"But what happens when this week ends?"

Gnawing my bottom lip, I met my friend's somber stare, her words echoing in the room, in my head, and in my heart. *What happens when this week ends?*

I was no longer looking at Kaitlyn. I was looking beyond her, into the future, something I rarely—if ever—did.

"Abram," she started gently, "it's Tuesday. We're leaving early Thursday."

Thursday.

Shit. I broke into a cold sweat.

It's too soon. We need more time.

A thought occurred to me. "If the snow lets us." I brought her back into focus. "We might be trapped here for several more days."

"Look outside." Kaitlyn shook her head, her gaze full of sympathy. "The sun is shining. Check the forecast. No snow for the next four days. If Melvin can plow the mountain road, Martin and the rest of the furloughed significant others trapped in Aspen will probably arrive today. We're leaving Thursday, at o'dark thirty. I think the plane leaves at six. You *have* to be in Seattle for Friday's concert. You and the band have been practicing for *months*, you're at the top of your game, the show is sold out."

I made no sign of agreement, even though she was telling me things I already knew to be true. Also true, Mona had finally been honest and I couldn't leave. Not now. Not yet.

She sighed. It was also full of sympathy. "Now that I've provided context, do you still want my advice?"

Staring at her, undecided, I continued gnawing on my lip.

"Abram?"

"If you're going to tell me to let her go, or that it's impossible, or that the timing makes it impossible, then no. I don't want your advice."

Her lips curved and her eyes warmed from stark to compassionate. "That's not my advice."

"Fine." My knee started to bounce. "Let's hear it."

"I think . . ." Kaitlyn sucked in another deep breath, held it.

I wished she'd stop trailing off her sentences. "Yes?"

"I think you should kiss her."

I blinked, confused, and waited for my friend to continue. When she didn't, I felt my face morph into a scowl. "That's it? That's your advice?"

"Yep."

"That's the plan?"

"Yep. I think that's the plan."

I rubbed my eyes tiredly. "I stayed up another hour, telling you everything, spilling my guts, for you to tell me to do something I haven't been able to stop thinking about in over two years?"

"Exactly."

Laughing weakly, I shook my head. "What? Why exactly?"

"My God, man. Kiss the woman. Kiss her senseless. Kiss her and mean it." She waited, looking at me like she expected me to have an ah-ha moment. When I didn't, she made a short sound of exasperation, adding, "You haven't kissed her and it's been over *two years*. Make a plan to kiss her, and then *do it*."

Maybe I was missing the obvious here, maybe I was too tired to be having this conversation. Whatever. I was so tired, my eyelids felt like paper.

"Never mind." God, I was tired. "I just want to sleep."

"Yes. You sleep. And then, you wake up, you find Mona, and you kiss her."

"Sure." I stood, swayed, and then stumbled to the bed.

"I'm serious, Abram. Follow the plan." Kaitlyn bumped me out of the way with her hip, pulling down my covers.

"I don't understand you, Kaitlyn. You're nuts, and your plan makes no sense."

"Flatterer. Here, let me tuck you in."

I practically fell into the bed. "I can tuck myself in."

"Do you need any warm milk? Should I leave a night-light on?" she fussed, sounding alarmingly like my mother.

"Go away."

"Fine. I will. Do you mind if I take your notebook? Check out the new lyrics?"

I hesitated.

"You know what? Never mind." Kaitlyn held up her hands, palms out. "I'll look later. But in the meantime, kiss her. Kiss the hell out of her. And then we'll move on to the next phase of the plan."

"Which is?" I asked around a yawn, dizzy, sleep irresistible.

"Securing an official clarification of expectations, with roles defined."

"Expectations? Roles?"

"Exclusive. Not exclusive. Boyfriend. Girlfriend."

I liked the sound of exclusive. Maybe her plan wasn't so bad.

"And then," she said, her words punctuated by the sound of the curtain being drawn, "phase three is—"

"How many phases are there?"

"The phases continue until you reach your goal, whatever that is." Her hands were back, and I felt her righting my covers, tucking me in with perfunctory movements. "Hopefully, the goal is happiness, for both of you."

Without thinking, I muttered, "I think I'd die happy if we made it to phase one."

Kaitlyn chuckled. It sounded farther away. I couldn't say for certain because I was already half asleep.

"Then you better draw up a will before phase four."

"What's that?" My words sounded slurred even to me.

"I'll give you a hint, it rhymes with trucking."

My eyes flew open and I groaned, glaring at my friend where she stood holding the doorknob. "Great. Thanks. Now I'll never sleep."

"And rucking. And mucking. And sucking. Actually, it involves sucking—"

I threw a pillow at her.

CHAPTER 14
FLUID STATICS

Mona

Upon waking, the first thought that popped into my head—the instant my eyes opened—was, *Did I tell Abram last night that I wanted to lick him like an ice cream and eat the fuck out of his cookie cone?*

Or did I dream that?

Staring at the ceiling, studying the vaulted beams of exposed wood, I realized that, no. It hadn't been a dream. And furthermore, the statement hadn't been the most shocking proposal I'd made.

Am I making you uncomfortable?

I loved you.

I'm still in love with you.

I'm so very, very much in love with you.

I'm suffocating, choking on air, because it doesn't smell like you.

Can I listen to your heart?

A rush of mortification—so intense it made me groan out loud—crashed over me. It was a nuclear blast of embarrassment, befitting the gamma-ray burst that was Abram (Harris) Fletcher's death grip on my psyche. Because I could, I ducked under my covers and squeezed my eyes shut, wishing for the wolves to actually come.

I don't know how long I stayed like that, replaying the evening over and over. The moment our eyes met across the dining room, how awful I'd been to Kaitlyn, how beautiful and meaningful his song had been, how brave and foolish it made me —*stupid bravery!*—and how he'd thrown the letter I'd been carrying around for years into the fire.

Into. The. *Fire.*

I'd been so angry. So angry. The closest I'd ever come to that kind of anger was the last time I'd been with Abram, when he'd forfeited the pool race in Chicago. I didn't get angry like that. I simmered, but I never struck out.

But Abram makes me SO ANGRY!

The rest of the evening—the drunken game of strip poker, Abram finding me, the disappointment in his eyes, my sloppy confessions, him leaving without a word after I'd asked to listen to his heart, me crying myself to sleep—made me sad.

Therefore, instead, I focused on the lost letter. I was tired of being sad, so sad. Between madness and sadness, I chose the former.

Tossing the mess of covers from my body, I stood and frowned at my surroundings. He'd been here, in this room, just a few hours ago. When my heart fluttered a little, achy, wistful, I told it to cease and desist. It didn't listen.

Therefore, I left. I rushed through getting dressed, intent on spending some quality cold time in the snow, and marched out of my room. I'd have to see him at some point, hopefully when I was too tired and numb to care that I'd revealed too much of myself, or that he'd repaid my honesty by burning my love letter, and later walking out on me.

I was almost to the mudroom when I heard Leo call my name. "Wait, Mona! Wait."

I turned toward the sound of his voice, and then twisted completely around when I saw he was jogging toward me.

"Leo. Should you be out of bed?" I felt his forehead as soon as he reached my location. He was still warm. "Why are you up?"

"I need to talk to you." His words and his expression were grim.

"Okay. Fine. Let's go back to your room."

Frowning his stern frown, his gaze traveled over me. "Where are you going?"

"Outside. For a walk."

"Here, I'll come down with you."

"You're not going outside, you still have a fever."

He gave me a half-eyeroll. "We can talk in the mudroom."

"Okay. If you're sure you—"

Leo nodded and brusquely walked past, leading the way.

I chalked his abruptness up to still being sick, so when we reached the lower room and he closed the door, I was surprised to see how annoyed he was.

"You know," he started, gritting his teeth, and then exhaled a humorless laugh. "Abram is a good friend of mine. I mean, a really good friend. He and I have been through a lot, and he's always been there for me."

Standing straighter, I flinched back a little, realizing that Leo must've heard what happened last night after Abram played his song. No one had asked me what was going on with Abram, not even Kaitlyn when she came over and sat with Allyn and I on the couch. She'd talked about satellite internet delivery and a non-profit organization that helped provide internet connectivity to underserved areas. You know, the normal stuff women talk about when they hang out.

I'd been thankful for her company and for her lack of Abram-related questions at the time, grateful for the distraction, even though I hadn't been totally distracted. I kept looking for Abram, hoping he'd come back, and unsure of what I would do if or when he did.

Everyone else kept their distance until Nicole suggested shots. Then, we'd all become fast friends. There was no greater bonding agent between strangers than alcohol.

But now I could see, even though Leo's friends hadn't asked me about Abram, they'd obviously asked him.

And Leo was pissed.

"Leo, I—"

"I get it, okay? I should've checked with you first before bringing everyone here. I knew you were going to be here, and I shouldn't have invited a house party."

"It's fine. It's honestly not a big deal. The house is huge, and I—"

"Why Abram?" he demanded, stone-jawed, his feverish eyes flinty. "Why him? He's my oldest friend."

I reared back. "Did—did Abram say something—"

"No. He's asleep. I haven't talked to him yet. Kaitlyn said he was up all night, so he's sleeping now. God, Mona." Leo growled, shaking his head and turning away to pace. "I really don't want to lose his friendship, okay? Can you understand that?"

"Yes. Of course." My instinct was to soothe my brother, especially since he was sick, but I didn't understand precisely why he was so agitated, so I tried again for clarification. "I don't understand why you would lose Abram as a friend, or why you think you're going to. Because we argued?"

I didn't add that, if Abram hadn't walked away from our nutty family already, after what Lisa and I had done, I couldn't fathom what would make him walk away now.

"Because!" He rushed forward, his eyes wide. "He's into you, okay? I heard what happened, and it was obvious to everyone—and everyone was there to see it."

That had me searching the walls around him, hunting for the puzzle pieces I was missing. "Wait. Wait a minute. You're worried about losing Abram as a friend because you think he's 'into' me?"

"Yes," he spat, gritting his teeth, his hands coming to his waist. "Could you avoid him? Please? Just until I get a chance to smooth things over? Or . . . just don't make it worse."

I stared at my brother, my stomach lifting quickly to my throat, and then dropping slowly to my feet with the comprehension of what he was saying.

A short, stunned exhale pushed itself out of my chest. It tasted sour, and I said and thought at the same time, "I can't believe you."

Leo glanced at me, his eyebrows suspending high on his forehead. "What? What can't you believe? That I don't want to lose a good friend?"

"How good of a friend could he possibly be if he let this—supposed feelings for me —impact your friendship?"

Gritting his teeth, he angled his chin, his eyelids drooping to administer a glare.

I wasn't finished. "If Allyn liked you, and you didn't like her—"

He perked up. "You think Allyn likes me?"

"Shut it, Leo. And listen," I whispered harshly.

He snapped his mouth closed and rocked back on his heels, looking feverish and exhausted and confused. And since he looked feverish and exhausted, I worked to harness my temper at his confusion.

I'd walked down here on a cloud of anger, clutching it close, because the only other option had been sorrow. Had I made mistakes with Abram? Yes. Did Leo deserve to lose his friend because of my mistakes? No. Obviously not.

But, dammit. "I'm your sister," I whispered, less harsh, searching my brother's gaze for some spark of understanding. "I would never do anything to hurt you, or Lisa. Or Mom and Dad. I'm your family. I want that to mean something."

He swallowed with what looked like effort and sighed. "It does, Mona. But—" he stopped himself, shaking his head as though to clear it. "Abram isn't the first, okay?"

"What does that mean?"

"It means I lose friends whenever they meet you. They meet you. They fall fucking crazy stupid for you. You shoot them down. They don't want to know me." He didn't sound angry. In fact, he sounded calm-ish, reasonable. He made it all sound so reasonable, and like it was my fault. "I don't want to lose any more friends, okay? Friends are how you make it in this business. It's all about who you know."

My eyes stung. So did my nose. So did my heart, and I asked the first question that popped into my mind. "Would you rather lose a sister?"

Again, he rocked back like I'd surprised him. Again, he looked confused. He struggled. I could see he struggled to respond, and it occurred to me that, had he been well, without a fever, he probably wouldn't be saying or thinking any of this. The temptation to soothe him, to apologize, to promise to avoid Abram—if that's what Leo wanted—surfaced once more.

But the words wouldn't leave my mouth.

Don't be too smart. Don't admit you're smart. Don't think you're smart. Be brilliant. Make some mistakes. Give your opinion. Don't make any mistakes. Stop trying to be perfect. Don't talk so much. Talk more. Don't be too nice. Be nice. Smile. Don't smile so much. Act like a man. Act like a woman. Be assertive. Don't be emotional. Be sensitive. Not too assertive. Be nice to my friends. Don't lead them on. Let them down gently.

I was so tired of walking a tightrope, at work, here, with my family, with everyone. Enough. I'd had *enough.*

Turning from my brother, I pulled on my hat and opened the door leading outside. I shut it. I didn't look back.

* * *

Four hours in the snow, making snow angels, listening to silence, and staring at the sky was just the kind of numbness I'd needed. But now I was freezing my nipples off and needed to pee.

Trudging through the snow, debating what to do with the rest of my day, and deciding something hot was in order, I made it back to the house just after two in the afternoon. I left all my snow clothes in the mudroom closet, my gaze lingering on the sweater I recognized as the one Abram wore last night while he sang "Hold a Grudge."

I hadn't been prepared last night to face the music (pun intended), but I was ready now. Tired and resigned, I was prepared. In fact, I was at peak detachment (i.e. preparedness).

Finished stripping off my outer layer, I swung by the kitchen to grab a bite to eat, and then I climbed the stairs to my room. The basement had a saltwater pool and a hot tub, and both of those options sounded absolutely divine. The idea of a few laps followed by a warm soak sped my movements, and after changing and wrapping myself in a bathrobe, it was back down the stairs, to the basement, past the studio, and to the pool.

The pool was a simple rectangle, and the space in which it was located ran the entire length of the house. It was a long, narrow room that smelled like salt, chlorine, and water. With lounge chairs at one end, the pool and then the hot tub until about three-fourths of the way down, a little shed-type structure at the far end and that's it, every sound echoed.

The shed was set away from the wall and housed a bathroom. Why the original owners had opted for a shed instead of a built-in closet and bathroom, I had no idea. Maybe they wanted to give the illusion of being outside? The walls were painted light blue, like the sky, so that was a distinct possibility.

Leaving my bathrobe on a lounge chair, and after grabbing some goggles from the shed, I walked to the water's edge and dipped my toe in the water. The temperature wasn't particularly hot, I estimated close to 302 degrees Kelvin (84 Fahrenheit/29 Celsius for all the non-physics nerds in the room). But it felt wonderfully warm given how cold my body was after the snow.

Using the pool steps, I submerged myself, my bikini shorts, and my swim shirt, pushing my hair out of the way as I surfaced and wiping my eyes. I'd just turned my attention to the goggles when I heard the door to the pool room open. Glancing up from the water, I did a double take, and then my muscles spasmed. I dropped the goggles.

It was . . .

He was—

"Abram."

His deep brown eyes were on me and his shirt was nowhere and those seemed like the two most relevant facts at the moment. Yes, he wore a bathing suit. But his chest —*my God, his chest.*

What looked like a single tattoo covered one side of his torso—the left side—disappearing into his shorts, swirling over his shoulder and down the entirety of his arm. A full sleeve, gorgeous ocean waves in black and gray and vivid blue.

A small, stunned, panting breath escaped me, and I backed up a step. Tangentially, I realized my mouth was hanging open, my eyes were approaching circular, and it was a good thing I was in the pool because I might have been drooling. And his shoulders? HIS SHOULDERS??! No one was prepared for the reality of his shoulders, least of all me.

His gorgeousness felt like an attack. I felt *personally attacked*. He wasn't Hallmark handsome, he was Turkish TV show handsome.

WHAT IS EVEN HAPPENING?!

"Hey," he said, and my eyes cut to his.

He wore a small smile on his lips and in his eyes, and I snapped my mouth shut, swallowing the thirst. But there was so much thirst. So much. So. Much. I was in very real danger of choking on my thirst.

As Abram made it to the pool, walking down the steps and toward me in fluid, unhurried movements, I realized I was not prepared. I mean, I'd been prepared for talking to him, or hearing him talk while I listened thoughtfully, contritely, and apologized for my drunken honesty-vomit. If we'd come across each other in the hall, as an example, or taken our discussion to the study again, I would've been more prepared than an Eagle Scout.

But now?

No.

No.

It was impossible to be prepared because it was impossible to be mindful when one's brain is addled by metric tons of lust. My lust was so huge, so substantial and unwieldy, it probably had its own gravitational field.

The water pushed me, swirled as he approached, the sound of gentle, lapping waves echoing in the cavernous, relatively bare room. And when he was just a few short decimeters away, he stopped. And then he waited.

And then he asked, "Aren't you going to say hi?"

"Hi," I said, the greeting weak, because apparently his body made me a weak woman. *Gravitational lust was a weak force. Good to know.*

His smile widened, his eyes that familiar shade of amber I remembered from Chicago, sparkly and twinkly and hitting me right in the nostalgia amblagada (which was the lesser known, fictional counterpart to the medulla amblagada).

With one more look, he dunked himself under the water briefly, returning to a standing position, but now fully wet. He was so beautiful, it hurt. It hurt so bad.

This is the worst.

I had a nagging suspicion that he was doing this on purpose, that this was payback for the night in Chicago when I'd shown up to the pool wearing a string bikini. He'd looked like he wanted to strangle me. If that's what this was, I applauded him, because his payback plan was a raging success.

And if he'd felt even half as turned on as I felt now? He deserved a standing ovation.

I swallowed, telling my eyes not to look at the droplets rolling down his sculpted chest, or pooling at his sternum. He wiped his beard and eyes and lips, and returned his eyes to mine, like they belonged to me.

"What do you remember?" The question was softly spoken, and he was closer now.

I didn't remember that happening—him moving closer—which made me wonder how long I'd been staring at him, but I did manage to say, "Everything."

"Everything?" He lifted an eyebrow, studying me, his voice low.

"Yes."

"Are you sure?" With this question he drifted closer.

"Yes." I nodded, sobriety finally penetrating the lust fog, because I did remember. With the memory came embarrassment. "I'm sorry."

"You're sorry?"

"Yes."

"For what?"

"For making the mess in the living room. And for—uh—if what I said made you feel uncomfortable last night, I'm sorry."

He nodded slowly, his hands moving back and forth under the surface of the pool, like he was caressing the water. I was now jealous of the water.

"It didn't make me uncomfortable," he said at length, his tone deep and thoughtful, and then asked, "So you're not sorry for what you said."

"No. I'm not sorry for what I said," I responded immediately, telling the truth even though I could feel the heat of mortification climbing up my neck. "I take full responsibility for my actions and my words. I am to blame."

Yesterday, he'd asked me to be honest, *for once*. This was me being honest, for twice. Once last night, again today. No one could claim I wasn't an overachiever at accepting responsibility.

"Even the part where you said you loved me?" The question sounded equal parts curious and taunting. Or maybe not taunting. Maybe . . . defiant?

I angled my chin. "Yes."

He angled his chin in a movement that mirrored mine. "That you're still in love with me?"

"Yes." My voice cracked, I cleared my throat, ignoring the fluttering in my stomach, and repeated more firmly, "Yes." *Ugh. This is hard. So hard.*

"I see." His chin lowered, his lush amber irises seemed to warm, maybe with amusement? "How about the part where you asked to listen to my heart?"

I winced a little and, unable to hold his gaze any longer, I stepped away and dropped my eyes to the floor of the pool. I spotted my goggles. "Yep. I remember that, and I'm not sorry I said it, because it was true. And you wanted honesty. As such, there you go. I remember all of it. Thanks."

Why was he doing this? Was he trying to torment me? What was the point?

"What about us kissing?"

My head whipped up. "What?"

What! WHAT!?! I missed us kissing? If I missed us kissing, I was going to be SO ANGR—

"Calm down." He moved closer, giving me a full smile now, looking like he was trying not to laugh. "I'm joking. We didn't kiss."

A gush of air escaped me, my shoulders slumping, my forehead coming to my hand. *Thank God.* But also, *darn.*

Abram's eyes were on me. I felt them. I also felt the water push and swirl again. Between my fingers I saw he'd come closer.

"Mona."

"Yes?" I shivered. The way he said my name, it was the auditory equivalent to being stroked.

"Will you be brave with me?"

My eyes stung, I shook my head, and I continued to be honest. "I'm so tired of being brave."

That seemed to give him pause. His hand came to my arm, curled around it gently, and smoothed down to my elbow, his palm hot against my chilled skin. Other than shaking his hand that first day, was this the first time we'd touched since Chicago? It felt like . . . it felt indescribable. A terrifying relief was the closest description I could summon.

Abram tugged on my arm, bringing me closer, his other hand sliding against my cheek and lifting my chin. My fingers fell away from my face. I braced myself. I felt like I might crack, splinter from the hum of uncertainty and anticipation.

I don't know what I expected, but when our eyes locked, his were an odd combination of kind and covetous. "Then will you let me know you?"

I pressed my lips together to keep my chin from wobbling. "Why? To what purpose?"

The question seemed to amuse him. "I need someone to listen to my heart." His face inched closer. "And it only wants to beat for you."

Wha—

Bah!

Argra!

DAMN POET!

It was no use. I couldn't stop the tears. Wherever fear meets hope, that's where I was. I wanted to believe him. I wanted it so very, very badly. But he'd been intensely angry with me just days ago. *Too fast. This is all happening too fast. And I know better. He is a wildly famous musician! You will be just one of his many consorts!!*

"Are you going to hurt me?" I blurted, knowing I sounded broken. Gripping his wrist, I gave myself permission to enjoy the strength of him, the solid sturdiness, even if it ultimately turned out to be a lie. "Because if this is payback, you win. You win. Consider me punished. I surrender."

His eyes grew impossibly soft, concern etched itself between his eyebrows. "No."

No.

What he really should have said was, *Not yet.* Because, eventually, he was going to leave, or I was going to leave, and it was going to hurt.

"I don't understand what's happening. You said—" I sniffled, shaking my head, blinking against hot tears, "You said you regretted it. You said you weren't—that you didn't know me, and that you didn't—"

"Shh. Don't cry. Please don't cry."

Abram brought his other hand to my opposite cheek and pressed his forehead against mine, our stomachs, hips, and legs brushing, warm accidental touches that set my pulse racing. I couldn't think.

"Mona, I *don't* know you, not really. You keep everyone at an arm's length. But you've given me glimpses, scraps, and they've only made me hungry for more."

His right hand slid down my jaw to my neck, curling around the back of it; his left hand smoothed over my shoulder, to my arm, and gripped my waist, pulling me to him evocatively; one of his legs moved against mine, bracketing it, and he angled his body such that all those accidental touches now felt powerfully purposeful.

I felt myself shake with the effort to hold still, but not because I wanted to push him again. For once, for the very first time, I was surrounded and overwhelmed by another person and my instinct was to draw him closer, ever nearer, sink into him, merge our bodies together, accept his strength and cocoon myself within.

Abram's nose nuzzled mine, his lips brushed my lips with the faintest of touches, and he whispered, "Let me in."

CHAPTER 15
FLUID DYNAMICS

Abram

She was shaking.

The plan had been to find her and kiss the hell out of her. But she was cold, and shaking, and crying, and it wrecked me.

I made a new plan. I wrapped my arms around her, my intention was to hold her for as long as she'd allow, but Mona surprised me by lifting her chin and pressing her lips to mine.

Fuck. . . YES.

Without inhaling, my lungs filled, and I heard a single note between my ears, perfectly pitched, traveling down my spine and heating every nerve ending with carnal, electric *want*. I'd wanted this for so long, it seemed there'd never been a time I hadn't thought about it, fantasized about this moment with her.

Her hands gripped my sides, her nails digging into me, anchoring me, as though to ensure that—should I withdraw—I wouldn't leave unscathed. As punishment? I found I didn't care, or couldn't, because her lips parted and I wanted *in*.

My tongue swept inside. She moaned, sucking, swallowing, her mouth slick and soft and fiery hot. I moved instinctively, walking her backward, charging forward as though I could enter her this way, gain access to the furtive parts of her through strength and force. And she, rather than stumble backward, jumped slightly and wrapped her legs around my waist.

Fuck, I was hard. My mouth alternately devoured and sipped her. *So hard.* My body selfishly sought relief as her back met with the wall of the pool. I rocked against the apex of her legs, spreading her wider, and she tilted her head back to gasp, shivering again.

But then her mouth immediately returned, fused to mine, and she tilted her pelvis—up and down—using me, rubbing herself on my cock through the layers of our bathing suits.

This is insane.

A spark turned inferno. My skin hindered me. I grew frustrated by the constraints of my body. It only imprisoned, subjugated and diminished this transcendent craving, reducing the wonder of it to something merely carnal, physical.

Her breath hitched and she broke away to suck in air while her body chased friction, bouncing clumsily, riding the length of my shaft as sparks and flares and bursts of hot promise ignited at the base of my spine.

But I wasn't inside her, and I wanted *in*, every barrier removed. I wanted inside her, all her secret places. I wanted her open, exposed, bare, and hot, and wet, and panting . . . and I pictured her that way. Even with my hands on her now, even with her clothed pussy sliding over my dick encased in my board shorts, I saw her naked, reclined, reaching for me, wanting *me* to be *inside.* That's what I saw. Not this imperfect, clumsy, hurried grasping.

This is insane.

A corner of my mind told me that this wasn't part of the plan. I'd hoped for a sweet moment, a step toward something lasting. Not this lascivious spiral we'd been sucked into, humping like mindless animals.

But maybe that's what we were.

Everything about this—how she grabbed me, how hot I burned, her nails digging into my back and sides, scratching, biting at my mouth, how I rocked against her greedy strokes, held her confined, reached my hand beneath her swim shirt to grab and pinch and twist one of the softest parts of her body—was animalistic and base, depraved and instinctual. On a physical level, it felt fucking amazing. But . . .

Is this what you want?

She blinked at me, like she was startled, and I realized I'd said the words out loud to her, a question meant for myself.

I flexed my muscles, tensing, thrusting against her open legs. She shuddered.

I repeated, "Is this what you want? For us?" I massaged her breast, circling the peak mercilessly with my thumb. "You wanna fuck?"

Her eyes dazed, a puff of breath leaving her, she whimpered, and she said, "No," like it cost her, like she wasn't sure.

But a no is always a no.

I swallowed, torn between relief and brutal frustration, and relaxed my hold. We were both breathing hard, and the effort required to remove my hands from her glorious skin felt like slicing my body in half. But I did. Reminding myself that I wanted *in* helped, made stepping away easier as her legs slipped from around my waist. I backed away, my hands on my hips. I wanted to conquer and be conquered, to be broken and reassembled using her pieces.

I retreated. For now.

Looking at her from across the pool, watching her suck in air, gripping the edge, her gaze still dazed and hot and conflicted, I knew taking Mona now wouldn't do a damn thing other than make us feel good—really fucking good—for one moment. I didn't want one of her moments, I wanted all of them. I wanted an invasion, not a visit.

"What are you thinking?" she asked abruptly, her searching eyes moving over me.

I cleared my throat. "I probably shouldn't say."

That made her frown, so I quickly added, "It involves you being very naked."

Her frown cleared, and the side of her mouth twitched. "Very naked? As opposed to just a little naked?"

I wasn't ready to smile, because my dick hated me, and I spoke to stall, just for the sake of speaking. "Yep. My cousin's friend was a lingerie model at some ridiculous shop in the Northeast, and one time she told me there are stages of naked."

Mona's eyebrows pulled together, but not in a frown. "Stages of naked? What stage is fully naked? I mean, with no clothes?" She sounded curious.

"Stage five."

Her eyes moved up and to the right, to some spot over my head. "Then what's stage one?"

Sexy lingerie.

I cleared my throat again and shook my head, needing to clear it. "I'll tell you later."

"Why? Is it bad?"

"No."

"Will I hate it?"

"I hope not."

That made her smile. "I think I figured it out."

I laughed, shaking my head again. Her smile widened and she wrapped her arms around herself, like she was cold. We needed to get out of this pool. Surreptitiously, I tucked my erection up and to the side, into the waist of my shorts, and tried not to wince at the action. I didn't want it tenting my wet suit. She'd already felt it, so I didn't think Mona needed to see how she affected that part of me.

Also, I didn't need my dick leading the way.

"Come on." I waded toward her gingerly, cock throbbing from how I'd concealed it, my hand outstretched, my voice rough. "Let's go."

She glanced between me and my fingers, stepping forward to grab them. "Why?"

"You're still cold."

"I don't feel cold," she muttered.

"Your skin is cold." It was. Her fingers were chilled where they tangled with mine. "Let's go warm you up." Tugging, I led her to the pool steps, careful to stay in front of her just in case my erection slid free of the waistband.

"Where are we going? The hot tub?"

My steps faltered and my balls ached. "Hot tub?" *What the hell?* Was that my voice?

"Yes. Right over there."

I swallowed around the thick band of lust and glanced at the hot tub, but only allowed myself a glance. Otherwise, I wouldn't be able to get the resultant image of Mona out of my brain, and tonight's lyrics would be brought to you by the words horny, hot, and tub. For an unknown reason, I felt like punching something.

"Bad idea," I rasped.

She studied me, her gaze beautifully earnest. "If you don't like the one in here, I have one in my room too."

Oh God. "What?" And what the fuck is wrong with my voice?

"It's actually on the balcony, not in the room."

My body quickly pocketed this information, hoarding the knowledge for later, just in case we were to find ourselves in her room and struggling with boredom. By the end of the day tomorrow. *Torture.*

"I was thinking more like hot tea, or hot chocolate." I made my voice deeper to disguise the strain of speaking while my brain fought a losing battle against my imagination. "Something warm to drink."

"That sounds great. I guess I am a little cold," she said, her lips now a shade of purple. "If I'm cold, I love anything hot."

"Me too," I said, my voice rough.

Something hot would be more than appreciated, it would be necessary, especially after the cold shower I was about to take.

* * *

As she dried off, I wrapped my towel firmly around my waist, and then walked Mona to her room, relieved to find she'd brought a huge bathrobe to cover herself, and not just because she was cold.

We agreed to meet in the kitchen, drink something hot, and talk.

I didn't care what we talked about, I just needed to hear her speak, about anything. I suspected the last time we'd had a meaningful, genuine conversation was after I'd taken her to Anderson's Bookshop in Chicago. Now I wanted to know how much of that dinner conversation had been the real her, and how much had been Mona pretending to be Lisa.

I wanted to believe she'd been 100 percent herself, but I didn't *know.*

Mona was already in the kitchen by the time I'd arrived, pulling spices out of the cabinet. She looked up as I walked in.

"Hi," she said, swallowed, and gave me a small smile.

"Hey," I said, giving her a much larger one, and crossed to her.

I watched her carefully as I approached, how she reached for and gripped the counter behind her, how she tensed, but also lifted her chin, her eyes on my mouth.

She wanted to be kissed? Wonderful. In fact, *fantastic.*

Bending my neck, I gently slid our noses together—she'd liked that in the pool—and pressed my body and my lips to hers. *Soft. So soft. Velvet and satin and heat.*

A tension I didn't know I'd been carrying relaxed, and my mind quieted. Kissing her, I wanted more, but I also calmed. A new kind of restlessness surfaced. Anticipation.

The goalposts were moving: Talking without anger. Honesty. Forgiveness. Touching. Kissing. *What's next?* I couldn't wait to find out.

Immediately, she also relaxed, lips parting, and she sighed. Mona's arms encircled my neck, and I kissed her again, this time catching her bottom lip lightly between my teeth. I licked it, loving how slippery and hot and delicious she tasted.

She moaned—arching, pressing, straining—a hitching breath, a needy sound, and I knew it was time to back off.

Removing my hands from her body, I placed them on the counter behind her. But I wasn't ready to cede our closeness. Lowering my face to her neck, I whispered, "What are you making?"

"Hot chocolate," she whispered in return, tilting her head to the side, exposing her soft neck to me, her hands sliding to my biceps. "Do you want some? Or do you want tea?"

"Which do you prefer?" Unable to help myself, I placed a hungry kiss where her graceful shoulder met her equally graceful neck, inhaling something mild, and sweet like cream. "You smell good."

"It's just soap." She was still whispering, and every time I spoke against her skin her body arched in a lithe, reflexive movement. She continued, "And I love both tea and hot chocolate. But I have to be in the mood for hot chocolate, and I am, so I'm making it."

"I'll have what you're having." I placed one more kiss just under her jaw, and then pushed myself away. She smelled too good, she felt too good, she tasted sublime. I could've spent all day with my nose in her neck, her body flexing and rubbing against mine. But the frenzy between us, the urge to touch and be touched, didn't need to be stoked. We needed space, and conversation.

Gathering a steadying breath, I turned from her, closed my eyes to gather myself, and reluctantly crossed to the stools at the end of the island.

Place granite between you. Good idea.

The stool creaked under my weight and I watched Mona move around the kitchen, a little wrinkle between her eyebrows. She pulled out a can opener and a can of sweetened condensed milk, setting both in front of me.

"Will you open that, please?"

"Sure." I was happy to. "What's this for?"

"For the hot chocolate." Mona placed a saucepan on the gas range, the burner clicking three times before catching.

"You use sweetened condensed milk?"

"Yes. I also use unsweetened cocoa powder, which is why I use the sweet milk. This isn't my favorite hot chocolate recipe, but we have all the ingredients, so . . . "

"You have hot chocolate recipes?" I grinned. "What's wrong with the powdered stuff?"

"Nothing. But I like to make the good stuff."

I finished opening the can and pushed it toward her. "You make the good stuff every time?"

She grabbed the can and scraped out the thick liquid with a spatula. "Yes."

"Fancy," I teased.

Her eyes lifted, connected with mine, and she promptly returned to her task. "I rarely have hot chocolate, so I want to make it count."

Considering this, I watched her place the ingredients into the saucepan—the milk, the cocoa, cinnamon, cardamom, orange zest, a pinch of salt—and a thought occurred to me.

I hadn't decided whether or not to share the thought when she said, "You look like you want to say something."

"I was just thinking." I tugged on my beard, just under my bottom lip. "I'm not saying this is the case, but maybe you only like having hot chocolate so rarely because you only drink the kind that requires a lot of work and cleanup."

She stood at the range, stirring the mixture with a whisk, splitting her attention between me and the hot chocolate. "It's not that much work."

I moved my eyes to the orange and the zester and the measuring spoons and the spices. "Not everything worth having requires a struggle. Sometimes, things that are easy are also very, very good."

Her lips quirked to the side. "You say that, but just wait until you drink this." She nodded to herself. "Then you'll be singing a different tune. Struggle can sometimes make the end result so much better."

"The end result is the end result. A struggle doesn't change it."

"Ha! I disagree."

I leaned my elbow on the countertop, placing my thumb beneath my chin and pressing my index finger along my bottom lip. "How so?"

"Because then you know you've earned it."

My eyebrows jumped. "Does everything have to be earned?"

Mona kept her eyes on the saucepan, and it seemed like she was working to keep her features free of telling expression. "Not everything. Just most things."

"Really."

"In my experience," she said quietly, her lips thinning.

I blinked at her, because a great deal of Mona DaVinci had just come into focus, and this clarity had me asking, "You expect people to earn a place with you? To prove themselves?"

Her frown was immediate, and she looked confused as her gaze searched mine. "What?"

"You expect people to struggle? To earn a place?"

Now she reared back, looking genuinely perplexed by my conclusion. "No. Of course not."

"Then what did you mean? 'In your experience'?"

"Just that—" she shrugged, stirring the hot chocolate faster "—I don't want anyone to give me something I don't deserve. I want to feel like I've earned what I have, then I know it's mine." She sighed, and then huffed a laugh devoid of humor. "And, believe me, I understand the irony of my statement. Here I am, in my parents' mansion, surrounded by luxury I had nothing to do with."

I want to feel like I've earned what I have.

Huh. . . *well, damn.*

A conversation I'd had with Melvin the evening Mona had arrived resurfaced in my memory, felt pertinent to the conversation she and I were having now. Suddenly, it was difficult to breathe.

Mona brought her own food. She made her own bed. She cleaned up after herself.

"Did you pay for your own college?" I asked.

Mona gave me a funny look. "Yes. Kind of. I had a scholarship."

"And now? Grad school?"

"Yes. I have grants, and scholarships."

"What about living expenses?" I was being tactless, but now that the suspicion surfaced, I needed to know. "Who pays those?"

Mona closed one eye, scrunching her face, and peeked at me through the other. "I do. Why?"

Of course.

"What did you get your brother for his birthday?"

She swallowed. "A few things."

"And what did he get you?"

Her lips thinned again. She didn't answer.

I stood. "And your parents? Did you get them anything?"

She shrugged.

"And they sent nothing, right?"

Mona tucked her lips between her teeth and when she lifted her eyes to mine, they were cool, aloof. "What's your point?"

The urge to wrap her in a hug had my feet moving before I'd told them to and I gave myself a mental kick for having it backward. Mona didn't expect anything from anyone. She'd saved her sister, because that's who she was.

Which meant what for us?

Did she think she needed to earn me? Conversations, interactions between us—both here and in Chicago—reframed themselves, and one in particular struck me as important.

"When we were in the pool, in Chicago," I started carefully, trailing my fingers on the kitchen counter as I moved slowly closer, absorbing every shift and change behind her gaze. "When we raced."

Mona straightened her spine, her attention darting over every part of me except my eyes. "What about it?"

"What were you trying to earn?" Her anger at me, when I'd forfeited the race, had never made sense. I stopped swimming because I didn't want to fight with her, and also because seeing her in that bikini had been torture.

Currently, Mona pressed her lips together, swallowed again, and when she spoke her voice was gravelly, quiet. "If you remember, the bet was that whoever won got to stay and do laps, and the other person had to leave. I wanted to earn the right to stay and swim laps."

"But that wasn't the reason why you were angry. What were you really trying to earn?" I'd made it to where she stood, still stirring the hot chocolate, but I didn't touch her.

She huffed another laugh, this one sounded nervous. "It was—I was being silly." She turned off the stove, wiped her hands on a towel, her movements fidgety.

"Tell me."

"You want honesty," she said, and I got the sense she was talking to herself, reminding herself. "If you want to know the truth, fine. I made a secret bet with myself too. That if I won the race, then I'd, uh—" she crossed to a cabinet, finishing her sentence with her back turned while she pulled mugs down for the hot chocolate "—I'd tell you the truth, right then, about who I was and why I was there."

I flinched, stunned, blinking rapidly, feeling like I'd been slapped. Holding my breath for a moment so I couldn't—*so I won't*—yell, *are you fucking kidding me right now?*

Instead, I waited. I stalled. I tried to think of as many words as possible that rhymed with *regret*—which ironically included *bet*—and then I switched to the word *resentment.*

I waited until the edges of my vision cleared, and then I did my best to match my volume to hers, since what I really wanted—what I really fucking wanted—was to rage. "But you didn't. You didn't tell me."

How different would things be now if I'd just finished that damn race? She'd been winning. She was so fast and fierce, and it had turned me on to the point of torment. I hadn't wanted to fight with her any more. I'd wanted to lift her to the edge of the pool, pull the tie on that flimsy bikini, and taste her, make her come with my mouth and fingers, right there. And then I'd—

Stop.

Back up.

Take a deep breath.

Shit.

There was no hiding from that night. I'd dreamt about her and that night many, many times; and we did many, *many* things in those dreams; but none of those things included fighting.

"I didn't tell you because I didn't win. You forfeited and I didn't earn the right to tell you," she said, making it sound entirely reasonable in retrospect. But at the time, she'd been angry. She'd been furious.

I didn't earn the right. . . My bones ached, my breath became shallow with the effort. What happened to her to make her this way? Make her think she wasn't deserving? That she needed to earn the right to tell the truth and take what she wanted? And what would've happened if I'd pushed her?

What if I'd kissed her? What if I had lifted her to the edge and untied the bikini? What if I hadn't been patient?

And what does this mean for us, now?

Mona's shoulders were stiff, and she seemed to take a few deep breaths before returning to the range and to me. She didn't look at me. She served the hot chocolate and handed me my cup first.

"Thank you," I said quietly, my fury slowly morphing to frustration, and then to grief.

Looking at her now, at her lovely face, so deserving of every beautiful, wonderful thing, I couldn't help but think back to real Lisa, not Mona-as-Lisa, and what she'd told me about making other people happy.

They have to do that for themselves, she'd said. Was she right? I had no idea. I hoped not.

Setting aside my mug, I took Mona's cup from her hand, drawing her hesitant and beautiful gaze to mine. I wrapped her in my arms and placed a lingering kiss on her neck. I held her tightly and I stroked her back.

"You deserve everything," I whispered.

Instead of relaxing, she held me tighter.

I hoped Lisa was wrong. I hoped, if you love someone enough, it was possible to show them what they deserved, and be their source of happiness.

CHAPTER 16
ATOMIC MASSES

I awoke to the sound of a heartbeat, and I smiled.

Blinking open my eyes, I carefully lifted my head from Abram's chest, doing my best to make as little noise or movement as possible while propping my chin on my palm and gazing down at him. He was divine. And he was 100 percent asleep.

What time did he come to bed?

After hot chocolate, the conversation had become much lighter and easier. I hypothesized Abram was trying to stay away from heavy topics after grilling me about whether I paid for my own school and whether my family reciprocated birthday gifts. They didn't, but I honestly didn't mind. I was a hard person to buy gifts for—as my sister and my mom's personal assistant in charge of shopping had told me countless times—and I appreciated the fact that they didn't send me things just to send me something.

It was fine. I was fine.

And I was grateful he'd dropped the topic. I'd wanted to spend time with him, get to know him, not discuss my family.

We'd talked about so many things, including how I didn't like cereal, or anything that grows soggy, and that my favorite element on the periodic table was sodium. Then, he'd made a periodic table Chuck Norris joke, and I'd laughed with more gusto than I'd expected, surprising myself. Which led him to telling his entire arsenal of Chuck Norris jokes for at least a half hour. I laughed so hard my face hurt.

Lila came in at that point to start dinner and Abram asked her if she could make ours to go. That earned him a look from me.

"What?" he'd asked, drinking the rest of his hot chocolate, his gorgeous brown eyes dancing.

"If we're both missing, people are going to notice."

"Let them notice." He placed a soft kiss on my forehead, followed by another on my cheek, and then the corner of my mouth, his beard brushing against my face. *Holy particle accelerator, Batman.* My stomach fluttered mercilessly.

And then he'd followed up the kissy-face treatment with, "I only want to be with you."

He was too good with the words. *Damn poet.*

I glanced at Lila, who was trying not to be too obvious about watching us. Regardless, I felt myself smile.

We had our meal in the solarium on the second floor, just the two of us, but I made a point to leave a note for Allyn under her door. I wanted to give her a heads up. She'd integrated with the group just fine, genuinely seemed to be having a good time, but still. I'd been the one to invite her. I worried I was being a bad friend leaving her alone for dinner again.

Abram proved to be an excellent distraction from my worries. I didn't typically mind quiet. I've never been one of those people who felt compelled to always fill it, and Abram didn't seem to be either. But, between the two of us, there was no break in conversation, no spots of silence. Every void was filled, every empty place occupied, and it didn't occur to either of us to check the time until I suppressed my second yawn.

"It's late," he said, and my stomach dropped as he showed me the time on his phone. "And as much as I want to keep you up all night talking, you need to sleep."

"What about you? Don't you need to sleep? You should sleep. We could both sleep." We'd been sitting on the couch under the lemon tree, facing each other, holding hands over the back of the couch. It was SO AWESOME!!!!

I thought I was already melty and relaxed, but his small, sexy grin liquified me. "Mona DaVinci, do you want to sleep with me?"

I tried not to smile, but I failed so hard. "Honestly? Yes. Sleeping with you in Chicago, in the theater room, is one of my fondest memories." At this point, after the day we'd had, confessing these small truths didn't feel brave anymore. With every confession, he made me feel less and less self-conscious, always confessing something in return.

I almost forgot that we were doomed. *Doomed like a dying star.*

"It's my heartbeat, isn't it? That's what you're after."

Yes. It's your heart I want. "Yes. It is. And your body. I really love your body."

"I really love your body," he said, like it was an easy and natural thing for two people to admit to each other, making my own heart do a wonderful and painful flip-flop. "But I need to write before I can sleep."

"Okay." I nodded tiredly. "I can stay up for a while longer. If you don't mind the company, I can read while you write. I finished the books I brought, but I have two journals I need to read before I leave."

Abram's gaze dropped suddenly and so did his smile. Before I could ask him about it, he said, "How about you go to sleep, and when I'm finished, I'll come up and lie down with you? No pressure."

I was already nodding enthusiastically before he'd finished. "Sounds great!"

And that's what we'd done. He'd tucked me in with a toe-curling kiss, and then left. But now he was here.

As I looked at him, sleeping so deeply, I realized, in addition to still wearing his jeans and long sleeve T-shirt, he was lying above the covers. Smiling at his strangeness, I took a moment to study his face, working to memorize every detail. I then placed my head on his chest again and listened to his heart.

I'm going to miss this. A lot.

Sadness abruptly weighed down on me, felt as tangible as the blanket covering my body, and I squeezed my eyes shut. The Abram chant sounded between my ears, telling me to be honest, telling me this was fleeting, telling me to be cautious, reminding me that I was leaving on Sunday.

I tried to reason with my reason, asking myself, *What is the harm in staying a little longer? Will listening to the cadence of his heart now make leaving him later more difficult?*

YES!

Absolutely. Yes.

Dammit.

Allowing myself to linger, to grow used to this closeness, would just make everything worse in the long run. I needed to get up. I needed to keep living my normal life. I couldn't pause it, like I'd done the last time, because reentry into reality would feel impossible and I'd crash.

If I were smart, I'd start distancing myself now.

. . . Just another ten minutes.

My heart squeezed and I held my breath. Yesterday had been wonderful, and I would treasure it and whatever time we had left. *Always.* But smart Mona was right. And unfortunately, smart Mona was also the primary decision maker.

With great care, I lifted away from Abram's glorious heart and body, and rolled out of the bed. The effort required made my pulse hammer between my ears. Standing, I hurriedly turned back to Abram and covered him with the blanket, I didn't want him to be cold.

And then I walked quietly to the bathroom and began going through the motions of my normal day.

* * *

I left Abram a note on the side table. On the envelope I wrote, "DO NOT BURN," hoping it would make him laugh. Though I was still a little sore about him burning my letter, and I sorta mourned the loss of it, I recognized now that I'd dodged a bullet.

My first draft of the new letter read,

~~Abram,~~

~~Dear Abram,~~

My dearest Abram,

I hope you ~~slept well~~ had sweet dreams. When you wake up~~, and if you feel inclined, please~~ come find me. I'll be in the solarium reading until the afternoon, and then I think I'll go outside and take advantage of the sun and the snow. I'll be by the sledding slope. Maybe I'll build a snow fort! But ~~I'm happy to modify my plans if you'd prefer to do something else~~ I'm up for anything ~~if you want to spend the day together~~.

~~Regards,~~

Missing you.

Love, Mona

The final version didn't have all the strikeouts, obviously, and it struck me as reckless. I'd fretted over the word *love* for far too long, but eventually committed to it. It felt like the truth, so it stayed.

I didn't see anyone as I walked down the stairs and halls leading to the kitchen, but I did hear conversation coming from the living room. I wasn't avoiding anyone, but I was hungry, so I decided to stop by the kitchen first, eat, and then seek out Allyn.

As it turns out, the two activities weren't mutually exclusive. Allyn was sitting at the kitchen table next to Leo, and the way they seemed to be so entirely engrossed in each other, and whatever they were talking about, made me smile. Even though I was still annoyed with my brother about our conversation yesterday, I wished him nothing but the best, and Allyn was *the best.*

"Hey, Mona." Kaitlyn's greeting had me turning toward her voice.

"Oh. Hi, Kaitlyn. How are you?" I hadn't spotted her when I first walked in. She was standing by the refrigerator, holding a carton of half-and-half.

"Great!" she said, her smile bright. "I don't think you've met Martin yet?" Lifting her chin, she gestured to a man, another person I hadn't immediately noticed upon entering the kitchen.

He was on the same stool Abram had sat on yesterday while I made hot chocolate, and the first thing I noticed about him was that his eyes were the most startling shade of blue-green. *Like an aquamarine.*

"Oh, hey there. I'm Mona, Leo's sister." I walked forward and extended my hand. He glanced at it impassively, took it, gave it a perfunctory shake, and let it go.

"You're Mona DaVinci," he said in a way that made me feel like he was contradicting me. "That would make Leo *your* brother."

I lifted an eyebrow at him. His lips curved at my confusion, and said bluntly, "We were just talking about this before you came in. In newspaper headlines about the two of you, it always reads something like, 'Mona DaVinci *and brother* are spotted having breakfast at blah blah blah.'"

"It's true!" Leo chimed in cheerfully from his spot at the kitchen table, his eyes full of pride. "Some of my friends call me *and brother.*"

That made Allyn laugh, Kaitlyn shake her head, and Martin smile.

I rolled my eyes at Leo, relieved to see he seemed mostly recovered from his cold, and that he didn't appear to be upset with me about our tense conversation yesterday.

"I'm Martin Sandeke," he added, giving me an assessing look, so I'm sure he didn't miss the recognition flicker behind my eyes.

"You're Martin Sandeke?"

He nodded, his expression bracing.

I glanced at Kaitlyn, recalling our conversation about how her fiancé had started a non-profit organization for helping rural areas gain easier access to the internet.

And suddenly, all is revealed.

Before I could stop myself, I blurted, "Your dad is an asshole."

I knew Denver Sandeke. He was the CEO and majority stakeholder in Sandeke Telecom Systems, the country's largest telecom company and arguably its largest unapologetic monopoly. He'd worked to block any binding measures on net neutrality. He'd also lobbied heavily against the launching of low cost, low maintenance satellites that would serve the dual purpose of providing inexpensive internet service to underserved areas AND helping scientists with space exploration.

Suffice it to say, I loathed him.

Leo and Allyn gasped, but Martin grinned, and then he laughed.

Kaitlyn also didn't seem surprised by my statement either, shrugging and lifting a hand in the air toward me. "Yes. Yes, he is." To Martin she said, "I told you that you two would get along." And then to herself she mumbled, "You're basically the same person."

Even though Martin didn't seem upset, a rush of embarrassment crested on my cheeks and over my ears. I apologized, profusely, but he continued to be delighted by my outburst. Eventually, he changed the subject to my opinion on anti-laser masquerades, and then drilled me on what we (physicists) knew about merging neutron stars, seeming intensely fascinated by the subject.

Soon, I forgot that I'd made an idiot of myself, and settled into the conversation. Kaitlyn set a cup of coffee down in front of me, along with sugar and the carton of half-and-half, and two hours later I was stunned to discover so much time had passed.

This? Discussing subjects about which I was an expert? This was easy. So easy. This was the center of my rocket. Perhaps I'm pointing out the obvious, but I was always perplexed by people who found this part of me impressive. It's easy to do something when you find it effortless. I mean, that's the definition of easy.

"We should do a double date," Kaitlyn announced to Martin during an extremely short pause in the conversation, like she'd been biding her time to make the proclamation. "The four of us should go out the next time Mona is in New York."

Martin's eyes narrowed on his fiancée. "You're sneaky."

"I am." She grinned.

"What? Why are you sneaky?" I picked up my mug to take a drink and discovered it was empty. Clearly, drinking without thinking was becoming a habit of mine.

"Martin doesn't like Abram," Kaitlyn said. Just like that. Like she was saying, *Martin doesn't like tacos*, which—for the record—seemed equally nuts to me.

"What?" I asked, ignoring the fact for a second that Abram and I would never be double-dating with anyone, and focusing on the impossibility that anyone wouldn't like Abram.

He slid his blue eyes to me. "We don't have anything in common," he said, and I got the sense that this was Martin Sandeke trying to be tactful.

"You both have penises." Kaitlyn hit him on the shoulder lightly and I was suddenly very glad my coffee cup had been empty.

Martin also looked like he was trying not to laugh, and he leaned closer to his fiancée, lowering his voice, "Other than that, we have nothing in common."

Kaitlyn leaned around Martin and focused her attention on me. "I've been trying to get these two to hang out for over a year. Now that Abram is leaving on tour, it'll never happen."

"That's not the only reason it'll never happen." Martin said, *not* under his breath, making me quirk an eyebrow at him.

"What's the other reason?"

Martin glanced at me, his expression frank (I had a feeling his expression was always frank), and said, "Kaitlyn's pregnant."

My mouth dropped open and I asked unthinkingly, "Is the baby Abram's?"

WHAT? MONA! YOU DOOFUS!!

Kaitlyn sucked in a breath, and then tossed her head back to laugh, hitting the counter with her palm.

Martin's lips twisted, like he also thought my question was funny (but maybe also not funny), and he shook his head. "No."

"Oh." Again, embarrassment climbed up my face and I glanced around the kitchen, hoping Leo and Allyn hadn't overheard my stupidity. They weren't anywhere and must've left at some point without me noticing. "I'm sorry. That was, that was—"

"It's fine." Kaitlyn grinned at me, wiping her eyes. "I needed that laugh. Thanks for that." She sniffled, still chuckling.

"Uh, I guess, uh, I don't understand then." I glanced between the two of them. "What does Kaitlyn being pregnant have to do with Martin not hanging out with Abram?"

Martin straightened on his stool, his eyes flickering over me. "We'll have the baby. I'm not going to have time to hang out with anyone, especially not some rock star with groupies all over him, and—"

Kaitlyn elbowed Martin, sending him a stern look. "You know he's not like that."

Martin scoffed. "*All* men are like that."

Her eyes hardened, and she challenged, "Really? Are you like that?"

I couldn't help it, I watched this interaction with interest, hanging on every word. I suddenly wished for popcorn, or a large houseplant to hide behind.

"Of course not, not for a long time and never again. You know how excited I am about the baby, *our* baby. I can't wait. You know better than to ask that. Which one of us is the one pushing for the house? So we'll have a yard?"

Her expression seemed to soften, a small smile curving her lips, but then he added quietly, "But I *was* like that. And your friend Abram is about to travel the world with a fucking harem."

She flinched and said firmly, "Abram has changed." Her gaze darted to me, then away.

"Come on, he's never going to settle down. Remember when you asked him where he wanted to live after the tour? If he was coming back to New York? He said he had no idea, that he had no plans. He just did that underwear modeling thing, soon there will be posters of the guy *in his underwear* everywhere. That's not a guy who's changed. That's a guy who is just getting started."

Underwear modeling?

Martin's words made my heart do strange things in my chest, but my brain seemed to be nodding along, like it wasn't surprised by any of this. *Yep, yep, yep. I agree.*

"You don't know him." Kaitlyn sounded angry.

"So you keep saying," Martin mumbled, clearly disbelieving, and clearly just—in general—disliking Abram.

For the first time since I'd met her, Kaitlyn's face was devoid of humor, and she was staring at Martin like she wanted to singe his eyebrows off with a hot poker.

And that was my cue to leave.

"Well." I stood, making a show out of looking at the clock over the ovens. "It was nice talking with you."

Martin lifted his chin in my direction, and I detected a glimmer of something like devious satisfaction behind his eyes. "You too, Mona."

I looked at Kaitlyn—just briefly—and gave her a tight smile. She seemed to be experiencing many emotions, and I had no doubt that as soon as I left the kitchen, she was going to have a few choice words for her fiancé.

* * *

I marched around in the snow, stomping it down for no reason other than to feel it crunch and compress under my boots. I was extremely agitated. But I didn't have a right to be. Therefore, I stomped.

Maybe I'll start an avalanche and it can match the avalanche of feelings IN MY HEART!!

I sighed, glaring at the horizon, talking myself back from the edge.

Drama llama green isn't a good shade on you, Mona. It brings out your pores.

Try as I might, and despite how exhausted and cold I eventually became, I couldn't escape the agitation caused by accepting my fate. We, Abram and I, were a red giant. A dying star. And that was that.

I sat on the snow, breathing hard from my last bout of stomping, and drew my legs up. Resting my elbows on my knees and clasping my gloved hands together lightly, I stared at the cloudless blue sky.

You know what? I can do this.

Abram and I had a few days left before Sunday. It was only Wednesday. We could fill these hours with a lifetime of memories. Not every happily ever after lasts forever. Why couldn't ours be days instead of years?

I can do this.

I'd had sexual contact with men without being in a relationship. In fact, I'd never been in a romantic, committed relationship, so this—with Abram—should be easy. I'd done it before. Why not with Abram? It made so much sense.

I'm going to do this.

But just like those encounters, what I needed from Abram was his explicit consent. Of course, first I would define my expectations and boundaries, he would define his expectations and boundaries, and then we'd enter into our brief arrangement fully informed. Perfect!

Consent was good. Consent saved people heartache. It removed doubt and disorder and hopefully would dispel this nebulous agitation.

Good. This is good. Good plan.

Movement in the corner of my vision caught my attention and I turned my head. As though I'd conjured him, Abram was there, walking toward me, his hands in his jacket pockets, a lazy smile on his face.

Goodness. I sighed.

I watched him come, enjoying every movement of his body, every moment of his approach. I took a greedy snapshot, saving the image for later, when I needed it.

"Hey there," he said, his voice still sounding sandpapery with sleep. Abram sat next to me in the snow and immediately leaned close to give me a kiss, his hand fisting in my coat to tug and hold me closer.

When our mouths met, he tasted like mint, and his beard tickled my cold face, and warm lips were soon replaced with hot tongue, and that's when my body decided to climb onto his lap. Lifting to one knee, I straddled him, grabbing the front of his coat like he'd done with mine, tugging and holding him closer.

Yeah. We made out in the snow. I felt him grow hard beneath me, through underwear and snow pants and maybe leggings. It frustrated me. Unlike my bathing suit, there were too many layers to yield any real friction or satisfaction. But his mouth made up for the constraints of my clothes, the heat of it moving from my lips to my jaw to my neck to my ear, increasing the temperature of my entire body, my breath hitching, my mind frenzied.

And then, just like he'd done in the pool and in the kitchen yesterday, he stopped. He breathed against my neck for several seconds, sending ticklish shivers racing along my clothed skin, and his hands were gripping me through my puffy coat. Even with the fabric and feathers between his fingers and my body, I felt the strength of him, of them, how he held me.

"Thank you for the note," he said, his voice strained.

He was still hard, pressing against my inner thigh. The man's self-control was impressive, and frustrating.

"You didn't burn it?" I took a deep breath, inhaling his delectable scent, and then leaned back to look at his face.

Abram was smiling. "You told me not to. You wrote *DO NOT BURN* on the outside of the envelope."

Delighted with his grin, without considering my words I said, "I missed your smile. It's infinite-dimensional." That wasn't even the right way to express the concept, but my ability to form words, coherent, intelligent phrases, didn't feel necessary at present.

His smile grew, and he laughed. "Infinite-dimensional?"

"Oh yes. Thank you for it." I moved my arms to twist around his neck. "And I missed it, a lot. Your smiles in photos—and even when I first arrived—they weren't. But this one, up close, and without meanness, definitely is."

"My smiles were mean?"

"Yes. Since we're talking about it, I also remember you being funnier," I teased.

"What?" He continued to grin at me, sounding mock-offended.

"You're not a very funny person anymore."

"How can you say I'm not funny? You were *begging* me yesterday to stop telling jokes."

"Yes, but those were Chuck Norris jokes. Those are universally funny." Now I was laughing.

Abram flashed his teeth, making a face like a snarl. "Is this a mean smile? How can a smile be mean?"

"I don't know, but it's something you've perfected. Mean smiles, no jokes, broody eyebrows. You're like an arthouse movie but without the nudity."

He laughed, *hard,* at that, and so did I, loving his face right now. I decided I loved his face best when he laughed.

Eventually, tilting his head to the side, he said, "Well, I can fix that."

"Good. Because, like I said, I really miss your smile. And you—"

"I meant the nudity."

I barked a laugh, and his answering chuckle sounded low and sinister.

"Very funny," I said, shaking my head at him. "Now you're a comedian."

He smiled, just a small one, but my heart lifted at the sight. Though it was small, it looked meaningful, intentional, like a gift just for me. My breath caught and, again, I sighed.

"Am I smiling?" he asked, his eyes on my lips. "Is it mean?"

"No," I responded, dazed. "It's a good one." It was the best. I took another greedy snapshot, saving the image for later.

When I needed it.

CHAPTER 17
SELECTED RADIOACTIVE ISOTOPES

Mona

We made snow angels. Together. It was fun. His were huge.

He'd also brought food with him in a bag I hadn't noticed earlier. My Abram-tunnel vision was apparently a strong force.

Abram spread out a picnic of hot broccoli and cheese soup, warm, crusty sourdough bread, and hot tea laced with the barest hint of whiskey. He warned me before drinking it, pointing out that he'd brought un-spiked tea as well. I was freezing, so I'd had the winter tea.

We spent several hours in the snow, having *the best* time while I struggled to find just the right moment to bring up my proposal. My *fling* proposal, to be precise. But whenever a break in conversation occurred, I swallowed the words, bargaining with myself, reasoning that I could do it later.

Ten more minutes.

But then the perfect moment presented itself. We'd just finished the picnic and were packing up, quietly working side by side. Our previous conversation had just wrapped up—about his sister and how she was engaged and getting married soon—and I had my chance.

And so, sucking in a breath for bravery, I asked, "Do you think you'll ever want to get married?"

Ah. Comet balls!

That wasn't asking him about a fling. That was literally *the opposite* of asking him about a fling.

He smiled a small smile, his attention on his hands as they packed the bag. "To be honest, I've never really thought about it."

I nodded, my blood rushing between my ears. I couldn't think. How could I save this conversation and redirect it toward fling territory?

Abram added, "I read an article about you once where the interviewer asked that same question." He lifted his eyes, they ensnared mine. "You said, 'Irrelevant. Next question.'"

"Oh. Ha!" I tried to laugh lightly, but it sounded forced. "They always ask me that, and it irritates me, because no one asks any of my male colleagues. It's always, 'What will you do when you have kids?' and I'm like, 'The same thing I do every night, Pinky. Try to take over the world.'"

He grinned at me, shaking his head like I was *too much* of something wonderful. "I loved that cartoon."

"I would judge you if you didn't." Returning his smile, I gave into the urge to grab his coat and pull him forward for a quick kiss. Because I could.

But when I went to lean away, I discovered he'd caught my jacket again and I couldn't move.

Staring at me, his gorgeous brown eyes serious and searching, he said, "Mona, I want to see you again."

A spike of blissful happiness was followed quickly by a spike of dread. I blinked, bracing myself, it was now or never.

Here we go.

"Of course." I nodded, my throat full of fire. "Actually, yes. I want to talk to you about that. I'm—" I uncurled his fingers from my coat "—I'm glad you brought it up."

"Good." His tone was firm. "I wanted to bring it up yesterday, but I didn't want to ruin our time together. Mona . . ." Abram opened his mouth, closed it, opened it again, his gaze felt both eager and restrained. "Mona, I leave tomorrow morning. We have to be at the airport by 4:30 AM."

. . . Oh.

Abram's face, less than two decimeters away, blurred, my vision becoming gray, cloudy. I wasn't crying or close to it. I'd cried my quota for the last ten years over the past week. If I cried today, I would no longer be able to label myself "not a crier," and that felt like an essential part of my identity.

But, given this news of his imminent departure, I probably would cry at some point. *And then I'll have to call myself a crier. I won't be "not a crier" anymore.*

. . .

Okay. That's fine. I'll just be a crier.

I made a mental note to invest in Kleenex.

"Mona?"

My name coming from Abram's lips brought him back into focus. Apparently, I was nodding for some reason.

"Of course." I continued nodding. Then I stood, studied the ground where we'd had our picnic for any left items, and then turned toward the house.

"Mona, talk to me." He was right there, walking at my side while I swallowed reflexively and worked to paste a convincing smile on my face.

"Yes. We should definitely meet up again," I said, trying to force a little cheerfulness into my tone.

He must've suspected something was off because I felt intensity behind his eyes as he continued to watch my profile. "What's wrong?"

"Nothing."

"Mona. Honesty."

"Nothing. Not really." Now I shook my head. "It's just, I don't know why I thought I would have more time with you before you had to leave."

His hand on my arm brought me to a stop and he tugged, encouraging me to face him. "I wish we had more time too. But we'll see each other. I'll have breaks during the tour. I can come visit you."

"In Geneva?"

Abram frowned, his fingers flexing on my arm. "What?"

"I'll be in Geneva until at least June. Maybe longer."

He stared at me, blinking several times. "Geneva, as in Switzerland?"

"Specifically, at CERN, at the European Laboratory for Particle Physics."

I studied him while he absorbed this news, noted how his eyes lost focus and they darted around at nothing.

"I didn't realize that," he said quietly, like he was talking to himself.

"I didn't tell you. Or, I mean, it didn't occur to me to tell you, meaning we've only really been on speaking terms for about thirty-six hours and I honestly thought for some inexplicable reason that you would be here through Sunday. So . . ."

He stared at me. I stared at him. We were surrounded by a mountain of snow, but it felt like—instead of surrounding us—it stood between us.

But we can have tonight. We can—

"Mona."

"Hmm?"

The muscle at his jaw flexed, his stare now determined. "We'll make it work."

I nodded, but the nod was a lie, so I stopped nodding and turned back to the house. His hand on my arm slid down to my gloved fingers, squeezing them.

We walked in silence, holding hands, for a while, reaching the house, removing our wet boots and outer layers in the mudroom. The silence continued as we walked up the stairs, each footstep sounding like the seconds ticking on a clock.

We made a detour to the kitchen where we dropped off the picnic stuff. Lila was putting the finishing touches on dinner and shooed us away when we tried to clean our dishes. She was so nice. I liked Lila.

Eventually, too soon, we reached my door. I placed my hand on the door handle, Abram at my shoulder, his hands in his pockets. I didn't turn the handle.

I'd never experienced the sensation of time running out. Yes, I'd had projects with due dates—big ones—and deadlines. But it never felt like this. That whole "sands through the hourglass" thing made so much more sense to me now. Each grain of sand was a moment, a final moment.

The meal we'd shared was probably our last meal, together. Holding hands as we walked through the snow would be the last time we held hands. This would be the last time I opened my door with him standing next to me. Tonight he would come inside my room, we would be together, and the final—the very last—moment would follow.

And that would be the end.

Give me another minute. I just want one more minute.

Keeping my eyes forward, I said, "You should come inside."

"Yes." His answer was immediate. "Yes. I'll come in."

I opened the door. I walked inside. He followed. He closed the door. I turned on him. I grabbed him. I kissed him.

He kissed me back.

Smart Mona reminded me that we hadn't yet discussed expectations and boundaries. He hadn't consented. But, you know what? Neither had I. At no point had I consented to feeling like my heart was being ripped out of my body, that tomorrow didn't matter because he would be gone. Thinking about the day after that, and the day after that, and the day after that felt overwhelming, like attempting to comprehend the vastness of space.

It stretched on, forever. There was a hypothetical end, to the universe, to me, to all this pain and longing and damn *yearning*, but it remained just that. Hypothetical. Beyond my reach or understanding. I couldn't fathom it.

But I could fathom now.

"Mona, what are you doing?" He caught my hands as I reached for the button of his pants, so I redirected them under his shirt, to the hard, glorious planes of his stomach and chest and back. He felt so good, hot, hard, necessary.

"I want you." I kissed his neck, his jaw. "Don't you want me?"

Time moving. Always away, always forward. Once lost, lost forever.

"There's no rush," he said, but his hands moved under my shirt too, lifting it, rushing to palm me through the fabric of my bra. "We can—" I felt his Adam's apple move with a swallow, his fingers pulled down the cup, massaged me, he groaned, "—take our time. This isn't goodbye."

This isn't goodbye.

My throat closed at the words. This was goodbye. In the morning, he'd be gone. His tour was twelve months. He'd be surrounded by women who desired him for his talent and body, and maybe even for his glorious heart. They would be gorgeous, and clever, and tempting, and probably lovely, good people.

Monogamy isn't for musicians. They will feed his voracious creative soul.

"Wait." Abram caught my hands again, lifting his mouth. "Wait. Mona. Stop."

I did. I stopped. I dropped my chin to my chest and I took a deep, bracing breath.

"What is going on?"

"I told you, I want you."

"No. You're frantic."

"I frantically want you." I pulled my hands out of his grip and turned away, pacing to the window and opening it. "It's stuffy in here," I mumbled.

He watched me as I breathed in the cool air, saying nothing.

He watched me as I turned and walked to the bed, saying nothing.

He watched me as I sat on it, folding and refolding my hands, and he said, "You don't believe me."

"About what?"

"This isn't goodbye."

"It is goodbye." My voice was robotic, because if any situation deserved a divorce of emotion from facts, it was this conversation.

"Oh? Really? You don't want to see me after this?" He sounded so hurt.

I rubbed my chest, because the hurt in his voice echoed in the chambers of my heart. "I would love to see you after this. I would love to see you any time you want to see me."

He seemed to pause here, as though trying to parse through what I'd just said, as though it were a riddle.

Eventually, he demanded, "Then why do you think this is goodbye?"

"Because—"

"Because you'll be in Geneva? That's not an issue. Distance won't be an issue. We'll make it work."

I covered my face, rubbed my eyes, and then dropped my hands. "Because monogamy isn't for musicians."

The room fell eerily silent, almost like he'd disappeared from it. Or maybe I'd disappeared.

Even if I was speaking to an empty room, I felt compelled to say, "A year is a long time. I know . . . I know what tours are like. I went on several with my parents. Lisa and I always got along with my dad's friends. They'd take care of us backstage. One woman, Vivviane, taught us how to braid our hair into crowns."

I lifted my eyes to Abram. He was still watching me, but his expression teetered between anguished and bracing. I suspected he already understood where I was going with this story.

Even so, I continued, "It wasn't until I was eleven and my mom visited me at a science summer camp with one of *her* friends that I added one and one together, and I realized one plus one makes several more than two. After meeting her boyfriend, after she confirmed who and what he was, so many other things made sense—about the women I'd seen with my father when he'd taken us on tour, about why my parents never seemed to both be home at the same time, about the women who some-times spent the week with us in Chicago, to keep my father company, while my mother was out of town."

"Mona—"

"They've been open with us about it, and I don't judge them for their lifestyle. In fact, they've always made a point to be sex positive with us, which I've appreciated. Sex should be fun. It should be equally beneficial for both parties. Reciprocation is a must. Clear consent, communication of expectations ahead of time, and safe words are essential. And, on that note, what's your safe word?"

Abram's forehead wrinkled, his dazed expression telling me he was having trouble keeping up. "You want to know my safe word."

"Yes. I do."

"Why?" he demanded, the anguish in his stare replaced with suspicion.

I was glad he'd burned my letter, *the letter*.

In addition to brimming with hot feelings, it also contained the hopes I'd had for our future. Ever since I'd driven through that neighborhood with him—his parents' neighborhood—the recollection of those pretty houses with picket fences, and US flags, and gardens, and toys in the front yard had become the centerpiece of my imagined future.

My childhood had been so chaotic, and those houses, each looking so similar, exuded order and consistency. If he'd read the letter I'd been carrying with me for over two years, full of impossible dreams, then I wouldn't have been able to say the words that were on the tip of my tongue. He would've known what I really wanted.

"I'd like to have sex with you," I said, folding my arms. "And if you want to have sex with me—no pressure—we should talk about it, before we do it, make sure we're both on the same page, you know?"

Abram, staring at me, his lips slightly parted, stood as though a statue for a count of four seconds. I know because I counted. And then a little puff of air left his parted lips, one of disbelief.

"You want to have sex with me," he repeated, not a question, more like restating my take-out order, to confirm.

"That's right. I'd like a fling. But, obviously, I'd like your consent first."

Something behind his eyes shifted, grew darker. It reminded me of the sky when a sudden storm gathers, the light changes, the mood shifts.

He was angry. I'd made him angry.

Confirming this, through clenched teeth, he said, "I do not consent to a f—" he stopped himself, like he'd been about to say something he didn't want to. Breathing out, he finished, "To a *fling*."

I likewise gritted my teeth, a cloud of fury encased my brain. "Well. Fine. Fine. Okay then."

"Mona—" He took a step forward.

I lifted a hand to stop him. "No. That's, I mean. That's it then. Right?"

"No!" He began pacing in front of me, pushing his hands through his hair, loosening it from the tie that held it back "Stop trying to put us in a fucking box!"

"Oh? You want space?"

"Mona—"

"I get it. You want to fly, right? You need freedom. For your creativity. For your—"

"Mona!" he snapped. Actually, he exploded, my name sounding like a command. "Shut. Up."

I closed my mouth, pressing my lips together, and moving my eyes to the wall behind him. He crossed to me, knelt in front of me, covered my hands with his, and I flinched at the contact.

He noticed, his eyes flashing hurt, but he didn't pull them away. "Listen to me. Listen. I'm in love with you."

I scoffed, shaking my head, shifting my gaze to a spot beyond him. "You said yourself, you don't know me."

"I don't want anyone but you."

"That's kind of you to say. Thank you." I gave him a tight smile but not my eyes, removing one of my hands to pat his. "And, as we've established, I also want you."

He exhaled, it sounded beyond frustrated. "No. I'm not—this isn't—*goddamnit!*" His hands moved to my arms and I finally looked at him. His eyes were wild, his voice a deep growl. "Listen and believe me. I've done that. I've tried that. Maybe it works for some people. I hated it." He shook his head firmly. "When you left, and all I could think of was you, all I wanted was you, but I thought I was crazy, I tried filling the hollowed out spaces with women. With alcohol. With violence and aggression. With anything that might distract me from the blinding absence of *you*."

Ugh!

My eyes were stinging, and my emotions were banging at the door with a battering ram. *Let us in! We want to hurt you!*

"Abram—"

"What I'm telling you is this—" His fingers flexed and he bent his head, forcing me to maintain eye-contact. The courage and determination within his gaze stole my breath, it seemed endless, boundless, immeasurable. "I am not built that way. Being sober isn't hard. Keeping my temper comes naturally unless it comes to you asking me to consent to a *fling*. I haven't been with anyone in over a year, and I don't miss it. I don't miss women. I don't crave women. I've never craved women. I crave *you*. There is no substitute, there is no additional accessory required. But if you don't feel this way about me, if you don't, you have to tell me. Now. Right now."

It was no use. Feelings bashed through the last barrier, pitchforks in hand, and punched smart Mona in the face. She was down for the count, leaving stupid Mona to throw herself into Abram's arms. I bawled. He caught me, cradled me, brought me to his lap on the floor, stroked my hair, kissed my face, held me close. He was so warm.

"I love you," he said. "Trust me," he said.

What else could I do?

I did.

* * *

I looked around the empty room, my gaze focusing on dust dancing in a beam of sunlight. A reminder.

There was so much, in life, in the world around us, that we rarely had a chance to see, but it didn't make those things any less real. We might experience and have access to the by-product, but rarely the thing itself.

Invisible forces, energy, quarks, radiation, dust dancing in a sunbeam, Abram.

Abram wasn't here. I couldn't see him. But I could remember his words, his smile, his touch, the sound of his heart. When I left Aspen, I would download and listen to his music. He was real.

Nodding at the truth of this, and trying to find comfort in it, I fought against the rising wave of tears. I took several deep breaths, blinking my eyes, and promising myself I wouldn't cry. *I won't cry,* not until I made it to the bathroom for a box of tissues. And then I would cry like crying was my job.

Tossing my legs over the side of the bed, I paused to drape a blanket along my shoulders, smelling it because it smelled like him. And that's when I spotted an envelope on the side table.

The outside read, *Do not burn,* but it wasn't my handwriting. My heart leapt, and then fell, and then recovered enough to settle someplace in the vicinity of my throat. He hadn't woken me when he left. We'd lain together, talking, holding each other, sometimes kissing, until I'd fallen asleep.

And when I awoke, he was gone.

I snatched the envelope and stared at the black ink on the white paper, the remarkably elegant cursive, and I opened it, feeling greedy for even a small portion of him.

Within was a piece of lined white paper that looked like it had been ripped out of a notebook. I unfolded the paper, taking care to press the crease neatly open, and I read the words.

Thoughts come easiest in the night.
In a room of light,
I see only the absence of you.
Darkness, though I cannot see,
Embraces me.

I'm blinded, yet my view is clear.
It feels possible that you are near, present, here.
So when you view your evening sky
Reach out to the night and there I'll be.
This is not goodbye.

—Yours always, Abram

LAWS OF PHYSICS
PART 3: TIME

CHAPTER 1
INTRO TO MODERN ASTROPHYSICS

I didn't know enough about spiders.

For example, what did they do during the winter when flies were scarce? Did they sleep/hibernate like bears? And what's the deal with hibernation? How does one get in on that action? Sleeping for long periods, as though time doesn't exist. *Then again—*

"Time doesn't exist."

"What?"

In the fuzzy distortion of my peripheral vision, I saw Lisa turn toward me. She'd been sitting at her square kitchen table, working on her laptop since I'd *meh-ed* all her suggestions for leaving the apartment today. I think she was relieved.

I sat in her living room, somewhat reclined on a big, brown leather couch that was too large for the space. It wasn't that the room was small, the couch was just too big, messing up the feng shui. Lisa had filled her apartment with fancy and colossal Williams Sonoma monstrosities, whereas what she really needed was some Ikea in her life.

My elbow bent, my cheek pressed against the underside of my forearm, I peered at the window.

"Time doesn't exist," I repeated, watching the spider in the corner of the glass pane as it did nothing. It wasn't dead, the web was too new, but it was completely motionless. "I need to read more about spiders."

"What does time have to do with spiders?" My sister's tone was uncharacteristically gentle, almost wary. I hypothesized that my bursting into tears with the smallest amount of provocation over the last three days had made her cautious. Poor Lisa. She'd invited me to stay not knowing I'd transformed from *not a crier* to *a crier*.

At first, she'd insisted we go out and, at first, I'd been happy for the distraction. However, no matter where we went, disaster struck. Abram's voice singing "Hold a Grudge" in the restaurant and at the movie theater. A poster of Abram and Redburn's album cover at L stations and street corners. A young woman wearing a Redburn T-shirt. He was everywhere and yet nowhere—no calls, no emails, no attempt at contact—and the combination made everything worse.

I figured, at least in Lisa's apartment I would be safe from the onslaught of Abram propaganda.

"I'm thinking about exploring the viability of human hibernation," I said through a yawn. If it was good enough for bears, need I say more?

"I don't think spiders hibernate." The sound of Lisa's chair lightly scraping against the tile drew my attention away from the spider. My sister stood, stretched, and her slippered feet made scuffing sounds as she walked. It was past 11:00 AM and we were still in our pajamas. "Do you want tea? Or coffee?"

"They should." Everyone should hibernate. "Why haven't humans investigated hibernation as an alternative to living through nonexistent time?"

"Mona. Do you want tea?" Lisa's tone wasn't impatient, but it wasn't patient either. Again, I didn't blame her. I'd been crying early and often, and I hadn't yet fully explained why. I couldn't, because every time I tried, I cried.

Which had me wondering, which came first: the try or the cry? *A paradox.*

"Yes to tea, please."

I zoned out as she moved around the kitchen and out of view. A short time later, a tea kettle screeched. Sometime after that, she set a mug on the coffee table. At some point, she sat next to me on the couch and placed her hand on my back. I didn't remember her touching me, only that one moment her hand wasn't there and the next moment it was. Straightening from where I half-reclined on the arm of the couch, I twisted to look at her.

Her lips were curved into a tight, small smile and she inclined her head to the right. "Your tea is ready."

"Thank you." I glanced at the mug, but I lacked the energy to reach for it. Therefore, I stared at it, willing it to move into my hands.

"What are you doing?" she asked after another vague span of time.

"You don't want to know."

More moments passed. Lisa's eyes were on my profile while I stared at the tea.

Eventually, she huffed, reached for the mug, and placed it into my hands. "You seriously need to snap out of this. What did he do to you? You've been here for three days and it's like hanging out with a ghost."

"WooOOOoooOOOooo." I made my voice shake, the pitch go up and down.

That made her chuckle. But then, for the hundredth time, she asked, "When are you going to tell me what happened in Aspen?"

I brought the mug to my lips because a sting of tears rushed to my eyes. I knew the contents within the mug were too hot to drink. I took a sip anyway. I burned my tongue. I blinked back the tears.

"Mona, come on." Her hand came to my shoulder. She squeezed it. She sounded concerned. "This isn't you. You're a mess."

"I'm not a mess." I was a mess. The logical path forward had abandoned me. Every road led to disaster. *The wolves are definitely on their way.*

"You *are* a mess. One minute you're giving me monosyllabic answers, and the next you're crying at the airport! I'm worried. I've never known you to be like this, ever."

I released a watery sigh, my eyes losing focus, the white mug and its dark brown contents swirling together to become a nebulous blur. "My display of emotion within the airport is self-explanatory."

"Yes. The large poster of Abram Fletcher in his underwear was difficult to miss." Once again, her voice gentled. "I'm sorry. I didn't see it on my way in, otherwise I would have walked a different way."

"It's okay." It was okay.

Martin Sandeke, Kaitlyn Parker's churlish fiancé, had mentioned the existence of the posters in passing last week. We'd been talking in the kitchen the day before Abram left Aspen, and Martin had said, *He just did that underwear modeling thing, soon there will be posters of the guy in his underwear everywhere.*

I hadn't given the statement extensive attention, instead focusing on the second part of Martin's claim, *That's not a guy who's changed. That's a guy who is just getting started.*

There he was. Abram. At the airport. Gorgeous. *Spectacular.* Hand over his heart. His eyes on the ground. A bright white background. Lust in my heart. His hair was down (I'd never seen him with his hair down since he'd grown it out) and he wore no shirt, just black boxer briefs that left very little to the imagination. Even worse, the advertisement for underwear had been life-sized.

I'd been warned, I should have prepared myself!

I wasn't prepared.

Martin had been right, the posters were everywhere, and *everywhere* included the baggage claim at O'Hare. I'd wanted to take it out of the plexiglass display, roll it up, and steal it, especially when I spotted two other women do a double take as they walked by. One of them elbowed the other and they shared a look.

They shared a look about my boyfriend . . .?

No.

Wait.

Is that what he was?

That would make you his girlfriend.

No.

Maybe?

I had no idea.

Anyway, I couldn't stop thinking about the fact that people in the airport had seen Abram with his hair down, shirtless, *in his underwear* before I had. And that gave me the sad. Would I ever see him with his hair down? Would I ever see him in his underwear?

Only time would tell, and time was being evasive.

Presently, my hand moved to the folded piece of paper I'd been carrying every day, now in my PJ pocket, and I rubbed my finger over the outline of its folded corners. I'd replaced my beloved letter—the one that Abram had burned in Aspen—with the poem he'd left me on my side table. The original letter I'd carried was thick, three pages of hefty hopes and dreams. This one was much smaller, which felt appropriate because it contained just one hope, *This is not goodbye.*

Then why does it feel like goodbye?

"Hey," Lisa said, pulling me out of my reflections. "You know, I almost cried when I saw the poster too." I could tell by the shift in her tone that she was trying to be funny, trying to cheer me up. "O'Hare should take it down, otherwise the arrivals area will be full of swooning, weeping women."

Ugh. "Not helping."

"I'm sorry. I'm just trying to—" Lisa's tone changed. "Listen, he's famous. Okay? He's famous, he's a rock star, and he's a model, and he's hot, and that means he's going to be a sex object, an object of lust for thousands of women. Those are the facts. You can't burst into tears every time you see a billboard of Abram Fletcher in his underwear."

My head whipped around to my sister and time slowed. "There are billboards?" My voice cracked, because of course it did.

She scrunched her face, and her response seemed to take forever. "Forget I said that."

"You've seen billboards of Abram in his underwear?"

Now she winced, again taking forever to respond. "Just two."

I set the mug away and covered my face, my elbows on my legs, and shook my head. "I can't do this."

"I'm sorry! I shouldn't have said anything." Lisa's fingers encircled my wrist. Just like when she'd placed her hand on my back earlier, I didn't flinch. Flinching had been instinctual for so long. I had no idea why the reflex suddenly stopped in some situations, with some people, yet persisted in others. But I couldn't think about that right now.

Removing my hand from my face, Lisa wavered for a moment, and then used her leverage on my arm to pull me forward into a hug. "Oh, Mona. I wish you would tell me what happened in Aspen. He hurt you? I'll make him suffer."

Heaving another watery sigh, I bit my bottom lip to stay my wobbly chin and clung to my sister. "He didn't hurt me. He was wonderful. So wonderful."

She made a sympathetic sound. "You miss him? Is that what this is about?"

I nodded.

"You two are together?"

I hesitated, because I wanted to be precise. "I think so."

"You think so?" An edge entered her voice and I felt her stiffen.

I pressed my lips into a firm line and endeavored to work through the jumble of feelings and thoughts and second-guesses cluttering my brain. Were we together?

Abram's words from that last night echoed between my ears, *Stop trying to put us in a fucking box!*

Sucking in a breath through my nose, I finally answered, "Definitely. Maybe."

I felt her chest rise and fall. "Maybe. What the hell does that mean?"

Scrunching my eyes, I leaned away, but kept hold of her forearms. "It means we love each other, and I told him I'd be open to seeing him whenever he wants to see me, and he—"

"What?!" She gripped my biceps and shook me until I opened my eyes. When I did, I was faced with a pissed off Lisa. "No. Oh *hell* no. You are not doing this. I will not allow it. You are not becoming one of Abram Fletcher's groupies. You are Mona DaVinci, world famous scientific badass, strong woman, brainiac, and role model to women everywhere. This is not happening!"

"It's not like—"

"I get it." Lisa gave me another little shake, her angry whisper like steel, her eyes flashing. "I get the insanity, I do. He's so talented, right? And sexy, and the sex is incredible, and he makes you feel special and alive, right? But, guess what, I guarantee you are not special to him."

"It's not like that."

"Mona, come on, you are so much smarter than this. You are a literal genius. You are no one's groupie."

"No, listen to me, we love—"

She let me go with a derisive snort. "Please. Love? He's known you for what? Two weeks total over two years? Bullshit. That's not love, that's sex and infatuation."

"Lisa, you're wrong. We haven't even had sex."

That had her straightening her spine, blinking her surprise. "What?"

"We've kissed, but that's it. You don't know what it was like when we were together that week here in Chicago. You don't know what it was like in Aspen. He—we—it's like, I don't even know how to describe it. I've never felt so . . ."

"Alive?" The question held a note of mockery.

"No. Comfortable. Effortlessly comfortable, being myself. He *knows* me, somehow, in a way I don't even know myself." I grunted, and then growled at the insufficiency of my words. "I'm not describing this correctly. The thing is, it's not about sex. Most of the time we were together, we just talked."

My sister's eyes narrowed into suspicious slits. "Seriously, Mona, this whole week, you don't even sound like yourself when you talk about him."

"Who do I sound like?"

"I don't know. Someone else. Someone not you." Her gaze moved over my face, like she was looking for the sister she knew within a stranger. "I guess, let me ask this, do you want to change? Do you like this person he's made you into? This weepy woman who can't leave the apartment without crying over a *guy*? Because—in my mind— this weak, sad, emotional person is not who you are."

Nibbling on my bottom lip, I dropped my eyes to my hands in my lap, absorbing her words. "I don't feel like I've changed. Much."

"But you have." Her hand closed over mine again, and this time I flinched, reflexively moving out of her grip. "Look. You're my sister. Obviously, I love you and want what's best for you. If you want my opinion—and you can take it or leave it— then it's this: Abram is not good for you. I'm not just saying this because I'm worried about how twisted up and emotional you've been this week, I'm saying this because I have experience with guys like him."

"You mean musicians."

"Yes. Exactly. They're a different breed. They're leeches. He might say he loves you, but he really just loves himself and his music."

"He's not Tyler."

"Oh, really? Has he called you? Has he texted you since Aspen? It's been almost a week, right?"

I winced against the chilling stab of pain slicing through me. She already knew the answer to her questions. He hadn't called. He hadn't contacted me.

After several beats of meaningful silence, during which I worked to breathe around the ache, I glanced at her. "You know he doesn't have my phone number."

"Right. And he can't get it from Leo, like, anytime he wants." Lisa lifted an eyebrow, her tone heavily laced with sarcasm, her lips a thin line. "No, honey. You forget, I chased after the human trash bag Tyler for years. I've been you. I've made these mistakes. I know what you're thinking and feeling, and I promise you—if you'd just cut him out now and stop hoping for more—everything will be so much better. You'll go back to being the Mona we all know and love."

Thankfully, the sound of Lisa's phone buzzing on the kitchen table saved me from having to form more words. With an irritated huff, she let me go and walked to the kitchen. I swallowed several times and lifted my eyes to the ceiling, willing back another confounded wave of tears.

She was right. Abram hadn't called or texted or made any attempt at contact. But, even if he did have my number, he was on tour. One quick Google search two days ago also told me that he was giving nonstop interviews to media outlets, radio stations, and magazines. He was busy. Having watched my parents go through similar times in their lives, I knew how full his days were. Just like them, he (probably) barely had time to sleep, and just like them, he didn't have time for me yet.

You should call him.

This wasn't the first time the thought had occurred to me. It was an insidious little whisper, a prodding, pushing, haranguing voice, and it disregarded facts.

Fact one: I didn't have his number.

Fact two: I could call my brother to get it, but I had no guarantee he would give it to me. After my discussion with Leo in Aspen about Abram, how he'd warned me away, I doubted he'd want me calling his friend. Yes, I would probably be able to extract the number from him after many minutes—or hours—spent in hostage negotiations, but that was assuming I didn't start crying on the phone. If I cried on the phone, Leo would never give me the number. Since I couldn't stop crying, calling Leo would just have to wait until I was more "myself."

Fact three: I wanted to talk to Abram, more than anything, but he'd been the one who left this time. He was the one who'd insisted it wasn't goodbye. I had to be patient. I had to be practical. I would give him space. I would wait. But I promised myself, if a month or two passed and he still didn't reach out, then . . .

Then you will still want to see him.

GAH!

Was Lisa right? Was I becoming someone else? Someone pathetic? Over a *guy*? But Abram wasn't "a guy."

But is he "the one?"

I hated the term, *the one*. However, here I was, using it, because I needed to call him something relative to my feelings for him. And yet, he couldn't be "the one." He didn't meet the minimum requirements.

By his own admission, Abram had never thought of getting married. I wanted kids, a house, a picket fence, normalcy, consistency. My feelings for Abram hadn't made those dreams go away, they'd just shifted, settled around him. He'd now become part of that picture.

But what if he didn't want to be part of that picture? What if he didn't want any of those things? What if his picture was completely different than mine? What then?

I rubbed my chest with stiff fingers, massaging my hurting heart through my ribs, telling myself that it wasn't Abram who'd made me weepy, he wasn't the cause for my constant catastrophic crying. It was me.

I was the problem. Me and my quest for stability while falling in love with a *musician.*

"Yeah, come over and help me talk some sense into her." Lisa raised her voice, obviously wanting me to hear her phone conversation, and I glanced up. She was sending me a stony look, her eyes slightly narrowed.

I glanced at the phone in her hand. "Who is that?"

"It's Gabby. She's on her way, bringing over ice cream and wine, but also offered male strippers."

Ah, Gabby.

I reached for my tea. "No. No, thank you. I don't need the wine or the ice cream either."

We'd gone out with Gabby during my first two days in Chicago. She was an *excellent* distraction. Or rather, her constant gabbing, zaniness, and wacky stories were. I was glad she was coming over just for the distraction factor.

"Well, you're getting wine and ice cream because she already bought them," Lisa said to me as she meandered closer, and then to Gabby, "Tell Duke to stay on standby. Okay, see you in a little bit. Bye." My sister returned to her spot on the couch, leaving her phone on the coffee table.

Taking as deep of a breath as I possibly could, I decided it was time to explain the entire situation to my sister. The inability to speak without becoming a blubbering mess had been a major limiting factor. I would just have to get over it. I would accept the tears, rather than fight them, and I would tell her the whole story.

"I'll tell you everything that happened," I rushed to say before she could launch into another rant. "Truly, Lisa. Abram is not like that, he's not like Tyler. He's not like

Mom and Dad either.”

She gritted her teeth and released a humorless laugh, shaking her head. “He is exactly like Tyler—and Mom, and Dad—musicians and artists are all the same, Mo, especially the brilliant ones. They’re flighty, selfish, and vain. They might be brilliant, but they only care about themselves, their ego, and their music. They will suck the soul right out of anyone who loves them, and they use it to feed their own brilliance until your light is extinguished, until you’re left broken. And then they move on.”

“Let me just tell you what happened, okay?”

“Fine, but if he doesn’t call you soon, *groveling*, and begging for forgiveness for not making contact in *six days*, then I will junk punch him with my new taekwondo moves, and then break his femurs.”

For the record, I didn’t want Lisa to junk punch Abram, but for some reason her overprotectiveness warmed my heart and, you guessed it, made me want to cry. I blinked against the new onslaught, lifting my eyes to the ceiling.

“Okay, first, let me explain something.” I cleared my throat and endeavored to recenter my thoughts. “You first have to understand, time doesn’t exist. As such, I can’t be angry at Abram for not calling me.”

One of Lisa’s eyebrows lifted, her gaze became a glare. “*Riiiiiiight.*”

“No, hear me out. We talk about people being deep, we talk about feelings being heavy. I’ve been thinking about this for the past week and it made me wonder: Do heavy feelings have more mass? Do they have their own gravity? Fields we cannot detect with any scientific instrument because they’re calibrated for the physical world?”

“Mona—”

“Just listen. If time is the result of gravity shaping or warping reality—which it is, which is why clocks tick faster on a mountain than at sea level—then what impact do heavy, weighty feelings have on time? I hypothesize that sadness slows time, and happiness does the opposite. Make sense?”

She rolled her eyes. “Only you would overcomplicate something so simple. Forget about the rules of physics—”

“Laws of physics.”

“Whatever! The rules of life, of society and engagement say that—if Abram was serious about you, if you were important to him—he would have called you *the very next day*. You can't tell me the weight of your feelings is at all responsible for the force of the mass of the gravity of fucking, selfish, shitty boys being shitty to you, blah blah blah." She waved her hands through the air, working herself into a frenzy. "He hasn't called you in *six days*. I don't care about gravity and feelings. In every universe, six days is a ridiculous amount of time."

"Yes. But—"

"There is no but! Stop making excuses for him!" Lisa's voice had lowered to a sharp whisper, and it was clear my attempt at using logic to explain my behavior was angering her.

"I'm not making excuses. You're right, okay? Six days is long, fine. But it's not really about Abram, is it? It's about me. What I'm saying is, I am heavy with unfamiliar feelings. All this crying, it's not because of Abram, not really. I've slowed time to an eternal crawl, and I'm overwhelmed. Therefore, me and my heavy, unfamiliar feelings are the problem. Not Abram."

I reasoned that, perhaps once I adjusted to this new time—Abram-less Agony Time—I'd stop being such a mess. Unfortunately, the only cure for Abram-less Agony Time was more time, and time was the problem in the first place, and time didn't even really exist! AH!

I need a nap. And a cookie would be nice.

Lisa gathered a deep breath, looking like she'd run out of patience and maybe needed a nap too. "Mona, I love you. But you are making me crazy. You can't accept responsibility for other people being assholes. I know you really like Abram, I know he said he loved you, but there's a reason people say, 'Actions speak louder than words.' I *totally* get it. He's hot. Talented. Charismatic. Something special. But if he doesn't treat you like a goddamn queen, then it doesn't matter how special he is, he's not worthy of you! And one more thing—"

The buzzer to the apartment cut her rant short and she frowned, looking mildly surprised. "Whoa, that was fast."

"Is that Gabby?"

"It must be." She seemed frustrated by the interruption. Lisa stood, walking to the button in her small foyer. "This conversation is on pause, but it's not over, okay?"

I nodded, frowning, feeling increasingly muddled.

Meanwhile, Lisa pressed the button, unlatching the main door at street level. She then unlocked and propped open her front door before shuffling to the kitchen and calling over her shoulder, "Prepare yourself for some serious day drinking. This is an emergency and the wine will help you relax enough to tell us the real story of what went down with you and Abram in Aspen. Think of it as medicinal."

"I thought you didn't drink anymore?" I straightened from the couch and stretched, walking aimlessly back and forth in front of the coffee table. Slowly, I turned toward the entryway. My brain was scrambled, but I figured I might as well be useful and help Gabby carry up her provisions.

"I don't drink anymore." Lisa appeared at the entrance to her kitchen holding two wine glasses. "But Gabby does, and she's a frequent visitor. She bought me these as a housewarming gift."

Despite the brain scramble, this data made me chuckle. It sounded so much like Gabby, buying someone a gift for their apartment because she would use it. Reluctantly, I admired how good Gabby was at looking after herself, knowing what she wanted, making it happen, and being unapologetic.

However, Gabby was also generous in completely unselfish ways too, like the wine and the ice cream.

"Here." I shuffled toward the door. "I'll go help her carry everything up. Be right back."

"You're still in your pajamas."

I glanced down at myself, at my plain white T-shirt, and black and blue pajama pants. "Yeah?"

Lisa twisted her lips to the side, considering. "I guess, nothing. Go ahead. But if you see the cute guy in the apartment below mine, make it clear you're my twin sister."

"Oh. I see what's going on." I nodded, managing a small smirk, and backing up toward her front door. "You want me to say I'm *Lisa* and ask him if I smell. Do I have that right?"

A rueful grin pulled her lips to one side, and she opened her mouth as though to respond to my teasing. Her eyes then moved beyond me, her mouth snapped shut, and she flinched. "What the hell?"

I glanced over my shoulder and did a double take. My heart jumped to my throat. My hand flew to my chest. I stumbled back. Behind me, standing in the doorway, was Tyler.

And behind him was Abram.

CHAPTER 2
ELLIPTICAL ORBITS

Abram

Stepping around Tyler, I walked directly to Mona. I saw only her, and her stunned expression gave me no pause. I wrapped my arms around her body, lifted her off the ground, and kissed her lips.

She was warm, and soft, and tasted like peppermint and honey. I bit back a groan.

God, she felt good. Great. Celestial. *Heavenly.* I may have surprised her, but she responded immediately, enthusiastically, twisting her arms around my neck, opening her mouth and welcoming the invasion of mine.

It wasn't enough.

It was a crumb, and I was starving. Desire—to tighten my hold, devour, take, keep, cherish, to never let her go—obscured thought and sight, and I slipped a hand under her shirt to touch the silky skin of her back, sliding my fingers upward until they rested under her bra strap.

Mona lifted her chin, breaking our mouths apart, and I kissed the point of it, the elegant line of her jaw, the tender spot beneath her ear, the hot skin where Mona's graceful neck met the slope of her shoulder. I was so hungry for her, I couldn't stop myself from tasting every exposed inch.

"Abram," she said, her voice a breathless, disbelieving whisper, followed by a little laugh. Her fingers flexed at the back of my neck, pressing me closer. Every part of my body hummed and vibrated, unable to contain the immensity of now, of this divine feeling.

"You're here," she said, her soft voice full of wonder and happiness, soothing the ravenous panic holding me hostage for the past six days. It had been a peculiar kind of madness, not being able to reach her while pretending all was fine, pretending she didn't occupy my mind every second of the day. But receding now, it left a new kind of turmoil and urgency in its wake.

We had no time.

No, I corrected myself, *We have time. We have the rest of our lives.*

"I need your fu—your phone number." I spoke gruffly against her neck, squeezing my eyes shut and breathing her in, again and again, the heat and sweetness of Mona.

I'd missed her, and that was a gross understatement. I'd been speeding toward this moment for days and being with her now felt like the aftermath of a head-on collision. Stupefied, frantic, but determined to enjoy every shared second remaining. My hands were shaking.

We have time. Calm down. Calm down.

Mona laughed lightly, the sound melodic, beautiful, and she pressed a kiss under my ear. "Why didn't you just ask Leo? Or send me an email?"

Leo.

I worked to keep the darkness of my thoughts from showing on my face as I leaned away, letting her slide to the ground but unwilling to release her fully, fisting my unsteady hands into her T-shirt. "I couldn't find an email for you anywhere, and neither could Marie. She tried calling your department for me. They told her all media requests had to go through the PR department at the university and it would take two weeks to a month for a response."

"Ah, that's true. My email is on lockdown, otherwise it gets out of hand." She nodded contritely. "But what about Leo?"

"Leo." I forced my jaw to relax and I lowered my voice but couldn't completely disguise the intensity of my wrath. "Leo wouldn't give me your number."

Mona's hand moved to my face, her palm pressed against my cheek, the pads of her fingers softly stroking my beard. "What? Are you serious?"

"Yes," I ground out. "He said he was doing me a favor. So I flew to LA."

"You flew to LA?" I felt her body tense, and the moment realization dawned, her beautiful eyes growing impossibly large as they moved over my face. "You must be so tired and—but I wasn't in LA, I was—"

"Here. Yes. I found that out yesterday when I stopped by your department at Caltech and they told me you weren't due back until Friday," I rushed to explain, multitasking, using the time to devour the sight of her, soak and submerge in the reality of being here with her.

Calm down. We. Have. Time.

"They said you'd be leaving for Geneva on Monday," I continued, willing my heart and speech to slow. "But that you were in Chicago, visiting your sister this week."

I left out the part about Mona's department secretary being a huge fan of Redburn, but not enough to give me Mona's email or phone number.

"What's he doing here?" Lisa cut in, sounding pissed.

I glanced at Mona's sister out of the corner of my eye. She didn't seem to be paying attention to us. Her stare was firmly fixed on some point behind me, I assumed Tyler.

"I also tried calling Gabby for your phone number," I continued, needing to tell the rest of the story before explaining Tyler's presence. "But her number had changed."

That caught Lisa's attention and her stare shifted to mine, held. "Yeah, well, that's Tyler's fault. He wouldn't stop harassing her last year, asking for my number, so she had to change hers." And then to him she said coolly, "You can leave now."

I spared a glance for the rocker, turning over my shoulder. "You should go."

The blond lifted his chin, his slate blue eyes flickering between me and his ex. "Don't forget what you promised."

I sensed Lisa's stare as it bored into the side of my face.

"I won't forget."

With a head nod and one more distracted glance at Lisa, Tyler turned and left.

As soon as the apartment door closed, Lisa spun on me. "What did you promise?"

Ignoring her, I turned to Mona. First things first.

I stepped back, pulled out my phone, unlocked it, and offered it to her. "Mona, will you please do me the honor of entering your cell number into my phone? And your email address."

"Absolutely." My beauty wore a small, genuine smile, but I also noticed she seemed tired, pale.

Before I could study her in greater detail, she took my cell, lowering her face and navigating to messages. She sent herself a text that contained her email address, handed the phone back to me, then her cell chimed from somewhere in the apartment. I took a moment to read her email address and number, repeating it to myself.

"It's so great to see you." Mona seemed to hesitate before hooking her fingers into the beltloops of my jeans.

I looked up from my screen. Her grin had grown, her gaze warm and hazy and happy, but now I could see her eyes were puffy, like she'd been crying recently. This discovery settled like a punch to my stomach, added a restless frustration to my sense of urgency, and I felt my eyebrows pull together.

This. Right here. This was the reason I'd been frantic to get here, to see her. We had time now, we had all the time in the world *now*, but I knew—I *fucking knew!*—the clock had been ticking on her faith in me. I'd told her it wasn't goodbye, I'd asked her to trust me. But without contact for days, she must've been thinking the worst.

Fucking Leo.

"Hey." I returned the phone to my back pocket, repeating her number to myself one more time, and cupped her cheek. "Are you okay? I honestly came as soon as I could. I promise, if I'd had your phone number, you'd be sick of hearing from me by now."

Mona pressed her cheek against my palm, her eyes drifting shut as her smile grew soft, dreamy. "Yes. I'm better than okay." She sighed. "Now that you're here, I'm awesome."

This was exactly the reassurance I'd needed. Relief didn't crash over me. It gradually settled, like a soft, warm blanket thawing the freezing panic in my bones. The terrible truth was, I hadn't trusted Mona to trust me. Technically, we'd known each other for over two years, but in reality, it had only been twelve days.

If I'd been her? I would've been irate.

Tilting her chin up, I kissed her again, softly this time, just a quick taste even though a sharp, throbbing pulse beneath my skin demanded I do more, take more, touch more.

We have the rest of our lives. Take your time.

"I missed you." Unwilling to cede any distance, I spoke against her lips. "I'm not here for very long, so we need to make plans to—"

"Hey!" Mona stiffened at Lisa's shrill interruption, her eyes flying open. My mouth landed on her jaw instead of her mouth as she gave the third person in the room her attention.

"Abram," Mona's twin demanded, "what did you promise Tyler?"

Unwilling to give Lisa my eyes—not while this woman I'd been craving was finally *right here*—I brushed my lips against Mona's temple and nuzzled the soft texture of her hair, answering Lisa distractedly, "He said he knew where you lived and would take me here, so I said I'd play Pirate Orgy's new single as part of our set during a few tour stops."

I didn't know why I was explaining myself. This was a waste of time. I was here, Mona was here, I'd been thinking about nothing else but hoping she'd still want to see me. And if she did, I'd been obsessing about what I would do to and with her body and brain.

Discussing stuff that didn't matter with Lisa—because it was already settled and done—was pointless.

"Which tour stops?" Lisa sounded obstinate, like she believed she had a right to the information.

"LA, Chicago, New York, and Miami," I mumbled, while pulling Mona forward and against me by the fabric of her pajamas. I smoothed my palm down the length of her arm, entwining our fingers together. How many hours had I spent thinking about this? Hoping she would still let me hold her hand?

Too many.

We have time.

Mona, splitting her attention between me and her sister, whispered sweetly, "I missed you too." And that made me smile.

But Lisa made a sound of indignation. "LA? New York? Why the fuck would you do that?" And that made me scowl.

"Lisa." Mona's voice was beseeching, and I leaned away to study her profile. She looked fretful, unhappy. *Damn.*

Damn. Damn. Damn.

Curling my free hand into a fist, I gathered a steadying breath, filling my lungs before turning from Mona to face her twin. Never mind that I'd barely slept in almost thirty-six hours. Never mind Mona and I hadn't seen or spoken to each other in almost a week. Clearly, if I wanted to spend any time with Mona, the sister would have to be dealt with first.

"Let it go," I said, deepening my voice so I wouldn't shout. "It's done, and it has nothing to do with you."

Lisa seemed to clench her jaw at my statement, her lips tightening, but kept her eyes —shining with accusation—stubbornly pointed at her sister. "You know what he did to me. And now your boyfriend is going to launch his career?" Ignoring me and addressing only Mona, her voice had become softer, and yet definitely angrier. "Fuck that and fuck you! You know that's not okay. I'm your *sister!* Don't just stand there and let him—"

"Hey." A sudden and savage spike in temper, the single word erupted from me, sounding like a bark, and Lisa's startled glare cut to mine. "Back off."

Mona's sister angled her chin, her eyes narrowing into slits. "You don't tell me what to—"

"That's where you're wrong. I don't care who you are, no one talks to Mona like that. No one."

Lisa scoffed, sneering. "Oh yeah? You speak for Mona now? Give me a fucking break. She is one of the most intelligent, amazing, strong, capable people in the world. She's a *genius.* She doesn't need you intervening on her behalf. Mona can more than speak up for herself, and this isn't any of your business, *Abram.*"

"No. This isn't any of your business, *Lisa.* You're right about your sister. She is amazing, strong, capable, but she also has a huge and sensitive heart that you don't seem to have a problem kicking around whenever it suits you. I see you're angry. I get why. But your anger isn't going to change a damn thing. Giving Tyler's song a spot was my decision. Mine. Bullying Mona isn't going to change my mind. You talk to her like the queen she is or shut the fuck up."

That made her flinch, her eyes blinking, a crack forming in her stony exterior as though I'd touched on a vulnerability, a fear. "I'm not—I'm not bullying her." Her gaze, now looking agitated, shifted to Mona at my shoulder. "I would never do that, I would never—"

"Yeah. You are." Some protective instinct had me stepping to the side, blocking Mona from her view. She didn't need this, especially not from her own sister. "She's not responsible for your screwups. No one is responsible *but you.* You don't like it?

Too bad. You made the shit sandwich, now you have to eat it, all by yourself. Want to whine to someone? Call your brother. But back off Mona."

"Abram." Mona squeezed my hand, her voice—again—sounded beseeching, and my name on her lips, in her lovely voice, acted like a pin puncturing my swelling fury.

Turning, I stiffened at the sight of her conflicted gaze, and my stomach dropped. But I fought against the reflex to apologize. I was contrite, but I wasn't sorry. I'd never be sorry for defending her. Mona's sister—and her brother—they didn't know her, didn't understand how sensitive she was. They didn't take care of her or look out for her like she deserved, like she needed. They made assumptions that were unequivocally false, and it pissed me off.

I swallowed the reflex to say sorry, and I faced her fully. I brought her hand to my lips and kissed the tender junction between her middle and index finger.

"What can I do?" I asked.

Mona's lips pressed together, her steady stare looking no less conflicted, maybe even a little resigned. "Give me a minute to talk to my sister."

My hands tightened on hers and a jolt of alarm made it difficult to breathe. I wanted to deny her. I wanted to drag her out of this room and apartment. I wanted to bring her back with me to the West Coast for the rest of the week and take care of her.

I swallowed those reflexes too. Working my jaw, I nodded. I stepped forward and kissed her quickly. I pressed my forehead to hers.

And, with effort, I forced myself to say, "Whatever you need."

CHAPTER 3
CELESTIAL MECHANICS

Abram

I waited in the room where Mona was staying, a small guestroom with a sleeper sofa and sparse furniture. Tearing off and tossing my outer layer of winter clothes to the dresser, I pushed my hands through my hair and fastened it back. It needed a cut.

Though the space was cramped, I had an uninterrupted span of nine feet and paced—back and forth—while studying her phone number and email until they were branded on my brain. I would never be without a means to contact her again.

You will see her again. After today, you can talk to her any time you want.

As much as I told myself we had plenty of time, I couldn't shake the notion that we had no time. In just a few hours, I needed to be on a plane. Despite acknowledging that this afternoon was just the first of many I'd be seeing her during the tour, purpose obsessed me, I was determined: we needed to make plans.

Definite plans. Commitments of time. Promises.

Unfortunately, after the shit-show with Lisa, everything I'd wanted to share and discuss and resolve with Mona had been eclipsed, muddied by her sister's breath-taking selfishness. I couldn't believe how Lisa spoke to her, and that Mona allowed it.

You shouldn't allow her or anyone else speak to you that way. You are so much more and better and worthy than you allow them to treat you.

The words rolled around in my mouth, souring my tongue. I wouldn't speak them out loud. They would undoubtedly lead to an argument and I wasn't here to pick a fight. But it wasn't just Lisa, her brother was just as bad. Even now, days later, the memory of my last conversation with Leo had me seeing red.

"You'll thank me," he'd said, sounding convinced. I'd kept my temper up to that point, listening to him call her cold and calculating, emotionless. Every adjective out of his mouth made me want to reach through my phone and punch him in the face. "Just listen to me, I'm trying to help you."

"I'm never going to thank you for this, Leo. And if you knew your sister—*at all*—you'd know that she is none of those things."

"Abram, man, don't tell me about my own sister." He sounded irritated. "I've known Mona her entire life. She's *my sister*. She doesn't even like people touching her."

I snapped. "And why the fuck do you think that is, Leo? You think people are just fucking born that way? You think that's normal? Did it ever occur to you to ask her why that is?"

"Would you listen?" Now he was yelling. "I've asked her, okay? I asked her why. I asked if anyone hurt her. She said no, flat out."

She said no? That was a surprise. Had she been lying? No. She wouldn't lie. She wasn't a liar, I believed that now. Mona didn't lie unless it was to protect someone she loved, unless she felt like she had no choice. *So maybe—like she said in Chicago years ago—it really is just as simple as: Mona doesn't like unexpected touch.*

That didn't seem right either. I'd touched her unexpectedly without her flinching away.

Before I could think through this revelation, Leo exhaled loudly. "You're being a fucking psycho about this. Stop. Just fucking stop. My answer is final. I'm not giving you her number so you can make an idiot of yourself. And yeah, she's my sister, so I don't want guys harassing her, okay? That includes you."

I rubbed my forehead, shutting my eyes, working to get my temper under control. "Then why don't you call her and ask her permission? Can you do that? Please?"

"No!" he shouted. Then he continued, quieter, "I know you're mad now, but you'll see I'm right."

I laughed, my chest, throat, and mouth full of broken glass, because what else could I do? "You're an idiot."

He also huffed a bitter-sounding laugh. "Yeah, well, maybe I am, because I'll still be here, I'll still be your friend when you come to your fucking senses." Leo sounded tired, spent. "I'm just trying to save you from yourself, man. It's not worth the pain, okay? Call me when you see reason."

Not worth the pain.

Fuck it. The next time I saw Leo, I would punch him in the face. All those years, listening to him talk about Mona as though she had no feelings, feeding into this narrative about her being completely callous and inhuman-levels of resilient.

Before Aspen, I'd believed him. It was easy and convenient to think of her that way.

But now, I hated it. I hated how they and everyone else talked about her like she was this invulnerable, dispassionate alien thing, too perfect, untouchable, unknowable. At some point, Mona and I would have to discuss it, because I wasn't going to be able to watch their continued abuse without seriously losing my shit.

Something has to give.

Mona opened the door and my head snapped up. Before she could close it, I was on her again, reaching for her hand to draw her through the opening, shutting the door, and pushing her back against it.

Unthinkingly, acting on pure instinct, I fit my hands under her T-shirt, seeking her skin. Smoothing my palms up, down, and then around her sides to her back, I touched my lips to hers. My heart suddenly in my throat, my irate internal rantings about her shitty siblings faded to background noise. Suddenly, I didn't want to talk or think about them at all. I didn't want to give them another second of this precious time.

Later. We would talk about it later. *Much later.*

"Hey," she whispered, pressing her mouth to mine, catching my bottom lip with a quick nip, and then moving her inebriating kisses to my cheek, jaw, neck. "Are you okay?" she whispered against my ear. She'd also moved her hands under my shirt, pausing for a split second, and then pulling me closer.

I laughed, incredulous. "Are you kidding? I'm fantastic. Are *you* okay?"

She tucked her head under my chin, her ear over my heart. "I can't think of a time I've ever been better."

I laughed again, tightening my arms. Thank God she wasn't pissed at me. Thank. God. I'd almost convinced myself she would be. This? Her reaction to my sudden appearance? It felt miraculous. Exhaling a long, quiet breath, I gave myself this miraculous moment, holding her, her holding me, and worked to memorize every touch, sight, smell—

"You shaved your beard," she blurted, yanking me out of my reflections. The statement sounded accusatory.

For some reason it made me smile. "No, I didn't. We just cut it closer."

"A lot closer. It's basically gone."

"I can grow it back, if you want me to. It won't take long. Just say the word."

Mona wavered before saying, "I can't decide. I love your wizard beard, but I've missed your dimples."

My smile widened. "My dimples, huh?" If she wanted my dimples, they were all hers.

"Oh yes." She turned her face and placed a kiss on my shirt in the center of my chest. "I can't believe you're here."

"I can't believe I'm here either." I allowed her to lean back just far enough for our eyes to meet. Again, I noticed how puffy hers were, how red, and was assailed with a forceful and frustrated sense of helplessness. "Mona, please believe me, I did everything I could to find your number or Lisa's number. I had Marie use her contacts—a security firm here in Chicago—and they found nothing under your name, no driver's license, no utility bills. Only a passport with your mother's PA's phone number and the Chicago house address, nothing else."

She gave me a wry smile. "Yeah. Sorry. That's because—"

"You don't have to apologize. I get it, you don't want crazies tracking you down. My number and details are similarly obscured. But Leo wouldn't give me Allyn's last name, so I couldn't call her either. I just need you to know, I did everything I could to reach you as soon as I could."

"I could have called Leo for your number. I should have. I'm sorry too."

"No, no. It was on me. I asked you to trust me."

"I do trust you." She beamed up at me, but I didn't like the unsteadiness in her voice. It betrayed her words, made them ring false.

"Hey." Cradling her cheek, I traced the line of her cheekbone with my thumb, and whispered, "I promise, I will never give you a reason to cry."

Mona's lips pressed together into a wobbly smile, her eyes glassy.

I groaned. "What's this? Tears?" I kissed her eyelids.

She laughed and rolled her eyes at herself. "Sorry. I don't know what's wrong with me."

I had my suspicions. My guess was that these tears were about many things, not just me, not just us. Of course, part of her upheaval over the last few days was about us. A lack of trust. She didn't trust me, not yet, but it was clear she wanted to.

Mona swiped at her cheeks, her smile now brittle. "I can't seem to stop crying and I've never been a crier. It's like I came back from Aspen broken."

Broken?

I shook my head vehemently. "No. God, no. You aren't broken. Mona, crying, *feeling* doesn't make you broken. Stoicism does. Burying your emotions—from everyone, all the time—does." I kissed her quickly again. "Don't fight the tears. Maybe you're crying so much because it's the first time you've let yourself. Maybe they'll stop, maybe they won't. But you're safe with me. Let them come."

She sniffled, her eyebrows pulling together. "You don't think all this weeping makes me weak?"

"No. I think it makes you brave, because it also makes you soft, and sweet, and honest. And those might not be parts of yourself that you value—or other people see as valuable—but those are the real, raw, essential pieces of *you*. You deserve to share them with someone, and if that's me, I'm honored to be that person. I will always, *always* treasure this side of you."

Her wide eyes moved between mine, breathtakingly, exquisitely vulnerable. I knew it was selfish but seeing her exposed and defenseless mollified a primal desire I didn't quite understand. It made me feel stronger, essential, necessary in a new way. Maybe because I was now necessary to her?

Whatever the reason, it also made my protective instincts swell. No one—and I mean *No. One.*—was going to fuck with her. Ever. No one would hurt her. No one would make her cry.

Uh, she's crying right now.

Searching her face, I could see she was overwhelmed.

So, I made my voice mock-stern, saying, "Crying is allowed—cry all day, every day —but no more apologies," guessing she both needed and wanted a reason to smile.

She did. And seeing her true smile made me smile in return.

Sniffling, she lifted an eyebrow. "Okay. Crying is fine, but no apologies. What else is allowed?"

My grin grew, my eyelids drooping, and I slid my hand from her cheek to the neck of her shirt, pulling it to one side, baring her shoulder. "I can think of some things. But first, we need to talk."

Her smile faded somewhat, became dazed, her attention lowering to my lips. She licked hers. "How long do we have?"

I'd promised myself we wouldn't do anything until plans and commitments were made, but I couldn't help myself. Bending, I took my time biting, licking, and kissing the top of her shoulder. She shivered. She also tasted like heaven, and each swirl of my tongue increased the hunger.

"Two hours." My voice was low, rough against the wet spot. Trailing my lips closer to her neck, I took another soft bite. Now that her skin was exposed, I couldn't stop.

She started to moan. She stifled it, her fingers fisting in the front of my shirt as she offered more of her neck. "Only two hours?"

"I have to catch a plane. We have a concert tonight." Reluctantly, I lifted my head, capturing her eyes again so she could see my regret. In that moment, my responsibilities to my bandmates, to my record label and my fans, they felt like handcuffs and a jail cell.

Her gaze—a mixture of disappointment and worry—turned scrutinizing. "Abram, you're exhausted. Have you slept?"

"I slept a little on the plane from LA."

She flattened her hand over my heart. "You have to take better care of yourself. Tours are stressful and exhausting. Please promise me you'll get sleep tonight after the concert."

"I will try." *Try* being the operative word. Performing in front of thousands of people was an indescribable high. But four nights in, and the tour had only made the longing, my craving for her, worse. My attention and patience had narrowed, leaving room for nothing but filling my hands and mind and memory with Mona.

"You'll try?" She narrowed her eyes, one side of her mouth tugging upward.

"I will. But after a concert, all the energy, and I'm thinking about you, wishing you were there, knowing it's not possible. It's . . ." I slid my teeth to the side, unable to stop my self-conscious grin.

"What?"

"Hard." The word slipped out before I could stop it.

Her head tilted slightly to one side. "What's hard? Going to sleep?"

She has no idea what she does to me.

My grin became rueful and I swallowed, my eyes moving between hers. "Please don't make me say it."

Mona's eyebrows slowly pulled together. I could almost see the gears turning, and the hand still loosely fisted in my shirt slid down to the front of my pants, as though she were unthinkingly confirming a hunch. Her curious fingers gave me an investigatory stroke, but it was more than enough. I sucked in a breath through my teeth as my cock swelled, lengthened, hardened, greedy for her.

"You—you shouldn't do that." Not trusting myself to hold her and not tear her clothes off, I braced my palms and forehead on the door behind her, again willing my heart to slow.

"Ah! Sorry. Sorry!" Mona completely removed her hands from my body, yanking them away. "Sorry. I should've asked permission."

Lifting my head, I peered down at her. She'd covered her face with her hands and was peeking at me from between her fingers.

"No." The single word came out gruff, raspy. I cleared my throat, reaching for her wrist and pulling it away from her face. "No, Mona. Not permission. But, if we're going to talk at all, you shouldn't—do *that*—today."

She was nodding before I'd finished speaking. "Yes. Sorry."

"Please don't apologize."

"Okay, sorry—ah! I mean, okay. Okay." Mona rolled her lips between her teeth, still nodding, her eyes wide and remorseful, but also bright, like she found my situation a little funny.

A pretty, pink blush was creeping up her neck, and it was fantastically distracting. I wanted to pull the neck of her shirt to the side again, peek inside, find out where the blush started.

Instead, I stepped away—one step, and then another—clearing my throat again and forcing firmness into my voice. "We need to talk." It was as much a reminder to me as it was to her.

"Of course." Her voice was also firm, but her attention flickered quickly to the front of my pants, her cheeks now pink, as were her ears.

I shook my head at her, increasing the distance between us out of necessity. "Do you want to talk?"

Shit. Where had that question come from? There was no choice. We had to talk.

Mona, staring at me, her eyes slowly narrowing as she chewed on her bottom lip, didn't answer.

"Mona?"

"What are my options?"

My mouth dropped open and I exhaled a laugh. "What are your *options*?"

"Yeah." She took tiny steps forward, her eyes once more dropping to my fly, and then back up. "I mean, we only have two hours, probably less now. Other than talking, what are the options?"

I stared at her, struggling, standing between the steady voice of reason and a raging hard-on. My eyes lowered to her baggy shirt, simultaneously both wishing it were see-through and hugely grateful it was so shapeless.

"First, we need to be—we need to be on the same page here." I choked out, my leg and foot conspiring to take a half step forward.

"About what?"

"About us."

This had been phase two of Kaitlyn's plan, and I'd been kicking myself all week for not being more explicit about what I wanted before leaving Aspen.

"Okay. What page are you on?"

Crossing my arms, I gathered a deep breath. If Mona could be brave, vulnerable with me, then I could be the same with her. "If it wasn't obvious, I want to make sure I'm clear now: I am not interested in anyone else. I want a commitment from you that we'll be completely exclusive."

She grinned, her eyes brightening. "Fine. Done. We're exclusive."

EXCELLENT!

"Okay." I nodded, having a hard time not grinning like a fool. "Good."

"Good." She edged closer, and her goofy grin made me feel better about mine. "Anything else?"

What else?

"Um."

Her beauty was distracting, and I fought to regather the ends of my wits.

Just as she took another half step, I remembered. "Wait. Yes! We need to make plans, so we know when we'll see each other again."

But it was more than just making plans. If we did anything now, I really would drag her out of here, take her with me to the West Coast, keep her in my hotel room, hide her clothes, and eat her out for breakfast, lunch, and dinner. And snacks.

We have plenty of time, plenty.

The hard-on was winning.

"Yes. Plans. Of course." Mona twisted her fingers in the hem of her T-shirt, showing me a sliver of smooth olive-toned skin at her stomach.

I'm sure it wasn't purposeful or meant to make me crazy, but it was like waving a red flag in front of a bull. My body lurched forward, already consumed, while I stood perfectly still, besieged, so close to giving in.

"But—and hear me out—we could make plans over the phone, or via email. However, it's much, *much* harder to do other things over the phone." She paused for a beat, staring at me as though hoping I would read her mind, and then added, "And basically impossible via email."

I swallowed around the scorching, thick knot in my throat, unable to do anything about the one low in my stomach. *Yet.*

"Mona," I started, stopped, winced, closed my eyes, then began again. "Mona, I want you. The things I want to do to you, to your body, they require more than two hours and a ten-by-ten room. As much as I missed you, as much as I crave you, as much as I've fantasized about being close" *—bare and touching and fucking your brains out* — "we need to take things slow. Two hours in the cramped guest room of your sister's apartment? No. That will only frustrate the hell out of me."

I opened my eyes, stared at her pants, waited a beat, and then lifted my gaze. Her lips were parted, her eyes hazy, reminding me of that insane, primal moment between us in Aspen, in the pool.

The memory haunted me. I'd imagined so many different endings more than a thousand times. Fantastically filthy, wonderfully selfish endings. But I had zero regrets.

Gathering my self-control and a deep, calming breath, I shook my head. "And these things I want to do, they also require trust."

Her eyes sharpened, sobered, and she frowned. "I trust you."

"Do you?"

"Of course."

"Then why have you been crying?"

Her mouth snapped shut.

"No, Mona. You don't trust me. And you were right, in Aspen. We don't know each other."

She blinked once, hard, and took two stumbling steps forward. "I thought you said I should cry."

"Yes. Absolutely. Cry if you need to, but don't ignore what the tears are about."

"What? Abram—"

I held a hand out to stop her advance. "I've been thinking, and I know you have too. A little less than two weeks, twelve days. You can't trust someone you don't know, and trust takes time."

Mona's frown deepened, her lips pinching together. "We don't have time."

I laughed lightly, because her words were a direct echo of my desperate thoughts. But we were both wrong.

The one thing we finally, *finally* had was time.

"We have all the time. We have the rest of our lives."

"I'm confused. You want to be exclusive. Now you say you don't know me? Are you saying—are you saying you don't lo—that you don't feel the same as—as—" She crossed her arms, her chin jutting out, a flash of vulnerability and hurt behind her eyes.

It was the vulnerability that had me heedlessly crossing the short distance, as though yanked, compelled and panicky to touch her before she could build any walls between us.

"No. No. Absolutely not." I held her face in my hands, ignoring how the gentle touch made her flinch, and stifled the urge to take back my words. Instead, I committed to honesty, no matter how much the thought of losing her now scared the hell out of me. "I love you. I'm crazy about you. I want you, only you. But, Mona—" I touched my forehead to hers, "—God, I don't want to rush a single moment. I want a first date, and a second date, and a third, and a twenty-third, and an eighty-seventh. I want phone calls and text messages. I want to hear about a day in the life of Mona DaVinci, every day."

I leaned away, needing to see her eyes, my heart giving a sluggish, painful beat at the conflicting emotions there.

Despite my pledge not to rush, I hurried to add, "I want to get mad at you, and fight, and make up—I can't wait to make up with you. It's going to be *so great.*"

That pulled a hesitant little smile from her and she swallowed, her gaze less stormy. "That does sound nice."

I grinned at her reluctant reassurance and didn't miss how her attention shifted to the left side of my face, the deeper of my two dimples.

While she was distracted, I pressed my mouth to hers, stealing a tender kiss and whispered solemnly, "I want to take care of you, when you want me to, when you need it. I want to trust you'll be there, that I can count on you to take care of me too."

She sniffed, nodding, her fingers gripping my forearms. "That also sounds nice."

"Good." Cautiously relieved, I let go of her cheeks. Smoothing my hands down her shoulders to her sides, I pulled her against me. She came willingly, going soft, lax, just as she'd done before, and my body hummed happily in response.

Well, happily and hornily.

I felt myself calm. "No. My feelings haven't changed. I'm still insane about you. But . . ." I stroked her hair, kissing her temple, inhaling her sweet scent. "I want to be sane about you too."

CHAPTER 4
ATOMIC PHYSICS

"That takes us through September," he said, the bed depressing as he claimed his spot on the edge.

I nodded distractedly, *again* scrolling through the calendar app on Abram's phone for August and July, hunting for a possible span of time where we might be able to arrange a quick meet-up. We'd both set timers on our phones, a countdown to the moment I'd have to drive him back to the airport using Lisa's car.

I felt good-ish about February through June, but July and August were still a problem. We hadn't been able to find even one rendezvous over those two months. Abram would be in New Zealand and Australia and I would still be in Europe. No face-to-face time for over two months felt like a rendezvous dearth of ginormous proportions.

Of note, I did rather like the word *rendezvous* and planned to overuse it in the future.

"How long is the flight from London to Dubai again?" I gazed longingly at the seven-day period of free time he had between Brisbane and Perth in mid-August. Unfortunately, it just so happened to be the same week as my Spectroscopy Symposium in London, where I'd be presenting at three sessions and moderating two graduate-level panels. Dipping into my parents' travel fund to visit my boyfriend—especially when international tickets were so pricey—didn't sit right with me.

However, if I skipped avocado toast for the rest of my life, I'd be able to afford the plane ticket.

Abram covered my hand, drawing my eyes back to his. "We've spent a half hour on just those two months. Let's move on to September through November."

We were situated adjacent to each other on the twin daybed in Lisa's guestroom. It doubled as a small couch, but I'd left all the throw pillows piled up behind the headboard. I was sitting against the wall, my legs crossed, with just my regular sleep pillow behind my back. Abram sat on the edge, one foot propped on the floor. He stood at intervals to pace while studying the calendar app on my phone.

Keeping it real, Abram's pacing was a problem, because I loved, loved, *loved* watching his body move. Which meant that I was staring at him when I should've been studying his calendar. He didn't seem to notice my staring. Or, if he did, he didn't say anything about it.

"We have to move on." His brown eyes flickered between mine, and—just like all the other times we gazed at each other for any length of time—I had to remind myself not to tackle him to the ground, rip his clothes off, and kiss and lick and bite every square centimeter of his rock-hard physique.

Especially his bottom.

That's right. I wanted to sample his bottom. Every time he paced away, little pheromone pixies danced on my pelvis, gleefully, wickedly smashing my concentration into a million pieces of agitated yearning. I wanted to touch it, stroke it, massage it, *bite it*.

Whew.

Clearing my throat, swallowing, I sucked in a breath and tore my eyes away from his, fanning my T-shirt. "Is it—" I had to clear my throat again because my voice cracked. "Is it hot in here?"

The thing is, I wasn't this person. No one, not even me, would ever describe me as physically focused, or fixated on touching an attractive or alluring exterior. Ever. I actively rejected external beauty as a contributing factor to how or if or when I interacted with people. I'd never been tactile. I observed. I calculated. I analyzed. I didn't even like playdough as a child.

But with Abram, I couldn't stop noticing. I couldn't stop thinking. I couldn't stop *wanting*.

"Mona."

Think of the Queen! Isn't that what the British always said? What was the US equivalent? Think of the first lady?

I worried my bottom lip, breathing in through my nose, endeavoring to get my brain out of his pants. "Okay. Okay. Where are you going after Perth?"

"Mona." He leaned close, using his hold on me to pull both my hand and his phone toward his chest.

My gaze darted up and then away, cheeks heating, because if I looked at him again, I'd be—again—fighting the impulse to tackle him and we still had three months to—

"Mona, look at me."

I did. I gave him my eyes. I also held my breath.

His gorgeous amber irises seemed to glow as they moved over my face, dropped to my mouth, lingered there. They felt hot yet controlled, self-possessed, and for some reason the self-possession took my heat level straight to plasma.

"I think—" He licked his lips, taking his phone from my grip and placing it on top of the throw pillows piled by the headboard. "I think we need to do something."

"Something?" I asked, still not breathing so the words came out more like a hitching whisper. I didn't know if it was the lack of oxygen or Abram that had me feeling so dizzy.

Abram. Definitely Abram.

On my sixteenth birthday, I'd had an IUD implanted, a gift from my sex-positive parents. Lisa had received one too. Leo had received a reversible vasectomy for his.

Even with the IUD, I'd always used a condom for sexual intercourse as well as spermicide I would procure after triple-checking the lot numbers and packaging date. Anything older than three months, I would throw away.

I'd administered two blow jobs, again always with a condom, and the second one only because I was convinced I'd missed something the first time. Once, a guy attempted to conduct cunnilingus using a female condom. I'd insisted after discovering he hadn't been vaccinated against HPV. It wasn't enjoyable. I'd stopped him after the timer denoted the agreed upon two minutes was over, not liking how messy and wet on my thighs it had become.

I mean, saliva. Do you know how filthy the human mouth is? Disgusting.

I'd done many, many things with my seven sexual partners—working my way through a checklist of positions and techniques, toys and gadgets—and everything I was open to exploring had been attempted at least once. Notes had been made. Items had been crossed off. Second and third attempts at pleasant activities had yielded varied results, leading me to the conclusion that masturbation utilizing a LELO vibrator was the only consistent—and therefore worthy—method of satisfaction.

But with Abram . . .

I wanted to do it all again, try it all again, even the items I'd crossed off my lists.

"We have twenty minutes left, before I have to leave," he said, the words rough. His palm came to my knee and my body jolted at the benign touch. A small smile tugged his mouth to one side, his delicious dimple making an appearance, and his voice was low and rumbly as he asked, "Do you want me to touch you?"

"Touch me?" I squeaked, clearly incapable of brain function higher than a parrot. Forced to exhale because my chest felt like it might burst, not a half second later I was gulping air again.

"Yeah." His hand slid higher on my leg, sending hot spikes of twisting tension straight to my center, and he leaned closer, rising slightly above me, filling my vision, his warm palm shifting to the inside of my upper thigh.

My feet did something weird, arching and pointing uncontrollably, almost like they'd been tickled, the muscles of my legs and stomach flexing. I sucked in an involuntary breath just as his large hand stopped at my hip, his thumb drawing a firm line over my thin cotton pajama pants from my lower abdomen straight to my clitoris.

Well, that escalated quickly.

I gasped, my eyes closing, my head hitting the wall at my back, my hands fisting in the comforter on either side of me while my body dichotomously froze and melted. I couldn't breathe.

I can't breathe.

"I can feel you," he said, his voice still a growl as the pad of his thumb circled me through the two layers of fabric, pressing, searching. "You're so wet. Is that for me?"

"As the, uh." *As the prophesy foretold.* "And thus, I die," I choked out instead and tried to shrug, making a joke of it, because—OMFG—I was ten seconds from orgasming. Honestly and truly. My lungs were on fire, my body clenching around emptiness, my skin stretched too thin.

And I was mortified.

He'd barely touched me. There'd been no buildup. One small stroke followed by two barely there circles, and my body had gone zero to the speed of light.

I can't breathe.

Some abrupt instinct had me clawing at his wrist, my hand fisting around his thumb to stop the efficient circles. I was wound too tight, it—everything—felt overwhelming.

"I—I'm—"

"Shh. Let me." His lips were on my neck, making me shiver, and he pried my fumbling hands away, threading our fingers together.

And then he was guiding me to my back.

And then I was lying down.

And then he was there, over me.

I experienced a split second of pure terror, of fear, my mind telling me that *someone* was above me, covering me, holding me down, and I couldn't move. Then Abram came into focus, settling himself between my open legs. Abram's scent filled my lungs. Abram's hips spread me wider. Abram's mouth sucked at my neck, eliciting more shivers, and my terror was nearly eclipsed by the surfacing wonder of seduction.

Abram rolled his pelvis, and the hard length his erection pressed *right* where I needed. Fear diminished, waned, but didn't completely extinguish. It became a quiet whisper instead of a clamorous shriek, inexplicably amplifying my senses without overwhelming them.

I can't breathe.

But I did breathe. I inhaled him, the Abram fragrance that both calmed and excited me. It spread like a velvety cloud, invading and liquifying each clandestine corner and hidden space and secret desire. It communicated a history without words: security and safety, longing and need.

I gasped again, my back arching sharply, my hips wanting to move. "What—what— oh God."

He made a noise, it sounded frustrated, his breathing now labored, his body heavy— so heavy—above me. Holding my hands on either side of my head, he rocked, sliding up and down, stroking me through our layers of clothes. I couldn't move. I was wholly trapped, inexorably tangled up and in and by Abram.

I should've been feeling panic. I wasn't. I was no longer the Mona who didn't like to be touched or crowded. I was a cluster of nerves and dark wants, *wanting* this man to cover me, hold me down, take over. I enjoyed the loss of control, how my fear mingled with pleasure, heightening every sense and sensation.

This, what we were doing, definitely hadn't been on any of my lists. We were fully clothed. Our bodies were touching through layers, but my hands were confined. His mouth was still on my neck, his breath falling on my skin, causing goose bumps, tingles, shivers, and *heat*. So much heat.

The only time I'd done anything close to what Abram and I were doing now had been last week, in the pool, when we'd mindlessly attacked each other. Nothing about this should have been sexy. But it was. I shouldn't have wanted to be possessed and overpowered in this way. But I did.

It was *the most* spectacularly sensual event of my life. Yet, even as it happened, I knew this conclusion made no sense. It felt incomprehensible, indecent, scandalous, and the indecency quenched some hidden, unacknowledged thirst.

"I think I'm going to—"

Abram kissed me, stopping my words, his tongue coaxing, a complete contradiction to the hard press of his body. Releasing my hand closest to the wall, he leaned to the opposite side, still caging me in, stroking his fingers from my breast to my stomach and replacing his erection with his palm.

I groaned at the loss of him, of the heaviness and friction, until his hand slid inside my underwear and he parted me with his fingers.

I was sweating. My heart was racing. My mind was swimming. I still couldn't breathe, but his scent was everywhere. He was everywhere. He was inside me, his hand in my pants, moving rhythmically in a way that—in the moment—felt wholly illicit, forbidden. He captured my cries and moans with his mouth, keeping me quiet like my pleasure was a secret, just for him.

I came, a shock of fire searing my nerves, to my fingers and toes, bursting behind my eyes. His composure, power, and precision made me crazed, made me feel as though I was his toy, or his instrument, and he was in total control. Bafflingly, I loved it.

His fingers thrust more forcefully, deeper, rubbing and stroking, prolonging my climax until I was boneless, exhausted, spent, sore low in my belly, and left with a cavernous ache in my chest. His amazing body, big and powerful, hard and mercenary next to mine, petting me, telling me wonderful and wicked things.

You are so fucking sexy.

I love watching you come. I love the way you feel. I love watching you lose control.

Do you want me here? Do you want me inside you?

Next time, I want the taste of you on my tongue.

Or, were those my thoughts? Did he say them? Or did I wish for them?

As the last of the spasms shook me and before I could disentangle myself, I turned toward him. He was gone. He'd left the bed. Rolling off and immediately pacing away.

Discombobulated and disheveled, I watched him, his hands braced on the far wall, his shoulders rising and falling. I felt the lack of him, a cold shock. I surfaced by degrees—Mona, me, the thinking, reasoned part of myself—and a sharp spike of alarm abruptly snuffed out any lingering residual exhilaration.

Why would you let him do that to you?

Wait. Do what? Touch me?

He held you down. You couldn't move, and you liked it.

I blinked at the internal accusation, remembering the last several minutes as though watching them happen to someone else.

I'd liked that? I'd like him over me? Holding me down? I'd liked not being able to move? Being touched, possessed, controlled like that? He didn't ask. However, I didn't say no. I didn't ask him to stop. Asking him to stop had never even entered my mind.

A flood of disbelief was followed by a rising tide of reason, during which I attempted to explain and describe my own desires to myself as something healthy and normal.

But is it? Is it healthy and normal?

Yes.

No.

Maybe?

No. You were afraid.

Was I?

Yes. And you wanted to be overpowered, you liked it. He could've done anything to you, and you would've been helpless to stop him. Even now—thinking about the possibility of handing over control again—You. Want. It.

I did. Just the thought of Abram over me again, his weight covering me—but this time naked, entering me, taking his pleasure from my body—I was completely and wholly arrested by the mere notion. It made me breathless, achy with a new dazzling, blinding thirst.

Yes. I want it.

And yet, I shouldn't want to feel helpless, right? I shouldn't want to feel overpowered physically. I'd felt that way once, against my will, and it revolted me, it kept me up at night, it gave me nightmares.

On the other hand.

With Abram it felt different—the loss of control, the lack of explicit consent, the being conquered sexually, emotionally—and what did that say about me? Was I turning a difficult moment in my life into a fantasy? Just the thought made me sick.

My internal arguments were becoming circular. Disbelief and reason were pushed aside by a creeping sense of shame and guilt.

Is there something wrong with me? I shouldn't want this, should I? I shouldn't—

"Mona."

My name in Abram's voice pulled me out of my shadowy reflections, and I looked at him, comprehending my own position at the same time. I'd rolled to my side, my knees bent and pulled to my chest, my arms locked around my legs. He was kneeling at the side of the bed, his hand hovering over my temple.

"Are you okay?" he asked, his gaze searching. "Did I—I didn't hurt you, did I?"

The trepidation in his voice was a sobering bucket of ice water and I immediately shook my head, pushing myself up. "No. No, not at all."

He didn't look convinced. "What did I do wrong?"

"Nothing." I shook my head more resolutely. "You did everything right, you are great."

I'm the one who is wrong. I didn't tell you to stop.

Abram seemed to be watching me closely, but he still wasn't touching me. "I had to leave the bed, I was too—uh—worked up, and I only have this one pair of pants." His mouth curved in a self-deprecating smile, one that didn't quite reach his eyes and quickly waned. "Do you want me to hold you?"

Swallowing against a lump in my throat, not trusting myself to speak, I nodded. His hand covered mine in the bed, and—*damn it!*—I flinched, not meaning to and immediately rebuking myself for the involuntary response.

Abram's eyes widened and he moved as though he was going to withdraw, so I caught him, grabbing his arm and using it to pull him forward. Wrapping my arms around his neck, I slid to the floor, to my knees, and held on.

He hesitated only a fraction of a second, and then closed me in an embrace. But it felt careful, hesitant, as though to communicate I was free to come or go, and that frustrated me.

There's something wrong with me, I shouldn't want—I shook my head. I would have to think about this later. We had no time, and I'd just come apart under his skillful hands. Which meant our relationship was operating under a climax disparity. My confused turmoil would have to wait until the scorecard was even, and he was on a plane back to the West Coast.

"Hold me tighter," I demanded. "I need you to hold me tighter."

"Are you sure?" His strong arms flexed, but he didn't draw me any closer.

"Yes." I crushed him to me. "Please."

It must've been the please that did it, *thank goodness*, and I liquefied in his powerful embrace, loving the constricting feel of the hug, snuggling closer, smelling him, and admitting unthinkingly, "I already miss you."

I felt him smile against my shoulder, placing a kiss there. "I already miss you too."

"How much time do we have?"

Abram sighed. "Not enough."

Moving my hands down his shoulders, I worked my arms inside his embrace, placing a kiss on the underside of his scruffy jaw, and slid my fingers to the front of his pants.

"Whoa—" He released my body to capture my hand before I could reach for his fly. "Wait—Mona—what are you doing?"

I stroked him over his pants with my free hand and a wild thrill raced down my spine at the feel of him, so hard, so ready. I'd never been a big fan of male sex organs, but —in this moment—I wanted to take out an ad in all the newspapers announcing my everlasting devotion to his.

"I'm going to give you a blow job."

"Whoa, okay, stop." He caught my roaming fingers, his breath a gasp. "First of all, we don't have time."

"I can be fast."

"Hold on. I don't want you to be fast. Like I said before, that would only frustrate me."

I kissed his jaw again. "But—"

"No."

I grunted, my hands going slack in his grip, and I leaned away to capture his eyes. "It's not fair to you."

"I'm not worried about fairness," Abram said on a laugh, his gaze wary, like I was tricky, or had magical powers and couldn't be trusted.

"But I—*you know*—and you didn't. You didn't get anything out of it."

"Believe me." His stare softened, warmed, and he released me, sliding his fingers into my hair. "I *definitely* got something out of it. I will be writing poetry about that moment for the rest of my life."

I grunted again. "You should let me reciprocate."

"I don't want you to reciprocate."

"I feel like . . ." *Like I haven't earned it.*

Once more, he seemed to be watching me very carefully, and when I didn't continue, he prompted, "Like?"

"It feels like an injustice, that only I should have this experience. Alone. And the next time we'll see each other isn't for three weeks."

Abram's eyes narrowed. "Is that what it's really about? Because you don't owe me anything."

"I know that," I said automatically.

"Do you? Do you know, do you understand, that I'm always going to want to pamper and please you? That making you come, seeing you blissed out and hearing you panting is like a drug for me?"

My stomach twisted delightfully at the picture he painted even as my spine straightened at the use of the word *drug*. "I don't want to be your drug."

"Too late." He grinned, his glorious left dimple completely adorable, almost distracting me from my concern.

"Can't I just be your person?" I asked, my eyes flickering between his and the thought-derailing dimple on his left cheek.

"Can't you be both?" Abram slid his nose against mine, giving my lips a tender kiss. "Can't I be both for you?"

"No. I don't think so," I said honestly, tilting my head such that I had his eyes again. "Drugs are altering. Addictive."

"That seems just about right." Another grin, a chuckle, and his arms came around me.

"But, Abram, I don't want to alter you. I want you—who you fundamentally are—to stay intact. And being someone's addiction automatically implies an unhealthy dependence. And—"

He stopped me with another coaxing, seductive kiss, his hands sliding into the back of my underwear and massaging my bottom, muddling my brain. *God, that feels good.*

Wait. *What were we talking about?*

I had no idea.

Must not be important.

Relative to his mouth moving against mine, his hands in my pants, the press of his erection against my belly, and the building "bliss" (as he called it), whatever I'd wanted to say didn't seem terribly important.

I kissed him back. I floated on the high that was Abram's mouth and hands, taste and smell. And when we were interrupted, it was the alarms we'd set on our phones.

He had to go.

Our time was up.

CHAPTER 5
KEPLER'S LAWS DERIVED

Mona

I spent the entire drive back from the airport and the climb up Lisa's four flights of stairs calculating and recalculating the number of hours, minutes, and seconds until I would see Abram again. Was I doing this to avoid dwelling on my earlier shame-confusion? Perhaps.

Pushing aside cloudy uncertainty had been easy while Abram was here. Our time was short. Therefore, reason told me I shouldn't waste a single second on self-assessments and second-guessing a *fantastic* orgasm.

I mean, fantastic orgasms don't grow on trees. And if they did, they'd be avocado trees, where the flowers bloom only once a season as female, and then forever after as male. They're a fruit miracle.

But now, now that he was gone, now that I'd walked him as far as I could, wrapped him in my arms and kissed him one more time, and waited until he waved at me from the other side of security, now I had no excuse. Except, I really needed to double-check my numbers with a calculator, just to be sure. Or maybe I'd make a countdown on my phone.

Yes. That was the right answer.

I was going to *hard core* make a countdown until Abram-time on my phone, or maybe using one of those countdown apps. Perhaps I'd even order a scrolling style marquee for my temporary housing in Geneva.

Nope. You need to save your pennies for plane tickets.

On that note, I decided sorting through my simmering shame-confusion would have to wait for a while longer as I had discount travel alerts to set up. Perhaps I would poke around a bit, see if I could fly out now for a visit. Where was he this week? Portland? San Francisco? Las Vegas? So close to LA.

After checking on tickets, I should probably check my emails, take a peek at the backend data processing requests I'd put in before leaving for Aspen, finish my lit search of two of my upcoming papers, and then—*whoa, look at the time!*—I should go to bed early. A good night's sleep was the key to being well-rested, and being well-rested was the key to Satan's liquor cabinet—

Wait. No. That's not right.

I frowned at the exterior to Lisa's apartment door, twisting the key in the lock, pushing it open while I considered what being well-rested might be the key to, and came face-to-face with Gabby.

AH! "Ah!"

"There you are!"

I flinched, retreating one step into the hallway, but she was fast. Before I knew what was happening, she'd pulled me through the door, shut it, and tugged me into the living room.

"You startled me. How did you—"

"I could hear you coming up the stairs. You have the gait of an elephant." Gabby waved one hand in the air while steering me with the other. "Come. Sit. Tell us everything that happened." Before I'd thought to extract myself from her grabby hands, she'd deposited me onto the couch, picked up a glass of wine, and pushed it at me. "Take it and spill."

"Don't spill the wine, spill the story," Lisa clarified, juggling three bowls as she walked out of the kitchen, a big, anxious-looking smile pasted on her face and aimed at me.

The last time I'd seen Lisa was this morning, when I'd asked Abram to give us a minute to talk. She'd been visibly flustered and rushed to offer the use of her car before leaving the apartment in a hurry to give us some space.

I was a little surprised to see her now.

"I put out the sundae stuff already." Lisa placed the first of the three bowls next to me on the couch. "Therefore, you have your choice of a banana split or whatever you want."

"Ta-da!" Gabby stepped to the side, revealing a coffee table covered in ice cream sundae toppings.

I had to swallow because my mouth was abruptly watering. *What time is it? Is it lunchtime?*

As though reading my thoughts, Lisa said, "It's ice cream and storytime," shoving a bowl at Gabby. "Don't forget to take your Lactaid."

"Thanks, mom." Gabby accepted the bowl and turned to kneel next to the table. "Okay, Mona, let's hear it. What's going on with the Redburn front man? Yesterday you were crying at a bus stop over his band's poster, and today—according to Lisa— he's kicking in the door and giving you movie kisses. Consider me *shook*. Last time I heard, he was still a manwhore. Fill in the blanks, please."

Manwhore?

My gaze drifted to my sister where she was perched on the other side of the sofa, her eyes wide and watchful, biting her lip as though trying her best to hold her tongue.

"Abram isn't a manwhore."

Gabby shrugged. "Okay, a goodtime guy."

"He's not that either." I cleared my throat, and then took a sip of the wine. It was nice. Not too dry. Good balance. "And I'm not really sure where to start."

"I'm sorry!" Lisa's sudden exclamation drew my attention. "I'm so sorry. I was—I was a complete asshole when he showed up here with Tyler. Tyler makes me so angry! But I—he—I mean, Abram was right. I shouldn't have talked to you that way. And I'm sorry. So sorry. So, so sorry."

I stared at my sister, surprised, perplexed, and yet also warmed by her unexpected apology. For Lisa, it was practically gushing.

Gabby cut in, "Assuage your guilt later, Lisa. Let Mona talk." She then turned to me. "Start with what happened in Aspen. Lisa already told me about your phone call, where you asked her permission to tell him the truth. Did you? What did he do? What did he say? Tell us everything."

I took a deep breath, and then I took another sip of wine. Well, it had started out like a sip, but it ended up being a gulp.

Licking my lips, I sorted through all the details of our latest week together, the hurt, the misunderstandings, *the burned letters,* our first kiss, and I blurted, "Do you like to be dominated during sex?"

Both Gabby and Lisa reared back, their eyes wide as they shared a look and I glanced between them, wondering what on earth and the Sagittarius Arm of the Milky Way I had been thinking. *Why would you ask them that?*

Before I could dial back the random, Gabby said, "Is Abram into that kind of stuff? Does he, I mean, is he, like, a dom?"

Her voice was free of judgment. Even so, I was shaking my head before she'd finished her first question.

"No. That's not what I mean. I mean, do you like—or I guess, do you think it's healthy—to like it when a guy holds you down? Or if he's over you when you do stuff? Even if he's heavy and physically stronger than you? Do you like that? Or is it wrong to like it?"

Gabby and Lisa shared another look, with Lisa speaking this time, "I don't have a ton of experience with lots of guys—as you know, there was and has been no one before, during, or after the T-bag—but . . ." Her eyes moved up and to the right, like she was searching her memory. "Are you talking about missionary? I liked that position okay. I thought other positions were better, though. Is that what you're asking?"

I gathered another deep inhale, trying to figure out what I was asking, when Gabby beat me to it. "Are you worried that liking something you've done with Abram— while *intimate*—makes you somehow screwed up?"

I nodded, because that was a decent approximation of my question.

"Hmm." Lisa seemed to be considering. "I don't think sex works like that. I mean, I don't know for sure. But sex is like, I mean, aren't we tapping into a different part of ourselves? It's like, not something you can apply logic to, you know? You like what you like, and as long as it doesn't hurt someone, or it's not illegal, then I'm pretty sure anything goes. Don't you think?"

Gabby didn't wait for me to respond, instead asking, "First, did he do anything to hurt you?"

Now I shook my head vehemently. "No. Not at all."

Gabby's gaze flickered over me, and I got the sense a suspicion was forming in her mind. My heart quickened as a result and I finished the rest of the wine in three large gulps.

"Mona."

"Gabby," I rasped, my throat tight, experiencing one of those odd moments where you know what's going to happen, what another person is going to say, but you're powerless to stop it.

"Is this about that thing that happened when you were fifteen?"

Our gazes locked, her green eyes intense. Mine were probably cagey.

"Is there any more wine?" I asked. Now my heart was hammering.

"You should slow down." Gabby motioned to the bowl beside me, her tone firm. "Eat your ice cream and answer the question."

"What am I missing?" Lisa sat forward on the couch, reaching for a spoon and dusting her chocolate ice cream with peanuts. "What happened when Mona was fifteen?"

Gabby made a choking sound. "You never told Lisa?"

I had to clear my throat. "I told you, nothing—"

"Holy shit, you still believe nothing happened? I swear to God, Mona. Get a fucking grip. You were assaulted!"

"What?" Lisa whisper-shrieked, dropping the peanut spoon with a clatter.

I stood up, setting my bowl on the table, turning toward the kitchen first, then the front door, and then the bathroom. "I have to—"

"No, you don't." Gabby also stood, placing herself in my path and grabbing my shoulders. "Tell your sister. Tell her. Or don't but tell someone! Why do you insist on carrying this trauma around? As my therapist always says, you have to confront trauma or else you'll never be able to move past it."

"Okay." I nodded, not really hearing her, my mind in disorder, my hands trembling, but my voice was perfectly calm as I said, "But first I need to pee."

Gabby released me, shaking her head and lifting her arm toward the bathroom. "Go, then."

I sprinted toward the bathroom, catching the first part of Lisa's whispered, "You need to tell me what the hell happened before I . . ."

Once I was safely closed within the small rectangular space, I leaned my back against the door, gulping in wine-flavored air, and fought a fresh wave of tears. My hands were still trembling. I was sweating. My heart was still racing.

And this time, inexplicably, for whatever reason, when I repeated to myself that nothing actually happened, the words felt like a lie.

* * *

"Mona?"

I stirred, my back straightening at the sound of Lisa's voice. I had no idea what time it was, just that I'd been sitting on the closed toilet lid for such an extended period, I'd passed the excuse "needs to pee" a long while ago and firmly entered "may require serious medical attention."

"Open up," she said.

Staring at the closed door, I debated my options. I'd heard Lisa and Gabby's murmuring voices, and then I'd heard the front door open and close. And now, some minutes later, Lisa was standing outside, and I was extremely reluctant to let her in.

"Mona." Her voice was gentle, and I thought I heard her place something on the door between us, maybe her hand. "Gabby told me what happened at school, when—when you were fifteen. Open the door."

Those tears I'd fought so hard to dispel threatened another appearance. I swallowed convulsively, blinking, fighting the stinging behind my eyes, and stood. I didn't want to cry. With Abram I would. But with Lisa? She'd said they made me weak. Therefore, no. I didn't want to cry with her. I needed to get a handle on these zany feelings before I could face her.

Then she said, "You know that you're not to blame, right?"

I covered my mouth with my hand, breathing in through my nose, waiting for the wave of emotion entropy to pass.

"You're allowed to be mad," she continued, her voice quiet yet firm. "You're allowed to call it an assault, you're allowed to say you were terrified, and you're allowed to admit that it—what he did—had an impact on you. Admitting the truth doesn't give him power over you." She sounded like she was quoting someone, which made me wonder if Gabby had coached her.

Lisa made a soft sound. "Mona, open the door."

Letting my hand drop, I shook my head. "I don't want to talk about it."

"Come on, Mona. Why not?"

Try being honest. Abram's voice, the ghost of Aspen past, filled my ears, spurring me to confess. "Because I don't want to cry."

She paused, as though considering this, and then said, "I won't make you talk. But how about, if you open the door, I will teach you a trick that will help you not cry."

That had my attention.

Eying the doorknob, I quickly unlocked it, hesitated, and then twisted it to open the door a centimeter. I then stepped back and crossed my arms. My sister peeked inside, her gaze wary, and she gave me a little smile.

"Hey."

I was busy pressing my lips together—because I was now a crier—and said nothing.

Stepping completely inside, Lisa's stare moved over me, as though I were somehow different, or she was searching for visible bruises. She then bent down to open the cabinet beneath the sink and extracted a black rectangular bag.

"Sit down," she said, motioning to the closed toilet lid and unfastening the gold-toned zipper of the bag.

"Where's Gabby?" I asked once I was seated.

"She left."

I nodded faintly, watching as she pulled a brush from the black case. "What are you doing?"

"I'm going to do your makeup."

"Why?"

"Because you don't want to cry."

I lifted an eyebrow. "And makeup will stop me from crying?"

"It's a great deterrent. If you have makeup on, crying will ruin it. It's helped me keep my shit together." She lowered her eyes, took a deep breath, and finally finished, "It's helped me a few times."

I stared at my typically prickly sister, sensing that she considered this statement a secret, a valuable weapon that might be used against her. It was a window—albeit, a closed window—into a softer, gentler core than she showed the world.

Nodding, I uncrossed my arms and said, "Okay."

Lisa's gaze cut back to mine, her eyebrows jumping. "Really?"

"Yes."

"Are you serious right now?"

"Yes."

"You're actually okay with me doing your makeup?"

"Sure." I shrugged, admitting the truth, "It actually sounds fun." Compared to talking about *the incident,* everything sounded fun. Even a colonoscopy. Even a mammogram. Even a root canal. Even all three occurring at the same time.

"Who are you and what did you do with my sister?" Lisa gave me a smile I suspected was supposed to be teasing.

"I wear makeup."

"But you don't wear it often." She shifted her attention to the contents of the bag. "And you don't wear much."

"True. But that's only because it's not high on my list of priorities. Like, eating zucchini isn't high on my priority list, but that doesn't mean I don't enjoy a good stuffed zucchini every once in a while."

"Are you pulling my leg?" She scrunched one of her eyes, making a face. "I thought you hated makeup."

"No. I didn't—okay, I don't. I never hated it, but—admittedly—I used to judge people who wore a lot of it all the time as being superfluous. Now I don't."

"Why not? Here, close your eyes." She approached me holding a brush she'd dabbed in eyeshadow. "What changed?"

"I guess." I did as instructed and closed my eyes, feeling the gentle swiping over my closed lid. "I guess it happened when I was pretending to be you. I had to wear eye makeup, and then I began looking up tutorials because I wanted to make sure I was doing it right. And then I found I actually liked it."

"And yet you still don't wear makeup."

"It's an expensive habit."

She snorted. "Yes. Very."

"Plus," I debated whether or not to continue. Ultimately, I decided on honesty. It had served me well recently and I fully committed to it. "If you want to know the truth, there have been a few times where I get one eye done and then I get distracted, forget, and show up to work with makeup on just one eye."

"No, you don't." I heard the smile in Lisa's voice as she switched to my other lid.

"I do. At least four times that I know about."

"Oh my God, Mona! You crack me up!" The eyeshadow brush stopped moving, so I opened my eyes, watching my sister hold her stomach as she laughed. "You are so cute sometimes, I can't stand it."

I felt a smile tug at my lips. "And the worst part is, no one says anything to me except my friend Poe. Everyone just lets me walk around with one eye done. It's infuriating."

"Maybe they think you're making a fashion statement?" She dabbed at the corners of her eyes with the back of her hand, sniffling.

"No. They're just cowards."

"Ha! Cowards. I love it."

"Think about it. If you see someone with spinach in their teeth, you tell them. If you see someone with yogurt on their face, you tell them. If you see a person with eye makeup just on one eye, you tell them."

"See, now, I would tell someone if they had yogurt or spinach, but not the eye makeup. I would assume it was purposeful and move on."

"Coward."

"No." She grinned at me. "Not a coward. Shut your eyes again so I can finish the other side."

I did, and she continued thoughtfully, "I'm giving people the space to be themselves. When is the last time you asked someone about their makeup? I mean, if you noticed something strange."

"I've never noticed something strange, but if I did, I would tell them."

Lisa was quiet for a few seconds, and then asked, "Don't you think that's because you never notice people?"

"What? That's not true."

"It is true. You never recognize people, even if you've met them a hundred times."

"You suffer from gross exaggeration syndrome."

She chuckled. "Fine. Maybe not a hundred times. But I've introduced you to people more than once and you never recognize them the next time you meet them."

"Like who?"

"Like my friend from boarding school who helped me play that prank on you during your graduation."

A stunned jolt had me reaching out blindly, my fingers connecting with her wrist and moving her hand away so I could open my eyes. "Wait, what?"

"Yeah. Evelyn? From the newspaper? You'd met her three times before she called you to confirm the "details" of the interview. She was so worried you'd recognize her voice and figure it out, but you didn't."

I stared at Lisa, incredulous. "So, you knew her? And she was in on it? The whole time?"

"Of course. What did you think? That I actually pretended to be you and gave an interview to your university paper saying those crazy things?" Lisa smirked, dabbing her brush in the eyeshadow palette again.

But when I said nothing, she glanced at me. She blinked, flinching back, comprehension sharpening her stare. "Oh my God, you did. That's what you thought."

"It's not important." I twisted my lips to the side.

"Like hell it's not." Lisa snapped shut the eyeshadow palette, tossed it to the black case, and placed her hands on her hips, her gaze darting over me. "How could you think I would do that? That would've been hugely damaging to your reputation, made you look like a fool."

I swallowed, but said nothing, sorting through all the assumptions I'd made about my sister.

"Mona, you—" She huffed, glanced over my head, then shook hers.

"What?"

"You are intensely frustrating sometimes."

"Thank you."

Lisa made a short growling sound. "Why are you thanking me?"

"I don't know. I feel like I need to say something and I can't say, *in this economy?* It doesn't make enough sense in this context."

A reluctant laugh tumbled from her lips and she sat on the edge of the bathtub, her gaze moving over me. "What can I do to make this happen?"

"Make what happen?"

"Prove to you that I love you?"

I bit my bottom lip, reminding myself that I couldn't cry because I was wearing eye makeup. Surprisingly, it worked, and one of Abram's statements from earlier floated into my brain.

Cry if you need to, but don't ignore what the tears are about.

Gathering a deep breath, I cleared my throat, and said, "I don't want you to prove that you love me."

"Then what do you want?"

"I want—"

"What can I do?"

"I—I want—why didn't you ever tell me what happened with Abram? In Chicago? That morning after I left." *Whoa. Where had that come from?*

"What do you mean?" She gave her head a subtle shake.

"He told you that he loved me." I didn't mean for the words to sound like an accusation, but they did.

Lisa met my stare for a protracted moment. "Mona, if you remember, you didn't want to talk about it. Every time I brought him up, you said you didn't want to discuss it and would sing "Bohemian Rhapsody" until I changed the subject."

"But I didn't know that he told you he loved me!"

Her eyes clouded with remorse. "For what it's worth, I did try to tell you, a few times. But, you're right, I should've made you listen. I'm sorry. I didn't know what to do. I was such a mess back then. And I honestly didn't believe him at the time. I truly, truly didn't. And when he seemed to move on so quickly, I took it as proof that I was right not to believe him."

My stomach sank, remembering the pictures of Abram and other women I'd found during my initial online searches after Chicago. I rubbed the ache at my sternum. He'd already explained, but still. I was never going to be able to think about Abram with someone else and feel "okay" about it. I wasn't like my parents that way. I never would be.

"Anyway," Lisa continued, "Now, it's clear to me that I was wrong. And I'm sorry I didn't push you on this, make you listen."

Frowning, I grunted at my wayward contemplations and silliness. "No. You're right. I didn't let you tell me."

"I could've emailed you, then you would've read it before you realized what it said."

"No. I was being a stubborn moron." I needed to let this go.

Universe, take note: this is me letting this go.

Her gaze moved over me, assessing. "I am sorry."

"I know. I am too."

"I'm also sorry I always seem to be making mistakes and doing the wrong thing with you."

"You're not."

She gave me a look, like *come on.* "Mona. Be honest. I irritate you."

"No! What? It's not like that. It's—"

"What?"

"I want you to—to treat me like—like—"

"Like?"

"Like you like me." Gah! That sounded trite. Unfortunately, it was also the truth.

She blinked at me, her gaze clouding with confusion. "You don't think I like you?"

"Do you?"

Lisa opened her mouth, hesitated, and blinked, as though surprised by her own thoughts. Closing her mouth, she frowned at me, swallowing and shaking her head. "Don't be ridiculous," she said, but she looked ashamed, her gaze shifty, her posture stiff.

Her outward display of guilt helped my own thoughts crystalize. "I think, you and I, we've spent a long time not knowing each other. I think we've made assumptions about each other that might not be true."

She considered this for a moment, then asked, "Like what? What do you assume about me?"

"You're bossy. And stubborn."

"But I am. And so what? I know for a fact you deal with bossy, stubborn, *arrogant* people all the time."

"Those people aren't my sister."

"So what? What difference does that—"

"Because I don't care about what *they* think. I'm not scared of losing *them*."

Lisa snapped her mouth shut, flinching back, her eyes growing large at the vehemence in my voice.

But for me, the floodgates had opened. "You push your experiences on me, like I'm responsible for them, like I should be able to read your mind, or like I shared those same experiences, and completely disregard that my life was—is—different than yours. That doesn't mean my life is better, or harder, or easier. It's just different. You think that I'm emotionless, or that I should be. But I'm not. I don't *want* to be emotionless."

Lisa blinked, her eyes watery, and shifted them to some point over my head.

"I want to believe you love me, and part of me does," I admitted quietly, the words sticking in my throat. "But another part of me is constantly worried that you don't, not enough. I wonder, if I do something or say something you don't like, will you ignore me again?"

Her face crumpled and she closed her eyes. My heart gave an aching lurch. A rush of heat flooded my neck and cheeks. Now I felt like a big jerk, and I wondered if I'd said too much.

"Lisa." I struggled with the impulse to take it all back.

She swallowed, sniffling, shaking her head, her eyes still closed. "I don't know what to say."

I couldn't think of what to say either.

Were things so broken between us? These last few years, we'd made progress, hadn't we? We spoke. I knew her daily, weekly, and monthly routines. I knew how she liked her coffee. I knew who her least favorite teachers and subjects were. But how much did I know—really, really know—about my own sister?

In a way, it was ironic. I'd spent twelve days total with Abram, but felt like I knew him better, felt more confident with him, trusted him more than I did Lisa. If I were honest with myself, I had similar feelings toward Leo, and my parents. Similar concerns.

Do they love me enough for me to be myself with them?

My heart gave another painful twist, one that nearly robbed me of my breath. I hoped they did, but looking back, looking at their actions, or lack of actions, I faced the facts I'd been ignoring for maybe my whole life.

I couldn't be certain. I didn't trust it. I didn't trust them.

Watching my sister's struggle with her wobbly chin, none of my words felt right.

At a loss, I decided to repeat something Abram had said to me at a critical time between us, something that, in retrospect, had made all the difference to me.

"Lisa, will you be brave with me?" I reached forward, covered her hand with mine, and waited until she met my eyes. "Will you let me know you?"

CHAPTER 6
RADIO ASTRONOMY

Abram

She picked up on the second ring. "Hello?"

My leg stopped bouncing. *Finally.* "Mona."

"Abram! How are you? How was the flight? Did you sleep? And the concert? Did you make it back in time? Did it go well? Are you all done?"

I closed my eyes and lay down on the bench of the stretch limo, covering my forehead with my arm. Her intoxicating voice washed over me, covering, surrounding, lifting. Relief. Sweet, sweet relief.

"It is so good to hear your voice." *Finally.*

I spoke into the darkness, holding the phone to my ear. This moment was the very first moment since I'd left her ten hours ago that I felt like I could breathe.

She didn't say anything for a moment, but I could almost see her smiling. I could certainly feel it, and an answering slow, spreading smile claimed my mouth. This was how it should have been for the last six days.

"Thank you," she said, definitely smiling. "It's good to hear your voice too." I heard her move, or something rustle in the background. "Do you feel like talking? Or are you too tired?"

"Not too tired. Tell me . . ." I began, not quite sure how to ask my next question. I didn't want to put her on the spot, but I was worried. "How were things after I left? With your sister?"

A moment of near silence followed, during which I could make out the faint sound of her breathing. My jaw working, I struggled to keep a lid on my temper, but her silence led me to assume the worst.

No one fucks with Mona. No. One.

"Mona—"

"It was good."

A short, surprised breath fled my lungs. "Good?"

"Yes. Good. We spoke. We talked things through, I think. It wasn't an easy conversation, and tears were shed. I know how you're a fan of tears."

I chuckled, stunned. Actually, I wasn't stunned. I was disbelieving.

"She was nice to you?" I asked.

Now she laughed. "Yes. She was nice to me."

Huh.

For some reason, I couldn't let it go. "Are you sure? You know, you could come out here, meet me in San Francisco. I'll be *very* nice to you."

"Yes." I heard the shy smile in her voice, and I imagined her face wearing it. "I could, and I thought about doing that."

My heart swelled, ballooning with hope.

"But I think, after my conversation with Lisa today, it's important for me to stay here."

I tried not to be jealous or resentful of Lisa. I tried and tried and tried and would likely have to try again tomorrow.

"Okay. Well, the offer is an open one." I stretched my arm over my head, bringing my hand back to scratch my beard. "Any time you want to join me on tour, please do it."

"You sound tired. Your voice is scratchy."

"That's because we did four encores." I yawned, relaxing a little. *Finally.* "I'm not tired."

"You, Abram Harris, are telling me a falsehood."

"I would never." I yawned again around my grin. "Are you always going to call me Abram Harris?"

"Probably. Is that a problem?"

"No. I'm not complaining either. I'm Mr. Fletcher to everyone these days, he feels more like a role I'm playing rather than really me."

"I get that." Her voice was low and soft in my ear, and the constant ache of our separation became something else, something warm, less painful. "People have been calling me Ms. DaVinci since I was little. Can I tell you something? I don't even like my name."

"Mona DaVinci? I can't imagine why."

She chuckled, and then exhaled. "I've always thought about changing it."

I settled more firmly against the bench, shutting my eyes, grateful we'd spent so much of our time together in Chicago sorting out when we would see each other over the next few months.

As convoluted as it was—twenty-four hours in New York, three days in London, forty-eight hours in Miami, another thirty-six hours in London—we were making it work.

Now that things were settled, now that we had plans and had made promises, now that I knew when and where and for how long I would see her until June, conversations like this one were possible.

"What would you change your name to?"

"You have to promise not to laugh."

Still grinning, I shook my head. "Nuh-uh. I'll laugh if it's funny."

"Then I shan't tell you."

"Shan't?"

"Affirmative."

That made me laugh. "Is it Wolf?"

"Is what *wolf*?"

"You want to change your name to Wolf?"

"Wolf? Where did you get that idea?"

"Because then we could talk about *the Wolf* coming, and it would take on a completely different meaning."

She busted out laughing, and so I laughed, and then we were laughing together. *God,* this was so great. So great.

"You are—" She couldn't speak, she was laughing too hard.

"What? What am I?"

"Never mind. I shan't tell you that either."

I loved her voice. I couldn't wait until the end of the month and our first scheduled meet-up in New York.

"By the way." She'd stopped laughing but the happiness in her voice remained. "Where are you? Still at the venue?"

"No. In the car, on the way back to the hotel."

"Oh. Is anyone with you?"

"No. Everyone else is still at the stadium. I left right after the last encore."

"Because you're tired."

"Because I wanted to talk to you." I stifled another yawn, clearing my throat. "Tell me about your day. What did you do after you took me to the airport? Thanks for driving me, by the way."

"You're welcome. And, let the record show, you got there on time."

"That's because you weren't driving like my Uncle Harry. For once."

She laughed again, and the seductive sound relaxed every muscle in my body . . . but one.

"You've only driven with me twice. That's not enough datapoints to make any meaningful extrapolations."

"I love it when you talk data to me. Say extrapolations again."

Her laugh was harder this time, and I imagined her blushing. "Tell me about the concert."

"Well." I yawned again, irritated because I didn't want to yawn at all. "It was fine. Vicious Pixies opened for us, do you know who they are?"

"No." She sounded regretful. "I'm not up on the music scene."

"That's fine. You don't need to know who they are for the story. Their bass guitarist showed up to the stadium around the same time I did, except he was totally shit-faced. High out of his mind."

"Oh no!"

"Oh yes. I filled in."

"Oh no!"

"Oh yes. It worked out though. No one realized it was me. I stood in the back, where the light was bad, and wore a beanie."

That made her giggle and I heard her typing on a keyboard. "I think it'll take more than a beanie and bad lighting to hide yourself."

I loved talking to her. Was this what it would be like all the time between us? So easy. Effortless.

"You'd be surprised. When I checked into my flight today, I walked right by two posters of me in my boxers. No one batted an eye."

"Oh, hey." A new edge entered her voice. "I'm glad you brought up those posters." Mona was quiet for a moment, giving me the impression she was gathering her thoughts.

"Are you?" I prompted, a little worried.

"Can I have one?"

I choked, my eyes flying open. "What?"

"Can I have one of the posters?"

I sat up on the bench and immediately regretted it, my vision swimming, and had to lay back down again. "Uh, I guess?"

"Thank you! That's excellent. Oh, and can it be one of the big ones? The life-sized ones?"

I laughed and I had no idea why I was laughing, maybe because this conversation felt hugely absurd. Maybe because I was insanely tired. Or maybe because she was so fricken cute.

"Mona, if you want a picture of me, I'll send you one. You don't need one from an advertising campaign."

"You'll send me a photo?"

"Yes."

Another contemplative pause before she asked, "Will you be in your underwear?"

I barked a startled laugh, and then I was laughing so hard, I couldn't breathe. She was also laughing, but it had an edge of self-consciousness, shyness.

"Fine, fine. You can wear clothes," she conceded, sounding embarrassed.

"Now, wait a minute." I wiped at the tears of hilarity, sobering slightly as an interesting proposition took shape. "Wait a minute. Of course, if you want sexy photos of me, I'll send them."

"Thank you, I do." Now she sounded prim, official, like we'd just agreed I'd send her a contract, or I'd confirmed a conference call.

Even exhausted and fighting another yawn, I was grinning. Yes. Absolutely I would send her photos. I couldn't wait to see her again in person. But if our prolonged separation meant that she'd be willing to send me pictures of herself? Well. That would definitely make the waiting more bearable.

"Here's the deal. I'll send you sexy photos, and then you'll send me some photos too."

Silence.

Dead silence.

I waited, pressing the phone more firmly to my ear. "Mona? Are you still there?"

"Yep."

"Is there something wrong?"

"No." Her answer was higher pitched than normal and sounded like a lie.

"You don't want to send me photos?"

"I'll send you photos."

Hmm. That was easy. *Too easy.*

I felt like I was missing something, so I said, "Okay. Then it's settled?"

"Yep. All settled. Where are you staying? What hotel?"

"Um." I thought about that, my brain full of static, and then shook my head. "Honestly, I don't even know. I'm so tired, I didn't ask."

She made a soft sound of sympathy. "I wish I were there."

"Why?"

She said nothing.

I rephrased the question. "Tell me why. Tell me what you would do if you were here." My words were a little slurred.

"I would have you rest your head on my lap as we drove," she answered immediately, and I learned something I didn't know about Mona. She didn't do well with vague questions. The more precise, the better. "And I would stroke your hair, give your head a massage, and watch over you until you fell asleep."

My scalp tingled at the idea. "Then what would you do?"

"Then, when we got to the hotel." I heard the springs of a mattress compress. "I would take a bath with you."

I stifled a groan.

Pain. Ache. Longing. I couldn't breathe. I could only stare at the ceiling of the limo, streetlights strobing through the windows, but otherwise I was enclosed in darkness. If I concentrated, it was almost like she was here, next to me, whispering in my ear.

"And I would sit behind you, with you between my legs," she continued, making me glad I hadn't interrupted. She sounded distracted by her own imagination and the last thing I wanted her to do was stop. "I would wash your hair, and your body, and give you a massage."

"What kind of massage?" My voice had gone from sleepy and slurred to strained, and I was suddenly very much awake, hanging on her every word.

She was silent for a beat, and I worried she might not answer, but then she asked in a less dreamy, very Mona voice, "Are we going to have phone sex?"

Hopefully. "We don't have to."

"I've never had phone sex."

I thought for a minute, realizing and saying at the same time, "Neither have I."

"Oh! That's exciting."

My grin widened and I closed my eyes again. "It is."

"Wait! I know a joke about it, though. Why should you always use protection when having phone sex?"

I pressed my lips into a flat line so I wouldn't laugh before she got to the punchline. "I don't know. Why?"

"Otherwise you might get hearing *aids*."

A beat of silence.

I rolled my eyes. "That's a terrible joke."

"Yeah. It's pretty bad. I was on a call once with the CDC and an immunologist told it. I think medical doctors have the most inappropriate jokes." She laughed. "But you know, they still crack me up. Does that make me a bad person?"

"What? No. No, you are not a bad person."

"I often worry."

"Why would you worry about that? You're one of the best people I know."

"I think it's good to worry about being a bad person. It's good to question yourself, you know?" She asked this question like she was confessing something about herself, a secret, and I wished *again* that my brain didn't feel so slow.

"You don't need to question whether you're a good person. Take my word for it, okay?"

"Have you ever read Bertrand Russell?"

"No. Who is that?"

"He was a mathematician. Anyway, he said, 'Those who feel certainty are stupid, and those with any imagination and understanding are filled with doubt and indecision.' I think that's especially true with knowing oneself. As soon as you grow certain of something, you've closed your mind to other possibilities."

I was too tired to give the words the consideration they deserved, so I said without thinking, "Then I guess I'm stupid for you."

A short beat, and then she replied quietly, "That's a relief."

"Oh yeah?"

"Yes. Because I didn't want to be the only one of us who was stupid." The tenderness in her voice had me imagining her face, her smile, her eyes.

My heart constricted painfully, I lost my breath for a moment, overwhelmed by how much I wanted . . . I just wanted . . .

I want her to be here.

Before I could catch myself, I said, "I miss you. So much."

Her laugh tapered, and I heard her release a soft breath before responding earnestly, "I miss you too."

CHAPTER 7
STELLAR PARALLAX

Abram

"Here you go, Mr. Fletcher." A PA hired by our manager, this one also happened to be his niece, placed a cup of tea in front of me, giving me a nervous smile. "I put honey and lemon in it, just how you like."

"Thank you," I whispered, distractedly picking up the cup while I flipped through the list of interview questions for later in the day.

Seconds later, the sound of items clattering to the ground had me glancing up. The items were photos of the band and black markers for signing them. She must've bumped into the stool where they sat, but she also must've done something else, like push the stack at an odd angle, because they were now everywhere.

"Oh God. Sorry." She squatted, flushing red, and worked to gather the fallen items. "Sorry about that."

I stood, sending a look to Charlie.

Charlie stepped up. "Don't worry. Abram and I will pick it up."

"It's fine." Her voice was high. Clearly, she was embarrassed. "I'm almost done."

She wasn't almost done. The photos had gone flying in all directions, falling like confetti. Thankfully, Charlie had already moved to her and helped gather the photographs. I crossed to where the markers had rolled—just under the couch—and bent to retrieve them.

As I straightened and turned, I caught her staring at me, her gaze in the vicinity of my stomach, her eyes dazed. Combatting a spike of frustration, I cleared my throat. Her gaze lifted. She seemed to smirk, her eyes heating suggestively.

What the hell? I grit my teeth.

"Hey. What happened?" Ruthie's greeting pulled everyone's attention to the door of our shared suite. We all had our own suites, but this one was larger. It was where the band gathered over these last few days—to meet, to give interviews, to take photos and whatnot—leading up to the LA concert.

Our guitarist, standing just inside the suite door, frowned at the mess, bending to pick up one of the photos near her feet. "Are we signing these or what?"

"Yes, yes. It was my fault," the PA said, pushing her hand through her hair. "I'm so clumsy."

"Don't worry about it." Charlie took the photos from her, added them to his stack, and brought them to the table. "I don't know why they were on the stool anyway. Could've happened to anyone."

Walking past the woman to the square kitchen table, I felt her eyes on me. Just as I reclaimed my seat and Ruthie took the spot next to mine, the PA tripped over her own feet as she walked backward. And then, instead of clearing the door, she bumped into the wall.

Finally, she turned, tucking her hair behind her ears and walked from the suite.

"She's got it bad for you, Abram." Ruthie kicked me under the square table. I shifted my gaze to her, and she lifted her chin toward the tea. "Did she make you that tea? I wouldn't drink that if I were you."

Charlie snorted, taking the chair next to Ruthie, which placed him across from me. "Why? You think she's going to drug him?"

Our guitarist lifted both her hands, palms out. "Hey, man. I'm just saying, the women lose their fucking minds over him. I've never seen so many bras on so many stages before, and bras are expensive. It's raining lingerie *every night*. That's not you, and that's not me."

Charlie shrugged good-naturedly, but mumbled, "I think it's a little bit you and me." His quiet words held an unmistakable edge of defiance.

Ruthie continued like she hadn't heard him. "If someone has lost their mind, there's no telling what they'll do. Alls I'm saying is, if I were Abram, I'd be careful. I wouldn't accept tea from any of the PAs." Turning to me, she poked at the teacup. "Wait for Melena to get back. Have her make your tea, just to be safe."

Melena was our chef, had a master's degree in nutrition, and was a registered nurse. Other than the three of us, she was the highest paid member of the crew, which made complete sense. She kept us healthy and well-fed. It was her tea blend that the PA had made. I was supposed to drink it three times a day.

"Am I missing something? Isn't Melena also a woman?" Charlie glanced between the two of us.

"Yes. But she's not one of the ones coming in here, tripping over her own feet, staring at him like he's cotton candy. I don't get boiled bunny vibes from Melena. Some of the other ones, however." Ruthie gave a little shiver of revulsion. "They give me the creeps."

I frowned at my bandmate. None of the PAs revolted me, but some of them worried me. Yeah, I was uncomfortable around a few, but not enough to complain. I didn't want them to lose their jobs, that didn't seem fair. So what if they had a crush? They were harmless.

Although, even though I was convinced they were harmless, I'd taken steps to ensure I was never alone with any of them. Hearing Ruthie's take on the situation did nothing to put me at ease.

Glancing at the tea longingly—because it helped, and my throat hurt, but what else was new—I removed it from the table and set the cup on the countertop behind us.

"Let's get these signed," I said, more of a rasp than a voice at this point. "We have that interview later this afternoon."

Charlie made a face. "Man, Abram, you sound like shit. Come on, you're being crazy. Just drink it."

"We don't—" I held up a finger, sneezed into a napkin, and then continued, "We don't have the show until tomorrow. I'll be fine by then, if you two do all the talking at the interview."

"Are you sure you're not getting sick?"

"I'm not getting sick." I blinked, my eyes scratchy.

"You know, Leo will be there. Tomorrow," Ruthie said conversationally. "He asked if you would be at the VIP thing after, cause' he's bringing all his Hollywood friends and they want to meet you."

Scowling, I reached across the table for a pen. "I won't be there."

Leo and I still weren't speaking. I didn't know if he was aware of my relationship with Mona, and I didn't care.

"Why're you so pissed at him?" Ruthie asked.

I opened my mouth to answer, but instead sneezed again. When I was sure no other sneeze was on the way, I responded, "I'm not pissed." *Damn.* My eyes hurt.

"I think you're getting sick." Charlie squirmed in his seat.

"I told you, it's fine." My phone buzzed in my pocket and I reached for it.

"It's not fine. I'll make your stupid tea," Charlie grumbled, standing, grabbing the cup. "Where does Melena keep this shit?"

I was only partially listening, the notification on my screen capturing most of my attention.

Mona: Finished early. Let me know if you have time to talk, would love to hear about your week. Miss you.

Staring, standing, smiling, and turning from the table, I unlocked my phone to read the message again. My heart thrummed with happy nerves. This was an extremely nice surprise.

Mona and I had spoken to each other every night until she'd left for Geneva. Since, we'd texted a lot, but talking over the phone had been spotty, now down to a weekly thing mostly because of the time difference and our schedules. But that was okay. We were making it work and we were set to see each other in less than two days. I planned to leave LAX via a chartered plane directly after the concert.

The promise of uninterrupted time with Mona, in New York, for twenty-four hours felt like a luxury life raft in this pitching sea of adrenaline highs and lows. The concerts were an intense high. Which made after the concerts—with no Mona—a huge source of frustration for no one but me.

"I'll show you where to get it," Ruthie said behind me, probably speaking to Charlie. "We'll be back with new *non-creepy* tea. And save your voice. Don't talk to anyone while we're gone."

Glancing over my shoulder to watch my bandmates leave, I navigated to Mona's number as soon as I estimated they were out of earshot. I dialed.

Two rings later, she picked up. "Hey. You're free? How are you? How long can you talk? Did I interrupt?"

I closed my eyes, smiling to myself. She did this. Every time we spoke, she answered with a *hey,* and then a barrage of questions. I loved it.

"I'm free. I'm better now. I can't talk long. You didn't interrupt me. But, Mona—"

"Abram. Your voice sounds bad, and you sound stuffy." She said this around a yawn. "Are you sure you're okay? Are you sick?"

"No." I cleared my throat, trying to deepen and firm it. "I'm not sick, I just need to rest my voice. What's going on with you? You sound tired."

"Should we be talking if you need to rest your voice? We can text instead. Have you seen a doctor? What does Melena say? Are you drinking your tea?"

"Stop. Listen to me. I want to ask you something. Actually, two things."

"Oh. Okay."

I could almost see her face. Her eyes were probably wide, a wrinkle between her eyebrows. Maybe she was biting her lip.

Her lips.

"First, have you been sleeping?"

She replied, "Yes."

That's right. I needed to ask specific questions. "Let's try this a different way. When was the last time you slept?"

"Uhhh, yesterday. I think. Wait. What day is it?"

She needed to take better care of herself. "Here it's Friday midmorning."

"So that makes it—"

"Friday night in Geneva."

"Then, yes. I slept Wednesday."

"Yesterday was Thursday."

"Then I slept the day before yesterday."

I shook my head, a frustrated grin on my face. "Mona. You have to take better care of yourself."

"I can't help it. I only get so many hours with the LHC, and then I have to go through the data. It's too much to backup, and my project isn't priority. And then there's the inevitable white whale hunt, which only seems to yield anything of value when I'm exhausted and my brain stops overcomplicating everything."

White whale hunt was what she called her process of choosing which hunch to follow, how to prioritize her time and energy searching for answers to the unknown, something about understanding or explaining quantum mechanics within the frame of Einstein's general theory of relativity.

Although, maybe that wasn't it? Most of the time, when she spoke of her research, it sounded like a different language.

Over the last several weeks, I'd come to the conclusion that Mona didn't sleep enough. She worked herself until she was exhausted or manic with exhaustion, and this was because Mona DaVinci both was and was not her genius.

Her genius was a paradox, terrifying in its complexity and beauty, but also severe, punishing, rigid in its demands of her. It didn't care about the frailty of the body. It didn't care about her relationships, even with herself. It explored, relentlessly, dragging her along—sometimes willingly, sometimes not—often at the expense of her health and wellbeing-.

"I understand the urge to work through the night and into the next day. I get it." I paced to the window, staring at the blue sky. "I'm not going to tell you what to do— obviously—I'm just going to say, as someone who cares deeply about *you*, I hope you get a chance to take a night off the whale hunt."

"I will. I'll be sleeping in tomorrow. I already packed, so I'll wake up, catch my flight, arrive in New York Saturday evening, and then I'll see you early Sunday." The unmistakable smile in her sleepy voice encouraged me to smile.

"Sunday."

"Yes. Sunday." She yawned again. I didn't take it personally. "I can't wait. But—uh —was there something else? You said two things?"

"Oh yeah." I nodded, almost forgetting. "I asked you to send me a picture of your-self, and you sent your faculty headshot from Caltech." I couldn't stop my smile from growing. When she'd sent it, I'd laughed on and off for an hour. I wasn't even mad. It was such a Mona thing to do.

It did, however, leave me unsatisfied. I'd sent her a few shots of me lying in bed, wearing nothing but my boxers, and she sends me a picture of her in a lab coat, smiling with no teeth. I wasn't looking for reciprocation, but, *man*, a candid maybe? A genuine smile?

She was quiet for a beat. Then she cleared her throat. "You didn't like the picture?"

"You are sneaky. You know what I mean."

"Are you saying it's a bad picture?"

Sometimes she was too fucking smart, especially when we debated. I loved it. I also hated it.

"It's a great picture, as you know. I've seen it in magazines, next to interviews of you. But I was hoping for something a little more candid."

"Candid? I can do that." The offer was made too quickly, which made me suspicious.

"Let me be clear. No pictures of you in a lab coat or at work. Or at school. Or doing anything for your charities."

She made a sound between a huff and a growl. "Those are the only pictures I have of myself."

I bit back a laugh, covering my eyes with my free hand. "God, Mona. I mean candid like, send me a photo of you, taken right that minute."

"Right that minute?"

"Yes. What are you doing now?"

"Uh, about to take a shower."

My smile vanished. I opened my eyes, my brain stuttered, and the hoarseness of my words had nothing to do with needing to rest my voice. "That'll do."

"Abram." She made another growling sound. "I can't send you those kinds of photos."

"What kind?"

"You know, me in just a towel."

"I don't need you to be in just a towel. If you don't feel comfortable sending a particular photo, definitely don't send it. I'm not trying to get you to do something you don't want to do. I want to see your smile, your real smile, not something your graduate program uses for promotional purposes."

"Fine. Then candid pictures of me. I can't send those." Her tone had me straightening, she sounded almost hostile.

"Why?" I asked softly, wanting her to know that I wasn't trying to push her, I just honestly wanted to know. "What am I missing?"

Mona sucked in an audible breath. "I've worked hard for my reputation. I've been so careful. I've never done anything that might jeopardize me being taken seriously."

She was solemn, severe. She sounded like a different person. Her voice was deeper, held a hint of dry antagonism, like she *dared* me to challenge her. I wasn't put off, but I was confused. It was a side of Mona I'd never seen in person, but one I'd witnessed last year when she'd given her testimony to congress. Basically, she sounded superior and aloof.

I waited for her to continue. When she didn't, I asked, "Am I asking you to do something that might jeopardize you being taken seriously?"

"Yes." Now sadness entered her voice, unmistakable melancholy, and my throat tightened in response. "Abram, this world I live in, it is an intellectual world, but it is not enlightened. Women are not seen as equals, young women in particular. And if you're at all attractive, it's an impediment. I've been called a distraction. Do you know what that's like? I've been called emotional when I raised my voice to match that of my male colleagues, I've been called bitchy and conceited and judgmental for recognizing my own intelligence, and not just by men."

As she spoke, she started to sound more like herself, but the despondency only increased.

"I have to demonstrate the appropriate amount of gratitude daily for being included on projects and grants that are full of my original ideas. I can't take for granted that I've earned anything, because I never will, because everyone—even other women— are just waiting for me to prove everyone right, that I'm too young, too sensitive, too female to be worthy of my place at the table. They want my ideas, my research, but not enough to change the culture or be inconvenienced. Not enough to entertain the notion that I'm just another person, just like them." Her voice lowered to a whisper. "I have to be faultless. I have to be perfect. I can't afford mistakes."

My heart in my mouth, I asked without thinking, "Am I a mistake?"

"No! God, no. Never."

"But sending me pictures of yourself, that's a mistake." I didn't know why, and I didn't understand the impulse myself, but bitterness had leached into my voice. Not even the rawness of my vocal chords could disguise it. And yet, I wasn't mad at her.

I was just . . . bitter.

"If—if your phone got hacked, and pictures of you in a bathing suit were leaked or published." Now her tone was soft, almost pleading. "Or—or the photos you already sent me, if those were leaked, would it be a big deal? Would it damage your reputation?"

"You already know the answer to that question. I'm on billboards in my underwear. No one would care."

"Oh, they'd care. But if any picture of me *not* looking uptight and professional were leaked, I'd never live it down. It would be 'Girls gone wild, rocket scientist edition.' Women—especially women in science, or politicians—aren't allowed that freedom without lasting consequences. It's not just my male colleagues who will judge me, it's everyone. And that's just the way it is."

I felt like putting my fist through a wall, growling, "The way it is sucks."

"I agree. But—" I could hear her breathing, it had quickened, like she was working herself up to say something difficult, and a spike of alarm had the hairs on the back of my neck standing up. Before I could interject, she finished her thought, "Abram, we live in two different worlds."

My bitterness morphed into anger, making me seethe. "I refuse to accept that. We live in the same world."

"Our paths are—they're very different."

"No. They're not. They're the same. We're on this road together, Mona. We're on this path together. And I want you—I want you to feel empowered, because you are powerful. You. Are. *Powerful.* Someone should be telling you that, making you believe it, every damn day. You feel like you have to hide part of yourself and it pisses me off. So, yeah, I need a minute here. Because I need to mourn the fuc—" I stopped myself, taking a deep breath, grinding my teeth, telling myself to calm down. "I need to mourn this world in which we live, where *gentlemen* and *ladies* exist who are less, so much less than you. And yet, because of how a flawed system is built, they get to decide how and when you share yourself with me."

"Abram! Are you on the phone?"

I glanced up at the sound of Ruthie's shrieking question. She stood just inside the doorway, holding a tray.

She also wore an impressive scowl. "That better be your priest, because Imma kill you now."

Suddenly tired, I gave my guitarist a quelling look and turned away, lowering my voice to a whisper. "Listen. I have to go. We have a—a thing. Stuff to sign and this interview later."

A few seconds of quiet, and then Mona said, "Okay. See you soon." She sounded distracted. I didn't like it.

"Hey. See you soon. I lov—" I'd wanted to say *I love you*, but she'd already ended the call.

Cursing under my breath, I turned to the table and sat down in front of the tray, ignoring Ruthie's death stare and navigating to my texts.

Abram: I love you. I don't need a picture, I just need you.

I didn't need a picture, not if it would be a source of anxiety for her, but she was wrong. We were in this together. If something affected her, it affected me. Reading back over the message, I decided to send one more.

Abram: What you have to deal with is ~~complete fucking bullshit~~ completely unacceptable. I wish I could do something to help and I shouldn't have ranted at you. I'm not mad at you, but I would like to punch some physicists right now.

Abram: Not you, obviously.

Abram: I miss you. You're incredible. I'm awed by you.

Staring at my phone, I waited for Mona to respond. Ruthie cleared her throat. Obnoxiously. I ignored her. Charlie came back in, took a seat, and began signing photos. Still, I stared, my stomach slowly sinking.

After a few minutes, I set the phone face down on the table and glanced at the tray. A mug, a teapot, cut up wedges of lemon, packets of honey, and a plate with some kind of cookie covered the surface. Ruthie must've been a butler in another life.

I poured myself tea, unable to shake a nagging sense of doom. Ruin set up residence in my chest, distracting and tight, telling me I'd fucked up.

But I'll make it right in New York. I'll—

"Do you like the *tea*?" Ruthie asked, somehow making the question sound like a threat.

"Yes. Thank you," I whispered, so as not to further provoke her ire.

"You're welcome. The cookies are sugar free and paleo," Charlie said. He reached for one of the cookies, shoving the whole thing in his mouth. "I made the tea. She assembled the rest and carried it."

"Fucking paleo asshats," Ruthie mumbled. "I hate those people."

"What? Why?" Charlie asked around another bite of a cookie. "Their snacks are pretty good. Clever. I like that they use dates in energy bars."

Blowing steam off the surface of the tea, I checked my phone again. Nothing. Now my throat not only hurt, it was full of glass shards of regret, making it nearly impossible to swallow.

"No, Charlie." She rolled her eyes. "I'm talking about people from the paleolithic time period. I can't stand those fuckers. With their stupid pet dinosaurs."

Charlie and I shared a look, because sometimes Ruthie was odd, and we couldn't tell if she was serious or joking. This was a woman who hated the most random things—like the word *chartreuse* and all-natural history museums—so there existed a very real possibility she actually hated people from the paleolithic time period.

Rubbing my sternum, I took a sip of the tea, set it down, and picked up a marker. "Pass me a photo."

"No talking, Abram," Ruthie chided, giving me a whole stack of photographs. "When you finish these, Charlie and I will take turns giving you more."

I nodded, grimacing, because the ache in my chest hadn't eased. *Was this our first argument?*

No. Our first argument had been in Aspen. This definitely wasn't that. I wasn't upset with her. I was upset with a system that rewarded hypocrisy.

My phone buzzed. Immediately, I snatched it up, almost knocking over the tea. A text.

Mona: I was saving this for New York, but I thought you'd like a sneak peek.

I frowned, reading the message again, searching for a hidden meaning. Then a picture came through and I almost dropped my phone.

It was Mona.

Standing in front of a full-length mirror.

Wearing a white string bikini.

It didn't matter that I had no voice, because I was now speechless, with profound lust.

"What's wrong with you? You watching porn or something?" Ruthie leaned toward me. "Who is that?"

I yanked the phone back, pressing it to my chest, glaring at her.

She immediately reared back, her eyes wide with surprise. "Sorry, sorry. Don't mind me, I'll just be over here hating paleos and signing photos, as one does."

Standing, I paced away from the table and toward the window, peering at the picture of Mona again, hungry for it. God, she was so fucking beautiful. So gorgeous. Her expression, smiling, confident, but with a hint of challenge, like she dared someone, anyone to make this picture of her something shameful. And her expression erased any worry I might've had that she'd felt pressured into sending it.

I loved it. I needed hours with this photo.

You'll have hours with her, and the bikini, in less than two days.

Two days.

Just two days.

Two days that stretched in front of me like an eternity.

CHAPTER 8
THE MAGNITUDE SCALE

Mona

Usually, if I'm booked on a flight and the airline offers a voucher to take a later flight, I am the first person to give up my seat. Discounts on air travel excite me more than well-timed puns and cookies combined.

Vouchers. *Vouchers.* Even the word sounds seductive.

But not this time. Nothing would induce me to give up my seat on the overbooked flight from Frankfurt to New York for a later flight, not even $800 in travel vouchers. Such was my commitment to arriving in New York as soon as the laws of thermodynamics would allow.

My plane was set to arrive around 9 PM. The plan was for me to check into our hotel, reserved under the names Abram and Mona Harris, and wait for his flight to land at approximately 6:00AM the following morning. Using the aliases had been his idea and made sense given how nuts the paparazzi had been over him in the last several months. Our hotel, called Inn New York City, wasn't one with which I was familiar, but he'd insisted on the location. I honestly didn't care, just as long as we were together.

The flight itself was uneventful, albeit slow, further buoying my theory that feelings influence perception of motion and the space-time continuum. Perhaps feelings were the key to unraveling the mystery of quantum gravity. *Hmm.*

Eventually, we landed at JFK safe and sound, and I immediately switched off the airplane mode of my phone, wanting to text Abram as soon as possible. I'd just opened my messaging app when a series of texts came through, the first one sent just after my flight had taken off, but the second one was from less than a half hour ago.

Abram: Can't wait to see you.

Abram: Call Marie at this number when you land.

Marie?

Frowning at the last text, my heart fluttering anxiously, I called Abram's number as instructed and turned toward the window at my right in order to achieve maximum privacy despite being packed into the very back of coach like osmium.

Three rings later, a female voice answered, "Mona?"

"Uh, yes?"

"Hi. It's Marie Harris, Abram's sister."

MARIE! How could I have forgotten awesome Marie?

Oh jeez. I quickly tested my breath, and then abruptly stopped myself when—obviously—I realized it didn't matter if my breath smelled bad. Unless they'd invested in olfaction-phonics and updated my phone without telling me, the status of my breath didn't matter.

"Hi, hi! Hi, Marie. It's nice to, uh—" SCHRÖDINGER! And all his cats, dead or alive. I couldn't say, *It's nice to talk to you again,* because when we'd first met, I'd been Lisa. Damn lies. Clearing my throat, I said the first thing that popped in my mind, "How may I be of service?"

"Uh, yes. Well, Abram asked that I call. He's here."

"In Michigan?" my mouth asked, just as my brain thought it.

"No. In LA. We're at the hospital—"

Hospital. Hospital. *Hospital.* Why did that word feel like being hit on the back of the head with a large, heavy, blunt object? All concerns about my previous lies vanished.

"—found him this morning. His fever was quite high, and an ambulance was called. Leo called me as soon as he found out and I arrived just an hour ago. They've been able to bring down his fever, and he's tested positive for the flu. The doctors were worried about a secondary infection, but the CT scan and blood work came back okay. The doctors say he looks good to be discharged tomorrow, but they want to keep him overnight for observation."

Hospital. Oh God.

My throat was choking me. "Is he okay? I mean, I know he has the flu, but is he—I mean—will he—is he—"

"They think he's going to be fine." Marie's voice was infinitely patient and reassuring and was exactly what I needed to hear. "Just to be safe, they're keeping him overnight and plan to get another blood draw in the morning. But, yes, he seems to be okay. Cranky, obstinate, and giving me dirty looks from across the room, but okay."

"He's there? Can I—is it okay for him to talk?"

"Yes. Absolutely. I just wanted to explain the situation first, answer any questions, to save him from having to speak unnecessarily, since he is *very sick.*"

I swallowed around a lump of guilt. I wanted to talk to him—desperately—but not if it would endanger his recovery. "If he's too sick to talk, I completely understand. It's obviously more important that he recover than—"

"No, no. It should be fine if you two talk. I just wanted to remind my brother that he is *very sick* and—under no circumstances—will he be performing tonight or flying to New York this evening. Here, let me put him on."

I heard a grumbly, angry voice in the background, and it mollified the sharpest edges of my anxiety. Being well enough to feel and express anger was far better than the worst-case scenarios I hadn't even realized I'd been imagining.

A brief silence on the other side was followed by the muffled sound of Marie saying, "Yes, I will keep it on speaker. And no, you can't hold the phone. Fight me."

And then Abram said, "Mona."

Suddenly, my eyes stung with a heated rush of disarrayed emotion. "Oh, Abram. You sound so sick. Don't speak, okay?" I closed my eyes, resting my forehead against the frame of the plane window. "Please don't worry about New York, don't worry about anything. Like you said, we have the rest of our lives. Concentrate on getting better and being well. I love you."

"I love you too."

I winced as he spoke. His rattled breathing and the sound of machines beeping in the background made my chest feel heavy and tight. Very little about his voice sounded like him, but it did make obvious how sick he was.

"We can text. I'll—I'll send you pictures, okay? Lots of candid shots."

Abram made a sound that I assumed was one of agreement or amusement. "No pressure, but that sounds great."

I winced again, because he'd said a lot of words, and speaking at all seemed to cost him. I wanted him to get better. Overextending himself on the phone—just so I could hear his voice—was not helping.

"Okay. No more talking. Put Marie back on. Go to sleep. Rest. I love you."

"I love you," he said, the last word sounding fainter.

A second later, the sound of the machines also faded, and Marie said, "Mona? Hey. Thanks for calling. You've definitely improved his mood."

"No problem, I—" I shook my head, opening my eyes and staring at the tarmac beyond my oval window. "I want to be there," I confessed, not caring how miserable I sounded, not caring that she was basically a stranger. "We were only going to have twenty-four hours in New York, but now I'm thinking about abandoning all my responsibilities for the next week and flying out to LA."

"I'm not advocating it, but can you do that? I mean, how big of a deal would it be?"

"I'd have to start my project from almost scratch, which means I might lose my spot in the program, which means I might lose my graduate funding." I would probably lose at least part of my funding. One of my grants was contingent on presentation of findings at the August conference. The math part was easy, getting time with the LHC was not. If I started from scratch, nothing would be ready for August.

But, strangely, uncovering the mysteries of the known and unknown universe didn't seem important relative to the reality of Abram being horribly sick.

"He's in good hands, Mona. I'll be here in LA until he's fully recovered. Our parents are coming later today. I promise, I won't let him do anything that will jeopardize his recovery and we'll keep you updated."

"I just—I need to—" I heaved a watery sigh. "I'm sorry. I need to be there. I think we're almost to the gate. I'll get a flight to LA as soon as I can."

"Mona—"

"You're not going to change my mind." I'd already been traveling for fourteen hours —Geneva to Frankfurt, Frankfurt to New York—what was another six or seven in comparison? No big deal.

"Take a step back and think about this, be rational. He'll be fine. You being here isn't going to—"

"I can't—I physically *cannot*—fly back to Geneva. I know myself, and I would regret it so much, the gravity of my feelings might cause the formation of a black hole somewhere over the Atlantic Ocean, and then we're all dead. As such, I'll text you as soon as I know my new flight data."

After a brief pause, she asked, "You're in New York?"

"Yes."

"Which airport?"

"Uh, JFK."

"I'll make a deal with you. If you promise to stay just for the original twenty-four hours, I can get you on a private plane leaving New York in—uh—forty-ish minutes, *and* a flight back directly to Geneva on the same plane. You'll have to make a short stop in Chicago to pick up my parents, but you'll definitely get here faster than a commercial flight."

I wrinkled my nose, pulling my bottom lip through my teeth as I considered her offer. "Whose private plane?"

"A friend's."

I shook my head quickly. "No. I can't promise that. What if Abram isn't better in twenty-four hours? What if he takes a turn for the worse? I wouldn't be able to leave then."

"Okay, if he's better, then you have to leave, go back to Europe as planned, and get back to work so you don't lose your funding. If he's sicker, you can stay."

A few sounds emerged from the back of my throat, all of which were disbelieving. "I'm sorry, but this doesn't sound like a deal. This sounds too good to be true."

"Do we have a deal?"

I didn't hesitate. "Yes."

Usually, I didn't accept gifts. And I never accepted anything without knowing the source, definitely not anything as luxurious as a flight on a private plane. But desperate times call for a relaxation of rigid ethical codes. I would have to sort through my overthinking on this subject later. *Much later.*

"Is that a promise?" Marie pushed, as though she sensed a statement of explicit promise was necessary.

"Absolutely."

"Good. I'll text you the details once I work things out with my friend. I'll also—hold on, Abram is trying to get my attention. Just a sec."

The phone went quiet for a minute, maybe two, during which I calculated the precise moment I would have to leave LA to make it back to Geneva on time. To my delight, we'd actually end up with more time together than if we'd met in New York. This realization was tempered by the reminder that Abram was extremely sick. I'd prefer less time and him well, not because I felt like I was missing out on quality time with him, but because I just wanted him to be better.

"Okay, Mona. Are you still there?"

"Yes. I'm here."

"Abram has a few stipulations for your visit, which I'm going to communicate. Item one: you can only come if you've had your flu shot. Have you?"

"Yes! I had it. I had it in November. Ha!" I did a little triumphant fist pump and accidentally hit my knuckles against the overhead reading light. I stifled an *ow*, also earning an irritated side-eye from the woman next to me in the center seat. Doing my best to ignore her glare, I cleared my throat and asked, "What else?"

"Item two: you will sleep while you are here whenever you are tired, and you will not spend all your time taking care of him."

"That sounds like two things, but sure. I'm fine with item two." I would definitely shower when we arrived.

"Item three: you will allow him to pay for a car to pick you up, your hotel room, and anything else you need while you're here."

"That seems gratuitous." I crossed my arms. We hadn't talked much about the money thing, but I felt like it was a conversation looming on the horizon. He had *a lot* more than me, and that was fine. But I wasn't penniless, I had pride, and I liked paying my own way. I liked knowing I'd earned what was mine, and that included experiences.

"He said you would have a problem with this one, so he said it was nonnegotiable."

"Define nonnegotiable? If he covers this visit, can I cover the car, hotel, and meals of our next rendezvous?"

"Hold on, let me ask. She wants to know—" Marie must've covered the phone because I didn't hear the remainder of her question. Less than a minute later, she was back. "He agrees. Also, nice use of the word rendezvous. I approve."

"Thank you." Her praise flustered me a little and I had to give myself a slight shake to refocus.

"Next item: you are not to sleep at the hospital. When you sleep, you have to sleep in the hotel. Basically, he wants you to get good sleep."

I made a sound of displeasure, but eventually said, "Fine. Anything else? Any other terms?"

"Nope. That's it. I'll be in touch with the details for the flight. Let me call my friend and get that ball rolling. See you soon."

"See you soon. Bye."

The call clicked off. I lowered my phone, releasing an expansive sigh. It did nothing to ease the knots in my chest and throat. I wanted to help. I wanted to help but was stuck on the other side of the USA, waiting to deplane. I was helpless.

I thought back over my last few conversations with Abram, searching for some clue, something I could do to help from afar. Perhaps picking up something from the gift shop? Personally, I liked snow globes. I wondered how he felt about the Statue of Liberty.

"Is your hand okay?"

Glancing at the woman next to me, the one who'd just given me the side-eye, I asked, "Pardon?"

"Your hand. You hit it on the reading light."

"Oh. Yeah. It's fine. I just, uh, got excited about something."

She gave me a small smile. "I once broke two fingers in my right hand closing them in a car door. It was awful, being one handed for weeks. But you know what? It made me realize how many selfies I took, because I just can't take them with my left hand." She laughed, shaking her head at herself.

Grinning, I found myself curious. "How many selfies did you take?"

"Oh, like, a few every day. But my boyfriend at the time—husband now—was always asking for them, so I think it just became a habit."

Ah!

AH HA!

Of course!

"Thank you," I said, already unlocking my phone and switching the camera around to face me. "You just gave me an exceedingly excellent and exploitable idea."

* * *

Abram was asleep when his parents and I arrived at the hospital.

Wait. Let me back up for a second, because I'm sure you're wondering. Seeing Mr. and Mrs. Harris for the first time in over two years was significantly less awkward than I'd feared it would be.

Pamela stepped onto the jet, saw me, walked over, and gave me a hug. "I'm so glad you're coming, but I worry for you, Mona. Abram says you're not sleeping enough."

Perplexed by her (shouldn't she be mad at me for lying to her about who I was years ago?), her words (like we knew each other extremely well and often discussed such things), and my body's reaction to both (which was to immediately return her embrace without nary a flinch), the profuse apology I'd planned stuck in my throat.

What is happening? What has just happened?

Stepping back, she held my shoulders and regarded me. "I also want to tell you how proud we were when we saw you on TV over the summer, giving those corrupt Washington jerks—excuse my French—a piece of your mind. But, honey, you look tired, and I don't mean that to be insulting, I mean that because I'm concerned. Here —" she let me go and reached into her bag "I brought muffins. This one is lemon poppyseed. Or, if you like, you can have blueberry."

"I like the blueberry," Mr. Harris said, standing a little bit behind his wife, giving me a matter-of-fact look. "She uses the fresh ones."

"It's because this one—" she pointed her thumb at Mr. Harris and chuckled merrily "—built me that greenhouse in the back. I can get blueberries in the winter. Isn't that something? Oh, I also brought you a de-stress mix of jojoba oil, lavender, and rose." Looping her arm through mine, she steered me toward the back of the plane and to a built-in couch. "They just added this couch last year, it's much nicer than sitting in the other seats."

She took a breath, so I took my chance.

"Mr. Harris, Mrs. Harris, I wanted to apologize for lying to your family when I attended your birthday party several years ago. I have no excuse, and I—"

"Oh, don't worry about that. You do have an excuse, a good one too, and Abram explained everything. It's like roses. You're still you. No matter what we call you,

you're still just as sweet. Now, I've been doing some steam distillation, and you know it takes thousands of roses to make just a bit of essential oil, but I got so many blooms the last two years, I managed a few drops."

And so it went.

Slightly shell-shocked, I spoke of essential oil extraction techniques with Pamela—as well as various other topics of interest to us both—while Mr. Harris ate his blueberry muffin and read the newspaper. All the while I fretted.

Their forgiveness felt too easy. Who forgives this easily? No one I knew. Definitely not the world. People don't just *forgive* anymore. Forgiveness, like everything else, needed to be earned, hard fought, won after proving oneself with huge, unwavering acts of self-punishment and atonement.

But for now, so as not to make the flight awkward, I decided to—as Gabby would say—*just go with it*.

Oh! Also, Pamela and I took a candid selfie and sent it to Abram just before takeoff. Sending Abram that photo yesterday had been a big deal for me, not because the picture was risqué, but that was definitely part of it. It was a big deal because I truly wanted to send my boyfriend a risqué photo. And so I did.

As I deplaned my Frankfurt to New York flight, I'd sent a text message of warning to Marie via Abram's cellphone, informing her that she should expect several candid selfies over the next few hours. It was the only action of potential value my brain could conjure to reach beyond geography and maybe, possibly help Abram.

Perhaps it would cheer him up?

I hoped so.

Anyway. Back to the hospital and a sleeping Abram.

His room was in the VIP wing—a very real thing in LA—and Marie had come out to gather us from security. We'd arrived late evening, therefore the paparazzi were minimal, really just one guy with a big lens, taking shots of us while wearing a perplexed expression.

Marie had also greeted me warmly, with a big hug, a sweet smile, and no mention of my prior offenses. For the record, she was just as lovely as she'd been years prior. A very weird voice in my head mentioned that it would be pretty cool if Abram and I got married, partially because Marie would then be my sister-in-law and Pamela would be my mother-in-law.

Not that I'm advocating marriage based on the groom's family. I'm just sayin'. You know. Throwing the facts out there, he had a stellar family.

IT WAS A VARIABLE! OKAY?

Moving on.

Upon entering his room, I held back with Marie, allowing Pamela and Mr. Harris the first approach, though my heart ached to see him in the hospital bed. It was too small for his big frame, and he looked pale. He never looked pale, so this was definitely distressing.

Neither of his parents woke him, they just took a peek and hovered for several minutes. Pamela made a sad sound. Mr. Harris put an arm around his wife's shoulders and whispered something in her ear. She nodded. Then Mr. Harris sniffled, and she bent her head toward his, giving him a kiss on the cheek.

It was so damn sweet. My eyes were misty. *They really love him.*

"Of course they do," Marie whispered, turning to look at me like I was strange.

"Yes. Right. Of course." *Yikes.* I must've spoken my thoughts aloud.

She continued her survey of me for a few seconds, then said, "How are you doing with all this?"

"Me?" I frowned at the obvious worry for me in her voice. "Forget about me, how are you doing? You must be exhausted."

Marie gave me a closed mouth smile, her eyebrows high on her forehead. "I'm not the one who spent the last twenty-four hours traveling. Mona, really, how are you? Are you hungry?"

I shook my head, her genuine concern disconcerting. "Marie, I—" I snapped my mouth shut, shaking my head harder, turning to face her fully, and whispering, "Why is your family being so wonderful to me? I lied to you, all of you. I want to earn your forgiveness, prove to you that I can be trusted, prove myself. I need to be the one—"

"Oh my goodness, stop." Once again, Marie was looking at me like I was strange, a little bubble of quiet laughter escaping her lips. "Abram said you were like this. But, honey, we don't want you to prove anything."

I eyed her suspiciously. "Then what do you want?"

She shrugged, her gaze flickering over my face. "I don't know. Kindness, I guess. Just be kind."

Swallowing around some unidentified thickness, I nodded. "Okay. I can do that."

"Good." Marie's smile grew, as did the warmth in her eyes. She slipped her arm around my back and held me next to her, hip to hip, turning us to face Abram again. "He wanted me to wake him up when you arrived."

I worked to keep my chin from wobbling, my mind in disarray. "No, no. Don't do that. He needs rest."

"That's what I decided too. I thought, instead, you could write him a note? Something for next to his bed? And then come back in the morning before he's discharged."

"Or, I could stay here."

Marie squinted at me. "You promised not to sleep at the hospital."

The potential for a debate helped clear my chaotic mind and rein in my emotions. "Correct. But I've been on Geneva time, so it's morning there. Plus, someone should stay. Plus, you've been here all day. Plus, your parents must be exhausted. Plus—"

"Okay, okay. You had me at Geneva time." Marie released me and covered her mouth to yawn. "You stay, we'll go, and we'll be back early in the morning." She stepped closer and embraced me again, giving me a full body hug, like she meant it. "Thank you for coming. He's been in a much better mood, been a *much* better patient, since you called from New York."

"No problem. I'm just—" I couldn't continue, choking back some emotion I couldn't identify. It was the strangest thing.

Obviously, I was worried for Abram. I hated that he was so sick, in pain, frustrated and disappointed. But I was also bizarrely happy, to be here, with this loving family who supported each other, who forgave so easily. It made me feel like, during this anxious time of crisis, everything was going to work out just fine.

Abram was an essential part of something real, meaningful, stable, safe. Which meant, by extension, so was I.

Taking a deep breath, I finished roughly, "I'm happy, so happy, to be here."

I felt Marie's cheek smile against mine and she held me tighter. "We're happy, so happy, that you're here too."

CHAPTER 9
THE QUANTIZATION OF ENERGY

Mona

Not going to lie, I spent a considerable portion of the night staring at him, unable to fully comprehend that, after so much time spent waiting and wishing and longing, we were together. But let the record show, I didn't smell him, though the temptation was a strong force.

I also took a shower, changed into fresh clothes, and got a good amount of work done, chasing a random hunch that ended up leading to a different hunch that ultimately yielded an extremely promising preliminary result. I ended up sending my calculations to Poe, asking him to double-check my math and assumptions. This was not unusual for us—sending notes, data, and calculations back and forth for comment—and he was the only one I'd trust with inception work like this.

After sending the email, I stretched my arms over my head, giving into a yawn, and glanced up to find Abram's eyes open and watching me. My body jolted, him being awake startled me. His mouth hitched higher on the left side.

"Hey, brown eyes," he said, sounding just as sick as the day prior. But his voice was soft, sleepy, and full of affection. Part of me melted, part of me tensed.

"Do you need anything?" I set my computer aside, closing it, standing, and stepped next to his bed. My hand sought his. Our fingers entwined. My other hand gently sifted through his hair, testing his forehead. "What can I do? Are you uncomfortable?"

He shook his head in a subtle movement, his gaze lowering to my lips. "I'm great."

I grinned. "You have the flu, you're not great."

"I'm so great."

That made me laugh, and I indulged myself by caressing his cheek, his stubbly jaw, trying not to frown when I noticed the slight green tinge to his skin, how his eyes lacked vibrancy. He turned his head toward my touch, his lips brushing against my knuckles.

"Thank you for coming," he whispered against my fingers.

"I'm not sure I had a choice," I admitted thoughtfully to his profile. "I think I might've gone crazy if I didn't see you for myself, make sure you're okay. Are you sure I can't get you anything? Some water?"

"Just you." He lifted his hand to mine and opened my fingers. He then pressed his cheek against my palm, closing his eyes. "Just you."

We stayed like that for a moment, holding still, *being* together. He took a deep breath and I heard the rattling in his chest, the crackle and wheeze as he exhaled. He winced, and then so did I.

Yes, I knew, reasonably, rationally, that thousands of people had the flu every year. It was rarely fatal. Most recovered with no lasting effects. And yet, Abram was in pain, now, in this moment. I wanted to alleviate it with a desperation I rarely felt. Emotion was the enemy of physicists—especially theoretical physicists, who spent more time chasing shadows than answers—and desperation had no place in my life.

But I felt desperate now, desperate to *do something*.

Therefore, hoping to distract him from whatever was making him wince, I asked, "How long have you been up?"

"Not long." He shook his head lightly, opening his eyes and giving them back to me. "You're very sexy when you're concentrating."

"Oh, well, thank you." I wagged my eyebrows. "Is it the cargo pants? Or the baggy T-shirt that caught your eye? Or perhaps the glasses?" I only wore glasses to read.

His lips twitched, like it took too much effort to smile again. "Hey, by the way. Thank you for the photo, but—"

"You're welcome. I hope you liked it."

"I do. But, uh, Mona. I don't want you to feel pressured to send me that kind of stuff. I've been thinking. I'm going to delete it, and you should too. I honestly just wanted to see your smile, I wanted—" he had to stop himself, covering his mouth as he coughed.

Gah. It sounded painful and it made me anxious for him. I passed him a cup of water. He took a sip. I placed it back on the adjustable tray table.

Needing to touch him, I placed my hand on his forearm. "Okay, first. Please don't delete it. I honestly wanted to send it."

His eyes narrowed slightly, the subtle curve of his lips telling me he didn't believe me.

"It's true. When you called me powerful, it struck a nerve. You were right. But you were also wrong."

Abram's eyebrows lowered over his eyes, making him look like that news eagle from The Muppets.

I didn't want him to waste his energy arguing with me about this, so I rushed to add, "I'm not powerful, not like I want to be. Think about it, how powerful can I possibly be if I'm constantly acquiescing to the very people who want to keep me powerless?"

His brow cleared, his eyes were hazy with fever, but I saw I'd said something that resonated.

"Therefore, I sent the photo. I could've sent you one of me smiling, just my face, but I didn't. I wanted to send you *that* one. And so I did." The picture made me feel sexy, and it reminded me of that moment between us in the pool, in Chicago, after he'd forfeited the race. The way he'd looked at me, I loved it. Just thinking about his eyes at that moment made my heart race. It was a memory I cherished.

"But." He tried to clear his throat, wincing slightly. "But if it ever gets out there—"

"I know the risks." I gave him a resigned smile. "I'm an adult. I'm aware of the possible damage it might do to my credibility, should the photo ever be shared. But if our phones are hacked and it goes public, I'm prepared to weather the storm. In fact, I've begun to think of it as an opportunity."

"Opportunity?"

"Yes. Someone has to be the woman who stands up and proudly says, 'Yes. I send my rock star boyfriend sexy photos of me. Why is that relevant to my work?'"

He made a weak sound that almost resembled a laugh. "Mona, if you change your mind—"

"I won't." I knew myself. For better or worse, when I committed to an idea or a cause, I was married to it in the old testament biblical sense.

Abram stared at me quietly, as though searching for some sign of uncertainty or regret. "Tell me something."

"What would you like to know?"

"What were you doing over there? What are you working on?"

Obviously, he was trying to change the subject. Which made me wonder whether he believed me about wanting to send the photo.

But since he was sick, I let the issue drop. "I was just sending off some preliminary work to a colleague of mine. Poe is a planetary astrophysicist, and my thesis is moving more in the theoretical physics direction and less planetary. Even so, Poe should be able to give it a glance and help me focus my energy in the right direction or tell me who I can trust to take a look."

"Good," Abram croaked, giving me another miniscule smile, his gaze moving over me with a sluggish, foggy quality betraying how awful he felt. "You seem energized."

"I think I made some good headway last night. It's like, so much of what I do is wandering around in a pitch-black room of indeterminate size, not knowing if I'm going in circles or a straight line or approaching a cliff."

"Searching the ocean for your white whale."

"That's right. I only have so much time, you know? I realize time is a faulty construct, which some argue doesn't even exist, but yet we've made it central to everything. I postulated at one point that time was not a single thing—a thread, if you will—but multiple threads, infinite threads *and yet* also beads, and feathers, etc., all woven together into a thick tapestry. Pulling one thread wouldn't change the overall structure of the tapestry as we know it, but it would change the reality for the feathers and beads that rely on that thread. Yes, it might allow us to bend space, but lose reality in the process. Generally, we see time as the past, present, and future, but what if it's both more and less?"

"How can something be both more and less?"

"Everything is both more and less. Everything is balance. My chromosomal arrangement is more XX, less XY. You are more musician, less airplane pilot."

His lips curved weakly, but a spark lit behind his eye. "I could listen to you talk about this forever."

"Then you're the only one." I grinned wryly. Seeing the light in his gaze did something wonderful to my stomach, making me feel both full and warm.

"I doubt that." Abram brought my hand to his lap, cradling it in both of his.

Considering, I sat on the scant sliver at the edge of his bed and amended, "Okay, yes. I do have a few colleagues who also enjoy theorizing with me."

"You mean philosophizing with you." He cleared his throat, his head seeming to sink deeper into his pillow.

"Of course, yes. Theoretical physics is married to philosophy. The nature of things, of reality. Perception."

"And art is the product of how humans interpret their reality."

That made me smile. "Look at you, smarty-pants. So, what you're saying is, physics and philosophy are married, and their child is art?"

"Or, the marriage of physics and philosophy *is* art."

I loved that. My smile deepened, my attention lowering to where he held my hand. He'd moved it to his chest, pressing my palm against his heart.

"Being with you . . ." he began, drawing my eyes back to his face. His were dazed, unfocused, like he was looking within and without.

"Being with me?" I prompted after almost a minute, curious, a bubble of something reluctantly hopeful expanding in my chest. So of course, a joke slipped out. "Is as the prophesy foretold?"

Abram's gaze sharpened on mine. He smiled, a real smile. His left dimple making its first appearance, stealing my breath before his words could.

"It's living artistry, Mona." Abram's gaze turned cherishing, earnest. "Being with you is like living in a song."

* * *

As the sun came up, I read the latest Lisa Kleypas novel to Abram. I'd already read it, but he hadn't, and I didn't mind at all. Eventually, he drifted back to sleep. A nurse came in to unobtrusively check his vitals. A doctor stopped by and asked if I was family. I explained that his sister and parents would be arriving soon. The nurse then returned with a food tray—for me—and then left again, informing me that I should call for his breakfast when he awoke.

Peeking at the food on the tray, I was surprised—but not really—to discover the fancy nature of my meal. Two poached eggs on avocado toast, a kale and rocket salad, a berry compote, freshly made yogurt, and cinnamon granola. The coffee came in a French press and the orange juice was pulpy, freshly squeezed.

Ah, Los Angeles VIP treatment. It was truly another world.

Marie and Abram's parents arrived just as I finished breakfast and was setting the tray outside the room. To my surprise, Leo was with them. My brother didn't seem at all surprised to see me. Confused, but not surprised.

We didn't hug. He made no move to do so and neither did I, a fact that hadn't struck me as strange in Aspen or at any point in the past prior to right this minute. But now, after being embraced by the Harris family, and seeing how they greeted each other, how genuinely they seemed to look forward to and enjoy each other's presence, I felt the lack of greeting between my own brother and me.

Almost immediately—as soon as we exchanged our tepid, polite hellos, and the Harris family was no longer within ear shot—he steered me a little further down the hall, away from Abram's room, and pulled out his phone.

"I thought you should know, you were photographed last night, coming in with Abram's parents. But they assumed you were Lisa. Let me show you the pictures."

Studying my brother's profile as he stared at the phone, and despite the unresolved tension between us since our conversation in Aspen, I had the sudden urge to hug him. Therefore, I did.

I gently pushed his phone out of the way, slipped my arms around his torso, and tried to mimic Marie's hug from last night. I wanted to hug Leo like I meant it. He didn't respond at first, and his body tensed like this might be an assault rather than an embrace. But as I continued to hold on, my big brother's arms encircled me, held me with an equivalent tightness ratio, and he pressed a kiss to my temple.

"Hey," he said against my hair. "Are you okay?"

"Yes." I tried to relax, turning my head against his shoulder and resting it there. "How are you?"

"I'm good." The tension left him by degrees until his big arms held me comfortably. "What's going on, Mona? Do you want to talk?"

"We should hug, I think. When we see each other, and just sometimes for no reason, because I love you, Leo. And I think I haven't been so great at knowing how to show you in a way that you understand."

I felt his cheek curve with a small smile. "I'm sorry."

"For what?"

"For being a dick."

Leaning my head back, I expected to find him smiling—since his voice held a smile—but he wasn't. He looked remorseful, serious.

"In Aspen?"

"Yeah. In Aspen. But also, I guess, for a long time. Lisa and I, we—uh—talked last week." He readjusted his hands at my back, I felt him lock them more completely together, and his eyes grew dark, heated with anger. "And she told me about what happened to you at school."

Oh.

Oh God.

Lisa told Leo?

Yes. Of course she did. She's worried about you.

I forgave my sister immediately, but wished she'd warned me. I wasn't prepared to discuss this with my brother.

Therefore, I tried to say, *Nothing happened,* but the words wouldn't form. I tried to draw a complete breath but couldn't. I stared at Leo, helpless to the rising anxiety. However, when it came, when the cold sweat broke out over my skin and panic reached eyeball level, it rose no further.

"I haven't been a good brother to you," he continued, sounding angry, solemn. "I've been pretty fucking blind about you, not taking the time to think about what you might need. I've replaced you, and Mom and Dad, and Lisa to an extent, with friendships, building my family elsewhere. Because Mona, I need family." Leo lifted a hand to my head and gently returned my cheek to his shoulder.

"I need people. I need a network, a community. I thought maybe you didn't. I thought you weren't built that way. But what I think now is that it doesn't fucking matter how you're built. You're my *sister.*" His voice now a harsh whisper, I could feel the restlessness in his body, the frustration. "You should've come to me, you should've told me when it happened. But that means I should've been—before that, way before that—someone you trusted. Someone you never doubted would help. Someone who put you above his friends. I should've been checking on you, letting you know I was interested, making it clear you mattered. That's all on me."

The panic slowly receded, with each breath I exhaled bits and pieces of the memory, of the strangling fear, until it simmered in my stomach instead of suffocating my lungs.

And my brother continued to hold me, petting my hair and making a suspiciously watery clearing-of-the-throat sound that—for some reason—made me smile.

"Mona baby," he said suddenly, breaking the moment, and I couldn't stop my laugh, because that's what he used to call me when we were little. "You need to see someone, to help you work through this."

Now I tensed. A second later, I removed myself from his grip. He let me go, but I could feel his eyes on me as I paced away.

"Uh, I don't think that's necessary." The last thing I wanted to do was talk about it. To anyone.

"Mona, I'm not letting this go. I have a list of good psychologists who you can do phone sessions with from Geneva."

I glanced at him. He'd withdrawn a piece of paper from his jacket pocket. Abruptly, the expansive hallway felt too small.

"I don't think I need—"

"Yes. You do. You're doing this." He reached for my hand and placed the paper in my palm. I didn't flinch. "I already made you an appointment with the first person on the list."

"But how will I pay for it?" I asked, using the easiest, most obvious excuse, and crumpling the list. "Insurance only covers so much. I can't afford—"

"You can." Leo reclaimed my hand and, using both of his, straightened the paper out. "You have your monthly allowance account—from Mom and Dad—and the money is all in your name. I bet it's just sitting there. I bet you've never touched it."

I scowled, because he was right. In addition to the travel account, our parents had set up accounts for each of us when we hit eighteen, depositing the maximum tax-free gift amount yearly as a fun money fund. It was one of their ways of demonstrating how much they supported us, in addition to all the other bank accounts.

Because *money* was how they supported us. Money. Just money.

"It must have over a hundred thousand dollars in it by now. Use that."

"I don't want their money," I whispered between clenched teeth, not knowing I was going to hurl the words at my brother until they were already out. The fervor in my whisper surprised both of us. I swallowed, trying to figure out why my heart was beating so fast, and why my mouth tasted like persimmons.

Meanwhile, Leo's eyes had widened, concern replacing the self-recrimination from moments prior. "Mona—"

"No. No. I don't want it. I don't want money from them." I stuffed the list of psychologists in my pocket, next to the poem Abram had written me in Aspen, mostly to get it out of my sight.

My brother's gaze softened, and he stepped closer, commiseration etched into his features. "I get it, okay? I mean, I really do. It feels like a payoff, right? Like, to them, the money replaces all the things they didn't give us, or couldn't."

Staring at him, I admitted nothing, working to tuck away these untidy emotions.

Abram inspired emotions? Yes. I was ready for those, I wanted them all, even the untidy ones.

My parents? No. I didn't want any of the untidy emotions or second-guessing they inspired. I loved them. They did their best. I understood that. No one was perfect. I wasn't perfect. They had responsibilities beyond their children. I understood that too. See? Look how reasonable I was. See how tidy and rational?

And yet, just the thought of taking money from "Mona's fun fund" made me want to throw a chair through a window just to hear the glass break.

Leo frowned, clearly frustrated. "Then let me pay for it."

"Leo, I don't need—"

"You do." He advanced, stopping abruptly when he seemed to realize that he'd backed me up until I was against the wall. Taking two steps away, he cursed under his breath. the line of his jaw was stern, but his gaze appeared apologetic. "You do. I wish this never happened to you. I wish it didn't take hearing about it to wake me up to how I've been a shitty brother. So, yeah, I'm going to hound you about this until you do it. And Lisa will, and Gabby too. Good luck avoiding this. Good luck dodging Gabby. You know she'll fly out to Geneva, and so will I. We're not letting this go. And if you don't do it, I'll tell Abram. I know him a lot better than you do, and he'll—"

Unthinkingly, I covered Leo's mouth with my hand, rocks in my throat. "You wouldn't."

He turned his head slightly to the side, lifting an eyebrow as though to say, *You wanna bet?*

I gritted my teeth, because I was angry. So angry.

He gently encircled my wrist, pulling it from his mouth and holding it. "Your hands are shaking."

"Because I'm angry," I seethed.

"Why?"

"You're bullying me into this."

Leo's mouth curved into a sad smile. "I love you, Mona baby. So, yeah. Whatever it takes. Because that's what family does. Because that's what love looks like."

CHAPTER 10
THE THEORY OF SPECIAL RELATIVITY

Abram

"What are you thinking about?"

I blinked, struggling to focus, looking for Marie and finding her leaning against the doorframe. "What was that?"

Marie's smile was soft. "I asked, what are you thinking about?"

My answering smile was flat. "Missed opportunities."

She chuckled, walking further into the hotel bedroom and taking the armchair next to the bed. "So, Mona?"

I grinned and glanced at my hands. "Yeah."

Mona had left eight days ago, keeping her promise to stay just twenty-four hours. Mona called every day since to check in, even if it was just for five minutes while she hid in a bathroom, stealing the time from her projects and work.

"You look better. Do you feel up to talking?"

"I do feel better. Yeah, sure, I could talk." My label cancelled the rest of my commitments for the week—interviews, appearances—so I could recover, and my fever finally broke last night. I still had a little cough. My throat wasn't bothering me much, thanks to Melena and her tea.

"So, let's talk. Abram."

"Marie."

"You look better, but you also look frustrated."

Inhaling deeply, because I finally could without coughing, I nodded. "I guess I am."

I was better, but I was unsettled. Restless. Dissatisfied. I knew Mona couldn't and shouldn't stay. But that didn't stop me from wishing things were different.

"What is this?" Marie pointed at my face, waving her index finger around. "Is this melancholy? Or ennui? Please tell me it's not ennui. Ennui is for dissolute dukes, not dissolute rock stars."

That made me smirk. "Maybe it's melancholy. Maybe it's *Maybelline*."

She laughed, which had been my goal, and rested her elbow on the arm of the chair, tucking her hand beneath her chin. "I'm glad you told me the whole story—with you and Mona—when you got back from Aspen last month. I was pretty confused over the summer, after seeing her on C-SPAN and CNN, thinking I was going nuts."

"Yeah." *I know how you feel.* "Thanks for your help trying to track down her number when Leo wouldn't give it to me. I appreciate your secrecy about everything, crazy as it is." I hadn't told her the *whole* story. Just enough to make sense of my desperate request.

"It is crazy," my sister agreed readily. "Thanks for trusting me with it, but how you and Mona met might be the craziest love story I've ever heard. And you know how wacky my friends are."

We shared a look and I grinned, thinking about her wacky friends.

"Anyway, sorry I couldn't help you uncover the number. Quinn and Alex were very impressed with Exotica and DJ Tang's security measures. They went to great lengths to hide their children's contact information. If we'd had more time, Alex might've been able to narrow down some potential options."

"But it makes sense, right?" I readjusted the pillow behind me. "They're just trying to keep their kids safe."

Marie made a face. "Eh, I don't think that's it. From what I know of Exotica and DJ Tang, I think it's more that they want to be able to text and call their kids without fearing their own privacy will be violated. They're extremely fastidious about public image. Speaking of which." She gave me a pointed look.

"What?"

"You should let Alex do the same for you. The last thing you need is your phone getting hacked."

Oh shit.

Staring at my sister, I was gripped with a sudden suspicion. "You looked at my photos."

Immediately, she shook her head. "I did not look through your photos. If you recall, I texted Mona from your phone that morning in the hospital, asking her to call me at your number. You gave me the phone, you unlocked it, you asked me to send the message. And that means the last photo she sent to you before I texted her—the one of her looking stellar in a bikini—was already in the chat window when you gave it to me."

Sometimes I forgot how great of a reporter my sister was. She had the most detailed memory of anyone I knew.

I shook my head, pushing my fingers through my hair. "Fuck."

"Abram, it's no big deal. I'm your sister. My job is to keep your secrets and love you unconditionally, and your job is to do the same for me. I don't care what you and Mona send each other. You should see the stuff Matt and I send back and for—"

"STOP." I buried my face in my hands. "Please, stop. I do *not* want to know about you and Matt."

My sister chuckled. It sounded sinister.

I wasn't laughing, because now I was concerned. Photos of Mona with my parents, coming to visit me in the LA hospital had surfaced, but the photographer had mistakenly assumed she was Lisa. Since we hadn't been photographed together—because there'd been no opportunity—rumors of my involvement with Mona's twin sister had already faded.

My family knew about us. According to Mona, Leo knew, but I hadn't talked to him since our disagreement. Obviously, Lisa knew, and if you didn't count Tyler or Gabby, which I didn't, that was about it.

It's not that our relationship was a secret. It wasn't. We just weren't advertising it. Keeping things quiet, being private, especially when everything was so new and we saw each other so rarely, seemed to be an unspoken desire we had in common.

But if my phone was hacked, and the photos we'd been sending each other were leaked, it would make national news *for sure.*

Lifting my head, I frowned at Marie. "Okay, do you mind? Can you ask Alex to help?"

"I already did." She picked an invisible piece of lint off her jeans. "It's being taken care of as we speak. The invoice will come from Cypher Systems, just make sure it gets paid. He's very expensive."

"Thank you. Whatever it takes. I don't want any pictures of her out there. It would be, uh, not good."

Marie's eyebrows flickered up a half inch. "You mean, it would be terrible. For her. And her career."

"Yeah. Exactly." I scratched my beard, which was now thick and bushy. I should have thought of this. *Crap.*

"Are you two keeping things secret for a reason? I get the sense that no one here knows about your relationship."

My sister's tone, like she was choosing her words carefully, had me inspecting her. "It's not a secret, but I don't think the crew knows. They might suspect." I thought back to the argument Mona and I had in front of everyone in Aspen, and how we'd missed dinner the last two nights. "Honestly, I have no idea. Charlie and Ruthie were in Aspen with us, but I don't think either of them were paying much attention. And, I mean, from the outside looking in, it's not like we make much sense. Plus, according to Leo, Mona has this reputation with his friends of being completely disinterested in musicians."

"Do you think dating you will impact Mona's career?" Again, her tone seemed suspiciously careful.

"What do you mean? In what way?"

"I'm not certain, because I'm not a stunningly gorgeous and brilliant twenty-one-year-old PhD student in astrophysics, who is also the daughter of two hugely famous —but also slightly ridiculous—pillars of the global music community."

"Are you asking if, by dating me, she'll have even more difficulty being taken seriously?"

Marie's gaze moved up and to the left. "I don't know. It's not like she's inconspicuous, no matter who she dates. But I do know, just from watching famous couples trying to navigate the media, how one of you acts or behaves will definitely make an impact on how the other is perceived."

"I guess that makes sense." I shared a glance with my sister.

She'd given me a lot to think about, issues I might've already been aware of subconsciously, but hadn't consciously considered. If how I behaved, the choices I made, had consequences for Mona, well, then I was determined that my choices would be stellar from now on.

"Hey." I gave Marie a grateful smile. "Thank you for your help getting my phone secured."

"No problem." She smiled sweetly. But Marie was sweet. "What are older sisters for? Oh! And before I forget, I asked Mona to be a bridesmaid."

I flinched, my head rearing back, not sure I'd heard her correctly. "You—you what?"

Marie cupped her hands around her mouth and mock-shouted, "I asked Mona to be a bridesmaid."

I rolled my eyes. "I can hear just fine, Hufflepuff. I'm just surprised."

"Why? She's great."

"Yeah. But you barely know her."

"Well, you're in love with her, which means so am I." My sister shrugged, her blue eyes twinkling. "And, may I say, you have exceptional taste in women. She is a friggin' *delight*."

"She is, right?" Unable to stop my grin, I dropped my eyes to my hands again, thinking about her goodbye kiss before she left. Obviously, she couldn't kiss my mouth. So she'd kissed the tips of my fingers—all ten—and my forehead, cheeks, chin, nose, and temples.

"You know who she reminds me of?"

"Janie?" I guessed, only because Marie's friend Janie was also brilliant.

She tilted her head back and forth, her eyes narrowing as she considered. "Um, yes, her too. But I was actually going to say Matt."

"Matt?" Again, I reared back, but this time I frowned. "Don't get me wrong, you love Matt, therefore so do I, but what about Mona reminds you of Matt?"

Matt Simmons was Marie's fiancé, a super good guy, and a nerd. Matt was great, really great, but he didn't make me want to write poetry until sunrise.

Marie chuckled. "Think about it, doofus. They're both in science, at the top of their field, in high demand. They both love to tell science jokes and puns, they both—"

"Wait a minute, wait a minute. When did you hear Mona tell a science joke?"

Marie gave me a smirk, it looked self-satisfied. "We talk."

My eyebrows jumped. "Who?"

"Me and Mona."

My eyebrows pulled low. "When?"

She glanced at her nails, saying loftily, "All the time."

I choked. Because—with the time difference and her schedule and my schedule—I could barely get Mona on the phone.

Marie laughed. "Okay, okay. Not all the time. But Mom, Mona, and me are in a three-way."

Wincing, horrified, I closed my eyes. "Please. Please never use the phrase *three-way* while referencing you or Mom ever, ever again. In fact, you're not allowed to use the phrase at all."

My sister laughed, good and loud, and a second later a pillow hit me in the face. "Get over yourself! A three-way text message conversation, you ass."

Now I was laughing, and I opened my eyes to locate the pillow she'd thrown, tucking it behind my back with the others. "Thank you. I needed another pillow." God, it felt good to laugh.

Mona makes you laugh.

My smile waned and I swallowed, breathing through the tight pain in my chest. *I miss her.*

"But back to what I was saying." She rested her cheek against her palm. "Mona and Matt, very similar."

"Other than being brilliant, into science and nerdy puns, I don't see the similarities."

"What about their parents?"

Lifting an eyebrow, I settled more completely against my pillows. "What about their parents?" I didn't know much about Matt's parents.

And, now that I considered things, other than what could be read in the newspaper, in magazines, etc. I didn't know much about Mona's parents—as parents—either. Leo didn't talk about them, but I always thought that was understandable. As Marie had said, they were hugely famous. I figured he wanted to protect them, like I would want to do with my parents.

"They both grew up with neglectful parents," Marie said, as though this was common knowledge.

Crossing my arms, I shook my head. "What are you talking about?"

Now Marie lifted an eyebrow. "Matt was raised by a series of nannies, housekeepers, and cooks. So was Mona."

"Just because a family has a nanny doesn't mean the kids aren't raised by their parents."

"Oh, I definitely agree! Just like, if a kid goes to daycare, it doesn't mean the parents don't raise the child. But in their cases—Matt and Mona—they were. They were neglected."

"How do you know this? I mean, about Mona. How do you know this about Mona?"

Marie seemed confused. "Uh, it's obvious."

Staring at my sister, I struggled to complete a thought, my brain was going in too many directions.

Taking pity on me, she leaned forward. "Look, tell me if any of this sounds familiar, okay? And this probably applies to Leo too. Mona feels like she needs to prove herself to people in order for them to be her friend or love her. True? You know how Leo is always doing people favors? Worrying about the status of his friendships? That's what it's about."

I scowled, but I didn't know why I scowled.

Marie continued, "But back to Mona. She doesn't open up easily, at all, and trust is super hard for her. In fact, she can count the number of people she trusts on one hand. Maybe three fingers. But once she trusts, she *trusts*. She bends over backward to make those people happy, worries she'll lose them if she does something wrong. So, she tries to put people in boxes, assigns labels to relationships, so she can lower her expectations, so she's never hurt."

My body ached. It had nothing to do with recovering from the flu. I had to clear my throat before I could speak. "That's, uh, that's pretty accurate."

My sister gave me a sympathetic smile. "That's Matt."

"So, what do you do?"

"What do you mean?"

"How do you, you know, make sure he's happy?"

She frowned, her mouth forming a subtle sneer. "Uh, I don't. Making sure Matt is happy is not my job. It's his job, and only if he wants to be happy."

I blew out a breath, frustrated. "How do you keep him from worrying?"

Marie shrugged again. "I can't. If he wants to worry, that's on him."

"Marie," I growled, gritting my teeth. "Come on. You know what I mean."

"Actually, I don't. It almost sounds like you think you're responsible for Mona's feelings. That's one hundred percent wrong. You're only responsible for your own feelings, just like she's only responsible for hers. If she wants to worry, that's her decision."

"But what can I do to help her worry less?"

"You're not hearing me, Abram. You do nothing. You love her—which you're going to do anyway—and that's it."

I didn't like that answer, and my sister must've realized it, because she chuckled, shaking her head as she stood and walked to the door. "The horse is going to do what it wants. You can't make the horse drink the water, even if it needs the water, even if it's miserable without it." She turned and walked backward out of the room. "Once you figure that out, and if you need to commiserate with someone about stupid, brilliant thirsty horses, give me a call."

* * *

Mona picked up on the first ring. "Abram! How are you? How was the concert? How many encores? You didn't push yourself, did you? Please be careful not to push yourself. Did you get the package I sent?"

A slow grin spread over my features and I fell back on the bed, covering my eyes with my forearm. "God, it's so good to hear your voice."

One beat of silence, then, "Uh, I think you called the wrong number. This is Mona, not God. Related, do you have His number? If so, please ask Him to reconcile quantum gravity with the theory of relativity. I'll wait."

I laughed. "You are a nut."

"As long as it's a do-*nut*, I'm fine with that. Hey, did you know, donut-shaped planets are theoretically possible? Great. Now I want a donut." Her voice and her cute facts relaxed my muscles and nerves and bones. My smile deepened.

This was perfection, almost. *Almost* exactly what I needed. Her being here or me being there was actual perfection, but this was pretty darn close. And yet, even as I relaxed, the shadowy thought, *I miss her,* made drawing a full breath impossible.

"What time is it there?" she asked.

I thought about looking at the clock on the side table, or at the screen of my phone, but laziness had me shaking my head. "I don't know. Almost two?"

"Yeesh. You sound so tired." In a quieter voice she added, "Please take care of yourself. Don't get sick again."

"I won't, I promise."

"You can't promise that. Germs have a mind of their own. And if it's a virus, well, let's just say it has a hive mind of their own." She chuckled at her joke and so did I.

"How about, I'll do my best. I can't wait to see you." I'd promised myself I wasn't going to say it until later in the conversation.

"I can't wait either! London in March. Have you ever been to London?"

"No. Have you?"

"Oh yes. My parents have a house there. We would go around Christmastime, if we went. The cook made yule logs, which were my favorite."

I frowned, removing my forearm from my eyes to rub at my sternum. *Our cook.* I'd wanted to ask Mona about her family, her upbringing, since Marie had raised the topic two weeks ago, but I didn't know how to start. Our phone conversations hadn't been exactly satisfying recently. One of us was either extremely tired or in a rush.

Before I could make up my mind whether or not to ask her about her family, she said, "So, speaking of London, I actually have a question about something related to the trip."

"Uh, okay. Shoot." After she asked her question, I decided I would ask how her conversation with Leo had gone at the hospital in LA. We hadn't discussed it yet, and it would be a good segue into asking about her parents.

"Great. So. About sex."

My eyes flew open.

"Tell me what you like."

I stared at the white ceiling of the hotel bedroom, thoughts and concerns and planned questions fleeing my mind as all blood rushed south. "You mean, phone sex?"

Were we doing this? Now? We still hadn't done it yet. I was tired, but I'd get untired real fast if phone sex was on the table.

"No, no, no. I mean sex-sex. Tell me what you like so that, when we see each other, I'll be able to do precisely what you like. Here, you can't see me, but I have a notebook for taking notes, to make sure I get it all down."

Most of my blood had abandoned my brain for my pants, so I think I can be forgiven for the slowness of my response. "You want to interview me and take notes? About what I like during sex?"

"Exactly. And then I'll tell you my preferences the next time we talk, because you sound really tired now and probably don't have pen and paper ready."

What the hell?

I made a face, speaking without thinking, "That's cheating."

"Cheating?"

"Yes, cheating." I sat up, mildly irritated. "No. I'm not telling you what I like. I want you to figure it out."

She made a noise, it sounded indignant. "But if you don't tell me what you like, then I might do something you don't like as much, and the sex will be mediocre."

"Yeah, I doubt it. I'm pretty sure I'll love it all." I bit my bottom lip, thinking about her face when we were in Chicago as she came, the feel of her silky heat on my fingers.

Now I was awake.

"Abram. I'm serious."

"So am I."

Another sound of indignation. "I need some direction. I want this to be good for you."

"Oh, I have no doubts it will be. But I'm not giving you instructions to follow. I'm not a recipe."

She laughed, it sounded surprised. "Okay. That was funny. But, look, like I said, I'll tell you what I like, and—"

"No. No way. Don't you dare. Come on, Mona. Give us a chance to be good at this. I don't want you to tell me."

"But—"

"That's the same as telling me what you got me for my birthday before I get a chance to open my presents."

"No, it's not. It's being communicative," she said through renewed laughter.

"Nope. You are *not allowed* to tell me a thing. I don't want shortcuts. I want to discover you. Giving me a grocery list takes all the fun out of it."

"It absolutely does not." She huffed, but her voice held a smile.

"No, Mona. I'm not a menu. You don't get to order what you want." Jeez. All these food references. *I wonder if room service is still open.*

"That's not—"

"It is. It absolutely is."

Mona made a strangled sound. "How can you be so laissez-faire about this? If we tell each other what we like now, and how we like it, we can skip over all the awkwardness and just get straight to the great parts. It would be very efficient!"

I bit back a laugh because she reminded me of Mary Poppins when she said, *very efficient!* Like efficiency was superior to seduction.

"Have things been awkward?" I asked. "You don't like what we've done so far?"

"You know what I mean." Her voice was quieter.

"I don't, honestly. And if we skip over all the awkwardness, we'll never discover anything new—about you, about me—and the discovery *is* the fun. Yes, maybe we'll have some bad sex, but nothing—*nothing*—is ever perfect, and that should be okay. I don't want you to be perfect, to get things right all the time. How boring would that be?"

She didn't respond, but I could almost hear her thinking, debating with herself.

So I added, "Think of it this way, if I only did what you *think* you like, then you'd never be pushed out of your comfort zone."

"Why do I need to be pushed out my comfort zone?"

"Because it's exciting."

She grunted. "It sounds unnerving."

"It might be. But it might blow your mind. Give us a chance to find out. Give us a chance to win big, and also fail spectacularly. And if we fail, know and trust that it's no big deal. We can always try again, and again. And again."

Mona was quiet for a moment, and when she spoke next her voice was more serious. "You know what? Fine. Okay. I see your point and it's valid. The idea of trying new things with each other, discovering each other sounds really, *really* good. But, two things."

"Okay."

"You should know, I have an IUD to prevent pregnancy, but I've never had sex without a condom. Even so, I've been tested for STDs and I'm negative, for all of them. How about you?"

Her candor, honestly, turned me on. I loved this about her, how direct she was about things that mattered. *So fucking sexy.*

But being turned on and tired meant I had to really concentrate on what I wanted to say. "Uh, so me: I've had sex without a condom, once, and regretted it. She didn't get pregnant and she didn't have any STDs, but I never did it again."

"Did you get tested after?"

"For STDs? Yes. I have none."

"But were you tested for HPV?"

"I was vaccinated when I was a teenager, so I don't think they tested me for that." All this clinical talk of STDs and HPV actually did help with my concentration.

"Okay. Good. Next question. When we have sex, will we use a condom?"

And, just like that, all the blood rushed south again. I'd never thought of myself as someone with an active imagination until Mona and Aspen. But every time she brought up sex between us, as though it was a forgone conclusion, I saw it. Vivid flashes of imagery, sights, smells, sounds. It was like describing a ten-course meal to a starving man. I could almost taste it, taste her.

I had to clear my throat before speaking. "Mona, if you want to use a condom, then we shou—"

"I don't. I don't want to."

Shit. Shit, shit, shit.

A spike of unadulterated longing shot down my spine. I had to press my hand against my dick. I hurt. Now I needed a cold shower. All this talking about it with her on the other side of the world was hugely, *hugely* frustrating.

She continued, "But if you want to, then you have veto rights. I guess what I'm saying is, we both have veto rights."

"Yes. Makes sense. Can I think? I'll let you know later?" A subject change was desperately needed if I was going to sleep at all tonight.

"Yes, yes. Absolutely. One more thing, before we move on from our planned sexual activities."

Fuck, fuck, fuck! I bit back a groan. She was killing me. Killing me dead.

But then she said, "I have hard rules, lines you can't cross. And I think, when you're not so tired, we should definitely talk about those."

Coming out of the lust fog, I said, "Yes. Perfect." This was definitely a sobering topic. "Tell me those. We can talk about it now if you want."

"We can talk later, but I just want to be really clear." I heard her take a few deep breaths, like she was working up to something. "Abram, pushing me about these lines will not be appreciated."

She couldn't see me, but I was shaking my head. "I absolutely do not want you to do anything that crosses your lines. I will never, ever push you on your lines. I consider them sacred. I respect you, deeply, and agree that discussion of boundaries is unquestionably important. And I'll tell you mine."

She released a relieved-sounding breath. "Good."

"*But*! Keep your favorites a secret, until I discover them. Then and only then, order from me like I'm a menu."

"Okay," she said softly, sounding a little shy. "I will. It'll be like a sexy scavenger hunt." I sensed she was pleased, excited, but maybe also a little uncertain.

The uncertainty concerned me, and I didn't want us to hang up until she felt certain. "I hope you know, you can always, *always* tell me, when we're together, or at any time, if anything I'm doing isn't your jam. My hope is that I'll be able to read you by your reactions. But if I don't, or can't, tell me. I will immediately stop, completely if you want, or move on to something else if you prefer. If things aren't spectacular for *you*, Mona, then—I guarantee—they'll be shit for me."

She laughed. "Spectacular, huh? I like the sound of that."

"Yes. Spectacular." I swallowed, closing my eyes against the imagery assault of everything that conjured, and my voice gravel, I added, "Let me discover you. Slowly. Over time."

CHAPTER 11
FAILURE OF GALILEAN TRANSFORMATIONS

Abram

Zero months.

Zero weeks.

Zero days.

Fourteen Hours.

And then, *finally*.

"Why're you always in such a bad mood?"

I moved my eyes to Charlie, watching him slip inside the green room. Beyond the open door, I spotted Stan. He lifted his chin in greeting, I lifted mine.

Stan was the security guard who'd been assigned to stand outside my door and was part of the team for the stadium. On our first day here, he and I had bonded over pinochle. We both played it. His landlady had taught him, my mother had taught me.

Last night, he'd brought his landlady to the stadium, I invited my mom, and we made a game of it over pizza from Giordano's. Best night I'd had in a long time.

Charlie closed the door, cutting off my view of Stan and reducing the noise emanating from both the stage and backstage. Lifting two bottles of champagne deftly in one hand, he grinned.

Drummers.

"Come on. Celebrate. We're in our hometown." He set one of the bottles down in front of me, right next to my feet propped on the glass coffee table and began removing the foil of the other bottle. "I brought the good stuff to get you started."

One and a half months. The last time I saw Mona in person. I'd been sick with the flu. She'd come to LA for twenty-four hours. I'd been delirious when she arrived, but only half-delirious when she left. Her visit had made all the difference, but the missed opportunities—to spend actual quality time together—haunted me.

"Nah, man. I'm good." I strummed three chords on my Dreadnought, the opening to "Hold a Grudge," but in D minor.

One week. The last time we'd spoken on the phone. Thirteen minutes, a quick call in the middle of the night, her time. She'd been so tired, I hadn't wanted to keep her up when she needed her sleep.

"No. Man. You are not good. You're depressing as shit. Ever since Las Vegas, you've been a real wet blanket. When are you going to get over that shit? Everyone thought it was funny but you. Come on, that woman was *gorgeous.*"

Keeping my face carefully impassive, I shrugged, because by now I'd realized Charlie wasn't ever going to share my ire about the situation in Las Vegas.

It was our first show after I'd recovered from the flu. After the concert, we were all backstage with the VIP ticket group, and this woman who I'd never met grabbed my dick and offered to give me a blow job. Since most people were drunk at this point, her offer spurred others to make similar offers until they started to sound more like requests, and then demands.

And that was the last VIP session I attended. My label was pissed. I told them to eat shit. Attending VIP sessions wasn't in my contract. Getting groped and propositioned by drunk fans, no matter how attractive they were, wasn't either. It didn't fucking matter if she was gorgeous. But everyone— Charlie and the crew who'd been present—made it clear that I was the strange one. I was the one who couldn't take a harmless joke. So, I kept my mouth shut.

Charlie popped the cork, sending bubbles cascading over his hand and onto the carpet. Shaking his fingers of the excess, he licked the back of his knuckles. "This one is for you. Here." Charlie held out the bottle.

I leaned forward. I took it. I set it on the floor under my legs. "Thanks."

Two days. The last time Mona sent me a candid picture. I kept opening it. A shot of her with one of my CDs at a music store in Geneva sent while I was asleep, giving me a huge smile and a thumbs-up along with the words, *I'm so proud of you!!*

And then I would scroll through all the pictures she'd sent, taking my time with each. My favorite was still her in the white bikini. But a close second was her in a lab coat, the front of it slightly open, just enough to show me she had nothing on underneath. The night after receiving that photo had been a long, frustrating one.

He grumbled, saying, "You know, I'm supposed to be the dark, broody member of Redburn."

"Oh yeah? What am I supposed to be?"

"The sexy one."

I cracked a smile though I felt no humor. "Maybe we've switched places."

Ten hours. The last time she'd sent me a text message.

Mona: We see each other in just twenty-four hours!! AHHHH!!!! If I get out of here on time, I'll text you to see if we can talk before my flight. I miss you.

I thought about the nature of those words, *I miss you.* Three words that fell colossally short of conveying the truth of their sentiment.

I miss her. I miss her. I miss her.

Charlie was right. I was depressing as shit and it was just getting worse.

It was the tour.

Every concert, the rush, the adrenaline, the energy of thousands of people singing my songs, chanting my name. And then afterward, nothing. The emptiness of praise that sounded like white noise, an ocean of bodies, people I didn't want, standing where she should've been.

In a way, I was glad Mona wasn't touring with me. I wasn't quite myself after a concert, after the last encore. A high like no drug I'd ever tried. I wanted . . . *things,* from her, only her.

But all would be better soon. I would be leaving tonight right after the concert, taking a direct flight to London. We would have three days. *Three days.* Just us, together for three days.

Thank God.

Since our phone call about sex and likes and dislikes, the conversations and texts weren't helping anymore. They left me unsatisfied and surly. I wanted to *touch* her. I wanted it so badly, my mouth went dry every time I thought about it, which was all the fucking time.

But I still wanted to talk to her on the phone when she called. Even if I was frustrated, and even if it felt more and more like a punishment, I needed to hear her voice.

I miss her. I miss her. I miss her.

"Nope." Charlie patted his lean stomach, making a show of sticking it out. "You know how I like that ice cream. I've never met a flavor I wouldn't eat a carton of. Besides, you're already on all those billboards in your designer tighty-whities. Too late for me to take that crown."

"Hmm." I nodded distractedly, glancing again at my phone where it rested next to me on the couch.

Recently, if Mona was able to talk, it happened about an hour before our central time concerts, 5 AM her time, 10 PM mine. But sometimes she was stuck at CERN, pulling an all-night shift, and she wasn't reachable. Even during the day her availability was spotty. Too many meetings, conferences, time with the instruments and resources and people she needed was difficult to secure. Too many *variables* as she called them. If she could make the call, she'd let me know with a text. *Any minute now.*

Charlie huffed, sitting down hard in the chair directly across from me. Leaning forward, his elbows on his knees, his eyes large and expectant, he shrugged.

"Well?"

I mimicked his shrug. "Well, what?"

"What the fuck is going on?"

"Nothing."

"Nothing? Nothing? Come on. We're on a world fucking tour. We're about to play Chi-fucking-cago. Do you know how many celebrities, Hollywood *actresses* are out there, dying to meet you before the show? We missed out on LA, so they all came here."

"We didn't miss out on LA. We tacked it on at the end of the tour. We're still doing LA."

"You know what I mean. Come meet some beautiful people."

I shrugged again, my eyes flickering to the phone. *No messages.*

"But you won't, because you're in here, waiting for a phone call." He didn't sound disgusted or exasperated. He sounded perplexed.

"That's right."

"Fine." He tossed his hands in the air, leaned back, and crossed his arms. "I'll bite. Who is she?" "Come on, Abram. Who is it?"

I smirked. "You know I'm going to say your mom."

Charlie squinted at me, his grin more like a baring of teeth. "You're fucking hilarious."

"Fine. It's your sister."

This joke was only funny to us, and only because Charlie has no siblings.

"Fuck you."

"No thanks. She already did."

"You know. . ." Charlie shook his head, looking reluctantly amused, but a second later, his stare turned thoughtful.

I said nothing, opting to instead quietly strum my guitar.

"It's not Leo's sister is it? I mean, the genius. Not Lisa."

I stopped playing, moving just my eyes to his.

He made a face. "Am I crazy? I only ask because you guys had that argument in Aspen, and then both of you skipped out on dinner the last two nights. It seemed like, uh, something was going on there."

Taking a deep breath through my nose, I considered my friend. We'd known each other for a long time. Yeah, he could be a real dick sometimes, but he'd always had my back. The truth about me and Mona was going to come out eventually. Maybe it was better if I preemptively told him.

Before I could figure out how to start, he said, "You should know, in Aspen, she told me she was hung up on some guy."

"Some guy?"

"Some guy she'd been with in college, I think."

"In college?"

"Or, uh, maybe in high school? I don't know, man. Honestly, I don't remember anything she said other than she was hung up on someone from her past. That trip is kind of a blur now." He laughed, presumably at himself. "Plus, after she shot me down, I kinda zoned out because it was fucking freezing outside and she was talking too fast. I didn't understand half of what she said. Something about dark matter and the space between planets? I couldn't follow."

That sounded like Mona. "Was this when we all went sledding?"

"Yeah. I asked her if she wanted to hang out and she just, like, started telling me all this physics shit."

"Huh." Thinking back on that afternoon, I remembered that I'd suggested she try to let Charlie down by being honest. In her very Mona-like way, she must've taken my advice.

"Anyway, what I'm trying to say is, if it is her, if you two hooked up in Aspen and are trying to keep it on the downlow now, then you should know, as of January, she was still hung up on someone else."

Clearing my throat, I lifted an eyebrow, working *really hard* not to smile at that. "Thanks for the information."

"So, is it her?"

"If it was her, would it bother you?"

"No." He shook his head, shrugged. "Why would it bother me?"

"You seemed interested in her."

"Uh, *yeah.*" His eyes rounded. "I mean, she's fucking gorgeous, right?"

I smirked but didn't answer.

"But Abram, there's a million gorgeous women. And that's my point, man. The last thing you want on your first world tour is to be in a relationship with DJ Tang and Exotica's daughter, unless you want to be under a microscope all the time. We might be famous, but that's a whole different ball park. They're level one billion famous, like in the stratosphere famous. People would go *nuts.*"

"I think it'll be okay. People might be interested at first. But then it'll die down."

"Holy shit, man." He reared back, gaping. "It's true?"

"We're—" I began, but was cut off by the swelling sounds in the hall mixing with the Vicious Pixies in the middle of their set.

Ruthie stood just inside, frowning at us both. "What are you doing?" She shouted over the ruckus. "Do you even know who is out here? Nico-fucking-Moretti! I swear!" She stepped inside, shutting the door, and made a beeline for the coffee table.

"I know," I said. "I invited him."

"You invited him?" Ruthie frowned at me, picking up the closed bottle of champagne and began working to remove the foil. "How do you know Nico Moretti? You two in the same underwear ad or something?"

I felt myself grimace at her joke, just a small one. *That stupid ad.* "His wife is friends with my sister." I'd had lunch with Nico and Elizabeth earlier in the day. In fact, we'd driven to the venue together after. They already knew I planned to leave right after the concert.

"Huh. Well, you should go say hi. He brought his hot actor friends and has everyone laughing. We go on in less than an hour and you two losers are in here doing what?"

Charlie lifted his hand toward me. "Abram is waiting for a call from—" he paused, studying me for a moment before deciding on, "His mystery lover."

"You mean your sister?" She twisted the wire holding down the cork.

"That joke isn't even funny. Fuck you."

"No thanks, your sister already did." Ruthie grinned at me, wagging her eyebrows. "He falls for it every time."

I smirked, shaking my head, glancing at my phone again. Any minute now.

"I'll tell you what, Nico is *hot*. If I weren't so into lady parts, I'd definitely be confused." Ruthie braced the bottle against her hip, twisting the cork and indicating to me with her chin. "You know his wife? She is also hot. Some kind of doctor, right?"

Nodding, I set aside the acoustic guitar and picked up the phone, touching the screen just to make sure Mona hadn't texted while I'd been distracted by my bandmates.

"See? See what I mean?" Charlie gestured to me again, and then let his hand fall to his knee with a slap. "He keeps checking his phone. Every night, it's the same. Fucking hell, Abram."

Glaring at Charlie, I gave my head a subtle shake. "Why do you care?"

"Because." Now he gestured to Ruthie. "Ruthie broke up with her girlfriend after Aspen." He pointed to himself. "I made sure to stay single. Even the roadies are unattached. Why would you do this to us?"

Examining my friend, I couldn't tell if he was serious or joking. "What am I doing to you?"

"You're raining on our parade." Charlie said this like it was obvious.

"How so?" I rubbed my face, scratching my beard.

"Listen, fine, be in a relationship. Okay. But people want to meet you. They come here for *you*. Your lyrics. Your music—"

"Kaitlyn's music."

"—and night after night, you're in your dressing room, hiding from everyone, waiting for a phone call. You've wasted the first two months of the North American tour. If your girl cared about you, she'd want you to have a good time. It's sad, man."

"It is kind of sad." Ruthie pressed her lips together, looking me over. "We're only young once. We only get this experience—of our first tour—once. You're missing out."

"See?" Charlie, again, made a big show of lifting his hand toward our guitarist.

"I don't feel like I'm missing out," I mumbled to no one, and it was only half true. I didn't feel like I was missing out on the drugs, and the sex with strangers, and the hangover sex with strangers. But I did feel like I was missing out on Mona by being *here*. If there were some way to do the practices and the shows without the rest of it.

Checking the time on my phone, I frowned. My stomach dropped. She never texted this late. *She probably can't make the call before her flight.*

"But I also think it's kind of sweet."

Ruthie's declaration had me glancing at her. "Sweet, huh?"

She gave me a small smile. "You look like a fucking porn star pirate fantasy, but you're a sweet guy, Abram."

I lifted an eyebrow at her. "Thanks?"

"It's a compliment. You should be flattered." Ruthie kicked my leg lightly with her boot. "Also, Charlie is right. You need to get laid."

Glaring at Ruthie, because she was right, I said nothing. But it wasn't just that I needed to get laid. I needed Mona.

Long-distance relationships totally sucked. Fantasies, jerking off, cold showers, vivid dreams, her pictures, more fantasies. I'd filled ten notebooks since Aspen. I had songs for decades. I'd sent a select few of the more complete poems to Kaitlyn and she'd been hugely inspired. She'd composed ten solid arrangements for the next album, we only needed four more, five tops.

Then what? Another album. Another tour? No.

No more tours.

A firm knock drew our attention to the door and had me gritting my teeth. Other than Charlie and Ruthie, who were always welcome, Stan and the crew knew not to knock. Not to enter. Not to seek me out or introduce me to some fucking VIP.

"Who is it?" Ruthie asked, glancing between us.

Our drummer shrugged, looking a tad defensive. "Don't look at me. I have no idea."

"Ohhhh." Ruthie made a wincing face, her wide eyes on me. "Someone is going to get fired, then."

Standing, I strolled to the door, fighting a spike in temper. Stan knew better. Taking a quick, deep breath before opening it, I reminded myself to stay calm. My fuse was too short these days. Everything and everyone pissed me off.

But then, upon finding Leo, his hands shoved in his pockets, a big smile on his face, my anger reluctantly diminished until I was more curious than irritated. I glanced between Stan, still at his post by the door, and Mona's brother. The security guard's face seemed carefully impassive, like both Leo and I bored him. *Hmm.*

"Leo," I said, not masking my confusion.

"Hey," Leo shouted over the noise, his grin widening. He looked like he was up to something. "Just in the neighborhood. Mind if I come in?"

I ignored the screams and voices calling my name from somewhere to my right, stepping to the side. "Please. Come in."

"Leo! Good to see you."

"It's Leo!"

Charlie was already on his feet, but Ruthie blocked the way, insisting on a hug. Giving stoic Stan one more searching look, I closed the door, reclaimed my spot on the couch, and picked up my guitar. Checking my phone again while my three friends exchanged greetings and banalities, I frowned at the screen. *No messages.*

"I'm so relieved to see you, man. If it had been anyone else, I think Abram might've lost his shit." Charlie chuckled, steering Leo to the chair where he'd been sitting earlier.

"Really?" Leo glanced at me. "What's going on, Abram? Isn't the tour going well? From everything I've seen—other than the rescheduled LA show—the reviews are awesome."

"Tour is fine." I strummed a series of chords, the beginning of a new song Kaitlyn had sent through. "What are you doing here? I thought you were in Miami."

"Uh." Leo's eyebrows jumped, and he glanced at my bandmates. "Hey, you two, do you mind giving us a minute? I have some, uh, business to discuss. Label stuff."

"Oh, sure. Yeah." Ruthie looked confused and I understood why.

The excuse of *label stuff* made no sense. Leo may have introduced us to our EP and label, but he didn't work for them.

"That's Leo's polite code for *leave us the fuck alone.*" Charlie backed away toward the door, opened it, and the building roar of backstage paired with the music of our opening act blared through. He motioned Ruthie forward. "Totally cool. We can catch up later."

"Yes. Absolutely." Leo pointed at Ruthie, then at Charlie. "See you after the concert. We'll hang out."

As soon as Charlie shut the door, the noise level returned to a faint hum, and Leo turned back to me, his smile falling away.

We stared at each other for a minute, but I didn't get the sense he was upset, nor did he seem contrite, like he was here to apologize for anything. The last time I saw him had been in Aspen, and the last time we'd talked had been when I'd called to get Mona's number. I was aware that he'd come to the hospital in LA, but he didn't stay to visit. I'd been too sick and he needed to get back to Miami. Mona had seen him, though, but she never told me what they'd discussed.

"How you doing, Abram?" He sounded honestly curious. "You look like you're recovered."

"Why are you here, Leo?" Yeah. I was definitely *in a mood.*

My dissatisfaction and frustration with life on tour was bleeding into every facet of my personality. Charlie was right. Ruthie was right. I needed to lighten up.

"The truth?" He shrugged, leaning forward to rest his elbows on his knees. "I promised Mona I would come."

I stopped strumming my guitar. "What?"

"She's worried about you."

I set the guitar aside, sitting forward. "What? She is? She said that?"

"I was supposed to go to the Cincinnati concert, but couldn't make it. So, I'm here instead." His stare turned scrutinizing. "She wanted to make sure you were happy, doing well, getting enough sleep. She said you've been kind of distant the last few weeks."

I pushed my fingers through my hair, and then brought them back to rub my forehead, eyes, and beard. "Shit."

"Don't be mad at Mona. It took me two hours of careful questioning to get it out of her, why she was so keyed up when we spoke." Leo huffed a little laugh. "It was kind of cute though. For the first time ever, she was asking *me* hypothetical questions about the opposite sex instead of the other way around."

"I'm not mad at Mona. Not at all. It's just—" I bit back a curse and said the words out loud before I could catch them. "I miss her." Glancing up, I locked eyes with my friend. "I miss her, man. It's like, I can't breathe. I'm drowning, suffocating in how much I miss her. I just need—"

Leo lifted an eyebrow when I didn't continue. "What do you need?"

I didn't know where to start. I needed to talk to her for hours, submerge myself in her brilliance and presence, debate and discuss, tease and laugh. I needed to not talk to her, sit with her, be quiet, together.

And yes, should things progress in that way and she was up for it, I needed to fuck her brains out.

I needed to taste every inch of her body, I needed her under me, above me, next to me. Reclined, kneeling, bending, on all fours. I needed her skin and sounds and lips and legs and neck and breasts and *everything*.

But I wasn't going to say that to her brother. She was right. I had been distant.

"I need everything," I finally said, and then laughed at myself.

"Oh? Is that all?" Leo also laughed, shaking his head. But his laughter quickly tapered. "You seem unhappy. And that's a shame. I mean, this is your dream, right? Playing your own songs, music, live, for tens of thousands of people. They adore you, man. They can't get enough. I think I can speak for Mona when I say she'd want you to enjoy it, not sit around and be miserable, missing her."

"It's honestly not even about missing Mona, not really."

Leo sighed. "Then what's it about?"

"What am I doing? What is this life? I want this?" I continued shaking my head. "I don't. I thought I did, but I don't. You're right, playing my songs is my dream. But the adoration, the chanting of my name, the echo in my ears, in my heart, it's a high and I hate it. It's like living inside a theme park for months."

I closed my eyes, leaning back against the couch. "At the end of the night, there is only me and an empty hotel room. Another city. Another audience. Another set. It's always the same. Even if Mona and I weren't together, even if she wasn't mine to miss, *that* wouldn't change."

"But if you were with someone else, someone who could tour with you and didn't have so many responsibilities, someone who made you their main priority, then *that* would change."

I opened my eyes, glaring at my friend. He seemed to be glaring at me as well, not with hostility, but with suspicion.

My friend. That didn't sound right.

My former friend? Possibly.

It took me a moment, and I had to swallow a few times, but eventually I was able to ask without shouting, "What the fuck does that mean? Hmm? Why would you even say that?"

A hint of a smile, there and gone, tugged his mouth to one side. "I'm just saying—"

"Fuck you. I love God and Mona and my family and music and words and that's it."

"That's it?" Now he was smiling. A stupid grin on his stupid face.

"Yeah. That's it." I'd had enough, and distrust lanced me, sharp and strong. I stood. "Wait. Why are you really here? What do you want?"

Leo also stood, still grinning, looking like he was trying to hold in laughter. "I told you already, because Mona—"

"Cut the shit, Leo. Did Mona also tell you to encourage me to replace her with a warm body? She's not replaceable, dipshit."

"Listen, calm down. Okay? Calm down." Now Leo did laugh, and now he was shaking his head. "Mona did ask me to come and check on you, and she is worried about you being unhappy when you should be having a great time. That was true. But the other stuff, that was me. That was big brother stuff, okay?"

I lifted my chin, inspecting him. "What the hell does that mean?"

"It means Mona is crazy about you, okay? She's—" Leo's eyes drifted to the wall behind me, like he was searching it for the right word "—completely crazy about you. Obviously, my sister fell for you in Aspen, and she fell hard, and I don't want to see you mess her up. I needed to, you know, make sure your intentions were honorable before I could give this thing my blessing."

Placing my hands on my hips, I narrowed my eyes on Mona's brother, not hiding my irritation. "Your blessing? Why would I need or want your blessing?"

Leo's demeanor instantly changed. He straightened to his full height, his eyes growing cold and hot at the same time, a subtle sneering curl to his upper lip. I knew that face. That was the face Leo made when he was about to threaten someone.

"You better believe you need my blessing, because Mona is my family. My. Family. *Mine.*" His voice was a rumble, and it raised the fine hairs on the back of my neck. I'd seen him angry, but I'd only seen him this angry once before, when another of our friends insulted Lisa in an extremely—uh—unsavory way. "And no one fucks with her, got it? No one. I will *ruin* you if you break her heart. You know I can, so don't doubt that I will."

Staring at my friend, I found myself fighting a smile. "Yeah. Okay. I see your point. Good talk." I was still irritated with him about how he'd treated Mona, but it was clear he was making an effort now to be a good brother.

Leo continued scowling at me, his aggression fading slowly, but doubt remained. "We clear?"

I smiled. "Mostly." Before he could get too upset, I added, "I believe you can ruin my music career, I believe that. But the truth is Leo, the only way you could ruin *me* is if you somehow convinced Mona to leave me."

The frost left his stare, and the heat diminished to warm affection.

"So, no." I turned, reached for my phone, and glanced at the screen. *No messages.* I tucked it in my back pocket. "I don't believe *you* can ruin me."

My friend's mouth curved into a pleased smile and he nodded. "Glad to hear it."

I missed having him as a friend. Leo was a good guy. Clueless sometimes, but someone who was truly trying his best. "You have anything else you want to add? Anything you want to apologize for? Now that you're here, sharing feelings."

"Nope."

"Nope?"

"Nah, man. I did what I did. I was wrong, yeah, but not about you. I was wrong about Mona, and I've already apologized to her."

"You apologized?" That surprised me.

Mona and I still hadn't talked about her family, though she always wanted to hear about mine. I had a suspicion Mona talked to my mom and sister more than she talked to me.

"I did. She deserved more and better than I was giving her."

"Huh." Inspecting Leo, I absorbed this information. When Mona and I were in London, face-to-face, I would make a point to ask her about her family, get her talking about her upbringing. I wanted to understand her, know her. Maybe I needed to do a better job of showing Mona the depths of my interest. "What changed your mind?"

"About Mona? Or about me being a shitty brother?"

"I guess both."

Leo stared at me, like he was searching for something behind my expression. Eventually, frowning, he said, "You'll have to ask her. It's not my—uh—story to tell."

"Okay. Fair enough."

"So, we good?" Leo extended his hand. "No more psycho phone calls?"

I snorted a laugh and rolled my eyes. "You know I can't promise that. You're the first number I call when I drunk dial. But I'll try to keep them to a minimum."

I accepted his handshake just as the door opened and we both turned toward the intrusion of noise. It was Charlie and he was bouncing on the balls of his feet, a bundle of nerves and energy, as per usual right before a concert.

"If you two are finished holding hands, we need Abram. Showtime."

"Right." Leo released my hand, giving me that grin again. "Well, see you after the show."

I shook my head. "I'm leaving right after the last song. I've got to catch a plane to London. But Charlie and Ruthie will be here."

Leo continued smiling but said nothing. He left with Charlie, but neither closed the door. No need. It was time for me to go to work.

And then London, Mona, three days.

I was just pushing my way through the backstage crowd, trying to find Melena to hand over my cell phone—she was the only one I trusted with it—and grab my mug of pre-show tea, when I felt my cell go off in my back pocket. I waited until I made it past the security rope where no fans were allowed before retrieving my phone and checking the screen.

My pulse stuttered. It was a message from Mona followed quickly by a candid shot.

I glanced at the photo first, but it confused me. She was standing in what looked like a darkened stadium, lights and stage behind her. She wore a dark dress, maybe blue, hair down, heavy—for her—makeup, and a giant smile. On one side was Allyn making a funny face and on the other side was Marie, grinning like she'd just done something brilliant.

Then I read the message and experienced a shock, current racing up my spine, wrapping around my heart, an electric tremor. I read it once, and then had to read it again and again to comprehend its meaning. Even then, even as I smiled widely, and my heart beat wildly, I read it again.

Mona: SURPRISE! I'M HERE!!! I'm sitting in the center section with your sister and can't wait for the show to start! LOVE YOU!

CHAPTER 12
THE LORENTZ TRANSFORMATIONS

"No," I called over my shoulder, shaking my elbow out of Charlie's grasping grip, knowing he couldn't hear me. But he'd get the picture. "No more encores. We're done." I handed my bass off to Geoff, one of our roadies, and darted around a group of smiling techs for the security rope at the side of the stage.

Melena said she'd be here. She'd promised to meet me *right here*, after the concert was over.

"Abram! Hey, man!" Charlie was suddenly at my shoulder, holding my bass and yelling in my ear over the persistent chanting of the crowd. "They're not stopping. They're nowhere near stopping. We got to give them at least one more."

I shook my head as I glanced around, searching for Melena and mouthing an emphatic *no*. I pointed to my throat. We'd already played nine encores. Nine. The most we'd ever done. My voice was raw, on fire. I would be paying for these extra songs for days.

"Come on." He held my guitar out, his eyes pleading and wild, like a druggy looking for another hit. "Come on. One more. This is Chicago. Our hometown. They love you. You owe them one more song."

Gritting my teeth, I glared at my drummer, but said nothing. I'd already given my answer. The pleading eventually morphed into frustration, and then rage. Charlie's jaw ticked in time with the chant, *Redburn, Redburn, Redburn.*

"Sometimes, you're a stingy motherfucker, Abram." He seethed, stepping back, wiping his upper lip.

Charlie's hands were shaking, his knuckles white where he held my bass in one hand. He was covered in sweat. So was I. I was hot and sweaty, and wired, full of adrenaline, just like him. And the high, the current and cadence of euphoria still held me in its grip. But I wasn't insane with it, desperate to prolong it, like he was.

I had something else, the thought of someone else making me crazy.

God, she was so close. *So close.* I'd gone off script, walking into the audience during Charlie's drum solo in the middle of our sixth song, unable to wrestle the anticipation into submission. Our security and lighting people scrambled, and I felt like an ass, but I needed to see her up close. I'd walked past the barricade, the guards, down the stairs, to her section, searching for her.

And there she was. Grinning at me. Eyes shining, looking so proud and excited. She also looked goddamn *hot*, wearing a skintight blue dress that ended mid-thigh, her hair down, red lips. My lungs on fire, it took everything, *everything*, every ounce of self-control not to grab her and kiss her gorgeous face off.

But we were surrounded by thousands of people, and that pledge I'd made to myself —that all my decisions from now on would be stellar ones, because my decisions impacted her—screamed between my ears. She deserved my circumspection and thoughtfulness, not a big, showy, dramatic, extremely public outing of our relationship. That wouldn't be romantic. It would be selfish.

So I'd taken a few photos with fans. I'd quickly signed a few shirts. And then I'd climbed back onto the stage and finished the concert, restless, eager for it to end. Yet also wanting to give Mona my best version of *our* songs.

Now the show was over.

Now it was our time.

So where the hell is Melena?

Movement behind Charlie snagged my attention and I pushed past him, Melena and one of the PAs running toward us, coming from the side hall leading to the dressing rooms and offices.

"Sorry." Melena stopped directly in front of me, holding a travel mug in one hand and a large water bottle with ice in the other, wearing a massive grin and shouting over the continuing chants.

The PA, however, bumped into me. And then brushed her body against me.

"Sorry, we thought you were going to do another song," she said, peering up at me, sounding breathless even though she was shouting.

I took a half step back. The PA swayed forward. Frustrated, I gently set her away with the palms of my hands, grinding my teeth.

"I'm glad you decided not to. Here." Melena pushed the travel mug into my hands, giving the PA an irritated look. Then to me, she said, "Drink this. It has something to numb the throat. You must be hurting."

Taking the mug, my eyes flickered to the PA who now was staring at me like I was food and she was starving. She licked her lips. *Give me a fucking break.*

Maybe it made me a dick that I didn't take the time to learn any of their names. Maybe if just one of them treated me like a person I would have. Regardless, I noticed she was holding one of my T-shirts and I frowned at it, and her, lifting my chin in question.

"Oh!" The PA shook herself, shoving it toward me. "I noticed the sweat, I mean, you're all sweaty. You look great but your shirt is sticking to your body and you're, uh, all, uh, wet. So I went to your dressing room and got it for you."

I scowled, my jaw working. How many times did I have to tell these people? I didn't want any of them in my dressing room.

She flinched back, presumably at my expression. "I thought—I thought you might—"

"Did you bring me a shirt?" Charlie asked, standing at my shoulder. "Or how about Ruthie? We're just as sweaty. Stop trying to fuck Abram, okay? Can't you see it pisses him off? Plus, he's got a girl already."

The PA blinked at me, and then at Charlie, her mouth moving without sound as a red blush climbed up her cheeks, visibly mortified.

I didn't have time for this. Ignoring both Charlie and the offered shirt, I tried to get Melena's attention. But she seemed to give her eyes a half roll, and shoved the water bottle at Charlie.

"This is for you," she shouted over the crowd. "It's my electrolytes mix. Where's Ruthie? I have one for her too. And if you have a problem with one of the PAs, talk to their boss, Charlie."

I reached for Melena's arm before she could dart off in search of our guitarist, released her when I was sure she wouldn't leave, and held my hand out.

She shook her head, her forehead wrinkling. "What?"

I made the universal symbol for phone with my thumb and pinkie finger since I couldn't risk shouting.

"Oh! Yes. I have it." She pulled out my cell from her back pocket. "I had it the whole time, never left my person."

Mouthing thank you, I snatched it and hurriedly marched past the trio, down the hall toward the dressing rooms, needing to get there before the backstage area flooded with fans and VIP ticket holders.

Stan was there, next to the door, and he turned as I approached. "Mr. Fletcher."

"Stan," I said, my voice raspy and tired. "I need a favor, man. I need you to go get someone for me. Her name is—"

"Mona DaVinci."

I drew back, surprised.

He pointed with this thumb toward the door. "She's already inside."

My brain stuttered to a stop, and I looked at the door. "She's . . ."

"Already inside."

Inside. The room. And suddenly, this steel door became a magical fucking portal to heaven.

"You going in?" Stan asked.

I nodded. "Yes." *This is it. Fuck, this is it.*

Was I ready?

No. I wasn't. I was still hopped up on adrenaline, the crowd was *still* chanting, but had switched to my name. If I went in there now, I would probably . . . *I will definitely do something selfish.*

"I just need a minute." Pushing my phone into my back pocket, I took a sip of tea, gathering my thoughts.

"Here." Stan reached in front of me, twisting the doorknob and then taking the mug out of my grip. "Let me get that for you."

Before I could stop him, he'd pushed it open. And—again—there she was.

She stood in profile, a hand on her hip, looking at something. But when the door opened, she turned, immediately smiling, her eyes huge and happy.

"Abram." She said my name breathlessly, hesitating a fraction of a second before launching herself forward.

Time skipped. She'd been across the room a minute ago, but now she was in my hands, her body pressed to my body, her mouth on mine, her fingers in my hair, and I was so, so right. I was definitely going to do something selfish.

Kicking the door shut, I turned her, pressed her against it, and feasted on her glorious mouth, demanding her tongue and drinking from her perfect lips. My hands traveled south, wanting the skin of her legs, my fingers curling into the fabric of her dress and lifting it.

She yanked her mouth away with a shocked gasp, her hands immediately gripping mine and trying to hold them still. "Wait, wait. You have to stop."

My mouth lowered to her neck and I bit it, wanting to consume her, taste every inch of her skin, rocking my hips forward urgently. "I need you."

"Abram!" she squealed. "We're not alone!"

We're not alone?

Breathing hard while my brain worked to make sense of her words, the sound of a throat clearing somewhere behind me had my back stiffening.

Mona ducked her head, whispering hurriedly against my ear, "Your—uh—sister is here with her fiancé. And so are Allyn and my brother."

Well, fuck.

Actually, no. Not fuck. No expletive existed that could adequately describe the magnitude of my frustration in that moment. Instinct told me to toss her over my shoulder. Leave. Find a room that didn't have a fucking housewarming party in it. Pick up right where we left off, with my hands up her skirt.

And when Marie said, "Don't mind us, we were just talking about the—uh—show. Not this show, the other show," and everyone laughed, I almost did it.

But we'd be photographed. Fans would have their phones ready and there'd be no escape. Everyone would know. Mona in her tiny blue dress, me looking like—what did Ruthie call it?—a porno pirate, covered in sweat, my shirt sticking to my body, my eyes a little wild. Not an image I imagined Mona wanted out there.

Mona.

My fingers tightened on the fabric of her dress. She was sifting her fingers through my hair, placing little, sweet kisses on my neck, murmuring words meant to calm and coax. "Let's visit. Just for a minute. Then we have three days, you and me. All the time in the world, right?"

Slowly, reluctantly, I gathered a deep breath and removed my hands from her, bracing them against the door and glaring down at this woman I loved, and wanted, beyond description, beyond the limitations of language.

"Ten minutes," I said, not sure if it was a threat or a promise. "Five if someone gives me a reason to kick them out."

Mona rolled her lips between her teeth and nodded, peering up at me, looking pleased and excited and a little dazed. "Ten minutes."

* * *

I wasn't much of a drinker anymore. But tonight, when offered whiskey by Leo, I downed the two-ounce pour just to take the edge off.

"Slow down," he said, grinning and taking my glass to pour me another.

Accepting the refill and looking over my shoulder at Mona, I took his words to heart. Slow down. *Slow. Down.*

Mona sat on the chair facing the sofa, talking animatedly to Marie and Matt. She seemed galvanized, like the show, the energy affected her too. And as I watched her, doing my best to slow down, I savored the sight. Her smile. Her bright eyes. Her laugh. Her voice, here, live, not carried across the planet over a phone.

I'd spent the last six weeks—hell, I'd spent the last two and a half months and the last two and a half years before that—wanting this. Just this. We were together, no secrets or lies between us, the promise of a great future on the horizon, and the reality of a great *now*.

And yet, amped-up from the concert, I was still shaky and preoccupied by selfishness.

"Great show, by the way. Nine encores." Leo poured himself a drink.

I nodded distractedly, my eyes still on Mona in her tiny dress. I wanted to take it off.

"Has Broderick been in contact about the next album? I ran into him and Kaitlyn in New York. They said you already have most of it done."

"Yep." My eyes followed the line of her toned legs to her feet. She'd taken off her shoes. She was barefoot. Her toes were painted bright blue.

"That's amazing, man. When did you find the time to write?"

"Here and there." I shrugged, watching with rapt concentration as Mona tucked one of her legs beneath her, the skirt hiking higher, showing me more thigh. My fingers tightened on the thick crystal tumbler as she leaned forward, her position highlighting the curve of her back and waist. My gaze traveled to the thin straps over her elegant bare shoulders, collarbone, the scooped neckline, the swell of her breasts.

I swallowed.

"Hey."

Reluctantly, I tore my eyes from Mona, glancing at Leo. He wore a frown, his eyes seemed to be narrowed with concern.

"Are you okay?"

Was I okay?

Was he really that dense? Had he never felt this way about someone before? Completely consumed. Destroyed. Rebuilt. Desperate.

No. I wasn't okay. But what could I say?

Sorry. I'm distracted by thoughts of fucking your sister, against the door with her tits in my mouth, or bent over the couch, reaching around to stroke her slick, wet pussy while she moans my name. If you weren't here right now, I'd be eating her out and loving every second of it. Forgive my preoccupation. What were you saying about the album?

"Your voice is almost gone, huh?" He nodded at his own assertion. "No need to talk if you can't."

I stared at him, breathing through my nose, working to regain control of anything. This was why I hated the minutes and hours after a show. I wasn't thinking straight. I wasn't myself. It was a peculiar kind of madness.

Did I want to take Mona against the door or bent over the couch? Absofuckinglutely.

But did I want that—here, in this random room, sticky and sweaty after a concert with thousands of people just feet away, the constant risk of someone coming in, interrupting us—to be our first time together?

No.

But in my current state of mind, I would. I definitely, definitely would.

Gathering a deep breath, I forced myself to relax my hold on the tumbler. "It's probably best if I don't speak at all," I murmured, returning my attention to Mona. But this time, she was also watching me.

She wasn't smiling. Her gaze was direct, sharp, and—if I wasn't mistaken—hot. Mona lifted her hand toward me in invitation, mouthing, "Do you want to sit with me?"

I shook my head. The only way for us to sit together in that chair was if she sat on my lap. Bad idea.

Her hand dropped, a slight wrinkle forming between her eyes. She looked anxious.

So I lifted my hand and mouthed, "Five minutes," making no attempt to disguise my meaning.

Five minutes.

One way or the other—either they left, or we did—we were going to be alone in five minutes.

CHAPTER 13
PLASMA PHYSICS

Mona

I checked my phone for the tenth time in two minutes, licking my lips, my mouth and throat dry.

Abram was looking at me, watching me. I'd felt his eyes on me earlier, but now I *felt* his eyes, the force of his intentions. I squirmed in my seat, my skin hot; the area between my thighs coiling, twisting, aching; my breasts heavy, sensitive. Unable to follow Allyn's funny story, or Marie's clever questions, or Matt's silly comments, just the act of breathing felt like a miracle.

Two minutes, twenty-two seconds left.

Twenty-one.

Twenty.

Nineteen.

There was a reason we'd snuck backstage before the last encore, and I'd been careful to bring others. The photos in LA of me—that everyone assumed was Lisa—were a sobering reminder that cameras were everywhere.

Hilarious in retrospect, I'd brought two condoms with me, just in case he wanted to do something here while we waited for the crowds to disperse, before we left for the hotel. I'd tucked them in the side of my strapless push-up bra and spent an inordinate amount of time reasoning with myself while getting dressed, trying to convince myself that I wasn't being presumptuous.

Therefore, in hindsight—now that I was here, and he was here, and I couldn't think straight, his eyes on me—my concerns about being presumptuous were hysterical.

I knew what he wanted as though he were speaking it aloud, over and over, whispering it in my ear.

The fine hairs on the back of my neck prickled and I rubbed the spot, checking my phone again. Two minutes, thirteen seconds.

I almost cursed. Was time moving backward? When would the five minutes end?! When would these people leave?!

Or, I debated, obviously not at all in my right mind, *we could just leave. Now.*

A laugh tumbled past my lips at the thought. Thankfully, it was well timed, as Marie had just said something to make everyone else laugh.

Then again, why not?

Why not just go?

Why stay if we didn't want to stay? Why care whether we were photographed? Why care who knew? Or when? Why not leave? So many questions, and I couldn't think of a single satisfactory answer other than *go.*

Go.

My eyes cut to Abram's. Collided. Crashed. He was still watching me, sipping something the color of brandy or whiskey. But it was *how* he watched me—like we were already alone—that made up my mind.

No more waiting.

I stood, in some kind of bizarre trance, seeing only Abram, and crossed to him. He watched me come. Someone, my brother, was talking to him. Wordlessly, Abram handed his glass off.

"Let's go," I said, taking his hand, holding it in both of mine as I walked backward, pulling him toward the door. He said nothing. Just looked. Just followed.

"Don't you want your shoes?" Allyn asked.

Abram stepped forward and, in one fluid motion, reached behind me for the door while using his leverage on my hands to twirl me, tucking me close against his side. He was strong and solid, and I loved it. He was also damp, and I loved that too.

"You guys." I heard Marie call to us. "It'll be peak crazy out there right now."

Too late.

He'd opened the door. People screamed his name—excited screams, not the killing kind—from somewhere to our right. The security guard stationed at the door looked to Abram, nodded once, and then turned.

"Follow me," the man said, walking down the mostly empty hall to our left. "Your car is ready."

Flashes went off. We passed people in the hall, too stunned to do anything but back up, stop, and gape. Echoes of the frenzied shouts and screams followed us. We encountered a broken bottle of beer and Abram scooped me into his arms without saying a word, his boots crunching over the glass, not breaking his stride. More flashes.

Then we were outside. The limo was there. New shouts. Fans catching sight of him and running toward us. Cameras going off, flashes, screams—still the excited kind— the thunder of a sprinting crowd.

Sights and sounds caught up with me, yanked me out of this strange daze. My heart in my throat as the guard calmly opened the door, Abram placed me gently inside, I slid down the bench, and he followed. The guard closed the door, the locks engaged, we were off.

Abram turned to me as the car lurched forward, threaded his fingers through my hair, his eyes darting over my face. "Are you okay?"

I nodded, strangely out of breath.

We're alone.

"Where to?"

BLARG! We're not alone!

"Old Town," I blurted before Abram could speak, announcing the precise address to our driver as I fumbled for the button that would lift the privacy screen. "Once you get there, drive around the block until we tell you to stop," I hastened to add before the screen completely closed.

But as soon as it did close, I turned to Abram, prepared to fling myself at him. I was too late. He'd already grabbed my arm, tugged me forward, and fused his mouth to mine. Off-balance, all I could do was hold on to his shoulders, open my mouth while awkwardly straddling his leg, and take the hot, ardent invasion of his tongue.

One hand pressed me forward at the small of my back, urging me closer. His hold rough, determined, his fingers digging into my hip, like he was worried I might disappear or flee. I felt the palm of his other hand on my thigh, equally rough and frenzied, pushing my dress up until it bunched at my waist, his fingers sliding between my legs and cupping me firmly through my lace undies.

I gasped. He cursed. The sound a deep, rolling rumble as he pushed the scrap of fabric to one side and stroked my opening.

"Your mouth tastes so sweet," he growled, biting my upturned jaw as I struggled to breathe. "Your skin is sweet." My hips rolled instinctively, seeking his circling strokes, his breath hot against my neck. "I bet this tastes like candy."

An overwhelmed, inelegant sound sprung from my lips as he entered me, stretching me with two fingers, making me pant, scattering my wits.

I couldn't think. I had plans, ideas, things I wanted, things I hoped for, but they'd vanished from my mind, leaving it blank. I'd become a creature of reaction. I wasn't used to this. Yes, the last time we'd done something, Abram had been in control. But in all my previous encounters with men other than Abram, I was used to calling the shots. I was the one who mapped out the course, set the boundaries and goalposts.

But this—the imbalance, the dizzying lack of control while he took and touched as he pleased—felt so good, so right and essential.

And yet, also mildly terrifying.

I loved it. I loved that I could smell him and me, his sweat and my sex. The fragrance pungent, and sweet. His mouth was at my breast, nuzzling, searching, and when he found my nipple, he caught it with his teeth, a sharp sting of pain making me cry out. And just like the last and only time he'd touched me, I was already close.

"Abram," I moaned, my brain paralyzed as I gripped his shoulders, frustrated with myself because I hadn't touched him anywhere. Yet my body was in motion, my back arching, pushing my breasts forward, my hips rolling, riding his fingers, everywhere heat, lava, fire.

And then his hand was gone.

"Come here."

"What? Where?" My eyes flew open. I hadn't realized they were closed.

"I want this off," he grunted to the strap of my dress, biting it and moving it off my shoulder, his stubbly beard scraping my skin. "Take it off."

Jerking at the hem, I pulled it over my head, only struggling slightly to free my shoulders before he was there, helping. I reached around my back for the hook of my bra and he covered my hands, stopping me.

I looked up and found his eyes on the swells of my breasts. Abram licked his lips. "No. Leave it. I like it, for now."

Moving me off his lap, he slid to the floor, opening my legs and kneeling between them. His mouth feasting on my neck, he reached inside the cup of my strapless bra with his index and middle finger to pinch and then pluck my nipple.

I cried out, surprised, and I felt him smile against my chest, bringing my breast completely out to soothe the offended peak with his hot mouth and tongue.

Oh. My. God.

"Abram."

"Hmm."

I cleared my throat, my body vibrating. "Will you do that again? Please?"

"What?" He tucked the abused breast back in my lingerie while reaching inside for the other. "This?"

Rougher than the first time, he pinched me, tugging harshly, and I gasped. Just like before, he soothed it with his tongue, drawing it into his mouth and sending churning, languid heat low in my belly, twisting between my legs.

Setting me to rights again, I whimpered, wanting more. He slid lower, holding my sides, kissing my stomach, swirling his tongue in my belly button and making my hips buck off the seat. Bracketing them, he used my position to pull down my underwear.

I tried to grab his fingers, but he was too fast.

"Oh my God, what are you doing?"

"I need you."

"Abram—oh—oh—oh God."

His hands had moved under my thighs, gripping my bare bottom and pulling me to the edge of the seat, his mouth there. Right *there*. Between my legs, licking, lapping, loud indecent sounds that made me wild.

Abram groaned, flexing his fingers on my backside and then slipping them from beneath me, down my legs to my ankles. He bent my knees, lifting my feet to the bench, spreading me wide, exposing me completely.

My fingers were in his hair, mindlessly grabbing and releasing, kneading and massaging his head and neck. I was so close, so close, *so close.*

"So close," I moaned.

Abruptly, he removed my hands from his hair and replaced his mouth with his fingers, a light touch. I heard a click just before the darkness was replaced with a flood of light.

"Open your eyes," he commanded as I blinked, endeavoring to adjust to the brightness, and caught the tail end of him pulling off his shirt, tossing it over his shoulder and advancing forward again, pulling me off the bench until I was kneeling with him on the floor.

His mouth fastened to mine, demanding, hungry. I tasted myself. I'd never tasted myself before and it made me crazy, making me feel reckless, naughty. Maybe a little vulgar. His hands moved over me, kneading, massaging and stroking my backside, lifting to unhook my bra and palm my breasts as it fell away. He groaned against my mouth, lifting the soft mounds.

"I'm tired of waiting," he said, a growl, and turned us both to set me on one of the long side benches that ran the length of the stretch limo. His touch grew frenzied as he grasped and caressed my naked skin. "I'm so fucking tired of waiting."

I wanted to say, *Me too,* but the words caught in my throat because his hands were everywhere and mine were fumbling stupidly for purchase. I reached for his pants, awkwardly unbuttoning and unzipping his fly, reaching my hand inside to cup him. Before I could feel the full, hard length, he pulled my hands away, freeing himself.

Abram shoved his pants down and I sucked in a breath, my hands hovering between us, not touching him even though I longed to do so. He was so beautiful. Thick and long and hard, his erection curved slightly upward, and—as a fan of anatomy—I knew that meant really good things. Really. Good.

My mouth watered in anticipation and a swirling heat pulsed between my legs. Entranced, I watched as he grabbed himself, rising above me, his immense, powerful shoulders and chest and arms filling my vision.

"Lie back," he ordered, spreading my legs with his knee, stroking my opening with his erection before guiding himself inside and thrusting.

I gasped.

Thrusting.

I gasped again. My body arched off the seat as he withdrew and then immediately pushed deeper, rougher. Repeating the motion, his fingers laced with my fingers and he held them over my head, against the leather of the seat, biting and sucking on my neck.

I felt like I was being devoured. Possessed. Dominated. It was all so familiar, but this time we were naked. This time he was inside me, deep inside, skin to skin, damp and slick, the sparse hair of his chest friction against my breasts. His hips rolling and pushing, stroking my body with his much larger, more powerful one, holding me down, covering me.

I can't breathe.

That same little fissure of fear ignited in my belly, making everything sharper, the sight of his glorious form brighter, more vivid. I loved it. I craved it. I welcomed it. He grunted, moving faster, the slap of his thighs against mine echoing in my ears, a purely carnal sound of sex and surrender. Taking, seizing, wild and rough, yet he moved with a skillful rhythm that matched my racing heart.

"You feel so good. Like heaven." His mouth was at my neck, biting and sucking, sending ticklish shivers down my spine just as he hit the right spot, the tight, aching center of my body, and I cried out.

I cried out, chanting *yes* and *please*, panting, splitting apart.

I cried out and the world disappeared except for where he moved, hitting the tender, twisting, secret place, my walls clenching, pulsing, until I completely shattered apart.

I can't breathe and it's so perfect and beautiful and wrong. You like this? What's wrong with you?

"Mona."

I barely heard him. He sounded far away, but I knew he was still there even as the stars continued to burst behind my eyes, even as the little whisper of fear became a louder voice of doubt, guilt.

You can't like this. You have no control, you can't like this.

Waves of pain and pleasure rolled through me as he moved faster, pushed harder, his body heavy, pressing me down.

"I'm losing my mind. I can't—I can't—" He groaned, tensing as his hips broke their elegant rhythm to pound deep, hard, covetous and mindless, and the force of his thrusts pushed me up the bench.

Abram's body curled, bowing forward, forming a cocoon of bronzed skin and sinewy muscle, and I breathed him in, raptly watching his face as he came, desperate to see his loss of control, tears pricking behind my eyes as I asked myself, if *he* can lose control, why can't I? Why is it wrong for me?

He's not afraid.

His eyebrows stitched together, he exhaled roughly.

Like it hurt.

Like it cost him.

"God. Fuck." His arms shook as he lowered himself to touch my forehead with his. "You're perfect. So perfect. I love you, I love you so much." His mouth crashed to mine and he released my hands, cradling my face, stroking my hair. Still inside me, he slid his hand lower, fondling my body, petting me.

"I love you," he said.

Or maybe I did.

I couldn't be certain.

"It's never going to be enough," I said.

Or maybe he did.

I couldn't be sure.

But I was certain that I sucked in a hitching breath as he gathered me to him and cradled me lovingly. And I was sure that the air I held within my lungs was to halt the beginning of a sob.

CHAPTER 14
TIME AND SPACE IN SPECIAL RELATIVITY

Abram

S*omething is very wrong.*

I'd held her, leisurely kissing the silky skin of her face and neck, fondling her luscious breast, enjoying the decadent softness and weight and the feel of her in my hand. The earlier desperation had morphed into elation, I was wholly and completely enamored. I'm talking fucking stars-for-eyes, cartoon-heart-beating-out-of-my-chest euphoric, convinced that this, being with her like this, so close, just us, exposed and vulnerable to and with each other was my heaven on earth.

In the moments after, thoughts of her happiness consumed me. I wanted and hoped I'd made her feel what I was feeling. I wanted her happiness, her laughter and joy, her contented sighs and smiles. But, almost immediately, it became abundantly clear that she *did not* feel what I was feeling.

She didn't push me away. She said nothing as I touched and tasted. In fact, she lay perfectly still. Even her chest didn't move. Slowly, much slower than I'd like to admit, I became aware that she was holding her breath, the beats of my heart ticking off the seconds.

I stopped kissing her, a prickle of unease between my shoulder blades. I waited, listening, certain I was being ridiculous. She'd been right there with me. She'd said *yes* and *please*, and when she'd come—*God*—she'd been so fierce, so beautiful.

Something is very, very wrong.

Abruptly, she breathed. Exhaling slowly, carefully, and then drawing in another breath to hold it. *What the hell?*

Lifting myself up, I searched her face. She wasn't looking at me. Her eyes were glassy, dazed, focused internally, her expression completely impassive. The warmth of euphoria was replaced with icy dread.

"Mona."

She seemed to give herself a little shake, her attention shifting outward, and she pressed her lips together. She was still holding her breath.

"Are you—what—what's wrong?" I wasn't going to panic. I wasn't. *I won't.*

"Nothing." She shook her head, her lips curving into an unconvincing smile, but her eyes betrayed her. They looked frantic. Sad, angry, confused, scared.

She was freaking out.

"You're lying," I thought and said at the same time.

The corners of her mouth turned down, her eyes shuttering, growing cold. "Can you give me a little space?" she said, her voice quiet and firm, laced with impatience, like I'd irritated her.

Space.

She wanted space.

She wants space.

I stared at her stupidly, feeling as though I'd just been slapped. The last time she'd asked for space, it hadn't been her. It had been Lisa. But since I hadn't been aware of that fact, I'd experienced the very peculiar sensation of feeling my heart fracture in real time.

This is all so familiar.

I remembered this. I remembered what this felt like, like being her garbage.

Except, this, now, this was her, and we'd just . . . I'd just . . . *shit.*

Stop. Don't panic. Just take a minute. Think.

Easier said than done.

Pushing myself off and away, I dropped my eyes to the floor of the limo, a balloon of confused dejection swelling in my chest, a rush of heat moving up my neck. I fought against both, telling myself to slow down. *Think.*

An object near her bra caught my attention and I squinted at it, something that looked like a piece of wrapped candy, or—*no.* Condoms. Two foil wrappers, glinting under the overhead light. I doubted they'd been left behind by a previous customer, the rest of the limo was too clean for them to be overlooked.

Mona brought condoms. Why would she bring condoms? Had she changed her mind about using a condom? Was that why she was upset now? Did I—*shit.*

I pushed a shaky hand through my hair. I'd been selfish. I'd been so desperate to have her. I must've pushed her or—

No. Wait. That's not how it was. She was just as desperate. What am I missing?

Mona was moving and I numbly lifted my eyes, watching as she searched the limo, her arm covering her breasts. Finding her dress, she turned away and pulled it over her head. Not looking in my direction, she held my jeans and boxers out to me, her eyes on the floor of the limo.

On autopilot, I took them, pulled on my pants, my preoccupied mind combing through the last twenty or more minutes, looking for a sign, for what I'd done wrong, or what I'd missed. *What the hell am I missing?*

Mona sat on the bench across from where we'd made love, frowning down at herself. She was moving her underwear between her legs, like she was trying to wipe herself off, like the evidence of what we'd done frustrated her.

Doing my best to ignore the flare of pained anguish in my chest, I spotted my shirt crumpled by her feet. I moved toward it, wanting to help, wanting to fix this, make it right. She turned her head at my approach, flinching as I came closer. The small action made me stop as a renewed wave of dejection filled my lungs.

I couldn't quite see. My senses weren't working as they should. My brain in disorder. All tools of perception were focused on the pain caused by every heartbeat and trying to figure out how to get through it. *God, this hurts.*

I cleared my throat, and I swallowed, and I moved back to where I'd been sitting, opting instead to tell her from a distance, "You can use my shirt, to—to clean up. If you want."

Mona stared at me, like she was trying to make sense of my words, and then she blinked several times, her back straightening, her mouth opening and closing. I watched her gather a deep breath, and then in the next moment, her chin wobbled.

Totally confused, but also absolutely fascinated, I studied her as she covered her mouth just as a sob escaped, tears filling her eyes and rolling down her cheeks. She shook her head. Her face crumpled, and she curled forward, bowing her head as she cried.

Stunned, I stared at her, completely at a loss. She'd just been so cold, aloof, composed. She'd wanted *space*. But now she was crying. *Crying.* Body-wracking sobs. My heart thundered between my ears, bouncing wildly against my ribcage, as though trying to reach her.

Did I hurt her? Fuck.

I couldn't breathe. I didn't know what to do, but I had to do something. I *had to.* I couldn't watch her like this from afar. I'd rather chew glass.

Carefully, slowly, keeping my eyes on her, I lowered to my knees. "Mona."

She hiccupped, shaking her head. "I'm so sorry," she said. "I'm so sorry. I ruined it."

What?

Fighting the instinct to just grab her and hold her close, I gathered an unsteady breath, as deeply as the ache in my lungs would allow, shifting closer. "Can I hold you?"

Instantly, she nodded. And then, before I could move, she flung herself at me, her arms wrapping around my neck, nearly strangling. Because I sensed she needed it, I held her tightly, leaning back to cradle her on my lap.

I second-guessed myself. I couldn't read her. I'd been wrong before. I couldn't trust that I knew what she wanted. Maybe she didn't want to be held tightly. Maybe she just wanted to hold someone.

"Hold me tighter," she demanded, as though reading my mind. "Please. Please forgive me. I'm so sorry."

I immediately complied, relieved for the explicit direction, and stroked her. "Is this okay? Can I do this? Does this—is this bothering you?"

My questions and uncertainty seemed to only make her cry harder, and then she growled, the sound frustrated. "Please, just touch me like you want. Don't—don't ask!"

I stared forward, my brain paralyzed by confusion. I was so confused. I wanted to ask her so many things, starting with, *WHAT THE HELL IS GOING ON?*

Instead, I swallowed them. I held her, stroking her back, kissing her shoulder, whispering words of reassurance.

And I silently simmered in the chaos of my mind and heart.

* * *

We drove around for at least an hour while she snuggled against my bare chest. Every so often, she'd squirm, like she wanted to get closer, and then she'd sigh, like she was frustrated by the limitations of our physical forms. But then she'd kiss me, my collarbone, my shoulder, my neck, and settle once more.

It did wonders to soothe my earlier dejection.

It did nothing to untangle my confusion.

It did a lot to increase my concern for her.

The hour was time well spent with my thoughts, reviewing every moment between us. Three in particular stood out as significant.

The first, when we were in Chicago during that original week and I'd found her in the dark, in the kitchen. I'd startled her, but her reaction at the time, even after she knew she was safe—sad, angry, confused, *terrified.*

The second, in Aspen, when I'd backed her into my room and stood between her and the door. The look in her eyes then—sad, angry, confused, *terrified*—reminded me of how she'd looked just after we'd made love.

The third, the last time we were in Chicago, in her sister's apartment, when she'd rested on the bed after I'd touched her, curling herself into a ball, her eyes vacant. Sad, angry, confused, *terrified.*

In the past, I'd wondered whether something had happened. What made her shrink from touch? But when she didn't recoil from me, when she'd seemed to welcome it, allow me to touch her freely, I'd—selfishly, stupidly—let the curiosity go.

But now.

Shifting in the seat, loathe to move her, I reached for the button to lower the privacy screen, cracking it an inch.

"Thanks, but you can take us to the address now."

"Okay, Mr. Fletcher," the driver said.

I lifted the window again, frowning at the direction of my thoughts and at the way Mona's body was now tense in my arms. I felt her swallow. She sniffed. She swallowed again.

"Are . . ." Mona started, stopped, cleared her throat. "Do you still want to stay with me?"

"Of course." But doubt had me asking, "Do you want me to stay with you?"

She exhaled loudly, lifting her head to look me in the eyes, miserable, remorseful, overwhelmed. "I'm so sorry. I love you, so much, and I'm so sorry."

"Please." I cupped her cheek with my palm, stole a quick kiss. "Please stop apologizing."

She nodded, pressing her lips together to firm her chin, but then blurted, "I'll do anything to make it up to you."

My heart heavy with worry, I frowned at her misery, trying to make sense of what had happened earlier and what was happening now. But I couldn't, and I wouldn't be able to unless she told me.

Gathering a deep breath, I slid my palm down her arm and lifted her fingers to my lips, kissing the back of her knuckles. "There is one thing you can do."

"Anything."

"You have to promise, before I ask, that you'll do it. That you'll give it to me, whatever I want." It was a dirty trick, but I was at my wit's end here. I needed her to talk to me, and the ends in this case justified the means.

"I promise. I swear, anything. I'll do anything." Her eyes were so wide, she looked so earnest and scared.

I thought back to Marie's statements about adults who grow up with neglectful parents and subsequently felt even worse about this manipulation. Just like Marie said, Mona was eager to prove herself, and now I was leveraging that vulnerability.

I kinda hated myself in that moment. But I also kinda didn't care. I needed her to tell me the truth, so we could figure this out, together. As long as I lived, I never wanted to see that look in her eyes again.

So, I gathered a deep breath, bracing myself, and asked, "Mona, why don't you like to be touched?"

She stared at me. And then she blinked rapidly, her eyes dropping. She pushed against my chest. I let her go. Climbing off my lap, she moved to the bench where she'd sat before, crossing her arms at her middle, not looking at me.

"I just don't like unexpected—"

"No," I said firmly, shaking my head, disappointed she wasn't telling me the truth. "No. That's not it. You're scared."

Her mouth dropped open and she gaped at me. "I'm not."

"Tell me the truth. Please."

She flinched. "I am, I am telling you—" She sucked in a hitching breath, the beginning of another sob, and then she closed her eyes. Her head fell back to the leather of the seat and she whispered, "Damn it."

"Why don't you want to tell me?" I asked softly, aching for an answer.

She shook her head, a humorless smile on her lips. "Because it's so stupid."

"Whatever it is, it's not stupid. If it makes you check out after every time I touch you, it's not stupid."

Her eyes opened and they cut to mine, held, devastating. Deep, bottomless wells of anguish. "I'm sorry."

"Stop. Apologizing. Please. Just tell me what happened."

Mona's chest rose and fell, breathing faster. I recognized this. She was working herself up to admit something difficult.

"I don't want you to look at me differently. I don't want you to treat me differently. I don't want you to think I'm crazy."

"I won't."

"But you might. Because what happened—God, Abram. It's nothing. It's so minor, especially compared to what other people go through. Nothing happened, and yet—and yet, I carry it around with me, empty luggage, and I have no idea why." Her voice cracked on the last word. I wasn't used to her sounding so helpless, so lost. I hated it.

Impulsively, I moved to where she was, knelt in front of her, and held her shoulders as well as her eyes. "Forget about other people, okay? If you stub your toe, you're allowed to acknowledge that it hurts like a motherfucker."

She laughed, a tear rolling down her cheek.

"If you break your arm, knowing someone out there in the world is starving and suffering shouldn't numb your pain. People say comparison is the thief of joy when it comes to success, right? But it's also the thief of compassion when it comes to suffering."

Mona nodded, sniffling, swallowing. "Okay, okay," she said, just as the car pulled to a stop.

Gritting my teeth at the inconvenient timing, I covered her hands with mine and squeezed. "Listen. We'll go inside. You take your time. If you need to sleep on it, fine. But before we do anything again . . ." I paused at the panicked look in her eyes, how her hands spasmed in mine.

"Abram." My name sounded like a plea.

"This isn't an ultimatum." I licked my lips, choosing my words carefully, gentling my voice. "This is me being careful with you."

Her face crumpled and she sounded angry as she whispered, "But that's just it. I don't want you to be careful with me. That's the opposite of what I want. And *that's* the problem."

Mona's words were a puzzle I was nowhere near solving when a knock sounded on the door.

I was resigned to the delay. "Come on. Let's go up."

She nodded, wiping at her tears.

Unable to help myself, I hugged her one more time, silently promising both her and myself that this was the beginning. No matter what she said, no matter what darkness or trials waited for us, or what events in her past held her hostage, my feelings for her would never change.

Tonight was the beginning, not the end.

CHAPTER 15
RELATIVISTIC MOMENTUM AND ENERGY

From the road, you would never know that the modest brownstone was an awesome twentieth-century Chicago-gangster-themed bed and breakfast. Situated in a quiet neighborhood, with single-family homes, parks, and coffee shops and restaurants at each corner, it looked like any of the other brownstones.

And that was exactly why I'd chosen it. Well, that and the huge bathtub, the relatively reasonable off-season price, and the milk and cookies available in the kitchen 24 hours a day.

My embarrassment was a great distraction from all the feelings churned up during our limo ride, and I did my best to not make the situation any more awkward for our driver. He was nice enough to give us his jacket, his shirt, and act like Abram's request was perfectly normal. The shirt was for Abram since I'd used his as a towel. The jacket was for me since my dress was torn. I didn't remember it tearing. But, then again, fabric cohesion had been the last thing on my mind when Abram helped me take it off.

I muttered only one anytime-phrase, "So, it has come to this," while Abram held out the jacket for me to put on, his eyes glinting with reluctant amusement.

But I still didn't have any shoes. Therefore, Abram insisted on carrying me to the gate where I punched in the code, and then to the door, where I punched in the other code. Once inside, he didn't put me down, instead whisper-asking me where we were going. It was late, and the rest of the guests and house staff were definitely asleep.

First, we had to swing by the kitchen to pick up our room key where the owner had hidden it. He then carried me up two flights of stairs. Our room took up the whole of the top floor. Walls had obviously been moved during the remodel, sectioning off the stairs from the rest of the space, with only one door accessing the entire suite.

Again, once inside, he didn't immediately put me down. He seemed to pause, glancing at the sitting area with a dark brown leather couch, the small mahogany bar in the far corner, the big screen TV mounted to the wall, and the black-and-white picture of Frank "The Enforcer" Nitti.

The gangster looked slightly confused, his eyes focused someplace above the camera, his hair parted to one side. If I didn't already know he was a gangster, I would've guessed he was a butcher. Or a baker. But not a candlestick maker.

As though suddenly deciding something, Abram carried me into the bedroom, twisted left, then right, conveying us to the bathroom before finally placing me back on my feet.

"There. You probably want to . . ." He pulled his hand through his hair, looking unsure and frustrated with himself. "Or maybe you don't."

I caught him by the hand before he could turn to leave. Swallowing around a lump of uncertainty, I held him in place and waited until he gave me his eyes.

I told him the truth. "I want to be brave with you."

His gaze softened, warmed.

So I quickly added before I could overthink it, "Will you take a bath with me?"

Abram's eyes widened, and he held still, looking caught, torn. "Uh."

"We won't do anything," I promised, giving him a beseeching half-smile. "It's just, I don't want to be alone, and we're both impressively dirty right now."

He chuckled, his eyes shifting to the side, glancing at the bathtub. And then he did a double take, noting roughly, "That's a huge tub."

I nodded, hope fluttering in my chest. "Yes. It is."

"Fuck," he said on a breath, the word one of deep despair, making me smile.

"Come on." I tugged on his hand.

His eyes came back to mine, even more conflicted, and his feet remained rooted in place. "No, Mona. No. I'll, uh. I'll come in later, after you're done."

I stepped back to him, holding his hand tighter, fear constricting my throat. "Please. Please stay with me."

"I will. I promise. But I can't take a bath with you without wanting to make love to you again. And, I'm sorry, but you scared the shit out of me in the limo. Once you tell me what happened, then we'll—"

"I was fifteen," I blurted, suddenly tired—so tired—of this between us. My brain switched to autopilot. "He was my chem lab TA. He found me alone one night in the lab and grabbed me from behind. He made me think he was going to rape me, though he never said the words. He let me go and said it was a joke. When I tried to leave, he grabbed me again, pinned me against the wall until I started to cry."

"Oh my God." The words tumbled out of him as he rocked backward on his feet, his large, shocked eyes darting between mine.

"But he didn't. He didn't rape me. He didn't hurt me. I had no bruises. He laughed at me, again. Said I was gullible, that I was just a little kid, that I reminded him of his little sister. He let me go. And that's it."

Abram swallowed convulsively, and I watched as the surprised confusion behind his eyes was eventually eclipsed by outrage and anger.

It was strange, telling him this now, how distant and removed I felt. When I'd told Gabby, I'd been shaky, sweaty, my heart had raced.

But not now. Now, it just felt like a fact. An ugly tale that happened to someone else but wouldn't stop following me around, making itself relevant to my life, insidiously inserting itself into my decisions. I wished it never happened, for so many reasons. Mostly though, I was frustrated with myself and how much power I'd given an event that didn't matter.

And I'd allowed it to ruin our first time together.

"Did you report him? Did you tell anyone?"

Shaking my head, exhausted, and abruptly feeling every speck of dirt and grime on my body, I crossed to the bathtub, turned on the faucet marked *hot*, and engaged the stopper.

"Come take a bath with me," I said, allowing fatigue to bleed into my words. "Please."

Considering me with a thoughtful and distracted frown, Abram acquiesced. I allowed myself to feel mildly relieved. I'd been afraid that telling Abram what happened would make him not want me anymore, as irrational as that sounded.

Except, the truth was, I was still afraid. I was still terrified that everything between us was going to change. He'd look at me differently, treat me like I was fragile, or crazy. Or he'd think I was overreacting, blowing the whole thing out of proportion. He'd tell me to get over it, like I'd told myself a thousand times.

Visibly distracted, Abram's fingers came to the buttons of the borrowed shirt. It was too small for his shoulders and too big for his waist. Meanwhile, numb, I shrugged off the coat, pulled off my dress, and climbed in the tub, adjusting the cold and hot water until the right temperature was reached.

I caught movement in my peripheral vision and turned my head to watch him push his pants down his hips, sparks of heat dancing in my lower stomach. My body came alive at the sight of his body.

Shame was quick to swoop in, reminding me that I'd just told him about what Leo had called *a trauma*. And now here I was, lusting after someone.

But he's not someone. He's Abram.

It didn't matter. Something was wrong with me. I shouldn't have lustful feelings so soon after speaking about *the event,* I shouldn't want to be held down while he took pleasure from my body, moving inside me. I shouldn't crave being dominated during sex. I shouldn't love it, but I did.

I faced forward again, cupping my hand and lifting it, watching the water spill around the edges until equilibrium was reached, leaving just about a tablespoon in my palm. Ah, what a perfect allegory for life. No matter how much I tried to hold on, ultimately, it would eventually slip through my fingers.

I looked up just as Abram climbed into the huge tub, his boxers still on. His mouth a frown, his eyes wary, he took the spot across from me.

"You take a bath with your boxers on?" I tried to make my voice light.

Abram studied me for a long moment before saying gently, "Tonight I do."

"You're afraid I'll attack you?" *What are you doing, Mona? Trying to turn this into a joke?*

Yes. Yes, I am. Maybe if I made it a joke then it would lose its power and I could move on.

His eyes narrowed, telling me he didn't think my statement was funny. In fact, it seemed to anger and frustrate him.

I swallowed again, my throat tight, my heart fluttering pitifully, wishing he would . . . *what?* What did I want? Did I want him to treat it like it was nothing? As I had? Did I want him to try to kiss me and make it better? Did I want him to grab me and devour me as he'd done in the limo?

"Was I too rough?" he asked, pulling me from my unanswerable questions.

"Pardon?"

"In the limo, when we were together. Was I too rough with you? Did I scare you?"

I shook my head but stopped. He'd been a little rough, and I'd loved it. But thinking about things now, I found it difficult to separate my feelings at the time from the guilt at having felt them.

"I was too rough," he said, sounding angry with himself. "I should've let you tell me what you like. I shouldn't have insisted that we discover each other. I'm sorr—"

"No. No, you weren't too rough. And I agreed with you, if you remember. I want us to discover each other. I want to give us a chance to be good at this. We're already good at this, we're great! It's just that it's—it's complicated."

He took a deep breath. "Complicated."

"Yes. Because I love you." My eyes stung with new tears, but I determinedly blinked them away, pulling my knees to my chest.

"That doesn't mean I get to do whatever I want to you."

"But I want it too. I like it rough. I—" I laughed, because I didn't quite know how to explain without sounding crazy, or wrong in the head. Sniffling, I said firmly, "I'm going to be brave, okay?"

He nodded, his eyebrows still knotted.

"Here is the truth, and if this makes me disturbed, then so be it. I've always been the one in control, with all my past partners. Always. But not with you."

He opened his mouth like he was going to say something.

I held up a hand, blinking against the stinging in my eyes. "Wait. Let me finish."

Abram nodded, clearly agonized by this data.

I took a deep breath, needing to clear my throat of emotion before continuing. "I love how you make love to me. I love it when you hold me down. I. Love. It. It gets me so, so hot. I love it when you're above me and I can't move. I love it when you take control and tell me what to do, order me around. However, after, I feel guilty about it, ashamed, and I can't stop comparing what happened when I was younger with what I enjoy, with you, during sex."

Abram blinked, distraught, his gaze moving over my head for a long moment, during which I regained control of myself, successfully winning the battle against the urge to cry.

"Have you talked to anyone?" His eyes cut back to mine. "A therapist?"

I hesitated. "Leo gave me some numbers a few weeks ago." It didn't escape my notice that everyone—Leo, Lisa, Gabby, and now Abram—seemed to think that my touch aversion in certain situations was related to *the trauma*. I still couldn't figure out why I flinched sometimes, and at other times I didn't, even with Abram. "I spoke to one of them—twice so far—but I just . . ." I shook my head.

"What?"

"It's like, I don't know this woman, and I'm going to tell her everything about myself? It seems very strange."

His mouth twitched. "Mona."

"Abram."

"That's what therapists do."

"I know."

"That's their job."

"I know."

His gaze moved over me. "Will you please talk to a professional about this?"

Ugh. Crap.

"Fine."

"I'll go with you if you want."

I splashed water on my face, hoping to wash off some of the eye makeup that I was certain had smudged under my eyes. I probably looked like a football player. "I'll, uh, let you know, if I need you to go."

Wiping my face of water, I gave him back my gaze. The bathtub was almost full, but neither of us made a move to switch off the water. I was too busy mediating a four-way battle between longing, hope, fear, and shame.

I longed for his touch, for things to be like they were before, between us.

I hoped he'd still want me.

I feared that he wouldn't.

Shame . . . well, that was a dead horse. I'd beaten it enough.

We were silent for a long time, long enough for anxiety to swell in my chest, long enough for me to await his next words with both dread and anticipation. I was terrified of what came next. But tonight was a night for bravery and recklessness. I'd come this far, I'd revealed this much. Therefore, even though I was nervous, I decided to rip off the Band-Aid.

Balling my hands into fists, I lowered my gaze to the surface of the water. "I already had your bags moved here. But if you need some time or want to stay at your original hotel for the next few days, or somewhere else, I completely understand."

Abram chuckled, it sounded incredulous. The laughter drew my eyes back to his and I found them to be equal parts tired, concerned, and frustrated. "Oh, my Mona. Do you really have no idea how I feel about you? Do you not understand that, even as I sit here, worried about you, livid and plotting revenge on your behalf, I'm trying to figure out how to prove you can trust me? Always. I love you with every part of myself, you've invaded every corner, every secret place, and I only want—I've only ever wanted—your happiness. If you want me to stay, then with you is always where I want to be."

I blinked against those confounded tears again, this time battling misery instead of apprehension. *Why does his beautiful profession of love make me miserable?*

"What can I do?" he asked, worry adding an edge to the softness of the question.

"I just . . ."

"What?"

"I don't want you to see me differently," I confessed to the water. "I loved how you looked at me, like you were hungry for me, like you wanted me all the time, like you're insatiable. I looked forward to it. Does that make me superficial and shallow?"

"Look at me."

Bracing myself, I did. His eyes glowed amber. Hot. Full of such raw desire and affection, it drove the air from my lungs and most of the wits from my brain.

"How am I looking at you?" His question was a deep rumble.

I couldn't answer, the words stuck in my throat, viscous with lust, heart humming happily. *Harlot heart.*

"I'm looking at you the same way you're looking at me. If you want the whole truth, and not to put any pressure on you, because that's the last thing I want to do, I'm—selfishly—trying to figure out a way to get inside your pants without making you feel guilty afterward. I'm conjuring ideas, wondering how you'd feel about dominating *me*, tying *me* up."

I had to swallow, because *lust.* "But, would you want that? Is that something you'd like?"

"Oh yes." His mouth curved, a flash of teeth, his dimple deeper on the left than on the right. But I knew it would be. "Yes. I'd like that very much."

"Even though you wouldn't be in control?"

"Uh, sign me up."

I couldn't help it, I laughed, shaking my head at him. "You want to be dominated?"

"By you? I would *love* it. Just think, I sit back, let you do all the hard work, sounds amazing. We could even get a blindfold and some handcuffs. I'd like that, you teasing me, making me crazy."

I laughed harder, tears leaking from the corners of my eyes, shifting my leg to kick him lightly with my foot under the water. "Now you're just being funny."

"I'm not." His voice, tired and raspy as it was, dropped an octave and he caught my foot, his hand sliding up my ankle to my calf, his touch calming and soothing the part of me that had been frantic about losing him. "Please, have your way with me. You're so clever and sweet. I bet you would come up with some very interesting, and probably educational, carnal activities. I swear, I am a million percent serious right now."

"A million percent?" I twisted my lips to the side, crossing my arms.

His eyes darted to my chest and then back up. He held my foot on his lap and was massaging the arch with his thumbs. "I've never been more serious about anything in my life. Except that I love you."

I huffed another laugh, but—after inspecting him closely for another few seconds—I believed him. My body *definitely* believed him, but it was biased, so it didn't count. My brain believed him. Most importantly, so did my heart.

Endeavoring not to smile like the sex-with-Abram-crazed lunatic that I was, I said, "Fine."

His eyebrows jumped. "Fine?"

"Let's do it." I pressed my lips together firmly.

"Yes, let's." He grinned, his eyes dancing. However, seconds later he blinked, and his stare sobered. "Also, you'll call your therapist? Talk to her about everything?"

Trying not to groan, I settled on a sigh instead, the reminder submarining my buoyed mood. But—strangely—not by much.

"Yes," I agreed, earning me a bigger grin.

"Promise?"

"Yes. I promise. I'll call."

CHAPTER 16
INFRARED, ULTRAVIOLET, X-RAY, AND GAMMA-RAY ASTRONOMY

Mona

I'm beginning to suspect that I have a tendency to overthink things (and don't roll your eyes at me, I CAN SENSE YOU ROLLING YOUR EYES!).

Take Abram and his desires, thoughts, and motivations as an example. It was morning o'clock. Or quite possibly afternoon o'clock. I couldn't be certain without looking at my phone or an actual clock, and this B&B didn't have one next to the bed. Anyway!

Here we were, nebulous time of day o'clock. In bed. Together. Except, when I woke up, instead of being tangled in each other like I'd been led to believe is standard for lovers upon waking, he was on one side of the bed, facing me, and I was on the other side of the bed, facing him. Also, we were both fully clothed in unsexy yet comfortable pajamas.

Uh, rather, let me amend that. Abram was always sexy. His Iron Man flannel PJ bottoms and no shirt were quite sexy. Whereas my pink cotton PJ bottoms with Albert Einstein sticking out his tongue rendered in cartoon, plus my baggy white T-shirt, were not sexy.

But back to nebulous time of day o'clock.

Blinking, I scowled at his handsome slumbering face. What, pray tell, did this bed distance and lack of tangling mean? Did it mean he'd changed his mind? Or that his subconscious didn't want me? Evidence suggested I ought to be in service as a femme pillow au extraordinaire. But I wasn't.

Were they not pillow material?

Twisting my lips to the side, I reached up, beneath my shirt, pushing it up, and tested my breasts. Grabbing and squeezing, I considered the value of a breast malleability quotient scale, where breasts could be tested and ranked for skin softness and general pliability.

Not that I wanted to give women another thing for society to tell them to fret over. But, if there existed women like me, who enjoyed having data to do with what they pleased, then I'd be very interested in a random sample normalized curve of bosom to suppleness ratio, and here is why: The last romance novel I'd read, and the seventeen before that, always included a scene where the hero and heroine woke up embracing, invariably with the man cradled against the female's chest.

Therefore, why wasn't Abram cradled against mine? Were they a non-pillowy shape? Not pliable enough? Where had they failed me?

First, an analysis was needed. Then a diagnosis of the problem. I squeezed and kneaded and inspected, endeavoring to think of words to describe them were I a heroine in a romance novel. Typically, racks were described as something like, *Her supple bosom,* but never something like, *Her jagged tits.*

Squeezing one and then the other, I closed my eyes and took a moment to diagnose.

Mona's malleable mounds.

No. That was just lazy alliteration, not an accurate reflection of my boob-truth.

"What are you doing?"

Tensing, my eyes flew open. I gaped at Abram's raised eyebrows and the sleepy, confused amber irises beneath.

A small smile curved his mouth and his stare brightened with suspicion. "Are you . . .?"

"I'm doing a breast exam." My voice was much higher than normal, so I cleared my throat, keeping my face impassive. "Always good to, you know, check out the—uh —good old mammary glands and whatnot."

His eyes narrowed, his lips somehow pursing but still smiling. "You're giving yourself a breast exam? Now?"

I nodded, trying on my academic face. "Of a kind, yes."

Abram seemed to be working harder to subdue his grin. "Okay, okay. That's cool." Taking a deep breath, he rolled to his back, pushed down the covers and his pajama pants to his feet, and gripped his morning wood.

I gasped.

I sensed him glance at me but didn't actually witness his eyes on my face. My attention was otherwise engaged. Watching him. Stroke. Himself. And, you know, panting. (Me. I was panting. The panting came from me.)

"Go on," his voice said. "Don't let my penis exam distract you from your breast exam."

I'd never watched anyone touch themselves before. Big, strong hand, long fingers wrapped around his thick shaft, smoothing down and up, down again in perfect rhythmic strokes, a sexy metronome. It was hypnotic.

Clearing my throat again, and obviously still panting, I nodded, rolling slowly to my back, eyes still fastened to his erection. My shirt bunching at my collarbone, I massaged and caressed Mona's suddenly sensitive malleable mounds.

I had to stifle a groan as Abram tucked his other hand behind his head, giving me a completely unobstructed view of his torso and chest. *So unfair.*

"Found anything?" he asked, his voice still deep with sleep and his efforts at last night's concert.

"No. Not yet," I panted (yep, still panting), my nipples now tight, hard beads against my palms, my stomach twisting and coiling and heating. "How about you?" I made the mistake of glancing at his face and found his eyes on my hands where I touched myself.

He looked almost angry, his eyes—sharp, feral—were at half-mast, his jaw tight. He licked his lips, his tongue darting out, and I had the most *intense* desire to shove off my pants and straddle his face.

Why don't you?

"Nothing yet," his voice scraped. "But I'm not finished yet." Then he groaned. "Mona, what are you doing?"

His eyes tracked lower, looking pained, and I followed his line of sight to discover I'd moved one of my hands to my stomach, the tips of my fingers skimming along the waistband of my PJs. My gaze flickered back to his, and I tested a reckless hypothesis, dipping my hand inside my underwear and pushing them down my hips.

Abram's breath hitched, ragged, unsteady.

"Pelvic exam," I said, just as I brought my knees up and parted myself with my fingers.

His eyes shot to mine, held, his head shifting forward on his pillow, like he was going to *do something*. But he didn't. He stopped himself. He glared at me, reminding me of a tiger behind the bars of a cage, making promises with his eyes. *If I weren't trapped, if I could touch you.*

I hoped my stare communicated, *Why can't you? Touch me!* I was so hot, wet, ready. I was *right there,* next to him. Why didn't he reach out? His lack of action clearly frustrated us both.

Instead, he swallowed thickly, his eyes drifting down again, first to my breasts, and then to where my fingers moved between my spread legs, heated, dazed. His jaw ticked. His breathing grew labored. He blinked. Hard. Like he was having trouble focusing.

And then, suddenly, Abram sat up, stood up, pulled up his pants, and left the room. A second later, I heard the shower come on, and my mouth dropped open.

!

So.

There I was.

In bed.

One hand on my breast, the other between my legs.

Bereft.

Listening to my gorgeous boyfriend take a shower by himself. *Probably naked!* Unless he wore boxers in the shower as well.

Growling, I also sat up, stood up, but I pulled my pants down. Whipping my shirt off, I marched after him into the bathroom, finding him—AH HA! *NAKED*—in the glass shower. I stopped short inside the door because his back was to me and his back was very naked, and I'd never seen a naked back like his before, if you don't count shirtless rugby players in spandex shorts (which I didn't).

Plus, this was Abram's back. Not anonymous sporty guy's back. Therefore, it was a spectacular force. Breathing hard, because I was turned on and angry, I placed my hands on my hips, and whisper-yelled, "Why did you leave?"

Abram turned his head, giving me just his profile, and then shook his head, turning away. "Give me a minute."

I took a step closer, so he could hear me better, not so I could get a better view of his ass because the shower was steaming up the glass. Not because worry had cut through the lusty fog in my brain and told me things between us were not functioning as per Mona-Abram relationship standards.

"Abram. Talk to me. Please."

He cursed, flipped off the shower, turned completely around while reaching for a towel to hide his glorious engorged erection. The action left me feeling uncertain, so I plucked a washcloth off the counter and used it as a fig leaf of sorts for my vagina, covering my breasts with my arms.

"Mona," he began, frowning at where I held the tiny square in front of myself. Shaking his head as though to clear it, he started again, "Mona. Last night, you shared yourself with me. I am so appreciative that you trusted me, thank you. And, because of what you shared, I'm doing my very best here, trying to keep my hands to *myself.* Which—" he glanced down at the tented towel at his pelvis "—I am incapable of doing while you're next to me touching yourself."

During his speech, I'd opened and closed my mouth many, many times, mostly planning to object, or question the validity of his logic. Conversely, as I listened and I realized the truth—that he was trying to be respectful and save me a visit to shame town—I snapped my mouth shut.

Glaring at me like I was a roast beef sandwich he'd been denied (the most exceptional of all sandwiches), he cleared his throat, stretched his neck, and waited.

At first, I didn't know what to say. I mean, he had a good point. But on the other hand, no. Hadn't he been the one to suggest me taking the lead last night? So why was he—*Oh!*

"Ohhhhhh!" I nodded, my nods slow and exaggerated. "I get it!"

He gave his head a subtle shake. "What do you get?"

"You want me to dominate you, tell you what to do."

Abram flinched, sucking in a breath.

But before he could speak, because that was my job now, I tossed the washcloth back to the counter and once again stood before him proudly, hands on my hips.

"Abram, my love, please step out of the shower."

He lifted an eyebrow over narrowed eyes, his lips parting and his jaw shifting to one side, a spark of something in his stare that had me grinning. *Was that defiance?* How wonderful.

Eventually, he did it. He stepped out of the shower, letting the towel shift to his hip where he gripped it in one hand.

His eyes struck me as sardonic and so did his tone as he asked, "What now?"

"We're going back to the bed." I mean, obviously, right?

I watched as he took a deep breath, like he was steadying himself. With reluctant movements, he began using the towel to dry his skin.

"No," I said, frowning.

"No?"

"Don't dry off. I want you wet."

He blinked again, like my words landed somewhere sensitive. His grin a tad incredulous, but also amused, he nodded and placed the towel on the edge of the tub. My gaze dropped to his erection and I licked my lips, the electricity of excitement making me restless.

Crooking my finger as I backed out of the bathroom, I motioned to him. "Come on."

Turning, I didn't wait to see if he would follow and crossed to the bed, standing at the edge of it, waiting for him to appear and nervously worrying my lip.

With the males of my previous acquaintance, providing directions before and during intercourse had felt a bit like giving a lecture, or explaining how to make poached eggs. But with Abram, I was a bundle of nerves, wanting to make this good for him, wanting to make it amazing like he'd done for me.

The main impediment as far as I could tell was my libido. I was already so incredibly turned on. Therefore, I concluded, I would just have to take things slow, get him worked up with foreplay in order to ensure his orgasm was pleasurable.

Go slow. I nodded at the assertion.

He appeared in the doorway, and I straightened. Realizing I'd been twisting my fingers, I stopped, scratched the back of my neck, and then pointed to the mattress. "Lie down. In the center."

Saying nothing, Abram strolled to and stopped just two decimeters in front of me. His eyes on mine, making my heart beat like crazy, and I recognized something about myself. The fear was back. Just like before, it made everything brighter, colors sharper, my skin too tight, my breasts heavy, so heavy, sensitive.

Huh.

But before I could give this realization much thought, Abram's eyes dropped to my mouth, heated. He swayed forward, like my lips were magnetic. The way he looked —again, like a tiger pacing in a cage—sent a sharp thrill from the top of my skull to the base of my spine. I shivered.

I actually owned a pair of tiger-print underwear and matching bra, and I'd brought it with me. *Note to self, wear sexy tiger underwear today.*

His eyes cut back to mine. His jaw worked.

"Lie down," I whispered, holding his gaze.

He did.

He lay down. In the center of the bed. His body visibly tense. His hands balled into fists. His muscles flexing. And his gorgeous penis. S*igh.*

Swallowing the thirst, I climbed onto the bed, now on all fours, and crawled to where he lay. Nudging his legs apart with one of mine, I placed a knee between his thighs, my hands on either side of his torso, and bent to lick the water from his chiseled abdominal muscles.

Oh yeeeeah.

Desire pooled low and insistent in my belly. He flinched, then groaned, his penis pressing tenaciously against my stomach, hard and hot, smooth like silk. I gripped it. He was rock hard.

I felt dizzy. My sex clenched around nothing, reminding me of how neglected it was, how empty, and—

Yeah, you know what? Forget taking it slow.

Impulsively, I straddled his hips and lowered myself, sucking in a relishing breath at the delicious, stretching invasion. This, clearly, shocked the hell out of him because his hands came to my thighs and squeezed.

"God. God. Mona—"

I bent forward, bracing my arms on either side of his head, and took his mouth. He groaned, immediately opening, chasing my tongue, obviously fighting the urge to take over as I rolled my hips, using him to rub just the right spot.

Abram's hands were moving, sliding up my sides, cupping my breasts, rolling my nipples between his fingers, and then tucking themselves beneath my arms to lift me higher so he could suckle one, and then the other, lavishing both with wet, hungry kisses.

Tingly, hot tendrils of electricity played tug of war between my pelvis and nipples, stretching, curling, making me slightly insane. The urge to sit up and ride him more completely was overwhelming. I needed him deeper, I needed more force, faster.

Placing my hands on his stomach, I straightened away, eliciting a frustrated growl from his throat, his eyes piercing as I shifted, using the hard plane of his stomach as leverage while also feeling him up.

"Say something," I demanded, because why the hell not? *He is mine to command*!

His lip curled into a feral smile, a baring of teeth, sending a renewed fissure of alarm down my spine to the back of my legs, making me hot. *So hot.* I was sweating with exertion and the thrill of uncertainty. I loved it and I was so close. I could feel the start of it, the deep ache teetering on satisfaction.

Abram's covetous eyes caressed a scorching path from my lips to my breasts and then further south, obviously watching us where we mated. "Thank you for the view," he said, his voice like gravel, his hands sliding to my hips. His fingers flexed into my bottom like he wanted to help lift me, help me go faster.

"Do you like watching?" I asked because I really wanted to know for some reason. It was *essential* that I know. Another shiver. I couldn't catch my breath.

"I like watching you." His hand came around to the front of my thigh, his thumb slipping between my folds. "I like this." He circled my clitoris and *OH GOD OH GOD OH GOD—*

"I like watching you come on my cock," he said through clenched teeth, sounding a little sinister.

His statement was well-timed because I was coming. So. Hard. My hips jerking, searching, seeking, needing to prolong the fullness and friction. My body igniting. I couldn't think, but intrinsically I knew he was coming too.

His hips pistoned, rolled, inelegant searching, just like mine. His head pressed against the pillow, exposing his neck, his powerful form in sharp relief. His hands moved away from my body, gripping the bedsheets and pulling. I heard a ripping sound. I ignored it, bowing forward above him, my hand on his heart.

Then I collapsed. I just freaking fell right on top of him, limp, my mouth at his neck, greedily gulping air as his hips still worked, seeking the last bit of his pleasure from my body. A moment later, I felt him go lax, also breathing like he'd just run a marathon. I felt fingers thread into my hair, grabbing a fistful to angle my head for a kiss.

Somehow, both of us breathing hard, our bodies completely spent, we were still able to kiss. Maybe because it was sweet. Tender. An unhurried, soft meeting of lips and tongue. Abram smoothed his hand down my back to my bottom, stroking it. He made a little sound in the back of his throat, something halfway between a growl and a hum.

Or maybe that was me.

No. That's him.

I fell asleep, right there, naked, on top of my purring tiger.

CHAPTER 17
THE NATURE OF STARS

Mona

I. Was. STARVING! when I woke up. But I was also sticky and alone. The former wasn't a surprise, but the latter was.

Wrinkling my nose, as I'd once again awoken without an Abram on my bosom, I rubbed my eyes and searched for my phone to determine the time. Honestly, I had no idea where it was. The night before had been a blur.

While I scoured every surface that could be scoured from my spot in bed, I noticed a folded piece of paper on the side table, one that had been torn from a notebook. My heart gave a little leap. Pushing myself to a sitting position, I snatched it, and chuckled when I discovered he wrote *DO NOT BURN* on the outside.

Dear Mona,

First, I love you.

Second, Marie called and said your phone was left in the greenroom last night. She picked it up for you so I'm meeting her now to grab it. I'm also picking up some food, because I'm starving.

Third, did you know this place has milk and cookies 24 hrs a day! I left you milk and a plate with oatmeal and chocolate chip in the mini fridge under the bar. EAT THEM.

Fourth, sorry I ripped the sheet. I told the owner and they'll send up a new one later today.

Fifth, I love you.

-Abram

PS I have to confess something. I watched you sleep while you were naked until my stomach growled so loud, I was afraid it would wake you up. Now, when I close my eyes, I see your naked body. Thank you for all the views. You are very sexy.

PPS I love you.

Smiling stupidly and reading the note more times than I could count, I eventually stood, refolding it carefully and tucking it inside my suitcase. On a happy cloud, I crossed to the bar, opened the mini fridge, and stood at the counter scarfing down cookies and gulping milk.

It was at this point I realized I was very naked. It felt a bit like Adam and Eve discovering their nudity, except without the creepy snake.

"What was in those cookies?" I mumbled to myself, hurrying to the bathroom and rushing through a shower, the promise of more food spurring my movements.

But when I finished and dressed—making sure to put on my tiger-print undies and bra—and Abram and the food still hadn't arrived, I was at a loss. The B&B's lack of Wi-Fi was supposed to be a bonus. No Wi-Fi meant less distractions. But I hadn't even brought a book! Without the distraction of my phone, access to email, or a book, I wandered around the large suite and inspected the photos of gangsters hanging on the walls.

After engaging in a staring match with a photograph of someone named Vincent "The Schemer" Drucci, an open notebook on the living room desk snagged my attention. Meandering to it, I peered down at the open page, recognizing Abram's handwriting immediately. I scanned the first few lines.

Your mouth tastes so sweet, your skin is sweet too

Hold still, my love, and let me savor you

Pushing lace aside I ask her, does this taste like candy, I wonder—

. . .

GASP!

I tore my eyes away and took a giant step backward, my hands flying to my suddenly hot cheeks, my skin—everywhere—breaking out in goose bumps.

It was sexy poetry. About *us!* Based on my body's crazy lava-like reaction to the first three lines—an explicit and direct window into his beautiful brain—I couldn't handle it. Catnip and love potion and a mixture of all aphrodisiacs in written word form and in Abram's handwriting.

Is this what life would be like with a poet? One minute I'm fine, minding my own business, and then the next I'm consumed by lava lust?

Good Lord. Have mercy. Amen.

"Oh no."

Startled, I turned toward the sound of Abram's concerned exclamation and I grimaced, my hands falling to my sides. "Ah! Sorry!"

"Who told you—wait, what? Why are you sorry?" Rushing across the room, he shut the suite door with his booted foot and placed three white plastic bags—of what I assumed was takeout—on the coffee table.

"I accidentally looked at your sexy poetry." My eyes moved over him, gobbling the sight of him up. He wore dark jeans and a black leather jacket over a button down dark blue shirt.

Oh jeez. I wanted him. Right now. Clearly, I was powerless against the power of suggestion where Abram was concerned, and especially when the suggestions were made by his poetry. If he ever turned his sexy poems into a song, I'd be ruined.

But Abram didn't seem to follow. "Sexy poetry?"

"Your notebook." I gestured to it, tangentially surprised it didn't burst into flames, what with all the hot, suggestive thoughts recklessly left on its pages.

"Oh." He gave me a distracted flash of his dimple, his eyes moving over me like he thought I was adorable. "No, that's totally fine. Read the whole thing if you want, it's all about you anyway."

"Oh my." My hands came back to my cheeks. *Lava-like lust.*

"Listen." Abram's gaze turned bracing and he encircled my wrist with his fingers, tugging me toward the couch. "Something's happened."

I allowed him to lead me. "What? What happened?"

"Last night, when we left the stadium, we were photographed."

"Oh. Okay." I twisted my hand so that our fingers tangled together, the smell of food finally permeating my senses. "Hey. Is that Mexican food? You didn't happen to pick up enchiladas, did you?"

He frowned. "Mona. This is a problem."

"Is it?" Now I frowned. "You didn't want anyone to know we were dating?"

"No. That is, I figured it would come out eventually, and I thought I was fine with it coming out now."

"But now you think everyone knowing is a problem?"

"Yes," he said emphatically. "Because it's not just about everyone knowing."

"Yikes. Did I accidentally flash someone? I knew that skirt was too short. So, Mexican food?"

He looked at me like he thought I was crazy. "No. You didn't—how can you be—" Abram growled. "Listen. This is important. You didn't flash anyone, most of the shots are blurry because it was dark. But they've got it wrong. They think it was Lisa with me, not you."

"Oh no." I grimaced. "I'll call and apologize to my sister."

"Mona. They—the websites, the newspapers, social media—they're having a fucking field day. They've dug up old pictures of Lisa, when she was with Tyler, and are making this into a shitstorm. Saying she's using me to promote his album, claiming that's why I've played his song."

"Obviously that's not true. How badly are they treating her? What did they say?"

"They're relentless, vicious. Saying she's not good enough for me, saying she's grotesque, ugly, saying she's a leech, a user, a gold digger and worse. It's brutal."

"Ah, crap. I'll call her now, let her know we'll get this all straightened out. Did you get my phone?"

He shook his head as though to clear it. "Yes, absolutely, we'll call Lisa, see what we can do to make this go away for her. She shouldn't have to go through this. But you're missing my point. If we tell everyone that it's actually you in the photos, that we're together, there's a chance you'll be ripped apart."

He lost me again. "Uh, yeah?"

Eyes flashing, Abram exhaled suddenly, clearly perplexed and frustrated by how well I was taking this. "And that's okay with you?"

Staring at him, comprehension slowly seeped through the barrier of my intimate familiarity with all matters celebrity. "Ah! I see. You didn't realize this was going to happen."

He seemed to choke on my statement for a few seconds before coughing out, "I thought, maybe, there'd be a few haters, outliers, whatever. But nothing like this. You were expecting this level of vitriol?"

"Yes. Well"—I waved my hand in the air—"not the Lisa part. And I can fix that for her. But the *Abram Fletcher's girlfriend being criticized for existing by news and social media* part? Oh yeah. I knew that was going to happen, and I knew it would be vicious. That's what always happens to women who date attractive male super celebrities."

Abram gaped at me like he'd never seen me before, and then he jumped up, paced to the other side of the room and ripped off his leather jacket with jerky movements.

Left alone with the food and an empty stomach, I slowly reached for the closest bag while keeping my eyes on him. I didn't want to be rude, as I could see he was going through a crisis of reality-fueled frustration, but I was extremely hungry, and my stomach demanded action. Reasoning with myself that I could be supportive *and* well-fed, I untied the top of the plastic bag, reaching inside to withdraw the first container of mystery takeout while hunting for utensils.

"I can't believe this." His hand was over his mouth and muffled the words slightly. "You wanted to be with me even though you knew this kind of cruelty might happen to you."

"Yes," I answered evenly, popping the container open. *NACHOS!* Licking my lips in anticipation, I dipped the cheesiest of the chips into a pool of salsa, and then shoved the whole thing in my mouth. Yum. So good.

Pacing back and forth, he scowled at me, quietly seething, "This is bullshit. You shouldn't have to deal with this. You shouldn't have to put up with being torn down simply because we're together."

"I mean—" Speaking around a mouthful of nacho, I had to swallow before continuing, "In a perfect world, yeah. This wouldn't happen. But this is just how it is."

"Why aren't you more pissed?" He stopped short on the other side of the coffee table, his eyes accusatory.

"Abram, I grew up around celebrities, rock stars, movie stars. I guess I'm used to it. You'll get used to it too." I meant my words to be comforting, hoping they'd make a positive impact.

They did not.

He exhaled. Loudly. If he'd been a dragon, I was certain I'd be on fire. His hands came up, his fingers stiff, and he shook them while making a growling sound. "This is so fucking *frustrating*!"

He paced away.

Surreptitiously, I quickly ate another nacho, chewing with haste and swallowing before he paced back. "Okay, okay. I can see you are very upset—"

"UPSET?!"

I rolled my lips between my teeth, standing and making a slow, careful approach. "And I appreciate you being upset on my behalf. But, my dearest love, I entered into this beautiful relationship with you knowing that, eventually, once we made our connection public, the peanut gallery was going to pick me apart. Everything about me will be public fodder. But that's okay, it always has been to a certain extent. I'll deal with it."

His eyes cut to mine, glaring at me like I was nuts.

"I'll let you in on a little secret." I took a few tiny steps closer. "The peanut gallery doesn't actually matter. All those haters? Who tear people down? They don't matter. And what they say doesn't matter. It'll just be more publicity for you, more noise. Your name will trend upward. My parents always say, 'All noise is good noise, unless it's mocking noise.' I don't think you'll be mocked for dating me, but I don't know for certain."

Abram shook his head. "I don't care about me, I don't care what they say about *me*. That's not the problem. It's what they say about you."

"But they don't matter."

"They shouldn't be allowed to say such hateful things."

"But since they don't matter, what they say doesn't matter either. It's like multiplying any number by zero. The peanut gallery is the zero."

He snapped his mouth shut, his jaw flexing. Breathing hard, his hands on his hips, once again he reminded me of a caged animal. But this time, it was angry helplessness I spied, not hunger.

I made a soft sound of compassion, closing the distance between us to place a hand on his scruffy cheek. "Oh, Abram. Please don't waste energy on this. Haters gonna hate, idiots gonna procreate."

He huffed a laugh, but his eyes looked sad, trapped. "I'm never going to be okay with this." Covering my hand with his, he brought my palm to his lips. "I'm going to fight the world for you." He sounded so fierce.

It made me smile. "Challenge all who besmirch my name?"

His mouth curved against my hand.

"You like that word? Besmirch? It's a great word, right? I dare you to use it in a song. You know another great word? Nachos." Turning my fingers, I caught his and tugged him toward the coffee table. "Come. Sit. Feast."

Abram allowed me to pull him back to the couch, and then he allowed me to gently push his shoulders until he was sitting again. Hesitating for a second but ultimately yielding to the impulse, I sat on his lap. Immediately, his arm came around me, one hand on my hip, the other on my thigh.

"I've never fed anyone before. Do you want me to feed you nachos?" I lifted a chip toward his mouth. "I can make airplane sounds."

Eyes still sad, he laughed, and his forehead fell to my shoulder. Again, he made a growling sound.

"Or train sounds? Choo." He shook his head, so I ate the chip. Turning, pressing my chest against his chest, I wrapped him in my arms. "It gets easier to ignore people who don't matter. I promise. Like any skill, it just takes practice."

"But what about your career?" He lifted his head, leaning back to capture my eyes as his scowl returned. "I think Marie tried to warn me about this. Charlie too."

"Physicists—and the science community in general—don't pay much attention to the chatter of pop culture unless it furthers their own careers. Me dating you might be the cause for some minor curiosity, and I'll probably have to put up with a slight increase in snobbery and pretentiousness. Eventually, they'll go back to hunting for puzzle pieces to the universe and struggling to find grant dollars to fund their research. Remember who my parents are. I've been dealing with their shadow most of my life."

Abram leaned further back, his eyes moving between mine, questioning. "I thought you were worried about candid pictures of you being made public. You said they could destroy your career. And, for the record, I don't like the idea of being a shadow for you."

"Oh, depending on the picture, they totally could wreck my career, or derail it. If that picture of me in the lab coat were released, I'd definitely lose a few of my grants and would have a hard time finding any funding. At least, for a while."

Aghast, he stared at me. "Then why did you send it?"

"Because I thought you'd like it."

"Mona."

"Abram."

"We should delete them. We should delete those pictures now."

"No. We shouldn't. You were right. Other people shouldn't be dictating how I share myself with you, so don't let them dictate how you share yourself with me. I came to terms weeks ago with the futility of conforming to pompous ideas of what constitutes appropriate behavior."

"You did? When?"

"When I sent you that picture of me in a bikini. I even told you in the hospital, but you might've been too sick to hear me. And actually, futility isn't the right word. It's *damaging* to everyone who comes after. It's damaging for Mona DaVinci to sit quietly and let others dictate her—my—personal life. Then what good have I done? History—the good kind of history—is seldom made by those who keep their head down."

His dimple winked at me as his eyes gazed deep into mine, like he was a little mesmerized. "You're the most remarkable person I've ever known."

"Ditto, Mr. Harris." I stole a quick kiss, grinning down at his handsome face. "But don't get ahead of yourself. I haven't done anything yet. It's not like I'm going to hand out bikini shots of me at faculty meetings. I'm just going to act like myself, do what I want to do. I'm going to be *honest.*" Tilting my head to one side then the other, I shrugged. "And if trouble follows, so be it."

* * *

I called Lisa while we ate the nachos. As I suspected, she wasn't too freaked out about the social media "shitstorm" as Abram called it, but she did surprise the Schrödinger out of me by offering to maintain the ruse.

"Just think about it," she said. A second later, I heard a microwave beep on her side of the call.

Abram and I swapped stares of disbelief, not because of the microwave beep, but because *what the heck?*

"Why would you do that?" I blurted, for obvious reasons.

"It's the least I can do for you after what you've done for me. And it doesn't bother me. We could just not comment on the pictures. It would buy you and Abram more time together without the press following you everywhere. Like I said, just think about it."

Abram frowned thoughtfully in a way that made me nervous. I glared at him, wanting to deter any temptation he felt to take my sister up on the offer.

"No. No way." I said this for his benefit as much as hers.

"Can you give us a minute?" Abram cut in and put Lisa on mute.

"The answer is no." I crossed my arms.

"She makes a good point about giving us more time. And if she doesn't mind, why not?"

"You can't be serious. You were the one who came in here less than an hour ago, huffing and puffing about how terrible the news was treating Lisa."

He gathered a deep breath and, holding my eyes, he nodded. "You're right. It's not fair to Lisa, and it's obvious she's trying to be a good sister here. I have to give her credit for that. But it's just, I love you. And I'm worried about you. You're more sensitive than people think, and you feel so deeply. I know you said you're prepared for this, but I'm worried. *But,* I also trust your judgment. If and when you want to go public, I'm all for it."

I understood his concern, and I wasn't looking forward to the glimpses of hateful pomposity I'd get from my place on the periphery, but I wasn't going to let Lisa be my stunt double, or my red herring.

Of note, as I inspected him, I sensed his worry, absolutely. But I was also picking up on some other vibes, like—despite his apprehension—he was relieved and happy I was opposed to Lisa's suggestion. *Weird.*

Anyway, in the end, we turned down Lisa's offer.

I then called my therapist's office and scheduled a new appointment. Since I'd now fully committed to the idea, I decided to make a list of items I wanted to discuss. For example, the flinching, why did I do it with Abram sometimes? I loved it when he touched me, so why would I flinch away at odd intervals? Also, if I felt fear both times we'd made love, why did I feel shame after he was on top, but not when I was on top? That made no logical sense. This therapist was going to have her work cut out for her. *FOR SURE.*

And then, since I was in a list making mood, I navigated to a few websites looking for some tips on dirty talking. I'd never done it before, but after reading three lines of Abram's sexy poetry and experiencing an electromagnetic burst of incalculable desire, the impulse was one I couldn't ignore. Dirty talking was clearly an electromagnetic force.

Now, all four atomic fundamental forces had been identified: his body made me weak (weak force), the urge to smell him was always strong (strong force), my feelings for him impacted time (gravitational force), and Abram's sexy poetry/his brain (electromagnetic).

While I composed my lists, Abram spent the next hour or so of the—early evening? What the heck time is it?—on the phone with his record label, and then his publicist, and then a conference call with his record label's publicist. They all promised to hammer out a press release for our perusal by tomorrow morning.

At one point they wanted to know if my parents' team needed to be brought in the loop. I shook my head, making a split decision based on the need for expediency.

Plus, my parents had a great committee of people looking out for their interests, and that was the problem. I wanted Abram's interests to be the priority, not theirs. If they got ahold of the story, they'd spin it to their own benefit somehow. Therefore, *no.*

When he finally got off the phone and we were able to sit down properly with our Mexican feast, I discovered that he had procured enchiladas and I fell a little bit more in love with him.

Over dinner, or lunch maybe? Whatever. Over food, conversation flowed easily, as expected. Whenever we'd spoken on the phone over the last several months, time had run out too quickly, our conversations never seemed finished.

Presently, he was finishing up a story about how one of the roadies showed up for pre-show rehearsals in his bathrobe and nothing else.

"He'd used the hotel sauna—the hotel was across the street from the venue—and forgot his room key, locking himself out of his room."

"Oh no."

"Oh yes. And when he went downstairs, the front desk wouldn't give him another key without his ID, which was in the room."

I laughed at this poor man's misfortune though doing so made me feel like a jerk.

"So he waited in the lobby, in his bathrobe, until someone with the show happened to be walking by, which was me, but I was already running late for an interview. So we decided to go to the venue—I got him in no problem—and see if anyone had extra clothes he could wear until we could make it back to the hotel and sort out the key issue."

"And?" I leaned forward, way too invested in the story.

"No one had any extra clothes. The poor guy had to do the sound checks in his bathrobe, and it was a windy day." Abram lifted his eyebrows meaningfully.

I covered my mouth, feeling badly about my laughter.

"But he took it in stride. I ended up giving him my T-shirt and just wearing my jacket."

My eyes widened, contemplating the kind of stir that must've caused. "How did that go over in the interview?"

Abram made a strange face, like he was trying to smile, but couldn't quite manage it. "It was fine." He pushed his rice around with his fork.

"Hmm. That sounds like a falsehood."

Rolling his eyes, he released his utensils and leaned back in his seat, saying as though bored, "The interviewer asked if she could touch my stomach."

I wrinkled my nose. "That's gross."

He shrugged, like it wasn't a big deal. And yet, something about his display of apathy felt off.

"How do you deal with it?"

"What's that?" Abram leaned forward again, picking up his fork and spearing a piece of enchilada.

"All the attention. My parents love it. I think nothing thrills my dad more—at least when I was younger, and I saw him interact with fans—than when a strange woman tells him how sexy and handsome he is. He honestly eats it up. But every time you and I talk about this facet of your job, it seems like you—"

"Hate it?"

I nodded.

"I do."

I frowned. "Except—and no judgment—why did you do those underwear ads?"

Abram's chest expanded with a deep breath and his gaze lifted to the ceiling. "You have no idea how much I wish I hadn't done those ads. It's like, especially since I did them, people assume I'm brainless. Or, they don't assume, they just don't give a shit. We have a few PAs who seem nice, but they make me uncomfortable every time we're in a room together. Always brushing against me when they walk by, even if there's a mile of space around us. I no longer go to VIP ticket holder meet and greets after this one woman—uh . . ."

His eyes widened and he blinked at me.

I lifted an eyebrow. "This one woman?"

He made a resigned sound. "Drunk, she offered to go down on me in front of a room of other VIPs, which inspired more people to make the same offer. Nothing happened, though. I just left, no big deal."

"God," I croaked, and I did my best to ignore the sour taste in my mouth. "I'm sorry."

He shrugged. I didn't like how much he was shrugging, and I'd almost convinced myself the tight feeling behind my eyes wasn't jealousy. Well, not really jealousy in the classical sense, because I trusted Abram. It was more like second-hand distress on his behalf.

A thought occurred to me, a worry, unsettling my stomach a little. *And maybe next time don't have so many jalapeños.*

"What's wrong?" Abram covered my hand with his. "Honestly, don't worry. It's nothing. It's like, what can I do other than avoid the PAs and ignore the VIP sessions, right?"

"Abram, I am going to worry. People shouldn't put their hands on you without your consent. That's not okay." In truth, it also made me uneasy because he sounded like me.

It's nothing.

Nothing happened.

No big deal.

He squeezed my hand. "The tour won't last forever. It wraps up this fall, and then I'll be done."

"Done? Aren't you already working on another album?"

"Yes, but we're not signed for two albums, just the one. I'll stipulate in my contract that I don't want to do a tour next time."

My mouth dropped open. "You—you don't want to do another tour?"

Abram shook his head, looking both determined and tired. "No. No more tours."

"I—I can't believe it."

"Believe it," he ground out, releasing my hand and reaching for his beer.

"This fall." I said the words like I could conjure the time jump just by reciting them. "Where will you go? Do you need to live in New York? To record the next album?"

"No. I'll go wherever you are." He said this easily, like it was already decided, like it was obvious.

And it made me giddy, so I grinned and spoke without thinking, "We should get a house!" *Ah!*

Immediately, I wished the words back.

But he was also grinning. "Yeah. Sure. Where? In LA?"

Now I was out of breath, because I hadn't expected his answer. "Are you serious?"

"Yeah. Why not?" He shrugged, like it was no big deal, and my heart deflated.

Bah. Of course. He wasn't thinking of a house like I was thinking of a house, as a place to raise a family, as a home, a future, stability.

"Yeah. Maybe. No big deal." I forced a smile and nodded, my attention focusing on my rice. "We'll see."

CHAPTER 18
THE INTERIORS OF STARS

Abram

Feeling a little cooped up after a day spent inside, and craving Stan's donuts, Mona convinced me to walk with her down to the donut shop. I didn't require much convincing.

When we made it to Stan's, after we'd ordered, after we'd sat down across from each other, I swiped some of her donut.

"For old time's sake," I said.

Scowling at my laughing eyes, she held the remainder to the side, supposedly out of my reach. "You are never invited again."

That just made me laugh harder. Excusing myself, I returned a few minutes later with six chocolate cake donuts, handing her one and explaining the rest were for tomorrow morning.

"By the way, what time is it?" she asked, patting herself down. "Shoot. I left my phone in our room. I keep forgetting to check the clock."

I shrugged. "I don't know. It's not time for you to leave yet, and that's all I need to know."

"Yes. We still have *two days.* Can you believe it?" She grinned at me, dancing happily in her seat.

I grinned back, pleased to see her mood had improved, but thinking three days wasn't nearly enough. I also wondered when she was going to tell me why she'd grown so quiet after dinner. She'd seemed preoccupied, but not distant. A little sad, a little resigned.

"I have plans for tomorrow," she said, pulling me from my thoughts.

"You do? Tell me." I picked up my own donut, toasted coconut, and took a bite.

"First, we'll go to Andersons and we'll do some leisurely book browsing. And then, dinner at that Italian restaurant where we had our first date."

My eyebrows ticked up an inch. "Our first date?"

"Yeah. You know, right after Andersons you took me to that place, and I had the lasagna."

"You're counting that as our first date?"

She looked at me as though I were odd. "Of course. Activity plus dinner makes it a date."

I laughed. "Mona, I think your hindsight is not twenty-twenty. That was the night you told me I was behaving inappropriately."

"So?"

"So, if it had been a date, then me making the moves wouldn't have been inappropriate."

She opened her mouth, lifting a finger, seemed to reconsider whatever she was going to say, and let her hand drop. "Okay. Good point. Then that means we haven't technically had a first date."

"What about tomorrow?"

"Now there's all this pressure. The *first date*." She made a face. "What did your parents do for their first date?"

"Um, let me see." I glanced over her head, trying to recall the story. "Ah, yes. The way my mom tells it, she *fancied* my father, but he was very quiet, shy. So, one day after a football game—he was on the team in high school, but his parents were really poor and all the money he made from his job went back to the family, so he could never go out with everyone afterward for food—she met him at his car with a picnic. She told him he could take it and eat it on his own, if he wanted. Or, they could eat it together. They ate it together."

Mona sighed. Deeply. "That's so wonderful."

I grinned, liking how her eyes were unfocused and dreamy. *She's such a romantic.* But then, so was I.

Before I thought too much about it, I asked, "How about your parents?"

She blinked rapidly, her eyebrows pulling together, and straightened in her seat. "I don't know."

"You don't know?"

"No. I never asked. They never said. I don't know. Anyway." Mona broke off a piece of her donut and popped it into her mouth, chewing and swallowing. "Did they tell you about their second date?"

She was attempting to change the subject, but I'd made myself a promise to ask her about her family more often. She needed to know she could talk to me about them, good or bad.

"Mona, why don't you talk about your parents?"

Her eyes dimmed. "There's not much to say."

"They're not interesting?"

"Oh, they're very interesting." Under her breath she added, "They're the most interesting people they know."

Hmm. "Would it bother you if I asked questions about them?"

"Why are you suddenly so interested?"

"It's not sudden. Not really. You never talk about your family, and in my experience —with my own family—they're a fundamental part of who I am. I'm interested in you, everything about you. By extension, I'm interested in your parents, how they contributed to who you are."

"Not every family is like yours, Abram. Not everyone's parents are directly involved with, or even interested in, their children."

"I find it really hard to believe your parents aren't completely fascinated by you. I mean, you're fucking amazing."

"As we've established." She flashed me a grin, there and gone, but her gaze remained troubled, or perhaps already exhausted by the subject of her family. "They're not interested in me." She took a deep breath and shook her head. "And that's okay. They're very busy. I understand that they have a lot of responsibilities and demands on their time. Being who they are, I consider myself lucky to—"

"You don't believe that," I cut in, because she was using her academic voice. It was the one she seemed to employ whenever she wanted to distance herself from the information she was sharing. "Why are you saying things you don't believe?"

"I'm—I'm not."

"You are. You don't believe anything you've just said. It's like you were reading from a script, saying the words you feel like you should say, even if they're all false."

She swallowed thickly, her eyes cagey, like she'd been caught.

I didn't want her to feel trapped, I wanted her to know she could share this part of herself with me and be honest. Gentling my voice, I tried to reach her. "You can say they're assholes, Mona. You can say they neglected you, if that's the truth. Or you can say they didn't neglect you, but that they weren't what you needed, if that's the truth. But trying to make the best of a situation in retrospect by telling lies about what actually happened, trying to reframe it, that's like—God—that's like putting a two-by-four in a fancy vase and trying to pass it off as a floral arrangement."

Her mouth twitched, and then she laughed a little despite looking like she didn't want to laugh. But she persisted in silence, saying nothing.

"What I'm saying here is, don't put someone else's spin on your life. Be honest, not just with me, but with yourself. Yeah?"

"Yeah." She nodded slowly, swallowing again. "That makes sense."

I waited, watching her, hoping my small smile was encouraging.

But she wasn't looking at me. Her gaze moved around the restaurant. She scratched the back of her neck, her cheek, the bridge of her nose. She twisted her fingers and sighed, taking another deep breath just to sigh again.

And I waited.

Eventually, Mona cleared her throat, and then blurted, "They're disappointing." Huffing a laugh, she leaned her elbow on the table, her forehead falling to her hand. "They navigate the world very well. They live firmly within it, and are praised for always saying the right thing, being upset and outraged at the right time. They set trends, are edgy but not foolish, and their charisma is suffocating. I don't actually know them very well, as people, but I don't think they know themselves either."

"What do you mean?" I kept my voice soft even though I ached for her and instantly despised them.

"I started to suspect, when I was in college, that my parents are more a product of the world than they are truly themselves. Every decision is made by a committee of experts—what they say, what they wear, who they're photographed with and where—and their interest in me—or Leo, or Lisa—is heavily dependent on how their committee votes. Sometimes I'm the right person for a photo spread, depending on the message they want to convey to the world. But sometimes I'm not."

Mona lifted her head, giving me her eyes back. They were tired, resigned, and I hated that Marie had been right about Mona's parents.

"Do you think that they might change? If you asked them for more of their time, that they might try?"

"No," she answered immediately, no hesitation. "They won't change. But you know what? Nothing changes."

"What do you mean?"

"Nothing changes. Not really. I mean, everything changes. Change is the only constant in the universe. Except, nothing really changes. Case in point, in undergrad, in my philosophy class—which I hated—the professor handed out a list of issues that were supposed to be problems with the world today, and they were spot on. Except, they were written thousands of years ago by a Greek philosopher."

"Huh. What do you think that means?"

"I guess . . ." Her eyes shifted up. "I guess, what's wrong with the world never changes. Selfishness, greed, brutality. There will always be stupid, brutal people. There will always be intelligent, brutal people too. And that's depressing."

"But what about the flip side to that?"

"The flip side?" She picked at her donut.

"Don't you think, if what's wrong with the world stays constant, then what's right with the world—love, compassion, honor, generosity—is constant as well?"

Staring at me intently, her breathing changed. She was doing that thing I was beginning to recognize as the precursor to discussing or saying something difficult.

I'd already braced myself for a big announcement by the time she said, "Abram."

"Yes, Mona?"

"I want a house."

I lifted my donut for another bite. "Okay." *Was that it?* Why would she get herself worked up about that? She'd already mentioned it.

"And a picket fence."

"A what?" I asked around my bite, frowning, certain I'd misheard her. It sounded like she'd said, *And a picket fence.*

"And a garden with roses. And a flagstone path leading through it. And a room—with a piano—that's big enough to also house a Christmas tree between Thanksgiving and New Year's. I want a dog and an alarm system. And a flag on a flagpole that's lowered to half-mast during national tragedies. And dinners together every night at six. And enough bedrooms so that, as my kids get older and need more space, I won't have to bunk them together anymore. But they should definitely share a room when they're younger so they can learn how to compromise. And I want to help someone with their homework and help them win the state science fair."

I blinked. Hard. "Wait. Slow down. Back up. You want—you want—"

"Kids. Not right now, but before my eggs begin to disintegrate. I could freeze them, true. But I'd prefer not to, for a variety of reasons."

I lifted a hand, laughing lightly and studying her sweet, earnest face. "Hold on."

"I'm not saying this dream of mine is a foregone conclusion. I'm not saying I expect you to want the same things I do. I'm just, you know, communicating what my dreams are, should you wish to have them as a data point."

"Mona. Stop. Let me ask something, okay?"

She crossed her arms. She uncrossed her arms. She glanced at her donut and began tearing it into crumb sized pieces. And then she nodded. "Proceed."

"Thank you. First of all, you want a picket fence?"

Her eyes narrowed, like it might be a trick question. "Yes."

I shook my head, making a face of distaste. "Why?"

Statue-still, Mona continued to regard me with doubt. "Because, I guess, I like the way it looks?"

I made a soft sound of disagreement, wiping my hands with a napkin. "We don't want a picket fence, believe me. They typically use pine, because you don't paint cedar, and then you have to keep repainting, and the wood rots, or the sections fall over. It's a real pain. We should get metal fence, aluminum, if you have your heart set on one, and assuming it's not for security reasons. I mean, a picket fence isn't going to keep anyone out. Aluminum is low maintenance and it looks nice."

Now she was looking at me like I was crazy.

I held up both hands. "If you don't believe me, just ask my dad. He doesn't talk much, but he'll have a lot to say about fences. And I'm sorry, but I'll never live it down if we get a pine picket fence. He'll be out there painting it every time he comes over."

She made a strangled sound. "Abram!"

I crossed my arms, giving my head another shake so she knew I was serious. "I'm not budging on this. You don't know how my dad is about home construction and landscaping. Every conversation will start with, 'Hey, so, can we talk about the fence?'"

Her hands came down on the table and she leaned forward. "After everything I just said, *that's* what you want to talk about? The fence?"

"Yes."

"Why?"

"Because it's the only thing I disagreed with," I shrugged, giving her a small smile.

Mona blinked like I'd blown dust in her eyes, and then leaned back in her chair again, her pretty lips parted. "You want to have a family? Kids?"

"Absolutely."

"And a house? In a quiet, suburban neighborhood?"

"I honestly don't care where we do it, but we can't have a picket fence."

She wrinkled the bridge of her nose, blinking again. "It's not about the fence. But you said, when we were in Aspen, that you hadn't given marriage much thought."

"I haven't. But you don't need to be married to have a family, children, a home."

"So you don't want to be married?"

"Are you proposing?" I grinned, lifting an eyebrow.

She made a face, clearly trying her best not to laugh, and asked, "Since when have you wanted kids?"

"Since forever." I scratched my beard, busy imagining what this dream of hers would entail, and I couldn't help but think about my own childhood. Moments I'd witnessed between my parents, how they'd shared their struggles and joys. Of course I wanted that.

Things hadn't always been easy for my family. My parents had struggled financially to make my dad's business work, and we'd had lean years. But I'd watched my mom and dad fight to make their marriage work, fight for my sister and me, fight for each other. Apparently, Mona wanted it too, presumably with me.

No. Obviously with you. She wouldn't have told you if she didn't want it with you.

Indulging my imagination, my mind drifted to scenes from our future. What would that be like? A house, kids, a home with Mona? *Beyond heavenly.*

Her gaze softened. "I had no idea."

"Well, now you do." My grin grew because she was smiling at me, her eyes dazed and warm and happy, and I lost myself a little in her gorgeous whiskey gaze. Truly, she was breathtaking.

I could get used to this, making Mona happy on accident, just by being myself.

Speaking of which.

On a sudden impulse, I blurted, "I need to tell you something."

She nodded eagerly. "Yes. Of course."

"So, I'm worried about you and what happens when the press release goes out tomorrow."

"Abram—"

"No, wait. Listen. I'm confessing here." I didn't believe this admission would make her happy but being honest felt important.

"Okay. Fine. Proceed." She didn't roll her eyes, but she looked like she was tempted.

I wavered for a second before admitting, "I'm glad you turned down your sister."

That got her attention. "Glad?"

"Yes. Relieved. Happy."

"Really?"

"Things are going to be significantly more difficult than I thought they would be. I'm going to fight the world for you. But part of me—the selfish part—really wants everyone to know."

Her smile wide, Mona reached across the table and entwined our fingers. "That we're together?"

"Yes. I want them to know that you're mine." I lifted the fingers I loved so much and kissed them, one at a time. "And that I'm yours."

* * *

We were most of the way back to the B&B when Mona said, "It's frustrating that people can't use the same adjectives to describe men that are used to describe women, and vice versa."

I glanced at her. "What? What do you mean?"

"Like, graceful. You call me or parts of my body graceful. And even though they apply to you, I wouldn't say so aloud." We stopped at the gate for her to enter the code.

"Why not?" I didn't see a problem with being called graceful.

"I wouldn't want to, I don't know, make you think I—bah!" The gate buzzed.

I opened it for her to walk through. "Do you think of me as graceful?"

"Y-yes," she said, stumbling on the word while we climbed the concrete steps.

"Good." We paused at the keypad for the door. "Because I am graceful."

Mona lifted her chin and grinned at me. "Yes. In so many ways." Her eyes seemed to grow hazy and hot, and I didn't need to guess what was on her mind.

I shoved my hands in the pockets of my jacket. Not touching her was hard. In fact, when she looked at me like she was looking at me now, a lot of things were hard.

Clearing my throat, I withdrew one hand to open the door to the bed and breakfast. "Then tell me I am. It's a beautiful word, with a beautiful meaning, no matter how it's applied, unless it's ironic or sarcastic. I think you should tell me how you feel, what you feel about me, and not worry about baggage that comes along with the adjectives."

"Beautiful?" She looked over her shoulder, waiting for me to draw even with her before continuing to the stairs.

"Thank you. I rather am, aren't I?"

She chuckled, her gaze sweeping down and then up. "Yes, you *rather* are. Let me see, what other terms, words, and labels can I apply now that the entire vocabulary is open to me?"

I bent and whispered in her ear, "Luscious?"

She almost missed a step, her grin wavering. "Absolutely."

"Sweet."

Her smile returned. "Yep. And kind."

"Thank you." That was a good one. Really good.

"Gentle," she said thoughtfully, just as we made it to the top landing. Adding in rapid succession just as I unlocked and opened the door, "Brilliant, lovely, tender, sexy, competent." She strolled into the suite.

I followed, shutting the door and leaning against it. "Competent?"

"Yes. Competent." She turned to face me, her hands on her hips. "And, honestly, I feel like it's the greatest of all compliments. So few people are actually competent."

I nodded. "Okay. I'll take it."

"How about curvy?" She turned her head to one side, walking toward me in a way that seemed more like a prowl, while watching me out of the corner of her eye.

"Am I curvy?" I shoved my hands in my pockets. The urge to always be touching her would be my undoing. *She needs space, and time.* I had no doubt we'd work things through and come out on the other side stronger. But for now, keeping my hands to myself was the only way to stay sane.

"Oh yes." Her eyes dropped, moving over my body slowly, stopping somewhere around the vicinity of my hips.

I grimaced. There was no mistaking the *curviness* in the front of my pants. "Want to watch a movie?"

Mona's gaze cut back to mine and she grinned, but also looked perplexed. "What? No. I'm appreciating you, and your superior exterior. Including all your curves." Slowly, so slowly, she stepped forward. Her stunning eyes hot with intent.

My lungs filled with fire. "Mona." I groaned through gritted teeth.

Her lips parted, her lashes fluttering, her body surging forward firmly. "I'd like to help you with that."

"We should do something else." I shook my head, balling my hands into fists inside my jacket, trying not to lose my mind.

She shook her head in a contrary movement. "What? No! In this economy?"

I exhaled a laugh but sucked in an abrupt breath as she fit her hand between us, stroking me over my jeans. "Let me help. I really, really want to."

Encircling her wrist, I pulled it away and behind her back. She quickly replaced it with her other hand, reminding me of an octopus. The next stroke more aggressive, she lifted her chin to place biting kisses on mine.

"If we only have two days left, we should make the most of it."

I pulled the second hand away and fought the consuming impulse to turn her and take her against the door. "But we'll have more than two days the next time." Unable to help myself, I stole a quick kiss from her soft lips. "A movie?"

"The next time is so far away." She nuzzled my neck, lifting to her tiptoes to suck my ear in her mouth. "I don't have a lot of experience with blow jobs, but I'd *love* to suck your co—"

"Mona!" No way was I going to let her finish that sentence, but I shivered as her tongue worked in my ear, and my brain finished the sentence for me. "It's not a good idea." My voice cracked. At this point, I didn't know if I was talking to her or myself.

"Abram." Her hot breath spilling against my neck pulled another shiver out of me, her hand somehow managing to break free to stroke me again. "I bet it tastes like candy."

I wanted to touch her, but I didn't trust myself. My hands hovered over her upper arms without making contact as hers unzipped my pants, reaching inside. *Oh—*

"Fuck."

"Maybe a little later." Her sexy chuckle slid over me, making me dizzy. "I miss you. I want you. And I want your big dick in my mouth."

I couldn't think. Words failed me. Her hand was now on me, tugging, massaging. I fully admit I was not strong enough to say no.

Mona rubbed her body against mine as she shoved my pants down my hips, lowering herself to her knees as she held my eyes. "Don't you want me?"

"Yes." It was really the only word in my vocabulary at this point. My next song would just be the word *yes*.

Hot, electric sparks of anticipation ignited at the base of my spine and I licked my lips, near panting, watching her, devouring the sight of Mona on her knees. Her hot, wet, sweet mouth an inch from my dick. She kissed the head and I clenched my jaw, flattening my palms on the door behind me to keep from fisting them in her hair, but *—oh how I want to.*

In the next moment, her lips closed over my cock, her hand sliding from my pelvis to my stomach, pushing my shirt up for her eyes. I took it off. And then I grabbed her hand, pressing it to my skin as her mouth sucked, so hot, so fucking soft.

I cursed, my fingers closing around hers. But then I released her hand, not wanting to hold her too tight. I was already so close. It felt like being on the edge of a blade, so frustrated by my inability to make this last, I physically hurt. But also greedy for the promise of a happy ending.

"Mona. I'm going to come. I'm—" I pressed the base of my palms into my eye sockets, trying and failing to control the jerking of my hips as I pumped into her mouth, falling off the razor's edge into an abyss of ecstasy.

So good. So fucking good.

I couldn't catch my breath.

My heart was pounding like mad.

And she was suddenly gone.

Opening my eyes and leaning heavily against the door, I heard a faucet run in the other room. *The bathroom*, my brain told me. I gave myself a minute to calm. The whole thing, from first stroke to finish, must've lasted less than three minutes, but I felt like I'd sprinted a mile. Eventually, my heart slowed, and I bent to gather my jeans.

"What are you doing?"

I lifted my eyes and did a quick double take. Mona had taken off her shirt and pants, leaving her in—no lie—a matching tiger-print underwear and bra.

Weakly, I straightened, unable to tear my eyes away. I choked on a spike of raw hunger, a powerful, visceral, scorching ache thrummed below my skin, everywhere. She advanced, and I held a hand out to stop her, wanting—no, *needing*—to see her this way.

Messy ponytail, eyes hazy, red swollen lips, neck flushed pink, black lace along the top curves of her breasts leading to the white, orange, and black animal print. Her chest rising and falling. The same black lace was at the waist of her underwear, and I think I blacked out a little as my eyes moved down her long legs.

"What?" she asked, her tone breathless, but also vaguely uncertain.

I blinked, my eyes cutting to hers. "And thus, I die."

She grinned, looking happy. *So happy.* "Come on, tiger." Like before, she crooked a finger, daring me to follow. And like last time, I had no choice. I would follow her anywhere.

"Take your pants off and come to bed."

* * *

We were naked.

I'd just taken her from behind—at her direction, and careful to keep my hands *only* on her hips, though the temptation had been strong to roam and stroke and grab as well as smack her glorious ass—and now I was sure I'd relive this day in my dreams every night for the rest of my life.

Tangled together, her head rested on my chest and her body pressed along mine. One of my hands was on her bottom, the other covered hers where it lay on my ribs. We were quiet. Neither of us had spoken for several minutes, each navigating our own thoughts, and I was reminded of that night in Chicago. The last night.

The first night, my brain corrected. I smiled, because it was. It was the first night we'd slept together and the first night she'd listened to my heart. I'd been so frustrated, but I'd also been concerned, determined to give her the space and time she needed to figure things out.

Just like now, except much less frustrated.

Mona stirred, her leg sliding higher on mine. "What are you thinking about?"

"Chicago."

Her arm on me tightened. "After The Blues Brothers?"

"Yes."

"Me too." I felt her smile against my chest, her hand curling on my body. "I wanted you, very badly."

I chuckled. "You have no idea."

"Uh, I think I have some idea. I mean, I was lying there trying to figure out how to cross dimensions and locate one where I didn't have to lie to you, one where we could be together."

"And now we're here." I dipped my chin to my chest as she lifted her head, our gazes meeting. "So I guess you did."

Now she smiled, her attention flickering to my left cheek and then back to my eyes. "Yeah. I guess I did." Resettling, she snuggled closer, inhaling deeply. "And your heart is just the same."

I bit my bottom lip, liking her compliment, and thinking back to Aspen, to the night she'd asked to listen to my heart. It had been a critical night for us, the first time she'd heard "Hold a Grudge," and she'd given me her letter, but I'd—

I frowned. "Hey."

"Yeah?"

"What was in the letter I burned?"

Mona was quiet for a beat, and then she busted out laughing, shaking her head and turning to hide her face in the crook of my shoulder.

Another automatic smile claimed my mouth at the sound of her laugh, but— suddenly, given her reaction—I really wanted to know. "Hey. Tell me." I rolled to my side, making her roll to hers, and I pushed my fingers into her long hair, angling her chin to give it a soft kiss. I then moved to her lips. Whispering against her mouth, I beseeched, "Tell me."

She grinned, her eyes bright. "I told you in Aspen, when you burned it. It was the truth."

"About what? About what happened in Chicago?"

"About how I felt. About what I wanted."

"What did you want?"

"Uh, interdimensional time travel, and—" Her hand on my ribs slid down to my hip and then up to my chest. "This."

Not following, my eyebrows pulled together. "What? Me naked?"

"Yes. Always. But mostly—" Her fingers over my chest flexed. "—this. This is what I wanted. This heart."

I swallowed around a sudden thickness and tightness and depth and breadth and gaping cavern of inescapable craving, tripping headlong into her, knowing I'd always be her fool. This time, I welcomed the notion.

"My heart is yours, Mona." I kissed her nose, my voice like sandpaper. "Always."

Her brilliant eyes moved between mine, glassy with emotion. She feathered her fingers into my hair, her touch gentle, cherishing.

"And my heart is yours, Abram Harris," she whispered. "Infinitely."

EPILOGUE
THE CONTINUOUS SPECTRUM OF LIGHT

Abram

Waiting for Mona's plane to land at Heathrow, I paced back and forth in front of the arrivals exit, tapping my fingers against my leg while I pretended to be on the phone. I'd cut my hair short and shaved my beard the day after the tour ended last week, and I'd been careful to avoid being photographed since.

I also wore a suit, hoping it would aid in my quest for anonymity, and because tonight was Marie's rehearsal dinner. I likely wouldn't have much of a chance to change by the time Mona and I made it to the castle.

So far, while I paced, I'd received a few interested double takes, but no requests for an autograph. Nowadays, this felt miraculous.

Mona was flying in for my sister's destination wedding. Years ago, Marie organized and planned her friend Janie's wedding. Now, Janie Sullivan had decided to return the favor. She'd called me with the idea a few months ago and I'd immediately offered to pay the hotel and food bill for all guests. Janie covered the air travel (she owned a private jet, long story) and flew everyone over to London. She also organized the Harry Potter themed bachelorette party last weekend that Mona attended, but for which I was—happily—absent.

Don't get me wrong. I liked Marie's friends, but all together in a group, they could be overwhelming. Especially her friend Sandra.

Matt, my soon-to-be brother-in-law, picked up the bill for everything else. Except the dress. My parents bought Marie's dress, mostly because it was the only thing we'd let them pay for.

When my sister had discovered what we'd done, she called me up crying. "You're crazy. Why did you do this?"

"Because I can," I said. "And because I love you. Don't make a big deal out of it, Hufflepuff." All the planning had been worth it, to make Marie happy.

I checked my watch and glanced at the arrivals board. According to the sign, the flight from Geneva had landed twenty minutes ago, and I knew she had no checked baggage. Since she'd flown over last weekend, her bags were still at the hotel. Assuming no holdups at customs, she should've been exiting the arrivals door, any minute.

Any minute now.

My phone buzzed in my hand, catching me off guard. Lowering it to check the incoming number, Mona's face filled the screen.

I answered immediately. "Hello?"

"Hey! How are you? How is Marie? Is she excited? Where are you? Are you here?"

I grinned, the sound of her voice taking the edge off the cold, granite block of missing her I carried whenever we weren't together, and wherever I went. After almost a year of mostly separation with short windows of meeting in random cities, I'd grown accustomed to the ache. What I hadn't grown accustomed to was the loss of breath each time we met again.

Or, as Mona would say, each time we met for a *rendezvous.*

The last six months had been full of highs and lows, with the worst weeks coming right after we went public with our relationship. I hated many of Redburn's fans' reactions to the news, how they talked about Mona on social media, how they picked apart her appearance, interviews she'd given in the past, making memes out of her pictures, and how they felt entitled to message me with their "thoughts."

But a few months ago, my producer, seeing that I was struggling not to feel betrayed by my fans' vitriol, said to me, "Be consumed by your art, Abram. Not the people who consume it." That had made all the difference. Like Leo's words about softness, it was one of the truest things I'd ever heard.

"Abram? Are you there?"

"Sorry." I was still looking for her in the sea of faces. "I'm here. Are you past customs?"

"Yes. And I'm past the arrivals exit. Did you get the bag I left at the hotel?"

"Yes, I have the bag you left last week. It's still at the hotel."

Mona had flown out last weekend, two days before I'd arrived, but hadn't been able to stay for the entire week. She was so close to the end of her tenure at CERN and couldn't spare the time. I couldn't leave the States until after several New York meetings about the new contract and album.

"Great! Glad you have the bag. Did you pick up the car?"

Frowning at a woman with long dark hair who was not Mona, I turned toward the elevators, searching for her there. "Yep. I have the car."

"I don't see you yet." She sounded distracted. "Should I wait on one of the benches?"

My forehead wrinkled as I twisted my neck, hunting for her. "Wait, are you in terminal three?"

"Yes. Terminal three," she confirmed just as an announcement sounded over the loudspeaker. I heard it echo on her side. Mona was definitely nearby.

"You don't see me?" I scanned the mass of people. The crowds in every direction would've made it difficult for a shorter person to see, but I was easily the tallest person in the arrivals area.

"Wait, you're here? I don't—ah! I see you!"

Turning in a slow circle, I shook my head. "I still don't see you."

"Now I'm hiding because I'm drooling. Good Lord, that suit."

I straightened, pleased, sliding a hand down the front of my jacket. "Do you like it? I had it made in New York."

"Do I like it? Does each action have an equal but opposite reaction?"

"Nerd."

"Sorry. Newton. Not the fig kind."

I laughed. "Mona. Where are you?"

"I'm here, but I need another minute to admire that to which I aspire."

"Nice rhyme. Come here."

"Not yet. Do that circle spinning thing again."

"I'm feeling a little objectified right now," I teased.

"Then your feelings are spot on."

I turned quickly, because I heard her voice in stereo that time—over the phone and nearby—my attention skimming the crowd, focusing on those closest until I found a woman staring at me. Except—

Wait.

"Mona?"

She wore a mischievous grin and fire engine red lipstick that matched her short dyed hair—no, not her hair. A wig. Her eyes were lined in thick black makeup, her body encased in a tight black shirt, a leather skirt, and black and white striped thigh-high stockings. On her feet she sported combat boots. Around her neck was a leather choker with spikes, and in the center of her nose was a ring.

"Hey, handsome."

Officially speechless, I stared at her. One hundred percent sure it was Mona, but still disbelieving my eyes, I unabashedly devoured this unexpected but not at all unwelcomed sight.

Her grin widened and she strolled closer, hooking a leather jacket at her shoulder over her black backpack.

Biting her tongue playfully, she wagged her eyebrows. "Looks like you're not the only one in disguise, Wall Street."

* * *

I couldn't stop staring at her legs. A big problem since I also wasn't used to driving on the left side of the road.

When Mona flew up last week for the bachelorette party, she'd taken the train out to the countryside and back to the airport without much issue. She'd been photographed just twice at Heathrow as she arrived, and only once in the Underground.

But this time, as we would be together, we'd implicitly agreed on renting a car. Once the news of our relationship broke last March, it seemed like traveling together on any public transportation—or even walking together on the street, no matter where we were in the world—ultimately led to mobs and disaster.

"Watch out," she said for the tenth time because it was my tenth turn. "Are you sure you don't want me to drive?"

"You can drive if you want." I shrugged, clearing my throat and struggling not to stare at her thighs again. Something about the combination of the thigh-highs and the leather skirt—*something about all of it*—made me want to do very, very bad things. "But then my hands will be free, and we might not make it to Marie's rehearsal at all."

Mona laughed, sounding delighted. "Okay, subject change. How are you? How's the new album? How's the band?"

"Great, now. We're almost ready for the studio. Charlie and Ruthie are looking forward to spending Christmas in Geneva, and you'll get to meet Broderick." After the wedding, I would be flying back with her to Switzerland and that was it. No more tour. No more concert dates on the calendar. No more meeting in random cities for only days or hours and then parting for weeks. We would be living together from now on. *Finally.*

I didn't blame Mona for deciding to stay at CERN through the fall semester. The work she did sounded exciting—well, she made it sound exciting—plus every time she stepped foot in the USA she was mobbed by paparazzi. We'd hired her a body-guard the last time we'd met up—in Miami—but, honestly, I didn't want her traveling in the States unless we were on the same plane.

Where I went, the band and support personnel followed. The new album would be recorded in Switzerland, with pickups and final mastering in LA after Mona and I returned to the States.

"How about you? Work? Grants? Those assholes still withholding your funding?"

One of the deepest lows came two months ago. According to Mona, the funding for three of her grants—which were fully awarded through the remainder of the fiscal year ending in June—had been suddenly halted, the grants managers claiming they required rereview of her progress reports.

That was bullshit. She insisted it could be anything—maybe she'd pissed off someone during the London symposium over the summer, maybe she'd irritated an important person at CERN, maybe one of her thesis advisors was frustrated that she hadn't returned to LA yet—who knows?

But I assumed the culprit was our relationship. She received the notice one week after we were photographed together in Rome having a romantic dinner at the Piazza Navona. She'd worn an unbelievable red dress and the press had gone nuts, calling her the "Philandering Physicist."

Philandering? What? Fucking idiotic nonsense. It didn't even make sense.

Currently, Mona sighed. Shrugged. Sighed again. "It doesn't matter. I figured out a solution. I should be able to defend my thesis in the spring without funding issues."

I glanced at her, surprised. "You got the Darwinger grant?"

"No," she ground out. "It went to someone else."

Motherfu— "Then how . . .?"

She scrunched her face, looking cute and indecisive, but finally admitted, "I'm using the fun money account my parents set up. I'm funding everything with that."

My hands tightened on the steering wheel as I absorbed this startling revelation, but I was careful to keep my expression and voice serene. "Oh?"

We'd been dating almost a year and I still hadn't officially met her parents. But I had been photographed with them. Twice. DJ Tang and Exotica had attended several of the same industry events as me, and we'd been photographed on the red carpet together—both times their publicist approached my publicist and said, *Let's make this happen*—but they didn't actually talk to me.

Although, her dad mumbled, "Smile like you mean it."

They'd swooped in, posed for the photos, and left without a backward glance. The next morning's headline read, "*One Big Happy Family*."

It was the strangest. When I told Mona, she hadn't seemed at all surprised, but she was embarrassed. I told her not to worry.

"Yes. I'm going to use the money." She exhaled the words, like they pained her. "I know you suggested it two months ago as a stopgap, but I needed to think about it. The thing is, as you know, my therapist and I have been talking weekly, and so I told her about the idea." Mona's therapist was one of my most favorite people in the world. But I'll get to that later. "Anyway, she and I were talking about stressors in my past, my parents, the nature of neglect in all its forms, and whatnot, and how I was so tense about the grants. And, well, she pointed out that we—all of us—are born with a different set of resources. Like you, for example."

"Me?"

"Yes. You came from a family with an abundance of love, but not always an abundance of financial security. She asked me which I thought was more important and if it made sense for you to reject your parents' love because other children—i.e. me— grew up neglected."

"Huh." See? The woman was amazing.

"We went back and forth for a while, because the issue is obviously not that simple. Money buys advantages that love cannot, and—anyway—after we discussed the nature of merit-based reward systems, bias in peer review grant awards, the problems with inherited wealth and so forth, I made a decision to use the money to finish my thesis, and I've committed to not feeling gross about it."

I wanted to say, *Hell. Yes.* But instead I simply nodded and said, "Okay."

Since Mona had started talking to Dr. Kasai last spring, she'd become so much more comfortable in her own skin, so much more willing to appreciate a moment rather than look for reasons to second-guess her enjoyment of it.

As an example, she loved being tied up. She loved blindfolds and handcuffs on either or both of us. The distinction Dr. Kasai had made clear for her, which Mona told me about when we'd met in London early over the summer, was the difference between giving control and losing control. Mona loved the idea that she was giving something rather than losing it.

"It's like, in my dream best-case scenario, I win the Nobel Prize in physics," she muttered fiercely, obviously still thinking about her funding situation and giving me the sense she was speaking to herself. "And the Darwinger Institute can choke on a dick because they then can't claim any credit."

I almost choked on air, sending her a surprised look. "Choke on a dick? Where'd you pick that up?"

Mona's smile was small but impish. "Your sister's friend Sandra used it last week during the bachelorette party. I've heard Gabby say it in the past. But after Sandra used the phrase, I warmed up to it."

Ah, Sandra. She was a handful.

The rest of the drive passed uneventfully, which was good. A few times, I caught myself staring too long while she talked, or glancing too often at the band of skin where her short skirt hit her legs. I'd also been distracted by my generous imagination, considering how best to make use of our disguises before the rehearsal dinner. . . since we were making such good time.

But when we arrived and were crossing the lobby on the way to our room, she stopped, squeezed my hand, and gave me a kiss on the cheek.

"Okay, I'll see you later."

"Wait. Where are you going?"

"I have to meet the other bridesmaids for rehearsal." She gestured over her shoulder with her thumb.

"The rehearsal isn't for another hour."

"Oh, no. I'm not talking about the wedding rehearsal. Well, I am. Sort of. It's a—but, well, you'll see tonight."

I caught her arm as she turned away again, disappointment landing on my shoulders like a shove. "Wait, wait. Mona, wait." I slid my hand down to capture hers again, staring deeply into her eyes. "Don't you need to change first?"

She grinned a slow grin at my obvious hint, and then she giggled, sounding gleeful. Stepping forward suddenly, she threw her arms over my shoulders and kissed me, her nails scratching the back of my neck, her tongue a hot, hungry slide against mine.

Before I could react the way I wanted—carry her off to our room—she caressed her hands down to my bottom, gave it a double pat, and then leaned away to break the kiss.

"See you tonight," she said, wagging her eyebrows. "Don't change the suit."

Turning once more, Mona left me to stare after her. I was too distracted, enjoying the view of her backside walking away to say anything else. She gave great view.

But as soon as Mona turned the corner, I shook my head, coming back to myself, and decided I'd try to find my parents, see if I could help with any last-minute arrangements.

Pulling out my phone, I sent my mom a text. But just as I finished, a flash of color caught my eye and I glanced up. I did a double take. And then I took a step back.

My cousin Anna, and my sister Marie, and all of Marie's close friends were walking across the lobby, and they were all attired in black leather, bright neon spandex, and various random wigs. Even Marie's friend Ashley, who was visibly pregnant, was similarly dressed.

I braced myself, straightening my spine, especially when Sandra—the handful—caught sight of me and smirked.

"Whale, whale, whale. Look who it is." Elizabeth Moretti stopped in front of me, her hands on her hips. She was wearing an insane amount of blue eyeshadow and what looked like a David Bowie wig.

My sister stepped forward first to give me a hug, pressing a kiss to my cheek and then using her thumb to rub off excess lipstick. "Did you get Mona? I was just about to text you."

"I did. She went that way." I tilted my head toward the room where Mona had disappeared and then turned to greet Anna, giving her a tight embrace.

Sandra rubbed her hands together. "Excellent. Excellent."

As soon as Anna and I separated, Janie Sullivan—who wasn't wearing a wig, her naturally curly red hair styled like she'd just survived a tornado—gave me a searching look. "There's something different about you, Abram."

"His hair?" Fiona Archer pointed to my head, looking me over with the disinterested attention of a mom surveying one of her kids' friends.

Janie narrowed her eyes, inspecting me. "No. His hair is the same, isn't it?"

I tucked my lips between my teeth. For all of Janie's brilliance, she was terrible with faces and features.

"Can we talk for a moment about the devastating loss of his glorious beard?" Ashley Winston Runous pointed to my jaw with one hand and rubbed her belly with the other. "Damn shame, Abram. Damn. Shame."

I chuckled at her, rolling my eyes.

"It's not his face." Janie scrunched hers as she said this, scrutinizing me. "But it is his face. There's something . . . different."

"The suit?" Anna tried, straightening my tie. "That's a nice suit, Abram. You look very handsome." My cousin gave me a big smile before adding, "Almost like a real adult."

"Har." I elbowed her.

"While we're on the subject, can I have the name of your tailor?" Sandra piped in. "You and Alex have the same build. It's hard to find suits that fit those shoulders. I agree with Janie, though. You look different, kid."

Lifting an eyebrow at her use of the word *kid,* especially since her husband was younger than me, I was about to make a charming joke and then excuse myself when a quiet voice said, "He's in love."

All eyes turned to Kat Caravel-Tyson O'Malley, who was wearing a black leather dress, a blue wig in long ponytails, and a small, knowing smile. "That's why he looks different. He's happy."

* * *

Apparently, even before Janie decided to throw my sister a destination wedding, The Bangles tribute band had been in the works. It was revealed just after dinner that the bridesmaids had been meeting over Skype on Tuesday nights, Chicago time, and Mona had tried to make the virtual practices whenever possible. She'd been reteaching herself the piano.

I knew Matt was a *huge* The Bangles fan. He'd even corrected me once when I'd said, "So, you're a huge Bangles fan?"

Matt had grimaced, shaking his head quickly, seeming to struggle for a moment, and then blurted, "I'm so sorry I have to be a jerk right now and correct you. It's *The Bangles*. You can't just call them *Bangles*, that could mean bracelets. I have nothing against bracelets. I'm just not a big fan of them like I am of The Bangles. Or someone might mistake your meaning as—*God forbid*—the Cincinnati Bengals."

He looked at me like he was pained, like correcting me physically hurt him, but he simply could not stop himself. And that's when I realized Marie was right. Matt and Mona were basically the same person.

Honestly, I was okay with that.

The ladies had their final practice in person. It took place during the hour prior to the rehearsal dinner itself. Marie and Ashley sang lead and harmony. Mona played the piano, and Anna—who was also the maid of honor—was on the drums. The rest of Marie's friends rounded out the band in various roles. Janie and Kat didn't play an instrument, so they played the part of backup singers with tambourines.

We all saw Marie and the rest of them in their getups during the actual rehearsal for the wedding. Matt and us groomsmen attributed the outfits to some kind of brides-maids bonding ritual. When the real plan revealed itself after dinner, we were all shocked and awed.

The great thing about having so many people in the tribute band was that they could take turns. Elizabeth Moretti also played the piano. She took over for Mona so that she could dance with me. Ashley sang lead vocals so that Marie and Matt could spin around the dance floor.

Later, much later, Matt requested a non-The Bangles song—"Careless Whisper" by Wham!—earning him a particular kind of look from my sister. But Ashley, Ashley's husband Drew, and I stepped up, making it happen for the couple.

By the end of the evening, it was pretty clear who the musicians were, but everyone had a great time pitching in and helping out. It was my favorite gig in forever.

"Such a great time." Mona used my hand to twirl herself. I carried her boots and she carried the rest of her champagne in her free hand. "What kind of tribute band do you want?" She glanced over her shoulder at me.

This time, stay.
Let me usher you to bliss.
Nothing else for me here
Just you gone, only memories remain to reminisce
Telling tales of your skin, your eyes, your mind, your kiss
Gasps and sighs and soft greedy sounds,
Amazes, razes, dazes, and astounds.
You
Never
Stay.

"Hey. Buddy. Eyes up here," she whispered.

I didn't lift my eyes. "In a minute."

Mona laughed quietly and continued pulling me towards our room.

I twist and turn and ache to touch
I promise I won't hurt you, I hope you won't hurt me much.
I see only you,
I know you want me the same way
The pull, the push, but too soon it's over.
I
Never
Stay.

It was late, but I didn't know why she was whispering. The entire hotel had been reserved exclusively for the wedding. The only guests on this floor were us, and most of the other guests were still dancing in the hall.

Whereas Mona and I had left just moments ago, after I'd bent my lips to her neck and whispered a few lines I'd been thinking about all night in her ear.

"No taste of you will ever be enough,
I try to take things slow, but you tell me you want it rough."

She'd shivered, her breathing changed, and—grabbing the lapels of my jacket—she pulled me off the dance floor mumbling something like, "VOILA! Electromagnetic desire."

Finally, we arrived at our door. Releasing her hand, I unlocked it, opened it, tugged her through, dropped her boots, shut the door, and pushed Mona against it.

Your eyes betray you, how they search for and find me
Burns in dreams, singes reality
Stealing my breath, my thought, my sanity
A moment without you, an endless eternity.
We
Never
Stay.

"Hello." I braced my hands on either side of her head, liking my view.

"Hello, Wall Street." Mona sipped champagne, and then decided to chug it, watching me over the rim. When she finished, she smacked her lips, dropped the plastic cup to the floor, and smiled. "What are we doing?"

An unhurried grin took my mouth, and my attention drifted to her lips, the neckline of her shirt, the swell of her breasts. My hands fell away from the door, lowering to the mesmerizing skin between the hem of her skirt and the tops of her stockings.

"I like these stockings." I fingered the band at the top. "You should wear them more often."

Mona bit her bottom lip, her hand sliding inside my jacket. "I like this suit." She tugged at my shirt. "You should take it off."

I smiled at her bossiness, getting ready to lift her skirt and play my part. But then I stopped, and I looked at her, and I committed to memory how divine of a moment this was. Here we danced on the precipice of something new.

After tonight, a tomorrow with Mona, and a day after that, and a day after that.

So this time, don't leave.
This time, tell me you'll stay.
This time, don't let life steal you away.

"Mona, my love." I kissed the tender skin below her ear.

"That's me." She tilted her head, giving me more access, her hands sliding under my shirt.

"No costumes tonight." I covered her left breast with my hand, seeking her heartbeat beneath. "I just want you."

Her fingers lifted to my jaw, angling my face just far enough away so that our eyes could meet and dance. Staring with me, she nodded, and lifted her chin for a sweet kiss. I gave it to her.

We would have opportunity for costumes and lady rockers and Wall Street tycoons later.

But not now.

Now, we finally had time.

The End

Scan me to receive new book updates and news from Penny!

Scan me if you'd like a signed copy of this or any Penny Reid book!

ABOUT THE AUTHOR

Penny Reid is the *New York Times*, *Wall Street Journal*, and *USA Today* bestselling author of the Winston Brothers and Knitting in the City series. She used to spend her days writing federal grant proposals as a biomedical researcher, but now she writes kissing books. Penny is an obsessive knitter and manages the #OwnVoices-focused mentorship incubator / publishing imprint, Smartypants Romance. She lives in Seattle Washington with her husband, three kids, and dog named Hazel.

Come find me -
Mailing List: http://pennyreid.ninja/newsletter/
Goodreads: http://www.goodreads.com/ReidRomance
Facebook: www.facebook.com/pennyreidwriter
Instagram: www.instagram.com/reidromance
Twitter: www.twitter.com/reidromance
TikTok: https://www.tiktok.com/@authorpennyreid
Patreon: https://www.patreon.com/smartypantsromance
Email: pennreid@gmail.com …hey, you! Email me ;-)

OTHER BOOKS BY PENNY REID

Knitting in the City Series

(Interconnected Standalones, Adult Contemporary Romantic Comedy)

Neanderthal Seeks Human: A Smart Romance (#1)

Neanderthal Marries Human: A Smarter Romance (#1.5)

Friends without Benefits: An Unrequited Romance (#2)

Love Hacked: A Reluctant Romance (#3)

Beauty and the Mustache: A Philosophical Romance (#4)

Ninja at First Sight (#4.75)

Happily Ever Ninja: A Married Romance (#5)

Dating-ish: A Humanoid Romance (#6)

Marriage of Inconvenience: (#7)

Neanderthal Seeks Extra Yarns (#8)

Knitting in the City Coloring Book (#9)

Winston Brothers Series

(Interconnected Standalones, Adult Contemporary Romantic Comedy, spinoff of Beauty and the Mustache)

Beauty and the Mustache (#0.5)

Truth or Beard (#1)

Grin and Beard It (#2)

Beard Science (#3)

Beard in Mind (#4)

Beard In Hiding (#4.5)

Dr. Strange Beard (#5)

Beard with Me (#6)

Beard Necessities (#7)

Winston Brothers Paper Doll Book (#8)

<u>Hypothesis Series</u>

(New Adult Romantic Comedy Trilogies)

<u>Elements of Chemistry</u>

<u>Laws of Physics</u>

<u>Irish Players (Rugby) Series – by L.H. Cosway and Penny Reid</u>

(Interconnected Standalones, Adult Contemporary Sports Romance)

<u>The Hooker and the Hermit (#1)</u>

<u>The Pixie and the Player (#2)</u>

<u>The Cad and the Co-ed (#3)</u>

<u>The Varlet and the Voyeur (#4)</u>

<u>Dear Professor Series</u>

(New Adult Romantic Comedy)

<u>Kissing Tolstoy (#1)</u>

<u>Kissing Galileo (#2)</u>

<u>Ideal Man Series</u>

(Interconnected Standalones, Adult Contemporary Romance Series of Jane Austen Reimaginings)

<u>Pride and Dad Jokes (#1, coming 2022)</u>

<u>Man Buns and Sensibility (#2, TBD)</u>

<u>Sense and Manscaping (#3, TBD)</u>

<u>Persuasion and Man Hands (#4, TBD)</u>

<u>Mantuary Abbey (#5, TBD)</u>

<u>Mancave Park (#6, TBD)</u>

<u>Emmanuel (#7, TBD)</u>

<u>Handcrafted Mysteries Series</u>

(A Romantic Cozy Mystery Series, spinoff of *The Winston Brothers Series*)

<u>Engagement and Espionage (#1)</u>

<u>Marriage and Murder (#2)</u>

<u>Home and Heist (#3, TBD)</u>

<u>Baby and Ballistics (TBD)</u>

<u>Pie Crimes and Misdemeanors (TBD)</u>

<u>**Good Folks Series**</u>

(Interconnected Standalones, Adult Contemporary Romantic Comedy, spinoff of *The Winston Brothers Series*)

Totally Folked (#1)

Folk Around and Find Out (#2, coming 2022)

<u>**Three Kings Series**</u>

(Interconnected Standalones, Holiday-themed Adult Contemporary Romantic Comedies)

Homecoming King (#1)

Drama King (#2, coming Christmas 2022)

Prom King (#3, coming Christmas 2023)

<u>**Standalones**</u>

Ten Trends to Seduce Your Best Friend

9 781942 874942